MW01318998

Talk About a Dream

By Glenn Marx

Talk About a Dream

© Copyright 2013

This book, or parts thereof, may not be reproduced without the permission of the author. For publishing information,
contact Glenn Marx, 2031 Scott Drive, Helena, MT 59601.

ISBN: 978-0-615-83540-2

Summary: A community newspaper owner relives a remarkable season of accomplishment by the Whitehall High School football team in 1986.

100 percent of the proceeds from this edition of Talk About a Dream will be donated to a Whitehall community project designed to raise funds for the Whitehall Star Theatre conversion to digital technology. The project is a collaboration among the Whitehall High School Interact Club, Town of Whitehall, the Star Theatre owners, community members and supporters of Whitehall and the Star Theatre.

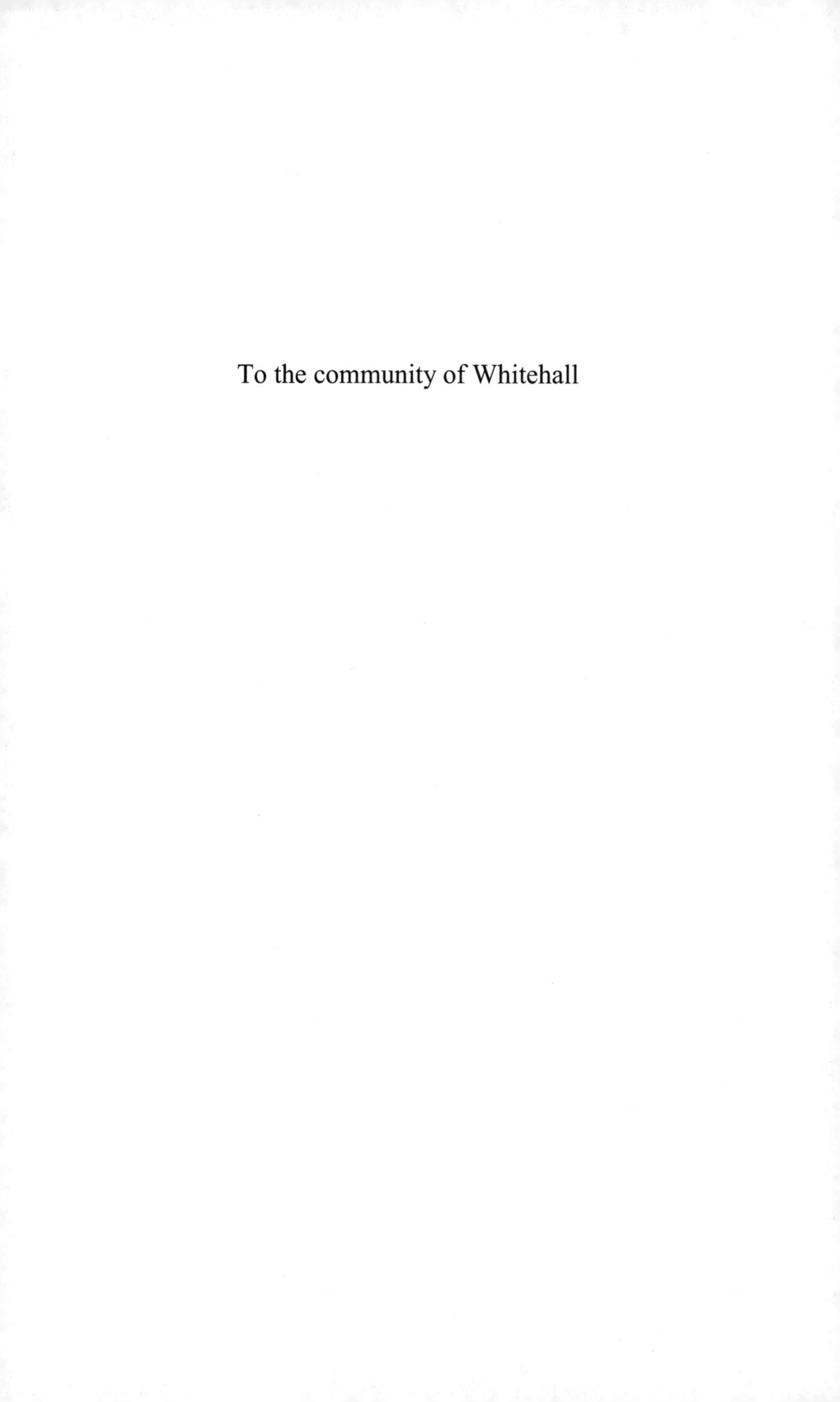

To the community of Whitehall

Pulling out of here to win

It's up to me, it appears, to tell the tale. And to be honest, I'm the perfect one, since I was there. I not only lived through it, I wrote about it every week.

Back in 1986 I was the publisher of the Whitehall Ledger, the weekly newspaper in the small Montana town of Whitehall, and when you're publisher of a weekly newspaper in a town like Whitehall, you're also the sports reporter and sports photographer. You're also the newspaper's columnist, the advertising salesman and about every other job associated with a newspaper, including janitor, and you work about seventy hours a week until you reach a point where the level of exhaustion consumes anything you have resembling energy and drags you down to your knees, which actually happened to me in 1991, when I more or less collapsed while covering a town council meeting.

I'm fine now, mostly. Except whenever anyone hears I'm from Whitehall, the first thing they usually comment on is the 1986 high school football season, and always – always – they tell me what they think they know or what they think they remember about Whitehall's team, and what they think they know and what they think they remember is always – always – wrong.

My son was a sophomore at Whitehall High School in 1986, and played a contributing role on a mystifying and mystical WHS Ranger football team that made an improbable, perhaps incomprehensible, drive in the state Class B football playoffs.

My daughter was in middle school then. It was increasingly obvious to her teachers, to school administrators and education officials that she was significantly above average in a lot of ways, in a lot of things. But it was just the three of us – daughter, son and me – and with the dizzying demands of the newspaper, life was essentially a blur. That isn't an excuse for anything, just an explanation.

And I'm not offering a revisionist theory or a justification for anything I've done or not done, or for anything that happened or didn't happen. My focus was on the business of running a weekly newspaper in 1986, and it took my entire focus for my business to financially and physically survive. I make no apologies for that, although, to be honest, maybe this whole book is an apology of sorts. Because even in 1986, as the events of that summer and fall unfolded, I was slow to understand and even slower to recognize the miraculous events and personalities that conspired in our little corner of Jefferson County to produce such acute astonishment and accomplishment.

That's another reason why I figure someone like me needs to tell the tale, and tell it right. Everybody *thinks* they know what happened, but only a few people really *know* what happened. And believe me, I *know* what happened. I was there before, during and after. I'm *still* there, in a way, except I don't own the newspaper anymore or live in Whitehall.

So what I'm going to be telling you here is the gospel truth. It's a tale told partly through the words of Bruce Springsteen, which is appropriate in that

Springsteen's music seemed to be blaring through the air and throughout the season. I figure only three people know the whole story – me, a coach we all called Jersey, and the school superintendent at the time, a guy named Ed Franklin. Ed passed away two years ago in a rest home in Great Falls, and Jersey simply vanished from Montana – and possibly from the face of the earth – as far as anyone knows.

Now that I think about it, I'm not only the best person to tell the tale, I'm the *only* person to tell the complete tale, the full story. I'm going to write the truth, but it's up to you whether or not you believe me. I can't make you believe this. I'm not even going to try. All I'm going to do is tell you what happened; exactly what happened.

Just don't think this is a story about football. It's not. It's a story about community, about determination, about sacrifice, about life, and about death.

But I should warn you right now, like Springsteen said, sometimes you got to have faith, and for you to believe this story, this is one of those times.

Chapter 1

If you stand north of Whitehall, up near the ridge of the open pit high wall of Golden Sunlight Mine, and look south, you see the Tobacco Root Mountains to the east and the Highland Mountains to the west, and in between you'll see the wide flat U-shaped Jefferson Valley curving slightly as it bends to the south.

What you also see, if you look at it from this vantage point, is a perfect wind chute north up the valley between the two mountain ranges that narrows and energizes the force-fed air current as it sweeps north and west. What the wind chute does, on most days, is take a gentle breeze in places like Ennis and Dillon and convert it into a gale force wind by the time it rips through Whitehall.

In about 1978, I think it was, when Amy and I were still married and Tony was just starting elementary school, we filled up our Subaru wagon and ventured north to Glacier Park for a rare and precious three-day weekend. During a stop at a West Glacier ice cream shop Annie, who was maybe four years old, started a conversation with the waitress by asking how far we were from Canada.

The waitress was grandmother-ish with a tight perm of coiled gray hair. She smiled in a friendly way, leaned toward Annie, and paused as if she was about to treat us to something truly remarkable. "Oh hon, you aren't further than 40 miles from the Canadian border right now."

Annie, with wispy thin hair and fierce brown eyes, had a swoosh of strawberry ice cream smeared across her knuckles. "Is there a marker there for the 49th parallel?" she asked.

The waitress gave a brief nervous laugh, cast a quick glance at me and a quicker one at Amy, then offered a slightly confused expression toward Annie. "There's a border guard, hon, if that's what you mean."

Annie, seated on her mother's lap, shook her head. "I mean the 49th parallel. It's a line of latitude that separates the United States and Canada," she said. "There's another one at California and Mexico, but that one's the 28th parallel."

The waitress offered an exaggerated smile my direction, lowered her eyes, kind of bowed, and retreated.

"Why do you do that to people?" Tony asked Annie.

"I don't know, *hon*," Annie answered. She licked the pink stain of strawberry from her hand. We knew already then that Annie was a smart kid, and almost everyone she talked to also knew it.

"Let's go," I said, and stood. That had been my singular role of authority in our little family foursome: deciding when it was time to leave the restaurant. It was typically done in haste to avoid domestic conflict.

It was in the adjoining gift shop while Amy bought the kids identical Glacier Park tee-shirts – a cartoon drawing of a sow and cub bear, the sow on all fours and the cub on its hind legs seemingly waving a greeting – when Amy paid with a check and the store clerk saw our address of Whitehall.

"My husband and I used to live in Bozeman and always traveled through Whitehall," the clerk said cheerfully. "One time we stopped there and the wind wasn't blowing. I hardly recognized the place."

I knew what she meant. A calm day in Whitehall, especially in spring, seemed unnatural, an eerie calm before a storm. Frequently a day will begin still and quiet, but as the sun rises the wind gathers strength, and before you realize the weather has changed you find yourself leaning – again – into a blustery, surly wind.

In April 1986 the wind blew so hard during the annual Whitehall Easter Egg Hunt a couple kids, young and on unsteady legs, were blown backward into the dry tall yellow grass after a sudden gust. The wind howled from the south, and the couple hundred kids who lined up along a rope bravely faced the blustery wind. Children carrying thin plastic IGA grocery bags held tight as the sacks snapped and popped against the rough ragged flurries, as if the bags were full, blown straight out and bulging.

The Whitehall Easter Egg Hunt was a tradition, and it was a tradition that took weeks to organize, days to fill and hide the eggs and arrange and display the prizes, and then about ninety seconds to actually complete. The kids moved in frantic waves north to south in the southeast end of the rodeo grounds like brightly colored locusts – some kids wore winter ski coats – through the bunch grass and horse droppings. The Whitehall volunteer firemen traditionally brought a fire truck to the event, and always let loose with a traditional siren wail at 10:30 AM sharp on the Saturday before Easter Sunday. By 10:32 AM the field was essentially swept clean of every egg. Toddlers, snot gumming up their nose and upper lip, appeared dazed by the sudden and complete conclusion of the event, and even later, when they had participated seven or eight straight years, the dazed expressions of elementary school students conveyed puzzled disappointment at the abrupt termination of the search. Parents, who annually shivered and shook after failing again to appreciate the severity of the cold and wind, hastily hoisted or hauled kids to cars and trucks and by 11:00 AM the rodeo grounds was desolate and empty.

By 1986 I was an experienced Whitehall Easter Egg Hunt veteran, which meant when I left home I was wearing a stocking cap, and starting closest to my body, a long-sleeve tee-shirt, sweatshirt, a hooded sweatshirt and a winter jacket. For seven straight years a picture of the Easter Egg Hunt – usually some kid wearing a bunny hat – adorned the front page of the Ledger the Wednesday after Easter Sunday.

The Wednesday after Easter Sunday in 1986 made it eight straight years, but if anything was noteworthy in that edition of the Ledger, it was a story of death, which always struck me as exactly the opposite of Easter, with its symbolism of birth and renewal. But in a weekly newspaper, as in life itself, death and birth are sometimes ironically connected.

That week the Ledger carried an obituary on page thirteen of Frank Stockett, who died at age sixty-three the evening of Easter Sunday. Frank had been at the Easter Egg Hunt, with his daughter and three grandchildren, who were visiting from Denver. Frank's daughter, Heidi, subscribed to the Ledger. Every week we mailed out about nine hundred newspapers to people who lived in over forty different U.S. states, and I knew the names of almost every subscriber. We sold another four hundred papers each week through our vendor outlets, which was about double the circulation of the paper the first week we owned it.

"Jesus H. Christ, let's get this thing rolling," Frank had blurted at about 10:25 AM, five minutes before the Easter Egg Hunt sprung into action, when we both stood out of the wind, near the fire truck and Brandon Bradshaw, a Whitehall Volunteer Fire Department firefighter. Brandon wore his knee-high rubber boots, pale green turnout and bright yellow helmet as he sat inside the fire truck, steadily checking his watch.

Frank wore an old lined windbreaker, the same one he wore each fall when he stormed along the sideline as Whitehall High School's varsity football coach.

"I'm freezing my ass off," he told Brandon, who nodded.

It was the last thing I ever heard Frank Stockett say. It was time to get the hunt started, and since Brandon was getting in position to ring the truck's siren, I had to get in position to take traditional pictures of the traditional event.

His son-in-law, Brady, a teacher at a private school in Golden, Colorado, found Frank's lifeless body the following night. The Stockett family and guests had gathered for Easter Sunday dinner, and afterward, they said, sometime around 8:00 PM, Frank had launched himself from his recliner, shuffled through the kitchen and out the side door to bring in an armful of firewood. It was probably twenty minutes later when Frank's wife, Lila, absently wondered about him. Brady looked outside and saw Frank's already stiffening body slumped against the woodpile, his mouth open and rigid as if issuing a final unheard and unresponded to command to a player or complaint to a referee.

When you own a small town newspaper, you find out almost everything about everyone. Or, as Amy would complain, anything about anyone. After the funeral, when a somber Lila came in the Ledger to place a "Thank You" ad to Scott Funeral Home and to "Everyone Who Sent Cards, Flowers, and Prayers," she told me about Frank's final moments. Lila and I chatted about the teamwork demonstrated during the funeral service, held in an overflowing WHS multi-purpose room, with several former pupils – Frank had also taught elementary school physical education for nearly three decades in Whitehall – in attendance, along with several former players participating in the ceremony. Frank had coached in Whitehall for 22 years, and I had intended to put his overall won-loss record in his obituary until I realized his teams had lost more – substantially more, it turned out – than they had won. For three wondrous years in the early 1970s the Whitehall Rangers had won a trio of conference titles and in 1973 got to the state Class B title game, losing to Belgrade 7-6. I knew the year, the score and the opponent because in the school trophy case there was a photo of the team and a younger and slenderer version of Frank together with a signed football that had the score written on it in white paint.

Since then, Frank's teams had, to put it kindly, struggled. Especially the most recent three years. In 1983, Whitehall went 0-8 and never for an instant led in any game. In 1984, Whitehall was again 0-8 and had three second-half leads, but each time let the lead slip away. In 1985, the team was loaded with seniors and was expected to possibly compete for a conference title, but a couple key players were injured early in the season and the team stumbled to an unfortunate and disappointing 2-6 record.

It had grown painful to interview Frank. As the losses mounted, as his team's performance worsened, as the bleachers grew more vacant and hushed, and as fewer and fewer boys even bothered to go out for the team, our interviews grew more terse and more tense. I got the impression Frank disliked me and my weekly football article, as if it was my fault in 1985 when the Rangers gave up 21 fourth-quarter points to lose 28-27 to a Big Timber team that only won one game all year. The anger behind his eyes was barely hidden during our weekly discussion, and sometimes his frustration erupted into what could have been interpreted as deliberate and sarcastic taunts.

After each home game we met in the coach's office – tucked away off the hallway just outside the Ranger locker room – and he gave me the game stats and after a loss, the quickest interview we both could arrange. By the end of the 1985 season it was hard to tell who dreaded the interviews more, Frank or me.

There was no sarcasm at Frank's funeral service. It was a solemn, locker room-like service. Players from his 1973 state runner-up team – including the former halfback named Bryant Sacry who played at Montana State University and in 1986 was a state representative from Gallatin County, and the former All-State linebacker named Chuck Glaus who over a decade later was still in the Army – stood behind the podium and talked about how Frank shaped their lives, and inspired them to be leaders and to accept life's challenges with resiliency.

I think they meant it. Or at least intended to mean it. I had a feeling Frank was a good winner and a sore loser, which if you think about it, is probably the way a coach should be. Coaches, even small town high school coaches, aren't supposed to tolerate defeat. Frank couldn't tolerate losing, couldn't tolerate admitting it or talking about it, and the only person he actually had to talk about it with was me. Frank simply, and perhaps tragically, lacked the energy, ability or intelligence to stop the losing.

Lila had asked me to say a few words at the service, and since I had no choice, I agreed. I said I admired Frank's persistence, his devotion to high school kids, and his commitment to education. And I mostly meant it. Both my kids had Frank as their elementary school physical education teacher and at what seemed like a years-ago parent-teacher meeting, one of the only conventional parenthood duties I actually attempted to fulfill, Frank told me Annie was the smartest kid he'd ever taught. Virtually every teacher in Whitehall had told me that at one time or another, in one way or another, that Annie was the most gifted child they'd ever taught.

"Lance, Tony's a good kid, you know that," Frank had told me as we sat, the two of us, alone in the bleachers of the elementary school gym, when Annie was still in elementary school. "But I've never seen a kid like Annie before."

"Yeah, she's always been smart," I said.

"Smart? Smart?" Frank raised his voice on the second "Smart," then lowered it. "She's dangerous smart. She's scary smart. She's *internationally* smart." It was perhaps Frank's most inspired use of the word 'internationally'.

Annie, 13 years old in 1986, wore a dark blue blouse to Frank's school funeral ceremony, and poured punch during the reception after the service. A day earlier she had forced me to accompany her to Dick's Department Store on Main Street in Whitehall so she could pick out a new pair of a dark slacks and dress shirt for me. Annie was 13 years old, and I pretty much did whatever she wanted. Most people, truthfully, did whatever Annie wanted.

She was the one who bought birthday cards for me to sign and send to my brother and sister, their spouses, and my various nieces and nephews. I could never remember names and ages of all the kids, but Annie dutifully retained all such knowledge, and even knew the dates of my siblings' anniversaries. It wasn't that I couldn't remember names and dates and anniversaries as much as that I didn't care and didn't have time to worry about that neglect.

When the funeral ceremony was over I drove back to the Ledger office. It was Thursday afternoon, a time of relative peace for a weekly paper. Laura Joyce Sabo, perpetually cheerful with a habit of punctuating every sentence with an abbreviated laugh, served as Ledger office manager, typesetter, proofreader and classified page editor. Everything else, I did. My primary official Thursday afternoon duty was to start the list of advertisements for the upcoming newspaper – called the run sheet – and try to get organized to make sure Friday was a productive day.

Laura Joyce was about ten years younger than me, and had me by a good forty pounds. She and her husband Bud lived on a small ranch about six miles from Whitehall west toward the Pipestone area, and they had a couple horses and raised a few cows, but he worked seasonally for a construction company out of Butte and she worked full-time at the Ledger. He weighed a good 75 pounds more than Laura Joyce, and for some reason wore tight-fitted jeans and western shirts, which didn't do him a lot of favors, looks-wise or fashion-wise.

"How was the service?" Laura Joyce asked when I walked into the Ledger office.

"Fine," I answered. "Some of Frank's old players were there and said some nice things about him. And about Whitehall," I added.

The Ledger office was heated by a large overhead furnace located in the back corner, above a corner of the layout table, and on chilly brisk days in winter and spring the smell of the heat always comforted me. The Ledger office itself, truth be told, comforted me. Home always contained responsibilities I either didn't want or couldn't handle, chores I failed to perform and surprises or problems I always sought to avoid. There was no consistency or understandable flow or stability to home life.

Work was much better. The volume of work was immense and relentless, but it was understandable and predictable. On Monday morning I sold advertising, and on Monday afternoon I wrote articles and laid out the individual ads. Monday night after supper was spent in the darkroom creating halftones for newsprint, and getting a modest start on layout of the newspaper. Tuesday morning, afternoon and evening were spent laying out the paper. Wednesday morning I took the paste-up sheets to Anaconda to the web press where the Ledger was printed. Wednesday afternoon we mailed the paper, hauled papers to the vending outlets, and transitioned from the old paper – just printed – to the new paper – one week away. Thursday morning I organized some of Laura Joyce's typesetting and made a list of articles, ads and photos for the upcoming week. Thursday afternoon I began the run sheet and usually did some writing and with Annie's guidance paid bills and made a bank deposit. Friday morning was set aside to write an editorial and other writing or picture-taking, and Friday afternoon was spent making sure Laura Joyce and I were caught up and ready for the onslaught of work on Monday. Friday night and Saturday were invariably spent at high school sports and community events, and on Sunday I wrote all the sports articles. This was the same routine, more or less, 52 weeks a year, every week, every year, at the Ledger. There were stretches where I would work 150 straight days, and within that stretch I would maybe work 100 nights. In my years in Whitehall, I never had more than three days in a row off work, and in an average year I probably worked all or parts of 350 days.

Amy never could figure out how or why I worked so long and so often. To the day she packed the one suitcase we owned and drove our Subaru out of town she never understood why the paper was so important to me.

"That's a handsome shirt," Laura Joyce said. "It's new, isn't it?"

"Yeah." I sat down at my desk and opened the large white folder that held the run sheet for the paper just printed. Annie would enter all the ads into files so she could do billing at the end of the month.

"Annie pick it out?" asked Laura Joyce.

"What?"

"The shirt. Annie pick it out?"

I lowered my chin and looked at the shirt. “Yeah. I had to get these black pants too.”

Laura Joyce cocked her head. “Just right for a funeral.”

“Yeah, thanks.”

“So Whitehall needs a new football coach,” she said.

“Looks that way.” I had also let my mind wander, just a bit, that direction. I figured the school would place an advertisement for the position within a week or so, and that the school board would probably try to make a decision and hire a new coach at the board’s May meeting. My guess was the new coach would be Wally Hope, a decently competent WHS assistant coach for years who seemed, given the alternatives, or lack of alternatives, a likely successor for the suddenly and unexpectedly vacated head coach position.

The school board met the first Wednesday of each month. The town council met the second Monday of each month. The planning board met the first Monday of each month. The watershed council met the third Wednesday of each month. The town Chamber of Commerce met the second Thursday of each month. I attended each meeting.

Whitehall folks saw me regularly at local meetings, events, games and almost anything that drew a crowd of two or more local people. Every now and then someone would ask me if I ever get tired of working so long and hard. My standard response was that the first sixty hours or so each week weren’t that bad, but it was the next ten to twenty hours that got me tuckered out.

Frank Stockett was dead now, and gone, eternally tuckered out. I mourned Frank a little longer, maybe fifteen seconds, then got to work. I started entering the name of each advertiser, size of the ad and the accumulated ad inches, pondered for a brief moment the prospects of weekly interviews with Wally Hope. I snuck a quick peek again at my new dark dress shirt and black slacks and wondered about the possibility of selling Dick Hogan at Dick’s Department Store an ad on Monday.

Chapter 2

Lyle O'Toole served as Whitehall School Board chairman, was president of the Bank of Whitehall, and represented part of what constituted Whitehall's middling upper crust. Lyle not only had a good job, he'd been to college, had once lived in a big city, had a nice home and a boat that had a motor on it. A few people in Whitehall had river drift boats and jon boats, but Lyle also had a new Ford half-ton pickup truck and would haul his boat and its outboard motor on a shiny silver trailer to Harrison Lake and Canyon Ferry and pull water skiers around in wide frenzied loops, a recreational activity well beyond the financial ability of most Whitehall folks.

Lyle had three daughters – one a high school senior, one a sophomore and one in eighth grade – and all of them were named after trees, or shrubs maybe, or maybe plants. Vegetation was not my specialty. The oldest was Holly, the middle girl was Aspen, and the youngest was Peach. Lyle wife's name was Rose, which might be a bush or a flower, or both. Rose looked maybe a year older than Holly, more like a fourth sister than a mother, and the O'Toole family was collectively so striking that not a single male in town knew how to react to them.

Lyle and I visited regularly – not just about bank advertising – but about the health and stability of the community as a whole. He was an early advocate for Golden Sunlight Mine, a gold mine owned by a Canadian company that in the early 1980s had started to dig, drill, and blast an open pit a few miles north and east of Whitehall that was growing increasingly visible from Highway 69, from I-90 and from virtually anywhere in town. Lyle thought Whitehall's location – located pretty much in the middle of a triangle formed by Bozeman to the east, Butte to the west and Helena to the north – anchored by an industrial giant like Golden Sunlight, would make Whitehall a prime location for economic development and population growth.

You'd never know that by looking around Whitehall itself. It did not resemble a prime location, or a prime anything. What it did resemble was a struggling town crumbling at the edges. The town's paved streets had no curbs or gutters, scattered streets were still gravel or just plain dirt and the part of town south of the railroad tracks was scarred, cluttered and ragged. Whitehall's abbreviated main street business section was partially located, simply enough, on Main Street. The buildings weren't old enough to be called historic, but were old enough to look rundown. From any of the four directions you entered town, you saw either junk, weathered and rotted buildings or depilated, crude, handmade billboard-like signs advertising businesses that were either no longer operating or were themselves housed in weathered and rotted buildings.

It was odd, then, that the first time I saw Whitehall, I liked the place. For some reason I felt immediately at home and immediately comfortable. Whitehall instantly seemed strangely familiar to me, despite the fact I had never seen it before and had never before lived in a small town. I never could quite share the confident and optimistic economic vision Lyle had for Whitehall, but I could verify, despite the town's crusty and worn appearance, it possessed some shrouded and intangible tenderness to it that maybe was more felt or sensed than seen.

On the evening of the third Wednesday in April 1986, I left Annie at home in her room reading a Popular Science article about the Challenger explosion, and Tony was outside in the driveway, with a couple friends, Brock Warren and Chance Nelson, shooting baskets under a darkening sky and a weak yard light. Brock had his boombox perched on the trunk of his battered Chevy Impala, and a cassette tape was blaring what I thought was the theme song from the movie *Top Gun*.

"You up for a game of Horse, Lance?" Tony asked me.

Since he was about age ten, my son has called me Lance. His friends also called me Lance, as did Annie. Neither kid has ever called me Dad. To my knowledge, no other Whitehall children called their father by his first name.

"I got a school board meeting," I said. I got in my car, a little blue Honda Accord that when parked looked like it had been abandoned, but to its credit it had never leaked a single drop of oil. "You might want to turn that down a little." I nodded toward the boombox. "See you in a couple hours."

"See you, Lance," said Chance as I backed out of the driveway. I was never sure if calling me by my first name was a sign of friendship or a lack of respect.

The school board was just completing the Pledge of Allegiance when I walked in. Lyle and I exchanged a brief nod of greeting as I took my seat in the front row, and Ed Franklin, the school superintendent, wearing glasses that were too thick, a tie that was too short and a white dress shirt that was too small, began his droning report about problems with the school's boiler, the need to re-stripe the parking lot during the summer, a new lunchroom rule from the Office of Public Instruction and an update about the senior class trip. The 47 students in the WHS Class of 1986 were in the final stages of organizing their senior trip to Seattle, a location that none of them outside of Holly O'Toole had ever seen. In all likelihood half the seniors couldn't place Seattle on a map. A few kids probably had no idea what country the Pacific Northwest was in and a few others had possibly never even heard of Seattle.

The senior trip was one of a handful of Whitehall rites of spring, along with an early home track meet, a spring stage play, the prom, final spring band and choir concerts and finally, with a hormonal and parental explosion of emotional joy and relief, the high school graduation ceremony. The school play had been performed a couple weeks earlier, the track meet had been canceled because of snow, but the prom, class trip, concerts and graduation ceremony were all coming within the next four weeks. One of the actual main purposes of the April school board meeting was to plan ahead and get the teaching and administrative staff in place for the upcoming school year, which started in late August. In addition to routine agenda items like library book approval, hiring of a new substitute teacher, early discussion of summer maintenance projects and hiring the summer maintenance crew was a board decision to continue the contract of its school superintendent through the 1986-87 school year.

Ed Franklin had been with the Whitehall school system – first as an elementary school principal – for over 20 years. If you looked up the word dull in the dictionary, you'd find a photo of Ed Franklin. He looked like a cross between a Mormon missionary and a tax auditor.

He was getting close to retirement age, and for much of his tenure in Whitehall he had affectionately been called Special Ed. The nickname's birth occurred on Ed's first day as principal when he met an arriving school bus early in the morning. Ed shook hands with the kids as they stepped off the bus, and introduced himself as the new elementary school principal.

One new arrival, a first grader at his first all-day session of school, shook Ed's hand and grinned. "You're Special Ed!" the kid proclaimed. "I'm supposed to see you for reading!"

Had it not been for the bus driver, who with great glee relayed the story all week, the greeting may have evaporated into history. But while everyone at school officially called Ed Mr. Franklin, everyone in Whitehall still knew him as Special Ed.

The only problem preventing Ed's reappointment as superintendent was that he and board member Daniel Purdy had a bitter dispute the previous fall about cheerleading uniforms. At the first home football game, a 44-14 Ranger loss, the weather was unseasonably warm and the WHS cheerleaders – with all three O'Toole girls front and center – wore a costume of sleeveless tee-shirts and pink shorts and performed a halftime dance routine to the song *The Heat is On*. Perhaps the sleeveless tee-shirts were a bit snug in front, perhaps the shorts were a bit brief, and perhaps the dance routine was a bit suggestive, but it hardly seemed a scandal until Daniel Purdy led a group of parents to bring a petition to the next school board meeting seeking to remove the cheerleading instructor – a first-year teacher named Betty Smithson who had no idea what the fuss was all about – and to require the school board to approve all cheerleading uniforms.

"You can't be serious," Ed told Daniel Purdy back in October 1985 at the school board meeting.

"Why can't I?" Daniel Purdy shot back. "Those girls disgraced the school, they disgraced the community and they disgraced themselves."

What Daniel Purdy should have realized was the father of a trio of *those girls* sat three chairs to his right. It wasn't the first time Lyle and Daniel Purdy skirmished at a school board meeting. Daniel Purdy owned the lumberyard in town, and also owned an exaggerated comb-over that somehow forced your eyes to gaze in confusion at his head as your mind wondered if Daniel Purdy really and truly thought combing thin wiry strands of hair across his scalp from the top of one ear to the other made him look less bald.

The skirmish didn't last long. By the time Lyle got done defending his three daughters, defending the school cheerleading program, defending the spirit of Whitehall High School students and defending the spirit of the Whitehall community, Daniel Purdy not only looked and sounded like a narrow-minded prude, which I think we all saw coming – in part because Daniel Purdy was, in fact, a narrow-minded prude – but when all was said and done Daniel Purdy also looked and sounded like a dirty old man, which no one saw coming, especially Daniel Purdy.

Daniel Purdy knew afterward that he had started a battle with Lyle O'Toole that he – Daniel Purdy – would never win and could never outlive. But six months later Daniel Purdy figured one way to retaliate against Lyle was to get Ed Franklin fired. Back in October, Ed had also stood up for the cheerleading program and the school, and more or less pulled the trigger on the verbal bullets that mortally and publicly wounded Daniel Purdy's character and reputation.

"I watched a group of spirited girls demonstrating talent and school pride," Ed had said during the debate. "What were you watching?"

Daniel Purdy failed to muster a response. His baffled expression suggested he realized what he had been watching. I knew what he'd been watching, because even though I was a parent and pushing age forty, I was watching the same thing. The difference was, I didn't tell everyone at the school board meeting about it.

The Ledger article in the final week of October 1985 must have offended Daniel Purdy, because after that he went from being an infrequent advertiser in the Ledger to essentially boycotting the paper. His subscription lapsed, and he was even disinclined to acknowledge my presence when he saw me around town. It was as if, to him, I didn't exist.

Ed, who plodded through each school day with monotonous efficiency, wasn't so lucky. Ed existed all too much, and Daniel Purdy's mission at the end of the 1985-86 school year was to get the school board to nonrenew Ed's contact and make him nonexistent within the Whitehall school system.

Most of the school board agenda items were completed – the board had voted to rename the football field Stockett Stadium and, as had been widely discussed during the weeks since Frank's death, had hired longtime assistant coach Wally Hope as head football coach – when the agenda item of "superintendent's contract" came up.

Daniel Purdy just couldn't help himself. He made a motion to non-renew Ed's contract, and Eric Johansen, a rancher from Cardwell, made a quick – and obviously rehearsed – second to the motion.

"Point of order," said Molly Ryan, a board member and single mother of a high school freshman daughter stricken with multiple sclerosis. Molly addressed Lyle. "I believe it is impermissible to make a negative motion."

"Correct," Lyle said. "It must be a positive motion." He paused, and put in order the papers on the table in front of him. "This is a personnel matter, and the right to privacy exceeds the right of the public's right to know. Mr. Franklin, you have the right to close the meeting."

There were maybe a half dozen people in the audience besides me. The "right to privacy" comment was a legal phrase meant to exclude the media, and most of the time it simply gave a board, council or committee the opportunity to conduct messy business behind closed doors.

"Let's keep it open," announced Ed. I knew he wanted to keep the discussion public. He had told me previously about his belief that to be successful bullies like Daniel Purdy needed to operate in secret. Expose their malice, he said, and their boldness vanishes. Ed was perhaps dull, but you'd be mistaken if you thought he was weak.

It was obvious that Eric Johansen, who had seconded the motion, was uncomfortable with the decision to keep the meeting open. Craig Hanson, a board member with two kids in elementary school, was a building contractor who had supposedly roughed up his wife at least once and to the dismay of many she'd declined to press charges. He shifted his eyes from Daniel Purdy to me, then back to Daniel Purdy. I couldn't tell where the fourth vote was – with four needed for a majority – to vote against Ed. Because in theory, Daniel Purdy would have never made his motion without having four votes lined up. Daniel Purdy was malicious and vindictive, but he wasn't stupid. He was, however, careless. He'd jumped the procedural gun, and his motion was in immediate trouble.

"I make a motion that we renew the contract of Ed Franklin, Whitehall Superintendent of Schools, for three years," said Molly. "And that Mr. Franklin receive a three percent increase in pay each year for the three years of the contract."

"Second," said Mark Johnson, an administrative officer at Golden Sunlight Mine, a WHS graduate and Montana Tech grad who moved back home from Alaska when the mine opened here.

"Discussion," stated Lyle.

Molly leaned forward, to be directly in Daniel Purdy's line of sight. "Mr. Franklin has been a valuable administrative employee in this school system for twenty years, and has dedicated his life as a professional educator so a generation of Whitehall kids have had the best public education possible," she said. "He has maintained strict adherence to state accreditation standards, involved the board and the public in all school policy issues and decisions, and has put together a first-rate faculty and staff."

I detected the slightest hint of a smile on Lyle's face. Daniel Purdy apparently wasn't the only one who had prepared for the meeting.

"I've been impressed with Ed and the school administration since I moved back to Whitehall," added Mark. "The school's a positive place, and that's important in any working environment. The grounds are well maintained, the school has made progress in national testing scores and with school access for handicapped students. I think when we have dedicated, respected and qualified people like Mr. Franklin working for the school district, we as a board have an obligation to retain those employees."

"I have letters of support for Mr. Franklin that I'd like to enter into the record," said Lyle. He lifted the sheets of paper off the table in front of him as if he'd scarcely noticed them before. "Let's see. Both Whitehall principals, Mr. McDougal in the high school and Mrs. Cullen in the elementary school, endorse Mr. Franklin. Past school board chairman and current county commissioner Cal Walker has written a letter of recommendation."

A half dozen or more letters of support or recommendation followed, nonchalantly thumbed through and commented on by Lyle, as if the documents were a mere collection of paperwork. In reality they were indictments against Dan Purdy. Lyle announced letters from the local special education cooperative, the Boulder School District Superintendent of Schools, various coaches, teachers, even a letter from the WHS junior class president. Lyle waved the stack of letters toward me and asked if I "wanted them for the paper," a gesture meant to infuriate Daniel Purdy. So I nodded an affirmative response.

The voice vote was 6-1, with Daniel Purdy alone voting in timid opposition. Lyle highlighted the damage to Daniel Purdy by claiming to be unsure of the tally, and asking for a roll call vote. Alone in the room and in the world, Daniel Purdy was required to sheepishly acknowledge his lone vote against Ed.

As the board members and audience stood and gathered their belongings for the trip home, I noticed Lyle make a quick gesture with his hand, and it was a gesture I knew all too well. His right hand formed an imaginary grip around something – possibly an invisible glass containing alcohol – hoisted toward his mouth.

I nodded. We'd meet for a quick drink or two – in this case a celebratory drink – at Borden's Lounge.

Borden's was Whitehall's signature building, built smack at the start of the twentieth century when the town was a fledgling train roundhouse and not much else. Railroad companies had built Whitehall in the late 1800s, and miners and ranchers and business owners followed the ever expanding train tracks, moving here from across the globe to find opportunity, a section of ground, a wife, wealth, and for some, simply someplace for a new start.

Borden's, with its distinctive brick exterior, was located on the corner of Main Street and Legion Avenue, and it had, consistent with the town itself, seen better days. The bar decor was unadorned western, featuring a pool table and country music jukebox, with dingy little bathrooms that never – not once – seemed as if they had recently been cleaned. Upstairs were a bunch of apartments or motel rooms or secluded hallways that were dark enough and sullied enough for lonely people who had drunk themselves to near oblivion and suddenly discovered they were in love, or perhaps in need of something resembling love.

Sally was one of those thin-waisted, pale-faced, middle-aged, red-lipsticked women with dyed hair sprayed firm and perfect and too much eye shadow, who seemed to survive solely on nicotine and thrive in front of bottles of alcohol. It seemed like every bar I've ever been in has a Sally working at it. She smiled when I entered, and immediately reached for a bottle of Rainier, the beer of my choice. I was, you could say, a regular.

I found a spot in the corner, on a stool at the north side of the bar, where people looking in through the windows on Legion Avenue couldn't see me. As if I could hide. In towns like Whitehall, everyone knows what everyone else drives, and my Honda told everyone uptown that Lance Joslyn, Ledger publisher, was drinking in Borden's.

"There a game tonight?" asked Sally.

I shook my head. "Meeting. Better get a Velvet ditch for Lyle. He'll be here in a minute."

In Montana, whiskey was typically the hard liquor of choice, and water was the mix most preferred. In the old days the water for mix supposedly came from a road ditch, so a whiskey and water in Montana was a whiskey ditch.

But it wasn't Lyle O'Toole who entered the bar next. It was Slack Henkel. Slack had more or less adopted me when I first moved to Whitehall. He was about thirty years old and lived with his mom and dad on their ranch south of town near the Jefferson River where they raised alfalfa hay and black Angus cattle.

Slack had been seventeen years old, according to the stories I've been told, and was in line to be the senior class salutatorian with a scholarship to attend Montana State University to major in civil engineering when less than a month before graduation he was mending fence just west of the Tobacco Root Mountains in a draw called Bone Basin.

There were some clouds south in the valley, people have said, but the weather wasn't threatening, and there was no real atmospheric indication of a storm. No one knows what happened for sure, but the best guess seems to be a bolt of lightning hit the ground somewhere south of where Slack was working, and the barbwire fence picked up the electric charge and shot it through the metal wires. No one ever saw a storm cloud, and no one ever saw a lightning strike. Slack's working partner, a classmate named Cam Scott, was walking behind Slack with a fence post pounder when he said Slack screamed and flew through the air. Slack had been thrown ten feet away from the fence. Cam said his first thought was that someone shot Slack, and Cam ducked, waiting for the next bullet. None came, but to be sure there wasn't someone sighted in on him Cam said he ducked and scrambled on all fours to reach Slack. Cam said he smelled burnt hair and flesh. Smoke smoldered at Slack's head, arm, and foot. Unconscious but breathing, Slack was laid out in the foothills five miles from the nearest telephone and twenty miles from the nearest ambulance. Cam said he lifted ad carried Slack to the truck for a frantic ride to get help.

The palm of Slack's leather work glove had blown apart from palm to wrist. His boot heel had exploded. His cowboy hat was singed and torn and had shot far uphill from where he fell. Speculation later was that Slack had his left hand on the fence wire, and the lightning ripped into his body through the connection between hand and metal. The lightning then shot through his left arm and into his body, where it split and exited through his head and through his left leg, possibly through the metal clasp on his headband and the metal nails in his boot heel.

Slack survived, but was permanently damaged. His short-term memory was now erratic at best, his eyes held a vacancy at times as if there was emptiness or confusion behind them, and the best way I can describe it – although not the most charitable way – was that Slack was simple, childish, without plans, without guile and without worry. His hair was already gunboat gray, and while he didn't really limp and his left arm wasn't really withered, the natural carry of his arm wasn't quite right and his left leg did not move in unison with the rest of his body.

Slack never graduated from high school, never studied engineering at MSU, never had a girlfriend, never drove a car, and never left his family's ranch north of Silver Star for a life of his own. Slack could sometimes be trusted with basic chores and responsibilities, and got to town on a fairly frequent basis. It was a Wednesday night, and his mother, Sue, a school route bus driver, ranch wife and a former county champion barrel racer, was bowling in mixed league at Roper Lanes. Some people were uncomfortable around Slack, and he could be difficult to converse with, in part because at times he seemed unable to make a distinction between what he thought and what he either said or thought he said. But we'd been friends since my first football game. Slack was part of the chain gang – along with his dad, Walt – and when I took pictures during games I patrolled the sideline, and Slack showed no hesitancy in striking up a conversation with me the instant he spotted me.

"Who are you?" he asked me.

I had no idea who he was, so I gave him my thirty-second summary of being the new owner of the Whitehall newspaper. I introduced myself and extended my hand to shake hands with him, but he didn't move. He smiled past me, toward the field lights in the distance.

Then he laughed. "Our football team is lousy," he'd said, practically shouting. "We couldn't even tackle my grandma," he'd said, and laughed oddly; little bubbles of spittle forming at the corner of his mouth.

An older man standing next to him had held up a hand, a gentle admonition to talk softer. I realized then something in the young man's eyes was absent, or, perhaps, muddled. I assumed then that he had been mentally handicapped at birth. Walt then introduced himself and Slack, and Slack and I have been buddies ever since. Sometimes he rides with me to away games, and sometimes after a home game he'll ride with me to an uptown Whitehall bar.

Slack wasn't stupid. I figured that out pretty quick, even before I learned of his injury. He was not sophisticated and he may have lacked tact, but he could be insightful and, in short bursts, downright engaging.

"Evening Mr. Slack," greeted Sally. "The usual?"

Slack pulled up a bar stool alongside mine. He grinned, pushed his cowboy hat up his forehead, and held his right hand like a playful pistol, and pointed it at her. "The usual," he repeated cheerfully.

Slack was always served *the usual* because had he been asked, he frequently couldn't tell you what he wanted to drink, and he was not allowed alcohol. His inability to consume liquor had never stopped me from consuming mine.

"Your mom bowling?" I asked him.

Slack nodded as Sally set a can of Squirt in front of him. He thanked her. Somehow Slack always remembered to say thank you. Sometime he said it three or four times, and meant it each time.

"Tell her Lance said hi," I said. It was always best to state your name early in the conversation with Slack.

"How come you're here alone?" Slack asked.

"I'm not," I said. "I'm here with you."

He laughed. It was amazingly easy to coax a smile or chuckle from him. "You were alone before I got here."

"I was with Sally then," I said.

Slack laughed again, and tipped his cowboy hat even further back. "She's always here!"

"Tell me about it," she said, smiled, and walked away.

"We got a new football coach," I told Slack.

"Who?"

"Wally Hope."

"My dad's name is Walt," Slack said.

"Your dad would probably make a better coach," said a voice behind us. Lyle O'Toole had come in from the corner door, a door that rested at a perfect angle off the sidewalk from the corner of Legion Avenue and Main Street.

Sally visibly brightened, and added a hint of energy in her stride. She didn't do that when I came in, but then again I wasn't the president of the bank, and I didn't have a big boat with an outboard motor.

"Drinks for my boys here," Lyle said, and Sally went to fetch another Squirt, Rainier and Velvet ditch. He pulled up a stool to my right, which put me in the middle.

"You're the banker," Slack told him. "You got all them daughters."

Lyle nodded. "You too, Slack? Every swinging dick in town knows those three girls."

"Including Daniel Purdy," I said.

"Shame on you," said Lyle.

"Shame on me? Shame on you. I'm pretty sure you permanently damaged his reputation," I said. "You publicly humiliated him in front of the school board, the school administration, the community newspaper and everyone else in the room."

"Yeah," conceded Lyle. He held his glass close to his mouth. "That was kind of fun, wasn't it?" He sipped his drink. "All I did is drape his own ignorance and arrogance around his neck, and let him pull the rope tight. I'd say he deserved it, but I'm not sure anyone deserved to look as foolish and depraved as he did tonight."

"Did you see the look in his eye when he realized he basically labeled himself a pervert?"

"Here's what I'm thinking about doing," mused Lyle. "The sophomore class is doing some fundraising by selling cookies, and I'm thinking I'll have Peach slip on her cheerleading outfit, walk up alone to Dan Purdy's back door and knock. And when he answers I'll have her say as sweetly as possible, 'If you got some money, I got something sweet here for you.'"

"You are an evil man," I said.

"Peach is beautiful," Slack pronounced, and blushed.

Lyle regarded Slack. "I'm warning you, brother, stay away from her. She'll only wrap you around her finger, and then break your heart. It's a family tradition. She's the most dangerous because she learned all the tricks from her mom and two older sisters."

"Her mom is beautiful," Slack announced with what sounded like awe.

"Watch it, cowboy, she's already been spoken for," Lyle said.

Slack chuckled.

"A toast to Ed Franklin," Lyle said, and the three of us touched glass, or in Slack's case, aluminum. "Slack, we hired ourselves a new football coach tonight."

"His name is Wally," Slack stated.

"Yep," said Lyle. "Word travels fast in these parts. Wally Hope. He was the best applicant for the job because he was the only applicant for the job."

"You could say he brings new hope to the program," I said.

"You could also say there's no hope for Whitehall football," said Lyle. "Has Whitehall always been this bad in football?"

I shook my head. Lyle was a large man, and had played some football for Rocky Mountain College in Billings. He had gained some weight, but not much, and still moved like an athlete. He played golf and water-skied, and every fall turned big game hunter. "Back in the 1970s Whitehall ruled, right Slack," I said.

"I'm so happy when we win," Slack declared.

Which was true, although I didn't realize it until right then. Whitehall's football team hadn't won much recently, but when it did Slack had barely been able to contain his undisguised glee.

"We used to be pretty good," I said. "In Class B the class sizes are so small that a couple grades of weak athletes and you're in trouble. A couple years ago we had one senior on the whole team."

"And he couldn't tackle," added Slack.

It was my turn to laugh. Slack was right, the senior, a kid named Dusty Walker, wasn't much of a player.

"But last fall we had, what, seven or eight seniors, and we still only won a couple games," said Lyle.

I nodded. "Last year was a disappointment," I agreed. "There were pretty high expectations for that team. But they never jelled."

"And they couldn't tackle," Slack said.

"Half the time they couldn't even line up right," said Lyle.

"But now we have new hope," I said brightly.

"Can Wally Hope coach?" Lyle asked me directly. "He seemed competent when we interviewed him, but he didn't exactly knock my socks off."

I considered the question. Wally Hope had been an assistant coach, more or less been the offensive coordinator, but he wasn't what you'd call an inspiring figure. I wondered how much the kids respected him. He wasn't a bad guy, but he didn't strike me as a big improvement – or even an improvement at all – in the head coaching department. None of which I intended to tell Lyle.

"The fact that he wants the job is a plus," I said. "I got the impression sometimes the last year or so that Frank wasn't really all that interested in coaching. Wally knows the school, knows the kids, knows the opposition, and he must know how to run an offense. He's been doing it for a long time."

"Nice try," Lyle sighed.

"He'll do fine," I said.

Lyle sighed. "He'll have to. He's all we got."

"What are you going to do to replace him as assistant coach?" I asked.

"Not sure." Lyle shrugged. "There's a guy who's student teaching in the middle school. Name is Conte or something like that. From back east somewhere. He's applied for the middle school English job that's open now with Lisa's retirement."

Lisa Betterman, with forty years in the Whitehall school system, had been my son Tony's homeroom teacher for all three years of middle school. She was retiring, and some of the faculty and administration would say *finally* retiring.

"I think I know who he is," I said. "Tall guy. He was at Frank's service, now that I think about it. He's from New Jersey. My daughter had good things to say about him."

Sally appeared in front of us, and her hint of raised eyebrows asked, *do you want another round?*

"Not for me," I said. "I better get home to the kids."

Lyle waved her off. "I'm good."

"Slack, you better get back to Ropers," I said.

Sally nodded, affirmation she'd make sure Slack made it safely to the bowling alley and his mom.

I had a five-block drive home. It was 11:30, but the lights were on, the kids were up, and the flicker through the windows broadcast to the world that our television was on.

I parked in the driveway, away from the basketball hoop. Our house had an unattached garage, but the garage was filled with old furniture and other junk I had been meaning – for about three years – to haul to the dump. The house, garage, basement and yard were all full of tasks and duties I'd been meaning to address yet had no intention of actually completing.

Tony was slumped on the davenport in front of the television, possibly watching a professional basketball game. He was using the remote to flip through the channels so rapidly it was impossible to discern what if anything held his attention.

I plopped down into the La-Z-Boy and told him he had a new football coach for next year.

"Hopeless, right?" Tony said, eyes on the television.

"Yeah. I guess he was the only applicant," I said. "I have a crazy idea. Why don't you watch one show on one channel at one time?"

Tony turned and regarded me as if I had just uttered complete stupidity. Apparently my suggestion was so idiotic it didn't even merit a response. He simply looked away and continued to watch television, flipping from channel to channel.

I saw a lot of his mother in him. He had a slight wave in his brown hair like her, and something in the pliant look of the eyes and shape of the forehead is clearly from her side of the family.

"You eat supper?" I asked.

He nodded, eyes on the television.

"How about your sister?" I asked.

"She's in her room."

"Did she eat supper?"

He shrugged. "Cereal, I think."

Cereal. Jesus. "She awake?"

"Not sure."

I looked down the hall, at her room. I could see a thin horizontal bar of darkness under her door. I had a sensation of vague guilt, or perhaps sharp and tangible guilt, a sort of never-ending guilt really, that suggested a proper father did not have to ask his kids what they'd made – nor not made – for dinner, and that a proper father did not come home from the bar close to midnight on Wednesday and find his teenage son and near teenage daughter alone, and without a parental clue what they'd done all night.

Chapter 3

It usually takes until the end of March in the Jefferson Valley for the slender but valiant green shoots to begin creeping out of a still partially frozen earth through compacted muck and in some cases, through crusted snow. Then one day, suddenly, you realize spring has clawed its way through winter's grip and you wonder why you didn't see it coming.

The signs are all there, visible and visceral, every year. The snowbirds from Alberta, towing their fifth wheels back from the hot Arizona desert, chug north along Legion Avenue on their return migration to Canada. The Canadians are as punctual as the sandhill cranes, bluebirds and meadowlarks, three of Montana's more enchanting and picturesque avian neighbors that magically appear each spring after wintering at points south. In the natural world, spring starts to nudge away winter when the frost leaves the ground and the smell of damp soil permeates the outdoors, but winter somehow still seems to be peeking over your shoulder. When the snowbirds flow north, you can finally be assured spring is actually here.

Every time I saw one of the Alberta license plates I had an internal pang of regret at life's mistakes, life's wrong turns. It wasn't as if I lusted for what amounted to three months of self-imposed isolation fighting stifling heat in what looked like a slightly upscale but equally cramped version of a trailer home. It was more like I wistfully wished for the barest opportunity to escape not my weather and not my circumstances, but to have an option – any option – to pursue if I wanted, or even to identify an option, even a bad option, if I felt like it.

But I didn't, and couldn't. I was locked in and locked down in Whitehall, and while I harbored no actual remorse about my life, I also realized that might have been a simple mindless rationalization, because the plain truth was there was not one thing I could possibly have done about my situation or my condition.

Mondays were when the internal pang of regret banged loudest. The Ledger routine required me to get up early – well before the kids – and be at the Ledger office by six a.m. I'd spend an hour or so writing, getting Laura Joyce's workload organized and maybe developing film before I'd return home for a quick stop to make sure the kids were up and ready for school. Some Mondays were too hectic, and there was no quick morning trip home. Three days during the workweek – Monday, Thursday and Friday – I'd try to get home when the kids left for school. Tuesday and Wednesday the Ledger had priority, and the weekends were unpredictable about who got up when and went where, except Annie was the first one awake. Annie awoke almost every morning at seven a.m. sharp, without an alarm clock, and arrived at school each morning at 8:01 a.m. sharp because the school doors were locked tight until eight a.m.

On the first Monday morning in April 1986 I arrived home and found Annie at the kitchen table, a bowl of Rice Krispies on the kitchen table, a spoon of cereal in her mouth, her eyes focused on the morning newspaper.

"Your brother up?" I asked her.

She nodded without looking at me. "In the shower."

It took something serious – presidential decree, nuclear explosion – to keep Annie out of school. It usually took something serious – shouts, threats – to get Tony awake soon enough to make it to school on time. Tony wasn't lazy, Annie once told me, he was simply under-motivated.

"Says here a bomb killed three people at a disco in Berlin," said Annie, still not looking at me. "A week ago a car bomb blew up a police station in Australia."

"Thanks for that cheerful update," I said. Annie didn't just read our area's daily newspaper – she devoured it, day-by-day, page-by-page, word-by-word.

"It's like bombs are now to rifles what terrorism is to war," she said.

That's the way it was in our family. I worried about making sure we got the school lunch menu in the paper, Tony was worried about school tardiness, and Annie was deciphering trends in international relations.

Annie was an exceptional child from birth, and was an exceptional student from the day she first set foot inside Whitehall Elementary School.

I can recall when Amy and I were still in our version of married, and Annie was probably two years old, riding in her carseat in the back seat of our old Taurus. We lived in Butte then, but were more or less planning the move to somewhere else. I was a public relations officer for the power company and Amy was an emergency room nurse at St. James. Tony was probably about five years old, dressed up in his bright red Pizza Hut little league baseball uniform. If you didn't know any better, you'd have thought we were a functional family, driving to watch a happy little leaguer play baseball.

Amy was fretting about something, or everything, it was hard to tell. Tony sat in the backseat opposite Annie, wearing his baseball glove, tossing the baseball into his glove as we drove to the ball fields.

"Don't throw the ball in the car," Amy told him. Then she turned toward me. As was my habit, I had failed to do something. I was supposed to have contacted our car insurance company about some paperwork, and I had run out of time, and opted to postpone the duty to a different day. "What's so hard about calling the insurance man?" Amy demanded. "I don't expect you to do much, but the insurance man was your idea, he's your friend, and you said you'd call him."

"I'll call him."

In the backseat, Tony tossed the ball into his glove.

"I told you to stop that," Amy told Tony. "When?" she asked me. "When are you going to call him? His name's Art, right? When are you going to call your buddy, Art?"

"What am I supposed to talk with him about again?" I asked.

"Oh for Christ's sake, Lance." Amy slapped the dashboard with an open palm. "Can't you be responsible for anything?"

"Mom?" asked Annie from the backseat. No one responded to her.

"I'll call him tomorrow," I said.

"Sure you will," Amy said.

"Mom?" asked Annie.

"Hang on, Annie," I said, eyes in the rearview mirror. I looked across the front seat at Amy. "I'll call him tomorrow, all right? Now relax."

Amy released a deep sigh. "Yeah, you do that. You call him. You don't even have a goddamn clue what to even tell him."

"Mom?" asked Annie gently behind me.

"That's why I asked you what I'm supposed to ask him," I said.

"Forget it. I'll call him. That way I know it'll get done."

"Mom?" asked Annie.

Amy whirled toward the back. "What! What is it?"

Annie paused, a little timid, slightly afraid. But Annie never was much timid or much afraid. "Mom, what's my destiny?"

"Your what?" It sounded somehow like an accusation.

"My destiny," Annie asked sweetly. "What's my destiny?"

Amy's expression soured. "You're a baby sitting in a carseat. Worry about your next box of apple juice, not your destiny."

"We're almost there," I said, turning into the baseball fields parking lot. "Tony's destiny is to hit a home run today."

It was another failed attempt by me to cheer up our unhappy foursome.

During a day in fall of 1985 so windy the Montana state flag above the bank broke loose from its moorings and was found in Cardwell – eight miles away – twenty-four minutes later, I was at the Ledger when I received a call from Martha Cullen, elementary school principal. It was obvious from her hushed and dramatic vocal tone the call was serious and not typical school news or Ledger-related, and the officially stated request was for me to meet her at the school sometime soon. I had already learned that whenever I was asked by the elementary school principal in hushed tones and professional earnestness to meet, the discussion could only pertain to one topic: Annie. The meeting was set up for a Thursday afternoon, the best time for a weekly newspaper publisher to take care of parental responsibilities.

When I arrived at the school and was welcomed inside Martha's office, two additional women – professional and city types in business dress clothes – were waiting for me. One of them was an elderly woman with a thick shock of gray hair and the other was a much younger woman a little on the plump side with the type of posture that made you want to tell her to relax, that whatever this was about couldn't possibly be as serious as her rigid carriage and firm stature suggested.

"Lance, come in," Martha greeted me. She had a big smile, more for her two out of town guests than for me. "This is Nancy Toups from the Montana Office of Public Instruction, and this is Diane Fordham from the University of Montana."

I nodded a greeting to each of them and sat. I wished I would have shaved that morning. I typically shaved on Monday, Wednesday and Friday; Monday because I sold ads, Wednesday because I printed the paper and Friday because two days without shaving made me look grubby. I could plainly see in Nancy Toups' eyes she believed I was plenty grubby after one day of not shaving.

Toups was the older woman, and Fordham was younger. I carried a blue plastic notebook that essentially was my Ledger reference guide – the two most recent editions of the Ledger, classified and display advertising rates, work items for the current edition of the Ledger and a list of article and advertising deadlines – and held it on my lap just in case the discussion related to a news article for the paper.

"Mrs. Toups administers the gifted and talented program at OPI, and Ms. Fordham is responsible for the gifted child education curriculum at UM," said Martha. She seemed a little jumpy; she was not the nervous type. She closed her office door behind me; Martha was proud of her open door policy, so whatever this was about, it was oddly but firmly private and meant to be heard only by the four of us.

I set the folder on the floor, under my chair. No doubt this discussion was about Annie. Every discussion in my life involving education and the word *gifted* or *talented* pertained to Annie.

"Did Annie tell you she was given a special series of tests recently?" Martha asked. All three women looked at me.

"I think she mentioned something about that, yeah," I said. Which was at best a guess, and quite possibly an outright lie. Annie hadn't said anything, or if she had, she told me when I wasn't listening – one of my more common parental transgressions. Or perhaps I had listened, and simply had failed to grasp the significance.

I was pretty sure the two ladies were here to tell me the significance.

"Mr. Joslyn," began Mrs. Toups. "Your daughter was given a special set of aptitude and intelligence tests. You had signed the forms authorizing these tests earlier this year."

I nodded as if I remembered. *Oh, those forms,* my nod meant to indicate. But I knew nothing about forms. Annie handled all that.

"Annie's pretty smart," I volunteered. Martha and practically everyone in the Whitehall School District were aware of Annie's impressive intelligence. I, however, knew nothing about any authorizing forms. What's the point of having a smart kid if she can't handle all the forms in your life? She was more or less the Ledger accountant. She could authorize all the forms she wanted.

Mrs. Fordham nodded. "Yes, she is, Mr. Joslyn. She's a very rare child, with a special gift. She's a genius."

"A genius?" I asked. It occurred to me right then that of course Annie was a genius. She had been a genius from the moment the doctor spanked her red-splotched bare bottom the day she was born at St. James. This was the first time, though, the intimidating label of *genius* had ever deliberately and officially been applied to her by someone who actually possessed a working definition of the word.

"She's a rare young woman," Mrs. Fordham assured me.

"The other day she tried to explain how fast in knots you could go and how many fathoms you could go, or something like that, if you had to outswim a shark," I said. "Or maybe fathoms are only used to describe depth." I shrugged. "She got me pretty confused. Knots and fathoms are nautical terms. I learned that much."

Mrs. Fordham's expression indicated she was thinking, *this guy's the parent of a genius?*

Martha held out her hands, as if to calm me down, but I think she was trying to keep herself calm. "Lance, we've always known Annie was an exceptional student. The district used some federal grant monies to contract with OPI and UM to develop the outline of a gifted and talented program for the Whitehall elementary and middle schools. We selected a handful of students to take an initial series of tests to first find out if the curriculum here could even lend itself to a gifted and talented program."

"Well, it can't be a surprise that Annie's a good student," I said. "She gets all A's."

Mrs. Fordham pursed her lips. "I'm not sure you understand, Mr. Joslyn."

"Lance," said Martha, "none of us understood."

"Understood what?" I asked.

"Lance," said Martha, "Annie's intelligence…" but she trailed off.

"Mr. Joslyn," Mrs. Fordham said, "your daughter's tests show she has the intelligence right now to enroll in college."

"Any college," added Mrs. Toups. "Any university in the nation." I got the impression Mrs. Toups was speaking to me only reluctantly, and would rather discuss this, whatever this was, with Annie herself, or at least with someone more intellectual than me.

"She's eleven years old," I told them, all three of them.

"Twelve, actually," corrected Martha gently. "She's twelve years old."

Was that right? I wondered. I wondered for a moment when her last birthday was, and when she was born, but I couldn't recall exactly what year she was born. "Okay," I said, "twelve." I sort of laughed at them. "But still, she's only twelve. You're not saying she should skip junior high and high school and go to college now."

Mrs. Fordham shook her head. "We're suggesting she *could* enroll in college, not she *should* enroll. There are abundant educational, personal, family, cultural and practical considerations here. The purpose of this discussion is not to necessarily pursue a single course of action, but to discuss the multitude of academic options that exist for Annie."

Mrs. Toups leaned forward, to make sure I understood. "Studies show, Mr. Joslyn, that maybe one in ten thousand children have Annie's type of intellect. But studies also show that although this level of intelligence is truly a gift, it is a gift with strings attached, if you will. Gifted children are academically advanced with remarkable intellectual abilities. These intellectual gifts vary greatly. Some children are gifted specifically in academics, or only within precise fields of academics. Some children are gifted musically or artistically, some have an advanced sense of social justice and some demonstrate immediate leadership characteristics. Some have all these traits, or a mixture of them. But gifted children can also be terrifically stubborn, self-absorbed, arrogant, conceited, sarcastic, bored and even show serious personality and behavioral disorders. These children need challenges and respond well to challenges."

"Lance, surely you've always understood Annie was destined to attend college," said Martha. "I'm sure you've already started a college savings account for her."

Not quite, I thought. I'd always *meant* to start a college savings account for her. "Of course," I said.

"Mr. Joslyn, Annie will receive a full scholarship to whatever institution of higher learning she chooses to attend," said Mrs. Toups. "I can just about guarantee that. I'm referring to the best universities in the nation."

"She's *that* smart?" I asked.

Three heads nodded. "I've never seen a child like her," said Martha.

"Her intelligence is rare, there's no doubt about that," said Mrs. Fordham. "Her test scores and her aptitude demonstrate a child who is truly gifted, but I should point out gifted students can struggle within a traditional public school system. They become bored, restless, troublesome. Worse, at times."

"Mr. Joslyn, if your daughter started her senior year of high school next year, in not just Whitehall but virtually any high school in America, she would almost certainly graduate as class valedictorian," said Mrs. Toups.

"Lance, has Annie sounded or acted as if she's bored or resentful about school or her studies?" asked Martha.

I shook my head. "She hasn't said anything to me." Which was true. But I hardly ever saw her. There was no time for her to tell me. Or she had told me, perhaps, but I hadn't been listening.

The two education experts eventually gave me some brochures and reports to read, and received my permission to talk later with Annie if they wanted to, and it was obvious they wanted to. As they placed the information in my hands, they briefly explained what each document contained, and to me it was all somewhat perplexing and overwhelming. As I left the room, Martha recommended I talk with Annie about our discussion, and she said she would discuss Annie's "situation" with other teachers, and meet later with me and Annie's homeroom teacher.

I figured it would be inappropriate to ask – since I didn't know, or had known and forgot – who Annie's homeroom teacher was.

That night during dinner of carryout A&W burgers and onion rings, I told Annie about my meeting in the principal's office.

"Toups struck me as something of an elitist," Annie said between bites of food. "Fordham was gifted and talented herself, and appears quite proud of it."

I wiped up some ketchup with the edge of my burger. "They're both pretty impressed with you."

"Have you ever wondered why I'm so smart?" Annie asked.

Annie wasn't an especially pretty girl, but she was nicely proportioned, with a sleek athletic body, not unlike her mother. Amy had run the 440 and 880 for the MSU women's track team, and Annie looked like she could be a runner. She had an unhurried, confident, graceful stride. At times, earlier in her youth, she could have been mistaken for a boy. But in the past year or so she let her hair grow longer, and although she was only twelve, her body was suggesting hints of budding female adolescence.

"I mean, I'm some kind of freak, if you look at it that way," she said. She loved onion rings. She was only going to eat half her burger – she could never eat a whole cheeseburger – but she was going to eat all her onion rings and most of mine. "I could have been born with a deformed arm, with terrible allergies, a neurological disease, mentally handicapped, a psychopath, blind, transgendered or something like that. Instead I'm a genius. I don't see why anyone should be impressed with that."

"Transgendered?" I asked. "What do you know about transgendered?"

"I'm a genius, remember. You want a tutorial on gender identity, sexual orientation and other culturally unconventional gender roles?"

"Why are you interested in that?"

"I'm not." She picked up an onion ring. "Geniuses know everything. That's what makes us geniuses."

I looked close, but there was no smile. Nor was she bragging. It was a fact. She was a genius. It was as if she had said she had brown hair. She did have brown hair. So what. She was a genius. You want that onion ring?

"I don't think transgendered is actually a word," I said. "I own a newspaper, so I know about words."

"The newspaper owns you," Annie said. "If transgendered isn't actually a word, it should be, or it will be soon."

"Probably not for twelve-year-olds," I suggested.

She tucked a length of hair behind her ear. "I'm not your average twelve-year-old. Think about this. I'm an accident. No one else is my family is smart like me. It's not hereditary. It's not like genius is in the family genes."

"Thanks for that."

"No, really. I'm smart. I know I'm smart. Real smart. But I'm *accidentally* smart. Some kids are left-handed, some have blonde hair, but I'm smart. That's how I was made. I've known that for a long time. Things come easy for me, and I realize that every day at school when I see how things don't come easy for other kids. But a blonde-haired kid usually has a blonde-haired parent. Left-handedness runs in families. Mom was…" she let the thought drift. "You're not a genius. None of my grandparents are smart like me. Tony's no genius. So it all means I'm a freak of nature. Somehow, when I was barely even a fetus floating inside the womb, developing in there day-by-day, week-by-week, some kind of strange concoction of chromosomes arranged themselves and when I was born my brain gave me an instant intellectual advantage over virtually every kid my age."

"I'm not sure chromosomes are actually concocted," I mused.

"Do you really want me to explain genetic codes and chromosomes?" she asked. "It gets real interesting, especially in the context of transgendered infants."

"No," I said. "I just want to eat my cheeseburger." I paused. "What's a fathom?"

"It's a nautical term. Six feet of depth. Why?"

"Does it have anything to do with a knot?" I asked.

"A knot? No. A knot measures speed, either on water or in the air." She scowled at me. "We went over this the other day."

"Want the rest of my onion rings?" I asked.

She reached over and slid them closer to her. "So what else these ladies tell you?"

She had to wait for me to chew my food. That gave me time to think about what I should, and shouldn't, tell her. I ventured a comment that left me exposed and vulnerable, and had the potential to irrevocably alter my life and her future. "They said you could start college in a couple years if you wanted. Maybe sooner. You're smart enough to start right now, actually."

She didn't appear impressed. "College," she mumbled.

"Any college," I said softly. "Any college in America, is what they said. They said you could start what would be your senior year in high school next fall, graduate as valedictorian, and head off to Harvard, if you wanted."

"Harvard?" she said. "Do you know where Harvard is?"

I pointed east.

"Try Massachusetts," she said. "Cambridge. Tell them that's not going to happen."

She had no idea how happy I was to hear that. I tried not to smile, but I couldn't help it. And I also couldn't stop myself from asking, "Why not?"

She was shaking her head even before I finished the two-word question. "I couldn't do that to Tony. Next fall he'll be a sophomore. I couldn't be his little sister, two years ahead of him in high school. Think of the crap his pals would give him about *that*. It wouldn't be fair. Plus, I want to go to high school. High school's supposed to be fun."

"Tony's having fun," I agreed.

"Tony could have fun in a Turkish prison," she said.

"What do you know about Turkish prisons?" I asked.

"What do you want to know about them?" she answered.

"Nothing." I leaned over and hugged her. "You're a good sister."

She allowed me to hug her shoulders, for an instant, then she reached for her plastic cup of root beer. "What else did the ladies tell you?"

"Well, they said genius kids like you are selfish."

Her eyes darkened. "And intolerant. Arrogant. Conceited. Angry. Yeah, I read all the same articles they did."

"Aren't they arrogant at Harvard?" I asked.

"That's what I hear," Annie answered.

We both chewed our food for a moment.

"The two woman said you'd get bored quickly in Whitehall because everything is so easy for you, and that you need a steady supply of intellectual challenges," I said.

"That makes sense, actually," she said. She sat back, looked around and motioned with her hands, as if displaying our kitchen. "But lucky for me I possess challenges galore around here. I'm the head of this household, you know."

Oh, I knew.

"Think about it," she said. "I have to be Tony's little sister and mom, which is a neat trick, not to get all Oedipus-like on you. In many ways, my role is more your mother than your daughter. I mean, I take care of you, and you know it. I'm the only kid in sixth grade who balances the family check book, makes out the weekly grocery list, does the grocery shopping, pays the bills and handles the meager collection of investments. Plus I'm the Ledger bookkeeper, accountant and financial planner. Do you even know what a dividend is?

She was right. It wasn't as if I required her to take on these duties, or demanded she assume these roles. She had more or less gravitated to those responsibilities, probably in pursuit of additional challenges, and she excelled at all of them. And I only vaguely knew what a dividend was.

"Let's face it, Lance, you're not big into this whole parental thing, are you?"

I lowered my eyes, and my head. So it came to this. My daughter couldn't head off to college at age thirteen because she refused to embarrass her older brother, and because her father wouldn't be able to function without her.

Her reality, I should have told her, bore no relation to her destiny.

The first true summer-like day in spring 1986 occurred on the first weekend in May, perfectly timed for the weekend of the Whitehall B-Y's 4-H Club Youth Rodeo. The weather was warm enough in the morning to suggest the possibility of uncomfortable heat in the afternoon, and winter coats and vests were discarded early in the day for thin western shirts and rolled up sleeves.

Rodeos are a photographer's dream, and youth rodeos are even better. You can't beat cowboy kids atop fleet ponies. Youth contestants in junior high and high school competed in the traditional rodeo rituals – barrel racing, calf roping, team roping, bull dogging – during a long, leisurely day at the Whitehall rodeo grounds, and it was a relatively simple task to take enough action and feature photos to fill two inside pages of the Ledger plus a large action photo that dominated the front page. Rodeo riders came from all over central and western Montana to compete, and I tried to blend in photos of Whitehall and Jefferson Valley kids with cowboys and cowgirls from distant places to showcase the geographic pull of the event and, I'll admit it, to sell papers. It seemed like the rodeo contestants were one big family who traveled from town to town and arena to arena, and if a kid from a town like Helmville got his picture in the Ledger we were sure to sell a half dozen extra papers when the Helmville parents found out – and they always found out – about the photo.

In past years, the little cowboys and cowgirls had ridden and roped through snow flurries, sleet, bitter gusty winds and driving rain, but this year they were removing their hats and wiping the sweat off their foreheads with the elbow of their long-sleeve cowboy shirts, and the flanks and necks of their horses glistened with sweat.

I appreciated and respected the cowboy culture, but I could never be a part of it. I bought me some cowboy boots once, and I bought me a cowboy hat. But the cowboy look didn't feel right, and I realized that in Montana you needed to earn a cowboy hat by roping or riding or moving cattle, and the first time I was on a horse years ago during a power company junket to the Bob Marshall Wilderness, I knew it would be the last time I'd ever be on a horse. I'm pretty sure the horse knew it too.

There were probably a couple hundred rodeo contestants – each of them wearing the mandated western shirt, cowboy hat and western jeans – and another couple hundred parents, relatives and spectators – most of them also wearing a western shirt, cowboy hat and western jeans – and me, wearing a WHS baseball cap, green Ledger tee-shirt, baggy jeans and hiking boots. It was clear I didn't belong there, which was okay, because the guy with the camera, I learned long ago, wasn't expected to fit in.

When you're a photographer, I realized early on, the sheer nature of your assignment separates you from everyone else. There was only one newspaper in Whitehall, and only one photographer. Everyone else was an observer or a participant; I recorded that participation and that observation. But as a photographer I did not participate and I did not observe the way everyone else did. At times, parents brought cameras to a rodeo, but they took poor pictures, while I took professional photos. Or, to be honest, supposedly took professional photos. Photography wasn't my specialty. I knew a good photograph when I saw one, and marveled at the photos in magazines like Sports Illustrated and National Geographic. But just because I knew a good photograph when I saw one didn't mean I could actually take a good photograph when I needed one.

My pictures were passable. Acceptable. I was a weekly newspaper publisher with a quality Canon 35-millimeter camera who took pictures that were three steps above pictures taken by parents with Instamatics. Step one was I had a better camera with a bigger lens. Step two was I always placed myself in a better position to take the picture. Step three was more secret and most important: I took *a lot* of pictures. What I lacked in talent I attempted to make up with sheer volume. For the B-Y's rodeo I would shoot over two hundred pictures, and would use maybe ten or twelve for the paper. I used black and white film only – color photography and full color pictures for the Ledger were too complicated, too slow at the printing plant, and too expensive – and tried to position myself as often as possible to take pictures where the sun lit up the faces of the rodeo riders.

Most of the time I stayed inside the arena near the rough stock chutes and hugged the fence line, with the sun at my back. As often as possible, I tried to stay close to a gate in case a quick escape was required. Two years earlier at a B-Y's youth rodeo a young male rider lost control of his horse in the pole bending competition, and three times he and the horse stampeded within a whisker of me. Twice as the frantic boy rode past me, a look of terror in his eyes as his horse galloped around the arena, he apologized as he stormed by me. "Sorry, sorry, sorry," he said as his horse ran north to south down the arena, and "Sorry, sorry, sorry" he moaned again as the horse ran back south to north before it was finally caught and gathered by the pickup men.

Another benefit of shooting photos along the fence was during down times I could visit with the parents and spectators who sat in lawn chairs in the end of flatbed pickups just outside the arena fence. If I was lucky, a parent or acquaintance would even offer me a cold beer or two to sip as the rodeo lengthened through the morning into the afternoon and approached early evening.

And I got lucky. During the barrel race, in which a rider navigates a pattern around a trio of barrels, Mandy Williams, or Mandy Phillips or whatever her last name was at the moment, the mom of Whitehall sophomore Cody Phillips, said I looked like I needed a cold beer. I admitted I probably did.

"Looks pretty goddamn dusty in there, Lance," she slurred. Mandy had apparently been drinking all day.

She worked off and on at the Whitehall hardware store and had two kids – boys in high school in both Whitehall and Harrison – with two different husbands, and was, apparently, single again. I had seen her at the spring high school music concert with a guy I hadn't ever seen before, then saw her a night or two later uptown at the Mint Bar with Gene Fenderson, a local rancher who, quite frankly, ought to have known better. At the rodeo she looked to be seated next to Ronny Kamp, a former rodeo cowboy who ranched somewhere up the North Boulder Valley.

"I think a cold beer would be an excellent idea," I agreed.

Mandy reached inside the cooler hidden in the shade under the pickup truck's opened tailgate, and handed me an ice cold Coors Light. Mandy barrel-raced at the county fair rodeo and in some of the area O-Mok-Sees and had the classic look of a rodeo queen a few years past her prime. Mandy looked young, until you looked close. The dyed blonde hair wasn't quite natural, the eye makeup was pasted on a little thick, the rump too wide and she had two buttons undone on her shirt that probably should have stayed buttoned. If you were a red-blooded male, she drew your attention, and if you had an ounce of brains, you then looked the other way.

Ronny Kamp maybe had an ounce of brains when sober, which had been the case maybe three or four hours earlier. A cigarette hung from the corner of his mouth, and when he greeted me my name came out *Lanch.* There was little doubt if I ventured uptown tonight I'd find Ronny and Mandy rubbing belt buckles on the dance floor at Borden's, two-stepping to a poor rendition of a bad song by the Statler Brothers. I had no plans to wander toward the bars tonight, but then again when it came to me and bars plans hardly ever had anything to do with it.

"Shit, isht hot," said Ronny. Ronny needed a shave and a shower – especially a shower – and probably a change of clothes. He wore his western shirt unbuttoned and open in front, with a tight black tee-shirt underneath. When he was sober, you always kind of thought he should have amounted to more than a struggling and broken down Boulder Valley hired hand, and when he was drunk you kind of thought he was lucky to have mostly stayed out of prison.

"Thanks for the beer," I told both Mandy and Ronny.

Ronny waved off the comment and more or less collapsed back into the lawn chair. Mandy stood along the fence; we were separated by just barely more than the thin rusted wire of the arena fence. She stood too close and talked too loud.

"Is the steer ridin' next?" she asked.

"Yeah," I said. "Right after the barrel racing. Cody riding?"

She nodded. "Hell, yeah. This is his fourth year…maybe his fifth year, ridin' steers here." She turned to Ronny. "Hey Ronny, is this Cody's fourth year or fifth year ridin' steers?"

Ronny had no clue. He couldn't possibly have had a clue. He had only been hanging around Mandy for a week and his attention probably never waived beyond her body. He probably couldn't even pick out Cody from a lineup of two kids. Mandy could have asked Ronny how many kilometers away the moon was and got a better answer.

"Howshd I know?" Ronny said candidly.

Cody and Tony were both sophomores in high school. They mostly ran in different crowds, but in a class with less than fifty kids all the classmates knew each other and most parents knew most kids in the class. Cody was a fair wrestler but not much of a student. He chewed tobacco, and when he wrestled the sweat would bathe his body in the scent of strained tobacco.

Chewing was against school policy and athletic training rules, but a student had to be actually caught with a chew in his mouth, not just smelling like it, to be in actual noncompliance. Plus, if push came to shove, chewing was perhaps one of the more innocent school policies and athletic training rules Cody routinely violated.

Tony was an above average student, played the trumpet in the school band, had acted in a couple of the school plays and played football and basketball for the Rangers. Wrestlers were a different breed; not worse, just different.

Ronny pulled his hat down over his eyes. A true rodeo fan, he intended to nap during the barrel racing. He probably needed a quick rest to gather a second wind, because he probably understood Mandy had certain expectations for later that evening, and the fulfillment of those expectations depended on Ronny's stamina and focus, which given Ronny's condition may have been considered questionable.

Mandy saw it, and shook her head. "I'm gonna have to cut him off," she said, more to herself than me.

I finished the beer, but didn't let Mandy know because I didn't want another one. The sun had moved east to south to west during the day, and the rough stock chutes were lined up on the east side of the arena. That meant to get the sun behind me, I had to stand in pretty much the center of the arena, and I wasn't completely comfortable out there. Rough stock animals – steers, cows, horses and bulls – depending on the rodeo and the age and experience of the riders, scared me to the point that more than once I feared I'd end up trampled or gored. Bulls stormed out of the chute stomping, jumping, snorting, twisting, snotting, shitting and kicking, and acted as if after they discarded the rider they wanted to kill the first person they saw. Sometimes that first person was me. I was the person in the arena who least belonged in there and knew least what to do if attacked. I figured I was supposed to run and duck and dodge, but I couldn't out-run or out-maneuver a bull. And I was pretty sure bulls knew it. I wasn't a cowboy. I wasn't a bullfighter. I wasn't a rough stock rider. I was barely a photographer.

And, I knew, had I been trampled or gored, a handful of spectators would be mildly amused by my misfortune. Their amusement wouldn't necessarily be malicious or insulting, but clutching a camera, wearing hiking boots and a baseball cap, it was patently obvious I didn't belong out there among the rough stock and at a real rodeo, and if I wasn't smart enough to get out of the way, that was my problem. Other rodeo fans would lament my getting trampled or gored because it would take time to carry me out of the arena, and rodeo fans disliked delays.

Fortunately, because the B-Y's rodeo was for youths, the rough stock was regular ranch steers, not colossal man-stomping bulls. So I was safer, and a little more confident in front of the chutes now than I was during the annual summer Frontier Days NRA Rodeo, where when the gate swung open bulls with names like *Widowmaker* and *Maneater* and *Psycho* come roaring out.

"Over there, isn't that the teacher…Jersey?" asked Mandy.

I followed her line of sight to the south, past the holding pens and the chutes for the timed event stock. I saw a tallish, slim man walking around the southeast corner of the arena, through and past the gathering band of team ropers.

"Could be," I said.

As he approached, it looked like the guy the kids called Jersey, but his real name was Jerry Conte. I didn't really know him, but did know he'd been a student teacher in the middle school this semester. Lyle had mentioned the school board was likely to hire him during the May school board meeting as the new junior high science and geography teacher and maybe junior varsity football coach. The high school and middle school kids usually harassed and horrified student teachers, in no small part because student teachers lacked the experience and confidence to be disciplinarians, even when necessary, and no one can sense weakness faster than a group of junior high kids.

Annie had Conte – or Jersey or whatever they called him – for a class, geography or geology or something like that, and she seemed to have no quarrel with him. Not all of Annie's teachers were as lucky. Annie could be somewhat disagreeable, especially when she'd been younger, and it could be argued that while Annie's genes supplied an overabundance of intelligence, the tolerance gene may have been somewhat shortchanged. Over the years – simply though passage of time – Annie has grown less weary of my perpetual shortcomings and her brother's lethargy, but she consistently expected – demanded – competency from professionals such as educators. She must have gotten competency from Mr. Conte, because two or three times in conversations she brought him up in passively positive ways, and although he didn't know it, that was a serious compliment.

As I watched him navigate through the group of horses and ropers, he walked at ease, as if he was comfortable around horses and cowboys. At rodeos I walked in perpetual fear of getting kicked by a horse, and I gave any horse – every horse – a wide berth if I walked behind it. And I knew, as I did it, every single rodeo fan who saw me knew I was afraid of horses. Mr. Conte strolled through the maze of nervous riders and restless ponies almost as if they weren't even there.

"I think he's here to see Cody," Mandy told me, holding her hand at her brow, in a type of salute, to block the sun. "I think he called the house last night."

"Your house?" I asked.

"Yeah," Mandy said. "Cody wasn't home. I think it was him who called. He asked if Cody was riding in the rodeo, and I said yeah, and he said thanks and hung up."

"He doesn't look like the rodeo type," I offered, squinting toward the sun as he walked out of sight behind a row of parked pickups.

"No shit," said Mandy. "Looks more like a preacher."

That wouldn't have been my observation, but it was possible Mandy had limited knowledge about what clergy actually looked likc. Her statement was likely based more on speculation than experience.

Thirty seconds later Mr. Conte approached the arena fence, and stood alongside Mandy. I may not have dressed like I belonged at a rodeo, but Jersey wasn't dressed like he even belonged in Montana. He wore a tight black tee-shirt, and a shiny gold necklace hung just low enough to contrast the shirt. He wore black jeans, black dress shoes, like loafers or something, and he had short dark hair with dark sideburns that went down lower than his ear. He wore sunglasses that were thin and horizontal dark boxes in front of his eyes. I had never seen anything like them. I thought it was possible no one in a Rocky Mountain state wore that style of shades.

Behind him, Ronny rustled a bit, and rubbed his eyes. "Ishat Johnny Cash?" he grunted, and then softly chuckled at his own wit.

"Jerry," was the answer. "Jerry Conte. People around here seem to like calling me Jersey." He reached over and shook Ronny's hand. A moment later Ronny burped, stood unsteadily, and staggered off, leaning toward the port-a-potties.

Jersey looked at me, and I nodded a greeting. "Lance Joslyn."

"He owns the paper," interjected Mandy. "I'm Mandy Brockton. Cody's mom. Cody Phillips." Her flirting was obvious, and it appeared quick as a spark.

Brockton, I thought. Mandy's last name changed more often than the seasons. I wondered if Brockton was her maiden name or if she'd been married briefly, and recently, to some guy named Brockton.

Jersey shook her hand but returned his gaze my direction. He had a gentle expression, as if he was slightly and sincerely impressed, or perhaps interested, in me.

"Lance Joslyn? You're Annie's father," Jersey said. Something about the way he said *father,* like *fahrthar,* announced an accent from a far away land. New Jersey, was my insightful guess.

"Oh, Annie," scoffed Mandy. "The brain."

Jersey seemed to ignore Mandy, on oddity among men. Mandy worked overtime to be noticed.

"Yeah," I said. "I hope she hasn't caused you any trouble.

"Oh no, on the contrary," said Jersey, which was undoubtedly the first time the phrase *on the contrary* had ever been uttered in Whitehall Rodeo Grounds. Again, something in the word *contrary* was a tipoff he wasn't from here. He smiled, a warm, considerate smile. "You must be very proud of her." The word *proud* didn't sound right. *Prahoid.*

I looked down, embarrassed I suppose, to accept a compliment for something I had nothing to do with.

"She's such a brain," Mandy said again, and sort of snorted, as if to close the subject. She seemed offended that two semi-youthful and apparently single men – one to her left and one right in front of her – were essentially ignoring her.

"Oh, she's far more than that," Jersey said quietly. "She's a gifted, thoughtful, kind and caring young woman. I thoroughly enjoy her in the classroom."

"Thanks," I said, because I didn't know what else to say. Mandy'd had enough. "You here to watch Cody ride?"

Jersey nodded. "Yes, ma'am. I hear he's quite the cowboy."

Mandy laughed. "He's practically been ridin' since the day he was born."

"And he's a wrestler, too, I hear," said Jersey.

"Fourth in state this year at one-nineteen as a sophomore," Mandy announced. Mandy was impossible to miss at a wrestling match. Loud, inebriated, gaudy, tinted blonde hair, she screamed her cheers not so much to encourage Cody, I always thought, as to encourage attention to herself.

"I wonder if Cody has ever thought about playing football," Jersey said.

She thought about it for an instant. "He ain't ever played," she said. "I suppose he's got chores around the ranch, and we ship cattle in the fall. Plus there's high school rodeo in the fall."

"Do you think he might be interested in playing high school football?" Jersey asked.

Mandy shrugged; I noticed what the shrug did beneath the tight shirt as the fabric stretched across her breasts, and Mandy noticed I noticed. "You'd have to ask him. I don't see how he'd have time for football."

Jersey nodded.

The rodeo announcer cheerfully proclaimed from the crow's nest that barrel racing was concluded and it was time for the steer riding competition, a crowd favorite because – from my viewpoint – there was a pretty good chance someone was going to get injured, which to me seemed the whole point of riding rough stock: Wear a cowboy hat and risk serious injury.

There were only three steer riders, and Cody was third to ride. I nodded a departure toward Jersey and Mandy, and headed out toward the center of the arena, with the sun at my back. Jersey remained alongside Mandy, and then I noticed Ronny was on his feet, standing on the other side of her, his hands head level draped over the fence. Mandy had to be pleased, I thought, literally surrounded by men, with her son about to take center stage in the arena.

The first cowboy slid off the steer immediately out of the chute, before his name was even announced and before I could get even a single photo. The next rider, a kid from Choteau, hung on for the full eight seconds, and then jumped off a moving, bucking live 600-pound steer as nimbly as hopping out of a stationary flatbed pickup. The scattered fans and parents gave him a nice round of applause. I took three pictures in eight seconds, and figured one of them had to be good enough to publish.

Cody was in the chute waiting as the previous steer was chased into the holding pen at the northeast corner of the arena. Cody wore a tan cowboy hat and a faded red shirt that had what looked like golden Indian symbols dancing across his chest. He wore that grim, intense expression common to all rough stock riders as he gathered himself, as the gatemen prepared the steer, in the final peaceful moments before the gate swung open for what people liked to call the kick and the spin.

"Our final steer rider is a Whitehall cowboy named Cody Phillips, and he's drawn himself a bad boy they call Cyclone," broadcast Bill Brown, the arena announcer. Steers didn't have real rodeo names like bulls or broncs did, but the names of danger, mayhem and destruction added drama to the ride.

"Com'on Cody!" screamed Mandy.

I focused on Cody, watched him give the final hopeful abrupt tense nod – *let's go* – and the gate swung open. The steer sprinted four or five sudden strides to his right – click, went my camera – and then swung its rear end around to the left as it bucked his rear legs high off the ground – click. Cody overcompensated by keeping his weight to his right – click – and when the steer twisted around to the right and bucked, Cody's weight was distributed outside the steer's mass, and Cody went flying – click – off the steer's right side. There were two rodeo bullfighters in the arena who both moved immediately – click – toward the steer and Cody, but they were a heartbeat too late. The rear legs of the steer landed flush – click – on Cody's lower back not once but twice, and the collective anguished and horrified moan from the audience was followed by total and absolute silence.

Mandy yelped as the steer stomped away from the stricken body.

One of the bullfighters knelt over Cody's body as the other bullfighter chased the steer further away. No one made a sound; it was so quiet I heard the gate at the metallic stock pen click shut when it closed after the steer was herded back into the holding pen. Mandy stood straight, rigid, her hands over her mouth, her focus on the bullfighter who hovered above her motionless and prone son. Cody laid face down in the arena dirt, his hat upside down about five feet away. A couple cowboys were running awkwardly from behind the chutes to aid the stricken cowboy unmoving on the ground. Then I noticed Jersey in the arena, already on his knees, already leaned frontward over Cody's upper torso.

He was dressed almost exactly the opposite of a rodeo cowboy – no hat, short sleeve shirt, clothes all the same dark color, jewelry around his neck – yet somehow, it didn't look like he felt out of place. I knew I looked out of place at a rodeo, and I knew I felt out of place at a rodeo, and I knew I looked like I felt out of place at a rodeo. But Jersey acted like he thought he belonged at a rodeo and now he acted as if he belonged in the arena at Cody's side.

The crowd remained quiet, and I moved a few steps toward Cody to see if I could determine the extent of his injuries. The only sounds I picked up were soft murmurs of whispering from Jersey or the bullfighters, and Mandy's whimpering off to my right. Mandy held Ronny's hand tight, more for show, I thought, than comfort.

The ambulance attendants scurried awkwardly across the uneven arena dirt-clumped ground and flopped to their knees next to Jersey and the bullfighters. The crowd was silent.

Everyone inside the arena, except for me, was crouched around Cody. I was a recorder, not a participant, and stayed a respectful distance away.

Rodeo crowds had seen pain and blood before; the cowboy motionless on the arena dirt, his hat laying empty on the ground, the initial medical response from a bullfighter, a quick follow up response by the local volunteer ambulance attendants, and more often than not, a stretcher, the body strapped immobile, the earnest vocal encouragement from the announcer to give the fallen cowboy a hand, and finally the flashing light of an ambulance as it rolled away from the arena. And I know rodeo crowds would take offense at this observation, but the unadorned truth was a large percentage of the audience had this thought in mind: Come on, get him out of the arena and get the rodeo started again.

Just before the ambulance attendants arrived, I caught a stirring of Cody's leg, and then some fingers. The ambulance attendants talked softly, calmly, to him a little longer – and apparently asked him to move various parts of his body, because soon the other leg and other arm moved – and then Cody sat up – applause – then stood up, helped up by Jersey – more applause – and then walked with a slight limp out of the arena, out the gate near the announcer's booth, into the dramatic waiting arms of his mother.

"That's one tough hombre, ladies and gentleman," cried Bill Brown through the loudspeaker. "Yes sir, they grow 'em tough here in Whitehall, Montana. Let's hear a big round of applause for Cody Phillips."

The crowd roared its approval, and then it was time for the final round of team roping.

Chapter 4

The worst day of the week for the Whitehall weekly newspaper publisher is Monday, and the worst Monday of the month is the second Monday – the night of the town council meeting.

Mondays are unpleasant because of one simple fact: There's too much work and not enough time to do it.

To help compensate for that dilemma, I usually got to work about six in the morning and usually stayed until early Tuesday morning. Home by Monday midnight was a typical goal, and typically didn't happen.

A first task on most Mondays was developing rolls of black and white film, and in 1986 that meant – in total blackness in the darkroom – rolling the film onto the metal film spools. Then set a timer for the developer and then the fix – unpleasant liquid chemicals that needed to be agitated properly – and finally rinse and dry the film.

It was after seven o'clock that Monday morning when I quickly scanned the rodeo film to see if I had anything good and as I held the 35 millimeter black and white negatives against the light it was clear there were a decent batch of useable shots, including a good one of Cody just before he and the steer had abruptly parted company. I scanned the next few frames and it looked – just by scanning the negative – that the steer had speared both its rear hooves in the small of Cody's back. Cody's upper body and legs were off the ground, with his lower body pinned to the ground in a kind of wide and shallow U-shape by the steer's back legs, which looked absolutely planted in the center of Cody's back. Yet Cody had stood and walked out of the arena. I shook my head. Cody was one incredibly tough kid, one lucky kid, or both.

By eight-thirty – there'd been no trip home to see the kids off to school – I had written articles about the rodeo, about the upcoming high school graduation and a short article about an upcoming meeting related to Golden Sunlight Mine's planned expansion. I had gone through Saturday's mail and weekend faxes to help Laura Joyce get started when she arrived. The Ledger's office hours were eight-thirty to five-thirty, Monday through Friday, and while the office was usually a busy place, no day was busier than Monday, deadline day.

Monday was chaos. Monday was the day the Ledger made its money. The more chaos, the more money, so in a way, we encouraged chaos. We sought chaos. We embraced chaos, even when the chaos overwhelmed us. Monday was the day people brought in and called in classified ads, brought in articles about anniversaries, meetings, community events, fundraisers and all the other community happenings that make a community a community. The more, the better. The more, the bigger the workload. The more, the longer into Tuesday morning I worked. During an average Monday there was a steady stream of people coming and going from the Ledger, and virtually every minute of every average Monday I was unavoidably behind schedule.

From a business income standpoint, it was a good problem to have. From a personal standpoint, it was frustrating and at times exhausting. There was simply not enough time, which made any waste of time – any needless interruption of work – exasperating. Yet, on Mondays, these wastes of time and needless interruptions were merciless and constant. At about eight-twenty, I opened the Ledger office window curtains, switched the cardboard *CLOSED* sign in the window to the *OPEN* sign, unlocked the front door, and was ready for business.

Laura Joyce arrived at eight-thirty sharp. She was punctual by habit, and she had been around the Ledger long enough to know what Mondays were like. She knew when she woke up every Monday work was already waiting for her, and she knew the work would pile up if she didn't get to it and get it done. My Tuesday schedule depended upon her accomplishing her Monday work something close to on time. Other days the flow of work was more predictable and less demanding; Mondays we were slaves to a relentless workflow we had no way to control.

"Morning," Laura Joyce called out when she arrived. One of her best traits was her cheerful disposition. I had always hoped she would take a little more responsibility at the paper and perhaps expand her duties to include some of the photography and writing, but she showed no interest in expanding her hours or duties. But she knew everybody in town, everybody liked her, she could type, she was responsible, and she was honest.

"How was your weekend?" I asked.

"Good," she said. She was already seated in front of her typesetter and organizing her desk basket of work. "Bud's cousin and wife are here from North Dakota. We went down to Virginia City on Saturday."

Laura Joyce had uttered one of my favorite Montana truisms when not long after she started working at the Ledger I asked her casually what Bud's real name was. She laughed and told me there were three things you never asked a Montanan: How many acres does he have, how many cattle does he have, and to a guy named Bud, what his real name is.

"How about you?" she asked. Her head was down, reading through the work awaiting her. She would arrange it by priority and length.

"Not much. Rodeo on Sunday," I said.

"We took Bud's cousin and wife to Borden's for dancing yesterday afternoon and they had a ball," Laura Joyce said. "God, was it hot in there."

"Yeah, it was hot at the rodeo too," I said. This was likely to be the first of a couple dozen Monday conversations in the Ledger about the weather.

"Bud's cousin's name is Skip, and we gave him a little tour of the town before we went to Borden's, and we saw everyone over at the rodeo grounds," she said. "Skip and Darlene loved Virginia City and the mountains and all, but they didn't think much of Whitehall." She frowned. "They thought the town was kind of dumpy."

"It might be," I said, "but it's located in Montana. That automatically makes it better than anything in North Dakota."

She laughed, which was a welcome addition to her best trait. She liked to laugh, and would seemingly laugh at anything you told her. "That's what Bud told them. But then Skip said he wasn't going to tolerate any more North Dakota jokes from someone who lived in a town without curbs and gutters."

Skip from North Dakota had us there. Whitehall was ninety-seven years old, in the beginning stages of planning the town's 1989 centennial anniversary, and after existing for nearly a century it still had a lengthy list of gravel streets. Curbs and gutters existed only on the state-funded and maintained Legion Avenue, the main east-west route through town. I wrote an editorial once endorsing new curbs and gutters throughout town and got absolutely zero support from anyone. We did get a letter to the editor from an elderly resident and town council member named Old Tom Langston who wrote that Whitehall didn't need and couldn't afford curbs and gutters, and that if I thought curbs and gutters were so darn pretty I should go back to California. Which made no sense, since I had never once set foot in California. I guess Old Tom's point was crazy ideas like curbs and gutters had to originate in crazy places like California, therefore I must have too. As a council member Old Tom opposed every expenditure of funds every time at every meeting. I would see Old Tom later at the town council meeting, and watch him vote no every chance he got, but first I had to go sell some advertising.

The Ledger made three-quarters of its income from display advertising, classified ads and grocery store inserts, and while the classified ads walked in the door – usually on Monday – and the grocery store inserts showed up seemingly by magic at the printing plant each Wednesday, display advertising had to be pried from business owners and religiously and tenderly gathered during a full Monday morning of ad stops.

I had thirteen stops to make – the bank, the convenience store, the hardware store, three restaurants or cafes, the grocery store, the Ford dealer, two agricultural supply stores, the tire shop, the flower shop, and the drug store – and had to get them done before noon. When my ad stops spilled over into the afternoon, and I grew irretrievably behind schedule, I grew more irritable and was essentially forced to fully abandon my kids until the following day, a Tuesday, in which I would only mostly abandon them.

So the trick during my ad stops was to be friendly, chat momentarily at each business, and get a decision about an ad. I was a lousy salesman, and didn't even try to talk anyone into placing an ad. I showed up, told them if anything special was going on that week that would boost the paper's circulation, talked a little about what kind of seasonal or special incentives their business might be offering, and left with or without an ad. A couple years earlier I attended a Montana Press Association workshop on advertising sales, and the instructor told us to design ads in advance of the ad stop, with the belief if the business owner saw an ad he or she was less likely to reject an ad recommendation. I didn't do that for three reasons: One, I didn't have time to design ads that might not run in the paper; two, that was a lot of pressure to put on my fellow Whitehall business owners; three, I was nowhere near that organized.

Selling advertising was a major part of my week, and generating income was a principal objective each week. I kept track each week of advertising inches, classified ad revenue, number of inserts and circulation sales, and was supremely motivated to make as much profit as possible from fifty-two editions of the Ledger each year. Yet, I had no idea about money management or the value of accumulating revenue. I almost never carried money, was largely ignorant of my bank account and had no care about earthly possessions. Annie served as my accountant and financial advisor and my indifference to the money I so diligently and so painfully earned each week was perpetually maddening to her.

My first ad stop each Monday was Whitehall State Bank. The bank advertised each week, and I had to get to Lyle early in the day, before his series of meetings, appointments and phone calls got in full swing. Lyle and the bank were supportive of the newspaper, and contributed to every special section or special edition we ever produced.

Lyle was reviewing a folder when I knocked on his office door, and he beckoned me in. "Monday," he said, "isn't it."

"All day," I said, and sat in a chair in front of his desk. It was nine-ten. I needed to be out of the bank by nine-twenty. It helped that Lyle was almost as busy as I was.

"Think it's going to be hot as it was yesterday?" Lyle asked me.

"Doubt it," I said. I opened a file I had with me that contained previous bank ads. I showed him the Ledger from this same week one year earlier, since banks tended to run ads based on cyclical activities and seasonal promotions like home loans, agriculture loans, or college savings accounts.

He looked at the ad from a year earlier. "You hear about Wally Hope?" he asked me. The question was put to me glumly.

I shook my head; an admission of failure. I always figured as the newspaper publisher, I was supposed to have heard about everything and everyone before anyone else heard. I had no news about Wally Hope, and my job was to have the news about Wally Hope. It was apparent that whatever Lyle was going to say next about Wally Hope, it wasn't going to be good. Could it be possible, I wondered, that Wally Hope had died?

"He took a job in Circle, as principal." Lyle, as school board chairman, was obviously not happy about that.

"Circle?" I felt utterly deflated.

"There goes our new football coach," Lyle muttered. "The old coach dies, and then the new coach moves to Circle. Personally, if those are the options, I'll take dead."

Montanans who live along or west of the Continental Divide – the mountains – look at eastern Montana with a special mix of distain and arrogance that for the most part is unfounded. Eastern Montana is drier and flatter than our mountain-and-valley section of Montana, but eastern Montana possesses a unique special beauty western Montana can't touch. As a kid I had camped on a bluff above the Yellowstone River somewhere around Glendive. I awoke in the middle of the night, and when I stepped out of the tent to take a leak I looked around and saw nothing but stars surrounding me. It was like I was inside one of those small handheld glass enclosures that you shake up and watch snow fall. I had never seen stars like that before, or since.

"Why?" I asked.

"Have you ever *seen* Circle?" Lyle asked.

"No," I said. "Why is he leaving Whitehall? He was just hired as head football coach?"

"It's a step up administratively, I suppose, to a principal's job," said Lyle. "And there's retirement. Teacher retirement is based on the last three years of salary, and he's getting a couple thousand dollars more per year in Circle. But good Christ, *it's Circle*. There is no possible redeeming feature in or near Circle, Montana."

Lyle was blustering as the school board chair, upset someone had the audacity to depart the luxurious pastures of the Jefferson Valley for, in his mind, the godforsaken plains of McCone County. The departure of a teacher and a coach meant more work for Lyle, and like most school boards in most school districts, his worry was more athletic than academic.

"That leaves us without a head coach or an assistant coach," groused Lyle.

Which wasn't good. People willing to or able to coach high school football in small towns like Whitehall were a fairly rare commodity.

"What about that Jersey guy?" Lyle ventured.

"What about him?"

"Can he coach?" Lyle asked.

"I have no idea."

Lyle shrugged. "Me either. He applied to be the assistant coach and was the only applicant, so we're stuck with him. But it would be nice to know if he knows anything about football. He looks like an oddball to me." Lyle paused, pointed to the Ledger from a year ago. "Go ahead and run that one." Meaning the bank ad from a year ago was okay to run this week. "But we're still short a head coach."

I'd done a little article about him when he joined the school as a student teacher, but I didn't recall anything special about him.

Lyle folded his arms across his chest. "I saw him at the spring school concert the other night and I gotta tell you, the guy looks like a mafia hit man. Dressed all in black, big gold chain around his neck. I heard he was at the rodeo."

I nodded.

"The rodeo? What the hell was he doing there? Does he even know the front end of a horse from the back end?"

"I got the impression he's not much of a rodeo guy," I said. "It looked to me like he was there to recruit Cody Phillips to play football."

Lyle expressed surprise. "The hell." He nodded once. "Cody Phillips ought to play football, now that I think about it." He hesitated. "Provided he can stay out of jail." Lyle leaned forward, his elbows on the desk. "Since when do Whitehall football coaches recruit anybody? One reason we've been so shitty is because half the kids who could or should play football don't."

My time was short, I had the ad, and it was time to move on. I stood up.

Lyle looked at me slyly. "See Mandy there?"

"Mandy?" I hesitated. "Yeah. Why?"

"Who was she with?"

I snorted, and grinned. "Exactly what business is that of yours?"

"Ronny Kamp?" he guessed, and I nodded. "Tell me that ain't a train wreck waiting to happen."

By ten-thirty I had four more ad stops completed – three ads approved and one friendly rejection – and got to the grocery store, located at the far western edge of town on Highway 2. My first five years in Whitehall the IGA had been owned by a local man who simply refused to advertise in the local newspaper, in part, I think, because he was upset the Ledger imported and inserted fliers from three Butte grocery stores – Buttrey's, Albertsons and Safeway – plus the Osco Drug Store insert.

But a few years earlier the store had been purchased by a young couple who'd previously worked in grocery stores over in Missoula. Mary and Ryan Jones had freshened and updated the store with a new shiny hard tile floor and a bright new lighting system, and like the bank, were weekly advertisers in the paper and supported virtually every community cause in town. Mary seemed to supervise the employees, and Ryan took care of the advertising. Ryan was an avid hunter, and the walls of his tiny office in the back of the store were covered with photos of him and animals he'd shot.

On good Mondays, he had a rough layout of the ad drawn up and sitting on his desk, and all I had to do was pick it up. I made my way through the store, nodding greetings to the half dozen shoppers I knew, and found Ryan in his office, on the telephone. I poked my head in, so he knew I was there, and then backed out. There's an unwritten rule somewhere that says: No matter what a business owner is doing, it is without doubt more important than talking to an advertising salesman.

But Ryan didn't keep me waiting long. He came flying out of his office, apologized for the delay – which was nearly no delay at all – and gave me the ad layout. Our habit then was for him to walk me to the front of the store. We were both business owners, both nominal community leaders, and it was good for us to compare notes to start each week. Ryan was a little older than me, black hair and a dark complexion, with a black mustache that reminded me somehow of Zorro.

"You look like you got a little sun over the weekend," Ryan said.

In fact, I had noticed my face showed a tinge of pink. It was mystifying to me how I could attempt to have the sun at my back all day taking pictures at a rodeo, and still end up with a sunburned face. "Hot day at the rodeo."

"Oh, yeah, Mary was there too," Ryan said. Mary had been an EMT in Missoula and was one of the Whitehall ambulance attendants.

"Yeah, I saw her when one of the rough stock riders almost got stomped by a steer," I said.

Ryan didn't say a word until we reached the front of the store, near the courtesy counter, which sat in front of the store's entrance.

"She told me about that," Ryan said. "The Phillips kid, right?"

I nodded. "Yeah, I took pictures, and this morning developed the film. I swear one negative shows the rear legs of that steer planted in the small of Cody's back."

Ryan nodded. "Mary said Cody's shirt was torn in back where the hooves or whatever landed flush on his spine. The kid's shirt was ripped – just sliced open – and Mary said she could see the smeared dirt where the hoof slashed the shirt. She thought there was a good chance Cody was going to have spinal damage." He smiled. "But when she lifted the shirt, there was nothing. Not a bruise, not a scratch, nothing."

"Yeah," I said, remembering. "He mostly just got up and walked away. Pretty amazing."

The ad stops were completed by noon. Laura Joyce always ate lunch at her desk on Monday; she was not a petite woman, and I got the impression that eating lunch at her desk was a highlight in her day.

I spent much of a Monday afternoon in the darkroom, creating half-tone photos for newsprint publication, while Laura Joyce took care of customers as they wandered in all afternoon. I could hear the muffled voices of visitors through the darkroom door. Kerry Sacry brought in the movie slick for the weekend film at the Star Theatre. One of the Loomis girls brought in junior high track results. Laura Joyce would type those up. Sonny Huckaba brought in a classified ad attempting to lease some spare pasture. Roselle Hanson came in with a classified ad to sell her daughter's trumpet. At least four women – one of them was a Giono and one was a Davis – came in with garage sale classified ads. A Carey brought in a 4-H meeting summary. A man brought in a classified ad attempting to sell a used pickup. I could tell them all by their voices. Rhonda Horst, an elderly lady with a thick German accent, brought in a classified ad to rent one of her spare rooms. She owned a large house not far from our home on the west side of town, an old railroad house once occupied by entire train crews, and people were forever moving in and out.

"Runt like ta otter vun," she said, meaning her past classified ads. "I be tellink you ven da take it out." For us at the Ledger, that meant TFN: the ad ran Till Further Notice.

Most of the people walking in the door on Monday spent money at the Ledger. That made Mondays more bearable, despite my apathy about making money and disinterest in spending money. My business financial goals were to make the Ledger profitable. My personal financial goals were more basic. Actually, I had no personal financial goals.

As a business owner, for a small town like Whitehall, I was a success. It was as a father where I was failing. I knew it, Annie knew it, and had Tony thought about it, he would have known it too. Every time I pulled up into the pea-gravel driveway alongside our worn out little house, the weight of parental failure seemed to pull me down, to literally oppress my stride and bearing, to the point where it seemed to hunch my back and stoop my posture.

I got home about seven p.m., and I had no idea what my kids had been doing since they were let out of school at three-fifteen. I saw them last the previous night. On this day, I would see my kids a total of twenty-five minutes. I would be at home until about seven-twenty-five, when I would leave again to cover the Whitehall Town Council meeting, and then after the meeting I would return to the Ledger and afterward call home and check on the kids, then write the town council article and get a slight jump on laying out the Ledger's twenty-four pages. I'd get home about one o'clock Tuesday morning, make sure the kids were in their beds asleep, then wake up the following morning at six o'clock, with the expectation the kids would arise on time, dress and eat properly, and get themselves to school on time. Amazingly, they almost always did, except for Tony, who seemingly took pride in arriving five minutes late as often as he could get away with it.

I opened the door and found Tony and a trio of his friends in the living room, watching a baseball game on television. I immediately smelled pizza, and saw two pizza boxes, each with a slice of pizza left congealed inside, spread open across the kitchen table.

"Boys," I said as I entered.

"Lance," responded Tony. Ace Lonigan, Morgan "Mite" Miteward and TK Carey each nodded a greeting. Mite always reminded me of a troll. The kid had a beard in eighth grade.

"Annie home?" I asked Tony.

He nodded toward her room. Her door was closed, but I could see a light on underneath the door.

"Did she have some pizza?" I asked.

Tony nodded. His dark hair was damp and brushed back. My guess was he had played basketball after school and had taken a shower. "You can finish it up, if you want."

"I might just do that," I said.

We might be haphazard and dysfunctional, but no one could say the Joslyn family didn't look out for one another. When one of us had food, we all had food. The Joslyn family also operated on faith and credit throughout the community. Since I sold ads all over town, and since the kids seldom had money and since I was the opposite of organized and the opposite of a provider, the kids could charge virtually anything they wanted virtually anywhere in town. Not only that, but since Annie actually paid the bills, I typically had no idea how much the kids had spent and what they'd bought. And they knew I had no idea, and still, to my knowledge, neither kid took advantage of my parental incompetence. And always, thanks to Annie, the bills were paid on time, which meant my credit all over town was good, and I had nothing to do with any of it.

In fact, when I entered Annie's room, she had the bank statement and checks spread out across the floor, the checkbook in her lap as she sat on the edge of her bed, near her desk. She routinely paid bills the second Monday of the month, and she never made a mistake.

"There's two pieces of pizza left," I said from the door.

She shook her head. "I already had some." She indicated the checkbook. "The Ledger's having a good April."

I nodded. The first three months of the year were usually slow not just for the newspaper but for most businesses in town, but when the weather warmed it stirred the local economy, and the next three months – April, May and June – were usually the best three months of income for the paper. Something inside me winced every time Annie commented on the financial aspects or monthly revenue of the Ledger, but she knew the only person she could discuss that kind of business with was me.

"Everything look okay?" I asked, and indicated the scattered checks.

"Looks great," she said. "Your investments are doing pretty well, too."

"What investments?"

"These investments," she said, and held up some documents I had never seen before. Or perhaps I had; I never really truly knew. She tucked some loose strands of hair behind her ear. "We talked about them last fall. We sheltered some income, remember, and invested some money in things like utility stocks."

"Oh, right," I said. *Utility stocks*? What the hell was a utility stock? I had no idea what she was talking about, although I did recall signing some forms at the bank.

"Did you hear what I'm doing my science project on?" she asked.

I paused. Was this something I was supposed to know? Had I been told once already and already forgot? I wasn't sure. She spared me the necessity of responding.

"Chernobyl," she said.

I was semi aware of Chernobyl, a Russian city half a world away from Whitehall, and thus of no interest to the Ledger and, consequently, to me. My only interest, when it came down to it, were things pertaining specifically to Whitehall. Chernobyl would make the Ledger when radioactive material from Chernobyl fell in Whitehall.

"Why Chernobyl?" I asked.

"It's the most significant nuclear disaster in history," she said. "Maybe that has something to do with it." There was only a slight trace of sarcasm in her voice.

I was going to ask how exactly she intended to transfer the tragedy of Chernobyl to a display in the Whitehall elementary school gym, but I had to quickly eat and get down to the town hall. Plus I wasn't in a mood for junior high sarcasm.

"Well, good luck with all that," I said, as if Annie Joslyn needed good luck on her science project.

She thought about telling me something, then opted not to, then went ahead and told me. "You wrote three checks to Borden's totaling $125 last month. On one of them your handwriting is so bad it's not even legible."

I meekly shrugged. "Anything else?"

"No. Go to your meeting."

"Okay, thanks. I'll call you after the council meeting."

Head down, sorting checks, she didn't respond. I closed the door, went into the kitchen, took the pizza slices, and sat down with the boys. As I ate, I tried to momentarily watch the baseball game on TV, but I watched for three full minutes and not a single thing happened. Then I saw one hitter ground out to the shortstop, one flew out to the centerfielder, and one popped out to the third baseman. At no time did any player on the field move at anything resembling full speed.

"Can there possibly be a sport more boring than baseball?" I said as I stood up.

Morgan looked at me, but said nothing. TK, I noticed, was wearing a NY Yankees tee-shirt.

"Tony, pick up the kitchen and get these boxes out to the garbage before you go to bed," I said. "I'll call you after the council meeting."

"I'll be waiting by the phone," he assured me.

That was the extent of my physical interaction with my two children for what would be about a forty-eight hour period. I left the house the way I entered it; burdened by the weight of parental neglect and failure.

Whitehall Mayor Luke Grayling had just finished approving the Whitehall Town Council meeting agenda and the handful of citizenry at the town hall already looked bored when I walked in. My regular seat, front row on the right side, was open, and as the mayor wrapped up explaining why one agenda item had to be omitted I took my accustomed chair and spotted Scott Lonigan, a council member and a local electrician, and Ace's dad, who nodded a greeting.

Town Secretary/Treasurer Rachel Brockton, a title also known as the town clerk, sat in the front of the room, facing the audience, between the mayor and town attorney, Chance Dawson, TK's cousin. The mayor and council operated for entertainment only; Rachel actually ran the town. She was pushing age sixty, had been town clerk for over three decades, and was the unchallenged authority in Whitehall town government. In the audience were the town marshal, a surly man with hooded eyes and a large bulbous nose named Henry Manfredini, and the town man, Gage Duncan. Gage's job could more properly be called the town public works director, since Gage's duties included driving the garbage truck and town snowplow, fixing potholes and tending the town's cantankerous and ancient municipal drinking water system. A handful of other town residents were in the audience – Dorothy Litchfield, who for some reason attended every town council meeting; Bruce Hankinson, an elderly gentleman who also frequented town council meetings; Young Tom Langston, son of Old Tom; and Daniel Purdy, the school board member who usually attended when he had a complaint about something – sat stone silent behind me.

"Okay, old business," said the mayor. "First on the agenda is the water tower north by the interstate."

"What's wrong with it?" asked council member Brandon Grant, owner of a motel and RV park on the east side of town.

"What's wrong with what?" shouted Old Tom Langston. Old Tom was a WWII veteran who looked more like a WWI veteran. He had a bad foot, a bad shoulder, a bad knee and a bad back, and he hadn't been able to hear clearly since the Nixon Administration. His son, Young Tom, came back from Vietnam in the 1970s with a black patch over his left eye and a perpetual scowl across his face. Young Tom worked for Daniel Purdy at the lumberyard. Old Tom and Young Tom lived together in a trailer home south of the tracks near the cement plant, and you got the impression from the outside of the place that inside the place was not maintained to any form of hygienic standards.

"The water tower," Rachel told him.

"I don't know," yelled Old Tom. "It was there last I looked."

"It's still there, Tom," said the mayor.

"What is?" shouted Old Tom.

Every town council meeting started this way, with Old Tom determined to participate, but after the first agenda item or so, the council more or less ignored him, and he more or less didn't mind. The reason he was on the council was because he wanted to be. If Old Tom had anything else outside the council in his life no one knew what it was. A typical town election featured two council positions on the ballot, and Whitehall was lucky to attract one candidate for each position. The council was essentially unnecessary anyway; Rachel made sure town government functioned. She was maybe five feet tall and maybe weighed 100 pounds. No one crossed Rachel more than once.

“We received two bids to clean and repair the water tank,” Rachel told the council. “One from a firm in Helena and one from the Harris brothers in Butte.”

“I vote no,” shouted Old Tom.

“There’s nothing to vote on yet,” the mayor pointed out.

“The Harris brothers are the contractors who helped clean the sludge from the settling ponds last summer,” Rachel said. “Scott Harris grew up south of here near Silver Star, and is Nettie Lewis’ brother from over in Pipestone.”

I knew what would happen next: The town council would go through the motions of selecting Harris Brothers as the contractor, and by appearances and by reading the minutes an average person would conclude the council had made a reasoned and researched selection. But Rachel had already, in her mind, chosen Harris Brothers, for her own reasons, and all the council would do was bless – officially and legally – Rachel’s decision.

“How’d they do on the sludge project?” asked Andy Zankowski, a council member and an employee at Golden Sunlight Mine.

Rachel nodded. “They did a good job.” She looked out into the audience. “Is that right, Gage?”

Gage, the town man, seated in the audience, stood to attention. “Yeah, Rachel, they did.”

Rachel nodded again, and Gage plopped back in his chair. I always thought it odd that his legal job title – in town ordinance and rules – was town man. I’d joked in the Ledger that if Gage was the town man, did that make his wife, Lou, the town woman? Were their kids, Linda and Boyce, the town girl and town boy? If the town hired a female for the job of town man would she be town woman, or still town man? No one, particularly Rachel, found my commentary humorous.

“What were the bids on the project?” asked Scott Forester.

“About the same,” answered Rachel.

“The same what?” wondered Old Tom.

Legally, the bids were supposed to have been opened publicly, and both bids read in their entirety. But Whitehall acted more informally. The town was essentially in compliance with most of the state’s exacting rules, laws and procedures, provided they didn’t interfere with what Rachel wanted to do or the way she wanted to do it. Rachel handled all bids, all correspondence, and whether anyone would admit it or not, all decisions.

“When can the Harris brothers start?” asked Scott.

“They’re flexible,” said Rachel. Translated, her answer meant the Harris brothers would start whenever she told them to.

“I make a motion we accept the bid of the Harris brothers to clean and repair the water tower,” said Jimmy Ford, a council member and an accountant who usually made the motions.

“I vote no,” called out Old Tom.

Rachel recorded the vote.

The council rolled through old business, new business and reports from town employees, and when it was time for the portion of the meeting for audience participation Daniel Purdy and his comb-over stood up. I detected immediate resistance, perhaps even defiance, from Rachel. They'd never been what you'd call friendly.

"It seems like every year I have to come here and complain about the way the town lets water drain down the hill behind the A&W and the mud holes in the parking lot by the lumberyard," said Daniel Purdy. If you looked close, you could see a glint of a reflection of the overhead lights off Daniel Purdy's scalp, under the combed over hair. "So again I'm tellin' the town to do something about that runoff."

"Hi, Daniel!" called out Old Tom, as if he'd just seen Daniel Purdy walk into the room.

"Old Tom knows what I'm talking about," said Daniel Purdy. "It's a mess every spring, and it's a mess right now."

Mayor Grayling looked at town attorney Chance Dawson, who looked at town clerk Rachel Brockton. The discussion at town hall about the runoff causing mud holes in Daniel Purdy's parking lot was a fixed annual spring event, much like the returning of the sand hill cranes to Lucy Chun's pasture south of town. Everyone in the room, including Daniel Purdy, knew what Rachel would say next and what the council would decide. He was determined to play it out anyway.

"The road north of the A&W is a county road, not a town road," stated Rachel with a clipped cadence. "If there is any runoff, you need to talk with the county about it. I don't know why we have to tell you this every year. And your parking lot is your responsibility, not the town's. Any water that gathers on your property is your problem."

"It's not my water," Dan Purdy argued. "It's yours. And you need to take care of it."

"Gage, are we under any obligation to address water runoff problems from county property to private property?" the mayor, asked.

Gage all but jumped to his feet. "No, Mayor, we got all the problems we can handle on town property."

"Chance, are we under any obligation to address water runoff problems from county property to private property?" Luke asked.

The town attorney shook his head. "No, we are not."

"My driveway is muddy too, but you don't see me whining that the town needs to fix it," said Hannah Brosovich, a council member who owned a hair salon on Legion Avenue a block from the Ledger. Somehow, sometime in the past, Daniel Purdy had offended her, same as he apparently had offended most everyone in town, except Hannah was less forgiving than most folks.

"Sorry, Mr. Purdy," said the mayor. "We don't have the resources to tackle water runoff problems on private land. We can barely keep up with the workload on town streets and alleys." He looked around the room. "Anything else tonight?" There was nothing else. "We're adjourned."

"We're what?" yelled Old Tom.

It was eleven o'clock when I called home, and I was surprised when Annie answered the phone.

"It's late on a school night," I said. "Aren't you supposed to be in bed?"

"I'm working on my science project," she said. "Did you know they think the radiation released from the nuclear reactor at Chernobyl was equal to one hundred times the radiation released from the atomic bombs America dropped on Japan in World War II?"

"As a matter of fact," I said, "I didn't know that."

"They think there was approximately 200 tons of uranium in the reactor before the explosion," she said.

"Wow," I said, because I thought she expected me to.

"Wow is right," she said. "About 30 percent of the reactor's caesium was released into the atmosphere. Radiation spread throughout Scandinavia, Poland, the Baltic states, Switzerland, northern France and even England. Do you have any idea how many people that is?"

Not only did I not know how many people that was, I had no idea what a Baltic state was and had never heard the word 'caesium' before in my life.

"A lot," I guessed.

It was going to be a late night for Annie. She could survive on less sleep than her brother, and once on a quest for knowledge she could pursue the quest until exhaustion.

"When is the science project due?" I asked.

"I don't know," she said. "I don't even have to do one, actually. I'm supposed to help Jersey judge the entries. I'm just sort of pretending I have to do one, because nothing like Chernobyl has ever happened before and people need to be aware of its significance. I sort of volunteered to help Trish with her project."

Trisha Ryan, school board member Molly Ryan's daughter, was a tenth grader with multiple sclerosis, and it was sobering to see her declining physical and mental abilities. She had been diagnosed a couple years ago, and from that point she had degenerated from a slight tremble in her hands to a stiff leg to a cane to a walker to a wheelchair.

"Midnight," I told Annie.

"Okay," she said. Her quick agreement meant she had absolutely no regard for my parental command that she be in bed at midnight. I thought about having Rachel the town clerk call Annie and demand that she be in bed by midnight. Everyone obeyed Rachel. But it was only me, a distracted, seemingly disinterested parent, and Annie knew I wouldn't be home until one o'clock or later.

"What do you think of this Jersey guy?" I asked.

"He's okay," she said. "He's a pretty good teacher. And he's a nice person."

Both were high compliments from Annie. "Can he coach football? I asked.

"I would certainly think so," she said. "How hard can it be?"

"Harder than you might think," I answered. "He seems like he's kind of odd."

"He's not from here, Lance," Annie said, in her tutoring voice.

"Got it," I said. "Where's your brother?"

"Watching TV."

"Are his friends still there?" I asked.

"No, it's just him." That's because all his friends have parents who work normal hours, have curfews for their children that are enforced, and are generally aware of where their kids are, who they're with and what they're doing. Had Tony been out of the house, I would have failed on all accounts.

"Let me talk to him," I said. "And I want you in bed at midnight."

"Right," she said, not meaning it.

"Lance," an unexpected deep voice said next. Is that Tony? How have I failed to notice a changing voice on my high school son?

"Homework done?" I asked.

"I didn't have any," he said. Figures; his sister was doing homework for a project she didn't have to do, and he was avoiding homework for projects he did have to do.

"Why not?" I asked.

"I dunno," he said, and I could all but see the shrug.

It was not an encouraging response, but there was nothing I could do about it. I had to finish writing the town council article, proofread the rest of Laura Joyce's articles, start laying out twenty-four pages of the Ledger and wax and cut to size over twenty photos. He either had his homework done or he didn't. He was essentially on his own, and he knew it.

"Okay, get to bed by midnight," I said.

"I'm going to crash now," he said. "I'm tired."

"Tell your sister goodnight," I said.

"Yeah," he said.

"You're on your own in the morning."

"We'll manage," he said.

I wouldn't see them the next day until after school, when they stopped by the Ledger. I worried about him, worried about his sister, but couldn't let that worry interfere with my workload. I stood up and turned on the radio to a Butte rock 'n roll station. Bruce Springsteen was singing a soft ballad about his hometown. I pondered the fate of my kids for about ten additional seconds, and then picked up an article about the upcoming PTA meeting as the start of an hour of proofreading. I was soon absorbed, content in my Ledger office, safely ignorant of anything and everything not immediately connected to my newspaper.

Chapter 5

The daylight hours crept a couple minutes longer each day as the rough and weathered surface of Montana emerged from winter and was reborn in spring green-up, and mid-May found Slack, Tony, Annie and me in my Honda Accord heading north early on a Saturday morning to the state Class B track meet in Helena.

The sun was behind us and to our right as we sped north up Highway 69, and off to our left the sunlight left a glow on the Golden Sunlight Mine workings. The low plane of the rising sun also lit the still snowy upper peaks of the Bull Mountains into crisp and etched rock faces. The Boulder River, high and muddy in spring, was nearly bank-full and as we drove upstream the Honda rolled along the narrow two-lane highway, the separated green pastures on either side of the road speckled with black calves and cows.

The Honda shimmied a little. A stiff west wind buffeted the car, but it wasn't the wind that caused the wobble. The Accord was starting to show its age; in addition to the shimmy one of the radio turn knobs had fallen off, the glove box didn't close tight and spots of rust were forming low on the quarter panels in front of the tires. Montana's changeable weather and rough roads are not charitable to motorized vehicles.

The Boulder Valley was as agriculture as agriculture could get. It ran about forty miles between the town of Boulder, a town of some institutional notoriety, and the blinking yellow light that hung south at the intersection of Highway 69 and Highway 2. Highway 2, once known as the Yellowstone Trail, was once part of a national network of roads that had connected America from coast to coast, but freeways like I-90 – completed through the Whitehall area in the mid-1960s – rendered the cozy cross-country two-laners mostly obsolete.

East of Whitehall along Highway 2, near the Jefferson River just before the river's main canyon section, LaHood Park sat perched on a bluff above the river, a historic and honorable destination hotel built nearly a century earlier. The hotel's glory years were long gone and short lived, and it was now empty and desolate, but during the period centered between the two world wars people could take elegant passenger trains to LaHood Park for holidays. A year or two after I'd arrived in Whitehall I saw a decades old book published in California that had listed America's top destination hotels, and the authors bestowed about ten photos upon LaHood Park. In the 1920s, men in tight black vests and women with bonnets and parasols paraded along the Jefferson River and up into the hills above where they explored a deep underground cave that later became a Montana state park. The hotel still stands on the south side of Highway 2, and the railroad tracks – essentially unused for the past decade – still run east-west between the river and the hotel. The hotel has a large awning that extends from the front door, and on the awning ceiling is what Whitehall town historian Roy Milligan termed in a Ledger article a "priceless display of Montana history." The underneath of the awning – you only saw it when you stood directly under the inside of the awning and looked up – was a one-of-a-kind hand-painted rendering of the coast to coast route of the Yellowstone Trail, with special details painted to highlight the Whitehall area. Old businesses in Whitehall were painted and advertised on the awning, and some of the telephone numbers were simple solo digits like *4*.

Most of the land in the Boulder Valley itself was owned by a couple families – the Careys and Dawsons – and cattle probably outnumbered people in the valley a hundred to one.

Slack watched a herd of cows and calves as they drifted behind us on our right. Slack was in the front passenger seat; the kids were in the back. Rides like this, to events covered by the Ledger, qualified as family time for us Joslyns. "Those are some fat calves," Slack said.

"You help them brand this spring?" I asked.

Slack nodded, and grinned. "Those Careys have a lot of fun after they're done branding."

Slack may or may not have actually helped the Careys brand this year. His memory could never be depended on for accuracy about recent events, but he certainly had helped the Careys in the past and he was absolutely right about the Careys' party after branding was complete. Branding was an annual spring chore throughout cattle country, and like many ranch areas the Jefferson and Boulder valley landowners staggered their brandings in late April and early May to ensure as many helping hands as possible for each branding. Brandings required several teams of workers: ropers, who lassoed and dragged the calves into the corral; two-person teams to wrestle and more or less pin the calves to the ground; people armed with the super-heated branding irons; a couple hands to perform castrations and a couple people with various syringes filled with vaccines. It was difficult, dangerous, physical work, but when it was over, the hosts felt themselves obligated to reward all the workers with food, beer and hard liquor. The Carey family rolled out quite a spread, food-wise and booze-wise. Sometimes the parties turned into rowdy large-group sleepovers, with entire exhausted families sleeping out in a shed, in an RV or under the stars.

The soil of the valley was revered, but the Boulder River water itself was a mess. Everything that could harm running water – old mine wastes, municipal discharges, riparian damage, sedimentation and siltation, shallow flows, algae blooms, water diversions and high water temperatures – harmed the Boulder River. Still, the Ledger had reported a surprising large number of brown trout survived in the lower part of the river, and in the upper sections of the river steady populations of brown, rainbow and brook trout somehow hung on.

A line of cows and calves, strung out in a long nearly single-file line, angled away from the road. The cows either had their head down in the newly emerging grass, or had their head up, mouth chewing, eyes gazing vacantly into nowhere.

"I wonder what cows think about," said Tony. "Do they know every spring that...I mean, are they aware...that year after year after year they're going to get bred, deliver a calf, then have the calf taken from them?"

"What about branding?" said Annie. "A branding iron has got to hurt, I don't care what kind of animal you are. And if you're a little boy calf..."

"Yeah," mused Slack, "but think about what a bull gets to do every year."

Annie emitted a slight giggle from the backseat, and Slack suddenly realized, or suddenly remembered, he was sharing the car with an underage feminine presence. He turned red as a radish, apparently by contemplating what a bull actually did, and doing that contemplation within close proximity of an underage feminine presence.

"I'm with you, brother," I told him. "How can you beat the life of a bull?"

We took a wide, gradual curve to the left, while the Elkhorn Mountains squared off to the north. Between the Elkhorns and our ribbon of highway was St. John's Church, with its tiny square cemetery, proud and strong, a monument to Christianity isolated and resolute in the heart of a rural ranch valley. Off to our left, the Bull Mountains crested underneath a sky the color of a metal bucket. About thirty pronghorn antelope grazed with indifference, spread out on the bench to our left. The valley held elk, visible in large herds mostly in winter, an occasional moose, a large population of mule deer and whitetail deer, and a true abundance of pronghorn. Pronghorn always struck me as smarter and calmer than deer. Deer jumped fences, panicked in traffic, and grazed nervously, always ready to bolt. Pronghorns crawled under fences, seemingly never crossed a paved road, and grazed as if they defied you to do anything about it.

On the sixty-five-mile drive to a track meet, between Whitehall and Helena, we saw waterfowl scattered in the Boulder River, pheasants in the borrow pit, a few dozen pronghorns, at least three different species of hawks, a pair of whitetail deer and in a tree line off I-15 between the Boulder Hill and Montana City, about a dozen mule deer. If you lived in Montana long enough, and if you weren't careful, you could take the abundance of wildlife for granted. I've appreciated all the wildlife I've ever seen. As a kid Tony possessed a genuine and gleeful appreciation for wildlife – either that or he was gleefully happy for me because nearly every time he saw a deer or antelope he joyfully pointed it out for my satisfaction – and would revel in our mutual joy.

The town of Boulder, like the town of Whitehall, was unkempt, even dreary. The weather patterns – split and splintered by a half-dozen area mountain ranges – favored Whitehall with sunlight and wind, and favored Boulder with moisture and clouds, and the low gray clouds rendered Boulder seemingly colorless as we drove through it.

Boulder was the county seat of Jefferson County, with the spire of the county courthouse partially visible from main street. Boulder was historically an institutional town, one of five or six Montana communities within the governmental pull of Helena or Butte that served as sites for prisons, state medical facilities or homes for the mentally ill. The collection of unnamed, unadorned and uninviting dirty red-brick buildings at the entrance of Boulder told of darker times when institutions were indifferent warehouses for the psychologically damaged or dangerous and mentally or physically incapable.

"The only reason Boulder was put on earth," said Tony, "was to make Whitehall look good."

"Both towns could be suburbs of Butte," I said. It wasn't a compliment.

"Boulder's worse," Tony said.

"Boulder has a Dairy Queen," Slack offered hopefully.

"A little early for that," I said. "We'll stop at Dairy Queen on the way home."

Slack's eyes brightened.

The state track meet was separated into two days, with roughly half the events on each day. Whitehall High School had a few kids compete on Friday – two girls in the 400-meters, a boy and a girl in the javelin, and a boy in the 300-meter hurdles – but I had to spend Friday selling ads for the annual WHS graduation section of the paper and could only get to Helena and the track meet for one day. Saturday had WHS girls competing in the 400-meter relay, 100-meter dash and shot put, and boys competing in the high jump, 400-meter run, pole vault and 1,600-meter relay.

The wind had downgraded to a breeze in Helena. By midmorning the temperature had drifted above fifty degrees but the sky over the mountains southwest of the city sagged low and dark with a fine mist of moisture. The kids had been smart enough to take their rain jackets, and Tony brought mine along for Slack. The three of them headed off toward the stands while – courtesy of my press pass – my camera and I were allowed down on the track.

A tall, gangly high jumper from Whitehall, a senior named Darby Jones, popped off a school record, Class B state record, and all-class state record jump of six-feet nine inches. I astonished myself by being in almost the exact right place at almost the exact right time. That was an oddity for me. I watched as Darby sped toward the high jump pit and launched himself in a majestic high twisting arc. He seemed to soar above everything, and to then float weightlessly above the bar. The brightly colored crowd in their shiny and slick raincoats erupted with cheers and applause at his jump. There was no doubt what was going to be the main photo on the Ledger sports page, with a front page lead, on Wednesday. A Whitehall kid had just made history, and the local newspaper was there to record it.

I was able to take a few pictures of Ace Lonigan in the pole vault – Ace fell shy of qualifying for the finals – and when I walked over to the finish line of the 1,600-meter relay I spotted, to my surprise, Jersey. He was poised comfortably along the fence outside the track just beyond the mark where the race started, ended, and batons were handed off. The hand-off of a baton was a favorite track photo, because it showed action and teamwork and – more importantly – because it was one of the rare opportunities to include two WHS Rangers in one track photo.

Jersey was standing more or less alone – parents wearing Lodge Grass and Cascade windbreakers were on either side of him – leaning against the fence, his hands in front, almost in prayer, his forearms resting on top of the upper fence bracket.

The runners were still warming up in sweatpants and windbreakers, so I had some time to visit before the race would start. As I approached Jersey the thought struck me that a month ago I had barely heard of the guy, and now he seemed to be every place I went. By default he was likely going to be the new Whitehall varsity football coach – the final decision on a largely nonexistent applicant pool was scheduled to come at the June school board meeting – and for that reason alone I figured I should re-introduce myself to him.

He saw me approaching and smiled, and extended his hand for me to shake. "Hello, Lance Joslyn, Annie's father," he said in greeting. The word *father* came out *fair-tha*.

I nodded. I was also Tony's father, but Jersey only taught junior high classes. Jersey wore a black leather jacket that looked as if it had been around awhile. He had on black jeans and black high top shoes that were sort of like tennis shoes, but weren't.

"Do I call you Jersey, Mr. Jersey, Mr. Conti, Jerry, or what?" I asked him.

"People in Montana tend to call me Jersey, I guess. Apparently there are not a lot of former (*for-mah*) New Jersey residents residing in Whitehall. Or from any other state, for that matter (*mat-tah).* I know of no other Whitehall area residents called by the state name of their birth."

"It didn't help that you student teach our collection of diabolical junior high kids," I said. "Plus," I added, "you *look* like a New Jersey guy. I have no idea what a New Jersey guy actually looks like, now that I think about it, but you look exactly what I imagine a New Jersey guy looks like."

"Well, thanks for that," he said, "I think."

"Let's just say it's a good thing you're not from, say, Alabama," I said. "You don't even want to think about what I imagine a guy from Alabama looks like."

He laughed. "If you say so."

"So what brings you to Helena and the state Class B track meet?" I asked.

"Same thing that brought me out to that rodeo the other day," he said. He looked skyward. "Although we seem to be having extremes in Montana springtime weather."

"Yeah, it was a hot bugger at the rodeo," I said. I also looked up and surveyed the solid, sagging gray clouds. "This isn't the other extreme from Montana spring heat, though. The extreme opposite from the rodeo would be a sloppy wet blizzard, and if we aren't careful that's what we're going to get tonight."

"In May?"

“Springtime in the Rockies,” I said, and shrugged. “It can snow any time of year. May is famous for snowstorms with snow so heavy it snaps trees and breaks power lines.”

He simply nodded, thoughtfully.

“The weather keeps the weak and vulnerable from moving here,” I told him. I hesitated. “You said you’re here for the same reason you were at the rodeo, but I gotta ask, why were you at the rodeo?”

He lowered his head, averting his eyes, and toed the fence with his boot. “Is this for the paper?”

I shook my head. “I’m just nosey.”

“I have a hunch the school board may hire me as the new varsity football coach,” he told me. “I think they would rather not, truthfully, but they appear to be desperate. They had to talk me into applying, to be honest, because I’m not qualified to be a high school head football coach. But no one else has applied.”

“Yeah, it was surprising when Wally Hope left,” I agreed. “I can’t imagine qualified coaches are standing in line to coach at a place like Whitehall.”

“Apparently that’s correct,” he said.

“We lost two coaches in what, five weeks. That’s on top of some crummy football teams the past few years.”

“So I hear *(he-ahh)*,” he said. He used the toe of his shoe to tap down a loose rock near the fence line. “I do not intend to coach a crummy football team.”

“No one does,” I said.

“See that kid over there, the one wearing the hood?” said Jersey.

It was Nate Bolton, a WHS junior. He was part of the boys 1,600-meter relay team, and was one of Whitehall’s better basketball players. “Nate?” I asked.

Jersey nodded. “He’s one of the fastest kids in school, one of the best jumpers in school and one of the best athletes in school. But he doesn’t play football.”

“He’s from Cardwell,” I said, as if that explained it. Jersey looked at me, his eyes expressing uncertainty. “Cardwell kids hardly ever play football,” I added.

“Why not?”

“I have no idea,” I said. “They just don’t.” Cardwell, a tiny collection of ranches east of Whitehall, had an elementary school that ended at eighth grade. It was a tiny school – five or six kids per class at most – and almost all the kids went to high school in Whitehall. Cardwell played other elementary schools and junior highs in basketball, but that was the only organized sport the Cardwell kids played and it was pretty much the only organized sport they played once they got to Whitehall. Every now and then a Cardwell kid played football, but standing there, talking to Jersey, I couldn’t think of one. Some of the Cardwell kids ran cross country or track, but mostly just to help their conditioning for basketball.

"We need kids like Nate and Cody Phillips to play football," said Jersey.

I didn't want to be the bearer of bad news, especially to a new guy who was trying his best, but I didn't see either kid playing football. Nate was a junior with only one year of school left, which meant he already had made a deliberate decision three straight years to not play football at Whitehall. Cody was a rough little one-hundred-thirty-pound hellion wrestler who barely stayed academically eligible for one sport, let alone two. A more realistic goal for Cody was for him to avoid incarceration until after graduation.

"I know both kids are long shots," he told me. "But Whitehall football doesn't have the luxury of giving up on kids."

"I'm not disagreeing with you," I said. "I'm just saying kids like Cody and Nate haven't accidentally not played football. They've deliberately not played football."

"Let's see if we can change that," Jersey said. "Let's see if they'll deliberately play football."

The runners began stripping off their warm-up sweatshirts and sweatpants, and I slid off the fenceline to get myself in position to take pictures. I looked for the sun to put behind me, but I couldn't find it. The clouds seem to have descended upon us, and I felt surrounded by near invisible tiny shards of ice.

Nate Bolton ran a strong anchor leg on the 1,600-meter relay for Whitehall but the Rangers still finished in sixth place, a couple strides from fifth. Watching Nate complete the race – his strong pale legs pumping through the final straightaway and finish line with a lean forward of a developed upper body – I found myself imagining him as a wide receiver or halfback on the football team, and I could see why Jersey was interested in getting a kid like that on the football field.

The sleet intensified slightly, and as I put my camera away I saw Jersey and Nate talking after the race. Nate was hunched over, hands on his knees, trying to catch his breath, and was listening to whatever it was Jersey was telling him.

The weather worsened throughout the afternoon and reached full storm status about two hours later as we climbed the Boulder Hill on the way south back home toward Whitehall. Fat snowflakes tumbled heavily earthward and deep, thick, slushy ruts in the driving lane made it difficult to see and challenging to navigate the switchbacks on I-15 up the hill. The snow accumulated enough depth between the ruts to scrape at the car's undercarriage, and I could feel the top layer of wet sodden snow through the soles of my feet as we sloshed down the road. It was hard to imagine that earlier we had been at a springtime track meet, with kids running around in shorts and sleeveless shirts and watched the Whitehall boys finish eleventh in state. Looking out the windshield on the way home, you'd have thought we were driving though a mid-January blizzard.

"Who was that guy all dressed in black?" asked Slack.

"Jersey," I said, eyes on the road. "He's a new teacher at the school."

"He don't look like he's from here," said Slack.

"He's not," said Annie. "He's from New Jersey."

"New Jersey?" asked Slack.

"It's on the east coast," Annie said happily. "By New York."

"Home of Bruce Springsteen," Tony added.

"Jersey is a *big* Springsteen fan," said Annie. "Last week in class he played *The River*, a song about two teenagers who got married because the girl was pregnant, and it was like all their dreams died at their wedding ceremony."

"Doesn't sound terribly uplifting," I observed.

"I saw on TV once how thousands of people were waiting for him and screaming and cheering when he showed up at an airport," said Tony.

"Like the Beatles," I said. Which got no response. "Beatlemania? *The Ed Sullivan Show*? You guys know anything about that?"

"Before our time," said Tony.

The storm rendered Boulder pitch black outside the scarce and timid arcs from streetlights, and Slack agreed to take a raincheck on a treat at the Dairy Queen. A plow had been through town and knee-high rows of piled snow lined each side of the road. We crossed the Boulder River bridge on the south side of town and ahead was a pale gray land of winter and snow.

I crawled at about 30 miles an hour along the river but once we climbed up on the bench south of the Elkhorn turnoff it was as if a switch had suddenly turned off. The headlights seemed to first glitter off snow, then skim off slick pavement, then find dry black pavement. A sweep of crystal-like stars shimmered overhead, and when I turned the wipers off the windshield was impossibly clear, as was the road ahead.

"We seem to have escaped the squall," said Tony.

"Montana weather never ceases to amaze me," I said.

"What do you expect us to have?" asked Annie. "North Dakota weather?"

"New Jersey weather?" Slack added.

I was at the Ledger office early the following Tuesday morning, starting to lay out the paper, when Merle Stoviack, an older man who I had seen around town at various events for years, came in the office and greeted me with a frail, halfhearted greeting.

Six months earlier, Merle had been in the Ledger with an obituary photo of his wife, Gwen. They'd been married over forty years. He was somber then, too, but made a point of stopping in after the paper was published to thank me for Gwen's obituary and to place a thank you ad. Merle was an old fashioned country gentleman, but as he stood in the Ledger that Tuesday it was obvious he was having some health problems. The color of his flesh was sallow, like a faded and wilted dollar bill. He had been an avid reader of the Ledger, and had faithfully showed up every year to renew his subscription and whenever and wherever I saw him, he would give me an encouraging word. I assumed he was here to renew his subscription again.

He took a deep sigh, and looked toward Laura Joyce, as if a silent request for this conversation to be private. The Ledger was a one-room office, separated into five distinct but open work spaces – Laura Joyce's desk, the subscription/circulation area, Annie's desk, my editor/typing desk and the layout bank – and there was no true privacy for interviews.

"Time to re-up?" I helpfully asked Merle.

He grimaced slightly, and shook his head.

"No, you're right," I said. I realized quickly that Merle always renewed his subscription around Christmas. "You're always due the end of the year. What can we do for you?"

"Lance," he said, "I need to cancel my subscription."

My stomach instantly went cold inside. It was possible I may have even emitted a slight audible gasp. From my view, it was the ultimate personal and professional insult, a journalistic humiliation, to have a subscription to my newspaper cancelled. Cancellations were rare, but when they occurred they did so with severe animosity. It had only happened twice since I'd owned the Ledger. Both times I understood the reasons. I didn't agree with those reasons, and I defended my actions that led to the cancellations, but I understood exactly why the subscription was cancelled. Merle was a considerate elderly man, a loyal Ledger subscriber, and my mind raced through a possible list of ways I had accidentally offended him. I couldn't come up with anything. "Are you sure?"

He nodded glumly. He wore the kind of glasses that magnified his vision. Behind the glass were the friendliest eyes in town. The eyes were downcast now, absent of humor or affection.

"Did I do anything wrong?" It was a painful question to ask.

And it clearly pained Merle to be asked. "No, no, no," he said quietly. He lowered his head. When he looked at me again his eyes held tears. His hands trembled as he reached in his pocket for a handkerchief, and he wiped at his eyes, readjusted his glasses, and swiped feebly at his nose. "I'm in poor health," he said hoarsely. He reached across the countertop and patted my hand. "I've always appreciated your newspaper."

There was a lengthy silence.

"Do you have to move, or something?" I asked, because I had to say something. "We can change your address and…"

Merle was shaking his head. "My eyes are bad." He spoke softly. "I can't read."

I leaned toward him. "Is it money?" I whispered conspiratorially. "We can work…" I started over. "We can keep…"

He held up a hand. His chin was firm. *Don't insult me*, his body language said.

My shoulders sagged. "Do you want a refund?" My voice sounded as if I was begging. "Your subscription has six months left."

He shook his head. “Of course not,” he said gently. I saw just a hint of humor in his big warm eyes. “Thank you for everything.” And he extended his hand, and as I shook it he patted my hand with his other hand. “I’ve always admired your newspaper. You remember that.”

I nodded, our hands parted, he turned, and was gone.

Merle’s visit to the Ledger haunted me all day, and I guess I understood what he didn’t have to say – what he wanted to avoid – that he was an old man in bad health with bad vision who faced a downhill future. But late that night, alone in the hushed Ledger office, when I updated the subscription list for mailing of the Ledger, I stubbornly left his name on the list. He’d get at least one more paper mailed to him.

Wednesday morning I was on the road at seven o’clock with twenty-four paste-up pages of the Ledger, a printed circulation list and two color photos I needed transformed into black and white halftones at the Anaconda Leader, which is where the paper was printed. It takes a large web press for newsprint like newspapers, and there were only a dozen or so of them in the entire state. The Ledger had been started up a few years earlier by the owners of the Anaconda Leader, who had spotted an opportunity in a growing town with a newly permitted gold mine. But absentee ownership of a small town business frequently fails, and the Leader owners wanted to jettison quickly out of Whitehall. The town businesses treated the Ledger with apathy, almost neglect, when Amy and I were announced as new owners, but within a year the paper was restored to profitability and stability, and had re-emerged as an important part of the community.

It took about three hours of post-production work by the Anaconda printing crew to get the Ledger pages ready to print. The pages had to be shot into negatives, the negatives had to be burned into plates, and the plates had to be bent and affixed to the rollers on the press. Once the press started to roll, and once the ink was uniform on all the pages, it took under fifteen minutes to print the fifteen hundred copies of the Whitehall Ledger. I loved the roar of the presses, the smell of ink and paper, and the satisfaction of watching the Ledger roll off the press.

There is something noble about publishing a community newspaper, and while at times I could physically feel the oppressive and numbing heaviness of exhaustion, and at times I all but abandoned my kids, the unvarnished truth was I took pride in what I did and how I did it. We made mistakes – every edition of the Ledger contained errors – and sometimes the mistakes broke my heart or made me curse my stupidity, but you could see our genuine and sincere effort on every page every week.

After I hauled the fifteen hundred copies of the Ledger back to Whitehall and carried in the newspaper bundles and mail sacks inside the post office, and after papers had been distributed to the vendor locations in Whitehall and Cardwell, I returned to the office to get ready for Thursday morning and gear up for another week. I almost always went home and took a short nap on Wednesday afternoons, Annie and Tony usually stopped by the Ledger office after school, and Annie always stuck around to fill out the postal report and calculate her weekly statistical comparison of circulation numbers, advertising inches and classified ad volume.

Mid-afternoon, back at the Ledger, I stopped next door at the pizza parlor for a pop. While I was there, Nina Finch, from the Whitehall Community Library, was finishing up a late lunch, and she asked me what I'd heard about Merle Stoviack.

I had the same cold feeling in my stomach from the day before. I hadn't heard, and I was certain I didn't want to.

Nina pursed her lips and told me what she'd heard from Brenda McGrew, the local emergency services dispatcher.

Merle had called up the local police number about ten o'clock that morning, and asked that Henry Manfredini, the town marshal, come over to Merle's house on Viella Street. Merle told Brenda he missed his wife every moment of every day. He said they'd had two sons, one living in Portland and one in Minneapolis. They were both great kids, and both had wanted Merle to move in with them, but Merle was sick with cancer, and his Gwen had gone and left him alone, and the loneliness was permanent. Merle didn't want to be a financial or emotional burden to his kids.

Brenda, the dispatcher, sensed Merle's despair and kept him on the telephone as she covertly sent Henry to Merle's house. But Merle saw the police car pull up along the side of the street. Merle's last words were uttered with gentle gratitude, perhaps even with a soft sigh of relief: "I see Henry now. Thank you." Just as Henry opened the door, he heard the pop of a gun, and found Merle slumped in a living room recliner.

Nina said Merle had written goodbye letters to his kids, taken care of personal business and his final act in life was to call to make sure someone promptly and officially found his body.

For just a second, I felt dizzy, unsteady on my feet. I almost sat down at Nina's table, but the dizziness faded. Beverage in hand, I crossed the narrow cement pad to the Ledger. I understood immediately that Merle's actions made a powerful and poignant newspaper story. I entered the Ledger and set a plastic cup of pop near Annie.

"You okay?" Annie asked.

I nodded.

Merle had carefully, deliberately and compassionately planned his own death. He did so because of his abiding affection to his departed wife, and he did so to spare his family lengthy emotional strife and hardship. His actions were touching and, in a way, tender. But they were also sad and sorrowful in a tangible, dreadful way. The story formed in my head without me thinking about it and without me wanting it to form.

And I knew I would never write a word about it for the newspaper. Merle's obituary printed in the Ledger would be a tribute to his life, not a reconstruction of his death. The grief of reliving Merle's final actions through a newspaper article would have been a callous intrusion and an unjustified invasion into his family's grief. Because of Merle's lonely and heartbreaking choice at the end of his life suggested a tragic conclusion, his life would have appeared as tragic, when in reality Merle lived a dignified and honorable life blessed with deep and unbroken family affection.

It would have been degrading to drag the details of Merle's death into the public spotlight. Merle and his family deserved better. Whitehall deserved better. Merle said he admired the Ledger. I thought I knew why.

This is a strange thing coming from a newspaper publisher: We all deserve privacy. There are things that happen to people that are none of your goddamn business.

Chapter 6

After five years of working in public relations for the power company, I'd grown frustrated with what seemed to me to be a trite and meaningless job, had grown tired of Butte's unbearable altitude and uncompromising attitude, and had been scouting around for other jobs, including the potential of moving to Whitehall and buying the Ledger.

Amy had no real desire to remain in Butte, but was not pleased with the idea of moving to a small town in a county so rural it had zero stoplights. We had been married for eight years at that point. We had two young children, but neither Amy nor I were finding much solace in our current and possible future employment and living arrangements.

One night I arrived home from work, and was climbing the stairs from the basement to the main level of our Butte split level home, stripping my tie through my shirt collar, when I looked up and saw Annie – already in her pajamas – beaming with excitement. Amy had been waiting for me to arrive home, and the instant I walked in the door she walked out, to a friend's baby shower.

Annie stood at the top of the stairs, her hands clinched under her chin, a giant grin on her face. "Mom's gone," Annie gushed. "Now you can do whatever you want!"

The comment spoke volumes about life with Lance and Amy, but what I remember most was how genuinely and enthusiastically thrilled Annie was that temporarily unshackled from my wife, I was briefly at liberty. Annie didn't say that she herself could do whatever she wanted, or that together we could do whatever we wanted or that Tony could do whatever he wanted. In her youthful and near-innocence, she was excited for me because *I* could do whatever *I* wanted. And Annie with child-like clarity thought the only reason I could do whatever I wanted was because Amy was out of the house, and unspoken was Annie's clear suggestion that I not waste this rare and glorious opportunity.

It has always been a good thing I had my genius daughter looking out for me.

I took a few minutes at the Ledger office to browse through the reading material given to me by the ladies from the Montana Office of Public Instruction and the University of Montana. The information consistently suggested that gifted children were arrogant, socially inept, stubborn, sarcastic and rude, easily bored, and unpopular. But while Annie could exhibit, at times, some of those attributes, she arguably did so with no more frequency than her brother, who had never been mistaken for a genius. Annie's mind fit all the categories of gifted – well read, wide in-depth knowledge about a wide variety of topics, excellent problem-solving ability, strong views and opinions, good communication skills, an unquenchable passion for knowledge – but her personality attributes didn't fit the profile of genius. I could sit and recollect specific examples of her intellectual talents, like the time when she was not yet two years old and we were together reading through a picture book about ocean creatures. She read the caption under a photo and said the picture was of a *good white shark.*

A mistake by Annie even then was seemingly impossible. "Annie, that's a great white shark," I said helpfully.

She pointed at the picture, kind of shook her head, and somberly said, "It's not that great."

What amazed me wasn't that she could read before her second birthday. What impressed me was that at age two she knew how to set me up for a joke. And what was sweet about it was that she wanted to make me happy by telling a joke. The constant tension between Amy and me gnawed at every discussion and decision in our household, and even as a baby Annie was perceptive of the dour moods and stressed silence and intelligent enough and caring enough to lighten the sense of domestic gloom.

But I had a hard time conjuring up specific examples of anything related to arrogance, social ineptness or rudeness connected to Annie. She was impatient at times, and still showed some traces of intolerance, but she had recognized her superior intelligence early and realized impatience and intolerance were not attributes that were going to help her accomplish anything, and above all, Annie valued accomplishment.

So it shouldn't have surprised me when on a cool and windy spring afternoon in early May 1986, when I left the Ledger office with Tony to take some pictures of the eighth and ninth grade science projects, I found Annie beaming again – much as she had at the top of the stairs at our Butte split level – as she met me at the elementary school gym entrance door.

The gym itself was a flurry of motion; the room was organized into a series of tables and exhibits, with students, parents and teachers slowly milling around the floor, inspecting each project display with varying degrees of real or feigned interest and awareness. The first display I spotted was the traditional baking power volcano spewing foam down its gray paper-mache cliffs. Annie walked with Tony and me through the aisle with projects on either side – earthworm survival projects, rabbit weight-gain projects, miniature spheres replicating planets suspended from yarn and hangers, an experiment measuring moisture and mold, something to do with friction. Wherever we went, whoever we talked to, with me stopping occasionally to take pictures, both kids received a steady flow of friendly and cheerful greetings not only from their classmates, but from teachers and other parents as well.

Tony wore his purple and gold Whitehall "W" letterman's jacket, and Annie wore a fleece-lined jeans jacket, and simply observing them both interact with their community and scholastic peers, you could not have identified the genius.

Lyle O'Toole, with his wife, Rose, and their picture-perfect blonde daughters – Holly, Aspen and Peach – were gathered handsomely in front of an exhibit that on first glance appeared to be another rabbit weight-gain project, but on closer examination the rabbits in the photos on the posters were blind, their scarred and disfigured eyes distorted and discolored.

"It's the vastly intelligent Annie Joslyn and some strange man with a camera," Lyle greeted us. Tony had already separated from Annie and me and had saddled up to Aspen.

"It's four beautiful young women with their grandfather," I answered.

"Annie, where's your science project?" asked Rose.

Annie shrugged. "I didn't really do one this year. I sort of helped out some other kids."

Peach, the youngest of the O'Toole girls, stepped back to show off her science project on the results, ostensibly, of product testing on animals.

Rose wore a buckskin vest, tight tan slacks and projected, without seeming to do so, radiant beauty. She nodded in awareness at Annie's disclosure. "I suppose it wouldn't make sense for Annie to submit a science project," said Rose. "That would be like asking Monet to enter a coloring contest."

I thought about taking a picture of Peach and her project for the Ledger, but the O'Toole girls were always doing something to earn their photo or name in the newspaper, and a photo featuring blind and mistreated rabbits might not be the kind of uplifting picture appropriate for a science fair. Peach and Annie were the same age and in the same class, but worlds apart in interest and appearance. Every red-blooded teenage male within sniffing distance of Whitehall – and that certainly included Tony – was unable to take his eyes off Peach or her sisters, while Annie was barely noticed by junior high boys. Peach was the kind of young woman that young men dreamed about. Annie was the kind of young woman who still could possibly be mistaken for a young boy.

"Isn't it just sick what cosmetic companies do to animals?" Holly declared.

Annie could have responded with a condemnation of cosmetics or a dissertation of the cosmetic chemicals themselves, with detailed examples of possible alternatives to product testing on animals. Or Annie could have lamented the use of cosmetics, which created the incentives for protect testing on animals. That would have been awkward given the elaborate layers of makeup adorning the quartet of O'Toole girls. But Annie simply agreed.

"Why do the companies do that?" asked Tony.

As if he cared. Peach and her older sister, Holly, who – I couldn't help it – always reminded me of a human Barbie Doll – closed ranks to explain with emotion and in detail the horrors of corporate animal torture.

Annie and I left Tony in Whitehall male heaven, surrounded by O'Toole girls.

There were probably a hundred people wandering aimlessly around the gym, slowly observing, and assessing and then discussing the myriad of science projects. Younger siblings, immediately bored or constantly in need of attention, either pulled – or were pulled by – their parents. A general din of conversation filled the air, and odd scents – grease, moist dirt, vinegar, sulfur, rotting fruit – drifted in and out as we surveyed the exhibits.

I saw Jersey, his trademark black shirt and black slacks, standing off to the side, more or less taking everything in. As a junior high teacher he was one of the judges, according to a Ledger article submitted by the school, and would soon be awarding ribbons to the project winners.

As we passed him, he gave Annie's shoulder a gentle touch. "Miss Joslyn, your efforts are greatly admired, applauded and appreciated."

Annie sort of blushed, which was odd, because if there was one thing in school she was used to, it was compliments.

"What's that all about?" I asked her, as we kept walking.

Her facial expression suggested she had no idea. It was obviously a patently false suggestion.

We turned a corner in the southwest corner of the gym floor and saw Trisha Ryan. She sat sort of scrunched in her wheel chair with her left shoulder slanted down and her waist oddly twisted to the front. Trisha was a high school freshman stricken with multiple sclerosis, but her health, and her class schedule, required her to do a mixture of high school and junior high class work. I frequently saw Trisha in the middle school area, and my guess was she had difficulty handling the full high school curriculum, and received special instruction. But despite those challenges, Ed Franklin had told me, he and Trisha's mother, Molly, were determined Trish would graduate after four years of high school with the rest of her class.

Annie had once explained to me the diabolical efficiency of multiple sclerosis. The disease essentially attacked the core of the central nervous system – the brain, optic nerves and spinal cord – and it was the body's own immune system that caused the damage. As Annie described it, with multiple sclerosis the immune system went on a physiological rampage and actually attacked healthy tissue, and the result was a degenerative descent into physical – but not necessarily mental – paralysis. Trisha's eyes at times seemed unfocused and distant, her speech could sound slurred and I'd seen her limbs shake with a slight but prolonged tremble, but Annie insisted Trisha's mind didn't fully mirror her physical deterioration. Since Annie was smart enough to miss parts of classes, Ed once told me, she was assigned or volunteered to partially tutor Trish and assist Trish in special projects like library research or school assemblies.

Molly was a member of the school board and perpetually hovered close to her daughter, but she typically addressed Trish in an adult conversational voice and best she could, treated Trisha as a mentally and physically fit teenager. Trish had been healthier as an elementary school student, but as she matured, the disease tightened its grip. Molly never said so, but I always got the impression she ran for the school board specifically to make sure her daughter was integrated into the school as fully as possible, with standard classes and instruction and full interaction with students. That may not have been consistently or completely possible, but the school district and Molly had reached some sort of accommodation that allowed Trisha to absorb as much of the high school experience as possible. At least a portion of that experience was the direct result of Annie's companionship, and once, a year earlier, Molly broke into tears when she attempted to tell me about her and Trish's appreciation for Annie's patience and efforts.

At the science fair, Molly and Trisha both greeted us with big smiles. Molly stood behind Trisha off to her left, and Trisha rolled her head awkwardly toward her mother and then the two of them exchanged smiles; Trisha's mouth formed an incomplete, almost misshapen, crescent, as if the facial muscles didn't work in unison with the intention.

Then I noticed Trisha's science project exhibit – The Chernobyl Meltdown – and the small nuclear reactor cones or towers or whatever they were called, built sturdily on a table, with charts and graphs on posterboard displayed colorfully on the table.

I snuck a peek back at Annie, who averted her eyes.

"Hello, ladies," I said to Molly and Trisha. I had to concentrate to maintain a normal tone of voice. The temptation with Trisha was to talk too loudly, too cheerfully and too childishly.

"Hi," answered Trish. She had a hard time regulating, or modulating her voice, and she sometimes slurred her words, but I could always understand her. I took basketball photos in the school gym from a spot along the baseline, and Trisha and her wheelchair were usually tucked slightly off the court, slightly off the aisle, near the main gym entrance. She always wore Ranger purple and gold school colors and she understood the game of basketball – knew the Whitehall players' names – and knew when and what to cheer. I recalled late in a game, with Tony at the free throw line in a close game, Trisha yelled out, "Tony, we need *both* of these!"

"What do you think?" Molly asked, waving a hand toward the Chernobyl display.

"Pretty impressive," I said, and again looked at Annie, who again averted her eyes. I looked at the display. "What's a radionuclide?" I asked, hoping I had the word close to pronounced correctly. One of the charts stated, *more than 40 different types of radionuclides were released during the nuclear disaster.*

"It's a radioactive atom," said Trisha, with the word *radioactive* split into five separate words and much higher pitched than the word *atom.*

"No kidding," I said.

Trisha nodded, her head tilted unnaturally, her eyes aimed low, seemingly toward my knees. "That's what Annie says."

"Look at this," exclaimed Ed Franklin as he walked up the aisle toward us. He wore a dark green suit, white shirt and a too-short tie that stopped halfway down his belly, and with his thick glasses and short hair, he could have passed for the type of nuclear physicist who built reactors. He pointed at the Chernobyl exhibit. "This is very impressive." He nodded, examining the exhibit. "A science project based on contemporary events, expertly documented and vigorously displayed. Excellent." He looked at Trisha. "Is this your work?"

Trisha lowered her chin and nodded with slow exaggeration, her head at an unnatural angle. "Annie's and mine."

Annie stepped out from behind me. "Trish read about the Chernobyl accident in a magazine and after we talked about it awhile we thought it would make a good science project."

"I feel sorry for all those people who died," said Trisha. "Some people who aren't even born yet could die from the...." she faltered.

"Fallout," Annie added softly.

"Excellent, simply excellent, you two," Ed said. It was hard to tell who was happier, Molly or Ed. "Excellent subject matter. Excellent research. Look at that chart on radioactive half-life. Excellent documentation. Excellent display. And the map showing dispersal of the radioactive clouds? Oh, that's superb. Simply superb. Nice work." Ed bowed toward Trisha and Annie, and moved on toward other exhibits.

"I'd say he liked it," I told Molly.

"Sure seemed that way," she agreed.

"Why don't I get a picture of Trisha with her display," I said, and motioned for Molly to escort Trisha to the table behind the twin reactor towers.

"Annie too," Trisha said, her eyes briefly aimed at the ceiling.

"Right, Annie too," said Molly.

"I better not," I told them. "I have to be careful about putting my own daughter in the paper. People get mad at me if my kids are in the paper all the time."

"Annie too," Trisha demanded. The word *too* was nearly shouted.

Molly waved Annie to Trisha's side, and Annie slid behind the table. I arranged them so they were positioned between the reactor towers with the word *Chernobyl* above their heads. I attached my camera flash, adjusted the aperture and shutter speed to be in synch with the flash, crouched, held my breath, encouraged a smile, and snapped the picture.

On an inside page of the Ledger that week was a three-column photo of Trish and Annie and their science project, with Annie looking uncomfortably straight into the camera as Trisha looked absently at a point below and just left of the lens. Two other photos from the science fair were in the Ledger, and the photo cutline noted that the project by Trisha Ryan received a blue ribbon and the science fair's BEST PROJECT award.

I was at the Ledger the following week, laying out the high school graduation section, when Ed called and suggested the two of us needed to talk.

"When?" I asked.

"Now," he said.
"Now?" I asked
"Now."
"Where?"
"My office."
"Now?"
"Right now."
"What's up?"
"We have something to discuss."
"Who's *we*?"
"Your kids, you and me. We're here in my office right now, waiting for you."
"Now?"
Moments later I found a clearly subdued and disconsolate Tony slumped in a chair in front of Ed's desk, and Annie was seated impatiently off to the side. There was a chair open between them, and when I walked in Ed gestured for me to sit down.
Ed got up, walked behind the three of us and closed the door. His pants were too short, with an unfortunate gap between the bottom of his slacks and the tops of his socks that revealed a pale white lower shin.
Tony clearly thought he was in trouble, which meant Tony *was* in trouble, since he had enough experience about trouble to know what it was and what it wasn't and when and how it pertained to him. I couldn't get a read on Annie, except she was definitely not happy. I couldn't figure out why Annie was here if Tony was in trouble. Ed sat back into his chair, and looked from Tony, to me, to Annie, back to me.
"We have an awkward situation here," Ed started. "In fact, what we have here is a first. I've been an educator for my entire adult life and I've never had a discussion like the one I'm about to have."
Ed paused and I tried to think of a question, but nothing came to mind. Whatever followed, I knew, was not going to be good.
Ed looked at Tony. "The thing is, near as I can tell, in a strict sense, there weren't any identifiable school policies or rules broken here. Maybe a dress code violation, if I really pushed it. But mostly just some bad judgment and even worse hygiene."
Tony looked pained, and Annie, if I had to guess her attitude, was disgusted. I knew from body posture she thought we were wasting her time; I'd seen the body posture many times before. Annie could waste her own time; neither Tony nor I were allowed to do so.
"Lance," asked Ed, "where were you when Tony got dressed for school this morning?"
"Me?" I asked. Maybe it was me, I thought, who was in trouble.
Ed pushed his glasses up the bridge of his nose. "Yes, you. You're the boy's parent, if I'm not mistaken. Did you know what he wore, or in this case did not wear, to school this morning?"

I didn't like the direction of the conversation, although I wasn't exactly sure what direction it was headed. I shook my head. "I got an early start at the paper. They usually get themselves off to school. What happened? Was he late?"

Ed shook his head. "No, not this morning."

I turned to Tony. "What did you do?"

Tony's response was a sheepish, apologetic lift of his eyebrows.

Ed sighed. "Tony here was in gym class, outside playing softball with all the other sophomores, when his sweatpants slid, ah, south," he said. He adjusted his glasses. "Which normally might not be that big of a deal. Except young Mr. Joslyn here was not wearing underwear today. Pretty obvious, apparently. It made quite an impression, shall we say, on the sophomore class, and a somewhat more devastating impression on the substitute gym teacher, *Ms.* Whitford. You're familiar with Ms. Whitford, Lance? Sixtyish. Never married. Mormon. *Perhaps* a tad bit on the conservative side. *Perhaps*. My guess is she's still having heart palpitations."

I whirled toward Tony. "You forgot to put on underwear?"

Tony was appalled. "I didn't *forget*. I didn't have any. They were all in the dirty clothes."

I looked over at Annie. She looked away in disgust, as if totally disassociating herself from Tony, the conversation and me.

Suddenly the thought occurred to me. I pointed at Annie. "Why is she here?" I asked Ed.

"I'm on the form," Annie said, not looking my direction.

"What form?" I asked.

"The parental notification form," Ed said.

I was momentarily confused. Annie, age whatever, was on the parental notification form? Wasn't that my job? I was, more or less, the parent.

"I'm the one who filled it out," she told me. "It sat around the house for a week, you didn't do anything, so I filled it out and turned it in. If Mr. Underpants here gets in trouble, I get notified first, and you get notified next."

I was *second*? He only had one parent, me, and I was *second* on the form? I looked, perplexed, at Ed.

"It is an unusual arrangement," he admitted. "But Annie is an unusual young woman, and quite frankly, you have an unusual occupation and collectively, you're an unusual family. I'd say this conversation is proof."

No argument there.

"You're always busy, and on Wednesdays you're always in Anaconda, so it just seemed easier for me to assume responsibility," said Annie. She turned toward Tony. "But I'm not responsible for your underwear." She turned and glared at me. "You have to be responsible for something."

"What's wrong with wearing dirty underwear?" I asked Tony.

"They're dirty!" he answered.

"Then grab a pair of mine," I told him.

"Yours?"

"At least they're clean."

"What do you have? Two pair? They're never clean," Tony answered.

"Whoa," said Ed. "That's way more information than I need right now. The three of you can continue this lively and, I'm sure, most fascinating, conversation at home. Tony, consider yourself sternly warned, firmly lectured and acutely punished. I never want to have this conversation with you again. Is that clear?"

Tony nodded.

I stood up. I thought I detected a slight smile crease Ed's face.

Annie was the first one out the door, followed by Tony, then me. It was still late morning.

"I can't believe I had to miss geology because you weren't wearing underwear," Annie said, not looking at either one of us, matching out of the door to the junior high portion of the building.

I assumed Tony headed back toward class. He vanished before I could ask him if he was wearing underwear, and then I realized that was a question I never wanted to ask my high school son. I took a left out the door, toward the teacher's parking lot and my car. The thought crossed my mind that I had better get Annie to do laundry that night while I finished laying out the Ledger.

Molly Ryan was one of the school board members who handed out diplomas to the WHS Class of 1986 graduates during the somewhat dull and dragged out graduation ceremony. Trisha was at the edge of the bleachers, sitting on the front half of her wheel chair, applauding as each senior walked up to, and across, the stage to receive their diploma. Another school year had come to a close. Another summer had begun. Another class of high school graduates was sent out into the world. In the bleachers and folding chairs mothers wept. Fathers sighed. Grandparents applauded. None of them could have predicted what would happen when school resumed in the fall.

Chapter 7

Each month in Montana casts its own distinct and unpredictable touch upon the landscape, but June is the crown jewel of Montana weather and mountain magnificence. It is June when the bite of winter departs in earnest, and although midday June weather can be excessive, the grass is a thick and fragrant fresh green, the rivers are high and wide and alive, bright white snow still covers the mountain peaks, prickly pear colorfully dots the pastures, the nights and mornings are cool and the sweltering and dry brown days of summer still lurk in the future.

In their end of the year report cards, Annie received her usual straight A's, Tony managed some A's mixed in with his B's, so as a reward for their diligence and for a rare out-of-town family treat the three of us – plus Tony's friends Cale and Mite – journeyed east and south on a June Saturday to the Paradise Valley and the destination resort of Chico Hot Springs. With the Ledger's summer recreation guide – a special section to promote tourism in the Jefferson Valley – printed and distributed, and with high school sports completed, a Saturday with no pressing responsibilities was heaven sent and none of us needed added incentive to take a break from Whitehall and work.

The Bridger Mountains were blanketed with snow the color of ivory twelve hours old as we sped along I-90 past Bozeman, and the jagged white peaks of the Absaroka Range seemed as sharp as sawtooths as we drove south along the Yellowstone River. The water ran fast, choppy and muddy, and the pasture on either side of the road was a lush green, with the hillsides to the west of us covered with a near fluorescent green of fresh fine growth. In forty days, maybe less, portions of those hills would be burnt to a color not quite brown but deeper than lifeless yellow by a hot unyielding sun and persistent dry wind.

Chico was a Montana tradition, a countrified hot springs resort a few miles north of Yellowstone Park. The power company had held frequent management meetings, planning sessions, team building seminars and employee training workshops at Chico, and more than once the combination of unnecessary consumption of alcohol and excessive warmth in the hot pools had left me alarmingly dehydrated and hung over the following morning.

In its early years, perhaps a century earlier, Chico had been a retreat for the ill and diseased. Several old black and white photos displayed in hallways throughout the main hotel held ghastly images of skeletal men and women and children tentatively peering out from waist-deep water as nurses or attendants looked on. The pool appeared cavernous then, almost as if in a grotto, and the word that always came to my mind as I looked at the grainy images of the sickly bodies was *consumption*. The sagging skin and protruding bones of the pale and fragile people in the photos gave the appearance of wasting away. The hot springs were supposedly restorative.

By the 1970s Chico had transformed itself into a trendy resort, with its restaurant universally recognized as serving the finest food in Montana. Chico also offered horseback riding, river raft trips and other pursuits designed for people who had time and money. We had neither. We would not be dining at Chico. We would frolic in the pool and dine at McDonald's in Livingston before heading back onto I-90 and the trip home.

I had taken photos of a Boy Scout pancake breakfast earlier in the morning, and had to take photos of a St. Teresa Catholic Church mother-daughter fashion show late Sunday morning. That gave me Saturday afternoon and evening to play, and gave us a rare family afternoon together.

At Chico the three boys quickly changed clothes and jumped into the deep end of the pool. They brought a small rubber football with them and horsed around like the immature young male adults they were, and I knew and they knew it was foolish to even attempt to stop or counsel them. They were going to screw around, no matter what I said or did, so I said and did nothing. Cale Bolling was tall and slender, an excellent forward on the Ranger basketball team and would probably start as a receiver on the football team. His hair was long and when he burst above the Chico pool water he emerged with wet hair plastered to his face down past his forehead and eyes to his nose. A quick swipe and headshake and the hair was swished aside in soggy layers. Morgan Mightward was shorter than Tony and a little stockier, and his nickname *Mite* was based strictly on his height and last name. Mite, age sixteen, to my continual amazement, had a beard thick as a Biblical prophet. He was a child with facial hair, a heredity quirk of some kind, and he even had a patch of frothy brown fur in a kind of cross shape on his chest. His parents were separated, but both lived around Whitehall and seemed to get along pretty well. His dad had what seemed to be a typical mustache, so I was never quite sure where Mite's prodigious facial growth originated. Mite played jayvee fullback the previous fall as a sophomore, and I figured he'd get some carries on offense and see some time on defense as a linebacker. Tony, with his short brown hair, showed signs of sunburn almost immediately. Tony played some wide receiver and safety as a sophomore, and had a shot to start both ways as a junior.

It came so natural that it came without thinking, this assessment of high school kids – boys especially – as athletes. Almost everyone in a small town who follows sports looks at kids as athletes, and kids as components of teams. In a small town, it's impossible to *not* look at kids that way. I watched them play junior high sports, and even then – without intending to think about it or even realizing I was thinking about it – I would project them and their classmates or teammates into individual high school football and basketball players and collectively as high school football and basketball teams. There were other sports at Whitehall – cross country, track, tennis, wrestling – but sports and to a degree the community itself revolved around Ranger basketball and football. When Tony and his class first took the football field back in seventh grade, not only me, but all the other parents, virtually automatically and essentially immediately envisioned them with the kids one year ahead of them and one year behind them and projected them on future high school teams. A couple years earlier the WHS football team was led by a group of seniors who as eighth graders had been undefeated in football and as freshmen and sophomores had lost only a couple jayvee games. That's why when that class of boys, the 1985 Rangers, won only a couple games it was such a supreme disappointment. That year was supposed to have been *our* year. In the normal up and down cycles of Class B sports in Montana, you only get so many *our* years, and we had wasted one.

This upcoming season, fall of 1986, the Rangers were not projected to be much of a football team, especially with – as Mite called him – a "third string" coach. The team did have a returning second-team all-conference quarterback in Colt Harrison who had the potential to play college football. The football team had been dubbed the Dangers because of the team's dull ineptitude, but as I watched the three kids fooling around in the pool, I thought maybe the team needed a coaching change to bring some new energy to the program. Frank Stockett was a good man who meant well, but he had the creativity of concrete. His offense was not only predictable, it was boring.

While the boys played catch and splashed in the middle end of the big pool, I rested with my arms outstretched outside on the ledge in the super-heated water of the little pool. Cale stood in waist deep water, pretended he was a quarterback taking a snap from center, and in slow motion pivoted, turned and rolled out to his right. He pump faked once, then froze as if posing for a photo, smiled, blew a kiss to imaginary fans, and threw the ball toward Tony. Cale had been imitating Colt, and it had not been intended to be a flattering imitation. Colt was a good quarterback, but he wasn't as good as he or his father, Hank, thought he was. Colt had the perfect quarterback look – socks up just short of his knees, thick cotton wrist bands, eye black, little towel tucked in the front of his football pants – and I always got the impression that from Colt's perspective looking good was as important as playing well.

Annie had been in the water awhile, then found a lounge chair on the deck and produced a book to read. It was either a book by Carl Sagan or about Carl Sagan; I didn't know which and didn't care. Annie wore a basic two-piece dark green swimsuit that turned black when wet, and while if you looked close you could see a hint of emerging womanhood, to me she looked for all the world like a lithe little boy.

I also couldn't tell her it was possible she had been conceived in the exact corner of the pool where I now sat. One chilly autumn evening, during a long-ago power company retreat, Amy and I had overstayed and overindulged at the post-meeting reception and in a burst of liquor-inspired mirth took a nocturnal dip. It was night, no one else was around, and the difference in temperature between the warm water and cold air created a thick layer of misty fog throughout the pool area. Amy sat on my lap to start with, and things got considerably more interesting after that. When her pregnancy was confirmed, we counted back the weeks, and both Amy and I recalled the bout in the hot springs pool. I was halfway tempted to tell Annie I had a theory why she was so smart. In the old days people believed the hot springs had curative and medicinal purposes. I could tell Annie, if I wanted, that maybe the reason she was so smart was because my sperm and your mother's egg were unnaturally heated by the hot springs, which caused the heated spark of conception for an unnaturally intelligent fetus. I looked at Annie, laying poolside on a lawn chair, flat on her stomach with the book under her chin, and knew there were near infinite categories of information for which her insistent quest for knowledge wanted comprehensive awareness, but I was all but certain how and where she was conceived was not on that list.

Annie was asleep – her head resting softly against the front passenger side window – before we even got to Bozeman. The three boys in the backseat were drowsy but awake, their stomachs full of McDonald's grease and meat and their bodies weary and red from their fun in the pool. The car rattled a bit and shimmied its way west.

The sun itself had disappeared in front of us, but below the horizon, seemingly under the ground far ahead into the distance, a dark orange glow turned the distant sky a surreal light blue. The mountains to the north and south as we went through Bozeman were tinged in the mute orange of fading light, and then, almost like a lamp switch had been flipped off, the light vanished, and the horizon offered nothing but silhouetted dark features as night engulfed us.

The lengthy afternoon combination of hot water and hot sun made me a little sleepy as well. I yawned, yawned again, tasted the bitter salt of the French fries. Behind me, Mite first, then Tony, then a few minutes later, Cale, each yawned.

"Did you know they don't have a precise scientific reason why people do that?" Annie said in the interior darkness. She apparently had merely been resting, not sleeping.

"Do what?" wondered Mite.

"Yawn," Annie said, sitting up.

"I thought you yawned because you were tired," Cale said cautiously. Annie's intelligence was intimidating.

"Some people yawn because they're nervous," said Annie. "And some people yawn because someone else yawned."

"We're all pretty sleepy," said Tony. "Sleepiness makes people yawn."

Annie nodded. I thought she might leave it at that, and she might have thought about leaving it at that, but she couldn't, and didn't. "Some animals yawn. Some don't. But all animals get tired. So yawning is distinct from fatigue, both in the human condition and animal kingdom. Just watch people sometime. Someone will yawn, and someone well rested will see the yawn, and themselves yawn. There's no behavior quite like it, really. Yawns are contagious. But they are psychologically contagious, not physically contagious. Here, try this." She turned toward Tony. "Okay, we're all tried. We've all yawned. I want you to look me in the eyes for sixty seconds and not yawn."

"You think I can't do it?" Tony said.

"Lance, can you time sixty seconds?" asked Annie.

I looked at my watch. "On my mark. Ready, start."

There was silence behind me, and I knew Annie and Tony had locked eyes. Within ten seconds Cale resisted the urge to yawn, but five seconds later couldn't resist, and yawned. We all laughed and the challenge was set aside. Within a minute Mite yawned, then Tony. Thirty seconds later I yawned, and did so again ten seconds later.

"How do you know all this?" Cale asked Annie.

Annie considered the question, then said, "I was in the library a couple years ago, I think, and I saw a picture in *National Geographic* of an African lion yawning. As I kept paging through the magazine, I realized I had yawned two or three times. I went back to the picture of the lion, just looked at it for a moment, and yawned again. I was pretty confident that if I hadn't seen the picture of the lion I wouldn't have yawned, but I had seen the picture and then couldn't stop yawning. I thought that was interesting. From there I looked up the word *yawn* in the card catalogue and found magazine articles about yawns. There were actually quite a few about the phenomenon of yawning. More than I had expected, anyway. As I read, I was surprised at what science *didn't* know about yawns. It's pretty generally accepted that sleepiness generates yawns, but exactly *how* a yawn is created and exactly *what* a yawn accomplishes – in a physical sense – are still somewhat of a mystery. It might have something to do with an, oh, a kind of oxygen depletion, I guess, brought on by fatigue or drowsiness. But that can't be true in all cases, because anxiety causes some people to yawn, and in many ways anxiety is the opposite of fatigue or drowsiness. And yawns are psychologically contagious not only in humans but in animals, and many scientists doubt a lengthy list of animal species are actually capable of psychological contagion. So, as you might imagine, there's quite a bit of debate about all this."

By then we were almost to Three Forks. There were no further questions.

Monday again. Monthly town council meeting again. Another seventeen-hour workday again ahead of me, which was discouraging enough, but it was June, I realized, school was out, and neither kid had a real job, which meant the kids were unoccupied all day. Annie and Tony both helped at times with the Ledger, but that was sporadic at best, and for a parent like me who had no real time to actually parent, summer vacation was a period of great worry and uncertainty.

As I quietly snuck out of the house in the dark of early morning and walked to my car under a bleak sky swept with moving clouds filled with more energy than I had, the thought struck me that while during the school year I couldn't always be certain my kids were wearing underwear, I could always be reasonably certain where they were. Another summer had suddenly and unexpectedly appeared – at least it seemed that way to me – which meant unless I took active steps to find out, I would literally never know where my kids were, what they were doing, and who they were with, for hours upon hours, days upon days, and possibly weeks upon weeks. *I have to do better than that*, I mentally, but sternly, scolded myself. And I meant it. But then I arrived inside the cocoon of the Ledger, and the massive tide of work rose like the crest of a wave and carried me through the relative safety of a hectic morning. If I was obviously too busy to parent, I couldn't possibly be blamed for poor parenting or non-parenting. With my chaotic schedule, it was patently clear to anyone and everyone that I was overworked and overloaded, that I was essentially a slave to the never-ending tasks associated with producing a profitable and professional community newspaper. I not only didn't have time to parent, I didn't have time to worry about not parenting.

But, because I thought I should, I did get home for lunch after my ad stops. Annie was seated in my recliner reading a different book – a beat up paperwork written by one of the Bronte sisters – and Tony was sprawled on the couch, shirtless, slightly sunburnt, wearing pajama bottoms, watching ESPN. Neither kid seemed to notice my arrival. I opened the refrigerator to find something for lunch and was appalled: outside of a box of ancient baking soda strategically placed, in theory to curtail odors, the fridge was empty. Totally empty.

"There's nothing in here," I said, mostly in amazement, mostly to myself.

"We know," said Tony, behind the magazine.

I held the door open, peering inside, gazing in disbelief.

"I mean, nothing," I said. "It's completely empty."

"There's some radishes, I think, in the bottom tray," said Tony. "Maybe they're plums. It's hard to tell. They've been in there awhile."

The bottom tray held vegetables and fruit, and I seldom ventured that direction.

"Shouldn't someone go to the store?" I asked. I opened the bottom tray. Something roundish and darkish was there, but I couldn't tell what it was. "Someone should probably clean the fridge, too."

"I'll go shopping if he'll clean the fridge," Annie said.

"Yeah, right," Tony said. "As if I'm going to clean a refrigerator."

"Why can't you clean a refrigerator?" Annie asked.

"Because I'd do a lousy job, and germs would still be everywhere, and we'd eat tainted food, and we'd all get sick and have the runs," Tony said.

"Are you saying you're too stupid to properly clean mold from a refrigerator?" Annie asked.

"No, I'm saying I'm too lazy to properly clean mold from a refrigerator," Tony said. "I'm smart enough to do it, and I'm even smart enough to know

I'll do it poorly. Therefore, I'm smart enough to know I shouldn't even attempt it. Give me some credit, will you."

"*Therefore?*" Annie said. "*Therefore?* What are you, suddenly a college English lit major at Swarthmore?"

"What's Swarthmore?" he asked.

I closed the refrigerator door. "I'm going to A&W," I told them. "You two sort out who does what, but when I come home tonight I want the fridge clean and filled with fresh food. And get another box of baking soda."

And I left. That was more and more becoming my role as parent. Discovering a problem existed, ordering the kids to fix the problem, then fleeing.

Rachel nodded a stern and stealthy greeting to me when I entered the town council chambers. I took my usual seat on the right side of the front row, and the meeting got under way with an immediate dispute about the agenda. The debate had something to do with a preliminary budget review meeting, but I was scarcely paying attention. The town's budget was essentially the same every year, with the same disagreements every year, and for a couple years when I first arrived in Whitehall I wrote lengthy series of researched and complicated articles about the budget that no one but Rachel read. They even bored me, when I proofread them. So in recent years I had merely summarized the budget in one article, and the article explained – as simply as possible – only the most pressing funding priorities or decisions approved by the council.

The mayor called the meeting to order at seven-thirty and I had been hoping they'd wrap things up quick so I could get back to the Ledger, call home and check on the kids, write the town council article and start laying out the paper with enough work completed to be home before one o'clock.

But Andy Zankowski, a council member who was also a capable and experienced administrator at Golden Sunlight Mine, understood budgets and budgeting, and since this was his first year on the council he was rightfully having a difficult time reconciling the town budget procedure with the actual town budget.

What he didn't know yet was that the town budget procedure was determined not by state law, budget protocols, administrative procedures or Robert's Rules of Order. The town budget procedure and funding allocations were determined outside any official meetings or discussions by town clerk Rachel Brockton, who sat next to the mayor, silent, listening to Andy's futile discussion wear itself out. Andy, who meant well, was frustrated with his inability to zero in on the exact question he wanted asked or the precise answer he wanted in response, and Brandon Grant – with two years on the council – agreed with Andy even though Andy couldn't have explained with precision exactly what there was to agree with.

After twenty minutes of meaningless and rambling conversation, Rachel touched Mayor Luke Grayling on his shoulder, whispered in his ear, and he nodded.

"We'll look into that," the mayor assured Andy, although no one – not even Andy – knew what the mayor had agreed to look in to, or thought he actually would. Rachel's dominance over the budget and town proceedings was not malicious or illicit. She just thought she could run things a lot better than a council of well-intended but largely inattentive and confused officials, and it was difficult to argue with her on that point.

The council didn't get into the *new business* portion of the agenda until nine o'clock.

"Tonight we're going to have first reading of a proposed nuisance and decay ordinance," said the mayor.

"What's loose?" asked Old Tom Langston. It was a challenge to figure out what was worse for Old Tom, his hearing or his health. He'd lost some recent weight, and he had a waggle of loose flesh under his chin at his throat. He wore slippers rather than shoes, and his feet were propped up on a special stool under the long council tables. I suspected the stool was brought from home by Young Tom, Old Tom's son, who looked as if his hair, cap and jacket had mopped up a quart of used forty-weight oil.

"Nuisance," corrected the mayor. "Nuisance and decay."

"Not since Thursday," responded Old Tom.

The mayor simply nodded.

Chance Dawson, town attorney, explained the purpose of the proposed town ordinance. He said the town had received several complaints of junk, garbage, debris, abandoned cars and worse accumulating on private property in Whitehall, and the odor, mess and general uncleanliness – plus some safety concerns – devalued the property of neighbors and ruined the appearance of the neighborhood.

"It's about time we address this," said Hannah Brosovich, a council member. "I've lived here my whole life and it's time we show some pride in ourselves and our community."

"This proposal is hostile to private property rights," said Scott Forester, a council member who was a retired railroad employee. "We can't tell people what to do with their own lands."

"Chance?" the mayor said, and turned toward the town attorney.

"Actually, we can," Chance said. "This proposed ordinance is based on several existing ordinances in other communities around the state. In fact, this is based – pretty much copied word for word, in fact – from the model ordinance we obtained from the Montana League of Cities and Towns."

"You can't tell me what to do with my property," argued Scott. His face took on a faint red glow as he spoke. "It's my property and I can do with it, or not do with it, whatever the hell I want."

"Chance," the mayor said.

"A property right is a limited right," the town attorney said. "There is abundant precedence in state and federal statute to constrain a property right."

"Constrain it my ass," Scott responded.

Rachel scowled; she did not appreciate foul language during her meetings.

"It's sort of like the right to swing my fist stops at your nose," reasoned Andy. "In this case, the right for me to manage my property stops before my property impacts or impairs your property."

"That's one way of saying it," agreed the town attorney.

Andy smiled. "I work at the mine, and believe me, we know about property rights. We own that property, but there are a lot of things the law says we can't do, and a lot of things the law requires us to do, on our own property."

"I vote no," interjected Old Tom.

"There's no vote yet," the mayor said.

"Why not?" asked Old Tom.

"Because no one's made a motion, and no one's going to make a motion because it's only first reading," said the mayor.

"That ain't American," asserted Old Tom.

"You can vote no next month," Rachel assured him.

"I wanna vote no now," Old Tom said.

"So noted," said the mayor.

By the time the meeting ended it was after ten o'clock. I was tempted to stop home and check on the kids, but I knew that would prolong an already late night of work. I called them when I got back at the Ledger. Annie answered the phone.

"So who cleaned the fridge?" I asked.

"I'll give you one guess," she answered.

"Why didn't Tony do it?"

"He said he would while I was at the grocery store," Annie said. "But when I got back he hadn't even moved off the couch. Come to think about it, I'm not sure he left the couch all day." She hesitated, as if mentally confirming her statement. "Long story short. The fridge is clean and stocked. You're welcome."

"That was actually pretty shrewd of him, wasn't it?" I thought out loud. "He deliberately took advantage of your noble and generous character to weasel out of a job. What a little shit he is. Put him on the phone."

"No, that's okay," Annie said. "I took care of it."

"You took care of it? Took care of what?" I paused. "Annie, how?"

There was no response.

"Annie, what did you do?" I asked.

She paused. "Nothing, really."

"Annie," I queried. "Is this something that's going to make him sick?"

"He's always got to learn the hard way," she said. "You'd think he'd eventually start to figure things out, but for some people it takes awhile."

"I don't like the sound of that," I said.

"How was the town council meeting?" she asked.

"Oh no, you don't," I told her. "What did you do?"

"This is between him and me," Annie said. "If I was you, I'd stay out of it."

"Put him on the phone," I said.

"Don't tell him," she told me.

"Put him on the phone," I directed.

I heard the phone placed on the kitchen countertop – placed a little too firmly, with a little too much emphasis – and then I heard Tony's voice.

"What are you doing?" I asked him.

"Watching TV," he said.

"How many hours of that do you watch every day?"

"Exactly? Tough question, Lance. Got to get back to you on that one."

"Did you clean the fridge this afternoon?"

I heard some kind of audible sound.

"What?" I asked.

"Not exactly," he confessed.

"Why not?"

"I meant to."

"Why didn't you?"

"I don't know. Annie beat me to it."

"What, you couldn't fit it in your schedule? Cleaning out the refrigerator is not a complicated proposition. Don't tell me you didn't have time."

"It's done. It's clean. Annie did it," he offered.

"So Annie went shopping, cleaned the fridge and put all the food away?"

Another audible sound.

"What?"

"I guess," he said.

"What did you do while she was doing all that?"

"I dunno." It sounded weak, and he knew it. "I gotta cut the grass later this week."

"So, what, you were resting all week for an hour of lawn work? Do you know how lame you sound?"

"Annie decided to clean the fridge herself. I would have done it later, but she said it had to be done right then, so she did it."

"Because you were too busy watching television?"

"I was watching a movie."

"You're pathetic," I said.

"That's pretty harsh, Lance."

"Are you wearing underwear?" I asked.

"Pretty sure Child Services frowns on those kinds of questions."

"Put your sister on."

"Annie!" he yelled. Either he shouted into the phone mouthpiece deliberately, or he wasn't smart enough to move the telephone away from his mouth when he shouted.

"Yeah?" Annie asked.

"Whatever it is you're going to do to him, you have my permission," I told her.

"Oh you nasty boy," she said, and hung up.

Brent Walker, a rancher north of Whitehall in the Whitetail Valley, was chairman of the Whitetail Water Users Association, a group of landowners who maintained a ditch to irrigate the bench land throughout the low, wide valley north of town. The old ditch headgate that had been around for generations – possibly since shortly after the turn of the century – had partially rotted and leaked, and the water users had prevailed upon the Bureau of Land Management to allow the installation of a new one. Work in a steam corridor is never an easy proposition, and with the BLM involved – the land immediately surrounding the headgate was public land – the job was even more complicated. It took years of governmental paperwork, environmental decisions, bureaucratic intervention, public hearings, redesigns of the headgate itself and even a district court legal determination before Brent and the water users were finally able to install the new headgate. The old headgate had deteriorated to the point that water leached through it and around it, was difficult and even slightly dangerous to operate, and more than once Brent had told me he was going to take some dynamite and blow the headgate into pieces smaller than a "BLM guy's brain." Finally, after a series of lengthy delays, the new headgate was getting installed, and Brent and the BLM invited me up to take pictures of the project.

Brent ran cows up on his ranch but also had some quarter horses. He called his place the Wind Dance Ranch, and all over Montana landowners gave their ranches names like Crosscut Ranch or Wolf Howl Ranch or the Shadow Ranch. Brent had a son named Tanner who was in the same class as Tony, and Tanner was an odd mixture of child: He was a tough little guard and linebacker on the football team, and was also a soloist in the high school choir and usually had lead dramatic roles in the high school plays. Brent was something of a notorious man himself. His first wife, Liz – Tanner's mom – left the ranch about five years earlier, when Tanner was still in elementary school. Within a week after Liz left, Lucy moved in, and Lucy was maybe – maybe – twenty-one years of age at the time. Lucy had black hair down to her waist, fancied bright cowboy boots, big belt buckles and wore oval loop earrings big enough to hold a parrot. More than once I'd bumped into Brent and Lucy at one of the town taverns, more than once they'd stayed too long and drank too much, and more than once I'd had to force myself to not contemplate what Brent and Lucy did in the privacy of their own ranch house while I slipped into my cold and shabby bed alone, a sorry role model for two children. I recalled one night in Borden's Brent joked he was going to rename his place the Lucky 21 Ranch.

The first time I met Brent, in fact, was at Borden's back when he was with Liz, at the time a chubby and cheerful redhead. I told Brent I had wanted to take some pictures of a rancher cutting hay, and he invited me to his place the next day. The late June afternoon sun was low in the southwestern sky, and photos of Brent and his swather grinding their way south were lit perfectly to toss long shadows across the furrows. I moved throughout the field, kneeling in the long grass, taking pictures that showed a cloud of dusty chaff surrounding the swather, with neat and symmetric rows of deep green hay cut and furrowed behind and to the side. And I crouched, and sat, in the tall grass, using some uncut hay in the foreground, dwarfing the swather in the background. I took maybe thirty photos, while Brent and the swather did slow, square turns in the field. When I was done I waved, and he stopped the swather. His face was dusty and greasy, his brown cowboy hat matted with chaff, and I noticed he had a holster wrapped around an iron rod near the swather seat, with a large handgun sticking out of the holster.

"What's the gun for?" I asked him.

"Snakes," he said. "This field is filled with rattlers."

"Shit," I gasped.

"Yeah," he said. "I figured you were either pretty brave or pretty stupid crawling around like that."

So when I arrived the afternoon of the headgate installation, I parked in the short dry grass between two pickups and even before I stepped out of the car I was on the lookout for rattlesnakes. Despite what you may think or what you may have heard, their rattle wasn't all that loud and sometimes they didn't bother to rattle at all.

I grabbed my camera bag, looked for and found Brent, and without even realizing it, I had already begun to think about the best photo or photos to tell the story, and had begun to formulate questions for Brent, BLM officials and the contractor about the new headgate. The BLM guys were in their tan uniforms and easy to pick out. Brent and the water users – all wearing cowboy hats – were clustered on a mound of dirt and gravel just beyond the spot where the headgate had been placed and was being installed. The contractors, a combination of Smith brothers and Davis cousins from Whitehall, had the area crowded with dump trucks loaded with gravel, a small crane, a combination of excavators and backhoes, and a cement truck. I took a couple photos of the backhoe lifting and dropping fill material near the water. The ranchers were clustered in one bunch, watching; on the other side of the ditch, BLM officials were gathered, watching.

"How's it going?" I asked Brent. I had to shout to be heard above the heavy equipment.

"We're gettin' there," he answered. "Look at them." He meant the quartet of BLM employees. "You'd think we were buildin' the Hoover Dam."

"It's just a headgate, for chrissakes," added Rand Bachman, a Whitetail rancher. "How many goddamn government employees does it take to stand around and watch us put in one stinkin' headgate?"

"Four, apparently," said Blaine Winston, another rancher and water user. Blaine was a college graduate, from Arizona State, and before he bought his Montana ranch he was an attorney in Reno for several years. You'd never know that by looking at him. He played the part of Montana rancher perfectly. His ranch was called the Roadrunner Ranch.

"Taxpayer money at work," grumbled Rand. For some reason, his place was called Three Diamond Ranch.

"We shoulda put this in after five o'clock," said Blaine. "Those guys look like clock punchers to me."

"It looks like the bastards are standing there like vultures, waiting for somethin' to go wrong," said Brent. "Like they want to shut us down."

I took a few more pictures with the equipment in the foreground and the BLM officials in the background as the area around the new headgate took shape. Soon cement would be poured into the form to stabilize the headgate structure.

"How's Tony?" Brent asked me.

"Fine," I said. "Lazy. How about Tanner?"

"Kid's got less common sense than a wood tick," Brent said.

"I always liked Tanner," I said. And I meant it. Tanner was always happy and friendly, and seemed to get along with everyone.

"Hell, I like him," said Brent. "I just wish he had a little common sense."

"How much common sense did you have when you were fifteen years old?" I asked.

Brent laughed. "I had plenty. Then I got my first hard on, and been in trouble ever since."

Three of the four BLM guys clustered around the backhoe and peered down into the fill material, conversed briefly, then backed up and conversed some more.

"I don't trust those little peckerheads," said Brent. He took off his cowboy hat, wiped his forehead with his forearm, and put his hat back on. "I was sure sad to hear about the passing of Frank."

"Yeah," I said. "I don't think anyone saw it coming."

"He wasn't a great coach, but at least he was a coach," Brent said. "I don't know anything about that new guy they hired." He looked at me. "You must know a little about him."

I shook my head. "Nothing more than has been in the paper."

"He ever even coached before?" Brent asked, as if the question was a complaint.

"Not much," I said. "He's played some college ball, I think, and he would have been the assistant coach, but when Wally Hope quit and went to Circle, the school board didn't have a lot of options."

"Christ," Brent said, and spat. "What did we ever do to deserve this? First, a coach up and dies. Then a coach moves to Circle. Circle, for god's sake. Why Circle? You don't move to Circle, you get sentenced to Circle." He spat again.

"I think both Tanner and Tony have a chance to start as sophomores this fall," I said, because I couldn't think of anything else to say.

"Yeah, and that's part of the problem," Brent said. "They're good kids and all, both of them, but neither one is really ready for varsity football. We hardly got anyone ready for varsity football."

"We got Colt Harrison."

"Oh, he's okay, I guess," Brent said as if he didn't mean it. "But the kids don't respect him. Tanner don't, anyway. Colt's parents thinks he's God's gift to Whitehall, but he's just an average player on a below average team."

"He's probably going to be All-Conference," I said.

"And we probably won't win a game," Brent said. "Hey," he said brightening, "what do you know about Cody Phillips playing football?"

I shrugged. "Not much. The new coach has been talking to him. Cody's a pretty tough little kid."

"Oh, he's tough, all right," Brent said, "and he'll be a good player, if we can keep him away from Manfred. Oh hell, what's their problem now?" Brent was looking across at the BLM employees. They were gathered around the headgate, and one of them was on his knees, gently scooping dirt away from what looked to be a rock. One of the BLM officials motioned for the backhoe to stop, and it was suddenly so quiet the world seemed to be without sound.

Brent took a few steps toward the headgate and gathered BLM employees. "Now what?"

All four of the BLM guys looked up at him. "We think we found something," one of them said.

"You couldn't find your ass if your balls had eyes," Blaine muttered quietly to Rand.

"We think this might be a bone," said the BLM official kneeling at the headgate. He gently took his fingertips and slid dirt away from whatever it was in front of him.

"This could be a major find," one of the other BLM officials announced. "This might be a Neanderthal man."

"Naw," said Brent. "It's just from one of the BLM guys from last year.

Chapter 8

The Ledger office was located inside a one-level L-shaped building on the corner of Legion Avenue and Division Street, and a goal had always been to get air conditioning some day. During the summer we stationed two large fans at either end of the office, and about 350 days a year the fans weren't really needed and the interior temperature wasn't really a problem. But a large white concrete slab led the way into and under the Ledger on the west side, and on hot summer days, when the sun eased past noon and direct unfettered sunlight hit both the cement slab and the west side of the Ledger office, the temperature inside could increase beyond comfort.

Montana is a state of meteorological extremes. No state in America has a wider gap of temperature than Montana. It can be, and has been, one hundred and fifteen degrees above zero in August, and five months later can be, and has been, sixty degrees below zero.

The Ledger building was actually set on top of a street corner that a few years earlier had housed a notable redbrick bar named Ram's, but a fire had wiped out a handful of the historic old structures. In their place a couple hastily constructed wood buildings – the building that housed the Ledger and another one that housed the pizza parlor – were poor and cheap examples of craftsmanship and architecture, were poorly insulated, poorly maintained and poorly designed.

Not far from our office was another edifice to poor construction. It was also a monument to greed and dishonesty, and it still stood as the tallest structure in town. After the turn of the century some businessmen swept into Whitehall and pledged to build a sugar beet factory if local agricultural producers would grow sugar beets. The businessmen even pledged a contracted price for the beets, and some Jefferson Valley farmers signed up. Investors back east approved the contracts, and impressively, a sugar beet plant was built. But it never operated. The power was never even turned on. It turned out the businessmen were swindlers who essentially stole money from investors and fled town. Not long after the crooks left town, so did the sugar beet factory. It was torn down, brick by brick, and hauled away by the truckload, reportedly to Utah, reportedly to swindle another bunch of greedy easterners. The large stack, however, was left behind, and still stood, a kind of tall round tombstone to Whitehall and Jefferson Valley economic opportunity.

On a warm early July Friday afternoon, the stack looming to the south, Annie toiled at what has more or less become her desk at the Ledger. Tiny beads of moisture formed on her forehead and upper lip as she prepared a bank deposit. Laura Joyce had left early, which she typically did on summer Friday afternoons – with my encouragement and blessing – when she was caught up with her work. Laura Joyce was paid by the hour, and if she had no work to do and was at work, she was being paid to do nothing. I worked far too hard for Ledger income to see it paid out for no purpose. Plus, Laura Joyce enjoyed taking Friday afternoons off, so it was mutually beneficial.

And, to be truthful, during the school year when classes were dismissed early on Friday and during the summer when she had nothing better to do, Annie would typically spend Friday afternoons at the Ledger, and I valued our time together at the paper.

"We need to get an air conditioner," Annie said. "It's eight-four degrees in here."

"I have no idea what an air conditioner costs," I said.

"You have no idea what anything costs. Besides, it doesn't matter. You can afford one. And you need one."

"How much money is in the account?" I asked.

"Enough," she said. She set her pen on the desk and looked at me. "You have no concept of money management, do you?"

"I have a concept of it," I said. "I just have no desire to do it."

"Money management is not that difficult," she said. "I keep telling you that, and you keep ignoring me. All you have to know how to do is count. And I know you can handle that, as long as there are not too many commas spread out within the digits."

"Did you just insult me?" I asked her.

"If you have to ask, then the answer is no," she said. "Let's do one simple thing. Take four thousand dollars from the Ledger checking account and place it in a money market fund. You'd triple your rate of interest with one easy transaction."

"I don't have a money market fund," I said. I didn't even know what a money market fund was.

She rolled her eyes. "I'm aware of that. Hence, the suggestion. You know, you're doing pretty well financially here at the paper. Surprisingly well, actually. Look," she said, and ticked the facts off with her fingers, "you have low overhead, manageable fixed costs and not much exposure to financial risk. The business is showing consistent slow growth. You have two bank accounts. A business checking account and a personal checking account. That's essentially nonexistent money management. You should diversify your portfolio," she held her finger and thumb a quarter-inch apart, "just a smidgeon."

"My what? Who do I look like, a Rockefeller?" I paused. "What's a portfolio?"

"It's just a collection of investments. Anybody can have one," Annie said. "I've been doing some research, and I'm going to have a portfolio before I graduate from high school. I could start a portfolio this afternoon, if I wanted."

"Here in Whitehall?"

"Why not? What, you think you have to go to Wall Street to create a portfolio? Get real, Lance. You can start one anywhere there's a financial institution. It's not that big of a deal. I intend to manage my money so it basically reproduces itself," she said. "Perhaps you've heard. I'm pretty good with numbers."

She always had been. As a baby one night she had crawled into bed with Amy and me, and at the time was so young she was still barely uttering simple words. She snuggled alongside me, alert and awake and mischievous, facing me and the digital alarm clock behind me on the nightstand.

"Tree, two, one," Annie had cooed.

In my drowsiness, it took me a moment to realize what she had done. I turned to look toward the nightstand. She had read the digital alarm clock dial. It was 3:21 AM.

"Amy, Annie can read the numbers on the alarm clock," I said.

"Good for her," Amy sighed. "Pat her on the head and tell her to sleep."

I saw through the darkness that Annie's little eyes were alive with fascination. It was beginning to dawn on Amy and me that Annie was a smart baby who did not sleep nearly as much as her brother, but we were still a couple years or so away from understanding that she was some kind of intellectual prodigy.

"Tree, tree, tree," I heard a baby's voice whisper with glee.

I had fallen asleep, with Annie still seated upright. The clock read 3:33 AM.

"You can do more than count, can't you," I whispered to Annie, whose eyes beamed with curiosity at the clock.

Not only could Annie read the alarm clock, I realized, she understood the significance of numbers. She somehow knew the numbering sequence between 3:21 AM and 3:33 AM were nonsequential but significant in their order. Had I not been so groggy, I would have been amazed. Instead, I reached over and turned the alarm clock so it faced the other way, because I knew *tree, four, five* was soon to be announced if I didn't.

Amy had resented working at the Ledger every minute of every hour of every day of every week of every month of every year she was in Whitehall. She had never been what you'd call cheerful, but on an average day at the Ledger she was silent at best, at times overtly unfriendly and at her worst, antagonistic. Days like this July Friday, when it was stifling hot in the office, she would silently seethe, waiting, searching for something to stir her anger.

"How much do you think an air conditioner would cost?" I asked Annie.

"Less than you'll make on legal notices this month," she said.

It had been a good month for legal notices. The county had been required to run a series of tax notices that took up the better part of two full Ledger pages for three straight weeks.

"I'm going to call Sacry Electric and tell them you want an air conditioner installed next Thursday or Friday," Annie said. "They'll figure out what kind and what size.

"Just like that? Buy an air conditioner? I don't think something like that should be so sudden."

"Sudden?" Annie cried. "You've been thinking about it for five years." She picked up the phone. "One air conditioner coming up."

"Annie," I said, "Are you sure we can afford it?"

"I don't know, let's check your portfolio," she said, and began dialing the telephone.

She spoke to Jim Sacry of Sacry Electric, and he said he'd be down to the Ledger sometime the following week to talk with Annie about models and installation. I listened to her portion of the entire conversation. Not once, it appeared, did Jim express uncertainty or hesitation about negotiating the purchase of an air conditioner with a junior high student, or ask if he should perhaps talk with me, the owner of the business.

"Done," she said, after she'd hung up the phone. She lowered her head, and worked her fingers over the calculator. Then she looked up at me again. "When I bring this deposit at the bank I'm also going to start a money market account."

"Can you do that?"

"I don't see why not," she said. "I do everything else."

"I mean can you do that, just start a money market account? You don't need a permit or something?"

"Jesus, Lance," was all she said. "You have the financial acumen of a child."

"This time I'm almost positive you insulted me," I told her.

The only thing I knew about fishing was the more beer I drank, the less the mosquitoes bothered me. Slack had a favorite spot on the Jefferson River in the canyon section east of Cardwell and LaHood Park, and we were at it the following Saturday when conditions must have been perfect because Slack – who cared if he caught fish – was reeling in fish after fish and I – who couldn't care less – even landed some stocky brown trout.

It was the July weekend before Frontier Days, the major community summer celebration in Whitehall, and I would have to work all day Sunday on laying out pages of the Ledger's Frontier Days special edition, which would be a thirty-six-page two-section paper with spot color on eight pages. I figured a little break on Saturday to fish with Slack would be a nice diversion, made even better by the oddity, at least for me, of actually catching fish.

We had headed out of town on Whitehall Street that morning and took I-90 east a few miles to the Cardwell exit, and as we left town I had looked south from the freeway and saw three or four boys on the football field. Shirtless in shorts, the boys were playing catch with a football, and one kid – who looked a lot like Tony – was jogging on the track with a guy who looked a lot like Jersey.

"What's going on over there?" I asked.

"Football," Slack said.

"Yeah, are those guys working out?" I asked, not really to get an answer but to verify that I was actually seeing people on the track and football field.

"It's too early for football," he said. For Slack, football meant fall evenings, part of the chain gang, holding on to a first down marker. "It's still summer."

He was right, but for a lot of kids in a lot of towns, football players worked out all summer, lifting weights and running in advance of August two-a-day practices. Whitehall kids had done summer conditioning a few years earlier when Coach Stockett was more involved and committed, but as his commitment diminished – and as the losses mounted – interest from players also diminished.

I tried to remember if I knew what Tony was doing that day, and I couldn't remember if I knew or not. A row of willow trees had been planted between the freeway and the field so my vision was partially obscured, but it sure looked like Tony on the track, and I thought I spotted Mite and Cale playing catch, and a couple other kids, as well.

"I wonder if we're going to win any games this year," Slack asked as we drove east past the football field.

"I don't know," I said, "but it's a good sign that we got kids out there working out and a coach out there with them jogging on the track."

"Who *is* the coach?" Slack asked. "Coach Frank died."

"Yeah, Coach passed away. The new coach is named Jersey, I guess. I suppose that makes his name Coach Jersey."

"Never heard of him," Slack said.

Yes, you have, I thought, and yes, you will.

"What I want to know," I told Slack, "is are we going to catch any fish?"

Slack grinned and nodded. "I am."

And Slack was right. In the Jefferson Canyon behind our fishing spot on the riverbank was a gaping hole in the rock wall where a couple generations earlier miners had carved out limestone for use in Butte, and west of us down river was a long tongue of red rock noted in the journals of members of the Lewis & Clark Expedition when they hauled themselves upstream on their way toward the Pacific Ocean. Better yet, in front of us was clear running water seemingly filled with fish.

Montana is internationally known for its trout, and fly fishermen from across the planet troupe to our rivers and mountain lakes each summer. Something about fly fishing always seemed effeminate to me, with the delicate nature of the cast and the intimate knowledge of the river and fish, only to release the fish you'd caught back into the river. The Jefferson River presented heavy water and big fish, and neither Slack nor I were much interested in delicate or intimate aspects of fishing. Nor were we interested in letting go any fish we caught. We both used Zebco spinning gear, and were tossing bright metal lures with treble hooks – the brighter the better and the bigger the better – into the water. This was fishing for men, and Slack hooted and hollered every time he hooked a fish.

"Slack, you know what I got?" I said, seated on a rock along the bank, can of Rainier Beer in my hand.

His cowboy hat was pulled down low to keep the glare of the sun from his eyes. “A fish?”

“Nope. I got an air conditioner, a money market account and a portfolio. All in one day.”

“What’s a portfolio?”

“Shit if I know,” I said. “I just like to hear the word tumble off my tongue. Portfolio. Tell me you’re not impressed. Portfolio.”

“Where do you get one of those?” asked Slack. He was drinking a plastic bottle of Squirt.

“At the bank. Annie took care of it. My portfolio’s making money for me right now as I sit here and drink beer. Tell me you’re not impressed.

I managed to land a few more fish, and as dusk shadowed the canyon Slack and I took our fish and brought them to LaHood, where we traded them for a couple steaks and for me, a few more Rainier beers. It was a logical and fair exchange: LaHood got to serve fresh trout appetizers all night during dinner, and Slack and I were properly rewarded for our efforts.

Steve Wendell, the owner of LaHood, who a couple years earlier had moved to Montana from California via Colorado, was tickled with the exchange, and even had us sample the trout we had hours ago pulled out of the river. I detected tangy spices, lemon and butter on the fillets, and the fish practically melted in your mouth.

“Why would anybody throw fish like that back into the river?” I asked Slack.

It was a tough philosophical and theoretical question for Slack to handle, so he just grinned.

We were grubby, so we ate at the bar, and not long after dark completely descended on the valley I noticed a few local ranchers walked in and took stools at the bar, and not long after that, it seemed, the bar was full.

The fish Slack and I supplied made us evening celebrities, and I pretty much lost track of time as Slack and I told stories of our prowess on the Jefferson River. Abundant other topics surfaced during the evening, and conversation veered from the sad neglect of county roads to the poor performance of the governor, from the invasion of tourists to the possible presence of a grizzly bear in the Tobacco Root Mountains, from the Whitehall High School football team to an alleged affair between a Boulder school official and an elementary school teacher. Plus, I was pretty sure everyone in the bar knew I had an air conditioner, a money market account and a portfolio.

“Watch out for the Rangers this year,” I told someone that night.

“Bullshit,” was the response from a Boulder Valley rancher. “You got no players, no coach, no program and no tradition. Boulder will beat you guys by fifty points, same as last year.”

It was hard to argue with that. The high school in Boulder, actually named Jefferson High, was simply called Boulder by everyone not residing in Boulder. Every year they beat Whitehall in football. The Rangers did fine against Boulder in other sports, but Boulder was dominant in football.

"We can't even beat Boulder's second string," Slack said, which was true but not necessarily helpful.

It was late by the time we vacated the bar and settled in the Honda for the ride home. As we pulled out onto Highway 2 to head back to Whitehall I realized the Honda reeked of fish, and that it was going to take a long time to get the stink out of the car. I could hear Annie and Tony complaining already. I reached over to roll down the driver's side window, and was directing Slack to do the same on the passenger's side when the headlights illuminated a large dark object in the middle of the road. I had no time to brake or swerve, and with an impact that sent Slack's forehead colliding with the windshield and my chest into the steering wheel, the front end of the car smashed into an animal as it simply stood in the middle of the road looking at us. After the collision the car weakly veered off to the side, into the borrow pit, and the overwhelming presence of heated antifreeze brought tears to my eyes.

In my mind, the immediate sequence of thought went: *We hit something. In the middle of the road. It must have been a deer. We hit a deer? We hit a deer. No, it wasn't a deer. It was a cow. It wasn't a deer. We hit a cow. Not a deer. We hit a cow!*

"We hit a cow!" I yelled.

"No shit, Sherlock," Slack answered, both hands holding his forehead.

We watched the cow limp off the road into the brush. It disappeared into the night. Montana has open range laws, which means if you hit a cow on any road under any circumstances and under any condition, it is your fault and not the fault of the cow or the owner of the cow.

"You okay?" I asked Slack.

"I got a lump on my head," he moaned.

I turned on the dome light and looked at him. It was a big bump. It was like he had a walnut under the skin on his forehead above his right eye.

"We better get you looked at," I told him.

I got out and inspected the damage. The front end was wrecked. I must have hit the cow squarely head-on. The bumper, both quarter panels, headlights, grille, everything was bashed in or ruined. But only a small pool of antifreeze slickened the pavement. The radiator rested under the hood at a crooked angle, and the hood itself was buckled into a low pyramid, but the radiator still held fluid and while one headlight was out the other one pointed up and away from the pavement, I could more or less see ahead of us. The battered little Honda started and wheels rolled when I put it in first gear. I eased the car ahead, and although I had to hold the steering wheel at an angle to drive the car straight, we limped the seven miles or so back to Whitehall. I stopped at the Ledger and called Dr. Terry Reiff at his home, who met us at the Whitehall Medical Clinic.

Terry was an affable guy from Missouri who still carried a bit of a *Missourah* drawl. He looked at my chest and quickly pronounced me fine, but spent considerable more time on Slack.

It seemed unbelievably bright inside the clinic examining room. I had to squint to see.

"You hit a cow?" Terry asked.

Slack nodded. I noticed how carefully Terry watched him nod.

"How can you hit a cow and end up smelling like fish?" Terry asked.

"The fish came first. The cow came later," Slack said.

Terry used a penlight and carefully looked into Slack's eyes and ears, and as he did so, he had Slack explain the place on the Jefferson where we had caught the fish. It was early Sunday morning by this time, and I had a hunch Terry was going fishing later that day, and I had a hunch where.

"He'll be all right," Terry told me. "He's going to have a headache for a couple days. His parents are on their way here to pick him up. I'll talk to them." His eyes narrowed slightly. He placed his index finger against my chest. "But you're supposed to be smarter than this. I should report you, and next time I will. Get out of here."

My bovine collision occurred late Saturday night, and by the time Monday morning rolled around the entire Whitehall world was aware of my accident. They had all heard variations of the truth, some versions disconnected to the truth, and there was lots of concern and questions about Slack's health.

"He's fine," I told all who asked. "He had a knot on his forehead."

During my stop at Rice Ford, I told Tom Rice I needed a replacement vehicle for my Honda. Tom was the opposite of the typically eager and cheerful car salesman. He was lanky and so lethargic the joke around town was that he wouldn't sell a car to just anyone, that you had to prove yourself worthy of a Ford before he'd show you around his lot.

"You whacked a cow with a Honda?" Tom said. "Cow won, didn't it."

"I'd probably call it a tie," I said. "We both sort of limped away afterward."

"Annie stopped by about an hour ago," Tom said. "She said you were interested in a new Escort wagon."

"Annie was here?" I asked. It took a moment to register. "A *new* Escort wagon?"

Tom nodded. "You just missed her. She picked up some brochures."

I closed my eyes and thought a moment. I had to ask. "You didn't sell her a car, did you? I mean, she didn't actually buy a car, did she?"

Tom laughed. "She's a kid. She's not even old enough to drive."

Not just any kid, I thought. "So the answer is no, you didn't?"

Tom continued to laugh. He shook his head. "No. I can't sell a car to your child."

That was a relief. Annie being a kid hadn't slowed her down much in Whitehall. I now had a portfolio at the bank, and for all I knew a portfolio was a lot more difficult to purchase than a new car. I had never owned a new car before in my life. Never. That was probably going to change. I was probably going to have a new Escort. If it came down to a battle of wills, Annie's will always prevailed. My bet was the new Escort was even going to come with air conditioning.

By the end of the day, Laura Joyce or I had talked to probably forty different people about the Saturday night collision, and by the time a special town council meeting rolled around that night I was pretty sure every single person in the town hall was aware my little Honda was essentially demolished after colliding with a cow. Most folks knew Slack and I had been fishing, and most folks assumed I'd been drinking.

Had I been as sober as a Methodist minister I still would have hit a black Angus cow standing in pitch black darkness on the eastbound lane of Highway 2. But I hadn't been as sober as a Methodist minister, and I would have undoubtedly failed a sobriety test. The kids hadn't said anything; they didn't have to.

I arrived at the town council meeting a little late and was surprised to find an overflow crowd had filled the council chambers. My seat in the front right corner of the room was taken; every seat was taken, in fact, and the mayor, Luke Grayling, and the town man, Gage Duncan, were setting up another row of folding chairs in back of the room. I followed the mayor as he carried two chairs in the back corner of the room, and when our eyes met I gave him a quizzical look.

"The damn nuisance ordinance," whispered Luke. "This is gonna get ugly."

Initially, the meeting rolled through the agenda with ease. As it did I scouted the audience and realized I only knew about half the people in attendance. Daniel Purdy was there, up toward the front, wearing his stained long-sleeved lumberjack shirt, the top button on his shirt buttoned, his rear end bolted to the edge of his chair as if he was certain the council was preparing to offend or eject him. Sally Logan, a young woman who meant well but couldn't quite figure out when she moved to Whitehall from Oregon she was no longer in Oregon, sat at the opposite end of the room, next to an elderly couple who had recently moved to Whitehall from Kalispell. I had met Sally only once, when she came in to subscribe to the paper, but she had reportedly been involved in a messy divorce out west. In Whitehall, there were not a lot of secrets. Accuracy, however, was just as scarce as privacy. She had at least two adult children; she had bought gift subscriptions for each of them at Christmas. As I looked closer, I could see a kind of division in the audience; a large turnout of folks seated around Young Tom would be against the ordinance, and a handful of others near Sally Logan had undoubtedly prompted initial consideration of the ordinance, and would support it.

It was a hot July night and, like the Ledger, the town hall chamber was not air conditioned. Actually, the Ledger would be air conditioned soon; an air conditioner was scheduled for installation on Wednesday, and just the thought of cooler air at the Ledger was refreshing. About a half hour into the town council meeting, the air was anything but refreshing; the place started to smell a little gamey, and a couple of the women turned their meeting agendas into fans and vigorously fanned the air in front of them. Young Tom's personal hygiene was almost certainly an unfortunate contributor to warm stale air in a small closed room.

"I smell fish," Old Tom blurted once during the proceedings. He sniffed the air. "Who smells fishy?" He sniffed again. His eyes prowled the audience, and I lowered mine when he looked my way.

An hour into the meeting, the subject of old business came up, and people in the audience started to shift in their seats and crane their necks to see around the people in front of them.

"It looks like we got a bunch of people who want to weigh in on this tonight, so I'm going to ask folks to keep their comments brief and to the point," said the mayor.

An older man with a scraggly white beard and scraggly long white hair suddenly bolted up from his chair. "No sir!" he shouted. "No sir, you can't do that to us. Americans fought wars to protect freedom of speech in this country and no communist mayor's gonna take that away from us."

I had never seen the man before in my life. It suddenly seemed much warmer in the room. The man remained standing, as if defying some imaginary voice that had told him to sit down. I had a hunch some of the unpleasant odor in the room could be directly attributable to him.

Young Tom stood up. He wore a greasy blue baseball cap with a U.S. flag stitched onto the front. "Harley's right," he said. He pointed at the mayor. "You have no right to tell us how long we can or can't talk. This is America, goddamnit, and I'll talk as long as I want to."

The mayor held his open hands in front of his chest. "Okay, let's calm down. And let's watch our language, all right. Let's show some respect and courtesy for everybody seated here tonight."

"I don't like the looks of this," Old Tom said, but no one was quite sure what he didn't like the looks of.

"The mayor is perfectly within his rights as an elected officer, according to Montana rule and statute both, to limit testimony," attempted the town attorney, Chance Dawson. "According to the Montana Code Annotated, the mayor—"

"Stick the Montana Code Appointed up your ass!" shouted the old guy named Harley. He didn't bother to stand this time. With his white-gray hair and beard, and his fiery eyes and throaty voice he looked and sounded like an unbathed and apocalyptic Santa Claus. "No socialist lawyer's gonna shut me down."

"Okay, let's settle down," responded the mayor.

If Luke had a gavel, he would have pounded it, but he had never needed a gavel before, and didn't have one now. Several conversations sprung up at once – among some in the audience and a couple in front among the council members, some of them friendly and some not – and Luke called out, meekly at first, to quiet things down. He was a little more forceful the second time, but the general din of noise continued. Rachel slowly rose from her chair, glaring at the audience, and by the time she was fully on her feet the room was absolutely and totally silent.

She then looked at Luke, and nodded; *you may continue now*.

The mayor was a nice man who worked as a local telephone cooperative administrative officer, but he was suddenly beyond his professional and political expertise, and it was apparent he knew it. He had never dealt with a crowd like this, an issue like this, or hostility like this, in his life. Possibly no one in the room had, and people like Daniel Purdy, Young Tom and Harley sensed that.

"Okay, let's try this," Luke suggested. "The council will take testimony from the public, and we'll try it without a time limit, and see how it goes. But please, be courteous and respectful of the council and the other people here tonight. When you testify, please stand up, state your name, and as succinctly as possible, your position on proposed Whitehall Ordinance 86-07."

Harley shot to his feet again. "The goddamn ordinance is unconstitutional!" he shouted. "You're trying to confiscate my property rights."

A slew of heads in the audience nodded, and it was obvious Whitehall Ordinance 86-07 was doomed. Luke would have done the entire Whitehall world a favor if he had simply accepted reality and pulled – at least temporarily – the proposed ordinance from the docket. Instead, the hearing continued.

"Please," Luke said. "Let's have decorum here."

Rachel glared at Harley. "Your name?" she stated flatly.

Harley paused. He didn't want to answer, but no one rejected Rachel, and even Harley, who had never been in the council chambers before in his life, knew that much. "Harley Vance, ma'am. I live on Jefferson Street."

"Thank you," Rachel said coldly.

And Harley Vance looked around the room, as if he was unsure what to do next, and sat down.

"I can assure Mr. Vance, the mayor, the council and everyone in this room that the proposed ordinance is legal and constitutional. The language within the ordinance is based on similar ordinances in Kalispell, Red Lodge, West Yellowstone and Missoula," said Chance.

"Missoula!" Harley bolted to his feet. "That's a den of communism!"

"Mr. Vance," was all Rachel said, and Harley Vance looked around the room, then gently sat back down.

"Thank you," Luke said. "Folks, this proposed ordinance simply aims to reduce the growing accumulation of waste, clutter, weeds and debris that is causing unsightly and unhealthy conditions in some areas of town. The ordinance builds in timeframes for appeals and mitigation so no one loses any rights. We're simply trying to create a more attractive and safer community."

Daniel Purdy stood up. He turned at an angle before he spoke. It was clear his comments were going to be directed to the audience as much as to the council. "I've lived here all my life, and I'm proud to call Whitehall my home," he started. "But I am ashamed of this mayor, this town council and this proposed town ordinance."

"Go ahead and talk, Danny," Old Tom urged. Old Tom had his left foot shoeless and perched up on a small footstool under the table.

"What's wrong with a more attractive community?" asked Sally Logan.

"I got the gout, lady," Old Tom answered.

Daniel Purdy ignored both comments. "This ordinance is just a socialist manifesto from a bunch of do-gooders who weren't even born here." He glanced at me, as if to direct me to use that statement in the newspaper article. I found myself wondering if Daniel Purdy knew what a *manifesto* was. I didn't. I was going to have to ask Annie. I wasn't sure I knew exactly what a socialist was, either, or what the difference was between socialism and communism. "They want to strip us of God-given rights and force us to live the way they want. What they're doing is criminal, in my opinion, and should not be tolerated. If this proposed ordinance passes, Whitehall will have what amounts to a Gestapo lawn police, who can fine us for not watering our lawn or cutting our grass, or having an old car in our garage or a pile of firewood next to our homes. I like Whitehall just the way it is, and if you don't, then I got just one word for you: leave. Get out of town and take your communist ideas with you."

Harley jumped up. "Goddamn right!" he shouted, and sat down again before making eye contact with Rachel.

Young Tom stood up. "See that flag there in the corner, Old Glory? That flag gives us ineligible freedoms and rights. And-"

"Unalienable," corrected Chance. "Unalienable rights."

"Who's an alien?" demanded Old Tom.

"That's what I said," an exasperated Young Tom yelled at the council. "Inalienable." I could smell the nicotine seeping from his agitated body and the cigarette smoke leach off his clothes from my spot in the back of the room. "I went to Vietnam and fought for that flag and those rights. And nobody, and I mean nobody, is going to take those away from me. Private property rights still mean something in this country, and it should mean something in this town. And if anyone thinks they can take away my private property rights without a fight, they got another thing coming."

Sally Logan stood up. "My name is Sally Logan. I moved here about a year ago, and live over on Rocky Mountain Drive. I'm afraid this proposed ordinance has been grossly misrepresented."

"She's a Bolshevik," Harley called out.

Sally was startled for a moment, but Harley never stood, or faced her, so she continued. "Nothing in this ordinance takes away anyone's private property rights. In fact, it reinforces property rights. It says, in essence, that your right to litter, pollute and ruin your property ends where my property begins. This ordinance simply protects my property – she pointed to people seated in the audience – and yours, and yours and yours, from the careless disregard of other property owners."

"What are you, a lesbian?" Young Tom demanded.

There are several versions of what happened next, but here's mine.

Sally grimaced for just an instant, and then shook her finger in the direction of Young Tom. Luke and Chance were both calling for order from the front of the room, but no one was paying attention.

Young Tom stood, and took a step toward Sally. A guy named Henry Branch, perhaps the only person in the room not interested in the proposed ordinance debate – he had a pending permit application to build an addition to his kitchen – reached out, in a helpful way, and sort of held Young Tom from behind, to keep him stationary. Henry was simply attempting to keep peace and protect Sally Logan, a woman he had never met before. Young Tom may or may not have been making an aggressive move toward Sally; he later claimed he wasn't, and that he had done nothing to provoke what he alleged was an assault by Henry.

But Young Tom did attempt to reach back and sort of punch or shove Henry Branch, which for Young Tom was a big mistake. Henry grabbed Young Tom in more or less a bear hug, and later said he did so for Young Tom's safety. Young Tom's cap fell off and his long stringy hair shook loose as he squirmed and, unfortunately, began to attempt to awkwardly and violently stomp on Henry's toes. The two of them, tangled up and off balance, tumbled forward and basically fell on top of an older couple named Miles and Lonna Simpson who were seated in the row ahead, and who were in attendance to support the proposed ordinance. I found out later they were next door neighbors to Harley Vance, and were not terribly happy about that fact, in that Harley's yard was largely a junkyard. Lonna Simpson was close to eighty years old and, weakened already by the stifling heat in the room, seemed to collapse when Henry Branch and Young Tom tumbled her direction. Her husband, Miles, who sort of resembled a vulture, immediately panicked, and blurted out something that possibly sounded like "she's dead."

Luke stood in the front of the room and attempted to calm people down, then started to rush toward the Simpsons. By then Sally Logan and Daniel Purdy were inches apart yelling at each other, and Daniel Purdy called her a faggot, and she slapped him flush across his check with such firmness it shocked his comb-over slightly out of place.

Old Tom stood to aid his son, but forgot about his gout, and yelped and fell over backward the instant he put weight on his left foot.

Young Tom, belly down on the floor, saw Old Tom topple backward. Young Tom howled, but Henry Branch, who hadn't seen Old Tom fall and was unaware of the family connection anyway, pinned Young Tom to the floor to, in Henry's mind, prevent additional mayhem or violence.

Sally Logan was angrily pointing a finger in Daniel Purdy's face, and Daniel Purdy slapped her hand away. She used her other hand to again slap

Daniel Purdy's cheek. Harley grabbed Sally Logan from the back, to "steady" her, according to his police statement, but Sally was younger and stronger than Harley Vance, and she had evidently taken self-defense classes back in Oregon because she whirled and brought a knee up into poor Harley's crotch so hard and so fast that it hurt even me, and I was six rows away.

Harley didn't merely collapse to the floor; he dropped dead weight like a stone. Sally brought her hands to her mouth in horror, and Daniel Purdy backed up a step, both hands guarding his crotch area.

Somehow Young Tom clawed free from Henry, and Young Tom crawled on all fours to Old Tom, who was flat on his back and motionless. A sense of order was slowly restored when people gradually began to understand that three people – Lonna Simpson, Harley Vance, and Old Tom – were possibly unconscious and injured there on the floor. Rachel had taken first aid and was an emergency responder, and although I didn't actually see her move, she was at Lonna's side with a small medical kit checking for vital signs. People cleared out of the way as Miles Simpson and Rachel knelt on either side of Lonna, who was awake and breathing, but not really moving. Young Tom had Old Tom propped up with his back against the wall, and Old Tom seemed to be, for him, breathing regularly.

Minutes later the Whitehall ambulance showed up and Lonna Simpson was carefully lifted and placed on a stretcher. Harley Vance, sweat streaming down his forehead, stood unsteadily, and for a moment he appeared as if he might vomit. He limped behind the stretcher as the attendants wheeled Lonna out of the room and into the ambulance, and Harley climbed in before the back doors of the ambulance closed, rolled to his side on the floor, holding his crotch, and joined Lonna Simpson for the trip to Butte and the Saint James Hospital emergency room.

The mayor adjourned the meeting.

Chapter 9

Sometime around 1972 the band Pure Prairie League came out with a song named *Amie.* For a few years I sang along every time it came on the radio or my car cassette deck, and it was understandable if not a cliché for Amy and me to pretend the song was our song. It took me a few years after she was gone to realize not only did I dislike the song, I had always disliked the song.

Amy and I had met in Missoula at the University of Montana. At the time she was majoring in a pre-nursing program, and I was in my final semester of my five-year collegiate career, more or less majoring in journalism, although I actually spent substantially more time bellied-up to the bar at the Missoula Club in downtown Missoula than at the college library. It was at the M Club, in fact, on a Saturday mid-morning before a home Grizzly football game, when Amy and I first met. We had a pretty standard romance, a pretty standard wedding, a pretty standard marriage and a not so standard separation.

I realized, after she left, that our relationship hadn't ever really lost the spark of magic affection, because our relationship had never really contained a spark of affection. On a rainy March afternoon, not six months after the wedding ceremony, I saw the wedding photo album sitting on the downstairs bookshelf in our house in Butte, and I looked at the guy in the tuxedo and tried to summon some kind of emotion, and couldn't. I didn't recall being happy. I didn't recall being sad. I barely recalled even being there.

The move to Whitehall was seen by Amy as an attempt to save our marriage, when in truth I had no idea our marriage needed to be saved, and if I had, I would have known the move to Whitehall only relocated our marriage, not saved it. For me, the move to Whitehall and the purchase of the Ledger was a chance to own my own business, publish my own newspaper, and have a measurable and visceral beneficial impact within a community. I had thought, since we'd had the two kids, Amy and I would more or less trudge through our marriage until separated by death. But in many ways it was something worse than death that forced us apart.

One night about two years into our stay in Whitehall I came home from a school board meeting and found Amy alone, in the kitchen, her suitcase standing upright alongside her chair at the table. The house was dark except for one dim bulb above the sink.

"I have to leave," she told me softly.

"You have to what?" I asked.

"Leave. I have to leave."

"Leave where?"

"Here. I have to leave here."

"For where?"

She sobbed once, and caught herself. She had straight blonde hair that she tucked behind her ears, but slight bunches of hair on both sides framed her cheeks. She always appeared slightly unkempt, as if indifferent to her looks or clothing. There in the half-lit kitchen, she looked dejected and defeated, somehow: Uncombed hair, shorts, baggy blouse, tennis shoes, all a poor fit for her and for the moment. She'd been crying. Her eyes were shallow, empty, or if not empty then simply resigned or indifferent, with thin gray pouches of gray underneath. She was thin, probably too thin.

"What's wrong?" I asked. I had seen this kind of emotional and marital drama from her before, and I was trying to walk a fine line between summoning genuine concern for her and at the same time wondering what was in the fridge for a late night dinner.

She lifted her head and looked me square in the eye. "Everything." I saw her throat gulp. "I'm leaving you."

I nodded. I realized she had never really looked me in the eye before. My mind was trying to assimilate her statement with her body posture and her attempt at resolve, and to buy time I opened up the refrigerator door. At first glance inside, it didn't look promising.

"Did you hear me?" Amy asked weakly.

"You're leaving me," I said, leaning toward the open refrigerator. There was essentially nothing inside it to eat. Cheese. Grapes. Grape juice for the kids. Milk. I took out the gallon of milk and set it on the kitchen counter. I poured a bowl of Grape Nuts cereal.

"I'm telling you our marriage is over, and that's your response?" she said, and sobbed once, or perhaps it was a half sob.

"Maybe we should sit down and talk this through," I offered. We had two kids, one not even in school yet, sleeping in bedrooms eight feet away down the hall. Amy had never accepted, or been accepted, in Whitehall, and it was largely because she'd never tried. But she couldn't leave, and my thought was we both knew that.

Before my uneaten cereal was soggy, she had set her spare house key on the table, told me she would be living near Missoula, and quietly left the house. In weak, hushed tones, she told me she'd told the kids she'd be gone for a little while, and told me that in a few weeks she would come back to get them and they would live in Lolo near her parents, Grandpa Earl and Grandma Jen, who lived in Stevensville. Amy's Subaru coughed once when she started it up, and even after I watched the tires crunch down the driveway gravel, and although I realized exactly as she slid the car from reverse to drive I'd always known it would end like this, I still had a hard time actually accepting her departure.

Tony was sixteen years old in 1986, and while he didn't have a real job, he did ride with me to Anaconda on summer Wednesdays to get the paper printed. The printers didn't care much for me but treated Tony like he was the print shop mascot.

Tony could do an uncanny imitation of Larry's hulking gait, agitated hand waves and involuntary little eye twitch, and the entire press crew – including

Larry, perhaps especially Larry – found the impression hysterical. Tony's mimicry had gotten him in trouble in the past, but it also bailed him out a few times, and it certainly lightened the mood at the print shop. I was known as a troublesome and difficult customer who was never satisfied with the quality of printing. That wasn't entirely accurate, because I was satisfied when the paper was printed consistently and properly. It was true I was frequently disappointed in the print quality of the Ledger, but not because I was troublesome or difficult, but because the print quality was frequently disappointing.

In addition to his services as an entertainer, Tony helped me stuff papers at the printing plant, haul fifteen-hundred bundled papers to the car in Anaconda and then about a thousand of the papers to the post office in Whitehall. He also helped deliver papers to the vendor locations.

Tony could legally drive at age sixteen, but we had failed to sign him up for driver's education, so he wouldn't be able to drive until his junior year. Driver's education in Whitehall was offered only during the summer, and signup had a defined time period during the spring. We missed the deadline of that defined time period. I had attempted to shuffle off the blame to Annie, but she adroitly argued she had brought the driver's education papers home from school, filled them out, and set them on the kitchen table for me to simply sign, which I promised her I would do. I was sure I would do that, and I was so sure I would in fact do that that I more or less claimed I had done that. The problem was I placed the signed forms in the car glove box, forgot about them, and by the time I discovered they were there and brought them to school, I did so precisely one week too late.

Tony was more or less on my side, in a way, and blamed Annie.

"Why didn't you take in the signed forms yourself?" he complained to her. "You know Lance always screws up everything."

His assertion was essentially correct. It was also correct that the more Annie was involved, the less likely it was that things would get screwed up. Given the consistent pressures from the Ledger, on the Lance Joslyn priority scale of life, regulatory forms involving the kids were somewhere between inconsequential and nonexistent. Because of that, and because the kids were now patently aware of it, my failure to file Tony's driver's education application would essentially be the final time I would ever be required to be responsible for any school or financial or personal official form for either of the kids. Annie was unofficially but absolutely delegated that authority, which was emphatically confirmed during Tony's dirty underwear dilemma.

As Tony and I drove home on a late July Wednesday afternoon from Anaconda, with fifteen hundred copies of the Whitehall Ledger stuffed in the back of the new air conditioned Ford Escort station wagon, I noticed Tony's neck and arms were sunburned. A few days earlier he and some of his buddies had floated the Madison River on inner tubes, and it looked like his neck was burned so bad it might peel. Amy would not have been happy; she was perpetually lecturing the three of us about the evils of the sun. He also had a smudge of newsprint ink above his eyebrow on his forehead.

The car still smelled new. It was the first new car I had ever owned. In a small town like Whitehall, everyone knows what everyone else drives, and everyone waves to everyone else. Behind the wheel of the new Escort I'd wave – a lift of my right index finger off the steering wheel – and some people either didn't think they knew who that was in the new Escort or saw too late to wave back.

"You got ink on your forehead," I told Tony.

"Does it make me look tough?" he asked.

I pretended to look at him while pondering his question. Solemnly, I shook my head. "It just looks like you have a dirty forehead."

The Bruce Springsteen song *Born in the USA* came on the radio and Tony reached over and turned up the volume. About a week earlier, when Tom at Rice Ford was showing Annie and me the car, Annie flicked on the radio, and *Born in the USA* had popped up on the stereo then.

"Coach Jersey plays this song all the time in the weight room," Tony said.

"You lifting weights now?" I asked.

He turned and showed me his bicep muscle.

"You guys lift weights at the school?" I asked. Perhaps his muscle was bigger; perhaps he just thought it was. Perhaps he just wished it was.

He nodded. "Almost every afternoon. Coach Jersey is there with a boom box, and he's always got Springsteen cranked up. I think Jersey knows every word to every Springsteen song."

"Who all lifts weights?" I asked.

"There's probably ten to fifteen of us in there. It's not always the same guys. I go pretty regular, but some of the kids have jobs and stuff. A lot of times we go out on the field and play catch, run patterns. Sometimes we run sprints or laps on the track."

Tony loved Burger King, so a typical stop for us on Wednesdays during the summer was the Butte Burger King just off Harrison Avenue. Tony usually ate a Whopper and onion rings, but as I stood behind him, the tune *Born in the USA* still playing in my mind, I heard Tony ask for two Whoppers. At first I thought he ordered for me, but then he stood aside; clearly it was my turn to order. He was digging in his back pocket for his wallet. Annie had trained him to always have money when he traveled with me.

"Two Whoppers?" I asked him.

He grinned, and the smudge above his eyebrow widened. "Gotta have fuel to burn."

We delivered the papers to the Whitehall vendor stops and afterward he went home and I went to the Ledger office. If you worked for a weekly newspaper, the afternoon the paper was published was a momentary period to collect your breath. I left Laura Joyce at her desk so she could get a leisurely start on the next paper, and Annie was at her desk figuring out advertising percentages for the mandatory postal report. Things were under control and I had a few minutes, so I figured I'd wander into the weight room at Whitehall High School. I was merely curious, and curiosity is an admirable, perhaps even a required, trait for a reporter.

It was still summer vacation. The main entry of the high school was unlit and deserted. No one was in the office itself, and the hallways near the office were dark and empty except for some large boxes and a few chairs. I detected a faint smell of paint, and something else, carpet shampoo, perhaps. Summer was maintenance time for the school, and Ed Franklin had the entire facility – classrooms, hallways, locker rooms, offices, gyms, parking lots, school grounds, fields – on a maintenance schedule. I heard a deep throbbing sound ahead of me, from the high school multipurpose room. I opened the doors and while the sound was clearer – and louder – no one was actually in the multipurpose room. The sound was coming from a storage room off the front of the room, right of the main stage. The noise got louder as I approached, and audible inside the throb of the music – which I could tell now was Springsteen's *Dancing in the Dark* – I heard the distinctive metallic *clink* of metal on metal.

I poked my head inside the door and was greeted by the crushing pulse of music, stench of young male sweat and hot, moist, almost suffocating, air.

"Hey, Lance," said Mite, his forehead glistening with sweat and a smile of white teeth between his youthful mustache and beard. He had to practically shout his greeting above the volume of music.

The music stopped, and it was as if I had been standing alongside railroad tracks as a train had roared past, and the lack of sound was almost palpable. But then another song kicked in, Springsteen again, singing about *Glory Days*.

A couple exposed ceiling light bulbs served as light. About a half dozen kids were inside what had been a storage room, where the multipurpose room tables and chairs were housed when not in use. I realized I saw, but didn't really understand what I saw, as I walked across the multipurpose room itself; lined up in rows along one wall were the sliding carts filled with folding chairs, and along the other wall were stacks of tables. The kids had to move out the chair carts to create enough room to lift weights.

I took a step inside the room.

"Welcome to the bunker," said Jersey.

He stood to my right, wearing a black tee-shirt with the word *Life* written in red script across his chest. His forehead was beaded with sweat.

"Does this place have *any* ventilation?" I asked. It was like being inside a bus with the windows rolled up on a hot day. I had been standing inside the room for barely a minute and I could feel myself starting to perspire.

Jersey shook his head. "It's much like a womb, isn't it," he said. "Or much like I imagine a womb to be."

"A little louder than a womb," I said.

Jersey pointed to a boom box perched on a shelf in the corner. "Yeah, the Boss. Many of the songs are anthems. Calls to arms, words to rally around."

Tony was in the middle of the room, lifting barbells. I saw him and nodded; he nodded back. The smudge was gone.

"Curls," said Jersey. "They strengthen the wrists, forearms and biceps."

Mite was off to the side, with a bar across the tops of his shoulders, behind his neck.

"Squats," Jersey said, indicating Mite. "Great for the thighs and quads."

Twin boys – identical twins named Jeff Collins and Scott Collins who since no one could tell them apart were both called JeffScott by everyone in Whitehall – stood near a bench that had weights coupled by two short twin posts.

"Bench press," said Jersey.

He turned away from me to JeffScott. "You guys posing or lifting? Come on, get going."

A couple more kids were inside. Dave Dickson, a small and slender freshman who looked more like a sixth grader, sat on the edge of a bench and lifted small barbells above his head. He almost looked young enough to need a babysitter. Another kid, a chunky sophomore named Bobby Bentmier, had sweated through his Ford Motor tee-shirt; it was fully sweat-stained dark gray except for one streak of light gray down each side along the ribs.

"Bobby's playing football?" I asked. Bobby was a good student and a nice kid with curly brown hair who liked chess and played trombone in the band.

"Bobby's playing football," Jersey repeated. "Look at him. He's a natural born defensive tackle. You gotta get kids his size on the football field."

Bobby was in the same grade as Tony and to my knowledge had never played sports before, not even in junior high. He was on the academic honor roll every semester but was soft and chubby, almost doughy. You could see it even through a sweated shirt in a weight room.

"You watch," Jersey said, either sensing or seeing my disbelief. "Bobby Bentmier is going to be a very good football player. A very good football player."

Bobby Bentmier was a good musician, maybe. Standing in a weight room, barbells in his hand, he looked like a good musician.

Tony's sunburn was so deep it appeared he was giving off radiation. It didn't seem to bother him, though. He focused his attention and breathed rhythmically as his arms pumped the weights. His bangs were glued by sweat to his forehead. The song *Born in the USA* came on and immediately Tony and a couple other kids were singing, shouting, "*Baaawwn inna Yewessay*!"

Jersey smiled. "Anthems. Calls to arms."

I nodded. The heat was oppressive. I needed to breathe, so I left.

In Amy's world, there were many enemies. The sun was one. Amy was a trained nurse, and she had learned long before we were married that sunshine caused cancer, and forever after that a primary goal in her life had been for her family to avoid the sun's deadly rays. The kids had been covered with hats in Tony's case, bonnets in Annie's case, long sleeve shirts all summer and layer upon layer of sunscreen for all of us, all the time.

I had the impression Amy viewed the sun as a diabolical foe plotting and scheming to strike down the unsuspecting, helpless or vulnerable. It was as if the sun was alive and organic, a thinking and sinister entity, exploiting the narrowest carelessness or error to cause damage.

Tony, during his days as a little league baseball player, had been repeatedly called out of the dugout by his mother for another application of sunscreen, until he finally attempted to ignore her. But Amy, at times, would not be ignored. At a game in Ennis, everyone at the field – players and parents from both teams – knew that Tony's mom wanted to apply more sunscreen to her apparently reluctant and unresponsive son. Amy, wearing a large floppy hat, continually insisted he step out of the dugout toward the fence along the right field line for another layer of sunscreen.

"Tony!" she called. Her fingers were intertwined with the chain link fence, and her pale, alert face was intently pressed against the metal fence wire. "Anthony Joslyn, you come here this instant!"

Some of Tony's teammates snuck nervous uncomfortable peeks at Tony in the dugout and toward his angry mother along the fence, attempting to avoid both of them.

I was seated next to Amy's empty lawn chair, immediately behind her as she stood at the fence. "Amy, come on, leave him alone."

She pretended to not hear me. "Tony! I mean it!"

"Amy, for Christ's sake, he's got four layers on already," I said, probably too loudly.

She whirled at me. "Sunburn kills people! Just because you don't care if he gets cancer doesn't mean I don't care," she said. "He's my son, and I'm going-"

Tony was standing along the fence, quietly, passively, ready to accept his punishment, more sunscreen. It was liberally applied, along with a stern lecture from Amy.

Germs were another of Amy's enemies. Our house, a one-story perfectly square enforced box built in the early 1920s, was never clean enough. Germs hid everywhere; in the refrigerator, in the sink, in the bathroom, the bedrooms, in the dirty clothes hamper. The kids were little germ-producing factories, in Amy's mind, and when they were infants she would follow them around the house, spraying disinfectant on chairs, floors and toys.

Strangers were enemies. Every stranger was suspect. As were some acquaintances.

My God, Amy, I'd think years after she'd left for Lolo, you should see how the three of us live now. I failed to apply sunscreen to either kid, the house had degenerated into a germ manufacturing plant, and the kids were essentially totally unsupervised, which meant I typically had no idea where they were or who they were with, and if one had been snatched by a kidnapper or molester it might take a few days before I'd notice.

After closing up the Ledger on Wednesday, I went home and searched the kitchen for something that could modestly be interpreted as something suitable for dinner. Sausage and mayonnaise sandwiches was a possibility. Annie had disappeared after work at the Ledger, and she was either at the library or not, or at a friend's house or not, and her plans for dinner were uncertain at best and more likely unnecessary. Tony was gone, probably with friends after his workout, so I figured I was on my own. I opened the mayonnaise jar and smelled it. No mold on the sausage. I looked for cheese, but couldn't find any. I took out a loaf of bread, spread some mayonnaise across and noticed the crust was covered with green and yellowish fuzz. The garbage can under the sink was full, but I shoved hard and stuffed the bread on top and closed the cupboard door.

I spread mayonnaise on a piece of sausage and chewed, but I thought I should be able to do better than that. The sausage seemed somewhat spongy, which I assumed was not a good sign. I found a can of chili, a couple cans of baked beans, some IGA creamed corn, a jar of olives, peanut butter and a plastic container of honey as hard as a baseball bat. I would have thrown the honey away but since the garbage basket was full, I stuck the container back in the corner of the cupboard.

I was always hungry on Wednesday nights. It had something to do with getting the paper out, with being able to relax, and because Mondays and Tuesdays were typically so hectic I had to eat on the go or miss meals entirely.

So this Wednesday night it was off on a solo trip to the Whitehall A&W. I walked in and saw Tony and a gang of kids from the weight room stuffed in the corner booth, and across from them were Annie, Molly Ryan and Trisha, Trisha's wheelchair rolled up to the outside edge of one of the tables.

There was the Joslyn family, all three of us, independently dining out.

Joan Jones, the A&W owner, stood behind the counter taking orders. Joan was an energetic forty years old, a successful business owner and community leader, and a fairly frequent Ledger advertiser. She was always amazingly upbeat. About a year earlier there had been a small grease fire in the A&W kitchen and the Whitehall volunteer firefighters were called to put it out. I wrote a small article about the fire and interviewed Joan, and she almost seemed enthusiastic about the fire, as if a grease fire was an entertaining and agreeable event in the life of the Whitehall A&W, and she had gushed praise that the fire department risked their lives to battle the blaze. All for a fire that could have fit inside a shoebox.

"Those your new wheels, Lance?" she asked.

We both looked into the parking lot at the Escort. I nodded.

She whistled. "Sweet," she said.

"Joan," I said, "it's an Escort station wagon."

"It's a cute little car." She paused. "You haven't hit a cow with it?"

"Not yet," I said.

"Not sure I'd want to hit a cow in that little car," she said.

"I'll try to avoid it," I said.

"Heard you had a rowdy town council meeting the other day."

"You could say that," I said. "Turned out everyone's pretty much okay."

"That's what I heard." She couldn't hide a smile. "Heard Harley had a bit of a limp for a few days."

"He won't be calling anyone a lesbian for a while," I said, and ordered my food. "How's my tab?"

Joan allowed no credit at her restaurant, but made an exception for the Joslyns in part because as a family we were so financially dysfunctional and in part because as publisher of the newspaper, she always knew where I was and knew I would always make good on my debt.

"You're fine," she said. Joan motioned toward Annie, who smiled a greeting my direction. "That kid just amazes me," said Joan.

"Yeah," I said. "Did you know I have a portfolio now?"

She was clearly impressed, or feigned being clearly impressed. "Well, congratulations."

"To be honest," I told her, "I don't even know what a portfolio is."

"She does," Joan said, indicating Annie.

I looked back toward my daughter. "In fact, I think she told me I have a diversified portfolio."

"If I was you, I'd stay on her good side," Joan said.

"Tell me about it," I answered.

Chapter 10

I opened my eyes and the light in the bedroom window told me the sun was already well up in the southeastern sky. The inside of my mouth tasted like rust. I had stopped by Borden's the night before after taking pictures at the county fair in Twin Bridges. I should have known better; I did know better. It was about nine o'clock when I got there, and I almost left about ten o'clock. Almost. Mandy, all baubles and perfume and noise, staggered in alone. She needed a Saturday night dancing partner, and she was clinging to my shoulder before I realized she was there.

Annie was gone, off to a weeklong summer science camp offered through Montana State University. The only two things I could verify about the camp were that she received a financial scholarship of some kind to attend, and that a visiting Japanese professor picked her up at the Ledger the previous Tuesday. She wouldn't be back until Friday night.

Annie had not been all that excited to attend the camp, but summer in Whitehall could appear tedious for a young female academic. Part of the science camp took place in Yellowstone National Park, I thought, or maybe it was Glacier National Park. Another part of the camp took place in Spokane or Seattle, or maybe Salt Lake City. I'm pretty sure it was a big city that had started with an S. She'd told me about it but I must not have been listening carefully. The professor was a tall, lean Asian about forty years old who seemed far more excited about Annie's presence than Annie did about his. He met Annie at the Ledger Tuesday afternoon and I was already behind schedule – I had to get two sections laid out – and the fair manager was in the office proofing a full-page fair ad when the Asian professor came in.

"I'll be back on Friday. Not this Friday but next Friday," Annie had told me. "I circled it on your desk calendar. You got food in the fridge. I did laundry yesterday. You should be fine."

I nodded. "Okay, thanks."

She introduced me to the professor, but I didn't catch his name, and didn't ask her to repeat it. It either had a Hu or a Woo, or both, in it. Laura Joyce and the fair manager were both watching, and I detected either genuine interest or amusement – I wasn't sure which – from both of them. I wasn't exactly sure what they were interested or amused about.

Annie had packed her clothes in one of Amy's old backpacks. I didn't realize until she had hoisted it on her shoulder that I had no idea what she had inside it, and had never even thought that I should help her pack or express an interest in helping her pack.

"Do you have everything?" I asked her. It seemed like the kind of question a parent was supposed to ask.

"Nice try, Lance," she answered.

"Do you have money?" I asked her.

She nodded. "Do you?"

I shrugged. How would I know?

The professor wore glasses with thick black frames. His black hair fell straight across his forehead, and almost touched the top of the frames. In passable English he told me he respected Annie's intellectual abilities and then laughed, complimented her intelligence again and laughed again, and then they were gone. He held the door open for her as they walked out, and Annie walked under his arm without ducking. He nodded his departure before he closed the door.

"Who'd that guy say he was?" asked the fair manager.

I paused. "Some MSU teacher."

"Jolly sort, isn't he," said Laura Joyce.

"Isn't he the professor conducting some sort of micro-something, microbiology maybe, experiments? At the Berkeley Pit?" asked the fair manager. "I think he's some Japanese scientific hot shot. He's a Japanese scientist, not a MSU teacher. He was on TV the other night, on the news. I'm sure that's him."

"Wouldn't surprise me," said Laura Joyce.

"What's a guy like that doing in Whitehall?" asked the fair manager.

Laura Joyce snorted. "Probably here to get some help from Annie," she said, and laughed.

There was no laughing Sunday morning. The pounding in my left temple throbbed with each individual pulse, as if someone was actually and maliciously banging bluntly on the inside of my head.

At times like this it was pretty easy to feel sorry for myself. I had to drag my weary body out of bed, wash up, and sometime during the day – sooner better than later – haul myself to the Ledger for a Sunday five-hour shift of developing film, writing, and preparing for Monday. It was already mid morning, it was already hot, and I was already defeated. My clothes from last night reeked of bar smoke. The clothes were piled into a heap on the floor, and Sunday was laundry day. Annie was in Seattle or Yellowstone Park or someplace with an Asian scientist who'd been on television, which meant Tony or I had to do laundry, which meant I had to do laundry, because Tony would expend twice the energy to avoid doing the laundry as it took to actually do the laundry. Which further meant laundry wouldn't get done, because I couldn't face it on Sunday and would not have time to face it on Monday or Tuesday. That meant my room would stink until Wednesday night.

It was too hot to stay in bed, but I couldn't quite rally myself to get up. What finally got me moving was not the heat but a desperate urgency to first urinate and then gulp aspirin. Why did I do this to myself? Why couldn't I stop doing this to myself?

I swallowed a handful of aspirin – it hurt to focus my eyes or to count – and held my hand under tap water in the bathroom sink and drank. The water was warm; stale. An overgrown shrub that I'd always meant to trim grew along the wall outside the bathroom and provided some shade to that side of the house. It meant the light was muted and the temperature in the bathroom was slightly more comfortable. The floor of the bathroom felt cool on my bare feet, and in an attempt to absorb as much cool as possible, I laid down on the floor. The space between the bathtub and sink was just about shoulder width, and the floor was long enough that with my feet out in the hallway just a little I could lie down, face up. The floor felt cool to my legs and back, and my head felt better lying flat than standing up. My face was aimed toward the ceiling and I could see all four dismal corners. Above the bathtub and shower, the corners were corroded and moldy and flaky with some sludge-colored grime. Bubbles and cracking in the ceiling paint exposed what looked like soggy and rotten wood underneath. I had to roll my eyes backward, toward my eyebrows, to see the corner by the window. It was mushy, coated with a spider web that looked sturdy enough to catch a sparrow.

I should be ashamed, or embarrassed, I thought. I battled the putrid poison in my belly; fought the urge to vomit in a bathroom that reeked of disgust and misuse. There was no excuse to have sunk this low. I knew, without looking, the bottom of the bathtub was a stained, scummy mess. The shower backed up to about your ankles when you took a shower, and what filth didn't make it down the drain added to a ring of crud around the tub and deposited a dark hairy clump at the drain. Annie had once complained our bathroom could be a Superfund site. Once a month or so she scraped and scrubbed the tub, but with indifference or worse from Tony and me, Annie and the tub had no chance. The water pipes banged and clanked and rattled and were in grave need of a plumber. Virtually every appliance or fixture in the entire house was in grave need of maintenance, repair or replacement. The sink was probably better than the bathtub, only because the sink drain wasn't as plugged. Dried clumps of toothpaste clung to one side of the sink, a grimy green Dial soap residue discolored the other side. The bathroom pipes were partially plugged so when the toilet flushed they rumbled, rattled and squealed, and it was inevitable that at some point in the not too distant future a water pipe would shake loose or burst and an unimaginable filthy overflow would flood the floor.

I turned my head and my eye was nearly level with the floor: Dirt, hair, toenails, small black droppings likely from a rodent, and a greenish mold concentrated at the baseboard from when the toilet had overflowed. A Q-tip was on the floor behind the toilet.

Every room in the house told essentially the same story: Neglect. Inexcusable and miserable neglect.

My life was work and sleep. Tony failed to recognize or appreciate the value of sanitation. Annie viewed the situation as hopeless, and was disinclined to invest her energy into hopelessness. So the rooms were filthy. The window glass on every side of the house was chipped or cracked. The glass on at least two windows was fixed in place with packing tape. At least two window screens were busted in. Not a single door closed tight. Some light switches didn't work. Some light bulbs had been burned out for months. An ugly pattern of stains cut across the living room carpet. One of the legs on the coffee table was busted and the tabletop slanted toward the television. The La-

Z-Boy recliner was stuck with its footstool down. A bunch of electric outlets mysteriously failed to provide electricity. The floor lamp had no shade. Our freezer was frozen over with a fuzzy carpet of thick white ice.

Outside was the same story. The lawn was a combination of weeds and dirt. Patches of weeds undercut the gravel driveway. The only tree in the front yard was a small dead rust-colored pine tree. The doorbell was broken. The porch light was burned out. The front step handrail was loose. The bushes were filled with litter. The exterior paint was faded, cracked and peeling.

It was all too much. Just too goddamn much. There was no place to start, because everything around the place needed repair or replacement. The work needed to restore the place was overwhelming, so restoration was never undertaken. The truly depressing thought was the certainty it never would.

How did it get to this, I wondered. How could it have gone this bad, this wrong, this filthy, this broke? Kids should not be raised in this kind of squalor.

I rubbed my eyes. I worried about what had happened with Mandy the previous night. We had danced, drank, we'd been in back, outside in the alley. My mind was foggy, and perhaps it was best that way.

I woke up to someone shouting my name. My eyes jerked open, in pain. I lifted my head, barely, and groaned.

Tony stood in the hallway, a smaller kid behind him. It was the Dickson kid, Dave Dickson.

"Jesus, Lance," Tony said, "We thought you were dead."

I blinked. My head felt like it was filled with concrete. I was still on the bathroom floor. My mouth was filled with paste. "Not quite," I said, and cleared my throat. "Just resting."

"What are you doing down there?" Tony asked.

I couldn't move my neck. I grimaced, then groaned again, as I slowly, with effort, sat up. "This is the coolest place in the house." It sounded more like an apology than an explanation or a response. I gently massaged the back of my neck. I was wearing only my underpants. I cleared my throat again. "What time is it?"

"I don't know," shrugged Tony. "After lunch." Outside of the alarm clock in my bedroom, we didn't have a working clock in the house. Unless the television was on, and you knew what time the show you were watching started, there was no way to tell the time. Annie wore a watch, but she and her watch were in Singapore or Glacier Park or somewhere.

I had been lying on the floor for over two hours. I rubbed the back of my neck. My head and body ached, and after I sat up I knew I needed to rest before I stood up.

"We thought you were dead," Tony said again. He sounded relieved. "Man, you were really out of it."

I sat up and could feel my skin tingle as the blood and heat started to flow within my body. I imagined the blood had been pooled, puddled in the body parts flush against the bathroom cold tile floor. I moved my shoulders, in part to make sure they would, in fact, move. They did, barely.

"I better eat something," I said, mostly to myself.

"Want me to make you a sandwich?" asked Tony. "Dave and I are going to grab some sandwiches then head over to the Kountz Bridge."

I nodded, once; it hurt too much to nod twice. "Yeah, thanks."

The two boys left, and unsteadily, I stood up. The room spun, and little black dots exploded in front of my eyes. I grasped the sink to steady myself. I looked in the mirror. Tony was right. I looked like a dead man.

I was still at the Ledger about ten o'clock that night when Cal Walker, a Jefferson County Commissioner, dropped by. He'd made a habit of attending the Sunday night show at the Star Theatre, and when he stopped at the Ledger afterward he usually brought me popcorn and a Pepsi.

Cal had been a surveyor and building contractor before he was elected county commissioner, but he instinctively and intuitively understood the concept of politics. He was conservative and connected to Republican Party leaders in Lewis & Clark, Jefferson and Madison counties, and while he wanted to make it seem like he was just dropping by for a friendly chat, there was always a purpose for his visit and always a hint or message or fact or rumor or suggestion he wanted to drop or deliver or discuss or verify.

Cal had a distinctive knock. The *Closed* sign was up, but my car was parked on Legion Avenue in front of the Ledger. He knocked once loudly, and then twice quickly. It was perhaps a statesman-like knock.

"Anyone home?" was always the first thing he said upon entering.

"Come on in," I said.

He backed in, one hand holding a blue plastic cup and the other holding a small bag of popcorn. With both hands occupied, I'd often wondered how he managed his signature knock.

"Thought a guy working this late deserved a little treat," he said, and always said something like that.

The instant I smelled the popcorn I immediately craved it, and so I stood up from my typewriter and walked over to the front counter, where Cal had set the pop. He handed me the bag of popcorn.

"Look at that," Cal said, and indicated the new air conditioner. "You're gettin' right uptown, aren't you?"

"I have to admit, it's pretty nice," I said. Summer days and summer nights at the Ledger were far more tolerable with the air conditioner. This Sunday night, dehydrated and hurting with a hangover, the air conditioner was particularly welcome.

"Feels downright pleasant," Cal said. "Something tells me it wasn't your idea."

"Annie," I said. "She said it was a good idea."

"As always, Annie's right," Cal said. He paused. "You walk down here?"

"No," I said. I thought a moment. "Oh, I got a new car. The white Escort wagon."

"That's yours? I was wondering whose car that was. Didn't recognize it."

Cal was like most small town folks; he recognized vehicles as readily as people. He drove a black Ford half-ton pickup with oversized NAPA mud flaps on the rear wheels. Cal lived west of town along Highway 2, about two miles out from the IGA. He was not a small man; in his youth, I suppose, he could have been burly. He was probably over sixty now, proportionately overweight, with a stomach that protruded over his rodeo belt buckle. He always wore a dark felt cowboy hat.

"New car. Air conditioning. Must be some money in newspapering," he said. He settled into Laura Joyce's chair, and twisted the chair to face me.

I shoveled the popcorn into my mouth. "The car was Annie's idea, too," I said. "That, and I hit a cow."

"Heard about that," conceded Cal. "You and Slack, wasn't it. He banged his head up."

"Yeah, he had a knot on his forehead," I said. "Damn cow was smack in the middle of the road. I saw it a split second before I hit it."

"Someone told me you'd been fishing," Cal said. Cal made the Whitehall loop on a regular basis. He knew what was going on, who was responsible and why it happened. He had regular – monthly, probably – conversations with me, and probably had visits like this with a dozen more folks in the Whitehall area.

"Slack and I caught a mess of trout on the Jeff," I said. "Then we stopped at LaHood," I said a little softer, "and celebrated."

"Right," Cal said, and frowned.

Cal was a serious Baptist who abstained from alcohol and tobacco. When he ran for county commissioner during his first campaign he had a candidate forum with his opponent, a guy named Larry Ellis, and when the forum started Cal opened with a prayer, and asked God to bless the audience and also bless Larry Ellis. Larry Ellis never had a chance after that.

"I thought I saw Tony at the show tonight," Cal said. "That kid's getting big. He's turning into a man."

"He didn't do anything stupid, did he?" I asked.

Cal shook his head. "He was with one of those O'Toole girls. I can never tell those little darlings apart." He paused. "This one was young, blonde. Put together pretty well, if you catch my drift."

Aspen, I thought. "I think they're an item, as they say."

"She's a younger version of her mother," Cal said.

I nodded. "All three of the girls are."

"Didn't see Annie," Cal said.

"No, she's at science camp somewhere," I said. "She'll be back on Friday, I think. I hope."

"Oh yeah," Cal said thoughtfully, as if recalling something. "I read about that, in the Bozeman paper, I think. Or maybe the Helena paper. A Japanese scientist of some kind, right? About a dozen kids from all over the country were going to Yellowstone to study geysers or something, then on to Laramie. Annie's name was in the article. Looked like it was all high school kids and her, if I remember right. She was the only Montana kid and the only junior high kid."

"Seems about right," I said. I had no idea about the Bozeman newspaper article, and no idea about Annie being the youngest and the only Montanan. But I wasn't surprised.

"The article made it seem like being selected was a pretty prestigious honor," Cal said.

I nodded, as if as a parent I knew everything, something, anything, about the camp and the scientist.

"You going to put something in your paper about it?" Cal asked.

He knew the answer to that. "She doesn't need another article in another paper about how smart she is."

"She's something special, Lance, and deserves to be recognized," Cal said. "The whole town should be proud of her."

"Sometimes I think people resent her," I said, and it was true, some people did. She was smarter than every son and daughter in Whitehall, and every mother and father knew that.

Cal nodded. "People can be a little small in their thinking. That doesn't diminish her accomplishment."

The popcorn was gone. I was hungrier than before I'd taken the first handful. I also had a good hour of work left to do, which meant I needed Cal to say whatever it was he came here to say.

"Thanks for the treat," I said. "I didn't realize how hungry I was until you showed up."

"You work too hard," Cal said. "A guy shouldn't be at the office working on a Sunday night in August. Life's too short for that. Especially after he was out late dancing on Saturday night."

"I stopped by for a beer after the fair," I said. "Big mistake."

"Mandy Phillips?" Cal asked.

I shrugged. Was there anything about Whitehall he didn't know?

He adjusted his hat. "You know better than Mandy Phillips."

Yeah, I did, but I didn't necessarily need to be told so. I was tempted to ask him what he knew about Mandy and me, because he might have had more details than I had, but I had a hunch when it came to Mandy Phillips and me, details were not my friend.

He stood up. "You see the crews working on that new bridge yet, over the slough by the Mayflower?" he asked.

"No," I said. "I thought that wasn't going to start until next spring."

Cal winked. "We found ourselves a little extra bridge money, and it got directed down here. Over the slough this side of the Mayflower Bridge."

"Great," I said. "I'll run over there and take a picture later this week." Which is exactly what Cal was hoping for.

He moved toward the door. "Oh, and I wanted to compliment you. That ruckus a while ago at the town council. You could have turned that into a black eye for the whole town. Most publishers would have. I appreciate the way you handled that."

I had put the article about the scuffle on an inside page. It could have been prominent on the front page, and that would have meant a good week for the Ledger in sales, but a bad week for the town and, ultimately, what was bad for the town was bad for the Ledger. No one turned out to be injured, and no one seemed inclined to press charges or sue anyone.

Cal was just about out the door. "Tell Annie congratulations for the science selection." He looked directly into my eyes. "I'm planning to read an article about her in your paper on Wednesday."

The temperature hovered above one hundred degrees Thursday afternoon when I drove east toward the Mayflower Bridge, a span that crossed the Jefferson River and conjoined Jefferson and Madison counties. Everything north of the bridge was in Jefferson County, everything south was in Madison. Residents in both counties on either side of the bridge argued which side of the bridge boasted the worse roads, and as I eased my new Escort down the Mayflower Road toward the bridge construction I thought it was probable the washboard roads north of the Mayflower had earned bragging rights. The dry August heat had baked the gravel and dirt into fine powdery dust that lifted in brown flinty clouds as I slowly dodged the rocks and holes along the road. The oil pan of the Escort scraped at least one upended mini boulder on the road and the tiny wheels of the car strained to roll through some of the larger and deeper potholes.

The main Mayflower Bridge was useful, but not as necessary as it once was. In the early 1900s the Mayflower Mine had been one of the larger underground gold mines in Montana. It slipped into the hands of various owners at various times, not all of them competent. But the mine had employed hundreds of men over the years, and the Mayflower Bridge over the Jefferson River once served as the major route of transportation for the employees and the commerce at the Mayflower. The mine was enormously profitable in fits and starts, depending on the quality of the ownership and the price of gold, but it closed suddenly in the 1940s, during World War II. The country no longer needed gold as much as it needed other metals for the war effort, and the mine was all but abandoned overnight by the old Anaconda Company, which put its resources and employees to work mining precious WWII metals in other parts of Montana. Legend suggested Mayflower miners had been in a new ore vein with gold nuggets the size of your fist the day the mine closed, but most mines are closed under suspicion and rumor. The instant the mine pumps stopped and the mine tunnels were abandoned the water began to rise in the adits, and within a few months every inch of the underground mine had been flooded by the simple act of water rising to the natural level of the water table.

In the 1970s into the 1980s there were local rumors of the Mayflower Mine reopening, and some day, I suspect, it will. Unlike most gold mines that ceased because the gold was mined out, the Mayflower closed to make the company more money mining other metals elsewhere. Many are convinced there's gold down there in the Mayflower. And, oddly for Montana, it's all under water.

The Mayflower isn't the only gold mine near Whitehall with an intriguing history. East of the Mayflower Mine, in the South Boulder drainage of the Tobacco Root Mountains, the small village of Mammoth is all that remains of a once prosperous gold mine along the South Boulder River. Mammoth is a collection of scattered cabins and homes, built haphazardly among trees on the east side of the river, where mine managers and employees were housed in the 1920s and 1930s. Some of the cabins and homes have been modestly restored and later used as summer cottages. Driving up into Mammoth from the south a large mine tailings impoundment of toxic waste sits on the east side of the road. Nothing grows on the large red mound of poison waste rock and spoils, but no one seems to care. There's a crooked and hand painted sign reading *KEEP OFF* between the road and the tailings, but there's no fence and no environmental cleanup.

The gold mine in the South Boulder wasn't as financially successful as the Mayflower Mine, but it was a viable operation until a violent spat between mine management and the workforce erupted. The disagreement turned ugly in a hurry, and employees actually blew up the company's small dam on the South Boulder that had created the hydropower necessary to generate enough electricity to operate the mine's mill. With no power, the company couldn't mill the gold, with no gold there was no profit, and without profit there was no mine. The employees had literally dynamited themselves out of work. The mine never reopened and almost certainly never will.

The Mayflower Bridge improvement project was hard to miss. They'd built a small bridge that crossed a Jefferson River slough – a side channel to the main stem of the river – and a collection of heavy equipment, including a crane, was parked on both sides of the slough. A handful of workers – orange hardhats, white tee-shirts – were milling around the site. I spotted the county road foreman, a guy named Dave Perry, off to the side. Dave lived in Boulder and while Whitehall people seemed genetically programmed to complain about a lack of county services in our end of the county, Dave and Cal were pretty good at directing transportation money, equipment and projects to the southern portion of Jefferson County.

"Hot enough for you?" Dave greeted me. His shirt was stained with sweat down the spine and in the armpits. Dust, mixed with sweat, turned into slight lines of gray grit on his face.

"It's gotta be a hundred," I said. A haze of dust from the gravel seemed to have followed me out of the car and hovered around the bridge.

"At least," he said. "And there's no breeze down here."

The slough was narrow and protected by willows and cottonwoods growing on each side of the river, so had there been a wind there would still have been no air movement along the water. The heat was oppressive, and I could taste the dust.

"You get a new car?" Dave asked.

I nodded. "It barely survived the Mayflower Road getting here."

"Yeah, the road's next on our to-do list," Dave said. "We beat the snot out of it getting all this equipment in here. It's gonna be a month or so. You might want to let folks know that."

I nodded. "Sure. I'll put that in the cutline with the photo."

I got the basic information I needed – cost of the project, timeframe for completion, contractor, funding source – and moved closer to the action for photos of the crews working.

Dave was standing at his white county pickup, gulping water from a large plastic bottle, when I walked towards him on the way back to my car. I had sweat trickling down my temples and inside my shirt along the spine, my shirt was wet where I'd slung the camera case across my shoulder, and I had only been there for fifteen minutes.

"Rangers got a football coach yet?" Dave asked me when I approached.

Dave was a Boulder – Jefferson High – sports fan. His kids, two girls and a boy, had participated in sports at Boulder, with all three of them running on state cross country and track championship teams. Every game between Whitehall and Boulder that I'd ever attended, in both Whitehall and Boulder, Dave was there, wearing a purple and gold Boulder Panther shirt or jacket.

"Yeah," I said. "A new guy. Everyone calls him Jersey."

"I've been seein' Whitehall kids on the football field working out."

I nodded. "My kid's been lifting weights and running. He's never done that before."

"Good for him," said Dave. "You gotta do that these days to compete. What's this new coach like?"

I took my index finger and wiped the sweat beads off my forehead. "Got me. He was the third choice, I think, after Frank passed away and Wally Hope left."

"Did I hear that right?" asked Dave. "Wally went to Circle?"

I nodded.

"What in God's name for?"

"More money."

"There ain't enough money in Circle," Dave said. "So what's the deal…this Jersey guy was the only choice you had left?"

"Pretty much," I agreed.

"Bummer. That was too bad about Frank, but he wasn't much of a coach," Dave said. "You guys should have been a lot better last year than you were. It was like Frank gave up. You guys had talent, but no spark, you know, no desire."

"Well, we had those injuries."

Dave shook his head. "All teams have injuries. You guys had no passion. And now Wally heads to Circle? Circle's not a place to seek. Circle's a place you end up at. I gotta tell you, Lance, things got to be *awful* bad in Whitehall for a guy like Wally Hope to move to Circle."

"Wally left because of salary and retirement," I said. "He'll be retiring in a few years, and his retirement income is based on his final three years of employment. He'll be a principal in Circle at higher pay."

"No offense, but that's bullshit," Dave said. "Wally was assistant coach for what, fifteen years? He finally gets a chance to be head coach and what's he do? Flees to Circle? That's gotta say something about the football team in Whitehall."

I shrugged again. "I don't know about that. Wally didn't have anything to lose by coaching here. You've seen how we've played the last few years. It couldn't get much worse."

"Yes it could," said Dave. He gulped some more water. "Boulder'll be okay this year. My guess is we'll win the conference and make the playoffs. But you guys might not win a game, and we'll beat you by fifty points. And that's why Wally left town."

He didn't mean it spitefully, or as an insult. And he wasn't alone in his assessment. "We'll see," was the best I could come up with.

"It's good to see the Whitehall kids working out," Dave said. "But I heard no one applied for the job after Wally left town. Think about that. No one. Not a single existing or former coach around the state put in an application to coach Class B football in Whitehall. That speaks volumes about your program here. You got a rookie coach who more or less had to take the job."

"We'll see," I said again.

The next day the temperature on the Rocky Mountain Bank clock read one hundred and three degrees, and it seemed hotter than that. A strong southerly wind blew hot air like a fan in front of a furnace.

Late afternoon Rhonda Horst, the elderly German landlady, wearily walked into the Ledger. Her hair was curled in tight spirals to her scalp, and she wore sunglasses with lenses the size of hubcaps. I figured she was there to extend, begin or end a classified *For Rent* ad. She owned a big house on First Street and she had converted the second floor to a fleet of what she called *schtewdeeo* apartments, and she owned a trio of trailer homes on Whitehall Street. People were forever coming and going from her apartments – the trailer home tenants seemed pretty regular – and she was faithful about placing and paying for classified ads.

I stood up at my typewriter and walked to the front counter, and grabbed one of our classified ad forms.

"Accht," she told me, and lazily waved at the direction of the ad form, "not dat today."

Laura Joyce looked up from her typesetter as if waiting for what happened next. Rhonda sensed it, and waved her off as well.

"So haht," Rhonda said. She looked up at the air conditioner. "At da drug store dey toldt how cool dis ist here."

She held a small bag, probably a medicinal prescription from the drug store pharmacy.

"Do you need to sit down?" I asked her.

"Ya," she nodded. "I sit."

I sort of escorted her to the little table in the corner of the office where I conducted interviews or discussed display advertising. I pulled out a chair, and she grimaced, and lowered herself into the chair.

"Are you okay?" I asked.

"Ya, so oldt." She laughed briefly. "Goot fer nothink."

"You want a drink of water?" I asked.

She nodded. "Vater, ya."

Laura Joyce beat me to the bathroom and fetched a cup of cold tap water.

Seated, Rhonda raised her eyes and tilted her head, a silent way of acknowledging kindness. She sipped the water, then dipped her fingertips in the cup and patted her temples.

"I'm not so much goot in dis heat," she said.

"No one is," I said.

"Accht," she said.

"You're not exactly a kid anymore, Rhonda," said Laura Joyce.

"No, I'm no kit," agreed Rhonda.

I wondered how old she was. She was tiny and thin, but certainly not frail. She hired a handyman named Tanner Ross to keep her properties up, and at Borden's over beers he had told me stories of her helping him unload a sink, steady a ladder or repair a gutter drainpipe. But the face behind the oversized sunglasses was pale and wrinkled, and I noticed a slight tremor in her hand when she had her fingertips in the water. She could be sixty, I thought, or ninety.

"Vere is dat schmart lietal girl?" she asked.

"Annie? She's at science camp," I said. "She gets home sometime today."

"Goot," Rhonda said. "Und dat boy?"

"Not sure where he is," I said. "Probably causing trouble somewhere."

"Acht," she said, waved away my comment. "He good kid."

"They're both great kids," Laura Joyce said.

Rhonda nodded. "Oh dat feels goot," she said, indicating the air conditioner.

"It might be too hot for you to walk home," I said. "You sit here as long as you want and take it easy. Laura Joyce will be glad to drive you home whenever you're ready."

I looked at Laura Joyce, who nodded. "You bet," she said.

"A minute I sit," Rhonda said.

"Sit as long as you want," I said.

"Ridt be goot," she said. "I ridt in your new Eshcort?"

Chapter 11

It was a sweltering mid-August evening when Tony showed up with the Bozeman Chronicle and Great Falls Tribune – two area daily newspapers – and read parts out loud on the Saturday night before football practice started the following Monday.

We had been to the Star Theatre – the three of us – and saw the movie *The Three Amigos* and the kids refused to believe me it was a parody of the best Steve McQueen movie of all time, *The Magnificent Seven*. Annie tried to tell me *The Magnificent Seven* was a remake of a Japanese movie, which was ridiculous, I told her, because *The Magnificent Seven* was a western, and the Japanese knew nothing about westerns, and all Annie could do was sigh.

So, bellies filled with popcorn and Pepsi, later on a Saturday night, Tony decided to read us the news. Insects flitted and jittered outside in the breathless air, and more than a few flitted and jittered in our house interior as well. The inside walls of the living room held heat from the daylight sun and were warm to the touch. We had a fan going in the living room, but all it did was move around the hot air.

Annie sat in the recliner reading a library book about the universe, or maybe just the solar system, I couldn't tell, and I lacked the energy to ask her. She had her hair pinned up to keep it off her neck. She was shoeless, and I noticed her toenails were painted a deep crimson. I had the television on, waiting to watch the news, not because I particularly cared about the news, but because I didn't particularly care about anything.

The kids would watch *Saturday Night Live* when it came on, and I would watch the first ten minutes or so and then doze off. I did my best to stay awake, and if I made it to the fake news broadcast I felt I had accomplished something.

"Oh come on," Tony moaned from the kitchen table. "Listen to this." We had a three-way light bulb in the lamp above the table, but it only worked on the low setting. I'd been meaning to change the bulb, but hadn't quite gotten around to it. Tony adjusted the paper so the light was aimed better on the page. "Oh, God. Listen. This is the Chronicle. It predicts Ennis to win the conference and Whitehall to finish last. It says here we're going to lose *every* game. O and nine! Listen." He launched into a pretty decent impression of football broadcaster John Madden. "'The Rangers lost an experienced head coach, Frank Stockett, who passed away last spring. Then they saw an experienced assistant coach, Wally Love, suddenly vacate the head coach job for a move to eastern Montana. The Rangers, who had three wins in 1985, will be led by first-year coach Jerry Conte and outside of All-Conference quarterback Colt Harrison will be short of experience on the field as well as on the sidelines. Harrison completed seventy-eight passes in his junior campaign for nearly nine hundred yards and seven touchdowns, but his three top receivers, leading running back and most of the offensive line graduated last spring. Defensively, the Rangers gave up a league high three hundred and eighty points last year, and it looks like more of the same this fall.'"

"Sounds about right," Annie said, hidden behind the book. That might have been Jupiter on the cover. Or maybe not.

"What?" Tony said. He scrunched the paper. "We will not give up more than three hundred and eighty points this year. I guarantee that. That's a promise."

"Grammatically, it's redundant to issue a pledge with a promise in association with a guarantee," said Annie. "The guarantee pretty much stands on its own two feet."

"I don't know what you just said, but there's no way we're going to give up three hundred and eighty points this year," Tony said.

Annie put down the book. I wondered, scientifically, what the difference was between the universe, the solar system and the Milky Way. I knew Annie knew, but it was a sultry late Saturday night and I didn't want to contemplate the universe. I didn't even want to contemplate *Saturday Night Live*.

"We're not going to lose every game, either." He put down the paper. "How many square feet are in a hectare?"

"Is the answer there, in the paper?" she asked.

He nodded. "In some guy's trivia column. You ought to have one of these in the Ledger, Lance. So, Professor Joslyn, how many square feet are in a hectare?"

"I don't even know what a hectare is," I said. I hesitated. "It might have something to do with the Bible and the ark."

"What makes you think I was asking you?" Tony asked me.

"It's a kind of international measurement of land scale or size," Annie told me. "It has nothing to do with the ark. Lance, you might be thinking of a cubit, which is something else entirely, or you might not be thinking of anything at all. I'm surprised you're still awake."

"Give me five minutes," I told her.

Annie looked into the kitchen at Tony. "Your question asks for the exact number of square feet?"

"Yep, exact number. It's written right here."

"I'm not sure I know the exact number," she said thoughtfully. "It's somewhere around 107,000 square feet. No, wait. 107,639 square feet."

"Nice guess," Tony muttered.

"Is she right?" I asked.

"Of course she's right," Tony complained. "She's always right."

"Not always. You just said I was wrong about the Rangers giving up three hundred and eighty points this year," she pointed out.

"Yeah, you're wrong about that. Flat wrong. Dead wrong."

"So is there a wager lurking behind your confidence?"

"What, you wanna bet? Bet what?" Tony asked.

"Let's have a little wager on the number of points scored on the Rangers this year," Annie said, deliberately temptingly. "Let's see, three hundred and eighty points in nine games is a little over forty two points per game." She paused. "Wow. That's a lot of points for high school football."

"It ain't gonna happen," Tony said. "I'll bet you anything."

"I'm not sure you two should be betting like this," I said.

"Right, Lance, like it's up to you," Tony said.

And like I cared.

"You want to bet, here's a bet. If we hold opponents to under three hundred and eighty points Lance has to buy me a car next summer," Tony said.

"What?" I asked, stunned. "I'm not part of your bet. Why would I buy you a car because she loses a bet?"

They ignored me.

"And what if you guys give up three hundred and eighty or more points?" Annie asked.

"Impossible," Tony stated.

"What if you do?" Annie chided.

"Name it," Tony said.

"Really?" Annie said.

"Name it," Tony answered defiantly.

"You have to get Dave Dickson to take me to the prom," Annie said. "We'll double-date with you and Aspen. And none of you can ever tell anyone I'm there because you lost a bet. If you tell anyone, and I mean anyone, or if Aspen blabs, I'll absolutely and completely ruin the rest of your life. I mean it. Your life will be devastated. Total destruction. I will make sure each day of your existence is absolutely miserable. And I could do that."

"Oh, I know you could," said Tony. He pondered the bet.

"I know what you're thinking, buddy boy," Annie said. "You're thinking Dave and I are going to crimp your style with Aspen O'Toole." Annie shook her head. "I'm telling you this for your own good. Drop her. She's way out of your league, Tony boy. She's at least three rungs above you on the social, cultural and sexual grid. She's worldlier now than you'll ever be in your entire life. Trust me on that."

"I might be more worldly than you think," Tony smirked. "And what do you know? You're in junior high. You don't even know what worldly is."

"What grid?" I asked.

"Lance," Annie said, as if speaking to a child. I thought she was going to keep talking, but she didn't.

Tony pointed his finger at Annie. "You're on, Professor Hectare. We got a bet."

"Tony," I said, "think this through. This is a losing proposition for you. If you lose, the outcome requires you to do something. If you win, the outcome requires *me* to do something, and I haven't said I'd do it. In fact, I haven't even been asked. And *if* I was asked, the answer is I won't do it. I'm not going to buy you car. Okay, is that understood? I will not, repeat, will not, buy you a car. I just bought me one. I can't afford another one."

Tony looked at Annie, as if I hadn't even spoke. "So we're on?"

Annie nodded. "We have ourselves a bet."

"Wait a minute," I said. "I could have sworn I just said something important. Didn't I just talk? Didn't I just say something? Tony, I'm warning you right now. Don't do this. This is a losing proposition."

Tony grabbed the Tribune. He was shirtless, and maybe it was just the shadows in the living room, but he looked like he had muscles he didn't have last time I saw him with his shirt off. "This is preposterous," he said. It was an imitation of someone, but I couldn't tell who. "The story about the Rangers in the Trib is even worse."

"Worse than zero wins?" Annie asked. "How can it get worse than no wins? Do they project minus zero wins?"

"Listen to this crap." There was no imitation now, just a steely anger in his natural voice. "'The 5B conference title is up for grabs, with Ennis, Boulder and Townsend expected to compete for the top spot. Whitehall seems to have the cellar clinched this year, thanks to an exodus of coaching and talent. Longtime Rangers coach Frank Stockett passed away, and heir to the head coach job, Wally Hope, turned down the position. With eight starters gone from a 1985 squad that went 3-5 and failed to live up to expectations, the Rangers' best friend in 1986 may be the Mercy Rule, which calls for a continuous clock when a team trails by thirty five or more points in the second half.'"

"That's a cheap editorial shot," Annie said. "It's totally unfair. Accurate maybe, but totally unfair."

"The Tribune will pay for that," said Tony. "This is how the article ends. 'The Rangers return talented quarterback Colt Harrison, an All-Conference player who completed seven touchdown passes last year and ran for three more. But the cupboard is now empty for the Rangers, and despite the heroics of Harrison the Rangers are going to have a tough time getting into the end zone and the win column. The Rangers will finish last in the conference, and despite a relatively easy nonconference schedule it's hard to find a team Whitehall can beat this year.'"

"I'm going to take both these papers out in the backyard and piss on them," said Tony.

"I promise the Ledger article on Wednesday will be better than that," I said.

"Well, I would hope so," Annie said haughtily.

"Both these papers even pick Big Timber to finish ahead of us, and Big Timber lost every game last year," Tony complained. "We thumped them last year. Even I got to play."

"The Ledger will predict you won't come in last place," I said. "But I'm not predicting I'm going to buy you a car. In fact, I'm predicting I will not buy you a car. In fact, I'm pledging a promise that I guarantee you I will not buy you a car."

"Lance, you're just babbling," Annie told me.

Moments later the telephone rang, and Tony jumped to answer it. "Hello," he said. "Oh hi, Aspen," he said loudly, and then turned his back to us and spoke softer.

I have no idea how long he spoke. He was still on the phone when *Saturday Night Live* came on, and later when I woke up, Annie was in bed and Tony was in the recliner, eating a bowl of ice cream and re-reading the newspapers.

"We will not lose every game, we will not give up three hundred and eighty points and I *will* get a car," he told me the instant my eyes opened.

My pre-season football preview interview with first year head coach Jerry "Jersey" Conte took place late Monday evening, after his first day of practice had ended. In the morning the players took quick physicals and were issued helmets, shoulder pads and other equipment. In the afternoon they wore tee-shirts and shorts and after calisthenics the kids ran sprints, ran pass patterns and then ran a mile on the track. After that they'd done grass drills and footwork drills. Tony stopped by the Ledger for a few minutes – I think the air conditioner had something to do with that – told me about their practices, and said they'd done a lot more running under Coach Jersey than under Coach Stockett.

I met Jersey in the coach's office just outside the locker room at seven o'clock. School wouldn't start for another couple weeks, and at night the building was dark and deserted. I entered the school at the main entrance, and my footsteps echoed as I walked down the empty and shadowy hallways to the coach's office, which was the only room in the building with a light on.

Jersey was inside the office, speaking on the phone. He wore a silky black tee-shirt and black slacks. A pair of sunglasses was tilted so the lenses were high on his forehead.

We made eye contact, and he nodded. "Hang on a minute," he said into the phone. He put the receiver against his chest. He turned to me. "Did you hit a cow?"

"Not recently," I said. "Just the one a few weeks ago."

"But you did hit a cow?" he asked. The word *cow* had that Jersey accent to it. The phone was cradled against his chest.

"Just that once," I said. "It was in the middle of the road."

Jersey shook his head. "A cow? Man, that never happens in Jersey."

"Montana's got a few more cows than New Jersey," I said.

"Hang on," he said. "I'll be right with you."

I stepped outside the office to give him privacy while he was on the phone. I hoped the conversation wouldn't last long. I had to do the interview, write the article, and then start laying out the paper. This was our back-to-school edition, twenty-eight pages, and I'd be lucky to be home by one a.m.

Outside, in the hallway, it was completely silent. I could hear bits and pieces of what he was saying. I tried not to listen, then realized I was trying kind of hard to listen. His nasal east coast inflection seemed to have waned slightly since I'd talked to him in the spring, but it was still there. Certain words had a dull and drawn sound in them you didn't hear much in the Rocky Mountain west.

"What I'm saying is you didn't treat these kids with respect," Jersey said. "These are fifteen, sixteen, seventeen-year-old young men, and they deserve to be treated with respect. You didn't respect them as individuals, as athletes, or as competitors."

He said something about not wanting to write a letter or another article. I missed part of what he said after that, and I crept up closer to the door to hear what he said next.

"I didn't call you to ask for an apology," he said patiently. "I just want to make sure you understand the power of your words. You have an obligation to these kids. It's easy to humiliate someone who fails. It's much more difficult to encourage someone to succeed." He paused. "Right, yes, that's all I'm asking. These Whitehall kids will do their very best every play of every game. That effort deserves respect." He paused again. "Right." Another pause. "Sure, anytime. Thank you."

I heard the phone placed in the cradle, and stepped in the office just as Jersey finished running his tan hand through his black hair.

"Oh boy," he said, "another newspaper reporter."

"Oh boy," I answered, "another coach."

He moved an upside-down football helmet off the only other chair in the office, and placed it on the floor by a mesh bag filled with footballs. I sat down across from him. "You don't dress like a coach," I observed after I sat and opened my notebook.

"What do I dress like?" he asked.

I shrugged. "I don't know. Not like a coach, though."

He smiled. "Like what, then?" he asked pleasantly.

I shrugged again. "I don't know. Like someone from Europe, maybe. Someone from Belgium, I think."

Jersey thought about it. "Belgium?" he said softly. "Belgium. Lance, have you ever met anyone from Belgium?"

I shook my head. "Not to my knowledge."

"Have you ever been to Belgium?

I shook my head. "I've never been east of Minnesota."

"Do you know how people in Belgium dress?"

I shook my head. "Not a clue."

"Could you point to Belgium on a map?"

"Probably not exactly. In Europe. West, I think, along the ocean. West of Germany, I bet." I spoke softer. "You know, the whole World War Two invasion thing."

"Right," said Jersey. "So you think I dress like people from a country you've never been in, like people you've never seen, like people who live in a country you couldn't find on a map."

"Maybe not Belgium, then," I admitted. "Maybe, I don't know, Italy."

"Italy?" Jersey said softly. "Lance, have you even been..." but he trailed off. Which was fine with me. He sat up straight. "How do you want to do this?" he asked. "This will be my first real newspaper interview."

"Gotta be at least your second," I said, and indicated the telephone.

"Oh," he said. "No, that wasn't an interview for attribution. That was simply a conversation with a reporter."

"That's basically what we'll do, except what you tell me will be published in the newspaper on Wednesday."

"Yippee," he said without emotion. "Let's start, and if I say something stupid either tell me to say something else or ignore it and don't put it in the paper. How's that sound?"

"That's sort of how Frank and I used to do this," I said. "Frank seemed to be perpetually mad, and he'd sometimes say things when he was angry that he would later wish he hadn't said. So I edited his comments and more or less avoided what he said when he was mad."

Jersey ran his hand through his hair again. "I'm not the angry type, and no offense, but let's go ahead and start so we can get it over with."

"No offense, but I'm as anxious as you are to be done here. So let's start. How's the team look? I know you've only had one day of practice and you're a new coach, and you can keep your comments pretty general if you want. But I have two weeks to write two preview articles. Football this week, cross country next week."

Jersey hesitated. "How does the team look?" he repeated. "Well, I haven't really had a proper chance to evaluate them yet, but I've seen some things I've liked."

"For instance?" I asked, writing his quote down on paper.

"We've got a solid quarterback in Colt Harrison, a two-year starter who brings lots of experience to the offense," Jersey said, who made *starter* sound like *stahtar*.

"Will your offense be built around him?"

Jersey shook his head. "We won't build our offense around one particular player or one particular position. We'll build our offense around our overall team strengths, and although Colt is one of those strengths, we've got other things going for us."

"Like what?" I asked. "Everyone else is new. You really don't have any quality starters back." My *starters* had a shade of *stahtars* in it.

"We have a lot of enthusiasm," said Jersey. "We have some kids who expect to excel, and we expect them to excel. Football is a team sport, and it takes eleven guys to do their jobs each play for the play to be successful."

"I know it's early, but do you have any idea who your starters will be?"

He shook his head. "I'm not thinking about *stahtars* yet, and won't for another week. Right now we're working on conditioning. We're doing a lot of running."

"Tony said a lot more running than under Frank."

Jersey nodded. "That's what I've been told. Between you and me, I don't really know what I'm doing yet, so the kids run. I've been a football coach for one whole day now, and a lot of these kids I met for the first time today. I need to learn more about them, I need to learn more about high school football, I need to learn more about coaching high school football, I need to learn more about my assistant coach – Coach Pete – and I need to learn more about talking with reporters. I obviously have a lot to learn. So do the kids. We'll learn it together, and in doing so we'll get stronger, smarter, faster and better. I hope we have some fun this year and win a few football games, but if we don't, we'll still forge bonds and perform as a team."

"Do you want me to quote you saying that?" I asked.

He sighed. "Probably not the part about me not knowing what I'm doing. But you can write that I know I have a lot to learn. And you can write that the team members have a lot to learn. Because that's the truth. We're installing a new defense and offense, and it's going to take some time for all that to come together. But as a team, we *will* learn it. And together we *will* get stronger and better."

I wrote it all down. "Anything you've seen so far that you're particularly pleased with?" I asked. "Anything individually?" Names in newspapers sell newspapers. I wanted some names in the article.

"I like the spirit and the enthusiasm of these kids," he said. "Individually, I like the determination I'm seeing in kids like Cody Phillips. I like the speed and hustle of Nate Bolton. I like the effort I'm seeing from Bobby Bentmier. Tanner Walker's a solid kid. Dave Dickson's got a sparkle out on the field. Your boy, Tony, plays with passion. The Collins twins are working hard. Logan Bradshaw stands out on a football field."

"Hardly any of those kids played varsity football last year," I pointed out.

Something in his expression made it clear he was aware of that. "We have a nice blend of experience and enthusiasm," he said.

"I think I'll put that in the headline," I said. "Something about Rangers having a blend of experience and enthusiasm."

"That'd be fine," said Jersey. He leveled his eyes at me. "To be painfully truthful, Lance, I don't care what you write, as long as you treat these kids with respect. They've earned that just by putting on the uniform. I can't promise you we're going to win a lot of football games. I can promise you we will play with pride, play with emotion, honor the game and respect each other and our opponents. By the end of the year our opponents, and the Great Falls Tribune, are going to respect us."

Respect. It can be a confusing, vague concept.

Amy left Whitehall, left her family – husband and two small children – on that chilly fall evening, and one of my many failures, she'd told me, was an inability to respect her. About two weeks after she'd left, she called late one night when I was at the Ledger to tell me she planned to return to Whitehall to pick up the kids so they could live with her near Missoula.

I didn't resist her claim on Annie and Tony. She was their mother, and it seemed natural for children to be with their mother; all children, and any mother. Plus, the Ledger workload required me to work every day and most nights. I didn't have time to parent. Tony was in fourth or fifth grade then, Annie was just starting school and had already been identified as a child with well above average intelligence. Despite not resisting or rejecting Amy's intention to take my kids to Missoula, and despite my yearning to focus on Ledger duties, the night she called she managed to bait me into a brief but bitter argument.

I had never respected her, she had told me. I had never given her credit, never treated her as my equal, never treated her as a professional. Yes I had, I countered. I told her we were equal partners as parents and in everything relating to our marriage.

She responded with one of her deep, mournful sighs. She could always sigh with a flourish, with true intensity, as if deeply, distressingly, wounded. Her sighs told the world she was strong enough to bear it, strong enough to tolerate the injustice, the persecution. I'll remember her sighs forever, and that particular sigh has been impossible to erase.

Amy called the house a couple times that fall and talked with the kids, and called on Thanksgiving, and everyone understood she would be returning to Whitehall within a month to pick up the kids before Christmas for a trip to their new home and new life.

But in early December that year, Amy's mother, a small stoic woman with dyed hair that seemed to be maroon in color, called me at the Ledger. Apparently, Amy wasn't feeling well, and just then wasn't *up to* the kids moving in with her. Tell the kids she loves them, Grandma Jen instructed me to tell them, and I could hear the grief in her voice. She started to weep, said Amy needed some time, and the conversation ended abruptly.

So Christmas that first year it was the three of us. It wasn't much of a Christmas. Amy had always done the Christmas shopping in the past, and by the time I realized Christmas shopping fell to me by default, it was too late. We had the Christmas Stroll edition and the pre-Christmas edition of the Ledger to publish, and I had no time for shopping. So on Christmas Eve, the kids and I went to Whitehall Drug, Dick's Clothing Store, the IGA and a couple other stores in Whitehall and Annie and Tony each picked out five presents for themselves, two for each other and one for me. Merry Christmas.

Then in late January, I received a call from Grandma Jen telling me a psychologist or possibly a psychiatrist or possibly some other kind of doctor had placed Amy in residential therapy. Six months later, Grandma Jen, in a weary voice saturated with regret and sadness, told me a lawyer would be calling to start divorce proceedings, and a lawyer did call, and divorce proceedings were started. When the lawyer called he talked for over an hour, but I barely heard him. I didn't really listen. The legal need for separation, division or divorce apparently had something to do with Medicare, co-payments, private insurance and medical treatment. I didn't understand, and I didn't care. He talked and talked, and I heard him, but didn't listen. He assured me a divorce was financially best for everyone, including the children, perhaps especially the children. Doctors called after that, as did insurance people, government people, another lawyer, more government people and more doctors. I did whatever they told me to do. I never questioned what they said, never challenged what they said. I just went along with it, all of it, did what they wanted, signed what they sent, agreed to it all, did everything Amy's parents requested. But what haunts me still is that I never once asked Amy herself what she wanted me to do or what she wanted for herself. Not once did I demand to speak to her or see her, to take her back home to Whitehall with me or hear from her own lips what she wanted to do with her life or what she wanted me to do with our children. I would have respected her wishes, but I failed to respect her by failing to even ask what her wishes were.

The sky had a dusty brown tint to it as I drove the three blocks from the Ledger to the Ranger practice field on a late Friday August afternoon to watch the tail end of practice. A forest fire had started near Dillon, about sixty miles from Whitehall, and prevailing southwesterly winds carried heat and smoke into the Jefferson Valley. The sun, a bright orange bulb, hung suspended in the western sky, the color of bright light shining through an orange construction cone. The temperature was above ninety, and the breeze felt as if it was hot enough to be from hell.

Whitehall was ending its second week of practice. On the following Monday school would start, and on Friday night the Rangers would open their season with a nonconference game against Columbus, a playoff team for three straight years that was projected to again win their conference.

I looked for – and found – Tony right away. He was lined up on defense, in the secondary. He had his shirt cut off above his belly, his socks pulled up almost to his knees, and white wristbands on each wrist. The team looked a little ragged, with kids wearing purple jerseys, white jerseys, gold jerseys and even a couple red jerseys and at least one green jersey. It looked like the offense was all wearing purple, but the defense wore a little of everything. If twenty-two kids were out on the field, my guess was WHS had about thirty-five players on the team, since a dozen or so kids were scattered either on the sideline or well behind the offensive huddle. Colt Harrison stood tall as quarterback, and on the first play I saw him rifle a pass to Nate Bolton – the

Cardwell track runner – who was quickly tackled by Cale Bolling, a lanky defensive back.

Pete Duffy, a retired Jefferson County deputy sheriff, was the Ranger assistant coach. He hadn't been officially hired yet – and wouldn't be for another week until the school board met – but his hire was in little doubt. The school had advertised for an assistant coach for two weeks, received no applications, and after no one applied, Lyle O'Toole and Ed Franklin each talked to a couple possible candidates and all of them declined to be a part of Ranger football. Finally, Ed and Lyle teamed up on Pete, who took the job only because he really had nothing else to do, because he owed Lyle a favor, because Ed had been good to Pete's own kids when they were in Whitehall schools and – this was a key aspect of the arrangement – Pete received a promise that coaching football would in no way intrude on his annual elk hunt in the Blackfoot Valley. Pete took the job strictly as a favor to Ed and Lyle, had never met Jersey – had not even ever heard of Jersey – and had Pete not taken the job, said Ed, the school had nowhere else to turn. Ed himself was going to have to coach the junior high team and Jersey had to do double duty as the jayvee head coach.

Pete was a short, barrel-chested redhead who years earlier as a deputy sheriff had been shot in the hip by a high school kid who claimed the trigger had been pulled by accident. The story was that Pete stopped the kid for speeding on Highway 69, and the kid – so drunk he could barely hold himself upright – pulled a pistol out of the glove box as Pete approached from behind the car. Pete said he leaned into the car and saw the beer cans and a pint of blackberry brandy and then saw the kid's left hand lift a gun that then fired through the door into Pete's leg. Pete said he yelped and went down, and the kid screamed, opened the door, screamed again when he saw Pete bleeding on the pavement, then took off running. Pete said he was sprawled on the pavement but could see the kid running down the highway about fifty yards before the kid stopped, dropped to his knees, and retched what looked like blood – foamy beer and blackberry brandy – onto the shoulder of the road. Pete said he must have passed out for a minute or two, because when he woke up the kid was seated next to him on the pavement, stinking of vomit, shirtless, holding a puke-stained shirt on Pete's wound, and stayed until help arrived.

Pete still walked with a lurch in his stride, as if his left leg wasn't quite as long as his right leg and wouldn't quite help support his beefy body squarely. On the Ranger practice field he stood behind the defense, baseball hat pulled low, stark white legs sticking out under Ranger purple shorts. He stood at an angle, almost as if he was leaning on his right leg as a brace. The armpits, back and collar of his gray tee-shirt were soaked with sweat, and somehow just standing there he looked frantic.

Colt Harrison completed another pass, this one to Logan Bradshaw, who caught the ball in the flats, squared his shoulders, and rumbled down the sideline.

"Goddamnit!" bellowed Pete. "Where's my D-end on the left side!"

One of the twins, it looked like, half of the JeffScott tandem, meekly raised an arm.

"Goddamnit!" Pete yelled. "Which one are you?"

The response must not have mattered.

"Goddamnit, JeffScott! How many times do you have to be told! You line up opposite tight end, you hit him when he gets off the line. Give me a tight end! Who's a tight end!" Someone I didn't recognize raised a hand. "Well, get over here, for chrissakes!" Pete said. Pete grabbed him and pushed the player down into a three-point stance. "Okay, now run a pattern!"

The player must have asked which pattern.

"I don't give a good goddamn which pattern! Just try to get off the line." Everyone watching knew what would happen next. Pete had the kid outweighed by at least thirty pounds. The player lifted slowly out of a three-point stance and Pete dropped a shoulder into him. The kid stopped on impact and fell virtually straight back on his rump. "See!" Pete shouted at JeffScott. Pete helped the player up. "Again!" he shouted. The player got off quicker this time, and Pete shoved him off stride but didn't knock the player down. "Good job!" shouted Pete. "What's your name, hombre?"

The name must have been Tuck, so he must have been Tuck Fredrick, a sophomore who looked like he was too frail for high school football.

"That a boy, Tuck," Pete bellowed.

The offense ran a few more plays – including a fumbled snap and a fumble by the halfback – before I heard Jersey say his first words as a coach: "Okay, gentlemen, let's run some sprints, shall we?"

The team spread out on the goal line, facing west, into the dull orange glow of coming twilight. Jersey stood about midfield.

"On the whistle, men," said Jersey.

The shrill single squawk of the whistle started a multi-colored stampede east to west. The players stopped at Jersey. He blew the whistle again, and it triggered a stampede to the west end of the field. Another whistle, another stampede, with more separation between the first place runner – a tiny kid wearing a gold jersey – and the last place runner, who looked a lot like Bobby Bentmier. Poor Bobby looked like he wished he were anywhere else on earth besides on a football field running windsprints. The players were breathing loudly as they rested a moment.

"This is where games are won, men," Jersey said. "This is how you get better and stronger and make the player next to you better and stronger. And this is how you make the player across from you – your opponent – weaker."

Whistle. Stampede. Whistle. Stampede. The players were huffing and puffing along a line with Jersey in the middle. He stood tall, with sunglasses, black hair, black sideburns, black tee-shirt, black slacks, black socks and black shoes. He didn't appear to be uncomfortable, despite the heat.

"This is where you gain an edge, Rangers," Jersey told them. "Stand up straight. No hands on thigh pads, no leaning over. Stand straight, stand strong.

This is where you gain a physical edge, a conditioning edge, a psychological edge. A winning edge. Right here, right now."

Whistle. Another stampede. The players stopped at the goal line, turned slowly, and faced west, toward Jersey.

Whistle. A slower stampede. The players lined up facing west. They all panted, heaving for breath.

"This is what builds strength," Jersey told them. "This is what builds determination. This is what builds character. This is what builds a team."

Whistle. The stampede, for some of the players, was now an exhausted jog. A couple players were stumbling and a couple could barely get their bodies moving forward.

They ran six more fifty-yard sprints – or something resembling running – before they were finished. Tony had finished in the top five or six kids in each sprint.

Jersey blew two quick chirps on the whistle and the team gathered in a sweaty, exhausted and poorly formed untidy circle around him. He stood tall and calm and comfortable in the middle. Behind him, Bobby Bentmier took a knee, and threw up.

Jersey pretended to not see or hear Bobby.

"Good job, gentlemen," Jersey told them. "The harder you work, the more fun you'll have. Football is not a complicated game. We're going to work hard, we will finish strong, we will win football games. I know it, and you know it."

A handful of players croaked out a weary cheer.

"No practice tomorrow, but take care of yourself this weekend. Eat right and get plenty of sleep. We practice at three-thirty on Monday afternoon, right after school. Full pads, so be ready to hit someone. I'm proud of you, men, and you should be proud of yourselves. Bring it in." He held his hand up, and sweaty arms and hands reached toward his. "Ranger pride!" he shouted, and the kids shouted – with a hint of muted weary emotion – "Ranger pride."

The sun had dropped behind the large red, white and blue Town Pump sign on the west side of Whitehall Street. Helmets in hands, walking in small clusters of wet and sagging bodies, the players trudged off the field. Jersey and Pete conferred on the field, in the shadows, and I waved to the both of them.

I caught up to Tony, whose face conveyed his fatigue. Sweat glued his hair to his head. He cleared his throat and spat a wad of phlegm just as I approached him from behind.

"Hold your fire," I told him, "I'm right behind you."

He whirled slowly. "You got any idea what we're having for supper tonight?" he asked.

"I was about to ask you the same thing." Which was true; I tracked him down after practice in part to see what we were doing for supper. I couldn't help but notice no other parents were trailing after kids asking them what they had planned for dinner.

He grunted. “Where’s Annie?”

I shrugged. “Home, maybe. I don’t know.”

“You know what would be good?” Tony said. “Some watermelon. I think I could eat a whole watermelon all by myself.”

We were almost at the locker room. “Okay,” I told him, “I’ll go pick up a watermelon at the IGA. We gotta have more than that, though.”

“You and Annie figure it out. Get a big watermelon, though.”

He disappeared into the door leading to the locker room.

As I walked back toward the parking lot I came across Pete, who was gathering up footballs and shoving them inside a mesh bag.

“How do they look?” I asked.

“Not as bad as they did a week ago,” he said. Bubbles of sweat dotted his temples. “I wish that Bentmier kid would stop throwing up, though. Every time I smell puke my hand automatically reaches where my gun should be."

Chapter 12

The school crosswalks were repainted with bright yellow paint, the fleet of cleaned yellow buses crawled across the countryside, kids were afoot on town sidewalks sharply at eight a.m., high schoolers cruised in cars and pickups down Legion Avenue and through the A&W parking lot one final time before the warning bell: school had officially started in Whitehall.

It was the final Monday in August of 1986. It was an odd Monday morning in that I stayed home rather than head to the Ledger, in part to make sure Tony got the school year off to a good start and actually arrived at school on time, and to get to the school myself to uphold a Ledger tradition – pictures of the new teachers the morning of their first day of school in Whitehall.

"I can't drive you to school this year," Tony complained to Annie, and then for some reason impersonated President Reagan, "because someone – we won't name names here – because someone named Lance couldn't get driver's education forms in on time."

"Do you ever get tired of whining?" asked Annie.

"I want to drive a car. Is that so wrong?" he pleaded.

There officially were three new teachers this year: a new high school librarian named Sam Longley, a new elementary physical education teacher named Mary Kristofferson – replacing the legendary Frank Stockett and his three decades of teaching experience – and Jersey, who had been hired as a full-time middle school English teacher. Jersey was also Annie's homeroom teacher.

As I poured myself a bowl of cereal Tony scanned the sports page of the Butte newspaper and Annie studied the paper's front page news section.

"You know the second guy to have an artificial heart, the guy who died a few years ago after over six hundred days with the new heart?" Annie asked, her head lowered toward the newspaper. She was eating something out of a plastic cup of what I initially thought held sour cream. Upon closer inspection I learned it was vanilla yogurt.

No one responded, so Annie gave up on us. I never did find out what point she was going to make about the guy who had died after living over six hundred days with an artificial heart. She found something else of interest: Bruce Springsteen had a new girl friend, according to the newspaper, and that she, Annie, thought Jersey would be interested to know that during homeroom.

"Since when do you eat yogurt?" I asked.

"She's an actress, apparently," Annie said, meaning Springsteen's girl friend. "Somehow I can't picture him happy with an actress."

Annie wore an outfit that I suppose was a kind of peasant dress; light red, but not pink, and went from her shoulders to practically her ankles. Tony needed a haircut. His hair hung over his eyes as he sort of stood eating a bowl of cereal – he had one knee on a chair seat, his other foot on the floor – and he looked sloppy, especially for the first day of school. I could recall my first day of school every year. My mother made sure I had a new dress shirt and new dress slacks, new underwear, new shoes, a new haircut and new school supplies. I couldn't be absolutely certain Tony was even wearing underwear let alone new underwear, and I was certain he wasn't wearing new clothes.

"You look like a bum," I told him.

He didn't even look up. "I'd dress a lot better if I had a car to drive."

"Technically," Annie told him, "you do have a car to drive. What you lack is a driver's license to legally operate said car."

"Go irritate someone else," Tony told her.

She more or less obeyed him. "Lance, you, of all people, have no justification to insult someone else's clothing."

I looked myself over: jeans, golf shirt, hiking shoes. "What's wrong with the way I look?"

Tony kept reading the paper. "Let him have it, Annie," he told her.

"You've had those jeans for what, five years?" she said. "The shirt is faded and stained with French fry grease. And those shoes? Come on. Nobody wears those waffle-stomper things anymore."

I simply looked down at my boots. They looked like sensible shoes.

"And the hair, Lance," added Tony. "Do something with that hair."

"What's wrong with my hair? I've had this hair since high school."

"Yeah, that's the point, Lance," said Annie.

Tony had finished the cereal and had moved on to Pop Tarts – two at once, like a Pop Tart sandwich with nothing in between – and washed them down with a can of 7Up.

"That doesn't seem like much of a breakfast," I told him. "Maybe you should eat some of Annie's yogurt." Yogurt, to my recollection, provided tasteless nutrition.

"If I could drive a car I'd go to the IGA and buy some fruit or something," Tony said.

"Right," I said, "you want a driver's license so you can buy more fruit."

Annie looked up from the paper. I noticed she was wearing a light shade of lipstick. I wondered if that was something new, something I should comment on, or something I was supposed to ignore.

"Yeah, it's lipstick," she said. "I'm in middle school, and it's okay for me to wear lipstick. I might even start to wear earrings pretty soon." She looked my way in defiance.

I knew I should say something, but I had no idea what it was.

Tony pointed at me. "Great comeback, Lance." He lifted his head and belched. "Keep it up, Annie, and by the time you're twenty you might need a bra." He folded the paper and exited the kitchen. "I better get ready. Tanner's going to give me a ride."

Annie opted, wisely, to ignore him. "Did you see this, about Lake Nyos?" she asked me.

I looked at her, and thought about the lipstick. What did lipstick mean? What was Lake Nyos?

"Right," she said, "It's a lake in Cameroon, near Mount Oku, which is volcanic. Almost two thousand people died when carbon dioxide basically flooded the air. Two thousand people. Think about that, Lance. One minute they're herding cows, tending crops, feeding children and then an unseen natural poison seeps from the bowels of the earth and kills everything. Everything. People. Livestock. Bugs. Wildlife." She shook her head. "How do you explain something like that? Who decides who lives and who dies, and why? Is it fair? Can it possibly be fair? No, Lance, it cannot. So who justified the unfairness? Who has the authority or the audacity to explain the rationale of life and death surrounding Lake Nyos?" She looked at me again. "Don't worry. We'll go to Dick's later this week and get you some new clothes. You're due. Truly." She looked at me. "Maybe we'll get you to a barber as well." She folded her portion of the paper, neatly refolded Tony's portion of the paper, and brought all the dishes to the sink and rinsed them. "We better get going, Lance, or we're all going to be late."

Ed Franklin was at his traditional *Special Ed* opening day post, just outside the bank of heavy metal doors to the elementary school on Division Street, greeting each child on the first day of school. The sun was bright on the east side of the building, and Ed had to squint through the thick lenses of his black-framed glasses to cut the glare. Dressed in a suit that was in style during Prohibition that bunched in the shoulders as if it had been hanging in a closet since then, he shook tiny hands, patted tiny heads, returned hugs from first and second graders who viewed Special Ed as a friend and chased down and greeted middle schoolers who viewed him as an adversary or embarrassment and had sought to avoid him. All received a smile, an awkward but heartfelt verbal accolade, a gesture of encouragement.

There was a sense of freshness, cleanness, of agitated energy, to the annual first day of school that had no comparison to anything else in life. Maybe it was the internal conflict created by the mostly freshly-dressed and scrubbed-clean kids, the anticipatory thrill of something new after another predictable summer vacation, the wonder of again seeing all the classmates and the inevitable nervousness about new academic challenges combined with the certain knowledge that despite the first day jitters and undercurrent of expectations this was *only school* and nine months of tedious boredom followed the initial and fleeting expectations and exhilaration.

"Annie Joslyn, my goodness, look at you," Ed cooed. He said, more quietly to me, "All three new teachers are together down the hall, in Mr. Conte's room, waiting for you." Just like that, I'd been excused. Behind me, I heard Ed promising Annie "new challenges and new responsibilities" this year.

It was chaos in the elementary school hallways. Parents were tethered to wide-eyed children by the tenuous holding of hands. Teachers and staff were giving instructions or directions, sometimes with a hesitant tone of uncertainty in their voice, as if they were partially guessing. The hallway walls were filled with decorative and colorful greetings and warm messages of hope and assurance. I navigated my way down the cluttered hallway to a door with a *Mr. Conte* stenciled sign above it. Inside were a few kids and parents, and Jersey, wearing black slacks and a dark gray dress shirt. A young man who looked barely older than a college student stood next to Jersey, and off to the left, talking to an overweight mom who loomed over her overweight elementary school son, was a woman with long black hair who was wearing a dress similar to the one Annie had on.

I immediately scouted the room for appropriate backdrops for the pictures of the teachers. They were the school's and thus the community's trio of new instructors, they would play a pivotal role in the lives of Whitehall school children, and the photos that appeared in the Ledger were more or less their proper introduction to the community. I wanted the new teacher photos to denote school and academics and personality, so I scouted for backdrops reflecting a scholarly and interesting impression. It took about one second to find the perfect background for Jersey's photo: He had a large map of the state of New Jersey stapled to a bulletin board in the back of the room. I also spotted a globe, which would work just fine as a prop. Someone, possibly Jersey himself, had written a large *WELCOME* on the chalkboard, which was an ideal message for this picture and this day.

In the back of the room, in the corner behind a small American flag hung on the wall, I spotted another potentially interesting background for Jersey's photo. Taped to the wall was a poster of Bruce Springsteen, his back to the camera but his head twisted in profile, a large U.S. flag forming the background of the entire poster. There was something arresting about the poster, about Springsteen's posture and facial silhouette, something patriotic but impertinent at the same time.

The woman with the long black hair finished her conversation with the overweight mother-son combination. The mom was June Dunkle, a ranch wife from south of town near Point of Rocks who, if I remembered correctly, was actually part of a local weight watchers organization in Whitehall.

Jersey caught me ogling the Dunkles. "Ten years from now that kid's going to be an All-Conference offensive tackle," Jersey said.

"Ten years from now he might be big enough to be the entire line," I said.

The young man beside Jersey stuck out his hand. "Hi, I'm Sam Longley, the new librarian."

"Lance Joslyn, publisher of the Ledger," I said. Sam Longley gave me a blank expression. "The newspaper in town," I added, and Sam nodded. He had obviously never heard of the Ledger and was unaware there was a community newspaper.

The woman drifted toward the three of us. "Lance Joslyn," I told her. "I'm the publisher of the community newspaper."

"Ah," she said carefully, "the media."

"Not like the real media," Jersey assured her.

"No," I said, "I'm more like the pretend media."

Jersey laughed. "More like a kind and gentle media. A compassionate media. A thoughtful and caring media."

"This I have to see," the woman said.

"Lance, this is Mary Kristofferson," said Jersey.

I had done brief biographies of the three of them when the school board had hired them earlier in the summer, but this was the first time I had met Mary and Sam. Sam, I knew, graduated from Montana State University the previous spring, had been born and raised in Thompson Falls, and was the son of the school superintendent at Thompson Falls. He had sort of frizzy short hair, and wisps of fuzz grew from pale cheeks. He looked a couple years older than Tony.

Jersey had graduated from Western Montana College in Dillon, had student taught in Whitehall the previous spring and was a New Jersey native. He was not a youth fresh from college; he was clearly older than Sam Longley. Information about parts of his life was missing.

Mary was a Minnesota native who graduated from a Saint Paul high school, attended one of the Concordia Colleges somewhere in the Midwest, taught for a few years in a couple small Minnesota towns, taught for a few years on the Northern Cheyenne Indian Reservation east of Billings, and accepted the job here. She had long brown hair, and stood oddly straight, her back firm, and her shoulders were flat and struck me as slightly masculine. She wore glasses, and she was almost as tall as me.

"Nice to meet you," I told her. She made no gesture to shake hands. "Well, let's get this done before the bell rings and the new school year has officially begun. I always take pictures of the new teachers. We'll start with you, Jersey, if that's okay with everyone."

Mary Kristofferson's eyes widened for an instant, as if in shock or fear, and I thought I even heard an audible gasp. She was clearly and suddenly alarmed about something, but Jersey was asking me where I wanted to take the picture, so I turned and indicated the New Jersey map.

"*Joy-see*," he said and smiled.

I took three or four photos of him, and then positioned Sam near the globe. Sam has a broad easy smile, a natural calm with a camera pointed at him.

"Okay, your turn," I told Mary. She seemed less distraught than moments earlier, but I'd taken thousands of photos of hundreds of people, and could tell when someone was uncomfortable, and she was uncomfortable. I tried to think of ways to relax her, to take an edge off her stiff and proper posture. She offered me a weak, tentative smile that failed to mask the fear in her eyes and facial expression.

"How about if you stand in front of the chalkboard, with a big *Welcome* behind you," I suggested.

Wordlessly, she nodded. She backed up a stoic, anxious step, as if walking in a dark lonely corridor.

“Okay, good, good,” I said, doing my best imitation of someone trying to make someone else relax. I could have used Tony. He could coax a genuine glow from anyone.

I motioned her a little to her left, a little more, a little more, than motioned for her to be still. She was at the left edge of the frame, with the *W* in *Welcome* extending behind her to the right. I got a big smile from Jersey and from Sam, but Mary looked with stark terror toward the camera. “Okay, here we go, big smile,” I encouraged. She stared with a lifeless, cold gaze into the camera. Her expression suggested she was expecting something awful to happen. It’s only a camera, only a photo, I wanted to reassure her, but reassurance no longer seemed appropriate at that point. Her discomfort was painful. “Big smile,” I said again, and took one, two, three photos, each time allowing the flash to recharge, each time providing a new opportunity for her countenance to soften. It never did; she had endured the photos.

I nodded a thank you, and she left the room. Sam smiled, shook my hand, and took a deep breath. “Here we go. My first day as a teacher,” he proclaimed, and left the room with obvious exuberance.

Jersey was already in a conversation with a parent, so I exited the classroom and the disorderly hallways out of the school, down the steps and toward my new Escort. I left all the energy behind me, at the school.

It was Monday morning, not even eight-thirty. I was already at least an hour behind schedule.

It was the following night – a Tuesday evening in late August that contained just a hint of a chill and a realization in the early nightfall that suggested summer was slipping away – when the school board met for a special meeting to approve the budget and school library book and textbook list.

Usually it was only the school board, Ed, the elementary and high school principals, a teacher or two and a parent or two, in the room for board meetings. I had noticed there were a bunch of cars in the parking lot. I figured they were there for some other school function, but when I got into the meeting room it was stuffed full of people.

I looked at Ed; he slid his glasses up the bridge of his nose, gently shook his head, and scanned the papers in front of him. Chairman Lyle O’Toole nodded toward an empty chair in the front row, but I opted to stand in the back of the room, behind the audience and facing the board members. A couple people in the front row – perched regally in the plastic chairs – were some of the community religious types. Two of them, Ginny Wilcox and Lorna Baxter, had tangled with the Whitehall Town Pump a few years earlier about the racy magazines displayed for sale at the store. Ginny and Lorna prevailed, Town Pump pulled the magazines, and truckers and local teenagers had to head over the hill to Butte or up to Boulder to buy dirty magazines. It was obvious by the eye contact and short discussions they had with other members of the audience that the two of them had orchestrated the turnout for the meeting.

Lyle opened the meeting with the Pledge of Allegiance, and as we all stood, right hands over hearts mumbling the words, I thought of the Springsteen poster. There was something about that poster I kept thinking about, but I couldn't figure out what the something was. It was troubling, almost.

The budget – a combined three-quarters of a million dollars for the high school and elementary school – took less than twenty minutes to discuss and approve. There was a hesitation before the book list approval motion was made, and a stirring in the audience as people shifted weight in anticipation of the discussion.

"Is there a motion to approve the book list?" asked Lyle.

Daniel Purdy cleared his throat. He wore a sweater for the occasion, another indication summer was slipping away. He had shaved – probably just an hour or so before the meeting – and his face was still red. He'd probably showered as well; the comb-over was neatly in place, with a little more life in it. "I make a motion to approve the book list as presented, with the omission of *The Confessions of Nat Turner*."

"Second," said Doris Hinkle, a little too quickly for it to be spontaneous or unscripted.

"Discussion," said Lyle.

"Let's hear from the public first," said Daniel Purdy.

"Why not," Lyle said grandly. He looked directly at Ginny. "Are there any comments from members in the audience?"

Ginny stood. The word that best described her hair was *elaborate*. I'd never seen her with a hair out of place. It would take some kind of catastrophic natural event, I thought as she stood, a nearby volcanic eruption perhaps, to muss that hair. The bangs kind of puffed out in front, but in back the hair was long with a curl at the bottom. If the Barbie Doll had a grandmother, she would look like Ginny Wilcox.

"Thank you, Mr. Chairman," she started. "There is a significant contingent of people here who object to the contents of this book, *The Confessions of Nat Turner*. The book, as you know, is proposed for the junior high English curriculum by a new teacher here named Mr. Conte."

All eyes were on Ginny, which she appreciated. My hand was writing what she was saying, but my mind was wondering about Jersey and this book. I had a vague understanding or remembrance about the book, about a slave uprising in the South before the Civil War. Nat Turner led the uprising. Several white landowners had been killed, and Turner was captured and executed, if I remembered correctly. I tried to remember if I'd read the book or read about the book, and couldn't recall.

"The book graphically details the murder of innocent people by a deranged slave named Nat Turner, which by itself is enough to question its presence in the Whitehall school system," Ginny said. "But this slave, Nat Turner, a man clearly mentally unbalanced, claims throughout the book to be a man of God. He brutally slaughters innocent white men, women and children, and claims to act in the name of God. As if God approves or accepts his murderous behavior."

"Did you actually read the book?" asked board member Molly Ryan.

"I most certainly did," snapped Ginny. She held up the book. It didn't look all that dangerous; a paperback with an orange cover. "I read every page of this book. Not all of it is offensive. But major sections of it are patently blasphemous and obviously inappropriate for young readers. This is a violent and vile book and has no place in this school." She sat down.

"Thank you," said Lyle. "Anyone else?"

Brenda Atkins, the librarian at the Whitehall Community Library, stood with substantially less confidence than Ginny had. I hadn't even seen Brenda in the room, but Brenda, who defined the word *plain,* was easy to miss. She wore large glasses with thick brown fames and the big glasses somehow made her head look smaller and her slender body look skinnier. I had never heard her speak – had never even seen her – at a public meeting before.

She also had an orange copy of the book. "Pulitzer Prize winner," she read softly from the cover of the book. People had to strain to hear her. "A triumph. The most profound fictional treatment of slavery in our literature." She flipped it over to the back cover. "The book of the year. Magnificent. Achieves a new peak in the literature of the South. The finest American novel published in many years. A masterpiece." She looked up meekly toward the school board. People in the audience scowled in obvious disagreement. Some people shook their heads in opposition, or possibly in denial of her comments. "This is a novel. It is not a history book of facts. Nat Turner is not a hero in this book, and his actions are very disturbing. But this is not an anti-religious or an anti-Christian novel. The mixture of religion and slavery was extremely confusing in the South during the early nineteenth century, and the issue of race and religion can be confusing even today."

"We don't need a lecture," Daniel Purdy interrupted. He glared at Lyle for approval, but Lyle simply sat back in his chair, arms folded across his chest.

But the brief conflict spooked Brenda. "Censorship is dangerous," she said timidly. "Banning books is wrong. This book is a classic." For a moment it appeared she was going to say something else, but she suddenly sat down.

Up popped Lorna Baxter. Lorna had three children graduate from the Whitehall school system, and had one last kid at home, a boy named Brian, in Annie's class. Lorna and her husband, Richard, both worked for the Forest Service in Whitehall and three of their children were all valedictorians of their class. I got the impression Lorna and Richard resented Annie and me, because as long as Annie was in Brian's class he had no chance of upholding the Baxter family valedictorian tradition. Worse, I think, from Lorna and Richard's perspective, was that Annie came from a broken home and a dysfunctional family, and something like that shouldn't possibly be placed above their son. The final insult, I suspected, was the Baxter family was prominent in the Lutheran church, and it was absolutely unfair in their minds for an upstanding Christian family like the Baxters to have to bow in any way to a heathen family like the Joslyns. They had a point, but it wasn't my fault Annie was a genius and Brian wasn't.

"Mr. Chairman and members of the board," Lorna said. "What we have before us is not an abstract or theoretical discussion. What we have before us is a book, *The Confessions of Nat Turner,* a fictionalized account of a slave rebellion in which fifty-nine people – fifty-nine people, Ms. Foster, according to this book jacket – are mercilessly and maliciously slaughtered. The leader of this murderous gang of killers is – again, according to the book jacket, Ms. Foster – *the preacher* Nat Turner." She turned from Brenda to the board, as if the board was a jury, which in a way, it was. "There is raw violence in this book, graphic pornography, sexual depravity, blasphemy and worse. This book is not a textbook. It is an abomination. It should be and must be removed from this school."

No one else stood immediately. While there was tension and opposition in the room, there didn't seem to be outright hostility – at least not yet – so I doubted we were going to have a brawl like we'd had at the town council. Thus far, the anger was directed at a book, not people, but I was slightly worried what Lorna and Ginny might be capable of if the board rejected the plea to remove the book and did, in fact, approve it for middle school English.

"Anyone else?" asked Lyle. His eyes found someone to my left. "Mr. Conte. Be my guest."

I leaned forward to look, and there was Jersey, near the door. I hadn't seen him arrive. He must have recently left the football field; he was wearing black slacks, a black tee-shirt and a black baseball cap, and a whistle hung on a black shoelace worn around his neck.

Jersey moved forward, amidst murmurings in the audience. He found an open space more or less between the front row of the audience and the tables in the front of the room where the board members sat, and then moved to the side, so everyone could see him. He took off his cap, and held it in both hands in front, about belt high.

"*The Confessions of Nat Turner* is about many things," he said, with the word *Nat* sounding almost like *not*. "It is a controversial book, with complex themes about life and death, and about things more important than mere life and death. It was written by William Styron, an author who has deservedly earned international acclaim. This book is serious in its scope and intent, but this book should not and will not divide this community. I appreciate Brenda's comments – I appreciate all your comments – and without question censorship is at times more than appropriate, it is essential. Suitable materials should be available at suitable times for students. And unsuitable materials should not be available. I think we can all agree on that, and what we all agree on when we do that is called censorship. So what we're talking about here is the degree of censorship."

I was trying to keep track, and thus far Jersey had appeared to agree and disagree with Brenda, and then also seemed to agree and disagree with Ginny and Lorna. I couldn't tell whose side he was on, and he *was* one of the sides.

"In some cases, censorship is a fear of the unknown, or just plain fear," Jersey said. "Never underestimate the power of fear. Fear, like faith, can move mountains. Fear, like hate, can also destroy bonds of community. It would be a good idea, I think, to remove *The Confessions of Nat Turner* from the middle school English reading list and replace it with *Call of the Wild*, a book which offers perhaps less controversial life lessons and moral guidance, but lessons and guidance nonetheless."

There were more murmurings, and Ed and Lyle exchanged looks in the front of the room. "Are you sure you want to do that?" Lyle asked Jersey.

Jersey nodded. "With all my heart." *Heart* sounded almost like *hot.*

"Ed?" asked Lyle.

Ed hesitated a moment. "I can defend *Nat Turner*, Mr. Conte," he said, "and you know I can defend *Nat Turner*. And I know you can defend *Nat Turner.*"

"But not the repercussions," said Jersey.

Ed leaned back in his chair, and adjusted his glasses. He shook his head glumly, and glanced toward Lyle. There would be no further defense. *The Call of the Wild*, a book with its own thread of violence and depravity, was about a dog turned killer, not a slave turned preacher turned killer. The vote to replace Nat the slave with Buck the sled dog was unanimous. Ginny and Lorna stood, victorious and radiant. Jersey slipped out of the room unnoticed.

But as I thought about it, Ginny, Lorna and Daniel Purdy hadn't really accomplished anything. All that had happened was that one middle school book was substituted for another middle school book. Jersey hadn't lost anything. And he hadn't really bowed to pressure. He modified his own school curriculum proposal, when it came down to it, to spare us an ugly community and academic confrontation. He took one, you might say, for the team.

After the Wednesday trip back from the printers I had to haul and distribute all the newspapers to the post office and vendors. Larry, the printing plant manager, had been grumpier than normal, and Dan – the lead printer – had some problems with ink distribution so it had been a trying time in Anaconda. Tony's wit would have been a welcome intrusion into the Wednesday production schedule, and my pedantic attention to detail and perfection was not helpful.

It was mid afternoon before I completed the vendor route. I figured I'd earned a nap. Long days and late nights at the Ledger had taught me the value of a ten-minute afternoon nap, and at times my body craved – lusted – for a brief reprieve on the davenport at home. Wednesday afternoons were particularly good for napping; even the briefest of breaks was still a break and helped to separate the week that was just completed – with a newspaper freshly published and distributed – and the week that was just beginning, with the new newspaper – published seven days into the future – in its infancy. I'd gotten to be something of a nap expert. At times I could drift into sleep in under thirty seconds. I had even fallen asleep while chewing food, and had woken up ten minutes later with a dry mouthful of lumpy food still waiting to be swallowed.

My habit was to sleep face up on the living room couch with a news magazine folded open across my chest. The sun was to the west that time of day, and the north side of the house was cooler in the summer.

I stretched out on the couch, disappointed the paper had been slightly late this week and because of the production problems about three hundred copies of the paper had some offset impressions on the bottom of pages six and seven. But it was time to let go of the paper that was just published and begin planning work on the product that would be published in seven days. Looking up from the couch, I saw remnants of a wispy spider web in one corner above me sway with the movement of air, and the delicate and translucent web strands seemed to pulse from an invisible and unfelt breeze. To the web's left was a round water stain where the roof had leaked. The web looked to have been deserted long ago, and I briefly wondered if the spider moved to a drier location.

Some weeks the nap was so necessary – and so pleasurable – that I couldn't even finish a full paragraph of a magazine article before dropping into sleep. Sometimes as I nestled myself down on the couch I could actually feel the fatigue of a seventy-hour workweek gather in one place inside in my brain behind my forehead, and I imagined I could actually feel the fatigue slowly dissipate as I slept.

A noise jostled me awake, and I slowly blinked my eyes awake in time to see Annie's back as she crossed the living room to her bedroom. My mind struggled to stir into comprehension. School must be out, which meant it was three-thirty in the afternoon, and time for me to head back down to the Ledger. I groaned, and still face up on the couch, tensed and stiffly stretched my arms and legs, my arms over my head almost like a referee signaling a touchdown.

Annie's schoolbooks – a tidy pile brought home more from habit than need – had been set on the kitchen counter. I spotted an advanced math book, a thick book about geology and a small orange paperback. I didn't even have to look to see its title. Nobody told Annie what she could and couldn't read.

"Did you sleep your fatigue away?" Annie asked me. She'd changed into a tee-shirt and jeans.

My fatigue was her little private joke. When she had been a child I had explained to her my concept of workweek fatigue settling behind my forehead and dissipating with sleep. She discounted my theory, but said if I *believed* my fatigue could be collected and dismissed, and if I *believed* it strong enough, then it could happen. She had explained her response in the same voice a parent might explain belief in unicorns to a child.

"I'm good for another ten hours," I told her.

"Is that fatigue I see wafting toward the ceiling?" she pondered.

To prove I was an utter idiot, I looked up toward the ceiling.

She mercifully ignored my stupidity. "I have a form from school here that you need to sign."

"Me? I thought we had an arrangement that stipulated you exercised power of attorney for all parental educational forms."

"Nicely done, Lance. That was a complete adult sentence you just articulated." She sat in the recliner across from the couch. "You don't have to actually sign this form, but you do need to be aware of it," she said. "It calls for your actual physical presence. You get to be a chaperone at the middle school fall dance."

"Right," I said, "like that's going to happen." Me? A chaperone? Not a chance.

She sat to my right, her body in profile, and I couldn't help but notice again her slender body was maturing; she wore a brown Yellowstone National Park tee-shirt and her budding breasts were evident behind lettering across the shirt. I wondered again if I was expected to have that parent-to-child talk about human reproduction, or if Annie already knew everything about it, in the same way she pretty much knew everything about everything.

"As a matter of fact, it is going to happen," she persisted. "Parents have to take turns volunteering. Would you rather make sloppy joes or a salad for the fall banquet, maybe help decorate the stage at the dance?"

I grimaced.

"That's what I mean," Annie said. "I think we can both agree that I can't chaperone my own dance, so the system has us in a quandary. They have assigned me a task I must re-assign to you. There is no alternative. I have to find duties you can physically and mentally handle, and I've found one. Even you can stand around in the back of a room."

"Appreciate your vote of confidence," I said. I sat up on the couch and rubbed my eyes.

"I think I can still see some fatigue," Annie said. She slipped a single sheet of paper from her folder, handed me a pen, I signed the sheet, she took the sheet and took back the pen.

"When's the dance?" I asked.

"Later this month. It's on a Friday night. I'd tell you the date now, but you'd forget before you even got down to the Ledger. I'll give you plenty of warning."

She gave me more credit than I deserved. If she told me the date of the dance now, I'd forget before I even stood up.

"I'm a lousy parent, I know," I said. "I'm lucky to have you two for kids."

Annie corrected me. "You're not a lousy parent, Lance. You're not a parent at all."

She hadn't said it maliciously. "Not at all?" I asked.

She contemplated the question a moment. "It's like the three of us – you, Tony and me – are all in this together. We get along fine, and we seem to be doing okay as a family, in a basically non-traditional kind of way. But I wouldn't exactly say you're an authority figure."

"I guess it's a good thing you don't need one, then," I said. "Who else are chaperones for this dance?"

"Jersey and the new teacher, Miss Kristofferson."

Poor Miss Kristofferson, I thought. Not because she had to chaperone a dance, but because of the photo of her that had just appeared in the Ledger. I had taken three pictures of her in Jersey's classroom, and not a one of them was in any way flattering. Only one was even marginally presentable. Her pained expression was one of pure dread, or even agonized panic. From the look on her face, you'd have thought I had been holding a gun instead of a camera.

"How can Jersey chaperone if he's got a game that night?" I asked.

"It's a home game. The dance starts right after the game ends."

"Man, that's going to be a long night."

"You'll probably need a nap that day," Annie said, waving her arms. "You know, to dissipate all that fatigue from inside your forehead."

I figured Thursday afternoon, the day before the Rangers opened their 1986 football season on the road against Columbus, would be a good time to take Tony out for dinner and get him a steak. The plan was for Annie and me to pick up Tony after practice and drive out toward the Jefferson River canyon at LaHood.

Annie and I worked until five-thirty, as did Laura Joyce, who spent all afternoon typing Madison County Fair 4-H results, when we turned off the air conditioner and closed up the office. The county fair results provided a short but significant circulation boost for the Ledger. Laura Joyce probably typed in the names of close to a hundred Jefferson and Madison county 4-Hers, plus their categories and ribbons they'd won, and I'd have to print fifty extra papers the following Wednesday to make sure vendors were amply supplied. Each 4-H kid kept an accurate scrapbook of his or her ribbons, projects and awards, and each kid needed documentation – like a newspaper article – of each accomplishment.

Each week, the Ledger aspired to do three things: Accurately chronicle the history of Whitehall one week at a time, frame policy or government issues so the community was informed and could make an intelligence decision, and fill scrapbooks. The Ledger was a community booster and the paper supported everything – all levels of sports, all types of music and drama, every type of academic honor, all promotions, all awards, each business accomplishment. Every time a Whitehall person succeeded in anything we published and promoted the success, and while we were required to report on conflict and tragedy in the name of historical accuracy, the Ledger stressed recognition and appreciation of triumph and achievement. Bad news and conflict sold papers in the short-term, but good news and a sense of progress and community identity were good for the paper in the long run.

Annie and I locked up the Ledger, got in the Escort, and when the engine started the radio came on, and suddenly Springsteen was singing a song called *My Hometown* about a father and son relationship based on the concept of community. I'd heard the song a few times, and turned the volume up as we backed out of the parking spot.

"Lance is a Springsteen fan," Annie said, with a hint of surprise, and possibly admiration, in her voice.

"This is a great song," I said. "He's singing about tradition, community spirit, family bonds, neighborhood strength, and the hopelessness of bigotry and racial strife. All in three minutes."

"You're as bad as Jersey," said Annie.

"He's big into Springsteen, isn't he?" I said.

"You could say that. He knows every word to every Springsteen song. He knows stories about Springsteen, stories about Springsteen songs and stories about Springsteen stories."

I turned onto North Division Street; we'd park in the faculty parking lot, near the football practice field. "How do you know all that?"

"I got him for homeroom, remember?" Annie said. "Every morning in homeroom he does a little current events quiz and then plays one Springsteen song on the record player. He either lectures about the song before or after he plays it, and he says pretty much every day that Springsteen is the only musician in the 1980s whose music will have lasting merit. Except his version of *lasting* always comes out sounding more like *losting*. He likes that phrase, *losting merit.*"

"Nothing wrong with lasting merit," I said. "Has he ever talked about this song?" I pointed to the radio, as if Annie needed help identifying which song I meant.

She shook her head. "Not yet. I'm sure he'll get to it, though."

When we got to the parking lot the football team was still on the field. A long practice the day before a game was a little unusual, and a two-hour-plus practice certainly qualified as a long practice. Just as we stepped out of the car, a chorus of whistles blew from the field, and the team trotted off from the practice field to the game field. I figured the team was going to practice extra points – the only goalposts in town were on the game field – and then head to the showers.

But the players divided themselves into two groups, one lined up across the field on about the twenty-yard line, and the other along the sideline, stretching from about the twenty-yard line to about the forty-yard line. Annie and I crossed the practice field to the game field to find out what was going on. Jersey stood on the field at about the forty-yard line, and by his body movement and gestures I could tell he was talking to both groups. Annie and I got to the sidelines and I stood next to Pete. His shirt was soaked, and trickles of sweat ran down his temples and cheeks. Pete stood by himself, clipboard held against his good hip, on the sideline at about midfield.

"I didn't know coaching was this tough," I told him.

"Me neither," Pete said. "This is way harder than people said it would be."

"Well, at least you're having fun," I said.

Pete scowled. "That explains why half the Ledger is wrong every week. You can't see straight." He took a step toward me, and clearly he was going to tell me something in confidence. "He don't let me cuss no more." He opened his eyes wide, as if telling me, *yeah, you heard right.* "No cursing. No swearing. Half my vocabulary was cuss words."

"Whose idea was that?" I asked.

He lifted his chin toward Jersey. "Whose do you think? The reverend over there. He says we have to set an example in both word and deed. Trust me, you don't want to hear the whole story. I got a full lecture from him."

"No more swearing." I pondered the thought.

"Not in front of him and the kids. That's harder to do than you might think."

I looked out toward the players, still lined up in two groups, one group on the field and one along the sidelines. "What exactly are we doing here, out on the field?" I motioned toward the players.

"Same thing we did yesterday. We're practicing lining up for the national anthem." Pete turned toward me, and said softly, "He's got a thing about the national anthem."

I strolled closer to the field, so I could better hear and see what was going on.

"Okay, just like yesterday," I heard Jersey call out. "Helmet in the crook of the right arm. All of you, now, helmet in the crook of your right arm. Good firm bend of the elbow, right, right, just like that. Left arm straight down along your side. Feet together. Arm straight. Your index finger should be more or less aimed pointed at your outside ankle. Back straight. Eyes at the flag." Jersey paused. "No one moves while the anthem is played. No one moves. Not a muscle," he shouted. "We will stand at attention and honor our flag, our national anthem, our country, our school, our team, our opponent and our sport. We will stay at attention until the song is completely over. No feet shuffling. No eyes roaming the stadium. No shoulder gyrations. We stand at attention. Are there any questions?"

There were none.

"Okay, assume the position," Jersey called out.

"That's your line, Pete," I said.

He shook his head. "Real cops never say that."

Tony was in line along the sideline. He told me he was starting as a wide receiver and at cornerback. Like the rest of his teammates, he stood ramrod straight, helmet firmly in his right elbow, eyes aimed straight at the scoreboard.

"Which kids are on the field and which kids are on the sideline?" I asked.

“Juniors and seniors are on the field, the rest are on the sideline,” Pete said. “He’s big into highlighting seniors. The only reason why juniors are on the field is because we only got seven seniors, and it looks dumb to see only seven players on the field.”

“He’s not afraid of doing things different, is he?” I asked.

“Different?” Pete said. “How’s this for different? We know how to line up for the national anthem, but don’t have a punt return play.” He let that sink in. “We ain’t once practiced punt returns.”

“Might not be a problem against Columbus,” Annie said. Pete and I both looked at her. “Columbus may never have to punt.”

Chapter 13

We left in the Escort immediately after school let out – Slack, me, Annie and her friend, Natalie Dickson, the younger sister of Ranger freshman football player Dave Dickson. It had been awhile – since the night the Honda was demolished after a collision with a thousand pounds of beefsteak – since Slack had been allowed to consort with me. I knew the reason why, even if no one verbalized it. Slack's parents, Wally and Sue, were not pleased I had endangered their son's life, and were not about to let me do so again. With Annie in the backseat, Slack's parents figured I'd behave myself, even if I had to force myself to do it, and although no one said anything, I knew this was a shot at redemption, a chance to prove myself trustworthy.

We exited Whitehall heading east, and on the way out of town drove past my favorite sign in town, a neon art deco reproduction of an Indian chief's war bonnet headdress, at The Chief Motel. The war bonnet headdress was lit in a bright red and yellow and blue, and the colorful, and inappropriate, expression *Me Like 'Um* was written as if a quote from the Indian chief. It was either a lighthearted wild west artifact or a bigoted slur, I figured, and it seemed improbable a business could exist by promoting bigotry.

Slack rode shotgun, and he had a two-day bearded stubble with just a hint of tobacco juice on his whiskered chin. I was tempted to suggest he rub it off on his sleeve, but decided there wasn't much of a point in it.

"This car is even smaller than your other one," Slack said as we drove east on I-90. "And that one was small."

Slack and his family – and almost everyone else in Whitehall, or in Montana, for that matter – drove pickup trucks. The Escort would probably fit in the back of Slack's family's Ford half-ton pickup, but I'd always been partial to compacts. They got better mileage, they were easier to park, were cheaper to own and operate, and they just seemed to fit me better. In the school faculty parking lot, maybe a quarter of the vehicles were pickups, because most of the teachers lived in town. Half of the kids, though, were ranch kids, so the student parking lot was mostly filled with pickups. In front of Borden's during a typical lunch hour, you'd find a majority of vehicles were pickups and at a 4-H meeting you find that nearly all of the vehicles out in the parking lot were trucks. Montana was truck country.

It was also chew country. Slack usually had a chaw tucked under the front of his bottom lip, and probably half the males in and around Whitehall chewed tobacco sometime during the day. I don't know how they did it. I tried chewing twice, both times I got dizzy then I got sick.

"This might be the tiniest car I ever sat in," Slack observed, looking around the car as if contemplating buying it.

"Four is a little cozy, isn't it?" I said. It was the first time all four seats of the Escort had been occupied. We weren't cramped, but we had close to a four hundred-mile round trip to make. Fortunately, the two people in the backseat combined maybe weighed two hundred pounds.

Slack continued his visual survey of the Escort's interior. "I'm thinkin' this might be the tiniest car ever made," he said. He had his cowboy hat in his lap. He had to; if he wore it, the hat's crown hit the ceiling. His forehead was marble white, his face red bronze. His hair was plastered to his head where the hat rim rode. It was as if he was wearing an invisible greasy headband.

The Escort labored up the Cardwell hill east of Whitehall, and three cars passed us as we cruised toward the crest at about fifty miles an hour.

"She gets pretty good mileage," I told Annie, making eye contact through the rearview mirror. "But she doesn't have much oomph."

"What's oomph?" asked Slack.

"Power," I said. "Horsepower. You know, giddyup."

Slack roared with laughter. I wasn't sure why. I made eye contact with Annie, who smiled shyly.

The sky ahead of us grew gray as we motored past Belgrade and Bozeman. We stopped in Livingston at the McDonald's for an early dinner; Slack pulled out a folded and refolded ten-dollar bill from his pocket and stubbornly insisted on buying his own food. He pointed to the Escort tires before he got back in the car. "You got baby wheels," he said, grinning.

We got back on the freeway and bugs fluttered and pulsed in the headlights and instantly perished on the windshield. Behind us, the sun descended behind a bank of glowing orange clouds, and ahead of us the gray twilight darkened by shades of purple, brown and black the further ahead we looked. It was a perfect night for football. A breeze barely stirred. On some flat pastureland to our right, just before the foothills that evolved into the Absaroka Mountain Range, a couple pronghorn antelope stood absolutely still, as if posing.

There's something special about a road trip to a high school athletic contest. The anticipatory excitement builds as your mind wanders through the possibilities, and if you're smart you'll allow your mind to wander through daydreams and reminiscences. Montana's long distances and sparse traffic were made for daydreams. Montana's scenery – viewed from almost any road almost any time of year – is breathtaking. The wildlife can be remarkable, and on a drive from Whitehall to almost anywhere for any reason you can almost always depend on seeing deer, pronghorn, raptors, waterfowl, sand hill cranes and more. I searched the land for wildlife, and I never grew tired of it.

"Did Annie tell you about the spelling bee?" asked Natalie from behind me.

"What spelling bee?" I asked.

"She didn't?" gasped Natalie. Natalie gushed with glee. "She didn't tell you?"

"Oh big deal," Annie said.

"Annie's going to compete in the school spelling bee, and then she's going to win the county spelling bee so we can beat Boulder in *something* this year," Natalie trilled. "It is *so* cool."

I looked at Annie in the rearview mirror. "I thought they held you out of spelling bees." Annie, as a fourth grader – her first year eligible to participate – had won the school and county spelling bee, and since it was apparent she would win every year if allowed to compete, school officials decided she would help organize the competition rather than actually participate.

"Mr. Franklin asked me if I wanted to compete, since it was my last year of middle school," Annie said.

"And you said yes?" I asked. It didn't seem like her.

"He asked me in front of everyone in homeroom, and they all wanted me to compete and beat the Boulder kids," Annie said. She tensed her chin. "I really didn't have an option."

"We were cheering for her," Natalie said. "We were, like, chanting, '*Annie! An-nie! An-nie!*'"

"Let me get this straight," I said. "Your own school superintendent used peer pressure *against* you?

"That's one way of looking at it," Annie conceded.

"What's another way of looking at it?" I asked.

She shrugged. "Well, you could say that I had an opportunity to help spur school spirit and boost school pride, and his best chance of nudging me to accept that opportunity was to challenge me publicly."

"When she uses words like that it makes my head hurt," Slack told me. He had a wounded look in his eyes; his stubble at the corners of his mouth now contained slimy drips of runny brown juice.

"That's exactly how I used to feel," I told him. "But I'm pretty much used to it now."

"It's okay, Slack," Natalie said, and laughed. "Annie drives everyone crazy, at least once in a while. She can't help it."

Dusk was vanquished by the bright football field lights, and we got to the game about five minutes before the Columbus High School band played the Star Spangled Banner. The Rangers, wearing their white road jerseys with purple numbers, stood solid as statues throughout the national anthem, while the Columbus kids – wearing dark green – nervously shuffled feet, rotated torsos, rolled shoulders and jiggled wrists.

Slack, Natalie and Annie headed to the bleachers and joined the small group of Whitehall fans – essentially a handful of parents and family members of players – who'd made the 190-mile trip to Columbus. Whitehall had struggled the past few years, Columbus was perennially ranked among the top ten Class B football teams in the state and was a virtual certainty to make the playoffs this year. Columbus was expected to coast to a win at home tonight against an inferior team, and Whitehall to Columbus and back was an incredibly long drive to see a team lose.

Trisha and her wheelchair were parked on the inside lane of the track, and her mom, Molly, gave me a little wave as I moved toward the sidelines to take pictures. Mandy Phillips and some guy I may or may not have seen before were off to the side, and I detected a tiny glint of a metal flask exchanged between them. She hooted and hollered when the Rangers lined up to receive the opening kickoff, but it seemed a forced and phony cheer. She jumped as she hollered and the guy she was with – a guy with a ponytail and a beard and a beer belly – steadied her to keep her from falling.

I found a spot on the Whitehall sidelines, and the first picture of the year was of a junior running back named Scott Atkins as he caught the opening kickoff. It was Whitehall's first play of the season, and Scott's final play of the season. He caught the ball, drifted to his left looking for an open lane up the field, and a Columbus player who'd sprinted untouched thirty yards down the field smashed into Scott just as he turned to head upfield. The brutal snap of plastic shoulder pads crackled in the night. The snap might have also been Scott's collarbone, which was broken in the collision. The ball popped out as Scott crashed to the ground, and two green-jerseyed Columbus Cougars fell on it as their teammates cheered and celebrated the turnover and the violence of the tackle.

The game was delayed a few minutes as Scott was tended to on the field by a Columbus medical trainer, who helped him to his feet and tenderly escorted him to the Whitehall bench. Scott's shoulder was wrapped up and he sat, dazed and tearful, his shoulder pads off and his baggy jersey hanging loose, in the exact same spot on the bench for the rest of the game.

Three plays later, Columbus was in the end zone. Columbus fans cheered but it was a dull, spiritless cheer. It was as if they scored too fast, too easily, and the game was going to be even more lopsided than expected. Perhaps the muted cheer indicated they believed they knew what was coming and held back some of their enthusiasm because they knew there'd be plenty more opportunities for cheering before the game ended.

Tony, wearing number twenty-three, was apparently the second string kickoff returner. He was standing at about the fifteen yard line awaiting the next kickoff. Part of me was hoping he'd return the ball for a touchdown and part of me was just hoping he'd survive the play without needing medical attention. The ball sailed over his head into the end zone, which seemed like a fairly satisfactory compromise.

Quarterback Colt Harrison handed off to halfback Nate Bolton on a play that may have been designed to go off-tackle. It was impossible to say because a Columbus defensive lineman hit and wrapped up Nate in the backfield the instant he took the handoff. Colt completed a short sideline pass to Cale Bolling, who was clobbered after the catch. All four Columbus defensive linemen joined in on a sack of Colt on an attempted pass on third down and long.

Jersey paced the sidelines calmly, somberly, and he looked almost like a casual observer rather than a head coach.

"Punt team," I heard him say, barely loud enough for the team to hear.

A couple Whitehall kids trotted off the field, and a couple kids trotted on the field. Colt was the punter. He fielded the snap from center and was able to avoid the first Columbus player, who sailed past Colt as he more or less improvised a fake punt. The second and third Columbus players were impossible to avoid, however, and Colt never had a chance to get the punt off. The Columbus players whooped it up as they left the field, and the Whitehall kids, heads down, slunk to the sideline as if seeking anonymity.

We in Whitehall had seen this before. And we knew what happened next. The lead grew larger and larger, until the start of the third quarter, when the mercy rule meant the game would last only sixteen merciful minutes.

The Rangers trailed 42-0 at halftime. According to the statistics I kept on the sideline, Whitehall had amassed one first down, a total of twenty-nine yards of total offense, and had turned the ball over three times. That meant Whitehall had more turnovers than first downs, and had less yards of offense than Columbus had points. Columbus had scored on six of seven possessions, and the only time they didn't score was when a ball carrier dropped a pitch in the backfield that Tanner Walker recovered. Even by Whitehall's minimal football standards, this was ugly. The Rangers weren't even competitive. They weren't even close to competitive. The goal for Whitehall in the second half was downgraded to diminish the embarrassment and possibly score a touchdown on the opposition second and third string players.

Annie, Slack and Natalie were standing just outside of the concession stand crowd at halftime. Slack had added a couple bright white popcorn crumbs to his stubble stains.

"What's wrong with Whitehall!" he greeted me.

"Pretty much everything," said Natalie.

Annie nodded glumly. "Not a real impressive debut, is it."

"A what?" asked Slack.

"We're off to a bad start," I said.

"No kidding," said Slack.

"Tony's made some nice tackles," Annie tried.

Tony had made some tackles, but the problem was they had been thirty yards downfield.

"Poor Jersey," sighed Annie.

I gave her a puzzled look.

"He was afraid of this," she said. "He said that Whitehall didn't match up well with Columbus."

"Match up?" asked Natalie. "That's like saying a rabbit doesn't match up against a wolf."

Slack had to give that some thought.

"If we don't play better, we won't match up well with anyone," I said.

"We'll play better," Annie said. "Jersey's positive of that. He was worried about the start, though."

"Worried? He should have been petrified," I said.

I got a couple Cokes for Slack and me, and Annie and Natalie each had an ice cream sandwich. Someone bumped me from behind and spilled pop on my hand, and as I fetched a napkin to clean up I bumped into Colt Harrison's parents, Hank and Kathleen. Hank, an accountant in Butte, advertised in the Butte newspaper but not in the Ledger, which I should have been broad-minded enough to ignore. Kathleen sold Tupperware or kitchen products of some kind, and tried way too hard to look professional. Most of the WHS students drove beat-up cars or trucks to school. Colt drove a red 1985 Ford Mustang.

"Well, what do you think?" Hank demanded. He had a hot dog in one hand and a cup of coffee in the other.

"They got a ways to go," I admitted.

He grunted. "Ways to go? Hell. This is embarrassing." Hank glared at me as if expecting me to defy him. His face was pinched and ugly with anger. He had a head of wavy black hair and somehow even his hair looked angry. He looked like he wanted to fight someone.

I nodded, as if in agreement, and oddly, felt a little as if I was somehow betraying someone, probably Jersey, Coach Pete, Tony and the whole team.

"Who's this joke they've got for a coach?" asked Hank. "Has this guy even seen a football game before? He looks like an idiot out there."

"This is his first game as head coach," I said, as if apologizing. "He was worried about a slow start."

"Slow start?" Hank almost choked. It was possible, I thought, the man might die of a stroke right then. If he collapsed, I realized, I'd have a tough decision: mouth-to-mouth, or let him die. "You're full of shit. Slow start? Look at the goddamn scoreboard!"

For some reason, like a fool, I did. Involuntarily, absurdly, I'd looked over at the scoreboard. That made my mind up for me. No mouth-to-mouth. If he had a stroke, he was getting no assistance from me.

"This is an embarrassment, an abomination!" He was so animated he spit soggy bits of hot dog bun as he spoke. I moved a half step to my left to get out of the flight path. "What the hell has this team been doing during two weeks of practice?"

I opted to not comment on the team's impressive ability to line up for the National Anthem.

"Goddamn," growled Hank.

"Maybe they'll play better in the second half," I said. "I better get out there." I motioned toward the field and fled, escaped, from Hank's hostility.

Whitehall did play better in the second half, against the Columbus reserves. Smaller, slender kids in sometimes ill-fitting green uniforms played in the entire second half, and the Ranger starters played the Columbus second and third string almost even, but gave up one touchdown on a long run and another touchdown after a Whitehall fumble. The Rangers fell behind 56-0. The Columbus third string, or possibly the fourth string – scrawny sophomores and freshmen, most likely – played the fourth quarter, and the younger kids made the kind of mistakes – fumbled center snaps, offside penalties and collisions in the offensive backfield – third and fourth string players typically make. Columbus fumbled the ball away three times in the second half. Midway through the fourth quarter Whitehall moved the ball down field, and with less than two minutes left in the game Colt completed a pass to Cale, who avoided a tackler at about the ten yard line and scored. I heard a couple weak cheers from the smattering of Whitehall fans behind me. Tony was the holder on the extra point, and the center snap sailed not only over his head but way over the kicker's head as well.

The final score was 56-6. You could look at the loss two ways. The second half was competitive. Or, had the Columbus starters played the entire game the final score might have been 84-0.

I put away my camera and drifted toward the mostly empty bleachers, and spotted Annie, Natalie and Slack.

"Remind me never to sit by Colt's dad at a football game," Annie said as I approached.

"Did you say anything to him?" I asked.

I paid attention to her response. If she had said anything, it would have been an unfortunate attempt to antagonize him. She was as good at antagonizing as anyone, and he was as easy and tempting target as she'd find. That was a bad combination.

She smiled. "I behaved myself." We took a couple steps toward the car.

"Please don't pick a fight with someone like him on a night like this," I said, my hand on her shoulder.

"Well, look on the bright side," she added. "As least he doesn't know Whitehall never practiced a punt return play."

"I think her bet with Tony looks pretty good, too," Natalie said. "Annie was actually hoping the Columbus first stringers had played a little longer."

It was a long, dark ride home to Whitehall. Before we climbed the hill on I-90 west of town to climb out of Columbus, Slack was asleep, the right side of his head against the window, his mouth open as if in a crooked grin.

A cold beer would have hit the spot. Just one. Just to help pass over three hours of lonely and depressed driving through the Montana night. I almost stopped in Big Timber, but didn't, and almost stopped in Livingston, but didn't. At Livingston, I spotted a license plate starting with 51 – Jefferson County's number – and thought through the darkness I saw the guy who'd been with Mandy speeding past us, but he went by so fast it was hard to tell.

After we'd crossed the long bridge spanning the Yellowstone River at Livingston the thick pungent stink of skunk hit us seconds before we drove past the black furry body lifeless in the passing lane.

"Whoa," I muttered.

"Skunks actually have two ducts, more like nipples, really, near their anal glands," Annie said. "Think about skunks. Think how they evolved. Most animals survive by fleeing to safety, are expert at hiding with camouflage or cover, can repel an attack with aggression or reproduce in such large numbers that predators can't really impact survival rates. But the skunk doesn't do any of those. Which is interesting, because you have to wonder…did the species evolve the anal ducts and obvious repellant odor because it had no other defense, or did it have the repellant odor first which obviated the need to develop other defense mechanisms? The odor is basically a collection of compounds, thiols and acetate derivatives of-"

"Jesus Christ, Annie," I said. "It's a dead skunk, okay. Just one goddamn dead skunk."

Ninety minutes of silence later, we were back in Whitehall.

One loud knock, two quick taps on the door on Sunday night at the Ledger, and I knew it was Cal Walker. Better yet, I knew he had popcorn.

"Anyone home?" Cal said as he opened the door.

"Come on in," I called out from my desk.

Cal backed in, turned, and held up a bag of popcorn and a plastic cup of pop. "Figured a guy working on a Sunday night deserves a snack."

"I won't be working much longer," I said. "I'm pooped." I had interviewed Jersey – which didn't take long – and had already written the football article.

Cal handed me the popcorn and pop, licked some salt or butter off his hand, and maneuvered out Laura Joyce's chair. "Looks like the Rangers had a tough time in Columbus."

I nodded. "You could say that."

"Well, keep in mind those Columbus boys know how to play football," Cal said. "Baker knocked 'em off last year in the playoffs, and some folks say it was the Class B game of the year."

"Columbus is pretty good, yeah, but it was hard to tell how good." I sipped some pop. "Not sure they ever broke a sweat." I ate a handful of popcorn. "Might be we're that bad."

Cal shook his head. His cowboy hat was tipped back slightly on his head. He was jowly, with a belly that threatened to burst through his shirt. When he shook his head, it seemed a consequential movement. "Too early in the season to say that. First game under a first-year coach, right? You gotta cut the kids some slack."

My mouth was stuffed with popcorn, so I just nodded.

"I watched Boulder play, and believe me, they made their share of mistakes," Cal said.

"Cal," I said, "they beat Townsend 38-7."

"Game was closer than the score," he said. "Some of the Boulder fans were muttering on the sidelines, and I told them to lighten up. It was the first game of the year, for heaven's sakes."

"What would the Boulder fans do if their team got beat 56-6?" I said.

Cal ignored the question. "I hear Hank Harrison's all bent out of shape," he said.

I nodded. "He jumped me at half time. I thought he was so mad his heart was going to explode."

"He's going around saying either Whitehall gets a new coach or he's pulling his kid off the team," Cal said.

It was like words had a force of their own. I froze for an instant. I hadn't heard anything about what amounted to an ultimatum. Had I been in the bars on Saturday night, a not infrequent occurrence, Hank's threat would not be news to me now.

"You think he's serious?" I asked.

"As a heart attack," Cal answered, and smiled. "You know Hank. He's got a pretty high opinion of himself and his kid. Hank gets a little riled up, and the whole world's gotta know it."

"I didn't know it," I said, an embarrassing admission from the local newspaper editor.

"You're not exactly high on Hank's list," Cal said.

"I can live with that," I said.

Cal let out a slight chuckle. "Roger that." Cal had lived in Jefferson County his entire life outside of a stint in the Army, and every now and then he felt more or less compelled to show off his stint of military training.

"Where'd you hear all this?" I asked.

"At church this morning," Cal said.

That was one major difference between Cal and me: I gathered intelligence at bars and he gathered much of his at church. Oddly enough, usually the rumors and news were fairly consistent between the two locations.

"Hank and Kathleen poured coffee at fellowship before the service this morning, and Hank made his displeasure known far and wide about the Whitehall football coach."

"What's his alternative?" I asked. "Whitehall hired the only applicant for the job."

"Hank doesn't recommend solutions," Cal said. "What Hank does is bitch."

"You think he's going to do anything? Get Jersey fired?"

Cal shrugged. "He might try, but look at this realistically. He'll go complain to the athletic director or principal or superintendent, and that'll go nowhere. You can't fire a guy from a job no one else will take."

"So what'll Hank do?" I asked.

"Fuss and fury, be my guess," said Cal. "He might raise a shitstorm so bad the coach quits. You might want to keep your eye on that. I think Hank might get hooked up with Daniel Purdy, and the two of them together could do some damage."

"Shit," I muttered. "That's all those two can do – damage. They never support anything, help anything, build anything. All they like to do is bitch and whine."

"Who does Whitehall play next?" asked Cal.

"Shelby, here in Whitehall."

Cal cocked his head. "It might be a good idea for Whitehall to win that game. Or at least play well enough to make a game of it."

I shook my head. "Not likely. The kids looked pretty inept against Columbus. Shelby isn't as good as Columbus, but they beat us by four touchdowns in Shelby last year."

"Is the coaching that bad?" asked Cal.

"It isn't just the coaching. It's everything. Vince Lombardi couldn't get this team to play real football. Maybe in a few weeks they'll figure it out, but they looked absolutely clueless on Friday."

Cal stood. He never stayed long. When the popcorn bag was empty, he figured I wanted to get to work, which was right. He slid Laura Joyce's chair to her desk. I stood up as well; I had to go into the restroom to wash the salt and butter off my hands.

"I heard you had an interesting encounter with Mary Kristofferson, the new teacher," Cal said. He giggled then, almost like a child.

"What do you mean?"

"You took her picture, right? I saw it in the paper."

"It wasn't much of a picture."

Cal snickered. He was almost out the door. "Wanna know why?"

"Wanna know why what?"

"Why it wasn't much of a picture."

"Why?" I asked.

"Remember what you said that morning. You told her you took pictures of all the new teachers," Cal said. He could barely contain himself. "She thought you said nude. That you took pictures of all the nude teachers."

Enjoying himself, Cal ducked out the door.

Chapter 14

September isn't fall in Montana, and it's not summer. September is in a category by itself, with warm afternoons and frosty mornings, when on an early departure from Whitehall in the Escort taking the paper to be printed in Anaconda I'd scrape the car windows, wear a jacket and gloves and ramp up the car heater, and mid-afternoon back in Whitehall taking the paper to the vendors I'd strip down to a tee-shirt, with warm sunshine pouring in the open windows.

Daily temperature extremes are so common in Montana they are not considered extreme. In September – with the slivers of willow leaves curling and shifting from the color of a lime to the color of corn – the temperature trend started downward, from August days so hot and dry your energy wilted and your appetite wobbled to October days with a cold wind from the mountains so crisp and fresh you could all but taste the snow.

September is also the month people turn serious. Summer vacations and summer frivolity are over, and an obligatory sense of responsibility is resurrected. It is something genetic, something programmed deep inside us through evolution, I think, perhaps something to do with daylight hours shrinking and the need to successfully hunt and gather grows into life and death. September is when animals begin growing winter coats or begin gathering or storing winter survival foodstuffs. In the animal kingdom, in places like Montana, if you don't prepare for winter, you don't survive winter.

The pace was faster in what passed for downtown Whitehall after Labor Day, as if people had more places to go, more important places to be, and less time to get there. The leisurely and extended Main Street summer sidewalk discussions were converted into quick nods or simple waves of the hand as people charged ahead to visits at the medical clinic, discussions with the insurance agent, a trip to the dentist, an appointment at the bank, a purchase of livestock winter feed or supplements, a meeting at the town hall or a discussion with a teacher.

A representative for every civic group or community club – the Rotary Club, Kiwanis Club, Whitehall Booster Club, Whitehall Saddle Club, Chamber of Commerce, Garden Club, Extension Service and more – stopped by the Ledger in September with a request to run an article announcing and promoting its September meeting. Most of them suspended operations in the summer, and with a somber and prompt sense of urgency resumed their duties with a serious September gathering. A semblance of summer weather continued through the middle of September, but the relaxing attitude of summer, of tranquil mornings and lazy afternoons, ended abruptly and annually after Labor Day.

Maybe, I thought once, it had something to do with the simple act of putting away shorts and wearing long pants.

At the school, the enthusiasm of the first day had faded into routine. The high school students had drifted into the dull day-to-day sequence of fifty-minute classes punctuated by brief hallway freedom, and the elementary school kids were beginning to realize that this school year was pretty much the same as the previous school year.

One of the school fall traditions was the spelling bee, an event organized each year by middle school math teacher Brad Knight. Brad was a burly, boisterous guy with a bushy brown beard and a single eyebrow that stretched from temple to temple. His wore baggy shirts and sweaters, and wore his slacks low, below his wide belly girth. His thighs were so doughy his legs seemed to bend slightly inward, the opposite of bow-legged. His appearance was deceiving, though, because he was devoted to hunting and shooting, and if an animal was huntable in Montana, Brad tracked it, called it, baited it or shot it. A few years earlier after a bunch of guys staggered out of the bars after a night of drinking, we somehow ended up at Brad's house with the expressed purpose, apparently, of watching a video demonstrating the art of elk bugling. Brad's house was filled with the heads of dead animals. Elk, deer, antelope, bighorn sheep and moose mounts stared glumly from the walls, from every direction. There was a dead trout in the bathroom, a dead turkey in the hallway and a dead snowy white mountain goat in Brad's guest room. He had a gun case in the living room that held enough weapons to arm a small African country. Before I finished my first beer, the bugling started. I watched Brad's eyebrow all but flutter in takeoff as he grabbed what seemed to be a tiny plastic trumpet and the spectacle – sight and sound – turned so surreal I got unsteadily to my feet, lurched away from the dead animals and stumbled my way out of the house. It was well past midnight and I was afoot, but I staggered home though the darkness and even safely in my own bed had a nightmare, if I recall, that contained the horror of Brad's sinister eyebrow combined with a dead elk and a shrieking artificial bugle.

Brad enjoyed organizing the spelling bee, but he also viewed it as a task that he needed to get out of the way as early as possible, before big game rifle season got under way. For Brad, the early autumn and upland bird and bow season turned in seamless transition to snowfall, rifles and big game season and shotguns and waterfowl, and if possible, a late season deer hunt somewhere. More than once I'd seen him at The Corner Store in Whitehall filling the car with gas on a Saturday or Sunday morning, decked out in either a fluorescent orange cap and vest or camouflage hat and shirt, off somewhere to shoot something. He was apparently immune to cold weather. On chilly early winter mornings I'd be wearing a winter coat and gloves as I pumped gas in the morning cold, but Brad would be sleeveless, wearing a thin orange vest, leaning leisurely against his jeep as he pumped the gas.

The way the Whitehall Elementary School spelling bee worked was each class – grades four through eight – held its own spelling bee, and the top three kids in each class – fifteen in all – qualified for the school spelling bee. The event was held in the high school multipurpose room, with the entire elementary school student body and staff in attendance. I usually took two photos, one of the group of fifteen finalists, and one of the school spelling bee champ.

Trish, seated in her wheelchair, made her way to the front of whatever room she was in, and she occupied a spot just off the far right side of the stage.

"Howdy, Trish," I said as she moved past me.

She flashed me an oddly big, awkwardly angled, smile. No one I knew had reason to smile less. Her illness wasted her strength, withered her limbs and eroded her abilities, but it had not defeated her spirit. I could never be sure how much her optimism was the result of her worsening mental abilities, but her smile was present and persistent, and projected with what looked like genuine and sincere empathy.

"The Rangers didn't play good in Columbus," she said. Her cadence floated dreamily, in lifts and slurs, but she was capable of communicating her thoughts with unmistakable certainty.

"No, they sure didn't," I agreed.

As the elementary children filed in – quietly, orderly, class-by-class – I spotted Special Ed near the entrance. I walked against the grain, so to speak, passing kids barely up to my waist, toward him, and pulled him a few strides away from the entrance door.

"Annie's going to compete?" I asked him.

"Yep." The bottom end of his tie was so short it couldn't even see the top of his slacks. In both fabric and color, the tie reminded me vaguely of Christmas present wrapping paper. The bottom of his pants cuff was a full inch above the top of the heel on his shoe.

"How come?"

"A couple reasons," Ed said. "This is her last year in elementary school, and she deserves a chance to participate. She shouldn't be punished for her intelligence."

"Okay, that's nonsense," I said. "What's reason number two?"

"Boulder's going to kick our ass in football again this year, so we're going to kick their ass in spelling."

"In spelling? Do you have any idea how stupid that sounds?"

"I try not to think about it, actually," he said. "If she wins, you know, you'll have to put her picture in the paper."

"I already have to," I said. "All of them up there," I indicated the stage, "are in the group photo." I paused. A thought struck me. "How many Whitehall kids will qualify for the county spelling bee?"

"Four," Ed said. "Four from each elementary school in the county." He paused. "Why? What are you suggesting?"

"I'm not suggesting anything," I said. "What are you suggesting?"

He shook his head. "It's interesting," he said. "She's a sweet kid. When you read the literature on talented and gifted kids, she fits the intellectual and academic profile exactly. The quest for knowledge, the insistence on perfection, all that stuff. But her personality is almost the opposite of standard talented and gifted. She's quite thoughtful and considerate, you know, very tolerant and patient."

"Yeah, she is, but people will assume she's elitist and boastful if she wins the spelling bee," I said. "People will resent it, and resent her. You know that. So why make her go through this?"

"She can't be blamed because other people are petty and narrow-minded," Ed said.

"Of course she can," I said.

"This is her last year in middle school, Lance, and she's going to go out in style," Ed said. "So just relax."

To my left, Mary Kristofferson entered the gym, surrounded by her students, and when I nodded a greeting she looked the other way. She wore long turquoise earrings that swung abruptly as she avoided looking my direction.

"Nude teachers," Ed whispered, chortled, and moved away from me toward the stage.

Brad stood on the stage at the podium, arranging a thick stack of cards, as fifteen timid kids joined him and sat tentatively on gray metal folding chairs. The chairs were set up in three rows of five, facing the audience, to Brad's far left. Between Brad and the chairs was a tall, isolated and intimidating upright microphone.

I took a few flash photos of the fifteen contestants, then put the camera back in the case and moved to the back of the room. I always figured the kids had enough stress and anxiety at the microphone without someone pointing a camera at them.

Brad explained the rules, told a weak joke to break the tension, made sure the judges were ready, and gleefully started. Brad had an immutable jolly disposition, and he was a perfect emcee for the competition.

"So, let us begin, shall we?" he said.

"We shall," a voice said behind me. I turned to see Jersey, wearing a black long-sleeve silky mock turtleneck, black slacks and a thick gold chain around his neck.

"Do you have any clothes that aren't black?" I asked him.

He thought about it a moment. "Not many."

"Why is that?"

He thought another moment. "I never really thought about it."

"You have all black clothes by accident?"

"I didn't say that," he said. "I said I never thought about it."

"I think less about my clothes than you do yours, and I wear clothes that aren't black," I told him.

"Don't take offense at this," he said, "but if you think about what you wear *and* about what I wear, you're thinking about my clothes a lot more than I am. And, truthfully, you look like you give your clothes virtually no thought, so quite frankly I'm surprised we're standing here talking about fashion."

"Is black your favorite color?" I tried.

“Lance, let me ask you a different question. Look over there at Ed. I think a relevant question is, *Can you explain that tie*? ”

“My relevant answer is, *No, I cannot*.”

“I think a predictable follow-up question is, *Why would someone ever wear that tie*?”

“Well,” I answered, “he’s Special Ed. Maybe that’s a special tie.”

Six of the kids were gone after the first round, and four more were gone by the end of the third round. Annie and Brian Baxter, whose mom, Lorna, had successfully removed *The Confessions of Nat Turner* from the school library, were the only two eighth graders left in the competition. Lorna and Richard, Brian’s father, were seated in the audience. Two seventh grade girls were still in the running, as was a sixth grader named Jordan Kling, a tough little runt with a bad haircut and a chin full of pimples.

The next word was *truant*. Annie spelled it correctly.

Brian’s word was *magnificent*. He got it right.

One of the seventh grade girls spelled *juxtapose* right, but the other girl spelled *incorrigible* with an *a* toward the end instead of an *i*. The crowd issued a quiet and collective gasp, and she sighed, and silently left the stage, exited at Brad’s far right. That left four, the final four, the qualifying four for the county spelling bee.

The word for Jordan was *catastrophic*.

He licked his lips nervously, absently scratched his scalp above his ear, and cast his eyes up toward the ceiling, as if the word was properly spelled out up there. He held his chin for a moment, and tilted his head. He wore a baggy tee-shirt that had probably been worn a few years earlier by his two older brothers, a pair of jeans with a hole in the left knee, and a pair of dirty tennis shoes that had duct tape on one of the toes. “*C*,” he ventured into the microphone, *a-t-o-s-t-r-o-p-h-i-c.*” He ended on a hopeful, slightly higher pitched, and almost inquisitive, *c*.

“Sorry,” Brad said, and sadly shook his head. “That’s incorrect.”

The kids in the audience let loose a collective gasp, and then the room was absolutely silent.

Little Jordan Kling closed his eyes and sort of puckered his face. “Fuck,” he moaned softly to himself, except when you moan something to yourself when you’re standing directly in front of a microphone you haven’t moaned anything to yourself at all. You’ve broadcast it to everyone. Accidentally, to be sure, but clearly and firmly, without a doubt. I was standing in the back of the room, and I heard the word as clearly as if Jordan had spoken it directly into my ear.

“Whoops,” Jersey said behind me, looking toward the stage.

Jordan was as shocked as anyone. His eyes flew open, then he quickly covered his mouth with both hands as if that could stop the distribution of the sound of the word, or possibly the repercussions. But the damage had been done. Jordan kept his horrified hands over his horrified mouth. Jordan knew there were going to be repercussions.

Older kids in the audience were buzzing with snickers and younger kids were buzzing with confusion, and then, to Jordan's right, Martha Cullen, the elementary school principal, was sternly moving her right index finger with the universal beckoning *come here* motion. Jordan sighed, dropped his head, and Martha's entire hand moved in the universal mandatory *get over here* motion. Jordan trudged her direction like a convict toward the hangman's noose.

Brad was doing his best to hide his laughter; the glee in his eyes was unmissable, and his eyebrow was wriggling. He looked down, and kept arranging his cards as Ed and Martha attempted to restore order. Brad looked up once, as if to restart the festivities, but he was grinning and immediately lowered his vision again to the cards.

After everyone calmed down, one seventh grade girl misspelled *decadent* and another seventh grader eventually misspelled *Teutonic,* which left Annie and Brian left to battle for spelling bee champion.

Brian was dressed for church; polished black dress shoes, creased slacks, dress shirt, his wet hair combed neatly across his forehead. Annie seemed to be dressed like an underfed but tidy peasant.

Annie spelled the word *nectarine* correct and Brian spelled *wanton* right. They each spelled two more words correct.

Her next word was *catatonic* and she spelled it *c-a-t-i-t-o-n-i-c*.

Brad leaned back away from the podium, as if surprised or puzzled. "No," he said, slightly confused, "incorrect."

Annie smiled wanly and shrugged.

The audience erupted with gasps, urgent whispers and a physical stirring; Annie's failure was a shock, and it brought the crowd to the height of spelling bee drama.

"That was deliberate," Jersey told me softly.

"Maybe," I said.

"No, she absolutely did that on purpose," Jersey said. "She could spell that word in half a dozen languages, including Latin. She's taking one for the team here, isn't she?"

"Latin?" I asked. "What team?"

"She knows it's more important for Brian and his parents for him to win than it is for her and her family," Jersey said. He shook his head. "She also knows people are tired of her intellectual accomplishments. They shouldn't be, but they are. She took a dive. That is one amazing kid."

I nodded. She *was* amazing. How in God's name did that happen? It was the greatest mystery in my life, and I was no stranger to mystery.

Brian had to spell one more word correctly and he'd be the Whitehall spelling bee champ. The word was *translucent* and Brian got it right, and I went to the front of the stage to take a picture of his big smile and perfect hair for a two-column photo in his hometown newspaper in front of two joyful and radiant parents.

That afternoon I had to take a trip north to Boulder to attend a county commission budget meeting. I tried to limit my journeys to Boulder to a minimum, and while I typically more or less ignored the varied and multitudinous government meetings in the Jefferson County Courthouse, some meetings I was more or less obligated to attend, and adoption of the county budget was one of those obligations.

Cal Walker had called specifically to remind me about the budget adoption meeting, and I'd agreed provided he buy me a burger afterward at the Boulder Dairy Queen.

The sun was over my left shoulder as I passed the flashing yellow light by the state highway sheds and headed up the hill north into the valley. The sun lit the red rocks west of Highway 69 as if the light were somehow underneath the rock shining up through the ground. The red sandstone, embedded in the hillside to my left, glowed like burning embers. To the west of the highway, the Boulder River valley bottom was a maze of bright orange, yellow and red as sunlight amplified the fall colors of the leaves. Beyond the river bottom to the east the sun struck and defined the trees and brush and rock outcroppings in the mountains with such clarity it was as if you could see individual needles in the conifers from miles away.

It was fall, for sure. The irrigated hay fields along the river and the evergreen trees were all the greenery that remained from summer in the Boulder Valley. The lower hills were a bleached straw color, and seemed to await, even embrace, snow cover. A trio of mule deer – two does, and a buck standing guard – grazed down to my right, between the highway and the river.

Every now and then, on a simple drive to a place like the county courthouse, I would realize, again, how lucky I was to live in Montana. At times, the overwhelming sense that I was blessed, absolutely blessed, to call this place home would stir inside me almost like a fever. The stirring always struck me while in a car. I had lectured Amy and kids repeatedly how fortunate we all were to reside in Montana, and apparently I overdid it, because Amy would sigh with resignation and the kids – Tony especially – would mock my discourse.

"Don't ever take this – *all this* – for granted," Tony would say, imitating my voice and my passion for the landscape. "Look, kids, there's a tree. And look, there's a rock. And another rock. And another tree. And a bird. And a grasshopper. And a gopher. And another rock. And a cow. And another cow. And look – there's *lots* of cows!"

Despite his ridicule, the stirring of pride and awe was within me still, and I felt it as I wound my way north to Boulder and the county budget meeting. The valley to my right shimmered in the sun, the leaves along the river fluttering and holding and reflecting light. To the west, a large group of pronghorn antelope stood just beyond the fenceline, their heads up and still, pretending not to be alert.

I didn't hunt, fish, ski, hike or float, the five best reasons to live in Montana. Hunting, fishing, skiing, hiking and floating were all holy grails of outdoor recreation in the west, and Montana offered the best of all five. Hunting and fishing defined Montana, as if branding the state with a sense of purpose. But it wasn't sense of purpose that defined Montana for me as much as sense of place. I didn't have to be on a river, a ski lift, a mountain trail or standing alongside something I shot to appreciate Montana. I appreciated Montana most through the windshield of my car, alone on a deserted road, with light and shadows dancing wistfully along the horizon. And the thought I frequently had from my view through the windshield was this: *Why would anyone want to live someplace other than Montana?*

After an intolerably dull and detailed discussion, the county commission finally got around to voting and unanimously approved the county budget, which when all was said and done looked remarkably like the budget the year before and the year before that. After the meeting I told Cal I voted unanimously for a cheeseburger and chocolate milkshake at the DQ.

"You don't care much for county commission meetings, do you?" Cal asked during dinner. Somehow he got twice as many fries as I did. Perhaps it was a county commissioner perk.

"You have to admit, you're pretty boring," I said. "No fisticuffs, no personal animosity, no drama." I pointed my plastic fork at him. "What you ought to do is discuss a proposal to abolish maintaining gravel roads. Now that would get lively."

"Just because county commission meetings are boring does not mean county commission meetings are unimportant."

"Even if you're right, which you are," I said, "boring is still boring."

"Sometimes I get the impression you have the attention span of a nine-year-old," Cal said.

"An above average nine-year-old," I corrected.

"Maybe," Cal said. "Maybe not."

"Are you saying the Ledger is shortchanging the county commission?" I asked.

"No, you're saying the Ledger is shortchanging the county commission," said Cal. "You're explaining *why* the Ledger is shortchanging the county commission. You're shortchanging the county commission because we're boring."

"You're not only boring, you're boring and you're a ninety-mile round trip to see you be boring," I said. "That's strike one and strike two."

"What's strike three?" asked Cal.

"The burgers at the Whitehall A&W are ten times better than at the Boulder DQ," I said. "However, the beer up here is just fine. I'll buy you one at Sig's."

"Not a chance," Cal said firmly.

Light gray faded to dark black on the early evening drive home to Whitehall. Stars grew in intensity from slightly visible to tiny bright diamonds against a black backdrop. The fencelines on either side of the road disappeared into the night, lit only in ghostly shadows on the outskirts of the Escort's headlights.

At home, Tony and a handful of his buddies were watching television, and an unofficial tally recorded four boxes of pizzas – some empty, some with a few cold and congealed slices still inside – scattered across the kitchen table and countertop.

Dave Dickson, wearing a University of Montana baseball cap, the JeffScott twins, Tanner Walker, Morgan, with pizza crust crumbs in his beard, and lanky Cale Bolling all looked comfortable seated or sprawled in the living room.

"You boys ready for Shelby?" I asked them.

"You got that right," said Cale.

"Oh yeah," said Tony. "We're ready."

"Where's Annie?" I asked Tony.

He nodded toward her room. "She's having a tough night," Tony said. He clearly intended to say no more.

I looked at the line where her door and the floor met, and it was dark. The lights in her room were off. It wasn't even eight o'clock yet. I looked at Tony to ask him a question, and he declined to acknowledge me.

I knocked on her door, heard nothing, and entered. The clock dial was the only illumination in the room. I shut the door behind me.

"You sleeping?" I asked.

"Go away," Annie's muffled voice cried. She sounded as if she was partially, if not mostly, face down, and spoke into her pillow or the bedding.

I sat on the edge of the bed. I found her hair, and it felt damp; she'd been crying. Annie never went to bed early, never sent me away and never cried. Even when her mom left, she didn't cry; and later, when she understood with clarity and certainty her mom was never coming back, she didn't cry.

"What's wrong?" I asked.

"Go away," she whimpered.

"What's wrong?" I asked again.

"You saw it," she whispered angrily. "You were there."

I almost asked *where* but caught myself. The spelling bee. I had seen her fail at the spelling bee. That was another thing Annie never did: fail.

"The spelling bee?" I leaned toward her. It was absolutely black in her room. I wasn't exactly certain where her face was. Heat seemed to surround her body. "I thought you missed that word on purpose."

She responded with an anguished groan.

I patted her hair, and used my fingertips to brush some strands behind her ear. Her face must have been buried flush against her pillow.

"Jersey and I both thought you deliberately misspelled the word," I said. "We figured you let Brian win."

The bed creaked as she moved. She groaned. "Of course I let Brian win," she said bitterly. "You really think I can't spell *catatonic*?" She had raised her head; she was so close I felt the warmth of her breath on my face.

"Then what's wrong?" I asked. What was I missing?

There was a long silence. She sniffed once, and moved again, and seemed to rub tears from her eyes.

"I will never, ever," she said, cutting off each word individually, her wet voice next to my cheek, "give Trish a reason to look at me like that again."

Instantly, I understood. Trish, who so admired the force and precision of Annie's intellect, had been in her wheelchair alongside the front row, ready to applaud and intrinsically share in Annie's spelling bee title. Annie's failure was Trish's failure, and Trish could not understand Annie failing anything.

"Do you understand?" Annie asked, as if accusing me of something. "*Never*."

"I understand," I whispered.

We sat together, silent, in the darkness, for a long time. Outside, in the living room, we could too clearly hear the boys' lighthearted banter. I was about to ask Annie if she wanted me to get them out of the house, but before I spoke I heard the soft rhythm of her gentle breath. I sat a little longer, brushed her warm and damp hair with my fingertips, eased myself from the bed, and quietly left her room.

Chapter 15

Hometown, small town, Friday night football.

No matter how bad your team is, or how good your opponent is, the anticipation of a home football game under the lights is a corporeal presence so alive you can feel it in your skin. It tingles. It somehow vibrates, like electric current.

Whitehall had lost its only game, and Shelby won its only game, a 48-0 win over Cascade. Shelby also had a two-hundred-pound running back named Chance Lonigan who was reportedly being scouted by Pac Ten schools like Washington State and Oregon. Lonigan had scored four touchdowns against Cascade and run for nearly two hundred yards in slightly more than one half of play, and in warm-ups in Whitehall he stood out like a man among boys: He wore number thirty-two, cruised and loped through pre-game drills like a thoroughbred itching to bust loose.

The wind blew straight from the west, and the flag unfurled and fluttered parallel toward the scoreboard on the east side of the field as the WHS band mustered passably through the Star Spangled Banner. Again, the Rangers stood in two inflexible lines, in rigid attention, as the National Anthem was played. Whitehall may lose the game, I thought, but we lead the conference in on field National Anthem precision.

Bill Herbolich, a WHS math teacher, had served as home football game announcer for at least a decade, and he started the year – you could hear it – with optimism in his voice. Herbie announced the starting Rangers lineup in their home opener with a rumble of enthusiasm, and each player received a nice round of applause.

Jersey wore a black long sleeve shirt, and the sunglasses were perched atop his head, like a crown. The sun rested atop the western horizon with a soft orange glow. The wind remained brisk, and rustled the trees on the west and north side of the field. The sleeves of Jersey's shirt flapped in the breeze as he talked with Colt. One thing you had to admit about Colt: He looked like a football player. Colt licked his fingers after he talked with Jersey, dried his fingers off on the towel, and with his helmet off, threw warm-up tosses on the sidelines while he nonchalantly accepted good luck pats on his shoulder and rump from players, managers and coaches.

Across the field, Slack, grinning, stood near his dad, Walt, one of the other chain gang members. Slack felt the tingle of hometown high school football. I could see it. He even felt it intensified, down on the field, surrounded by the opposing team, under the stadium lights.

Behind me, on the outside lane of the track, near the bleachers, Trisha sat in her wheelchair, smiling, absorbing the atmosphere and the surging emotions that surrounded her, her face flushed with excitement. She wore a purple Ranger sweatshirt and had a purple blanket on her lap, for when the sun disappeared and the temperature dropped. She seemed to be looking toward the field, but not looking exactly at anything on the field. I could never be exactly certain how much of the game, the plays and turnovers and penalties and scoring, Trish and Slack actually comprehended, but they both understood the thrill of the game, the sense of competition, the elation of accomplishment and intensity from the players.

Behind Trisha stood Annie with Natalie and a few other girls. Annie was looking out toward the field, but Natalie was talking with the other girls, and the other girls appeared absolutely disinterested in the game. They scanned the stands for friends and classmates.

To the north, on I-90, a trucker let loose a loud and cheerful horn blast, a good-natured burst of encouragement to the home team. The trucker horn blasts were something of a tradition for the high schools along I-90. From Montana, end to end, along I-90 and its brother, I-94, there could be over twenty high school games played across over seven hundred miles during autumn afternoons and evenings on verdant green fields, chalked with white and lit along the sidelines, and the quick *beep-beep* from a semi-truck was a comforting measure of goodwill and acknowledgement.

The Whitehall stands were over half full, and the exhilaration of hometown high school football reached its apex just before kickoff. The players were animated, pounding shoulder pads and exchanging high-fives. The crowd buzzed. The band played. The O'Toole girls and remaining cheerleaders bounced and kicked and shook pompoms. Jersey walked down the sideline, patting each player on top of the helmet. There was the euphoric feeling that *anything* can happen.

From the freeway: *Beep-beep*.

But then the game started.

Colt kicked off, and Lonigan caught the ball at about his twenty yard line. Eighty yards and thirteen seconds later he was untouched in the end zone and Shelby led 7-0. The score happened so sudden and so quick the WHS cheerleaders had their backs to the field and were still conducting the opening cheer to the crowd. Much of the crowd was still settling in the bleachers. At Whitehall, like most small town high school games, about half the fans sat in the bleachers and the other half stood beyond the sidelines behind a fence, either following the ball as it moved up and down the field or leaning against one spot at the fence the entire game. Most of the crowd along the fence were parents, family members or family friends of players, and parents were typically pretty intense fans. The collective anguished groan from Whitehall fans was disheartening. You could even hear an audible groan from Herbie in the press box. The first play of the first home game for the 1986 WHS Rangers was a touchdown for the opponent.

Tony broke a tackle on the Ranger kickoff return but went down at the thirty yard line under a barrage of Shelby players. The Rangers ran the ball for no gain, ran the ball for a two-yard loss, and Colt was sacked on third down and twelve. Colt punted the ball about twenty yards out of bounds, and on the first play from scrimmage Lonigan caught a pitch, got outside the defensive end, one of the JeffScott twins, who flailed haplessly as Lonigan burst past him to the sidelines, and ran fifty-three yards for a touchdown. The game was seven plays old and Whitehall was losing 14-0.

Jersey shook his head in dismay. Coach Pete was on the verge of apoplexy.

The silence and moans from the parents behind me sounded and felt more like mourning than anger. The quiet resignation of another losing game – and another losing season – was deafening. And depressing.

By halftime the Rangers were down 41-0. Whitehall had zero first downs, minus seventeen total yards, and had somehow managed to get a holding penalty on a play where five Shelby players joined for tackle behind the line of scrimmage. Lonigan had rushed for one hundred and forty yards on nine carries and had scored four touchdowns. His uniform wasn't even dirty.

At halftime I ducked behind and around the bleachers to avoid Colt's parents, although not everyone else either evidently wanted to or could. Hank held court at the base of the bleachers, a small cluster of fans and parents around him, and there was no doubt what his message was. I slid away from them in the shadows, and nearly bumped into Mary Kristofferson, who clearly hadn't seen me approaching.

I nodded a greeting, and without a sound she more or less nodded back. Since she'd improbably and momentarily, I'd hoped, thought I'd wanted pictures of *nude* teachers I'd seen her twice, and twice I had been unable to think of a cogent comment to say, and twice she had skittered past me in fear I might actually utter a word to her. I wanted to apologize, but I wasn't sure what to apologize for, and I wasn't sure I was even supposed to know what she'd thought I'd said or if she did know I knew what she thought I'd said if that would make it all worse somehow. If I was supposed to know, I wasn't sure if I was supposed to talk to her about it. So we passed, as quickly as possible, as quietly as possible, uncomfortably, in opposite directions, as far apart from each other as possible, in the darkness of the dirt path between the bleachers. Later that night we were scheduled to be two of the chaperones at a junior high dance, which seemed to be an awfully awkward arrangement. Right then I decided to find Annie and tell her she had to get me out of being a chaperone.

"Impossible," Annie said, when I found her, firmly shaking her head.

"Nothing's impossible," I pleaded.

"Lance, will you listen to yourself," Annie said. "You sound like a whimpering child. You're fully capable of being a chaperone. Anyone can be a chaperone."

"But not anyone *wants* to be a chaperone," I said.

"Quit whining," she told me. She rolled her eyes. "It's a junior high dance. You don't have to do a thing. You just stand in the back of the room, pretend you possess some semblance of authority, and make sure no rules are broken."

"Rules?" I asked. I really was whining now. "What rules? You know I can't enforce rules."

She shook her head in dismay. She flicked her fingers at me. "Go away," she told me. She smiled at Trisha, who let loose with a brief holler when the Rangers took the field for the second half.

"Can Slack at least help me chaperone?" I asked.

Annie shook her head, and I saw just a hint of dismay. "Sorry. You'll have to be a grown up tonight. The only people allowed in the building are junior high kids and the three chaperones. That means you, Miss Kristofferson and Jersey." She regarded me with something like pity. "The dance will last two hours. All you have to do is stand in the back of a room and do nothing. Okay? Stand in the back of a room and do nothing. I have confidence in you, Lance. You can do nothing. I'm sure of it. " She shooed me away. "Now go. Go take pictures or something."

I made my way back to the field, and the WHS pep band passed me going the other way. They had played the school song as the Rangers took the field, and were putting their instruments away before they left. You know it's bad, I thought, when the pep band heads home after halftime.

Mandy Phillips staggered my direction, and grabbed me as she stumbled. I smelled the liquor on her breath, and held her shoulders to steady her on her feet.

"Whoopsie," she giggled. "How's my favorite newspaper publisher?"

"Mandy's had a cocktail or two, hasn't she?" I asked, holding her steady.

"Maybe two," she admitted, and leaned into me.

She was dangerously and sinfully attractive, and had attracted many willing and even unwilling partners into brief trysts. Her hair had that unbridled look of brushed messiness, and her body was impossibly lean and hard. Her face betrayed her if you looked close, but with Mandy it was best to not look close and best to not think carefully. She wore a tight long-sleeve shirt and fleece vest, tight jeans and some kind of leather boots.

She leaned into me. "You look like you could use some company tonight," she said.

I probably did look that way. People walked past us in both directions, and there was absolutely no doubt what they were thinking.

I held her up, and took a step away from her. "I have to chaperone a dance tonight."

She was barely listening, but she heard one of her magic words. "Dance?" Her voice lifted a note. "Where?"

I smiled. "A junior high dance, Mandy. Here, at the school."

She gave me a brief derisive wave. "School," she grunted.

Her eyes made an unfocused appeal for kindness or generosity, but Mandy interpreted kindness as weakness. "I need to go take some pictures."

"Bullshit," she said with spite. "This football team is bullshit." She waved wildly and nearly fell down, but caught herself. "I keep telling Cody to quit bullshit football."

"See you later," I said. And escaped, with her complaining about additional bullshit as I fled.

The Rangers held their own in a quick continuous-clock second half. Colt threw a couple touchdown passes – one to Tony – and Whitehall lost 55-12. Shelby started the second half with reserves, and by the fourth quarter, just as had happened in Columbus a week earlier, small and timid third and fourth string players were on the field. Shelby scored midway through the fourth quarter and the Whitehall booth announcer Bill Herbolich dejectedly announced a touchdown scored by number forty-four for Shelby.

"If anyone from Shelby knows who number forty-four is, please let us know up here in the booth," Bill moaned.

It had come to that for the Rangers: Shelby was playing so deep into the depth charts their players weren't even listed in the program.

By the time the game ended there were only a couple dozen fans still scattered around in the bleachers and along the fence. When the scoreboard horn signaled the game was over not a single Whitehall fan applauded. The shrill blast of the horn was replaced with total and absolute silence. Everyone was glad to get it over with.

Slack and the other members of the chain gang – Walt and a guy named Brett Svenenson – hauled the yard markers across the field, and I stood and waited for them.

Walt wore a blue stocking cap and a silver Dallas Cowboy jacket. "I never thought I'd say this," he grumbled, "but goddamn, I miss Frank Stockett."

Brett, a tall blond Scandinavian, was an electrician at Golden Sunlight Mine and had three boys in junior high who'd likely be playing football on this field sometime soon. "There's not a lot of give-up in these kids," he said. "They outplayed 'em in the second half."

"Tony had a good game," acknowledged Walt. "He made a nice move to get open for that touchdown."

I nodded. Tony was wide open, and the closest defender was a scrawny little kid with a spotless and ill-fitting uniform who looked out of place on a football field.

"Yeah," said Slack. "Tony played great." Slack had a runny nose, and the glint of snot was visible under his nostrils. "Maybe we'll win next week."

"Maybe," Walt said. "And maybe next week I'll look like Tom Cruise."

The sarcasm was unrecognized by Slack and unappreciated by Brett.

"We play Cascade, I think," I said. "There." Another lengthy drive, this one an hour north of Helena. "They're beatable. Shelby beat them about the same way they beat us."

"Are you goin' to Borden's?" Slack asked.

He meant now, after the game. I shook my head. "I can't. I have to chaperone a junior high dance."

"Good luck," Brett told me. "Any of my boys give you a hard time, you have my permission in advance to take 'em out into the parking lot and knock some sense into them."

Slack laughed.

"Slack, you're going with me to Cascade, right?" I asked.

Slack nodded eagerly.

"Walt, you want to go?" I asked.

He shook his head. "That's a long way to go to watch a team like this."

Jersey was alone in the coach's office, leaning back in the chair at the desk, and he did not appear pleased. He was looking straight ahead, and was staring straight into a wall.

"Listen to that," he told me.

In the hallway, and in his office, noise from WHS players in the locker room that adjoined his office was muffled but audible. Someone had a boom box in the locker room, and it sounded like Kenny Loggins singing, but I couldn't be sure.

"Listen to them," Jersey said. "They're *happy*. They were outplayed, outscored, outworked and outhit on their home football field and they're *happy*." Clearly, Jersey was not. "How can they be happy?" He jabbed at the wall. "That locker room should be silent. Morose. Filled with dejection." He took a deep breath. "A loss like this is a time for introspection, for self evaluation, for reflection."

A couple male shrieks made their way through the walls.

Jersey bolted to his feet. "Let's go. I have to get out of here."

I followed him out the door, down an unlit hallway, down another dark hallway, and soon realized we were going to his classroom. He unlocked his door, flipped on the light switch, turned two front row chairs to face each other, and sat down as if he was attempting to punish the chair.

He leveled a look my direction. It was an obvious *get started* directive.

"Did you see anything out there you liked?" I asked. I tried to perpetually emphasize the positive. These were kids, after all; just kids.

He laughed, mostly to himself, and shook his head. "Anything I *liked*? Yeah, I liked the way that Lonigan kid plays football. He plays to win. He plays to conquer. That's how we need to play."

"Anything," I ventured softly, "you liked from the Whitehall kids?"

He thought a moment about the answer. "We executed far better in the second half," he said. "Colt hit open receivers and the line gave him some time to throw. Logan ran hard. The first half we were outplayed at every position on virtually every play. I guarantee you that is the last time you will see that from this team."

He kept his eyes locked on mine. I had noted his anger made his accent more prominent. He seemed to be glaring at me.

"You want me to write that?" I asked.

"Write this down," he said, and pointed to my notebook. "I guarantee the community of Whitehall will see a better football team the rest of the year. We will play harder, we will play smarter, and we will play better. We have a long way to go, but we'll improve. I promise."

I wrote it all down.

"It's going to be a hard week of practice, and we may make a few changes, but we will compete at a higher level the rest of the season," Jersey said. "Whitehall is going to be proud of this football team."

He talked some more about the game itself, and among a few other players singled out Tony for his play. He also mentioned Cody Phillips, Morgan Miteward and the twins, JeffScott Collins.

"I don't know if we can beat Cascade next week," Jersey said. "But it's going to be our starters against their starters the whole game. No mercy rule. Their third stringers will stay on the bench. Whoever scores is going to be listed in the game program. Cascade better be ready to play football next Friday."

The dance was held in the multipurpose room – the combination cafeteria, auditorium and gym in the high school – and it was decorated, apparently, in some type of an Egyptian motif. Why, I had no idea. Earlier in the week it had housed the spelling bee in which Jordan Kling had uttered the most famous word of the school year, and in which, to her everlasting shame, Annie had deliberately failed.

Both incidents seemed long forgotten. The room was reconfigured to replicate a desert landscape with something resembling a cavern or cave, and the dance floor in the middle of the cave, if that's what it could be called, was empty. A collection of kids were clustered in small groups – mostly either boy or girl groups – on either side of the room. Hugging the wall was something I'm sure was supposed to resemble a Pharaoh's, or mummy's, coffin. Fake spider webs were suspended from the bleachers and a smattering of well-intentioned hieroglyphics were magic-markered on imitation-sandstone paper. A few drawings of Egyptian queens were taped to the bleachers, as were drawings of camels and pyramids and the Sphinx.

Up in the front a couple older kids – Aspen O'Toole among them, wearing what looked like glitter in her hair – fiddled with a sound system. Aspen, age sixteen going on age twenty-four, also seemed to be wearing gold glitter eye makeup, and it took me a minute to realize she was dressed up as an imitation of Cleopatra. Tony, to my surprise, was up on stage as well, his back to me as he plugged in a speaker the size of a large suitcase. His hair was soaking wet from his post-game shower.

The junior high dance was a fundraiser for the sophomore class, and Aspen and Tony were both class officers, both had junior high siblings, and both also truly enjoyed dances. They appeared to be the sophomores in charge tonight.

"We seem to be on the shores of the Nile," said Ed Franklin, from my right. He wore a purple Ranger windbreaker, but underneath was a dress shirt and dress pants. No tie. For Ed, that was casual attire.

I nodded. “Do you have an idea why?”

“With two teenage kids, you don’t know?” Ed said.

“There’s a lot I don’t know,” I said.

“Well then, you’re in for a treat,” Ed said. “I had to supervise the gym decorating last night and this afternoon. It took them over five hours to get the Egyptian décor in place, and they played the same song over and over and over.”

“What song?”

“Believe me, you’ll soon find out.” Ed moved away, on to some official duty, somewhere within the school.

Mary Kristofferson arrived alone, and either she didn’t see me or did a convincing job of pretending she didn’t see me, because she immediately flowed toward the front of the room, and helped a quartet of small and slender junior high girls pour quart bottles of 7Up into a large glass container as partial mixture for some kind of punch.

The first song over the stereo was one I recognized – a Bon Jovi song played frequently on the radio – but no one moved to the dance floor.

“The second best rocker from New Jersey,” Jersey said. He had changed clothes, and wore a black satiny-looking shirt with a high stiff collar. The cuffs at his wrists were tight, but the shirt kind of billowed at the sleeves. It was the only shirt of its kind, I was pretty sure, in Whitehall and quite possibly in all of Jefferson County.

I decided to move further away from the entrance, so people would stop sneaking up behind me and speaking before I saw them.

Jersey walked with me toward the middle of the room, a safe distance from the dance floor.

“It’s Italian,” Jersey said.

“What is?”

“The shirt.”

“I didn’t say anything,” I said.

“You didn’t have to,” he said. “It was a gift from my grandmother, who, by the way, is Italian.”

“It’s a nice shirt,” I said. “I have one at home just like it, except red.”

Jersey laughed. “I bet you do.”

It was nice to see him laugh; thirty minutes earlier he’d looked as if he wanted to tear something apart. Along the sideline during the two football games, I’d seen his perpetual tense, grim expression, as if he was in constant receipt of bad news, which in a lot of ways he was. He did little yelling at players or officials – unlike Frank Stockett, who had screamed at someone after nearly every play – and buried his obvious anger and frustration with an occasional helpless and silent appeal skyward or dejected shake of his head. Coach Pete was a trembling figure of hostility on the sidelines, but Jersey seemed somehow resigned to what happened on the field.

“What does a chaperone do at these things?” I asked.

"The basics, I suspect," he said. "Make sure there's no drinking or smoking. Break up any fights. Keep kids from getting carried away romantically."

"Fights?" I asked. "No one told me this gig could possibly get violent."

"Don't worry, I got your back," he said. Back sounded liked *bayck.* His accent either came or went, or I was noticing it less.

"What do you mean, *carried away romantically*?" I asked. Annie had failed to warn me how complicated this was. "What does that mean, exactly?"

"It means whatever you think it means."

"Give me a brief explanation of what you think I should think it means."

He indicated a group of girls up toward the front. "Don't let anyone do what you don't want your own daughter doing."

Sure enough, there was Annie, with about five other girls, gathered up near the stage. Trisha was there, still wearing her Ranger purple sweatshirt, her wheelchair decorated, it appeared, like a chariot. Trisha had sparkles in her hair, and when I looked closer, so did Annie.

"What's with the glitter?"

"Do you know how to dance like an Egyptian?" asked Jersey.

"I don't know how to do anything like an Egyptian," I admitted.

"Well then, that explains it," Jersey said.

"Explains what?"

"Everything," he said, smiled, and left.

An Aerosmith song blared through the speakers, then a few songs I didn't know, although one of them was by Prince, who, if I recalled correctly, had a shirt he wore in a video that looked remarkably similar to the one Jersey was wearing.

A trio of girls started dancing to the Prince song, and Tony and Aspen jumped off the stage and started to dance. They did so, I thought, to generate additional dancers, but Tony was not shy around a dance floor. As a baby, naked on his back on the changing table, he would squirm and tremble at the first sound of a musical note. He'd always been moved, I guess, by music, but had never the slightest interest in learning to play any kind of musical instrument. When he was about five or six years old, and a niece of mine had been married at Big Sky, Tony danced the entire wedding reception – sometimes by himself – and enjoyed the night as much as anyone present.

Aspen slithered and shimmied to the music and I did my best to not notice. She wore a short tight glittering gold dress that in back was maybe two inches below her fanny. Watching her, the thought that crossed my mind was exactly the thought she wanted to cross the mind of every male in the building. Except I was a chaperone, and while I wasn't exactly sure what a chaperone was supposed to do, I was pretty certain what a chaperone was *not* supposed to think. Tony boy, I thought, you'd best be careful.

"You could be thrown in jail for what you're thinking," Ed told me.

"Goddamnit! Stop sneaking up on me," I said. "How do you do that?"

"Do what?"

"Sneak up on people."

"I'm a professional educator," he said.

"What's that got to do with being sneaky?"

"I gotta be sneaky to catch these kids. They're pretty sneaky themselves."

It made sense, although Special Ed had never struck me as being particularly crafty. "What am I supposed to do here?" I asked.

He shrugged. "Keep the kids out of trouble. You're also expected to dance at least one song."

I whirled to look at him, and I spotted Mary Kristofferson from the corner of my eye, who looked at me with alarm. I knew instantly, by her expression of barely concealed terror, that Ed had moments ago told her the same thing.

"You're making that up," I told him.

"I don't make anything up," he said. "There are certain obligations that come with the responsibility of chaperoning. We all expect you to get out there at least once and boogie."

It was surreal, if not outright bizarre, to hear the word *boogie* come from the mouth of Ed Franklin.

"Did you just say the word *boogie*?" I asked him.

"One song," he said sternly, in his professional educator's voice. "It's a tradition."

"I thought you said it was an obligation."

He moved away from me, stopped, and turned back toward me. "A traditional obligation."

Later, I stood alone along the bleachers, wishing for some kind – any kind – of alcoholic beverage, and the instant a song started through the sound system a shrill squeak of joy seemed to shriek from the girls, and all the kids, including Annie, immediately jumped toward the dance floor. The kids were all dancing, it appeared, like Egyptians, and the song was, apparently, *Walk Like an Egyptian*, which I'd heard on the radio and seen on MTV a couple times, when watching TV with Annie or Tony. Trish, on the edge of the dance floor in her wheelchair, was slowly and awkwardly moving her arms and hands and elbows in straight lines, much like I recalled the dancers did in the video. Annie was in front of Trisha, her back to me, but was making the same arm and hand gestures as Trish. Jersey, standing alongside Mary, was even doing an abbreviated version of the arm and elbow movement. Tony was on stage, dancing with Aspen and Aspen not only looked like Cleopatra but she could actually walk like an Egyptian.

I was the only person in the entire building, outside of Mary, who didn't know how to, or didn't care to, dance, or walk, like an Egyptian.

Annie spotted me, and beckoned me with a finger, and instead of fleeing, which would have been prudent, I merely and foolishly shook my head no. She walked like an Egyptian the ten yards or so in my direction, held out both hands toward me, and when I hesitated she reached forward and firmly took both my hands and not only backed herself onto the dance floor, but backed all the way to the opposite corner near her friends, with me in tow.

In high school and college, and as a newlywed, it had been fun to go out dancing. But after we were married awhile nothing was fun, and nights out dancing faded into the past. Once in awhile, after Amy had left, uptown at Borden's or the Mint when they had live music, I'd blundered out to the dance floor, but not often. And never sober, never with my glittered daughter, never surrounded by junior high kids and never ever like an Egyptian.

But what father can reject a daughter who wants to dance? So I did my best to not embarrass myself, to move as controlled as possible, and to limit whatever damage was bound to accrue by being out there.

Next thing I knew, Tony and Aspen were dancing next to Annie and me and the other junior high kids.

Aspen, grinning, slithered her hips in a circle around me. "Lance has got it down," she cooed, her eyes alive with mischief. I turned away from her, and saw Trish, still smiling, still moving her arms and hands in a partial imitation of the video.

Finally, the music started to fade, and mercifully, my dancing obligation was over. But the next song was a John Cougar Mellencamp song called *Rockin' in the U.S.A*. and before I could get off the dance floor Aspen grabbed me, Tony was moving alongside Annie, and even Jersey and Mary were out there dancing among the dozens of writhing little middle schoolers. Jersey executed, almost perfectly, a rendition of several 1960s and 1970s dance moves, that like an idiot, I also attempted, as did Aspen, and she knew the dance moves better than Jersey. I actually started to sweat, and when the song was over and I was about to exit the dance floor the opening chords of Springsteen's *Born to Run* roared through the speakers. Most of the junior high kids stayed on the dance floor and spun and shook and stepped. Annie pointed at Jersey and danced like I had never seen her move before, and she and Jersey actually appeared to pair up to dance. I could see Jersey mouth the words to the song, and I imagined he gave a pretty convincing performance of Springsteen actually singing. Somehow, I found myself dancing with Mary, and our tepid and formal movement paled in comparison to Jersey and Annie and Aspen and Tony, who, to be honest, all looked out of control. Jersey wasn't actually dancing. He pretended to play an imaginary guitar, and Annie spun frantic circles around him across the dance floor. That was my daughter, I realized with sudden awe, with her homeroom teacher, jointly possessed by Bruce Springsteen and rock 'n roll. I looked up at Mary, who looked toward the floor as our eyes met. When I looked away from her, I was shocked to see we were the only six people left on the dance floor.

Bruce stopped singing, and I smiled toward Annie, who was flushed with what…effort, movement, pride, euphoria? It was hard to tell. A slow song started, sung by a deep-throated foreign woman, and Tony, bless his big-brother heart, moved toward Annie and they joined arms. Jersey was smarter than me, and escorted Aspen to the punch bowl. Mary, as if bewildered, simply stood in front of me, eyes lowered. I took a half step off the dance floor, but she didn't move or look up. If she was done dancing, or disinclined to dance, she would have moved away, but she wasn't moving at all, so I took a tentative step toward her. She made the slightest gesture, the barest hint, to open her arms, and I took another tentative step inside. I put my hands on her hips, and she draped her arms around my shoulders. There was enough room to slip a basketball between our waists, but we were doing a decent imitation of two people slow dancing. We'd yet to say a word, yet to verbally acknowledge the physical awkwardness between us, but we shuffled in a tight harmless circle.

The music faded, and I met Mary's eyes. I was going to speak, intending to admit my poor dancing skills and obvious discomfort with the whole *nude teacher* mistake when I could tell by her expression she was interested in, and troubled by, something going on behind me.

Tony was holding a sobbing Aspen. Ed was behind them, grim and serious, all business. I moved the three strides toward Tony, and stood alongside him.

"What's wrong?" I asked.

"Mandy Phillips is dead," he told me.

Chapter 16

Mandy's death was a depressing cliché with little true compassion, and it didn't take long before thoughts ventured to her troublesome son, Cody, and his future. Mandy and her companion, a cowboy from Twin Bridges named Gil something, had been on Highway 41 between Sheridan and Twin Bridges heading north when her pickup veered into the borrow pit, then crossed both lanes of traffic into the other borrow pit, where it rolled and flipped end-over-end twice. Speed, according to the Montana Highway Patrol, was a factor, as was alcohol. It was a single-vehicle accident with no witnesses. Neither person wore seat belts, both were killed. Mandy's obituary was one column, with her high school graduation photo as the picture, in the Wednesday Ledger, and outside of her son and perhaps vague drunken recollections by a group of wayward males and a handful of other friends, she was largely forgotten before she was even buried. Her legal name wasn't Phillips. It was Horton. No one knew, and no one cared. End of story, end of life. That was the sad part.

The other sad part was Cody. With his mother gone, he lost whatever faint semblance of structure had been in his life. For all her faults, Mandy was connected to her son, and with that connection gone, Cody was connected to nothing. A rumor was Cody would settle in with Mandy's father, a mean-spirited old codger named Cap Horton, a man who once did a stretch in jail for beating a horse to death with a metal fence post. Cap was one of those people born a century too late; he had no use for laws or regulations and lived in a dingy little trailer home on a dry and brittle plot of land down by Fish Creek. He had an old truck, an old horse and an old attitude. He showed up in town a couple times a month and drank whisky alone in the bar, his sweat-stained and dirty cowboy hat low over his eyes. He seldom spoke or made eye contact, and shuffled off his stool wearily late into the darkness of night and the darkness of his soul. It was tragically possible for a kid like Cody to default into that kind of existence, trained by the malevolent old man, both of them tied together by blood and the loss of a daughter and mother.

The death was past tense and Cody's future was still unclear the day of the Jefferson County Spelling Bee, held with significant decorum and formality in the courtroom of the county courthouse in Boulder. It was Thursday, one day after the funeral service, and there were twenty kids competing, four from each elementary school in the county. Jefferson County didn't have a traffic stoplight in the entire county, but it did have five elementary schools. Whitehall was represented by Annie, school champion Brian Baxter, slender little Jordan Kling, who I was confident would be on his best behavior with a microphone in front of him, and Michelle Bradshaw, the long-haired seventh grade sister to WHS football player Logan Bradshaw.

Brian was carefully groomed, properly stoic and studious, and wore a pressed white dress shirt. Annie looked slightly disinterested, as if waiting for a movie that was frustratingly late in starting. Jordan clearly wished he were anywhere else, and probably should have been, but he was needed as a substitute when a seventh grade girl named Lisa Dawson – Chance Dawson's daughter – came down with strep throat and was not available. Michelle quivered with excitement, and with an abrupt and nervous gesture waved frantically to her family, who sat proudly – with Logan in tow – in the audience. Trish had ridden up in the Escort with Annie and me and I sat in the front row near the corner, with Trish and her wheelchair to my right. Tony was seated near the back, after the trip to Boulder with Aspen in her dad's pickup. Aspen herself wore a tight pink blouse, jeans so tight a freckle would have been a bump, and lipstick the color of, close as I could tell, molten lead.

The Jefferson County School Superintendent, an elderly woman named Martha Perry, was either the aunt or mother – I didn't know and didn't care – of Dave Perry, the county road supervisor. Martha had been county school superintendent, seemingly, since Montana had been a territory. She had to have been at least eighty years old, ran unopposed every four years for re-election, and for the life of me, I never could figure out what a county superintendent of schools did. I knew what a teacher did, what a principal did, what the school district superintendent did, what a school board member did, even knew what a school custodian did. But outside of swearing in new school board members and emceeing the county spelling bee, so far as I knew the county school superintendent did nothing. Still, Martha did whatever it was she did with overt correctness. Above all she was proper, official, formal. She was not a small woman, with solid stocky legs for an older woman. She wore thick black rubber-soled shoes and stood with a firm and unforgiving posture; I figured she could possibly hold the job another twenty years.

Standing in the front of the room, Martha cleared her throat, and the audience immediately quieted, except for a chubby girl in the front row who continued chattering to someone in the row behind her. Martha sternly looked in her direction until the room was absolutely silent. Once everyone was attentive and properly respectful, and once Martha had everyone's undivided attention, she offered us all a patronizing smile and welcomed us to the Jefferson County Spelling Bee. She congratulated all the participants, their families and schools, and patiently, and with great dignity, explained the rules for the event.

Maybe this is what Martha does all year, I thought, planning and executing the county spelling bee. She had all year to think up and look up challenging and tricky words for the contestants. She proceeded to detail her instructions and the intricacies of the rules so slowly and carefully, and with such professional articulation and precision, you'd have thought she was explaining how to elect a parliament or remove a pancreas. The room atmosphere was steeped with tension, and mentally I urged Martha to tell a joke or offer a slight quip or at least smile to lighten the emotional and mental load of the kids. But Martha was not the joking kind. There would be no humor at this spelling bee. Her eyes surveyed the contestants as if they were criminals.

She insisted on explaining every nuance of each rule as if it was an intricate military exercise involved in a Special Forces hostage rescue mission, and when she finally finished there was a collective sigh of relief and an anticipatory movement of chairs and body positions as she began to gather cards and notebooks for the first word of the evening.

Trisha clutched her right hand fingers in her left hand, and squeezed. She looked around with apprehension. This was the first time I had ever been responsible for Trish and the first time I had to handle the logistical and physical challenges of her handicap. Back in Whitehall, Molly, her mom, helped her into the backseat of the Escort, and helped me fold up the wheelchair and place it in the trunk of the car. There was ample room, but it was heavier and more awkward to handle than I had thought. Both Annie and I helped Trish from the car into the wheelchair at the courthouse in Boulder, and after I got the wheelchair out of the car and standing upright on its own I had to pull the wheelchair – Trish's back to me – up the half-dozen exterior courthouse steps, one forced step at a time. She was a good sport about it all, and didn't seem uncomfortable with someone like me, someone she only casually knew, as her guardian. Her apprehension was for Annie and the competition, not the situation.

I looked at her and smiled, but she simply kept squeezing her right hand. She'd seen Annie falter in Whitehall, and was distraught at the thought of it happening again, this time on a larger and more prestigious stage.

Annie's first word was *muticous* and she breezed right through it. I had never in my life heard the word before. Michelle, her long golden hair tumbling to her shoulders in blonde ringlets, stumbled over *therapeutic,* reversing the *e* and the *u*, and cheerfully sighed, then sat down. It was as if she was thrilled to be there, and happy to have it over with.

Jordan fell in round two, missing *crustacean*, and merely sighed – mouth closed – and rolled his eyes in dejection.

Martha's diction was perfect, and as each word rolled off her tongue it was obvious this was something she knew she was good at. I figured she had probably been praised for her diction her entire life, so she placed a high value on the skill, much like she would for punctuality or good manners. I tried to imagine what Martha did for fun; I came up nothing. Zero. Maybe this was it; the spelling bee.

Annie zipped through *parasitosis* and then *kunzite* and after three rounds only half the kids were left in the competition. Brian and Annie got through the next round, and when Trisha turned to me with a quick excited smile only eight kids were still in the running.

Two other kids dropped out, then Brian put an extra *s* in *rasbora* and to his shock, and his parents' disgust, he was gone, and finished in sixth place.

A couple rounds later the competition was down to three kids: Annie, a tiny girl with metal braces across her teeth who wore a frilly dress and ribbons in her hair, and a boy who thus far had not demonstrated a single mote of emotion. Annie smiled at Trish and me a couple times, mostly, I think, to reassure us; the girl in the braces was clearly relieved after each word she spelled correctly; but the boy showed all the emotion of oatmeal.

Annie got *scarificator* right and spelled *tachymeter* correct, but the boy was an *r* short in *ferraiolone* and sat down with the exact facial expression he had when he'd spelled all the previous words correctly. The audience, however, was more vocal. There was a definite gasp when he misspelled the word. There had been some previous gasps or muted groans, during the evening, but when three was reduced to two, it happened with a dramatic flourish.

The two girls got each word right, and I started to wonder if this thing was going to last all night, when the girl in the braces was given the word *tiralleur*.

She pondered the word. She pursed her lips, and scratched at her ear and then her cheek. It was apparent the correct sequence of letters to properly spell the word was not coming to her. But my eyes were on Annie. I knew her look of thoughtful but determined opinion. There was something she wanted to say, and when there was something she wanted to say, she usually said it.

She cleared her throat and faced Martha. *Oh oh*, I thought, *this is not going to be good.*

And it wasn't.

"You're pronouncing it wrong," Annie said with perhaps a bit too much confidence.

Martha's face froze. "Pardon me?"

Annie cleared her throat again. "You're mispronouncing it."

Martha's eyes bored holes into Annie. "I think not, miss." She said it in a profoundly challenging tone, as if to terminate all discussion.

Give it up, Annie, give it up, Annie, give it up, I thought. *Please Annie, give it up. God help us, Annie, give it up.*

Martha glared at Annie, and Annie glared back, but did not respond.

Martha shifted her attention a few feet to Annie's left, to the girl in the braces. Martha repeated the word, and the girl spelled it wrong. The group gasped, and Annie silently shook her head.

Trisha beamed when the girl missed her word; if Annie spelled the next word correctly, she was the county spelling bee champion. Annie didn't look over to Trish, and right then, I knew what would happen next.

Martha tersely repeated the word, *tiralleur*, repeated it exactly the same way, and Annie looked Martha squarely in the eye and just to make sure there was no mistaking the intent, she spelled the word the exact incorrect way the other girl had. Annie refused to win in what she would consider an unfair manner.

The gasp was nearly a shrill cry when Annie missed her word, and I thought Martha allowed herself the hint of a superior smile. Off to my left, in the middle of the second row, Lorna Baxter, Brian's mother, gave a smug, short clearing of her throat.

But the meek self-assurance of the girl with the braces was eroded, and she correctly guessed more than confidently spelled the next word, *inagglutinable*, but then added an extra *s* in *ponsasinorum.* Annie ripped through the word without hesitation and Martha glumly nodded, and Jefferson County had a new spelling bee champion.

Trisha squealed and clapped her hands once, and held them tightly together, almost in supplication. Annie smiled in our direction. When Martha stoically gave Annie the championship trophy, Annie leaned forward and whispered something in Martha's ear. Whatever it was prompted a sudden and harsh scowl from Martha, and she removed her hands so fast from the trophy you'd have thought the metal spread plague. Annie kind of laughed, then held the trophy up for Trish to see, and Trish again squealed. Annie beamed with delight, displayed the trophy toward Tony and Aspen, who both were standing and applauding. Tony whistled and Aspen cheered, and Annie nodded in their direction with satisfaction.

This called for a celebration, which in Boulder was either the Dairy Queen or a bar. The five of us – Annie, Tony, Trish, Aspen and me – sat around a table in the brightly lit interior of the DQ, the trophy tall in the middle of the table. Several people from the spelling bee – including the Bradshaw family – also rewarded their kids with treats, and all of them congratulated Annie.

"That will sure look nice in your room," Aspen told Annie.

Annie had a spoonful of strawberry shake at her mouth, and merely shook her head. She swallowed the food and said, "This can go in the school somewhere." She looked at the trophy. "What would I do with this?" She scoffed at the thought. "Mr. Knight can have it."

I laughed. "Brad would display it proudly."

"I'm sooooo happy!" Trish said.

Annie patted Trish's arm. "I'm happy too."

"What did you tell her, there at the end, when she gave you the trophy?" I asked.

"Nothing," Annie said quietly.

"No, you said something," Tony said. "You said something to piss her off."

"I just said the *ll's* are silent," Annie said.

"The what?" asked Holly.

"The *ll's* are silent. It's a French word. She pronounced *tirailleur* as if the *ll's* should be pronounced. They're silent."

"How do you know that?" Tony asked. "How can *anyone* know that?"

Annie responded with an expression of helplessness. "I have no idea."

It almost appeared, for an instant, as if Annie was going to start crying.

"We better pack it up, boys and girls, we got a long haul to Cascade tomorrow night," I said.

"Wooo wooo!" cheered Trish. "Go Rangers!" The statement drew a few disapproving looks from all the Boulder Panther fans in the dining room.

Tony helped me with Trish and her wheelchair while behind us along the main street of Boulder Aspen revved up the engine of her dad's pickup.

"You better be ready to do some cheering tomorrow, Trish, because the Rangers are definitely – d-e-f-i-n-i-t-e-l-y – going to score some points," Tony told her.

"Okay," she responded, with her way of making the single word *okay* sound as if it had three syllables. She slid out of the wheelchair into the backseat of the Escort. Trish seemed to be suddenly fatigued. The spelling bee drama had emotionally drained her.

"You okay?" I asked her as I buckled her in.

She nodded wearily.

I closed the car door and stood alongside Tony on the sidewalk. "Get home and get to bed. You got a big day tomorrow."

He looked back at Aspen and the truck. "I might have a big night tonight," he grinned.

"Don't be an idiot," I told him, although looking at Aspen, I saw how she could render young males brainless. "Go straight home," I said, but I knew and he knew he could do and would do whatever he wanted. I had to hope he knew he needed to get home. It was going on ten o'clock by the time we got out of Boulder.

There was no moon above but the roads were clear and dry ahead as we headed south down the Boulder Valley. On a short straightaway just past the Boulder Hot Springs the maroon O'Toole pickup sped past us, Aspen driving and Tony in the passenger seat. Tony waved gleefully as they shot past us, and Aspen gave a short bark of the horn. I wasn't going fast – under the speed limit – and Aspen hadn't done anything dangerous or illegal, but I wished they'd slow down. Their red taillights disappeared past the crossing of the Little Boulder River.

Mandy and her boyfriend had been drinking and speeding, but anyone driving nights in Montana runs a risk. Montana roads are narrow and dangerous, black ice could be lurking anywhere, wildlife and livestock were near invisible obstacles and the weather could change in a heartbeat.

"I'm sleepy," Trish said dreamily, with her singsong voice, from the dark backseat.

"You can sleep if you want," Annie said.

"I'm too happy to sleep," Trish said.

"I'm happy, too," Annie said. "And I'm happy you're happy."

"I'm cold," Trish said.

Annie reached over and turned up the Escort heater.

"I got a jacket back there," I told Annie. "Go ahead and wrap it around her."

I turned on the dome light and Annie unbuckled herself, reached behind me to the driver's side of the backseat, and sort of covered Trisha's lap and legs with the coat, a fleece jacket. I turned off the dome light and looked ahead just in time to see two deer standing in the borrow pit, just south of the Elkhorn turnoff.

"Stupid ass deer," I complained as we passed them. Had they been in the road, I would have hit them. There would have been nothing I could have done. Deer are virtually suicidal around roads and traffic.

"Relax," Annie said. "They didn't move a muscle."

"They have no concept of vehicles," I said. "None."

"Slow down then," she said. "The valley is full of them, and you know it."

On the way up to Boulder for the spelling bee, heading north with the setting sun to our left, we had seen several deer and antelope – standing alone, standing in pairs or in small groups and even in a large herd near the church – but the light was still decent and none had been grazing alongside the road.

"Why are deer so stupid about traffic?" I asked. "You can find dead deer on this road almost every day and pretty consistently on every road in Montana. You don't see dead antelope. You don't see a dead moose. You don't see a dead coyote, or an elk or a mountain lion or any other Montana wildlife."

"Occasionally you'll see a cow," Annie smirked.

"You think that's funny?" I said. "Cows are livestock, not wildlife, and they're not supposed to be on the road. They're so dark they absorb rather than reflect light."

"*Rather than*," Annie repeated. "Very scholarly, Lance."

"I'm serious." I peered through the windshield, bright lights on, searching ahead, left and right, for deer. "Only deer. Why can't deer figure it out the way all the other wildlife has?"

My question was met by silence.

"I'm serious," I asked. "Why can't deer figure it out?"

After hesitating, Annie looked my direction. "Are you asking me a question?"

"Yeah."

"I don't know," Annie said.

"You know everything," said Trisha, her voice drained of emotion or conviction.

"No one knows," said Annie. "Deer are crepuscular, of course, which is peak time for travel."

"What's a crepuscular?" I asked. "And don't tell me I didn't pronounce it right."

"Actually, you did fine," she said. "It means deer are most active during dawn and dusk, which is when a lot of people are driving to and from work, school, peak traffic periods. And right now we're closer to mating season, and bucks, like most males, are essentially brainless during the rut."

"That only explains why deer are moving around," I said. "It doesn't explain why deer can't figure out that cars and trucks are dangerous and that they – the deer – should refrain from running in front of them."

Annie paused. "What's that up there?"

I had just started wondering the same thing. Ahead on the road we saw vehicle lights flashing, flashing, flashing red. The lights were to our right, on the shoulder of the same lane we were in, and as we approached I saw it was the O'Toole pickup, and to the right of the pickup, standing in the borrow pit, our headlights found Tony and Aspen, in an embrace. Our headlights also picked up a deer, flopped in an unnatural pile of fur and legs, on the pavement, and the grille and hood of the pickup were buckled and broken.

"Oh no," I said, and pulled over onto the shoulder, ahead of the pickup.

"What are the odds of this?" Annie remarked.

"Ohhh, the poor deer," Trish said wearily.

"That's not going to be Lyle O'Toole's first reaction," I said. The Escort rolled to a stop. I took off my seatbelt and turned to Annie. "Stay put, all right? *Do not* leave this car."

Annie nodded. Trish was sobbing quietly.

Outside, Aspen was sobbing loudly. She was practically shrieking. I walked in the grass to the right of the pavement about ten yards back to where the truck sat and the dead deer bled. The deer corpse and Aspen and Tony were bathed in a steady pulse of red flashing lights.

"Everyone okay?" I asked.

"We're fine," Tony said.

"No we're not!" Aspen screamed, sobbing.

"We're a little upset," Tony added, and Aspen sobbed louder.

"But no one's injured?" I asked.

"We're fine," Tony said. He was holding Aspen, and her head was buried on his chest. She was sobbing so hard she was having difficulty breathing.

"You sure?" I asked. I stepped as close as I could to them and gave them both a good look. I didn't see any blood or bumps. The broken glass from the headlight casing sparkled in the light of the one headlight that worked. The puddled anti-freeze fluid turned the reflected light a soft green hue. The windshield wasn't cracked.

A car cruised past us slowly, its headlights on bright, and while the driver – maybe Brian Baxter's dad – surveyed the damage, the car didn't stop. In the bright lights I got a close look at the deer – one of the brainless whitetail bucks Annie had chided – with a nice little four-point rack, a gray tongue hanging out on the pavement, a bold black lifeless eye aimed my direction and a neck twisted in an impossible angle.

Aspen must have seen me looking at the deer. "Is it dead?" she asked between sobs.

"Yeah," I said, and she howled in what sounded like agony.

"It died sudden," I said, hoping to help. "It never knew what hit it."

"It seemed to come out of nowhere," Tony said.

"It didn't suffer," I said. Aspen was still sobbing.

The passenger side headlight was damaged, as was the passenger side of the grill. Had the deer been a stride and a half faster, or the truck moving a mile per hour slower, the collision would have been avoided.

Another vehicle – a pickup – crawled past, heading south, and stopped in the driving lane. "Everyone okay?" a male voice asked.

"We're fine," I said, and Aspen was mercifully quiet.

"Need any help?" he asked.

"I don't think so," I said.

"You sure?" the voice asked.

"Yeah," I said. "Thanks."

"Okay," he said, "Good luck." He drove off.

"I want my daddy," Aspen begged, trembling.

"Right," I said. "We'll get you home and-"

"I want him *now*."

She had issued a non-negotiable demand. It struck me Aspen was accustomed to receiving what she wanted, when she wanted it, and there was no doubt she wanted her father. Off to the left, on the east side of the highway, about two hundred yards ahead, I saw yard lights, and after thinking it through a minute, realized the lights were at the residence of Tom and Helen Carey, longtime residents of the Boulder Valley.

"Can you walk about two hundred yards? Up there, to the lights?" I asked Aspen.

Her sobbing had downgraded to sniffling, and in the darkness I saw her nod.

"Okay," I said. "The truck is far enough off the road for now. Tony, go sit in the Escort with Trish and your sister. All right? Keep them safe. If anyone stops and asks, we're fine. Stay in the car. Don't be wandering around out here."

"Maybe I should go with Aspen," Tony said.

"No, you stay here with your sister," I said. "I'd feel better if someone was with them. That's Tom and Helen Carey's place over there. I'll call Lyle. Believe me that's better than you or Aspen calling Lyle. You understand that, right?"

Tony nodded. There was no way Tony wanted to call Aspen's dad and tell him what happened, and I wasn't sure Aspen could actually speak. If she did, she would panic her family. No parent should be exposed to the shock of a sobbing, hysterical girl, attempting to explain a late night traffic accident on a lonely rural road. I'd make the call, and would reassure them their daughter was frightened but not injured. I also wanted to see Aspen in better light to make sure there were no bumps or bruises or scratches.

"Aspen," I said to her back, "I need you to walk with me down the road there to the light."

She didn't even lift her head to look and see where the light was. She stumbled her first step.

I steadied her. "Okay, let's go," I said.

"Why does she have to go with you?" Tony asked.

"I want to see her in the light to make sure she's not banged up somewhere," I said. "And I think Tom and Helen can give her some water or aspirin or something. They can doctor her up if she needs any, and if she doesn't need any, I'd like to get her calmed down before her dad shows up." I paused. "Any other questions?"

Apparently not. Aspen weakly moved away and I propped her up by holding on to her waist. This was going to be the longest two hundred yards of my life, I thought. She gained a little vigor as we walked, and steadied herself down the gravel driveway, and the Carey's yardlight looked like a beacon to me.

Before I could knock once, Tom was there, opening the door. He wore a plaid shirt and thick green pants held up by suspenders. He wore his hair in a kind of unruly crew cut.

"Lance, what the hell?" he said. He looked out beyond us. "Did you run over one of our cows?"

I shook my head. Tom looked at Aspen, whose head was lowered, aimed at the floor.

"Little young, ain't she, Lance?" Tom offered.

"Jesus, Tom," I whispered.

Aspen lifted her head, and I couldn't see the expression because it was aimed at Tom, but his face turned stone cold serious. His eyes widened in alarm. "Helen!" he cried back into the house. "Helen!" He looked at me and stepped aside. "Come in come in come in," he told us.

"Who is it?" I heard Helen's voice call out.

"It's Lance the Ledger guy," Tom shouted back. "He's got some girl with him."

Aspen and I were in the hallway and almost in the living room, and the heat inside was like a force. The instant I felt the warmth, Aspen started to shiver.

"Did Lance hit one of our cows?" Helen called out, and then showed up, tying a bathrobe belt. She was smiling, but when she saw us she was suddenly all business. She was short but lean and firm. She was a grandmother several times over, but her vigor hadn't faded a bit. "For goodness sake, Tom, bring them in the living room and get them seated."

"Should I call the sheriff?" asked Tom. "What happened? Is she hurt?"

"I don't think so," I said.

"I'm calling the sheriff," Tom announced.

"Tom," Helen ordered, and Tom stopped and stood motionless.

Helen looked at me. "I think we're okay," I told her. Helen helped Aspen and me to the couch.

I looked closely at Aspen in the brightly lit living room, and I didn't see any injuries. There was no blood or rips in her clothes, and no abrasions that I could see on her face or head. She had streaks of mascara below her eyes, and her face was puffy and blotched, but I saw no physical damage. Aspen must have known I was inspecting her, because she shook her head to say no, she wasn't hurt.

"We hit a deer," I told Helen and Tom. Aspen leaned against me. "The truck's pretty banged up. She needs to call her dad."

"The truck?" asked Helen. "What truck? I thought you had that sporty new Escort."

"I do," I told them. Despite the grave situation, it did not escape my attention that Helen called my Escort sporty. My guess was you had to be rural and at least seventy years old to think an Escort could be sporty. Or else you were being sarcastic, which was also possible.

"You hit a deer in that dinky thing?" asked Tom, amazed. He hesitated. "Could that thing even kill a deer?"

"It's her dad's truck," I said. "She was driving. This is Aspen O'Toole, Lyle's daughter. She and my son-"

"The banker's kid?" Tom asked.

I nodded. "Right. Aspen and my son were driving home from Boulder in her pickup when they hit a deer."

"Oh you poor thing," Helen said, and sat down by Aspen.

"So you walked here?" Tom asked. "How far'd you walk?"

"Good Lord, Tom, just get them some water," Helen demanded, and Tom was in the kitchen with the faucet running before Helen was done speaking.

I could see Tom's point, though. No one was bleeding, so the injuries couldn't be too severe, and it wasn't every night Lance the Ledger guy showed up at the Carey door with a slightly damaged – plus tear-stained and frightened – young and stunning blonde. Tom wanted to know what happened. It had to be a good story.

Tom had worn his flattop haircut – hair just a tad longer on the top than the sides – his entire life. Outside of his years in the military, he had lived his entire life in the Boulder Valley, and the Carey family owned much of the middle section of the valley. He and Helen had raised a half dozen kids or so in the ranch house we were in, and almost all the kids still lived near or in the Boulder Valley. The boys were all ranchers, and the girls all talked exactly the same – same vocal cadence, same inflections, same tone – as Helen. She was a classic matriarch of a classic Montana ranch family – strong, proper and regal – and she had a distinctive singing voice that had graced several Whitehall Christmas church choirs. We had apparently interrupted Helen's bedtime routine; she wore a bathrobe over a sweatshirt and flannel pajama bottoms.

Helen continued to calm Aspen, who sipped water and started to breathe in regular intervals, as I quickly recounted the events of the evening. During my summary, Aspen seemed to sit a bit straighter and looked to be controlled enough to talk with her parents.

"Annie?" Tom asked Helen. "Ain't she the smart one?"

"Her father is seated right there, you could ask him yourself for heaven's sake," Helen said. She then added, "And yes, she is the smart one. And she won the spelling bee."

Tom's face brightened. "She won it?" Tom even chortled. "So she's the one who told old Martha Perry she botched a word?"

Amazing. Word traveled quick through the Boulder Valley.

"Where is she?" Tom asked and looked toward his front door. "She out there? I want to shake that young lady's hand."

Helen rolled her eyes. "Martha gave Tom a bad mark back in fourth grade," Helen told me, "and he's never gotten over it."

"It was fifth grade," Tom corrected with some gusto, "and I haven't gotten over it because I didn't deserve it. She didn't care for the Careys and punished me for it." He had finished with a flourish of defiance.

"And that was about a hundred years ago," Helen added.

"How'd you hear about Annie correcting Martha at the spelling bee?" I asked. "The thing got over an hour ago."

"We don't miss much out here in the boonies," Helen said slyly. "Our daughter-in-law called us right away that one of the kids sassed Martha." Helen paused, and indicated Tom. "He was tickled about that, believe me."

Tom, tickled, grinned and nodded.

"This would probably be a good time to use your telephone," I said. I looked at Aspen, who nodded. "We need to call her dad."

The next day, a Friday, late afternoon we headed to Cascade. It was a little over a two-hour drive, first through the Boulder Valley – this time in daylight – then up past Helena, north through the Missouri River canyon, and finally past Wolf Creek where the valley widened and stretched itself from east to west. It was only Annie and me; Trish rode with her parents, who stopped in Helena to see Trish's doctor, and there was a seat for Slack on the team bus so he could ride with his mom, Sue, who drove the Whitehall team bus to the game.

Halfway through the Boulder Valley the Carey place sat on our right, and the accident from the previous night – marked by a distinctive rusty red blood stain on the pavement – was impossible to miss. The deer carcass was barely visible – just the legs and feet frozen in rigor mortis poking up in the borrow pit where Lyle and I had dragged it – but it would be awhile before the weather would wash away the blood on the pavement.

The night of the accident, after Aspen and I had called Lyle – and after she had conducted a reasoned and sensible conversation – she and I accepted a ride back to the truck and Escort from Tom. Aspen and I also accepted a plate of cookies from Helen, and Tom waited with us until Lyle showed up.

Tom and Annie chatted about Martha Perry for twenty minutes until Lyle showed up, his wife and both of Aspen's sisters in tow. There were many hugs, tears, whimpering and commiserating and worries among the women.

Lyle and I pushed the banged-up pickup further off the road, and it was well after one o'clock in the morning when we finally arrived back in Whitehall.

Now, as we drove north back through the Boulder Valley, Annie pulled out a hooded sweatshirt and stuffed it between the backrest and window and was settling in for a nap. She had spotted the stain on the road, watched as we passed the Carey ranch. The truck was already gone, either driven or hauled back to Whitehall and Ron Fuller's body shop. Little shards of glass glinted on the pavement, but that was really all that remained from the drama and trauma of the preceding night: dried blood and tiny specks of reflected light.

"Tom Carey's a nice guy, isn't he," said Annie, her head against the passenger side window.

I nodded. "Yeah, the Careys are good people."

"I going to let him have the spelling bee trophy for a few weeks," she said. "He'd get a kick out of that. Last night he held the trophy like it was a Nobel Peace Prize."

"He could put the trophy on the mantle by all his paintings and photos of cows," I said. The house held photographs and paintings of Carey cows and Carey kids, with more cows than kids. That seemed to be it for artwork. "He must really like cows. He's apparently not a big fan of Martha Perry, however."

Annie grunted. "He's carried a grudge since fifth grade."

Tom and Helen had eventually prospered, but like all farmers and ranchers in Montana, they'd had their lean years. I heard stories, mostly in bars in both Whitehall and Boulder, about the Careys that Helen and one of her boys more or less confirmed with off-hand comments about *trucker buffets*. Highway 69 between Whitehall and Boulder is a major trucking route because it cuts time and miles for over-the-road semis to drive through the Boulder Valley compared to the twisting route of I-15 between Butte and Helena. I-15 was the main north-south national route, and trucks from across North America carried every product imaginable here. The only place truckers ventured off I-15 was between Dillon – south of Whitehall – and Boulder. That meant every product imaginable went past the Carey place.

During the winter months the two-lane road surface could get icy and slick. A couple times every winter a semi-truck took a curve with a little too much speed and slipped off the road where it slid and stuck in the borrow pit or rolled over. When that happened, based on the stories from the Careys, the Boulder Valley telephone tree got busy.

It wasn't looting, really, what the Careys and Boulder folks did. It was more like rescuing or, as one of the Carey boys told me once in a bar, *liberating* perishables. Once a truck was either stuck in the ditch or flopped on its side, Boulder folks showed up to assist the driver with warm blankets, a libation or two or three, and maybe even an invitation to a local ranch for refreshments and warmth. Fruits and vegetables from California destined for Calgary and Edmonton made regular transport along I-15 and Highway 69, and it was not uncommon for a truck carrying exotic – from a Boulder Valley perspective – fresh fruits and vegetables to find itself imperiled in the Boulder Valley. One of the Carey boys told me about in the old days not only eating fresh fruit in the dead of winter but eating fruits he had never heard of, had never seen before, and eating out of cardboard cartons filled with it for weeks straight.

I could envision Tom and the Boulder cowboy gang using a crowbar to pry open the back of the truck and forming an efficient distribution line to quickly move the cartons of fruits and vegetables from the semi to the waiting pickups.

It didn't take long for the trucking companies and their insurance companies to improve the quality of the drivers, the trucks, truck security and law enforcement response, but there's something amusingly quaint about the knowledge that back in the 1950s and 1960s while most of rural America was surviving on canned foods and frozen goods during the winter, the backwater hicks in the desolate Boulder Valley were awash in cartons of pilfered persimmon, pluot, kumquats, mangos, Fairchild tangerines and other magical and unnamed fruits or vegetables.

On the way to Cascade I drove through Boulder without a stop at the DQ in part because Annie was sleeping and in part because she said she wanted to make a quick stop in Helena. Annie woke up as we decelerated through Boulder, and after a quiet trip through the upper half of Jefferson County she had me take the second exit in Helena, for a stop at K-mart. I sat in the car, and she was in and out in under five minutes, and emerged carrying a small plastic bag. I fretted for a moment, thinking it was some kind of feminine hygiene necessity, but before we were even back on I-15 toward Great Falls she had the bag opened and two small containers unwrapped – cassette tapes of Bruce Springsteen music – and *Darkness on the Edge of Town* was plugged into the Escort cassette player. The other cassette was an earlier release, *Greetings From Asbury Park*.

"Now we're talking," Annie said, and turned the volume in the Escort up higher than normal. She smiled. "Friday night football. Get your game face on, right Lance?"

On the cover of the cassette box was a photo of Springsteen, and he looked like a skinny kid. Tony had the *Born in the U.S.A.* album and on the jacket all the photos Bruce looked brawny, almost like an athlete or body builder. Bruce from *Darkness*, especially the back photo, standing alone in front of a closet wearing a white tee-shirt, was young, fragile and scrawny.

"He looks almost like a kid," I said.

"This is from 1978, so he's eight years younger," Annie said. "But don't let the photos fool you."

"Why's that?"

"These aren't songs from a kid or for kids. These songs come straight from his gut," Annie said. "He bares his soul, his vulnerabilities, his insecurities. It takes a lot of courage to do that."

"You've been talking to Jersey, haven't you?"

She nodded. "Springsteen's got a line from the song *Badlands* I think is especially appropriate for a night like this. *I wanna go out tonight, I wanna find out what I got*. That's every young man's dream isn't it, to go out and find out what they got?"

"I suppose." I remembered her excited shaking to *Born to Run* at the junior high dance, her joy, her expression of exhilaration, this serious intellectual prodigy of mine and her solemn academic disposition abandoned to the music. "Boys aren't the only ones who need the challenge, the test, to find out what they got."

"True," Annie said. "But boys measure the challenge, or the test, differently. With them, there needs to be blood and sweat involved, a winner and a loser. There needs to be someone or something conquered."

"Is that what Jersey thinks or what you think?" I asked.

She thought about it. "That's a good question." She reached over and turned the sound up a notch. "I'm not sure what Jersey likes to do more, listen to Springsteen or talk about Springsteen."

I would rather listen to Springsteen, which was what we did as we drove past the Sieben Ranch – spread out on both sides of the freeway – and entered the Wolf Creek canyon section of I-15. A tiny stream split the heart of the canyon as rockfaces and conifers stretched tall in the sky above us. Rock gray like the color of metal, rock burnt red the color of sunset and rock brown like the color of desert cut in and out on both sides of the road as we wove our way north through the canyon. The sun had fallen behind the cliffs to our left, but sunlight still spotlit the rocks high on our right, and again the feeling swelled inside me that anyone alive not living in Montana was missing something special.

The gravelly, somber voice of Bruce Springsteen filled the car's interior as we drew closer to Cascade. The music was sober and earnest, and at times Springsteen sang as if he was mentally or emotionally, rather than physically, suffocating. The lyrics from one song seemed to spill from the narration of a young man too weary or possibly too disconnected to even be frustrated about his lost youth, his depressed wife, his forgotten freedom, his long gone spirit. Another song seemed more defiant, as if the narrator had met, and either defeated or delayed, the same challenges the voice in the previous song had succumbed to. Or maybe it was all in my imagination, or my own interpretation, based on my own history, my own situation and my own problems.

The quick little sliver of Prickly Pear Creek water vanished and the placid, wide and flat Missouri River – sluggish after release from a trip through three dams around Helena – flowed as if the water was in no particular hurry with no particular place to go. The canyon broadened in the distance on both sides of the road, and as night fully descended, as the dark Missouri River water flowed without effort, a section of bright lights over a lush green field interlaced with white chalk lines emerged to our right and announced our destination: Cascade High School, where tonight the Whitehall Rangers would find out what they got. The cattle guard at the end of the off ramp rumbled our entrance to Cascade just as Springsteen ended a song about a darkness at the edge of town.

The Ranger players stood rigid during the National Anthem, a weak and spotty rendition played by the Cascade High School band, under the direction of a man who looked eerily like Richard Nixon. The weather was ideal for football, cool but not cold, barely a hint of a breeze.

Trish wore a satin purple and gold jersey over a jacket, and had a purple blanket over her legs and the wheels of the wheelchair. Her mom, Molly, stood behind her, a Styrofoam cup of steaming coffee in her hand. Standing alone behind a snow-fence around the outside of the field were Hank and Kathleen Harrison, each wearing matching jean jackets and black gloves, and each of them held a cup of coffee. I got a nod of greeting from Molly, and I waved back.

Maybe two dozen other Whitehall fans had made the trip through the valleys and canyons of southcentral Montana to Cascade. It was a contest of two teams who had combined for zero wins; the Cascade side of the field held more fans than the Whitehall side, but less than the Whitehall side at a Whitehall home game.

Slack, wearing his big gray cowboy hat, sat by himself in the bleachers. Sue wore a stocking cap and was on her way back from the concession stand, each hand holding a cup of coffee.

"Are we playing the skunks?" Slack asked me. He had already – or some time previously – spilled coffee on his Carhartt jacket.

"The what?" I asked.

"Skunks." He pointed to an emblem of an animal in mock attack painted on a sheet of plywood near our side of the bleachers.

"The Badgers," I said. "That's a badger."

He peered at it. Finally he shook his head. "That's a skunk."

"It looks a little like a skunk, but we're playing the Badgers, believe me," I said.

Sue arrived with the coffee. She looked chilly. She was tall with long gray hair, tucked under the stocking cap with a curl of the hair above her ears. She never got over the unfairness of what had happened to her son at the fenceline years ago. And she still distrusted me since Slack had been injured in my car accident.

"What's that?" Slack asked her, pointing to the painting on the sheet of wood.

"What's what?" she asked.

"That," Slack said, pointing again. "That animal."

She shrugged. "A wolverine?"

The Rangers got the ball first, and Tony had a good return on the opening kickoff. It was obvious early Cascade was not the quality of Columbus or Shelby. On the first play from scrimmage, Nate Bolton sliced through the right side of the line for about a twenty-yard gain, and Colt Harrison ran an option play that picked up another first down. It was the first time all year the Rangers had opened a game by actually moving the ball downfield.

Cale Bolling caught a short pass along the sideline, slipped a tackle, and ran another ten yards before he was forced out of bounds. Colt ran for six yards, Nate ran up the middle for five yards, and on third down and short Colt picked up nearly four yards on a quarterback sneak. Suddenly, it seemed, Whitehall was in position to score and take a lead.

Jersey called the plays and sent them in by shuttling in offensive linemen. The Ranger team, as a whole, looked more settled and more polished than the previous two games. And while I didn't fully understand or appreciate football formations or strategy, it seemed like there were more designed plays with Colt carrying the ball than in the past. Whatever play Jersey called seemed to work, and the chubby linemen, knees pumping and arms swinging as they hustled on and off the field, looked more animated and determined than previous weeks.

Jersey, rangy, dressed in black, held whichever player was bringing in the play by the inside edge of the shoulder pads, by the player's neck. Jersey was visibly taller than the players, especially stubby kids like Cody Phillips, Morgan Miteward and Bobby Bentmier, and would send in the play, look at the clock, look at the ground, look at the clock, then greet, grab and hold the player coming off the field who would carry in the following play.

The Rangers took their first lead of the year when Logan Bradshaw broke off tackle, cut straight up the field, and lunged into the end zone. Trish screamed a cheer, and Annie yelled her approval. A few other Whitehall fans hollered, and the reserve Whitehall players on the sidelines jumped and clapped and cheered. Jersey simply nodded once. I snapped what I hoped and thought was a good picture of Logan crossing the goal line, of Logan standing up with the ball raised over his head, and in an embrace with Nate in the end zone. The Rangers actually had something to celebrate.

Whitehall opened the game strong and led 14-6 at the half. Colt had run for sixty yards and a touchdown, completed seven passes for over eighty yards and kicked both extra points. The Ranger offense had nearly two hundred total yards, compared to Cascade's seventy-five yards, and Whitehall had thirteen first downs. All in two quarters. Whitehall hadn't had that many yards in the first two games.

"I'm going to lose my bet if Cascade doesn't start playing," Annie told me at halftime. She brought up the bet to antagonize me.

"Don't tell me you hope Cascade wins," I said.

"I hope Whitehall wins, but I need Cascade to put some points on the board."

"That was a stupid bet," I said.

"It's just a bet. A little friendly wager."

"That involves me buying a car," I complained.

"Oh come on. Think it through, Lance. You'll have to buy Tony a car sometime anyway," she said. "He's in high school and needs a car. Right? Isn't that obvious?" It was, now that I thought about it, but her question, apparently, was rhetorical. "All Tony does is whine about not having his license and riding around with Aspen driving. He says it's embarrassing. And it is, but not for the reasons he thinks. He's going to get his driver's license next summer, and unless you want to share your car with him – which you don't, okay, you don't – you'll have to get him his own car. That's inevitable. That's unavoidable. That's reality. That's a fact. So if he wins the bet, what's he won? Nothing, Lance. Nothing. He's not winning anything he wouldn't already get." She held her hands out front, as if pushing away an invisible person.

Colt scored another touchdown early in the second half – I got a good photo of him avoiding the final tackle before he got into the end zone – and Whitehall led 21-7 late in the third quarter.

Along the sidelines, I thought about Annie's explanation about the bet and the car, and I couldn't find any flaws in her logic. She had figured it out pretty well, and in a perverse way, she was actually looking out for me. She was way ahead of Tony and me, which shouldn't have come as a surprise.

Cascade scored early in the fourth quarter on a long pass to a wide open receiver to make it 21-14, and with four minutes left in the game Whitehall had the ball at midfield still up by a touchdown. On third and eight, Colt dropped back to pass and got hit from behind. The ball squirted loose and a Cascade player pounced on it. The turnover gave the Badgers the ball just inside Whitehall territory.

A Cascade pass was incomplete, a second pass was incomplete, as was a third. On fourth down and ten yards for a first down, the Cascade quarterback dropped back to pass, was chased by Morgan and both the JeffScott twins and was almost sacked for a huge loss, but escaped and scrambled for a thirty-yard gain down to the Ranger fifteen yard line. Three plays later, with less than a minute left in the game, the quarterback swept the wide side of the field and got in the end zone. With Whitehall still up 21-20 and fifty seconds left on the game clock, Cascade lined up for the win and a two-point conversion. Jersey quickly called time out, and gathered the defense on the sidelines. The faces and body postures of the Rangers were noticeably less confident than they'd been at the end of the half.

Everyone, except Trish, stood. She sat, her body angled forward, her hands clasped at her throat. Slack seemed to be expecting the worst. The Cascade quarterback dropped back, looked right, looked left, looked right again, and took off running. Just before he was tackled by Tony, the quarterback lobbed a desperation pass to the back of the end zone where a Cascade player jumped high into the night sky and hauled in the ball for a 22-21 Cascade lead.

The Cascade fans stomped and roared and clapped and cheered; behind me on the Whitehall side there was a collective groan and then deathly silence. The stadium was just off Highway 15. A truck *beep-beeped* its good wishes.

Goddamnit, I thought. These poor kids played too hard to lose again. This was probably their best chance all year for a win, they led the entire game, and they still lost. *Goddamnit.*

Before the kickoff, Jersey called the team into a large huddle along the sidelines, and every pair of Ranger eyes and every stooped and defeated posture held dejection and failure. Tony's head hung down, as did Dave's, JeffScott's and Cody's. It had been a tough week for Cody; his mom died on Friday, was buried on Wednesday, he was an orphan, and now his football team was still winless.

Tony took the kickoff and was gang tackled at the Whitehall thirty-five yard line. With thirty-six seconds left he caught a thirteen-yard pass from Colt, and Nate caught a short sideline pass to put Whitehall in Cascade territory with twenty-one seconds still left on the clock. After two incompletions, Colt hit Tony on a short post pattern to the Cascade twenty-seven yard line. Whitehall used its last timeout. With four seconds left, the Rangers had time for one last play. Jersey sent Cale in with the play, and Colt threw a pass to the corner of the end zone toward Tony. Tony dived for the ball but the pass sailed a little long, just outside the back line of the end zone.

The Whitehall fans issued a loud collective groan, but on the other side of the field, in the end zone, a penalty flag had fluttered to the grass. Holding, Cascade. The Whitehall players gathered in an excited huddle for one more final play while the Cascade fans and coach yelled and screamed at the referee. In protest, a couple Cascade fans even threw some crumpled up plastic cups onto the field.

A field goal was a possibility, but barely. It would have been about a forty-yard attempt, and I doubted anyone knew if Colt could accurately kick a football that far. It had to be a quick decision, and Jersey opted to go for the touchdown. Fans on each side of the field yelled and cheered. Colt got under center and called out the signals. Either Cody hiked the ball a beat too slow, or Colt pulled away a beat too fast; somehow the ball was fumbled and even though Whitehall recovered the fumble it didn't matter. The game was over. The Cascade players ran onto the field and jumped and cheered and celebrated. With the game on the line, with a chance to pull off a dramatic win, Whitehall failed to execute the most basic function in football, the center snap, and lost by one point.

I took off the telephoto lens and shoved the gear back into the camera bag. "Goddamnit," I complained to no one.

Later, after the Rangers had lined up and shook hands with the jubilant Cascade players and climbed on the Whitehall team bus I walked silently toward the parking lot. I almost had to push Hank Harrison out of the way as he stood in front of me and complained about not attempting a field goal.

"Kick the ball, win the game," he sneered. He was taller than me, and he sort of grabbed my jacket at the shoulder. "What's wrong with a field goal? Huh? Why not kick the ball and win the game. Colt can kick a ball forty yards. Easy."

A confrontation with Hank Harrison was not an attractive thought. He was furious, his anger focused on the failure of the coaching staff to recognize his son's talents. My frustration and disappointment was with the simple fact of another loss, another lost opportunity, another collapse, another failure of the kids to simply succeed instead of fail.

"It's only a high school football game," I told him, and walked away.

"Who appointed you official apologist for the new coach?" Hank yelled at my back.

But if it was only a high school football game, why did I slam the car door and fly out of the parking lot, and speed wordlessly and recklessly onto the interstate heading south, breathing in short huffs out of my nose?

Neither Annie nor I spoke all the way though Wolf Creek canyon, until we crested the hill north above Helena.

"Look at those lights," she said. "It reminds me sort of what I imagine Pompeii to look like, from atop Vesuvius."

"Pompeii? In Greece?" I asked.

"Italy, actually," Annie said, as if apologizing.

"Pompeii's in Italy?" I asked. "How long's it been there?"

She smiled and touched my shoulder.

"Let's look on the bright side," I said abruptly. "They led for three quarters. Out-gained Cascade in the air and on the ground. We scored more points tonight than in the first two games combined. Tony played well. Lots of Rangers played well. It was a close game. They played a close game. You gotta play in close games to learn how to win close games. The Rangers learned tonight. They improved. They grew as a team. They'll play better next week." I paused. "Does that about cover it?"

We flew down the hill toward the bottom of the Helena Valley.

"Maybe a bit defensive, perhaps somewhat of a rationalization, but yet, somehow appropriate," Annie said.

"Let's stop and get something to eat in Helena," I said. "The team bus is stopping at Kentucky Fried Chicken."

"I'm all for that," Annie said. "I've had to pee since Wolf Creek."

"Why didn't you say something?" I asked.

"I was scared to."

We smelled the Colonel's delicious blend of eleven herbs and spices before we even saw the red and white sign brightly lit twenty feet up in the sky. It was going on eleven o'clock, and as we approached, the place looked closed. The parking lot was empty, and no customers were seated inside. When we walked in, a kid was sweeping up the floor behind us in the dining area and in front of us, in the kitchen, it looked like they were scraping up, mopping up and closing down.

"You open?" I asked a skinny middle-aged woman at the cash register.

She turned and looked back at the clock. It was five minutes to eleven. "Five more minutes," she said.

"What about the bus?" I asked.

"What bus?" she answered.

"The Whitehall bus," I said.

Her blank facial expression made it obvious the phrase *Whitehall bus* was foreign to her.

"The Whitehall football team is on its way here to eat," I said. "They'll be here in about ten minutes."

"Or sooner," Annie added. She motioned outside, and the Ranger bus was just pulling in.

The slender woman, with a plastic nametag that read *Ellen, Assistant Manager* pinned to a baggy, greasy work blouse, frowned, looked behind her, then looked at me. "Wait a minute," she said with what sounded like remorse.

She disappeared in back, behind the pop machines and food display area into the kitchen, where she conferred with a chubby young man who looked as if he was cleaning gray metal vats or sinks. He looked from her toward Annie and me, the two of them talked a little longer, and together they walked toward me. The chubby guy looked maybe twenty years old, and he had wispy little blond hairs on his cheeks that you really couldn't call a beard. He was taller than me, though, and weighed more than Annie and me combined.

"Where you from?" he asked. "Whitefish?" His shirt looked slept in and stained with grease and flour. His glasses had slid too low on his nose.

"Whitehall," I corrected.

"And you got a bus here?" he asked. He sort of wrinkled his nose to position his glasses.

"I don't," I said. "Whitehall does. There are about thirty hungry football players out there."

"Did you call it in?" he asked, and contorted his nose again to slide his glasses up, I guessed, the bridge of his nose.

"I don't know," I shrugged. I looked at Annie.

"I assume they called ahead," she said. "Are there two Kentucky Frieds in Helena?" she asked.

The guy with the wispy beard shook his head. I could almost count the individual hairs on his chin. There were maybe twenty of them. "We're it," he said.

“You shoulda called it in,” the scrawny woman named Ellen said. She shook her head, as if answering an unheard question with a negative response. “We’re closing down now. Our fryers are down.”

Jersey and Pete entered the KFC first, followed by a few of the football players. The players still had wet hair from the showers after the game, and while the dour expressions of Jersey and Pete suggested coaches who’d lost a close football game, the players themselves seemed to have already gotten over it. A couple of the kids – Brock Warren and Chance Nelson especially – entered with what could almost be described as glee.

The beaky woman looked from me to Jersey and Pete, and back to me.

“This the bus?” asked the chubby KFC guy, whose name badge identified him as Alex. He crinkled his nose, perhaps for better vision, to see ‘the bus’ more clearly.

I nodded.

“You call in?” the beaky little woman asked Jersey.

“Pardon me,” said Jersey, who did not resemble anything near gleeful. Disappointment and gloom hung over him like a garment. “What was that?”

“You call in the bus?” she repeated.

Jersey looked at Pete, who shrugged. “We’re from Whitehall High School,” Jersey said. “Someone from the high school office, maybe even the superintendent, a gentleman named Franklin, called and told you we were coming.”

Alex and Ellen exchanged expressions of regret, ignorance and worry. Alex contorted his nose and eyes, and the lenses of his glasses seemed to be more aligned with his eyes. “We didn’t know you were comin’,” he said.

“No one tole us,” Ellen told Jersey’s feet.

“What are you saying?” asked Pete. Pete took one awkward step toward Ellen, who backed up a step. I wondered if either of them intended or even noticed the two steps. “We got thirty-plus kids here who need to eat, and eat now.” Pete’s face had turned from pale to pink.

Ellen simply sighed. Alex shook his head.

“What do you mean, no,” Pete said. His face was darkening from pink to red. “These kids need to eat, so you two think of something.”

Most of the kids had entered the building, Ranger jackets, wet hair, weary expressions, shifting weight as they waited.

“We’re closing,” Ellen said meekly. She looked like someone who had no business with any kind of authority. She looked up at the clock on the wall to her left. “Closed. It’s after eleven.” Something in the tone of her voice had assigned blame to us.

“Our kitchen’s down,” Alex said, as if apologizing.

“Then bring it back up,” Pete ordered. His face had turned the color of a plum. “You were supposed to have thirty-five box meals.” He turned to Jersey. “That’s what Ed told me.”

Alex contorted his nose and actually used an index finger to manually slide his glasses up the bridge of his nose.

"Alex," Jersey asked affably, "what are our options here?"

Alex scratched at his flimsy blond facial hair. "We got some odds and ends you can have."

"Odds and ends?" bellowed Pete. He brought one firm hand down on the metal countertop near a cash register. "Jesus H. Christ. There's a bus full of hungry football players out there, and we got seventy miles on a school bus before we get home. They need more than goddamned *odds and ends.*"

"Pete, do me a favor and get the kids back on the bus," Jersey said. "Round 'em up and herd 'em back on the bus."

"It's after eleven," said Ellen. "Everything's closed. McDonald's, Wendy's, Taco Bell are closed now." She seemed vaguely pleased about that. "Town Pump's open."

"We're not…" Pete was so angry he couldn't complete the sentence. His eyes were wide with pressurized energy.

A couple of the kids groaned, and Tony's eyes flitted a *can't you help* look my direction. I in turn looked at Annie, who was watching Jersey.

Jersey sighed. "No, we're not going to Town Pump," he finished softly. "Pete, round up the Rangers and load up the bus. I'll bring the food in a couple minutes."

"What food?" Pete said.

Jersey's expression was unmistakable, and it was directed to Pete: *Don't make me say it a third time. Get on the bus.*

Pete scowled at both Ellen and Alex, and whirled around on his good leg toward the players. He opened his arms wide, as if gathering them into a group. "Back on the bus," he proclaimed. "Let's go." The players groaned, and a few of them momentarily, mildly, verbally challenged the command. But Jersey's expression warned them to do what they were told. The players began shuffling out the door, and then it was just the five of us, Annie, me, Jersey, Ellen and Alex.

"Did you guys eat?" Jersey asked me.

"Us? No, not yet," I said.

"Give them what they want," Jersey told Ellen. "We'll take the rest."

"No," I protested. "Feed them. We'll go to Town Pump."

"No one's going to Town Pump tonight," Jersey said. "I'm going to wash my hands." He looked at Ellen and Alex. "Feed them. Put all the rest of the food into buckets. I'll write a check for it." He walked down the hallway along the side of the restaurant and out of sight.

"Come on, let's get the food and get out of here," Annie said. "He means it. I've seen that look before and heard that tone of voice before. Do what he says." She meant Jersey. I still hesitated. "Lance," Annie said, "We're getting some food and getting out of here." I still hesitated. Annie rolled her eyes. She turned from me to Alex. "Just give us two meals of something. Anything." Alex nodded, and immediately retreated back into the kitchen and started to stick food in two small cardboard boxes.

Alex gave us each a box and refused Annie's payment. "Sorry about the mix-up," he said.

"Shoulda called it in," Ellen said. She plopped two buckets on the steel countertop at the cash registers. One bucket was half full of chicken pieces, the other was about a third full of buns.

"You think that's going to feed a football team?" Annie asked her.

Ellen declined to answer. Jersey showed up, and she slid the buckets his direction across the countertop.

Alex looked down into the buckets, looked up at Jersey, and contorted his glasses so he could see Jersey through, rather than above, his lenses. "Sorry," he said.

"Not your fault, Alex," Jersey said. "How much do I owe you?"

"We don't take out of town checks," Ellen told him.

Jersey smiled. Of all the things he could have done, he smiled. He pulled a twenty-dollar bill from his wallet. "Will this take care of it?"

Alex was about to wave off the payment, but Ellen took the money. "I suppose you need a receipt," she sighed.

Jersey smiled again. "Don't trouble yourself, Ellen." He backed away from the counter with two half-filled buckets. "Thanks for everything." Jersey backed out the door into the parking lot and the waiting bus. "See you back home."

The door closed, and it was just Annie, Ellen and me. Alex had already returned back into the kitchen to finish clean-up.

"Ellen," Annie said. She motioned Ellen closer, and Ellen leaned toward Annie. "Ellen, tomorrow I'm going to call the owner of this place, and I'm going to let him know what happened here tonight. I have no idea who he is or what his name is, but I'll find out. And I'm going to try to get you fired. You deserve to know that. I'm going to make a serious attempt to make sure you don't do to anyone else what you did to us here tonight. And just so you know, Ellen, I don't fail. Ever. And I won't fail at this. I'll call the Colonel himself if I have to. Do you understand?"

"Annie," I said.

She ignored me. Her eyes bored into Ellen. "You *will* lose your job. Trust me, you'll be fired. Unless you do one thing, one little thing right now, Ellen." Annie paused. "Apologize. Right now. Just say you're sorry. Just look at us and say, with something like sincerity, *I'm sorry*. Just two words. Just say them like you mean them, like you care."

Ellen's face twisted into a soured glare. "We're closed."

I followed Annie out of the door and the parking lot lights turned off above us before we reached the Escort.

There's an old story about Montana that goes something like this. Years ago, when automobiles were still relatively new and some accessories had been added – accessories like headlights that flashed with a tap of the toe from regular brightness to intensified or concentrated brightness – one auto manufacturing company kept receiving complaints about the headlights of their vehicles suddenly burning out. A car would be driving along a Montana road at night and suddenly – poof – the headlights would in essence turn off.

Almost all of the complaints of this problem issued from Montana. The car manufacturer was at a loss, according to the story, because cars were manufactured along an assembly line and distributed at random, so it was impossible to designate a vehicle – car or truck – to Montana, and have a headlight problem for vehicles specific to Montana. Vehicles were randomly shipped to Montana the same way they were randomly shipped everywhere else. Therefore it should be impossible to have any vehicle problems specific to Montana.

Yet the reports of headlights burning out persisted. Finally, the manufacturer sent an automotive engineer to Montana to see if he could figure out what was wrong. The engineer conducted some tests, but found no pattern or cause. Finally, one night he jumped in a car and drove it down the highway, and later that night, to his surprise, the headlights suddenly burned out. He inspected the wiring, the headlamp itself, the molding, the fittings, the entire headlight casings and found nothing. He later took another new car and toured around the state at night, and again the headlights went out. This time he had figured out why. In Montana, you could drive hours with the headlights on bright, and something within the headlamp fixture itself wasn't configured for the heat of the headlamp generated after hours with the headlights on bright. Some tiny piece of metal or glass casing overheated and shut down the headlamp. It only happened when the headlights were on bright for an unexpected extended length of time, and one of the only places in America you could drive with the headlights on bright for that length of time was Montana.

Montana had a population of somewhere around 850,000, which probably equated to about 300,000 vehicles. Montana is 145,000 square miles in size, with about 12,000 miles of road. Take a late night drive on a rural highway and you could drive all night without passing another vehicle.

On the way home between Boulder and Whitehall, we never saw another set of headlights and I never had to turn the bright lights off. Annie was quiet but not asleep, and on the way through the Boulder Valley we saw deer, a skunk, the spot where Aspen had hit the deer, and a large white owl that swooped and swerved and just missed the windshield. Out of instinct I lowered my head as the owl veered over the car.

"Good thing you ducked," Annie told me.

It was the first we had spoken since Helena. We had simply been silent, listening to Springsteen, the volume turned low, isolated in our own thoughts.

"You're not going to get the woman fired," I told Annie.

"Lance, this doesn't involve you."

"You're not going to get her fired," I repeated.

She hesitated. "Do you miss Mom?"

There was no answer to that question, or perhaps there was a multitude of answers to that question.

“Are you ever lonely? For Mom?” she asked.

Never before had Annie or Tony directly asked me about their mother. They knew their mother was never coming home. Never could come home. They knew their grandmother and grandfather, Amy’s parents, from cards, birthday and Christmas phone calls, and once in awhile Amy’s mom would assure Tony and Annie that their mother loved them. Tony had taken everything at face value, and has accepted his mother’s fate and absence the same way he seemed to accept his own fate and existence. Annie took nothing at face value, but I had always sensed a reluctance on her part to discuss her mother. I had never expected her to bring up the subject in the context of my possible loneliness.

Yet, the truth was, there was something in Springsteen’s *Racing in the Street* about the narrator’s observation of his wife’s crying herself to sleep that made me think of Amy, her mental anguish, her fatigued sadness, her hollow, barren and lifeless eyes.

“Do you miss her?” I asked.

“That’s not an answer, Lance,” she said.

“I’m not sure I have an answer.”

It was dark in the Escort interior, and Annie was looking not away from me, but not toward me, either. She was looking almost straight ahead, just off to her left, out the driver’s side of the windshield. “Have you ever thought the reason you work so hard, day and night, all the time, is so you can escape an answer to that question?”

I drove another mile before I realized I could not answer her question. “I thought I was avoiding the responsibility of parenting by being constantly busy.”

“Consider that mission accomplished,” Annie said, but in the gloom of the dashboard lights I could see a hint of a smile crease her face.

“I’m proud of the way you two have handled this,” I said. “I mean that.”

“I know you do, Lance. You need to give yourself some slack. We know you love us. We know you care for us. We know you lost your wife. We know you’re incredibly busy. We know you’ll always be there for us. We know you’re doing your best. And we know right from wrong. We know how to behave. Tony’s a sweet boy. And I’m the town genius. Tony and I are good kids, and you should take some credit for that. You deserve credit for that. You’re ditsy sometimes, it’s amazing the decisions Tony and I make on our own, and our lack of parental supervision is nothing short of remarkable, but we know you love us and care about us. And that’s what’s important.”

I couldn’t talk, so I gently reached out and touched her shoulder.

“So,” Annie asked, “do you miss Mom?”

When Annie wanted an answer, she persisted until she received an answer. “I remember when we first got married, and everything was new to us, and everything was exciting and fun,” I said. “Going to McDonald’s was fun. Going to the grocery store was fun. Waking up together was fun. Going to bed together was fun.” I paused. “I miss that.”

"Sometimes I bring out the photo albums when you were just married," Annie said softly. "I just page through them. You and mom were like kids. Grinning. With all that long hair. You had a mustache."

"You had to then," I said, in a weak attempt at humor, "or you were sent to Vietnam."

"Mom wore her hair long and straight, and it was like silk," Annie said. "But there was always something about her in the photos. She never looked at the camera, and she never looked at you. You were always looking straight into the camera. Mom never could, I don't know, look it in the eye."

"The thing is we were happy at first," I said. "Then I started noticing things. Even before you kids were born there was something missing in her. I thought it was me, or our relationship, but I could never figure it out. I couldn't do anything right. We started to argue all the time, and I started to avoid an argument by avoiding her." I hesitated. "That was a mistake."

"You and mom have three photo albums while you were dating and three more right after you got married," Annie said. "Then everything steps. There's a few loose pictures, but no more albums. It's like life stops."

In some ways, I thought, life did.

"There's one of Mom bringing Tony home from the hospital, and in the picture she's not even looking at him. She's looking off the side."

I sighed. I remembered that picture. Jesus Christ, how I remembered that picture. She had refused to be in the photo. She claimed she was too fat. I wanted to take a picture of her with her new son. I insisted. I demanded. We quarreled. She consented to have her picture taken, as if she had been violated.

After that, it just grew worse. I never got a chance to tell her I was sorry. How sorry I was. Am. I didn't realize what was wrong with her. And it's that sorrow I live with every day. Do I miss her? I miss the Amy I married. But more than that, much more than that, I regret I never understood, never appreciated, never responded, and never told her how sorry I was. I needed to apologize, and she needed to hear that apology. But I failed. And that failure haunts me every day.

It was about twelve-thirty when I clicked the bright lights down as we entered Whitehall. Outside of a few cars parked in front of the bars, the town was dark and quiet. I brought Annie home and drove to the school to pick up Tony when the bus arrived and dropped everyone off in the school parking lot.

There were maybe fifteen unoccupied cars in the parking lot, spaced unevenly apart, parked in the rows of the student section, cars driven by football players that had sat in the lot all day since school had started that morning. Another ten cars or so were parked in the front row, closest to the school, occupied by either a parent or an older sibling, waiting for the team bus to show up.

Which it did, less than ten minutes after I got there. The usual routine was for the kids to sleepily drag themselves off the bus into the darkness, haul their gear into the locker room, and then slowly, one by one, make their way wearily to the awaiting vehicles. That's what I expected to happen, and it took me a few minutes to realize it wasn't what was happening. I was in the Escort, the motor running, headlights and interior lights off, waiting for Tony and after awhile the thought struck me that I'd been waiting a long time. He'd had plenty of time, even if he was tired, to drop his stuff off in the locker room and find our car. As I waited I realized he could have dropped off his gear and gotten a ride home with one of his teammates; I had told him I would wait for him, but it was possible he forgot. It had been a long day and he might have just rode home with someone else. Then I noticed other parents were stepping out of their cars, as baffled as me. It was as if the kids had stepped off the bus and disappeared off the face of the earth.

I turned off the car, and stepped out into the parking lot. All the student vehicles were still there, except the bus was gone. It looked as if no one who had been on the bus, or had been waiting for the bus, had left. I walked down the sidewalk to get a view of the locker room door, and saw the door swing open, and watched as a Ranger football player, still in uniform, open the door and trot away, into the darkness. Off to my left, toward the field, above an equipment shed, was a yard light, the only exterior brightness anywhere on the school facility. The player had moved off in that direction, so I crept through the darkness in the general direction of the light.

On the way I encountered a few more people, and the big white cowboy hat of Brent Walker stood out in the darkness. He was undoubtedly looking for Tanner.

"Lance?" he asked.

"Yeah."

"Where'd the kids go?" he asked.

"Got me," I said. "I saw one of them head this direction."

"I think someone's out by the field," he said.

"Let's go have a look," I said.

I heard some noise coming from beyond the equipment sheds, and Brent followed me as I more or less felt my way between the sheds. On the north side of the main shed, above the roof, was the yard light, which cast a wide but dim arc of light from the outside of the shed toward the west end zone of the football field. Behind that, across the street, the Town Pump Exxon sign lit up the western sky. When Brent and I got to the north side of the shed, just shy of the yardlight, we saw the kids lined up out toward the west end zone. They were arranged in four straight rows. They wore their football pants and jerseys, but no helmets or shoulder pads.

"What the hell they doin'?" asked Brent.

"I have no idea," I said.

They started doing jumping jacks. The area was poorly lit, and the players were lined up in a dark shadowy end zone, so we couldn't make out individual players or facial features, just a motion of bodies in the faint darkness.

"What's goin' on?" Brent asked.

"It looks like they're doing jumping jacks," I said, confused.

"How come?"

"Good question."

I could hear Jersey's voice, but he was too far away for me to make out the words. We were probably thirty yards or so away from the closest kid. I couldn't really even see Jersey. He must have been further away, totally out of the dim shading of light. His voice sounded weary, or maybe patient, or maybe even instructional. It did not sound angry.

The boys got down on the ground and did pushups. Then they did situps.

"I don't get it," said Brent.

"Me neither," I said, because I didn't. It was going on one o'clock in the morning, it was dark, and these kids had previously played a football game then had a two-hour bus ride.

Brent and I watched, dumbfounded.

The Rangers ran in place for a couple minutes, then started doing up-downs. They ran in place, flopped to the ground, got back to their feet, flopped to the ground, got up, flopped, got up, flopped. Over and over.

"Jesus," said Brent. "They don't deserve this. They were in the game till the very end."

"I think I know what's going on here," I said. "I don't think they're getting punished because they lost. I think they're getting punished because they don't care they lost."

"Because what?" asked Brent.

The kids kept doing up-downs, and some of them were slowing down on the *up* part.

"Last week, when Shelby came down here and beat us, I did my interview with Jersey after the game and he was all pissed off because the kids were screwing around in the locker room," I said. "He takes a loss pretty personally, and was upset when the kids didn't."

"I supposed I'd be pissed, too, if I was him."

Out in the gloomy half-light, the players were up, down, up, down, up, down. They were getting up to their feet slower and slower. Some missed an *up* before the next *down* came.

"I bet the kids were screwing around on the bus coming home," I said.

Some of them were unable to get up before the next flop to the ground. Still, down they went, up they staggered, down they fell, slowly they rose to their feet, then down again they flopped. As a group, they were starting to look ragged and disorganized and exhausted.

"Is he going to keep 'em here all night?" asked Brent.

They trudged now, barely moving their feet, dropping to the ground, and struggling up to trudge in place. Some couldn't get back up.

“What stinks?” asked Brent.

I smelled it. It was a familiar odor, but I couldn’t quite place it. Brent and I were both sniffing the air.

“It’s Kentucky Fried,” I said. The Colonel’s blend of eleven herbs and spices were especially tangy in the dark night air.

“Chicken?” asked Brent. “How come we smell chicken?”

“That’s what they had for dinner,” I said. “They ate in Helena after the game. What we’re smelling is their dinner.”

“Puke?” asked Brent. “You’re sayin’ they’re all throwin’ up out there?”

“Yeah, they are,” I said. “I hope Pete doesn’t shoot one of them.”

Brent sort of snickered. “I ain’t never seen anything like this.”

“Me neither,” I said.

Up slowly, down slowly. Barely up, wearily down. They moved sluggishly, painfully, pitifully.

“How long you figure they’re gonna be out there?” asked Brent.

“Can’t be much longer,” I said. “Jersey’s made his point.”

The hot, sticky stink of the vomit grew in strength, and then the players stopped moving, and then were staggering through the gloom in the distance off to our right, past the far arc of light, toward the locker rooms.

Chapter 17

In some ways, the act of publishing a small town newspaper hadn't changed since America was organized in colonies. In other ways, rural newspaper publishing was changing now more than any time since the invention of the printing press.

Even out in the American frontier of Whitehall and Anaconda what we did – and the technology we did it with – was improving. In the 1980s, spot color – even on newsprint press runs of 1,500 – was possible and affordable, and twice a month or so the Ledger was graced with a color, or even a combination of spot colors. For a patriotic Whitehall Frontier Days celebration the Ledger front page, back page, and middle two pages each contained a sprinkling of blue and red. Each color cost an extra seventy-five dollars, and each color needed its own plate and own ink font on the web press in Anaconda, and it took an extra half hour to develop the extra plates and accurately dial in the spot color, but we charged advertisers extra for the spot color in their ads and typically sold enough extra papers for the color to generate income.

In some of the Montana daily newspapers, full color photos – called four-color photos by printers – were growing more and more common. But the cost – close to four hundred dollars per photo – and extra time – one extra printing plate was needed for each of the four colors – made full color both cost and time prohibitive for Whitehall and Anaconda.

Just like newspaper publishers a century earlier, when we first bought the Ledger I had to type newspaper articles on a typewriter – an IBM Selectric – but technology had advanced to allow us to purchase a machine that aligned the print in columns ready for paste-up. Like newspaper publishers a century earlier, I had to lay out the newspaper with an assortment of newsprint copy, headlines and graphics, but equipment had advanced past the old 'hot type' from a plate to 'cold type' from a computer. Small town newspapers had initially been created by printers, who had little or no background in writing or journalism. As the metal block letters faded to newspaper storage rooms collecting dust, so too had the concept that printers published newspapers. I was no printer. I viewed myself as a journalist, trained and educated in public relations with an understanding not just of printing and business but of reporting and journalistic ethics.

Just like newspaper publishers a century earlier, my camera took black and white photos and I developed my own film and printed my own pictures in a darkroom. But technology had advanced past big block cameras, large and impractical film sizes and chemicals in trays to develop the prints. I used a thirty-five millimeter camera that held rolls of thirty-six exposures, and for less than three hundred dollars I had a processor, halftone screen and photo paper that allowed me to produce halftones – photos with the camera-ready screened dots for newsprint – in about ten minutes per photo. Anaconda also had a PMT machine – post mechanical transfer – that could transfer a color print photo into a camera-ready black and white halftone. The PMT machine, situated in the darkroom, was adjustable, which meant they could make any sized black and white photo into whatever size I wanted.

Laura Joyce and I – just the two of us – could produce a fully camera-ready standard twenty-four page Ledger in, really, a little over one day, essentially from Monday afternoon to late Tuesday night. Everything we did preparatory to the actual publishing process, gathering the news, writing the news, gathering the advertising and laying out the ads, handling the walk-in traffic and tending to the business aspects like updating the subscription lists, took far more time than the actual physical effort to take all the material and make a newspaper out of it.

The way I looked at it, on Wednesday through Monday afternoon, we gathered the pieces of the puzzle. Between Monday night and Tuesday night, I put the puzzle together. And just like a real puzzle, you can't finish the puzzle until and unless you have all the pieces to the puzzle. Laura Joyce and I tried to enforce the Ledger deadline of noon on Monday – so we had all the pieces of the puzzle and no more pieces were coming in – but in reality we almost never turned anyone away who had a time sensitive ad or article that had to get in the paper. If someone had a garage sale planned for Saturday, you had to get their classified ad the Wednesday before the Saturday, no matter when they brought the ad in or how frustrated you were about the flagrant violation of the deadline. When your newspaper comes out once a week, you have to be flexible, because you don't have the next paper coming out the next day. You don't have the next newspaper coming out for seven days. As a rural newspaper you serve the community, and you can't serve the community if you turn away articles or advertisements because they came in a couple hours late.

There would be days I'd be in the darkroom on Monday at four o'clock, well behind schedule already, and someone would come in with a long legal notice, an article about an anniversary they wanted me to write or some other lengthy intrusion to our schedule and I'd grit and grouse but invariably acquiesce because I either had to or because – in the case of the legal notice – I couldn't afford to turn away the money.

After the newspaper puzzle pieces – all the articles, photos, ads – were gathered, I spent roughly twenty hours fitting them on the designated number of pages. We were a tab sized newspaper, which meant we had to be a number of pages divided by four – because of the way the pages fit on the press – and either expanded or shrunk in increments of four. That meant if I'd planned to go twenty-four pages and couldn't fit the articles, ads and photos in twenty-four pages, the next size up was twenty-eight pages. About once every two or three months, I'd have a paper started during layout, and part way through the process realize I couldn't fit everything in, and have to expand the paper by four pages. That meant another four hours work, minimum, provided I had enough photos and articles for four full additional pages. Most weeks, it seemed, we had the perfect amount of material for a twenty-two page paper.

But twenty-two pages was not an option. It was either twenty pages and leave articles and photos out, or twenty-four pages and hope you had enough photos and articles to fill the four extra pages. Costs varied slightly, but I figured it cost about twenty-five dollars a page to print and mail the paper, so if I went four extra pages it was an additional one hundred dollars in production and mailing costs. That was not an incidental amount. And the extra four to five hours of work late Tuesday night were long hours after mental and physical fatigue had already set in. An expanded paper was a challenging combination: More work and more cost. We tried to have the Ledger content average half ads and half news and photos, and if that percentage held up for a twenty-eight page paper, the advertising in the extra four pages more than compensated for the additional costs and labor.

No matter when the Ledger was laid out – each photo, each ad, each headline, each article waxed individually to the layout paper – the pages had to be in a flat wood box and ready for delivery to Anaconda no later than seven o'clock on Wednesday morning. I had to be in Anaconda no later than eight o'clock, and there were weeks when the paper would be laid out at four or five in the morning and I'd barely have time to proof the pages, go home and shave, and get to the printer.

At the printing plant, the printers – Dan, Bryce, Mike and Larry – took over. The pages – in pairs of two – were 'shot,' or photographed, by Larry with a large stationary camera in a darkroom that turned the pasted up pages into negatives, like a large film negative. The film negative was by a separate process turned into a thin metal plate that was affixed to a cylindrical drum on the printing press. The press itself was about twelve feet high and forty feet long. At daily newspaper printing plants, the presses were sometimes three stories high and longer than a football field.

The plates on the press were greased with a steady flow of ink and the compressed rubber drums of the press were pressed to the plates, and this cylindrical collision of metal plate and newsprint created an 'impression' of the plate on the paper, and in the case of the Ledger, this collision took place fifteen hundred times per press run. At the printing plant in Anaconda, it took about three hours to shoot the pages, dry the negatives, burn and rub the plates, get the plates on the press and get the right amount of ink consistently on all the pages to start the count of fifteen hundred editions of the Ledger. It took less than twenty minutes to actually print the fifteen hundred editions.

It took another ninety minutes to label, stuff and bag the Ledger for the post office and the vendors, and if I got to Anaconda at eight in the morning and if everything went well, I was usually loaded up and on my way home back to Whitehall before two o'clock in the afternoon. The Anaconda printers had a different weekly paper – from Philipsburg – scheduled for the press after us, and had two additional newspaper press runs in the afternoon.

From the time the pieces of the puzzle were gathered in Whitehall to the time two days later when I brought fifteen hundred copies of the Ledger back home, there were about eleven different machines used and abundant opportunity for malfunctions, delays and breakdowns. Anything could go wrong at any time, and – at least it seemed this way – something almost always did. Sometimes it was only a minor unexplainable glitch, other times it was a major inexplicable breakdown. Always, though, we somehow muddled through it. The latest I ever got the Ledger back to the Whitehall post office was seven o'clock.

But even though we – collectively, both me and the Anaconda printing crew – always managed to get a newspaper produced, we were not always jointly happy about the product.

The printers accused me of being too demanding and too eager to complain, and I accused them of indifference toward quality and willing to readily sacrifice excellence for expediency, convenience or speed.

It was me who pulled the Ledger's two-page negatives from a processing bin after they had been shot, processed and dried. It was me who looked at the negatives corner to corner, from the middle out, to ensure consistency of the negative, looking for 'hot spots' or thin areas that could lead to non-uniform distribution of ink on the page during the press run. It was me who arranged the rows of flyers for insertion and made sure each flyer of each insert – about a thousand – was in the right order and the right configuration. It was me who stood at the end of the folder as the Ledgers came off the press, and it was me who pulled papers on a regular basis to make sure the ink was consistently distributed on each page. It was me who warned Dan, Bryce or Mike of print quality problems – the ink was light on the middle of page six, there was a gray strip across pages twelve and thirteen or some other problem – and it was me who inserted the flyers in bundles and carried the bundles to the car.

It was me, essentially, who was the quality control officer in Anaconda, which, to put it plainly, pissed off Larry – the foreman in the pressroom – and to an extent the rest of the printing crew. I had put it clearly and forcefully to Larry one morning after I discovered a wrinkled seam on most the papers produced during the press run. "Here's the deal," I told Larry. "I worked seventy hours this week to bring you the best quality product I could. I'm not going to let you screw up all that work during the fifteen minutes you got my paper on the press."

Larry had responded angrily. He told me that I was the only customer allowed in the press room, that they made almost no money on a small press run like the Ledger's, that I was an asshole perfectionist, and that I was the only newspaper owner who complained about the way Anaconda printed their paper.

Once, in mid-1985, after the Ledger had been printed, I had to make a telephone call to Laura Joyce. I stood next to a wall phone in the stairwell while talking to Laura Joyce, and I overheard Larry in his office, at the top of the stairwell, also talking on the phone. I heard Larry say they had finished printing the Ledger. Whoever Larry was talking to on the phone must have been asked how the print job went, because his answer was, "Must have gone perfect because we hear about it when it doesn't."

My attention to detail regarding the Ledger in no way carried over to other aspects of my life. The inconsistency is difficult to explain. I took pride in the Ledger, took pride in my community and believed with all my heart that the quality of the community newspaper was inexplicably connected to the quality of the community. But it was more than that. There might be a photo of someone like Irene Strauss from the Whitehall Garden Club on page six of the Ledger, and it might be the only time in Irene's entire life her picture is in the paper. Didn't Irene and her family deserve to have the picture printed with quality and preserved with quality when tucked away in a scrapbook or photo album forever? Why screw up quality in perpetuity to save a penny's worth of ink or two minutes some forgotten Wednesday morning?

"You're like Lance's evil twin," Tony told me one summer afternoon after I groused all the way between Anaconda and Butte on the way home because the ink on page six of maybe a couple hundred copies of the Ledger was a shade lighter than it should have been. "We got sour milk and rotten oranges in the fridge, half the lamps at home have burned-out light bulbs, our lawn hasn't been mowed all summer, I led the freshman class in tardies and out of all those details the only one that gets you bent out of shape is that the IGA ad is dark gray instead of black?"

It wasn't until late Saturday night, nearly a full twenty-four hours after the midnight gang's drills on the football field, when I next, sort of, saw Tony. I'd been at a fundraiser for the library, and when I finally arrived home Annie was in bed asleep. She had apparently spent some time picking up and cleaning up; the place was more or less presentable. I sat in the La-Z-Boy paging through a magazine as I waited for Tony to get home. I fell asleep almost right away, and awoke only when he closed the door to his room. I'd missed him. I looked under the door and his light was out. It was after eleven o'clock and I figured we both needed sleep, so I left him alone.

Sunday morning I got up and drove to Twin Bridges for a tri-county 4-H fall exhibition, where I took pictures of sweet kids in white shirts and thin black ties, standing shyly next to their exhibits, detailing such rural essentials as canning jam, livestock weight gain, noxious weed control and energy consumption of irrigation pumps.

From there it was off to Cardwell and LaHood, to take a picture of the three Hanson brothers – Melvin, Frank and Ernie – and their brides – Ethel, Delores and Violet – as the three couples celebrated a collective 150 years of marriage. Melvin and Ethel, both in their eighties, had been married for 58 years; Frank and Delores, late seventies, had been married for 55 years; and the 'kids,' Ernie and Violet, still in their sixties, were virtual newlyweds at 37 years. LaHood was packed with Hanson family members of all ages, all wearing their Sunday best, all cheerful, all *so glad* to see me and my camera.

Melvin's health wasn't good, and it was his daughter's idea to hold what amounted to a family reunion before he passed away.

The three Hanson brothers, ranchers along the Jefferson River between Whitehall and Cardwell, stood together stiffly, sipping whiskey to diminish the discomfort of essentially being on display. All three of them had pink scrubbed-clean and shaved faces, colorful neck scarves, western style corduroy jackets and blue dress slacks. Their wives all had elaborate spun hair, eyeglasses with large square lenses, necklaces with imitation stones big as gravel, wrinkled necks and fluffy new dresses.

Ellen, Melvin's daughter, had asked me to come out and take a picture of the six of them, and while I agreed I left the time of my arrival flexible. I got there in time for lunch, which included some kind of roast beef in gravy that was so good I ended up consuming a couple helpings.

Ellen said we'd take the picture right after lunch, although I was welcome to stay as long as I wanted. I assured her I was in no hurry, and simply continued to eat. It was during my second helping of meat, potatoes, gravy and homemade buns when Lucas, Ellen's husband, with his own second helping heaped above his plate, settled into the chair next to me. Lucas had never lived outside of Whitehall and although he knew everything about Whitehall, he knew little about anything else.

"Lance," he said, and nodded a greeting. He was maybe only ten pounds overweight, but every one of those pounds settled like a loaf above his belt buckle. Outside of that bulge he looked underfed. "Here to take a picture?"

My mouth full, I nodded. I chewed, swallowed. "Sometimes I think I should have a sign printed that says *Will take pictures for food*. You'd be surprised how often I get a free meal out of the deal."

"Nothing wrong with that," Lucas said. He mixed the potatoes and his gravy. He filled a fork, and looked up at me. "I heard about the spelling bee up at Boulder. That girl of yours sure is smart."

"Too smart," I admitted. Years earlier, I used to joke that she took after her mother.

Lucas nodded thoughtfully, as if the thought of the subject of intelligence was something to approach soberly. "You think she's a genius?"

"Maybe," I admitted.

"Someone told me the other day she could start college right now, if she wanted." He chuckled at the thought. "She ain't bigger than a minute."

"She's slight in size," I said. "But don't let that fool you."

Lucas smiled appreciatively. It was time to change the subject. "Saw the damndest thing this morning," he said. He pondered the statement a moment; had he been smarter, I would have thought he was deliberately building suspense. "I was at the Town Pump this morning early for coffee."

Nothing unusual about that. Sunday mornings were family time, and Town Pump was one of the more popular settings for casual before and after church gathering spots in Whitehall.

"I was leaving, heading out toward home when I saw a flock of birds out on the football field," Lucas said.

I stopped chewing, and looked closely at him. My surprise must have been evident.

"Yeah, I mean a *big* flock," said Lucas. "All kinds, too. Magpies. Crows. Robins. Even seagulls. *Seagulls*. All out there on the field, I mean *on* the field, walking on it, not flying around it or up in the trees." He paused. "So I stopped and watched, and it looked like they was all eatin' something. Well, I wondered what the hell was going on. I thought maybe they was eatin' bugs or worms or something. So I turned around, drove through the parking lot over there at the school, back by the field. I got out of the truck, and get this," he sort of chortled. "The first thing I smell is Kentucky Fried Chicken."

I couldn't hide my amazement.

He held up a hand. "I know, I know. Makes *no* sense." He laughed. "I can't explain it neither. But I smelled it for sure. I'll swear to that. And then I walked out on the field, and out there in the grass, all them birds is out there eating and walking around like they own the joint, like they ain't scared of nothin'. I walked out there, and they'd fly out of my way, but they wouldn't fly away, if you know what I mean. Just fly a few feet off to the side. And they're out there eatin' something. And I'm still *smellin'* Kentucky Fried Chicken. And then I *see* bits of what sure looks like chicken in the grass. I see 'em *all over* the place. Bits of chicken. All over the grass." He finished, a look of merriment and puzzlement across his face. He held up both hands. "Go figure." He shrugged. "Beats me how that happened."

My response was a facial expression that meant to convey, *beats me* too.

"Only thing I can think of is a trucker," Lucas said. "I figure maybe a trucker parked back there overnight, and dumped out some garbage or somethin'."

"Makes as much sense as anything else," I said, which wasn't an absolute fabrication.

I took the interstate back from LaHood and looked out onto the football field before I exited into town, but the end zone appeared bird free.

At home, Tony was alone and sprawled on the couch, watching football on TV. An empty can of Chunky Soup was on the kitchen counter. The house was no longer picked up. The Sunday paper was scattered in sections on the kitchen table, the living room floor, the couch and even under the kitchen table. A can of Pepsi was tipped over – empty, possibly – on the living room floor, a pair of Tony's shoes, one on its side and one upside down, were in front of the couch.

Tony wore a ragged old purple Ranger tee-shirt, faded blue jeans and neither shoes nor socks. I could see an ugly purple bruise on his arm just above his elbow, and a series of deep scratches on the outside of his wrist; the perils of playing a contact sport.

"How you feeling?" I asked.

"Fine," he said, without conviction. His hair was uncombed and untidy. He looked like he'd been on the couch for a week.

"Where's your sister?"

He didn't looked over at me. "Trisha's. She's going to eat over there, she said. I think they're going to the movie later."

"What about you?" I asked.

Belly down on the couch, he more or less shrugged.

I plopped down in the La-Z-Boy and realized with certainty a nap was on its way. I felt the fatigue gathering behind my eyes as surely as I could feel hunger or pain. I had ten minutes, fifteen at the most, before I'd doze off.

"Guess what was all over the end zone this morning," I said.

Tony shrugged again. "Puke?"

"Yeah, well, guess what else," I said. "Birds."

This time he looked at me. "Birds?"

"Puke-eating birds," I said.

Once the statement sunk in, he kind of smiled. "Really?"

I nodded. "All kinds of birds. Seagulls, even. They were all out there eating the chicken you guys threw up last night."

"Lucky them," he said.

"Why'd Jersey haul you out there?" My eyelids were already starting to get heavy. If someone offered me a thousand dollars to stay awake for the next thirty minutes, I couldn't have done it.

He shrugged. His shoulders looked bigger under his shirt; I noticed a juvenile attempt at growing sideburns. Was he shaving? I wondered since when and with what. I was pretty sure those were questions a father should be able to answer. And I would get answers to those questions, right after my nap.

"He must have said something," I said. "He must have given a reason or a warning or an explanation. I've never heard of a team getting off a bus at midnight and doing drills in an end zone."

"Yeah well, it came as a surprise to us too," Tony said.

"So the bus stopped and he politely suggested you line out on the field?"

"Not exactly," Tony said. "He was talking about defeat as failure, or something, that defeat is not something to accept." He paused. "He was pretty mad."

"And then he made you do up-downs until you puked?" I said. I yawned. A single tear of exhaustion crept from the corner of my eye. "I wonder if he's going to get in trouble for doing that," I wondered absently.

"He said he thinks he will, but he also said we had to purge the acceptance of failure from our systems. Something like that."

“You didn’t purge failure as much as you purged Kentucky Fried,” I said. “The amazing thing is you guys threw up all that chicken when you hardly had any chicken to eat.”

“What do you mean?” asked Tony.

“I was in the Helena Kentucky Fried Chicken joint and they just about ran out of food before the bus showed up,” I said. “I saw them scrape the bottom of the barrel for a barely half-filled tub of chicken and a handful of buns. There was maybe enough for four or five kids.”

Tony thought about it. “We had plenty of food.”

I shook my head. “You couldn’t have. There were what, thirty kids on that bus. Maybe, fifteen pieces of chicken were in the tub. You had maybe a dozen buns.”

It was Tony’s turn to shake his head. “I bet you I had five pieces of chicken myself. Mite was sitting right next to me, and he had at least five pieces. We all had plenty to eat. We were all stuffed.”

“Tony,” I said, patiently but confidently, “that’s impossible. I saw Jersey leave Kentucky Fried. He had two partially filled tubs. That was it.”

“What do think, I’m making this up?” Tony answered, somewhat defensively. “I was there. I was in the bus. We all ate. No one complained. We had plenty of food.”

“How many tubs?” I asked.

His eyebrows wrinkled with thought; his mother’s eyebrows had done that. “Tubs? I don’t know. It was dark. Maybe four. I think two went down the right side of the bus, two went down the left. We took food – chicken and buns – and passed it back. It went front to back. We grabbed some, and then it went back to front, and we took some more.”

“There couldn’t have been four tubs,” I said. “And even if you had a full tub of chicken, that couldn’t feed a busload of kids.”

“Well, it must have,” Tony told me.

“But that’s impossible,” I corrected.

“Jesus Lance, what, you’re the chicken police? It was dark. It’s hard to see in a school bus at night. We ate chicken. We passed buckets inside the bus. What do you want me to tell you?”

“I’m not talking about not being able to see in a dark bus,” I explained. “I’m talking about logic, about math and common sense. You can’t take one tub half-full of chicken and feed a whole football team. You simply can’t. It cannot be done.”

Tony began a rebuttal that involved his assurances and confidence about the volume of food that night in the bus, and had I not drifted into sleep, I’m sure the mystery of the Kentucky Fried Chicken would have been resolved.

Shawn Davis was a three-time world champion saddle bronc rider, a member of the Pro Rodeo Hall of Fame and a pro rodeo legend. He was also a

Whitehall native, and on Monday late afternoon – when I went to interview Jersey – I instead found Shawn, his big white cowboy hat tilted up on his forehead, giving an instructional pep talk to thirty high school football players.

They were gathered in the multipurpose room wearing tee-shirts and sweatpants, seated in the bleachers facing Shawn, the closest thing Whitehall had to a hero. Mondays for football teams were typically film sessions or light practices working on specific portions of the game – say, for instance, the snap exchange between quarterback and center – but there the Rangers were listening to arguably the second most famous Whitehall native of all time. Chet Huntley, the NBC news broadcaster, was also from the Whitehall area and was better known nationally, but Shawn was eminently more approachable and Jefferson Valley residents knew a lot more about saddle broncs than network broadcast news.

I'd only seen Shawn a couple times. He lived in Idaho and coached a college rodeo team, and was also the new general manager of the National Finals Rodeo. He was an incredibly busy man but his mother, a brother and other family still lived in Whitehall, and from time to time he'd show up in town and try to blend in with everyone else. He had allowed me to interview him a couple times, but it was pretty apparent when he came to Whitehall he came here to relax, not to do interviews.

Shawn had evidently been talking for a while. Some of the kids looked a little restless, and others appeared bored and inattentive. The twins, JeffScott, looked half asleep. I noticed Shawn's voice was level and somber; this wasn't a pep talk, I realized. It was a lecture. Tony seemed to be paying attention. Dave Dickson seemed to hang on every word, as did Cody Phillips, who himself had an affinity for rough stock and adrenaline. I wondered how long Cody would stay in school or eligible for football.

"Champions don't truly realize they do anything special to become a champion," Shawn said. He was short, broad shouldered, with a square chin and thin bowed legs. He'd been busted up some as a saddle bronc rider, but wasn't really hobbled. When he talked he didn't move much, or change the tone of his voice. "But champions don't become champions by accident. Champions don't become champions overnight. And champions don't become champions without sacrifice."

There were so many stories around Whitehall about Shawn Davis it was impossible to separate the legend and myths from reality. Supposedly he and some of his high school pals corralled an elk up in the Tobacco Root Mountain foothills and Shawn rode it. Another story had him breaking his back in 1969 and being told he'd never ride again and might not ever walk again. A year later he was back riding saddle broncs, and the next year he earned another trip to the National Finals Rodeo. There were stories about him breaking a wrist, rubbing it a minute, then climbing back on and riding a bronc the full eight seconds. There were stories about him riding racehorses at county fairs when he was in elementary school, and my favorite Shawn Davis story came from Boulder Valley rancher Jack Dawson, a rough stock veteran with decades of rodeos under his belt. Years earlier, when Jack and Shawn were kids just out of high school, a car full of Whitehall cowboys had competed in a rodeo somewhere in Wyoming. On the way back home, they took a shortcut through Yellowstone Park, and along the road they came across a bear cub. The guys had had a few beers, and one of them came up with the brilliant idea of taking the cub and throwing it in the trunk, with the plan of releasing it in a West Yellowstone bar.

The cub had other ideas, however. Not far down the road the guys heard a ruckus coming from behind them – a growling and a tearing and a clawing – and then there was a firm thump from the back of the backseat. There was more growling and tearing and clawing, and more firm bumps and then the bear's claws were visible through the backseat cushion. The cub was frantically clawing and chewing its way out of the trunk through the backseat, and was heading into the car interior. Two of the guys in the backseat were hollering for the car to stop, while Shawn, in the front passenger seat, as calm and comfortable as could be, leaned back and said laconically, "Jack, you better pull over. I do believe that bear wants to drive."

Like all rodeo rough stock riders, in his youth Shawn had the mentality that danger was fuel and injuries were inconvenient or inconsequential. He may have scoffed at the thought of fear, but Shawn was generally credited as being the first rough stock rider to actually train to gain strength and to physically prepare himself for competition. He lifted weights and stretched out during an era when as a warm-up most rough stock riders took a drag from a cigarette and flicked the butt out into the rodeo arena immediately before a ride. He was a rodeo legend and a rodeo pioneer, and he was a world champion. I'd met one world champion in my life, and he was it.

"The one thing champions know without some of them actually knowing they know it is this," Shawn said. "The difference between average and excellence is this much." He held his index finger and thumb a mere sliver apart. "This much. And the difference between average and excellence is three things. Preparation, determination and execution. That's it. Three simple things. Not easy things. But simple things. Preparation is just knowing what you have to do to be excellent, to be a champion, and doing it. Over and over, until you can't do it wrong. Determination is the discipline to make sure you do it over and over, and over and over some more, and over and over still some more, until you're prepared. And execution is the fun part. You're prepared. You're determined. The execution is simply performance. Champions perform like champions under pressure because they've prepared, they're determined to succeed, and the execution then comes naturally. Or seems to."

Some of the players were nodding their heads. The JeffScott twins were sleeping, leaning against each other.

"People ask me how I handled the pressure at the National Finals Rodeo all those years," Shawn said. "Hell, that was the easy part. There was no pressure. The hard part was practicing, all the training, all the practice rides, over and over, when it was cold, when it was hot, when it was wet, when I was sore, when I was tired, when I had other things to do, when I wanted to chase girls. But I practiced, over and over, and over and over some more. So when it came time to ride for a championship, I had prepared like a champion, I was determined to be a champion, and so I naturally executed like a champion."

"Do you think we can be champions, Mr. Davis?" asked Dave Dickson.

"Don't matter what I think," Shawn said. "What matters is what you think."

"Preparation, determination and execution," Dave answered.

"My dad told me you once put a bear in the trunk of a car and it clawed its way into the backseat and tried to eat you," said Tanner Walker.

Shawn laughed. "That was one determined little bear."

After a surprising upbeat interview with Jersey – he praised the kids for playing hard and smart the whole game, said he saw signs of progress and improvement, said the final center snap was an unfortunate mistake that wouldn't be repeated and said the midnight assemblage was a point about purpose and conviction – I went home for a quick bite to eat before returning to the Ledger for the night shift.

I walked in the house and set my notebook on the kitchen counter and before I could cross the short kitchen floor Annie popped out of her room and angrily stood in front of me.

"Why'd you tell Jersey?" she demanded. She stood defiantly, in a posture eerily resembling her mother's unfounded and unyielding hostility.

"Settle down," I didn't know what she was talking about. "Tell who what?"

"I am settled down! You told Jersey!"

She was, in a sad way, comically disturbing.

"About what?" I asked.

"You know what!"

I truthfully had no idea what. Since we'd parted ways in Helena I hadn't seen nor talked to Jersey until moments earlier, which meant whatever we talked about could not have made its way to Annie already.

"What did I allegedly tell Jersey?"

"About the Kentucky Fried lady. Ellen."

"What about her?"

"You told Jersey about her." Annie's voice bordered on shrill. I hadn't seen her like this for a long time. She'd always had an innate and advanced sense of justice and fairness, and when she'd been younger if she in her mind had been victimized – either unjustly or unfairly – she'd respond with shrill histrionics.

"I don't know what you're talking about," I told her, patiently, reasonably. "I never told anybody anything."

"You had to," she said. "How else could Jersey know?"

"Know what?" I hesitated, took Annie's hand, and led her into the living room. I placed her on the couch and I sat on the edge of my recliner. I tried my best to not think how much work awaited me at the Ledger and how little time I had to spend on this mini drama. "What is it exactly you're accusing me of?"

Her eyes glowed with indignation. "This morning in homeroom, Jersey said he wanted to tell us a parable, and he told our story – you and me – from the Kentucky Fried Chicken in Helena," Annie said. Her hair hung loose, unmanaged. "He didn't use names and didn't actually say it was the Kentucky Fried Chicken, but he told a story about, I don't know, forgiveness, tolerance, understanding, I suppose. But it involved a downtrodden woman and an angry young girl who wanted retribution." She pointed to herself. "*I* was the angry young woman in the story. He was looking right at me."

That would bother Annie, to have a type of flaw exposed, for all to view. "I never told him," I said. "I never even saw him until an hour ago. I never told anyone about Ellen and your, ah, discussion with her." I paused. I had an explanation. "Did you tell Tony?"

She shook her head. "Did you?"

I shook my head.

"Then how'd Jersey know?" she demanded. "Two people know what happened that night, you and me. And neither of us told anyone."

I gestured helplessly with my hands. I was still trying not to think about the work waiting for me at the Ledger. "I never told anyone. To be honest I mostly forgot about it. Did you tell Trish or Natalie or anyone?"

"No, no one."

There had to be an explanation. "Maybe the Helena Kentucky Fried Chicken called the school," I said.

She shook her head. "I asked. No one called. Plus, what would they say? Tell the mean little girl to leave us alone?" Annie said. She took a deep breath. "I had decided not to call them." Her tone softened. "I started to kind of feel sorry for Ellen."

That was a comforting admission, I thought. But there was still the mystery of Jersey's parable. "Let's think this through," I said. "Only two people in Whitehall knew about your altercation, or whatever it was, with Ellen. You and me, and neither one of us said anything about it to anyone." There was a hint of a question in my voice.

"Right," she nodded.

"The only other person aware of the discussion was Ellen, and we're doubtful she or anyone at Kentucky Fried called Whitehall or Jersey."

"Right," Annie nodded.

I leaned back in my chair. "Well, then, Jersey can't know. No one can know outside of the two of us and the Kentucky Fried people. I don't know what Jersey was talking about, but he couldn't have been talking about this, right? He couldn't have been talking about it because he couldn't possibly know."

She frowned. "Oh, he knew. I was the focus of an object lesson this morning. He made it obvious. To me, anyway, it was obvious. Maybe no one else in the room understood."

"Maybe in Helena he saw how mad you were before he left, and assumed you and Ellen had a dispute," I offered. "Maybe he called Kentucky Fried on Sunday." Once this was resolved, I could get to work.

"Maybe," she mused.

At least she was calmed down. Her body posture was more relaxed, her facial skin tone more natural, and she was talking in a more normal tone of voice.

"You want to figure out a mystery, figure out this," I said. I stood up. "Remember how much chicken the Kentucky Fried crew gave Jersey? One tub maybe half-full of chicken and one tub barely half-full of buns."

Annie nodded. "Yeah, I heard the team puked it all up later when Jersey made them practice."

"Yeah, but that's not the mystery. You saw the tubs, right? Each half full?"

She nodded. "Probably less than half."

"Right, less than half," I said. "Those two half-buckets fed the whole team."

She frowned. "That's not possible. We're talking teenage boys."

I held up my hands, to acknowledge her point. "I know. It's impossible for two half-buckets of chicken to fill a high school football team. But Tony told me they ate all they could handle."

"It's all too weird," she said, and stood. "Thanks for, you know, talking," she told me. "I know you wanted to be at work fifteen minutes ago."

Chapter 18

While there was some background consternation and annoyance, only one set of parents – Hank and Kathleen Harrison – officially complained to school officials about the midnight football drills after the trip home from Cascade. I halfway figured there'd be a universal parental insurrection against the coach and his unprecedented and unnatural moonlit football practice and disciplinary action, but in truth as many people found it amusing as did disconcerting.

But, really, there wasn't even much of a community conversation. Had there been, I would have been obligated to write an article about it. The Harrisons reportedly wanted Jersey fired, and Lyle, as board chairman and Ed, as school superintendent, officially and privately rejected the complaint without a full board meeting. The Harrisons, for reasons left unclear, opted to not publicly press the matter. It would have been easy for me to write a Ledger story about the midnight football player up-downs, the vomit, the parental anger and the school administration refusal to punish or terminate Jersey's tenure. Hank would have been an eminently quotable source.

It can be easy and tempting for newspaper writers or publishers to create or promote conflict, division and acrimony. Someone is always mad at someone or always challenging or rebelling against some established governmental entity or established group, and if there is one uniform group of people who are always eager to talk to reporters it is this group: malcontents. They believe the media exists to serve them.

Conflict may sell newspapers in the short-term, but conflict injures a community's sense of purpose and sense of pride. The reality is conflict is bad for the newspaper in the long-term because conflict is bad for the community, and whatever impairs or injures the community ultimately impairs or injures the community newspaper.

If I wanted to perpetuate conflict or acrimony all I would have had to do was start a conversation about any topic with Daniel Purdy, Whitehall's chronic malcontent. He sowed discord, spurred quarrels and created dispute with every step and every word, and enjoyed the attention his controversy spawned. Hank Harrison was somewhat smarter and smoother than Daniel Purdy, but they were a duo cut essentially from the same cloth. They weren't happy unless they were unhappy about something, as if the complaining was indispensable to their own sense of personal self-esteem.

At least that's what I told Ed at Borden's. We'd had a few beers; it was Wednesday, the paper was out, I'd been to a special Rotary Club dinner honoring Erv Hedegaard, the sweetest guy in town – a man who absolutely refused to complain about anything at anytime – and had seen Ed's nondescript Ford Fairlane parked uptown and figured I'd stop in to say howdy.

Four beers later, he was telling me the background story on Jordan Kling, the sixth grader who had horrifyingly – to him and everyone else – uttered the profanity heard around the Whitehall gym during the school spelling bee.

Apparently, the vulgarism uttered into the microphone in the school multi-purpose room was not his first brush with comic profanity.

"I think Jordan was in first grade, and I could see in his eyes the kid was a pistol," Ed said. "You have to remember, he comes from a single parent home, with a dad who's done time at Deer Lodge."

"Prison?" I had heard something about that.

"Oh, he's out now," Ed said. Ed wore a white dress shirt, gray dress slacks and a gray tie. If you took a picture of him, I thought, he'd look the same in black and white or color. "He works in Hardin, I think, at some grain elevator or something. But, yeah, he's been in prison. For stealing copper wire. The Milwaukee Road hit the end of the road, so to speak, in the 1970s, and they rolled up a bunch of the wire they'd used for electrification of the line. They stored it at the substation south of town over by Point of Rocks, and left it there. Randy, Jordan's dad, hears about it, breaks in, steals it, hauls it to Butte, and sells it."

"All at once?" I asked.

Ed nodded. "He wasn't a genius, okay. He was a lousy crook. He'd stopped at the M&M in Butte for a few celebratory brews and the cops got to his house before he even got home from Butte. They tacked on a drunk driving charge to theft or whatever it was he was charged with. He did a year, maybe eighteen months, but he's never come back here since he was released."

Sally swept by with two more bottles of Rainier. To my knowledge, neither Ed nor I had made any request. Ed nodded a thanks. Sally, lips glossed in bright red, eyes shadowed in shades of purple, definitely needed to be photographed in color. I'd always had trouble pinpointing her age. She could be forty, or sixty. If she was forty, I figured, she must have started working at Borden's when she was a teenager.

"He's probably embarrassed," I said. "Can't you see the cons sitting around the cells, asking *What you in for?* and being told, *Stealing copper wire.* Sounds pretty lame."

Ed agreed. His tie was always cinched tight at his throat. He and Jim McCrossin, a teacher at the school, were the only two people in Whitehall who wore ties. I was tempted to reach over and loosen Ed's tie. A cinched tie in Whitehall, at night, in Borden's, seemed somehow unacceptable.

"How you figure Cody Phillips is doing?" Ed asked me.

The question caught me by surprise. "Cody?" I shook my head. "I don't know. Where's he living?"

Ed nodded. "Mandy's old man's no good. You know it, I know it, everyone knows it."

I nodded. I did know it.

"Mandy never had much of a chance," Ed said, looking at his hand and the bottom of his beer bottle. "I know Cap's type. He's a bully. He's a physical, emotional and psychological bully." He looked me in the eye. "Cody doesn't stand a chance out there."

I nodded. “What are you thinking?”

“Cody’s seen his share of trouble, but he’s still got a chance, Lance. I can see it. There’s a good heart buried deep in that kid.”

I’d seen the trouble, but not the good heart. I figured it must be buried way deep. But Ed was a better judge of these kids.

“I’m not sure I can just stand back and watch Cap ruin that boy forever,” Ed said. There was a steeliness in his voice I’d not heard before.

“What are you saying?” I asked.

“I’m not saying anything,” Ed said. “I might need your help, though, all right?”

I nodded. I didn’t ask *help to do what?* I could tell Ed wasn’t ready to answer that question.

“So Jordan’s in first grade,” Ed continued, and leaned back in his chair. “He’s a tough little kid. Sort of a natural leader, you know, but he’s also a kid at risk, with his family situation and all. So I sort of take him under my wing, talk to him about his family, his interests. One day he says to me, ‘Hey, Special Ed, I know what the ‘A’ word means.’”

“The what?” I ask.

“The ‘A’ word,” Ed said. He took a few gulps from his beer. “I didn’t know what he was talking about, so I ask Jordan, ‘What ‘A’ word?’ Because, really, I had no idea what his version of the ‘A’ word was.”

Neither did I, now that I thought about it.

Ed grinned the whole time he told the story. He was one of those people who magically, amazingly, fortunately, found themselves in exactly the right job. Ed and his wife, Alice, had raised two intelligent, if somewhat homely, daughters who both were teachers in other parts of Montana. Alice had never worked outside the home, and Ed had never been anything other than an educator. He looked, sounded, and acted like an educator. He seemed to lack a personality, and he dressed like a 1950s shoe salesman, but both those images could be misleading. It was true you somehow had the impression he knew nothing of the world outside the walls of his school, but he also had a determination, a fierceness, to him when it came to his definition of academic success.

And to his credit, he habitually sought out the struggling kid, the ill-tempered kid, the kid with a learning disability, the kid from a broken home, and worked to give them special attention and recognition. He took failure personally, and when a kid dropped out of school, he blamed the school, not the kid. When a kid dropped out of school, he would say, “We lost one.” He viewed the world as an inhospitable place for a high school dropout, and with some degree of severity did whatever he could to keep kids in the classroom. Many of his special cases understood his efforts, and every school year a past student, now a young man and woman, would drop by the school simply to tell him hello and thanks, and to show him, I think, his efforts were not only appreciated but were also successful.

Annie was one of his special projects. She had practically unfettered freedom at school to explore her interests. Trisha was another special project. Trisha's multiple sclerosis caused partial paralysis, her physical constraints varied, and she had bad days and perhaps more tolerable days, and she presented a unique challenge to the entire school district. Ed had insisted the district meet that challenge, and he'd told me more than once he learns as much from Trisha and her illness as she does from the school district.

"So Jordan sort of winks, an honest, friendly little first grader wink and says, 'Come on, Special Ed, you know, the 'A' word.'"

Ed took a sip of beer.

"And I can't figure it out. 'What 'A' word?' I ask. 'Come on, the 'A' word,' he says. And he gives me a conspiratorial little elbow nudge. 'Come on, you know, the 'A' word,' he says. I get a little firm with him. 'I don't know any 'A' word.' So he leans toward me. 'Come on, you know, the 'A' word. Fuckin-A.'" Ed erupted in laughter.

So did I. Ed, in his white shirt and tie, this proper career educator, this stoic and stern administrator, was laughing the hardest I'd ever seen a grown man laugh in my life.

The Ranger football team, zero wins and three losses for the year, had to travel to Boulder for a Friday night conference game that would almost certainly be another Ranger loss. The Boulder Panthers were unbeaten and ranked seventh in state Class B football, and their game against us was their Homecoming. It looked to be another lopsided defeat, so Thursday afternoon after practice Annie and I picked up Tony and we went to LaHood to buy him a steak, sort of like a prisoner's last meal. Annie and I sat in the Escort, parked in the student parking lot, only a space or two away from the spot I'd parked when the Rangers performed what was becoming a mythical midnight workout.

Annie had her hair in some kind of a thick short braid. I never knew if I should ask about her changes in clothing, hair or appearance. If I did ask, chances are her response would include some kind of chastisement that I hadn't noticed the change earlier. I had commented on a dress once, and it turned out she'd had it for over a year and had even worn it for her school picture the year before. But if I didn't notice or comment, it was as if I was unobservant or indifferent. And the truth was I largely was unobservant or indifferent, but I didn't want to appear that way.

I opted to venture a comment. "How long have you had your hair like that?"

"My hair?" she asked. She appeared amused. "Since when do you notice my hair?"

"I notice," I said defensively. "I may not say anything, but I notice."

"It's called a French Braid," Annie said. "Natalie did it in study hall this afternoon. So it's new. Good job, Lance."

"Really?" I asked. I probably beamed with pride. "So this is the first time I've seen you with your hair that way, and I noticed and complimented you on it? You gotta admit, for me, that's pretty impressive."

"Technically, I should point out, you didn't actually compliment me," she said. "You asked how long I'd had my hair this way. That's an observation, not a compliment. You didn't say anything about how it looks."

"It looks fine," I said.

"Oh Lance, you're a charmer, you are," she said. She hid a short, shy smile. "Are you ever going to ask Ms. Kristofferson out?"

"What?"

"You heard me."

"Yeah, I heard you. But why would you ask that?"

"You danced with her," Annie said softly.

"I more or less had to. You dragged me out there. Literally, dragged. I haven't said a word to her since. Haven't even seen her."

Annie leaned away from me. "It was a question, Lance, not an accusation. It's not a crime to go on a date. You're allowed to do that."

"Allowed to do what?" Tony said. I'd missed his walk from the shower room to the car. His hair was slick and brushed back above his forehead. He carried his football cleats in one hand and his jacket in the other.

"Nothing," I said, and started the car's engine. The cassette player sprung to life, playing a song from *The River*, the newest in our growing collection of Bruce Springsteen cassettes. This one wasn't actually ours, apparently; Tony explained it was a loaner from Dave Dickson.

"Don't you think Lance and Mary make a nice couple?" Annie asked.

Tony's expression suggested amusement. "A couple?"

"Your sister thinks she's being funny," I said.

"Yeah, she's a riot," Tony said.

He had the kind of smile that made you feel good. He really was a handsome kid, I saw, as he ran his hand through his hair and sat back in the seat. He had thick hair, a little too long, brushed back away from his face. He had a slim face; a strong, square chin; and piercing blue eyes. He had a thin row of summer freckles below his eyes that were the remnants of a thick patch of freckles in his youthful years. He looked innocent, really, in a way Annie never had and never would. He took everything at face value, and Annie took nothing at face value. Tony's world was relatively and surprising simple, even within the complicated family arrangements the three of us had gravitated into, and despite the loss of his mother and all it represented, I'd never seem him brood or be rebellious as a result. He wasn't the thinker Annie was – but then no one was the thinker Annie was – and he wasn't the most ambitious kid I'd ever seen, but he was respectful, well-behaved and a hit with high school girls.

“Maybe I’m not being funny,” Annie offered. “Maybe Lance should ask Ms. Kristofferson out on a date.”

Then and there illustrated a major difference between the two kids. Tony laughed because he knew I enjoyed his laughter. Annie was essentially told to drop a conversation topic, but she didn’t want to, so she didn’t and wouldn’t.

“You’re a relatively normal man,” Annie told me. “Have you even been on a date since mom left?”

“Annie,” I said, and with a normal kid, I wouldn’t have had to say anything more.

“I mean a date,” she continued. “Not a drunken barroom tryst.”

“Annie,” I said sternly, “that’s-”

“Enough,” she finished. She held up her hands. “Fine. All I’m saying is that it’s natural for you to want another adult sexual relationship, and if you do, we’re okay with that. Right, Tony?”

“If you say so.” The last thing Tony wanted to talk about was his father’s sexual relationships, or more precisely his father’s sexual relationship deficiency.

At LaHood, he ordered a sirloin steak that was about the size of a car tire. Annie ordered chicken strips and I went with a halibut steak. Tony dug into his steak as if someone was poised to steal it from him.

“Did you tell him about Cody Phillips?” Annie asked.

Tony looked up from his food, his cheeks bulging with food, and shook his head.

“Want me to tell him?” Annie asked.

Tony nodded, and resumed cutting his steak.

I sensed danger, trouble, or both. No conversation involving Cody Phillips had ever been pleasant or upbeat.

“Cody’s been living with his grandfather. You knew that,” Annie said.

I nodded.

“No one really knew who Cody’s dad was, so when his mom died, he didn’t have anywhere else to go,” she said. “Cody showed up at school today late. He had a black eye and a bloody ear.”

“Goddamned Cap Horton,” I said.

Tony looked up, surprised. He looked at Annie, as if she should continue.

“Cody and his grandfather had a fight last night,” Annie said.

“And Cody did not lose the fight,” Tony added, one cheek puffed with food.

“Who told you all this?” I asked.

“I worked an hour in the high school office this morning,” she said. “I saw Cody when he showed up for school, and I heard Special Ed telling all this to Jersey.”

“What’s going to happen to Cody?” I asked.

“Mandy has a brother, I guess, but he’s in the Army in Germany,” Annie said. “For a while it looked like Cody was going to have to go to a state school in Miles City.”

"Jesus Christ," I muttered. Ed would not be happy with that. Pine Hills was not a benevolent institution. "Cody has to leave Whitehall? Because of goddamn Cap Horton?" I asked.

Annie shook her head the same time Tony looked up and shook his.

"So guess what?" Annie said. "Cody's moving in with Special Ed and his wife."

"No kidding," I said, stunned, even though Ed had all but warned me it was coming. "And Cody's okay with that?"

Ed and Alice, both in their sixties, had raised two bright and obedient daughters and sent them out into the world. The biggest worry they'd had about their two girls were their SAT scores. Adopting, for lack of a better word, a delinquent and impulsive high school sophomore into their lives and into their home was a bold and generous and dangerous offer. I wondered if Cody appreciated that.

"Special Ed laid down the law with Cody," Annie said. "I was right there. I heard it. It was like I was a witness. Like I was deliberately meant to be a witness. No truancy. No drinking. No chewing. No drugs. No screwing around."

"That'll be a big change for Cody," I said. He'd been essentially on his own, something not entirely foreign to the children in the Joslyn family.

"It gets better," Annie said. "Cody's got a curfew now. Cody…a curfew," she said, as if astonished. "He has to maintain a 'B' average. He has to keep his room clean. He has to keep himself clean. And he agreed to it all. He's sitting there, dirty and bloody from his fight with his grandpa, and he's promising Special Ed he'll work hard in school and keep his room clean."

Tony looked up. "He won't even be Cody anymore."

"That's an awfully nice gesture on the Franklins' part," I said. "It shows how much Ed cares about you kids."

Annie nodded, her eyes open wide. "Yeah, it may have been a nice gesture on Special Ed's part, but I don't think Mrs. Special Ed was all that thrilled about it. I only heard half of that phone call, and let's just say this same discussion about Cody we're having here is going on right now at Special Ed's house, except it's a lot more lively there than here."

Another Friday night, another drive to Boulder, another football game. Slack and Annie joined me in the Escort, driving through the North Boulder Valley darkness, Bruce Springsteen singing about the promised land.

Slack's big cowboy hat was perched in his lap. He had a chew of tobacco tucked under his lower lip and he held a plastic Budweiser cup he'd raise to his mouth and spit into every few minutes. He sat in the front passenger seat quiet and mostly still, and I found myself again wondering how much of his life and his lost world of opportunities he comprehended. Did he remember that summer day years earlier in the foothills of the Tobacco Root Mountains, mending fence, feeling the surge of lightning-charged energy rip through his body? Did he ever realize, in perhaps fleeting moments, that he had once been an intelligent and promising high school student with a bright and unlimited future? Or did the shock and raw jolt of electricity forever destroy his sense of past, his sense of promise? Did he ever detect the slight expression of dismay or grief his parents couldn't quite fully hide? Did he know what he was missing? I couldn't help feeling sorry for him. Did he feel sorry for himself? Did he know he had a reason to feel sorry for himself?

Annie had been tested and re-tested, her intelligence measured and quantified and computed locally, regionally, nationally and, as I understood it, internationally. Nationally recognized academic and educational leaders were tracking her intellectual capabilities. But Slack seemingly had little professional or medical appraisal of the damage lightning did to his brain and body. He had almost died, but didn't, recovered almost complete use of his arms and legs, but not quite. His reason, his wits, his intellect, his personality, his mental abilities, never came close to full recovery and never would. But I wondered to what extent his mind had been medically surveyed and studied to know exactly what was damaged and how bad. His physical deformities, a slightly withered arm and shoulder and a hint of an awkward gait caused by a stiff leg or maybe something wrong with his foot, were visible only upon close inspection and did not seem to hinder his physical work at the ranch. With supervision, he hayed, branded, fed, rode a horse and helped move cows. It was his intellect, his memory and his sensibilities that were truly deficient. The vacant stare in his eyes, the disconnected silly laughter, the inappropriate grin and the confused facial expressions marked him as damaged and disordered. To what extent did he and doctors understand that?

"How are your mom and dad?" I asked.

He smiled, said they were fine, raised the Budweiser cup and spat. It was a simple question with a simple response. Yet I couldn't help but wonder if at that moment he could have told me exactly who his mother and father were, what their names were, and how he had last interacted with them.

We drove past Tom and Helen Carey's place, and it was hard to tell if the headlights picked up a rusty red bloodstain on the highway pavement. I'm not sure I could still pinpoint with certainty the exact place to look. I spotted other bloodstains as I looked. Crossing Highway 69 was a death-defying trek for deer.

It was late September, with a dusky dark sky above dotted with faded stars and a fat bright yellow moon off to the east. Trees were shedding leaves, and the spindly naked upper branches were barely visible against the darkening sky.

The yearly cycle of local livestock operations – calving in February and March, branding later in spring, moving cattle to summer pastures, moving cattle from summer pastures, shipping cattle, feeding cows all winter into calving season – was fixed by nature, weather, moisture, federal grazing permits, financial and business and lending obligations and sheer necessity, year after year, for over a century now in Montana. Did Slack understand that? What did he understand about cattle futures, weight gain and the myriad intricacies of livestock finances? Could he tell a good year from a bad year? What would he do after his parents retired or died? What *could* he do?

It was more comforting to shift my thoughts. "You think we got a chance tonight?" I asked him.

He grinned, and shrugged.

"Boulder's pretty good," Annie said. "My guess is they'll score at least sixty points tonight."

Slack responded with a muted howl. It was possible he had forgotten why he was driving north through the Boulder Valley, or that he was even in the North Boulder Valley. "Sixty points!"

"Tony and I have a bet," Annie said. "I say the Rangers will give up at least three hundred and eighty points this year, and Tony says they won't."

Slack appeared to be attempting to contemplate the numbers.

"What is that," I asked Annie, "about forty-five points a game?"

"So far they're averaging over forty-four points scored against them," Annie explained, "but Cascade only scoring twenty-two put a damper on the average. I need the Panthers to find the end zone early and often."

"Goddamn bet," I griped.

"Oh Lance, relax. I'm not rooting against Whitehall," Annie said. "It'd be great if they won fifty five to fifty four, but the odds of that are not real promising."

"It pisses me off you're hoping Boulder scores," I complained.

"Me too," said Slack sluggishly.

"That a boy, Slack. See," I told Annie, "you even got Slack pissed off."

Slack giggled.

Had Slack gone to his high school prom, I wondered, the spring before the summer lightning storm? If he did, did he have any kind of recollection of it? If he did… did it haunt him?

We took a long bending curve to the right – the Jefferson County Fairgrounds to our left – and ahead, on our right, were the distinctive bright lights and slick green grass of a football field.

There were two high schools in Jefferson County – one in Whitehall and one in Boulder –and they had the same school colors: Purple and gold. How the only high schools in the county ended up with the same exact colors was something of a mystery. There were varied versions of which school came first and which school should be required to change its colors, but which school came first and which school should change colors depended on which school officials you asked. Maybe – maybe – there was another county in America with only two high schools that had the same exact school colors, but maybe not.

Two, maybe three, years earlier, I had suggested in the Ledger that Whitehall High and Jefferson High go head-to-head for a full sports year with a point system that allowed two points for each varsity win and one point for each junior varsity win. The winner got to keep the purple and gold, and the loser had to shop for new school colors. Not a single person thought the idea had merit.

It always bothered me the way Boulder consistently beat Whitehall in football, and it bothered me even more that the high school in Boulder called itself Jefferson High School. It didn't seem right that there could be two high schools in Jefferson County and one more or less claimed the title of the official county high school. There were two Class B high schools in the county, both approximately the same size, about forty miles apart, and it seemed snobby or elitist for one school to declare itself the county high school. Although, to be honest, had we ever beat Jefferson High in football, my suspicion was the whole official county high school name dilemma wouldn't have bothered me nearly as much.

Whitehall wore their road light uniforms – a faded yellow – and the Panthers wore dark purple. I counted twenty-seven Whitehall kids in uniform, and a handful in street clothes, afflicted with various injuries, on the sideline. Little Scott Atkins, his arm in a cast, banged up in Columbus on the first play of the year, looked tiny in his street clothes under his game jersey.

Boulder had at least fifty kids dressed and warming up. And with at least ten minutes until kickoff the Boulder bleachers and sidelines were already full, everyone wearing purple, with a large crowd still streaming in. I stood on the Ranger sidelines, and as I put new batteries in my camera flash I turned toward the Whitehall cheering section and counted a couple dozen fans spread out in the small visitors seating section. Trish was stationed off the corner of the bleachers, with her mother seated in the row alongside her. Molly was always close, but also attempted to not, as I heard her say once, hover. Various Whitehall parents were in attendance, including an already dour-looking Hank and Kathleen Harrison. Brent Walker stood smoking a cigarette along the fence. Ed Franklin was standing in the bleachers, and his wife Alice was bundled up and seated next to him. Cody Phillips had something to do with that, I figured. The handsome and dapper O'Toole family was present and scattered throughout the bleachers. The parents sat together, and each of the girls was seated in small circles of friends, and each O'Toole girl stunningly stood out in each circle of friends. Aspen was wearing Tony's purple number twenty-three home jersey, and even though it was three sizes too big it somehow looked good on her.

The Rangers stood statue-still as the Boulder high school band played the national anthem, and although it wasn't a terrible rendition, the WHS band had done a better job two weeks earlier against Shelby. The Rangers were more respectful, as well. The Panthers, across the field, stood around the sidelines in no order and in no posture, and starting hollering and whooping before the band stopped playing and before the cheerleaders retired the colors.

The Rangers got the ball first and moved the ball enough to pick up a couple first downs and get into Boulder territory. The drive stalled and Colt's punt pinned Boulder inside their own ten yard line. On their first play, Boulder's best player, Adam Collins, was stopped for a two-yard gain on a nice tackle by one of the JeffScott twins. Collins picked up three yards on the next play and was forced out of bounds by Tony. On third down Cody Phillips broke through up the middle and sacked the quarterback just outside the end zone. Tony fielded the punt at about the Boulder forty-yard line and ran straight up the field for ten yards before being tripped up. Colt hit Tony on a sideline pattern for a first down to the Boulder twenty yard line. But on the next play Colt was tackled in the backfield before he could hand the ball off, and eventually Colt underthrew Logan Bradshaw on a deep curl and Boulder took over on its own twenty five yard line.

It was an impressive start for the Rangers. The first quarter was scoreless, and Whitehall had close to double the offensive yardage of Boulder. Collins had fourteen yards on seven carries, and the Panthers hadn't yet completed a pass.

After another Boulder punt Whitehall got the ball on its own thirty yard line, and on first down Colt set up to throw a little swing pass to Logan Bradshaw. Collins stepped inside of the receiver, made an easy interception, and raced untouched into the end zone for a touchdown.

Whitehall got the ball and to their credit, responded. It was the first time in a few years a Ranger football team actually overcame adversity and put the ball in the end zone. The offensive line – the two JeffScott twins, Cody Phillips, Tanner Walker and Morgan Miteward, with help from Bobby Bentmier – opened up some gaping holes for Nate and Logan, and without a pass attempt the Rangers marched straight down the field to score and tie the game at 7-7. It was perhaps the most impressive Ranger drive in four years.

Boulder had a nice kick return and started their possession close to midfield. Morgan and Tanner stopped Collins on first down, and a second down pass was incomplete. On third down the Boulder quarterback pitched the ball to Collins for a sweep, but he pulled up and threw the ball. The halfback option pass was a simple play call, and never should have worked, especially on third and long. But the Ranger secondary, determined to stuff Collins on the sweep, got caught upfield. The Boulder wide receiver was fifteen yards behind the nearest Ranger defender – Tony – and hauled in the pass. Tony caught him near the goal line but the Panther receiver tumbled into the end zone. The extra point made it 14-7 Boulder.

Again the Rangers responded with an impressive drive. Logan consistently sliced off tackle for big gains, and Cale Bolling carried the ball a couple times – once for an eighteen-yard gain on a sweep – and with about three minutes left to go in the half Whitehall was on the Boulder fifteen yard line.

Jersey called some kind of an option or pitch play to the wide side of the field, and Boulder had the play defended perfectly. Colt should have tucked the ball in and accepted the two-yard loss. Instead, as he was being tackled, he attempted a desperation pitch outside to Nate. The ball got close to Nate's knees, and as he bent down to catch the pitch he got whacked by Collins. Nate flew backwards, Collins on top of him, and a Boulder linebacker picked up the loose ball and ran eighty yards for a touchdown and a 21-7 Boulder lead.

The Boulder sidelines – players and fans – erupted into near hysteria. On their side of the field there was cheering, clapping, shouting, stomping, whistling and the Panther Pep Band cranked up the volume on a quick burst of the school song. Had the Rangers scored, the game would have been tied at halftime, a significant accomplishment for Whitehall and a serious surprise in Class B football. But Whitehall did not score.

The Whitehall side of the field was silent as a crypt. Even Trisha hung her head in despair. The players on the sidelines moved like walking corpses, and the fans in the bleachers were mumbling glumly. Only Jersey, wearing a black turtleneck and tight black slacks, showed signs of life. He applauded the players as they trotted off the field, congratulated the offensive linemen and collected the players in a circle around him. He really didn't say anything special; he just told them they were playing strong, playing with intensity, and playing their best game of the year. He told them to forget about the scoreboard and concentrate on their assignments.

The half ended with Whitehall down 21-7. The Rangers had more total yards, more first downs, more passing yards and more rushing yards than Boulder, but because of two plays trailed by two touchdowns.

I had taken close to twenty pictures in the first half and thought I had a couple good shots, one especially of three Ranger tacklers pushing Collins over backward. I thought I also had a nice picture of Cale hauling in a pass along the sidelines.

The temperature had dropped since kickoff, and a slight breeze had chilled the air. I ventured toward the concession stand for some hot chocolate. I stood in line a few minutes, ordered, and when I went to pay realized I had no money. I panicked, looked for Annie, and saw Cal Walker behind me in line, chuckling.

"I got it, Lori," he told the woman in the concession stand.

I sheepishly stepped aside and let Cal step ahead of me. He ordered a coffee and a couple hot dogs, handing me the first hot dog Lori gave him.

"Here," he told me, "you look hungry."

I wasn't hungry until I had a warm hot dog in my hand; then I was starving.

Cal and I stood next to the condiment stand – a large wooden wire spool stood on its side – and as I squirted catsup on my hot dog he lathered mustard and dropped onions on his.

"Whitehall's outplaying Boulder," Cal said. He was wearing a long sleeve western shirt. I wore a tee-shirt, under a sweatshirt, under a Ranger windbreaker, and I was cold.

"This is the best Whitehall's played in five years," I said. "We're down by two touchdowns but we really should have the lead. That fumble really hurt."

Cal nodded. The circumference of his face seemed perfectly round under his cowboy hat. "I can't believe this is the same team that lost 55-12 to Shelby."

"We're getting better, I think."

"You should be, practicing at midnight." There was a twinkle in Cal's eye.

"You heard about that, huh?"

"We all heard about it," Cal said. He motioned toward the field. "Your kids don't need any extra drills tonight. This is the first time Boulder's been outplayed at home in quite a few years."

I sighed. "And we're still down fourteen points. Somehow that doesn't seem right."

"Sometimes the ball takes some funny bounces," Cal said. "Your boy's playing well. He really hustles out there."

"He gave up the TD on that halfback pass," I said. "That was third and long, too."

Cal shook his head. "That wasn't his guy. He was covering the wide receiver on the other side of the field. That was your safety's fault. Colt Harrison's a good player, but he's not as good as he thinks he is. He's making mistakes on both sides of the ball."

"He's the best we got," I said.

Cal kept shaking his head. "Maybe. Your option play should work, but he can't run it. I bet he fumbles twice more in the second half. You watch."

I did watch, and Colt actually fumbled three times. None of them were really his fault, and Boulder only recovered one of the fumbles.

Boulder took the opening half kickoff and drove into Whitehall territory, but then Tony picked off a pass tipped by Tanner and the Rangers got the ball close to midfield. Logan and Nate pounded the ball inside and without a pass the Rangers scored to make the score 21-14. Colt scored the touchdown on a quarterback sneak. The Ranger sidelines showed signs of life, and I saw Colt's parents – Hank and Charlene – hug and cheer and then hug again.

Trish, in her wheelchair, yelled, shook her head and punched the sky awkwardly with both fists.

On the next Boulder possession Morgan, Tanner, Cody and the JeffScott twins dominated the line of scrimmage and after three runs that actually lost yardage the Panthers had to punt. Cale scooped up the bouncing ball after the punt and brought the ball all the way to the Boulder thirty yard line. On third and long, a Boulder linebacker blitzed from the blind side and collided with Colt just as Colt raised the ball to pass. Colt went down face first, and the ball flopped out from his hand. Collins caught the ball near his belly and jogged into the end zone for a 28-14 Boulder lead.

Hank Harrison cupped his hands at his mouth and yelled for the Rangers to block someone. That was the only sound from the Whitehall crowd. Trish had an elbow on her leg, her chin in her palm, and her eyes aimed toward the ground. Slack's head was down, his cowboy hat pulled low so he couldn't see.

The score was still 28-14 midway through the fourth quarter when Colt and the Rangers put together another nice drive into Panther territory. On third and short, Cody and Colt somehow misconnected on the snap, but Nate dived at the offensive line's feet to recover the ball. On fourth down and three yards for a first down, Colt rolled out to the wide side of the field and under pressure threw a pass toward Tony. Colt was off balance when he released the ball and the pass was a stride, maybe a half stride, behind Tony. He tipped it as he reached to his left – behind himself – and the ball hung in the air just for a second. As he tried to stop he tipped the ball higher in the air and as he fell a Boulder defensive back jumped up, caught the ball, hurdled Tony, and cruised into the end zone for a touchdown.

Trailing 35-14 late in the fourth quarter, Jersey put in some of the Ranger reserves. The Boulder fans sang the *Na na na na, na na na na, hey-hey-hey, goodbye* song and I stood dejectedly, realizing a game Whitehall could have won was going to be another lopsided loss. Behind me, along the sidelines near the Ranger bench, something, some movement, caught my eye. Cody and Colt were nose to nose in an argument. Not nose to nose really, because Colt was six inches taller than Cody. But fiery little Cody, his hair messed up and soaked with sweat, his right hand taped up, bloody and grass-stained, his face red and puffy, was pointing his right index finger in Colt's face and after Cody angrily said something he actually threw a short, choppy punch at his own quarterback.

How pathetic is this, I wondered. We're getting thumped on the field, and on the sideline we're fighting like spoiled and sullen children. Who do the Rangers think they are, I wondered, the Whitehall Town Council?

Before either kid threw another punch three or four Rangers – including Tony – stepped in between the two players and separated them. Colt and Cody walked away from each other, down opposite ends of the sideline, each with a handful of Rangers surrounding him. With their attention focused on the field, I'm not sure Jersey or Coach Pete saw any of it.

With eighteen seconds left to go in the game, Boulder called time out. From the Whitehall twenty-eight yard line, on the final play of the game, the starting Boulder quarterback completed a long sideline route for a touchdown. It was the football equivalent of giving your opponent the finger.

The final score was 42-14 and a couple of the Rangers were so angry at the outcome of the game – and the final cheap shot touchdown – that they declined to shake hands with the Panthers and instead walked from the sidelines directly to the team bus. Colt, the JeffScott twins, Cody, Tanner and even coach Pete stormed off the field without shaking hands. It was a sad ending to a sad game.

Jersey shook hands with the Boulder coaching staff and each Boulder player. It was, I figured, a way for Jersey to put the game behind him. But I was wrong.

Chapter 19

Whatever animosity existed between Cody Phillips and Colt Harrison must have festered on what had to have been a tense bus ride home from Boulder, as the Rangers – bitter and battered – headed home to Whitehall.

Stepping off the game bus after a trip home used to be a routine thing for the Rangers. Not anymore. First was the midnight practice and next was a brawl.

Details were, you could say, sketchy. Tony wouldn't, or perhaps couldn't, tell what he heard or what he saw, but he and the rest of the Rangers must have heard and seen something. Cody and Colt apparently jawed at each other down the Boulder Valley and the instant they stepped off the bus in the Whitehall High School parking lot they started throwing punches at each other. Only a handful of people saw what actually happened, and I wasn't one of them. And of the handful who actually saw it, none of them would talk about it.

The fighters were quickly pulled apart by a group of players, but the two of them continued to argue and had to be physically and spatially separated from each other. Tony admitted he was one of the players who took Cody and hauled him into the locker room, where they changed clothes without showering and a small group escorted Cody from the locker room to his pickup.

Tony barely said a word about any of this to me. He also never told me that after Cody had jumped into his truck and sped out of the parking lot he had failed to arrive at the Franklins as planned, and wasn't found until early Saturday morning – and found by town marshal Henry "Manfred" Manfredini – back at the family trailer home he'd vacated when his mother had died. I found out later, from pieced-together information, that a group including Ed and Jersey had searched for Cody all night, and that there were some worries Cody may be gunning – literally – for Colt. That was one reason why Manfred and the Jefferson County Sheriff's office had been called in. It turned out Colt and his family had been in no danger; Cody had driven to the cemetery, slept in the truck across the road from his mother's grave, and gone back to the trailer.

I didn't know about any of all that until late Saturday afternoon, after Cody had been found and returned to the Franklin home. It was Jersey who told me, during the weekly interview. I had asked him to get the interview over with on Saturday so I could write the article Sunday, because I had to attend a town council meeting on Monday night.

I had met Jersey at the school Saturday afternoon, and he was waiting for me in his classroom. He hadn't shaved, his clothes looked a little rumpled, and when I commented on his appearance he commented on the search as if I had known all about it.

"Tony didn't mention it?" a surprised Jersey asked.

"No," I answered. "Is he okay? Cody. Is he all right?"

Jersey nodded. "Oh, he's fine. He's probably at Franklins right now, sound asleep."

"What was the fight about?" I asked.

"What was the fight about?" Jersey repeated. "I'll tell you what it was about. It was about a center and a quarterback who've fumbled too many center snaps. There's also some mutual frustration involved about losing four straight games. And Cody's an emotional mess, which is explainable and understandable. I feel for the kid. We all do. But do you know what this is really about? Class warfare. At its core, the fight wasn't about football. It was about class and status. Someone like Colt, an All-Star and child of privilege, doesn't think someone like Cody, a product from life's grittier base, should dare to challenge him. Cody doesn't know his place. That's the problem."

I had no response to that. Fortunately, I didn't need one.

"Which is patent nonsense, of course," Jersey continued. "But I'll tell you, we're close to being a pretty good football team. It may not look that way, but reverse five plays in Boulder last night and that would have been an incredible game."

"That was a bush league touchdown they scored to end the game," I said.

Jersey waved off my comment. "Yeah, it was, but so what. The Boulder coach expected to dominate the game and dominate the scoreboard, and that obviously didn't happen. To keep his state ranking he had to make it *look* like his team dominated the game and scoreboard, so he manufactured a cheap touchdown. That was our fault, not his." He gave another dismissive wave of his hand. "I have a lot of other things to worry about besides a coach running up the score on us."

"Like what?" I asked.

"Like team unity. We're building a cohesive team spirit. It might not look like it, but we are. We're figuring who plays best where, and you saw the way we ran the ball last night. We've made great strides the past month, and we're this close" – he held up his thumb and index finger a fraction of an inch apart, much like Shawn Davis had – "to being a good football team. We're not even close to playing to our potential and one major reason why not is this friction between Colt and Cody."

"Just those two?"

"No," he said. "You've lived around here a long time. You know it's just not those two. Kids long ago more or less picked sides, and the loyalty more or less falls along social status lines. I sensed something was holding us back but I couldn't figure out what it was. Until last night. When I saw Cody and Colt flailing away at each other, I realized we had a problem, but it wasn't until I saw two groups of kids neatly step in and separate the fighters that I saw the breadth and depth of the problem."

It wasn't exactly a revolutionary insight. All kids in all schools have some sort of method to rank themselves by status, and the Whitehall Rangers were not the first team to suffer from some kind of disharmony. Disharmony was more common than harmony, in fact, and it could be argued that Whitehall teams – even this Whitehall team – got along far better than most teams.

"So what are you going to do?"

He shrugged. And for the first time I detected a hint of fatigue in Jersey. The dark brown eyes held weariness, his shoulders slumped in almost a palpable form of dejection, and even his gestures meant to convey enthusiasm lacked any sense of animation. He had been up all night, true, and no doubt that contributed to his exhaustion, but he also wore the burden of responsibility as the head coach of a winless team that had lost four games, had just lost to the county rival by four touchdowns, had to host a good Townsend team in less than a week and had serious discord inside a team that had more internal strife than external zeal.

I didn't see Tony until Sunday morning. I got up first, about nine o'clock, and intended to have a bowl of cereal when I realized we had neither cereal nor milk. By the time I got back from the IGA both Tony and Annie were awake, and both stood at the kitchen counter reading portions of the Sunday Butte daily newspaper. Without looking, I knew what parts of the paper they were reading; Tony was browsing through the sports page and Annie was devouring the front page.

It was a late September Sunday morning and there were easily two dozen yard work or home repair jobs that fell into the *urgent* category in and around our home. The sun was out, the morning air held just a tinge of winter chill, and the wind was relatively calm. It was an ideal morning to rake leaves, remove brush and debris wedged in the lilac bushes, clear out the weeds and wind-strewn garbage, muck out the garage to see if there was some way possible to actually fit the car inside it before winter struck, dig out the supposedly flower – actually weed – beds around the house before the snow started to pile up. That was just the obvious yard work staring me down. The exterior of the house was, plainly, a disaster. The exterior badly needed to be painted. Before that, of course, it needed a coat of primer, and before that it needed to have all the chipped paint sanded and scraped off. It was at once depressing and exhausting to even think about it. The gutters were filled with leaves and debris from the trees, the drain spouts were plugged with God knows what, and on the southwest side of the house, which absorbed the brunt of the wind, the gutter twisted and shimmied during wind gusts, a precursor, I knew, of a dangling section of gutter and then a torn free and busted section of gutter down in the weeds. I could see it all coming, and there was nothing I was going to do about it.

Was there any part of the house and yard that did not need immediate maintenance? As I carried the bag of groceries into the kitchen I realized I could confidently answer the question with a negative response. Every aspect of the house and yard was in desperate need of maintenance, upgrade, repair or replacement. None of which would be accomplished or even attempted. The house defeated me. Mentally, I'd waved the white flag.

I never expected that of me. Back when Amy was around the place it may not have been a model of home and yard care, but neither was it the embarrassment it had become. I expected better of me. After breakfast, I'd head to the Ledger until mid afternoon, go home for dinner, and then return to the Ledger for the evening. I had no choice. There was a required volume of work that needed to be done, and it took a required amount of time to do it.

"Townsend beat Three Forks by three touchdowns," Tony told me, his head down aimed toward the newspaper.

"What's up with Colt and Cody?" I asked him.

"What do you mean?" Tony's eyes looked up toward me as I began to put away the groceries. He appeared a bit timid, or unsure of himself, and he reminded me of his mother when he did that.

"You know what I mean," I told him. "Jersey told me about it."

Tony arched an eyebrow. "What'd he say?"

"He told me about the fight in the parking lot, and about Cody disappearing for half the night."

Tony had an odd expression on his face. "That's all he told you?"

"There's more?"

"Remember, he owns the newspaper," Annie told Tony.

"What else happened?" I asked.

"Nothing."

"I think this falls into the whole *whatever happens in the locker room stays in the locker room* thing," Annie told me.

"What do you know about locker rooms?" I asked her.

"It really didn't happen in a locker room," Tony said.

"The term *locker room* in this case is not a defined physical location but more of a concept of togetherness, Tony. Whether whatever happened actually happened *in* a locker room is immaterial."

Tony wavered.

"Trust me on this, Tony," Annie said. "The less you talk about this, the better. It involves law enforcement, and neither one of you want to be involved with law enforcement."

Tony looked at me. "It'll all work out, Lance," he said, in a passable imitation of Jersey, "it will all work out."

"What will all work out?" I asked. "Law enforcement? What's going on here? Are you two conspiring to keep secrets from me?"

Annie looked above the newspaper, her eyes above the top of the page. "Of course we are. We've done it for years. It's for your own good, actually."

Tony gave me a friendly, patronizing, almost sympathetic, pat on the shoulder when he reached past me to grab the gallon of milk. "Let's just say it is in all our best interests if Cody stays away from Manfred."

"What's that supposed to mean?" I asked.

"Lance, have you ever thought about expanding your portfolio?" Annie asked me. She was partially hidden by the newspaper – the business section – but I could see what she was wearing. It was what she'd worn to bed; a baggy Disney long sleeve tee-shirt and what resembled red long underwear bottoms. She looked like some kind of a street waif.

"How much do you weigh?" I asked her.

She lowered the newspaper. "How much do I weigh?" she repeated. "What kind of question is that? You're never supposed to ask a woman how much she weighs." She put the newspaper down. "And by the way, when a young woman asks you if you want to expand your portfolio an improper response is to ask her how much she weighs."

"Do you even weigh a hundred pounds?"

"I am not going to dignify that with a response." She picked up the paper and held it in front of her face. "I think it's time we look at expanding your portfolio."

"I just got a portfolio," I told her. "How come I have to already expand it?"

"You need to diversify," she said. "You own a business, so you have a commercial interest. You own property, a home in Whitehall."

"Yeah, unfortunately it happens to be *this* home," Tony said. In front of him was a salad bowl full of cereal.

"True," admitted Annie. "Eventually you're going to have to invest some money in this place. But for now, like I said, you've got an interest in land, in commercial property, you have a checking account, a savings account, and just recently you've expanded and have a small amount of stocks and a money market account. But you're not making much progress on retirement plans, like a pension or annuity."

"It don't know what an annuity is," I pointed out, "but I do have the Escort." The cold cereal looked pretty good. I grabbed a bowl, a box of Kix, and made myself breakfast.

"You have the Escort?" asked Annie.

"Yeah. It's worth something."

"Do you even know what a portfolio is?" asked Tony.

"A vehicle is a possession, Lance," Annie said.

"Isn't a possession part of a portfolio?" I asked.

"Oh Lance," she said with dramatic remorse.

"Jesus, Lance," Tony said as he ventured into the living room couch.

"Don't *Jesus, Lance* me," I told him. "You wouldn't know a portfolio if one came up and picked your nose."

"Like you would," he answered.

"You're just jealous you don't have your own portfolio," I told him.

"Boys," Annie said. She sighed, and looked at me. "Anyway, I was thinking you've got a decent start, from a financial planning standpoint, but there are a couple investment opportunities you might want to take advantage of."

"Like what?"

"Land, for one," she said. "There's some property available between Bozeman and Belgrade that's actually part of an auction next Saturday. It's farmland now, but everyone knows the land between Bozeman and Belgrade won't be farmland forever, and is going to be far more valuable in the not too distant future than it is now."

I was stunned. "You want me to buy land over in Gallatin County?"

"As an investment," she said, nodding. "You wouldn't have to move there or anything."

I gestured toward the living room. "This place is falling down around our heads and you want me to buy *more* property? I run my ass ragged all day, every day, at the newspaper and can't even touch the work that needs to be done around here."

"You wouldn't even have to set foot on the land," Annie said. "You've wouldn't even have to see it. Just own it."

"Not a chance," I told her. "Not a chance. Leave my portfolio alone, if that's what you want to do."

"We need to do something," she said. "If you enjoy paying taxes, then don't do a thing. Just keep things as they are, and you'll get to pay all the taxes you can stand. You got three months to do something before Uncle Sam whacks you good."

"What do taxes have to do with my portfolio?" I asked.

Annie rolled her eyes.

Laura Joyce and I were swamped with work on Monday. The Jefferson County Commission called and asked to place a four-column legal notice, and with the classified page overflowing it meant we'd have to go twenty-four pages for certain. A half-page ad was faxed in from Bozeman – advertising a farm auction east of Belgrade that included twenty-four acres of land on the south side of I-90 – and Lacy Warren, Brock's mom, came in early afternoon and slowly, repetitively, and tediously, explained there was an important upcoming meeting at the school she and the PTA sincerely wanted to promote with an article I had to first gather the information about and then write. I had hoped to slide by with a twenty-page Ledger this week, and the four additional pages would add about ten hours to my workload. Patty's interview and article ate up another hour, which meant I had an extra eleven hours of work added to a schedule that already included an extra three or four hours because of the Monday night town council meeting.

Rhonda Horst brought in a classified ad for her rental property, and she also dropped off a plate of homemade chocolate chip cookies.

By early Monday night – before the town council meeting started – I'd written all the articles but hadn't even been in the darkroom yet. I had to attend the council meeting and write the article about the meeting, print, dry, wax, cut and place the halftones into the paper, and get a start on twenty-four pages of layout. I stayed at the Ledger a few minutes too long, and by the time I found my notebook, washed my face to help me wake up, ate four chocolate chip cookies for dinner and walked the three blocks to town hall, I was ten minutes late to the meeting. The Pledge had already been recited, the council was discussing approving the agenda – which included resignation from the council by Old Tom Langston – and Daniel Purdy was seated in my chair. He knew he was in my chair – front row, right corner – and if it had been anyone else it wouldn't have bothered me, but it was Daniel Purdy, and the only reason he was seated in that chair was an attempt to prove his prominence over me and the newspaper.

I sat directly behind him in the second row. He wore his lumberyard work shirt and hat, and he smelled like sawdust. Young Tom, reeking of cigarettes, his long stringy hair hanging on his shoulders, was seated next to Daniel Purdy. Only a couple other people were in the room. Gage Duncan, the town man, was seated toward the back of the room. Henry Branch, the guy who'd tried to play peacemaker during the town hall scuffle, was seated in the middle of the front row. Henry was adding on to his house, and probably still needed a building permit.

Outside of them, the room was empty. Perhaps people were fearful of additional fisticuffs. The scrum over the proposed nuisance ordinance had been concluded with only minor lasting repercussions. Lonna Simpson, the elderly woman who had been hauled by ambulance to the emergency room, had been held in the hospital overnight for observation and then released. She had apparently simply fainted, and emerged uninjured when she fell. Lonna and her husband, Miles, had supposedly talked to a Butte attorney about a lawsuit against the town, but Rachel Brockton, the town clerk, had scared off the lawyer. Harley Vance, the surly old man with a long gray beard, had also thought about pressing charges against Sally Logan, a woman who'd laid him low with a precisely placed and vigorously launched knee to his groin. But Rachel had warned him the town may have reason to press charges against Harley for instigating the ruckus, and it was Harley who wisely suggested a truce, in that he would forego a lawsuit if the town would drop any thought of charges.

The true victim of the fracas had been the proposed nuisance ordinance itself, which after the fight was never even discussed again let alone voted on. It simply vanished. And Old Tom could also be considered a victim. His gout pained him, and he was essentially deaf, but the role he and Young Tom had played the night of the scuffle was unfortunate at best and troubling at worst. Old Tom had decided to resign, and while no one ever said so, his resignation was likely Rachel's idea. The scuffle had made statewide news – from an article in the Butte newspaper that was picked up by the Montana Associated Press – and was an embarrassment to Whitehall. That meant it was an embarrassment to Rachel, and that meant changes were necessary. Old Tom's departure was chief in those changes.

The first order of business was Old Tom's resignation.

Mayor Luke Grayling presented Old Tom with a certificate of merit for his service to the community, a small wood key to the city, and thanked him for his contributions to the council and the town. Every departing council member received the certificate, the key, the pat on the back, and their picture for the paper, which I took of Old Tom as he held his key and certificate. It also meant I had to develop an entire role of film for that one picture, and had to do so later that night. Rachel joined in the brief applause for Old Tom.

"It's the damn gout," he complained. He sat down in the front row, in careful stages, awkwardly, painfully.

The mayor consulted his meeting agenda, and asked if there were any nominations to replace Old Tom on the council.

"It's this damn gout," Old Tom repeated. In front of me, Young Tom gestured toward his father, and Old Tom's eyes opened wide. "Oh. I nominate Daniel Purdy."

Shit, I thought. Daniel Purdy? This town can't do better than Daniel Purdy?

"Second," said Old Tom.

"You can't nominate and second, and you're not even an official member of the council," pointed out the mayor.

Old Tom lifted his hand and pointed vaguely. "Then I nominate Young Tom." He gave his son a proud and exaggerated wink.

The mayor pretended to not hear the second nomination.

"I nominate Daniel Purdy," said Brandon Grant. Jimmy Ford followed with a motion to second the nomination.

"Are there any other nominations?" asked the mayor.

I watched Rachel, and she barely lifted her eyes, but she did lift her eyes, and she did look directly at councilmember Hannah Brosovich.

"I nominate Henry Branch," Hannah said.

"Harvey who?" Old Tom called out.

Andy Zankowski seconded the nomination.

"Harvey who?" Old Tom repeated.

"Henry," the mayor answered. "Henry Branch."

Old Tom looked directly at Daniel Purdy. "Never heard of the guy."

Henry Branch shyly stood up. He cleared his throat. He looked briefly at Rachel, then spoke toward the mayor. "My name is Henry Branch. I'm a contractor, carpentry mostly, and have lived here about three years now. My wife's a cook up at the school. We got three kids, one in junior high and two in elementary school. I've never been on anything like a town council before, but Miss Brockton told me about the vacancy and thought I could help maybe."

"Thank you, Mr. Branch," said the mayor. He nodded Daniel Purdy's direction. "Dan, you want to say anything?"

Dan Purdy stayed seated. “You all know me. I own the lumberyard. I’m on the school board. I’ve lived here all my life.” For a moment it looked as if he intended to say more, but didn’t.

“I vote for Dan,” Old Tom announced, his hand in the air.

“Okay, let’s vote,” the mayor said.

The first vote was for Daniel Purdy. He got two votes. The second vote was for Henry Branch. He got five votes.

Daniel Purdy abruptly stood and more or less stormed out of the room. Rachel’s mouth betrayed a muted sense of mirth as she watched him leave. Then she handed the mayor the oath of allegiance, and he had Henry Branch stand and raise his right hand. I stood to take a picture of Henry Branch as he was sworn in – a second new picture to print in the darkroom – and then I sat down in my chair, in the right corner of the front row, that had been vacated by Daniel Purdy.

It was sobering, though, to watch skinny Old Tom slowly, tenderly, rise on his unsteady legs and aching feet. Young Tom waited for Old Tom at the aisle, and together they shuffled along the wall and out of the town hall.

It was after eleven o’clock before I had the film developed and pictures printed, and I finally got out of the darkroom for the week. Old Tom and Henry would both be featured on the front page of the Ledger: the outgoing and incoming councilmember. I still had a minimum of three hours of work still to do.

I grabbed another cookie, and noticed a small crumbly half moon around an edge was gone. I took a bite from the cookie and called home – at eleven-ten on a Monday night, a school night – and whoever answered the phone had to shout to be heard above the Bruce Springsteen music blaring in the background.

“Who’s this?” I requested.

“Who’s this?” the young male voice repeated.

“This is Lance Joslyn, the owner of the house you’re standing in.” I said it with as much authority and conviction and intimidation as I could muster.

“Oh, hi, Lance,” the boy said. Then I barely picked up his voice saying, “it’s your dad.”

“Lance?” It was Annie’s voice.

I had expected Tony’s voice. It was eleven-thirty on Monday, a school night, and a boy had just given Annie the phone. “Annie,” I demanded, “what-”

“Hang on, Lance,” she interrupted. I could hear the distinctive clank of the phone placed on the countertop, and then in the background the Springsteen music diminished in volume. There was another pause, and the phone was lifted off the countertop. “Lance?” Annie asked.

“What’s going on, Annie?”

"There, that's better," she said.

"What's going on?" I yelled. "Who answered the phone?"

"Cody."

"Cody? Cody who?"

"Phillips."

"Cody Phillips is over at our house?" For a lot of reasons, that sounded terribly dangerous and frightening. "What...why..."

"There are a few guys over," Annie said. "They were watching Monday Night Football, but it looks like it's over now. Some of them are rehearsing the play, I think, and I'm helping Cody with his homework."

"Play? What play? Do I need to come home? Goddamnit, Annie, I'm way behind this week and don't have time for this."

"Lance," she said in her authoritative tone of voice, and I could picture her expression; slightly humored, a twinge of a smile, eyes sympathetic and understanding, her unwrinkled forehead pensive, on the verge of a patient and meditative insightful lecture to an audience of one who really should know better. "Take it easy. Honestly. Cody's over, along with Chance," and I can tell she was looking over the crowd at our house, "Dave, Cale and Morgan. The twins were here, but they're gone."

"The twins? Jesus," I said. "Why is Cody there?"

"I'm helping him with some schoolwork," Annie said.

"Did anyone break anything?"

She paused. "Not so you'd notice. Lance, everything's fine. The boys stuffed their faces with pizza, watched football on TV and played Springsteen on the stereo. Cody and I are going over some of his history and English assignments, and Tony and Morgan are going over some of their lines from the play. Everything's fine. Nothing's wrong. You can come home if you want and eat some leftover pizza, but there's no corrective actions you need to take."

Corrective actions? I thought. Is that what normal parents do? Take corrective actions? If that was the case, my guess was Annie had probably accomplished that. There were probably pizza boxes laying all over the kitchen and the living room, and I had no time to deal with a mess at home. "What play?" I asked.

"I told you. The school play," Annie told me.

What school play? "Put Tony on the phone."

"Okay, he's right here." I heard a muffled *Tony* and could hear the telephone change hands.

"Want us to save some pizza for you?" Tony asked.

"Who's over there?" I asked sternly.

"Annie already told you," he said. "Cody. Morgan and Cale. Dave. Chance. Although it looks like Dave's heading out."

"Hell, Tony, that's a gang. What's a gang doing over at our house?"

"Annie told you that, too," he said. "We're not doing anything. We watched the Broncos on TV. Cranked up some Bruce, and now we're working on some of our play lines."

"What goddamn play!"

"The school play," he answered defensively.

"You're in the school play?" I asked.

"Yeah. Where do you think I've been every night for the past two weeks?"

I didn't have an answer to that. I tried to remember if he or Annie or anyone had ever told me he was in the school play. Then I tried to remember if I had any idea if I'd even noticed where he'd been the past two weeks. The remembering wasn't working. I wasn't coming up with anything. I vaguely knew about the school play – the high school did two each year, one in the fall and one in the spring – and Tony had never been in school plays before.

"You still there?" Tony asked.

"Yeah," I said. "What's the play?"

"*The Wind in the Willows*," he said. "It's a goofy play about…it's just a goofy play."

"Why would you want to be in goofy play?"

"I just thought I should be in a play, to you know, broaden my horizons," he said.

That didn't sound right at all. "Who else is in the play?"

"Morgan is." He hesitated.

"Wait a minute," I said. "Don't tell me. Aspen's in the play."

"What's that got to do with anything?"

"Nothing, I'm sure," I said. "So Aspen's in the play. What's her role?"

"She helps Mr. Toad escape from prison."

"Oh, I bet she does." I had work to do. I had to put Annie in charge. "Okay, go ahead and get back to rehearsal for a few minutes, but everyone is out at eleven-thirty. Eleven-thirty sharp. Hey, what's your character's name?"

"I play the god Pan. I only have one scene. Cale plays Ratty, one of the leads."

"Ratty? Jesus, what's this play about?"

"I have no idea," he answered, and I could tell he meant it. "There's a bunch of strange costumes and characters like Mr. Toad, Mole, Mr. Badger and Weasels."

"I want everyone out of there in fifteen minutes," I said. "Got it? Fifteen minutes. I mean it. It's a school night and kids are supposed to be home already. And you pick up the house and haul all the trash outside to the garbage. I mean that too. All of it. If the house is a mess when I get home I'm waking you up and you're cleaning it up. Put your sister on the phone."

She must have known the request was coming and had been standing next to him; she was on the phone in a heartbeat.

"It's a fun play really," she assured me. "And Tony is a very convincing Pan."

"I'm sure he is," I said. "You and Cody Phillips are doing homework?"

"Yep," she said. "He has to write an English paper, and I'm helping him with it. He's writing an essay about riding a rodeo bull. And he has a quiz in history tomorrow on the Great Depression."

Cody Phillips, at my house, with my daughter, approaching midnight. "Annie, you know about Cody."

"Not now, Lance," she told me.

"Finish up in ten minutes and get him out of there," I said. "That's an order. He's not supposed to be out this late, and you're not supposed to be hanging around with kids like that. Are we clear on this?"

"Kids like what?" she asked coldly.

"Don't start with me," I told her.

"We're almost done."

"Ten minutes, Annie. I'm calling Ed Franklin right now and telling him Cody will be home in ten minutes, and if he's not, to come over to our house and drag his ass out the front door."

"Don't bother. We're almost done. He'll be on his way home in five minutes."

"I'm trusting you on this, Annie."

"Lance, you trust me on everything, which is why the tone of this call is so offensive." And she hung up.

Midnight, Monday night. We had a back room at the Ledger where we stored clip art books and surplus copies of past editions, and we also had a small refrigerator with a permanently iced over frozen section. The fridge had been Amy's idea, and I think she'd picked it up for five bucks at a Whitehall garage sale. Laura Joyce kept Tupperware containers of food in it, and every now and then I'd find yogurt or cottage cheese or something as she fought a losing battle to stop gaining weight. I usually had a stash of pop stored in the fridge. I didn't drink coffee; I depended on the caffeine of Coke or Pepsi to keep my eyes propped open during late nights at the Ledger.

Some afternoons my body and head begged for a nap, and if a nap wasn't possible, a couple cans of Pepsi or Coke was the next best thing. It was probably in my imagination, but it was also my experience that a can of pop could also help ease a headache.

I had a headache on this late Monday night, I was bone weary, and I figured I'd earned a can of Coke. Cody Phillips, the definition of a young hellion, was at my house with my daughter. How do things like that happen?

I drank half the can of pop as I walked the short distance from the refrigerator to the layout bank, which was essentially a work area with a plywood backboard that slanted away from me as I stood. The work area held two two-page sections – four pages in all – and the remaining pages stood on the floor, braced by a waist-high wood cabinet behind me. When I laid out the paper, I would typically work on four pages at a time, which were right in front of me. Behind me, as I worked, were the other twenty pages. To my left and right on the layout bank were the pieces of puzzle that would fill the paper – photos and stories were to my left, ads were to the right. The stories were all typeset, in sharp, justified rows. Everything had to be cut, waxed and affixed to the pages. Everything had to be perfectly straight. Each ad might have a dozen or more different parts – clip art, perhaps a photo, different sizes and types of fonts – and each part had to be exactly straight on the page. Each headline, each photo cutline, each separate portion of the story, which we called 'type,' had to be perfectly straight. I stood looking at the layout bank and then turned to look at the pages propped up on the floor behind me. Twenty-four blank pages. I drank the rest of the Coke.

I knew what exhaustion felt like. It was obvious when the fatigue became too much. When I was tired – too tired – I saw things, usually out of the corner of my eye. When I was at the Ledger, late at night, either typing an article, laying out the paper or working in the darkroom, if I saw a fleeting tiny object out of the corner of my eye, and upon closer examination there was nothing fleeting, I knew it was time to quit. I always figured being so tired you saw things should be avoided.

Midnight wasn't really late. Not unhealthy late. I never saw imaginary things at midnight. I'd get home about two o'clock, get up at seven o'clock; five hours sleep, not quite enough, but close. I turned on the radio to a Bozeman oldies station and opened another can of Coke. I re-waxed and placed all the section headings – front page masthead, classified page, sports, opinion, community, farm and ranch – placed them on a blank page, and then placed some of the regular weekly columns in their regular weekly column spot. Next, I waxed and cut all the photos, and put them on the appropriate pages. Then I started to place ads, with the most important ads on the outside of the odd-numbered pages. By two-thirty in the morning I more or less had the foundation of the Ledger laid out. Mistakes occurred far more frequently after midnight. Fatigue truly contributed to errors. I had learned that the hard way. I also had three pages completely laid out.

Not a bad start. I had a decent shot of being done before midnight Tuesday night, which wasn't 'late' by Ledger Tuesday night standards.

I was the only car on the road for the six blocks to our house. The kitchen light was on – Annie's habit was to leave a light on over the sink for me – and the floor creaked as I entered. The kitchen was clean – or as clean as it ever was – and as I looked around it was hard to tell the place had been full of teenagers a few hours earlier. A couple Springsteen record covers – *Born in the USA* and *The River* – were propped up on the floor and leaning against the stereo, much like the pages of the Ledger were on the floor and leaning against a cabinet. The stereo was off. I took a couple pieces of pizza from the fridge, put them on top of each other, and ate them cold standing in the kitchen. I took off my shoes, pants and shirt in the bedroom, laid down, looked at the lighted dial on my clock – it was two-forty-one – and looked up at the black ceiling above me. I doubt my eyes were still open at two-forty-five.

Tuesday night ended just before eleven, and as I proofed the final pages for a final time – with Springsteen singing about a *Cadillac Ranch* on a cassette in the mini boom box – I spotted something small and dark scurrying across the floor. It seemed to scamper at the edge of my peripheral vision, but when I turned my neck for a better look I saw nothing. I shook my head. I needed to finish up and get home.

The high school drama club had written a small article promoting the upcoming play, *The Wind in the Willows*, Laura Joyce had typed it up without me knowing it until page paste-up. I put the article on page three, the second best page for news, behind the front page. The front page was spoken for this week – with pictures of an expressionless Old Tom and a somewhat somber Henry Branch, along with articles about the upcoming PTA meeting and an article about a grant received by the Whitehall Volunteer Fire Department. I always tried to get three articles on the front page.

I was awake Wednesday morning at six o'clock. The house was cold, dark and creaky as I snuck out of my bedroom, into the kitchen for a breakfast of Pop Tarts and milk, and out the door that didn't quite close right, which was one reason why the house was so cold on a late September morning.

I was weary, but not sleepy, as I guided the Escort west over Homestake Pass, through a foggy early morning in Butte, down the hill to Rocker, past tiny Ramsay, just south of Fairmont Hot Springs Resort and into frumpy Anaconda. Years earlier, Butte and Anaconda had been hustling mining towns filled with black and toxic air and polluted swirling water. It was a place where life was hard and people died young. As a façade to draw workers to the area the mining barons even had the audacity to bestow upon a town between Butte and Anaconda the name of Opportunity, as if this really was a place for opportunity, riches and independence. Which was attractive, if you were an impoverished and gullible Polish or Russian or Italian immigrant who didn't know any better.

I showed up at the back door of the Anaconda Leader at seventy-thirty sharp. Larry, a short man with hair black and greased as Elvis, was never more than three minutes between cigarettes. Among his jobs on Wednesday morning was to get the chemicals poured and heated in the processor which converted a solid black sheet of thin shiny negative film into a reverse image of the pasted-up Ledger page. He didn't say much most mornings, and when I walked in he only nodded. I set the box of twelve two-page paste-up sheets on the counter by the darkroom, and went back to the pressroom to sort and restack the collected grocery store and drug store inserts. We usually had four inserts each week, and those four inserts provided enough income to mail the paper, to fund the Ledger travel expenses and just about paid enough to take care of our monthly rent bill. The classified page income paid the printing costs of the Ledger, the subscription income paid for Laura Joyce's salary, and it was the display advertising income that, I guessed, generated the money for Annie to invest in my portfolio.

Dan showed up next. He was more or less the press manager and was nearly as wide as he was tall. His passion was fishing. He was always telling me he was coming over to Whitehall to fish the Jefferson and Boulder rivers, and was always disappointed when I told him I never had time to fish.

"How's Lance?" he asked when he saw me. He had asked me that exact same question every Wednesday morning since the first Wednesday morning I showed up in Anaconda eight years earlier.

"I'm good," I said each Wednesday. "How's Dan?

"Just right," he said each time as he walked past me into the newsroom, in the front of the building.

Bryce arrived next. He wore the same clothes every Wednesday except for one minor exception. In the spring, summer and fall he wore black jeans, a short sleeve shirt and a down vest; in winter he wore black jeans, a long sleeve shirt and a down vest. He was a press assistant, and had a quick laugh and a quick temper, and I'd made him so mad in the past that it was a rule if I had a complaint about the printing quality I was supposed to register that complaint with Larry or Dan, so they could ignore it.

The last one to show up was Mike. Mike had an obvious drinking problem. Some Wednesdays he showed up a pasty white color that you'd swear you could scrape off his skin. He wore thick glasses, had serious dental needs, looked like he had just rolled out of the backseat of a car and gave you the impression no matter how much you felt sorry for him you could never feel as sorry for him as he felt sorry for himself.

The three of them – Larry really didn't do much in the pressroom – got the paper plated by ten o'clock and fully on the press thirty minutes later. All Larry did after that was bunch and gather the papers as they rolled off the press. Whenever Dan got the press running a loud bell sounded – a warning to stand clear and be wary of rolling press banks – and the bell always sounded to me like a call to action, like the bell that starts the rounds of a fight. There is something purely magic about watching, smelling and hearing a Goss press produce hundreds of papers per minute. Wednesday mornings I was typically exhausted, but when that bell rang and the press got rolling I was instantly exhilarated.

Printing was still a weekly challenge. The paper eased through the press painfully slow as Dan and Bryce twisted knobs and dials to get the right ink density throughout the twenty-four pages of the paper. They were always too eager, I thought, to start counting 'good' copies of the paper, and usually the first hundred or so papers off the press were not as high of quality as they should be. Bryce always argued that on a press run of fifteen hundred like the Ledger it could take the profit margin of the print job to get the right ink density; in other words, just when they got it right, the press run was over.

If I had other options to go to print the paper, I would have considered them. The next best option was Livingston, twice as far away, twenty percent more expensive and I would have lost one if not two inserts with the change. I was stuck with Anaconda and Anaconda was stuck with me.

When the press run was over, I stood near the gathering table at the folder and paged through the Ledger page by page.

"What's wrong now?" Dan demanded.

Mike sauntered over to us, and Bryce stepped in behind me.

I shrugged. I held the paper open to pages seven and eight, where in the middle third of the pages the ink was just a shade lighter – just a shade – than the ink above and below it on the same page.

"Do you guys know what the difference is between average and excellence?" I asked them. They simply looked at me. I held my right forefinger and thumb an eighth of an inch apart. "This much," I told them. "This much is all that separates average and excellence. The keys to excellence are preparation, determination and execution."

I paused and looked at them. Bryce walked away to smoke a cigarette. Mike looked pained and embarrassed. Dan looked like he wanted to punch me, which he might have done had I kept talking.

Chapter 20

"Do you believe in God?"

The question came from Annie as the two of us were headed east out of Whitehall to watch the Rangers take on the Townsend Bulldogs. It had the potential to be a good game; the Rangers were winless in four games, and although Townsend had won twice they had lost to Cascade by two touchdowns.

Annie's questions were growing more and more profound, more and more challenging, and from my standpoint, more and more uncomfortable and unanswerable. It wasn't that I deliberately wanted to avoid answering them or wanted to deny her the opportunity to ask them as much as I wished she would ask them of someone else.

"Do you?" I asked in response. We had never been what you'd call churchgoers, even during the brief years when we'd been a functional family. In Whitehall, it seemed I either needed to sleep or work on Sunday mornings, and the idea of getting up, getting the kids presentable and getting somewhere on time not only felt daunting but most Sundays insurmountable.

"You don't, do you?" Annie said.

"I'm not sure I'd say that," I said. "I think there might be a higher being, a spiritual presence on earth."

"Might be? That sounds vaguely agnostic," she said.

"If you say so."

She arched her eyebrows, as if in warning. "You have more of a humanistic approach to religion, and I'm not sure that will get you to heaven."

"I'm not sure it will, either," I admitted. I wasn't certain I could define what a 'humanistic approach to religion' meant, but I was sure I didn't want to ask. "I'll say this. I never want to speak the words *there is no God*, because I think maybe there is and if He hears me saying He doesn't exist I'm afraid He'll do something to make sure I know he does exist. Or maybe get pissed and punish me."

"Like making you own a weekly newspaper?" Annie joked. At least I thought she was joking.

"Or worse," I said. "At times I think, How can there not be a God? How can someone look at a rainbow and not see God? But then I see preachers on TV looking like Las Vegas pimps shilling for money or am reminded about some of the Old Testament stories about David and dreams in Egypt or Joshua and his trumpet and I think it all sounds a little corny."

"Lance," Annie said, with a lilt of surprise in her voice, "you've been thinking about this, haven't you?"

"Not really," I said. "But something tells me you have."

She was silent for over a minute. We had just about concluded the trip east on I-90 and weren't far from the lonely Town Pump at the Highway 287 interchange. We were within a mile of exiting the freeway; then we would head north for about thirty miles to Townsend.

"Do you worry about going to hell?" she asked.

"Right now I'm worried about going to Townsend," I answered.

"What do you think hell is like?" she asked.

"For a weekly newspaper publisher, I imagine in hell every day is Monday," I said. We turned and drove north on the two-lane highway. The sky toward the east was black as pavement. To the west the sky was a dull lifeless gray.

"What do you think hell is like?" I asked.

She sighed. "I think maybe your response wasn't all that far off. Perhaps hell is our own worst fear. Or our own personal repulsion." She looked at me. "But I don't know. I want to think all this – this world, this life, this existence for all of us – is here by design and not just some kind of a cosmic or biological accident. But then I think, Where is hell, if there is one? Where's heaven? Is heaven only for Christians, or can people who have faith in other supreme deities get in?"

"I went to church some as a kid, and I could never figure out if God, Jesus and the Holy Ghost were all one part of God, or three parts of God, or three Gods, or what," I said. "If God sent his only son, Jesus, to earth, then who is the Holy Ghost? Is he God's brother, Jesus' uncle? And if you've got God and Jesus, what's the Holy Ghost actually do? And why is he even called the Holy Ghost? It's actually kind of a cool name, if you think about it."

"How did God get there?" Annie asked. "If God created the earth, who created God?"

"I have some questions about Satan," I said. "Was he really once a good angel who went bad? How could he go bad before Satan was there to actually tempt him? I mean, how does bad pre-date Satan?"

"Well," Annie pointed out, "part of being a Christian and believing in God is having faith. You're supposed to have faith, and it's the faith that gets you into heaven."

A little later we crossed the Missouri River, not far north of where the three forks – the Jefferson, the Madison and the Gallatin rivers – merged to create a great river that flowed through Montana then eastward all the way to the Mississippi. It was interesting to realize Lewis and Clark had traveled exactly under us on their way west to the Pacific.

"I'm trying to have faith," Annie said. "I want to have faith. But I'm not sure. How can you have faith when you see Trish, or," she hesitated, "Mom. Why have faith in a God that does that to people."

Annie desperately wanted to believe she was the way she was – a genius – for a purpose, and not from some random or accidental sequence of genetic code. She also wanted to believe physical or psychological tragedies that destroyed lives did so for some explainable and meaningful purpose. That at some point, in some fashion, everything would be corrected, justified and appropriate. She had earlier once ventured in the direction of wondering if her mother's condition was hereditary, and left unsaid the obvious implications. At some point in her life, she was going to have to come to grips with all that, and she was going to have to do it on her own. I was certainly going to be of no help.

"I have faith in you," I told her. "I know you'll figure all this out so it makes sense."

It must have been Townsend's Homecoming. The Rangers, with their dismal recent won-loss records, were a perfect Homecoming opponent because of the simple fact that schools liked to win their Homecoming game. We turned the corner by the gas station and saw all the storefronts were decorated with blue and white – Townsend school colors – banners, drawings, and slogans like *Shoot Down the Rangers*! with a drawing of a muscular bulldog wearing a football helmet holding a six-shooter as a purple and gold Ranger lay prone on the ground. We spotted the stadium lights and found a place to park a couple blocks away.

It was definitely Homecoming. The parade floats were lined up on the track near the bleachers, and a couple queen or princess candidates – all long dresses, eye makeup and awkward smiles – were standing in a nervous group near the concession stand.

It was decidedly less festive on the Whitehall side of the field. The Rangers were finishing their pre-game warm-ups near the south end zone. I spotted Trisha in her wheelchair on the south corner of the visitor's bleachers. Molly waved as I scouted the bleachers, and I waved back. Trisha and I exchanged waves, and Annie left my side to go sit by Trish and some other junior high and high school girls.

Ed and Alice Franklin were seated with a blanket across their laps. It was chilly, and the temperature would drop as the night wore on, but kids were running around in tee-shirts, and a lap blanket seemed a bit much. But Ed and Alice weren't true football fans, and were only at a road game to keep an eye on their boarder, Cody Phillips. Slack, with a parent on either side, was on the same bleacher bench as Ed and Alice, a few feet away. Sue and Slack waved, and I waved back. Mary Kristofferson sat with a small group of parents, with Lyle and the stylish O'Toole ladies behind her and the Harrisons stoically in front of her. There were fewer Whitehall fans at this game than at the Boulder game a week earlier, and it wasn't hard to guess why. As losses added up, attendance tended to go down.

The public address speaker made some Homecoming announcements that drew large cheers from the filled Townsend bleachers. With much pomp and strutting the Townsend cheerleaders marched the American and Montana flags to midfield, and the Townsend High School band launched a respectful rendition of the National Anthem. It was hard to explain, but I felt, sensed somehow, the confidence aimed at us from the Townsend side of the field. It was invisible but as palpable as smoke or wind. The Townsend players, coaches, parents, fans and even the cheerleaders – the entire mass of blue fifty yards away – exuded a strained but assured confidence.

I looked at the Ranger players, lined up in two groups – one on the sidelines and one on the twenty yard line – standing stoic and silent and still, eyes locked on the flag. It took Coach Pete all he had to hold himself motionless. You could see him concentrating, forcing himself to *not move.* The only movement among the thirty or so kids still in a Whitehall football uniform was the little towel Colt Harrison wore tucked into the front of his pants, which waved faintly like a tiny flag. The kids were impressive lined up at attention, demonstrating reverence to the song, the flag, the concept of a team and the honor of competition. Too bad they played too often like a disorganized band of misfits and couldn't even execute the exchange between quarterback and center.

I studied the Whitehall kids, and watched them with a personal knowledge that for many of them started back when they were in elementary school. Each Whitehall class had forty or fifty kids in it, and over the years I grew to know most by either name or face.

Colt Harrison, who looked like a Ken doll version of a high school quarterback. Tall, sleek, sideburns, groomed dark hair, white wristbands, high white socks and neatly tucked-in jersey. Colt was generally thought of as the best athlete in the school, and certainly he and his parents thought of him as the best athlete in the school. His performances almost – almost – met those expectations, but no one viewed him as a leader. Colt cared a great deal about Colt, and it was hard to tell what else he cared about. He played quarterback on offense and safety on defense.

Morgan Miteward, called Mite because of his short stature. He resembled a bearded gnome. Jersey, I'd noticed, changed Mite to Mighty, and Tony and the guys lately had been calling him The Mighty One. Only his teachers and Annie called him Morgan. Even his parents and siblings called him Mite. His legs were incredibly short and stocky, but he was barrel chested and sturdy and strong. He had something of a complexion problem, and the sweat from exertion and the padding of a football helmet converted his forehead into a mini mountain range of pimples. The beard did a decent job of hiding imperfections elsewhere on his face. He wasn't much of a student, apparently, and had academic eligibility problems throughout fall during football and winter during wrestling. His father worked at Golden Sunlight Mine and his mother was a waitress at the Town Pump. I talked to his mom a couple times when she came to the Ledger to place classified ads for spring garage sales, and it wasn't hard to see why The Mighty One struggled in school. He played guard on offense and linebacker on defense.

Tanner Walker, a gifted musician and singer who walked loosely, on his tiptoes, as if he had someplace he had to get to in a hurry. He had short hair with a cowlick in the middle, as if the circle of twisted hair above his forehead had been spun there recently and deliberately. He was a rare type of ranch kid who didn't look or act like a ranch kid. He wore sneakers, not boots. I'd never seen him in a cowboy hat and he wore untucked lumberjack shirts, not western shirts, and I'd even seem him wearing a reggae tie-dyed shirt emblazed with a psychedelic Bob Marley. He played guard and linebacker.

Brock Warren, an exuberant kid who enjoyed attention. He was loose and loud, and his mom told me once she and her husband had planned to have four kids until Brock had been the second child born, and within six months of his existence they decided they would have no more kids just in case they had another one like him. He was the kind of kid who if told not to do something, immediately did it. He wasn't a malicious kid, just hyper. He sometimes played running back and sometimes wide receiver, and on defense he played in the secondary.

JeffScott Collins, identical twins who had deep, manly voices and stout mustaches since junior high. They were impossible to tell apart, and according to their father had some sort of telepathic powers. Once, when Jeff was in elementary school and at the dinner table eating with his parents and siblings, he suddenly stood and said with absolute certainty that Scott had hurt his leg. Asked to sit down, Jeff bolted away from the table, out of the house, and ran down the street. Five minutes later he returned with Scott, who'd sustained a nasty and bloody gash on his leg after he'd fallen off his bike. The father told me other tales of the twins' *radar*, he called it, and I was tempted to write an article about it, but the twins were isolated enough because of their twinness and I didn't want them to seem any more strange than they already appeared. They rarely spoke, in school or out, were almost never outside of each other's sight, and because of their closeness didn't really have any other friends. They played on the offensive and defensive lines.

Logan Bradshaw, a burly, brooding brute of a kid who smelled of cigarette smoke – both his parents smoked – and likely so did he. He lived in the equestrian ghetto – 20-acre lots south of town with a dilapidated trailer home perched on hardscrabble ground with three morose and near-starving horses pawing the parched dirt for nourishment – and drove a rusted pickup truck that looked worse than the horses. His mom was overweight, chewed gum constantly and wore an unfortunate selection of paisley colored stretch pants that could not possibly have made the fashion statement she either thought they did or hoped they did. Logan's dad was a mechanic at the mine whose hands were dry, calloused, scarred and grease-stained for life. It was possible Logan's practice uniform, tee-shirt under his shoulder pads or any other attire he wore in connection to football never saw a washing machine all season. But when he had the football tucked in his arm he ran straight and hard and never seemed to be hurt, sore or tired. He played running back and strong safety.

Cale Bolling, a runner on the track team and forward on the basketball team who appeared to play football simply to get in shape for the other two sports. Cale was a ranch kid from south of town who had a gentle, even sweet, disposition, and who was probably the smartest kid in his class. Accomplishment and success came easily and naturally to him. He had a sister who graduated as a WHS class valedictorian and had been on the Honor Roll at Carroll College each semester, a tribute which had been proclaimed at every opportunity by the Ledger. Cale's mom was a nurse at St. James in

Butte and his dad raised purebred bulls that were advertised in state and regional stock magazines. Cale played running back and cornerback.

Nate Bolton, the fastest kid on the WHS football team and one of the fastest kids in the conference. He was so fast he looked fast just standing still. He was built for speed, with long strong legs and a graceful balance that allowed him to glide across a football field, down a basketball court and around a track. He had long blond hair that flowed behind him when he ran, and even his hair looked fast. His dad, Bradley, was a manager at the mine. Bradley was taller than Nate and he was one of Whitehall's only morning joggers. I'd see him from time to time running down First Street, which ran the entire east-west length of town, and I'd seen his name among the finishers in 10K races or distance races in places like Butte, Bozeman and Three Forks. Nate played running back. Since he wasn't terribly fond of contact, he didn't play on defense.

Dave Dickson was a two-hundred pound football player in a one-hundred thirty-pound body. He was the little kid on the sideline yelling at opposing players, harassing the referees and shouting encouragement to his teammates. He was a tough kid from a broken home; his father had long been suspected of beating Dave's mother and it was Dave himself, a tiny junior high kid, who took a piece of firewood and whacked his dad on the back during an attack of his mother. Dave and his mom, a shy and slender woman, lived in a large brick home near the high school. Dave's mom, Sara, worked as a clerk at the hardware store, and was always friendly when I'd go in to sell an ad. She was at every football game and wrestling match Dave participated in; he was a good 112-pound wrestler on the WHS team and had won some junior high wrestling titles. When he was a Little Guy wrestler, years earlier, I took some pictures of him and asked him his name and weight, and then asked him his record. He'd told me he was *undefeatedable*. Dave played on special teams and was the backup quarterback and a reserve in the secondary.

There were other players in and out of the lineup and in and out of the game, but these kids – along with Tony and Cody Philips – were the core of the team, and these kids were the ones who would – in words or actions – lead the Rangers to either victory or defeat.

After the National Anthem, the Ranger players broke from their rigid alignment, yelped and gathered around a frenetic Coach Pete while Jersey and Colt calmly discussed strategy near the bench.

"Get it up, get it up, get it up! Let's go. Get. It. Up!" Coach Pete yelled.

The players responded with cheers and shouts. They slapped each other on the side of the helmet and banged shoulder pads. Dave Dickson walked up to each player, held his hands waist high in front of himself, and each player slapped his hands. Cody Phillips head-butted the members of the defensive line, one by one. The only calm ones along the Ranger bench were Jersey and Colt, who stood side by side and could have been discussing gardening.

"Hey blue boy," Dave Dickson heckled a Townsend player who lined up on our side of the field for the kickoff, "You gonna be black and blue by the time this puppy's over."

There was a heightened sense of tension, of competition, at kickoff. This was a conference game, it was a Homecoming game, it was a game either team could win, and there was a mass of blue-clad fans in the bleachers and along the fence to cheer the Bulldogs to victory.

Which seemed pretty certain at halftime. The Rangers and Bulldogs, according to my unofficial sideline statistics, each had a little less than one hundred and fifty yards of offense, but Townsend had scored three touchdowns and were up 21-0. They'd scored on third down and long on a halfback option pass that shouldn't have been a surprise call, shouldn't have produced a wide open flanker and shouldn't have been the game's first score. Later in the first quarter Townsend blocked a punt and scored four plays later. They scored again early in the second quarter after a Ranger turnover – Colt fumbled when he was sacked from behind – and then just before the half Townsend had stopped the Rangers down by the goal line after an impressive Whitehall drive that produced – again – no points.

Thanks to all the Homecoming ceremonies it was an agonizingly long halftime. I would have sworn every kid enrolled in the Townsend high school was introduced during the ceremonies and made a ridiculously long stroll along the sidelines – with flashbulbs of parents' cameras popping all the while – in front of the bleachers. I stayed on the sidelines the entire halftime. I avoided an obviously frustrated Whitehall bleacher section – an audible groan filled the air after Colt's sack and fumble and after the Rangers had been stopped at the goal line before the half – and sat on the WHS bench working on stats to look occupied and diligent.

The halftime ceremony was so long the WHS players emerged from the locker room early and walked around the sidelines more or less killing time until the second half kickoff. It was eerie, to be among a football team, during a game, whose players seemingly had nothing to do.

Just to kill some time I walked over to Coach Pete – who despite the chill wore a purple Ranger tee-shirt and shorts – and asked him why Whitehall had such a hard time getting in the end zone.

"We got to stop fiddle-dicking around and block someone," he said tersely.

Twenty feet away up the sidelines, Jersey looked over at us and scowled.

Pete looked down, more or less at my feet. "Jesus H. Christ, how'd he hear that?" he said softly. "He doesn't like that word. Man, I got to stop cussing. Last week I cussed and he said something like, *There are two hundred thousand words in the English language, do you have to use that one?* I was tempted to ask him which word bothered him, fiddle or dicking, but I had a hunch he wouldn't find that amusing."

"Yeah, I got a hunch you're right about that," I said.

The Rangers were milling around, inactive and aimless, but I saw a grim determination in their eyes. I spotted Tony, and he looked belligerent, which was not like him. It was as if he refused to acknowledge me. It was Dave Dickson, a freshman backup, who told the players to get into six lines for warm-up drills, and amazingly, all the players did as ordered. They ran in place, did a couple somersaults, some jumping jacks, some trunk twisters and some leg stretches, and by the time the Townsend halfback and a shivering girl in a thin baby blue dress were crowned Homecoming king and queen and had posed for pictures, the Rangers had completed a lengthy series of warm-ups, had run some pass patterns and even some light contact tackling drills. It was possibly the longest halftime in the history of football. When it was over – or because of the lopsided score at the half – the Townsend side of the bleachers was depleted.

They missed a memorable second half.

Townsend got the ball to open the third quarter and drove to the Ranger nine yard line, where the drive bogged down and on fourth down and five yards a Bulldog player dropped a sure touchdown pass. On its first offensive play of the second half, the Rangers were flagged for an illegal procedure penalty.

Colt dropped back to pass on the next play and as he looked to his right a Bulldog defensive lineman smashed into him from the back. The ball went one way and Colt went the other, with the Bulldog player on top of him. It was as if the Townsend defender had tried to plant Colt in the ground. Cody fell on the ball in the end zone for a safety – two points – and Townsend was up 23-0. Worse, Whitehall had to kick off to Townsend.

And much worse, Colt wasn't moving. He was face down on the grass; his head wasn't twisted to the left or right. He was actually and perfectly face down, his facemask flat on the grass. Jersey and the Bulldog trainer converged on Colt from opposite sides of the field, and it was eerily quiet as both were on their knees alongside him. After a few moments Colt was rolled so he was on his back, helmet slipped off, face toward the sky, but that was as far as he got. The Bulldog trainer signaled the ambulance – parked at the opposite end of the field behind the concession stand – and the ambulance circled outside the field on the track and approached Colt from outside the end zone. A stretcher emerged from the back, and the trainer and two ambulance attendants carefully hoisted Colt up on the stretcher, and slowly carried him to the back of the ambulance. Jersey stood there in the end zone, holding Colt's helmet, and fans from both sides of the field applauded as Colt was lifted into the ambulance. He waved weakly once, and his parents had come out of the stands, treading careful and reverent toward the end zone. I saw Colt turn to look at them, and his mother held his hand a moment while the ambulance attendant and Hank spoke. It was so quiet I heard the ambulance attendant say the word *shoulder*, and I heard the ambulance door squeak and then slam shut. Hank and Kathleen more or less leaned against each other as the ambulance – with lights flashing but no siren – pulled off the field, off the track, onto a side street and then disappeared. Hank led his wife as they walked toward the bleachers, then veered away, and went behind a school building to the main parking lot.

The Whitehall side of the field was demoralized. You could see it, hear it, feel it. Except for Dave Dickson's chattering, it was a silent and sullen sideline. The game resumed with Whitehall kicking to Townsend. The injury and sight of an ambulance had pulled the emotion and energy out of the players, and on their second play from scrimmage the Townsend quarterback and fullback bumped into each other in the backfield. The ball popped out of the quarterback's hands and Tanner recovered the fumble.

It was Whitehall's ball, and for the first time in nearly four full seasons someone other than Colt Harrison was at quarterback for the Rangers. There was so much confusion on the Whitehall sidelines – a player ran onto the field after the Rangers broke the huddle the same time a different player was running off the field – that Jersey called a timeout and motioned the players over toward the sideline.

Dave Dickson, who was maybe five foot six inches tall and weighed one hundred and forty pounds with rocks in his pocket, was at quarterback. It was quite a contrast to Colt, who imitated the look of an NFL quarterback and communicated confidence and poise even standing still. Dave's socks were barely above his shoes, he wore no wristbands, no towel tucked in his pants, and communicated anger rather than confidence and anxiety rather than poise. He was almost a full foot shorter than Jersey as the two of them stood on the sidelines figuring out what was supposed to happen next. Dave was so small the bottom of his jersey numbers two and three were tucked inside his pants.

The offense huddled on the sideline, and because it was still so silent on the field and in the bleachers, I heard Dave's first words as quarterback of the Whitehall Rangers. "Anyone who thinks we can't win this game get out of the huddle right now!" he barked at them.

One of the linemen – maybe JeffScott – mumbled something in response, and Dave yelled at him then grabbed his arm and tried to drag him out of the huddle. Dave wasn't big enough to do it, and JeffScott stood his ground.

A referee saw the brief Ranger huddled skirmish, shook his head in disgust, blew his whistle, and ordered the Ranger sideline to run a play.

On the first play Dave whirled to his left to hand the ball off to Cale, who had gone the other direction to receive the handoff. Dave turned, saw there was no one there to get the ball, lowered his head and ran for a three-yard gain. The next play he took the ball, drew a defender to him, and pitched the ball to Cale, who picked up fourteen yards down the sideline. It was hard to tell which Ranger had the ball. I was taking pictures and much of the time I couldn't find the ball. Logan carried the ball four straight times, and then Dave faked a handoff to Logan and pitched it to Cale who beat a tackler to the corner of the end zone for a Whitehall touchdown. The Rangers were down 23-7 after Dave kicked the extra point. Later I found out it was the first extra point Dave had ever kicked in his life.

The Whitehall players had an actual bounce in their step as they trotted to the sidelines after the extra point. Dave all but danced off the field. He was shouting, punching the sky and jumping up to pat his teammates on their helmets. The third quarter was half over and the Rangers still trailed by more than two touchdowns, their starting quarterback was probably getting x-rayed in a Helena hospital, but a touchdown was a touchdown, and Whitehall didn't score a lot of touchdowns, so the celebration was merited.

On the next Townsend possession the Bulldog quarterback dropped back to throw and JeffScott knocked the lineman blocking him straight over backward. The quarterback saw him coming and let the ball go just as JeffScott jumped high in the air, his arms up stretched. Somehow the ball hit JeffScott flush on the hands, and stayed there. The ball stuck in his hands, like a block of lumber in a vise. JeffScott couldn't catch a ball thrown to him, or them, couldn't hang on to one if you handed it to him, but this ball wedged itself in his hands. He collapsed with the ball, and it was Ranger ball in Bulldog territory.

On second down Dave gave the ball to Logan up the middle for a three-yard gain. But Logan didn't have the ball. Tony did. And he was running untouched on the outside for a thirty-seven yard touchdown. Dave must have faked the ball to Logan, and handed it off to Tony on a flanker reverse, but I'd lost track of the ball. So, apparently, had everyone else, including all eleven players on the Bulldog defense.

The third quarter ended with Whitehall down 23-14, but judging by the two sidelines – and two sets of fans in the bleachers – you would have thought the Rangers were ahead. I caught myself thinking if the game ended 23-14 the Rangers would have something to feel good about.

On their next possession, Townsend moved the ball to the Whitehall forty yard line when on third and long the quarterback threw a deep pass down the sideline that Nate intercepted at about the seven yard line. In some ways it was as good as a punt, but the Whitehall fans and players erupted with cheers.

Townsend stopped Logan – who actually did have the ball – on first and second down, and on third down Dave dropped back to throw his first true varsity football pass. He moved a few steps to his left, and looked downfield. A tackler had him for a sack but Dave ducked and the Bulldog lineman simply grabbed air. Dave took off running downfield, dodged a chasing linebacker, slipped another tackle and got to midfield before he was knocked out of bounds. Coach Pete ran over and jerked him to his feet so abruptly it seemed Dave was lifted two feet off the ground. The Whitehall sideline was yelling and screaming – as were the fans behind them – and Jersey calmly held Dave by the shoulder and told him what play to run next in the same manner as you'd select a greeting card at a drug store.

Logan picked up four yards off tackle. Then he picked up a first down on what looked like the exact same play. Logan pounded the left side three more times for close to twenty yards. Logan ran hard and low, and delivered a blow harder than he received one. I could see some of the Bulldog defenders were attempting to hit him from an angle rather than head on. Dave carried the ball for six yards, and Logan led Nate around the end for a touchdown. Logan hit a linebacker so hard the kid fell backward and the back of his helmet was the first part of his body to hit the ground. The touchdown made it 23-20, and Dave's extra point was blocked. Actually, it was a poor kick; it might have hit a Ranger lineman in the back. There were still over four minutes left to play.

Townsend ran three plays – for a total of three yards – and punted. The Rangers had a little more than two minutes to go seventy yards.

They did it in less than a minute. After a completion, a short run and long incompletion, Dave threw a screen pass to Cale, who got great blocks from Cody, Tanner and Tony, and outran the defense forty yards into the end zone. Tony intercepted a desperation pass a few plays later and the Rangers had their first win of the year, a come from behind 27-23 win to ruin Townsend's Homecoming.

The three dozen or so Whitehall fans swept onto the field to congratulate the joyous Ranger players. Annie and a trio of junior high girls skipped onto the field to congratulate Tony and Dave, and, I noticed, Cody, and then various other players. Molly brought Trish's wheelchair to the front of the track, behind the Ranger bench, and I saw tears streaming down Trish's face and around her wide smile. Tony, wet and dirty, came over and high-fived Trish, Molly, all the O'Toole girls, except for Aspen, who got a sweaty, stinky hug.

Sara Dickson was also weeping, holding the hands of her agitated son near the bench. Her eyes held unadulterated pride. Jersey came up from the side, put an arm around Dave, and said something to Sara that made her smile, nod, and wipe away a tear.

Then Dave ran over to where I was standing. I had taken some pictures of the individual and collective celebrations, and knew one of them was going on the front page of the next Ledger.

"Hey, Ledger guy," Dave called out as he skipped past me. His eyes showed a hint of mischief. "You saw it," he yelled, "Do you believe it?"

"You bet," I told him.

"Then tell everyone what you saw," and he danced past me.

He let go a loud *Whoop!* and jumped into the arms of Logan. Dave was celebrating, but Logan looked like he could barely move. An exhausted Logan took his right hand and patted Dave on the top of his head.

Whitehall had won a football game. It was only a football game. It was only one win.

Why did it feel so good?

Chapter 21

The Bozeman Chronicle and the Montana Standard in Butte, the two daily newspapers that with varying commitment covered Whitehall high school sports, each downplayed the Ranger win over Townsend.

The Chronicle called both Townsend and Whitehall Class B 'bottom feeders,' an uncharitable choice of words I was certain Jersey would call and voice his concerns about. The Chronicle's story was three brief paragraphs that told how the Rangers' first win of the year spoiled the Townsend Homecoming. The Townsend coach complained about his team's lack of focus and inability to win close games, and disregarded the strong Ranger second half and astonishing comeback.

The Montana Standard in Butte attempted an article about the game from more of a Ranger viewpoint, but the Whitehall-Townsend game was one of over a dozen games called in to the Standard sports desk Friday night – a sports desk worked by novices or worse – and in a seven-paragraph article that contained maybe two dozen facts, the Standard managed to get half of them wrong.

According to the Standard, Dave *Dickens* was inserted at quarterback and kicked three extra points, and someone named *Dirkson* threw a touchdown pass; Cale *Bowling* scored two touchdowns; *Tommy Josling* scored a touchdown and recovered a fumble; coach Jerry (no last name) praised his team's attitude and desire and singled out *Dickson* and *Morgan* Bradshaw for their strong efforts. The Standard reported Whitehall next played Three Forks for its Homecoming, which was wrong in that the next Ranger game was against Ennis, and that the win mysteriously left the Rangers with a record of zero wins and five losses. Some of the errors were understandable, given the rush of games and scores and names called in barely before deadline with stories written by people totally unfamiliar with the game they're writing about. Some of the errors, though, made the Standard sports reporters look like they either didn't know or didn't care or both.

Which didn't bother me a bit, given the competition factor between the Ledger and the Standard. Every error made the Ledger look more competent. The little sister of *Tommy Josling*, however, found it all insulting.

"How hard can it be to have a phone book or team roster handy to get names spelled right?" Annie complained. She was utterly disgusted. "It's not a surprise for the Standard, is it, that they report on Whitehall football games? If a kid does something good enough to get his name in the newspaper the least the newspaper can do is spell the kid's name right."

Easier said than done. Mistakes in newspapers were something I was all too familiar with. We might be better than the Standard, but perfection was similarly elusive for us. God knows, in the near decade that I'd owned the Ledger, I'd made some doozies. I'd start an article on page one and send the reader to page twenty to finish the article, except the article actually finished on page twenty-four. Once, in a photo cutline, I referred to former Ranger basketball player Brandon Fox as Brandon Marshall, when I knew it was obviously Brandon Fox and never heard of a Brandon Marshall in my life. In an article in which Brock Sullivan, the son of Lawrence and Margaret Sullivan, was engaged to be married, the headline I wrote was *Lawrence Sullivan engaged.* Which was quite a surprise to Margaret, his wife. Evidently, Lawrence got quite a ribbing about it. So the following week we re-ran the exact same article with the headline *Brock Sullivan engaged*, and did so because I assumed the family wanted the clipping for a family scrapbook or for the family record. They probably did want that, but I also got a call from Margaret firmly asking me to publish a correction that stated Lawrence Sullivan is *not* engaged. Apparently, she was not as amused as her friends and neighbors were to find the local newspaper announcing the engagement of her husband.

I had always wanted to study a Ledger work chart and determine what portion of the workweek was spent after midnight, and compare that percentage to the percentage of Ledger mistakes that were made after midnight. My guess was that probably less than five percent of the workweek was spent working after midnight, but my theory was half the mistakes I made occurred after midnight. There was absolutely no doubt in my mind that fatigue manufactured mistakes. I was living proof.

The Ledger did not downplay the first Ranger win of the season. We teased the article on the front page and devoted two full pages to the article and photos.

Nor did I have to write an article that exaggerated or outright fabricated an imaginary glimmer of positive news from a lopsided loss to provide the Ranger lads with a crumb of honor. When the home team loses by fifty points and essentially is out of the game from the opening kickoff – which had happened repeatedly in recent years – I just couldn't report that the Rangers were an embarrassment and had no business being on the field with whoever it was that beat them, even if that assertion was undoubtedly correct. Such an article would be as unkind and mean spirited as it would be accurate and unpopular. So several times each season I'd have to manufacture or exaggerate some kind – any kind – of positive results from the game: Whitehall had a nine-play, eighty-yard drive to end the game (and make the score 49-7); the Rangers held the opponent scoreless in the fourth quarter (because the opponent's first string was drinking Gatorade on the bench and laughing as they watched the subs); Whitehall held the opponent to only thirty yards passing (because the opponent ran the ball for over three hundred yards); and my favorite, which I trotted out every year, in part because it sounded convincing, the lament that the opponent made enough big plays to win and the Rangers didn't (the Rangers were incapable of making any plays at all or of preventing the opponent from big play after big play).

No excuses or invented rationale were needed for the win over Townsend. The Rangers had staged a bona fide magical comeback against the Townsend starters to win a conference game on the road and improve to one win and one loss in conference play. A three-column photo of JeffScott – both of them, mirror images – jumping jubilantly, was on the front page. Pictures of Cale scoring the winning touchdown; Logan leaning forward, running over a Townsend defensive back (the photo couldn't be any larger than two columns because the force of the collision distorted the image and made both players look out of focus) and Jersey conferring with Dave were so prominent as to be unmissable.

I always figured the Ledger had three basic duties: *One) Frame issues so the community could make intelligent and reasoned decisions. Two) Report accurately the news of the week; the Ledger reported Whitehall's history one week at a time. Three) Promote the positive; fill scrapbooks with good intentions, good deeds and accomplishments.* The better we fulfilled those three goals, the better the paper was received and the more the paper contributed to the community.

The Ledger certainly fulfilled duty three with the article about the win over Townsend. Jersey's quotes praised the kids – especially Dave, Cody and Logan – to the point you'd have thought the kids had won a state title. Jersey singled out practically each kid in a Ranger uniform for individual praise, and each quote made the paper. The only downer was Colt, whose shoulder wasn't injured as bad as originally thought – it wasn't separated, only sprained – but Helena doctors said he would be out at least two weeks.

I was so eager to lay out the two pages containing the Ranger win that I stayed a little later than usual on Monday night. It was close to one o'clock in the morning by the time I got the pages to look the way I wanted – with the headline *Rangers roar back for big win* – as a banner headline. I was almost done, and was reaching for my can of pop when I saw something scurry along the floor, away from me, out of the corner of my eye. Time to go home, I thought; I'm seeing things.

Then I saw it again, except this time I actually did see it. A tiny slender dark gray mouse scurried in starts and stops along the base of the wall toward the bathroom. Like an idiot, I yelled at it, and it simply vanished. It was just suddenly gone. I crept closer, and saw, just above the carpet, a tiny slit in the baseboard. It wasn't more than a sixteenth of an inch across, but without a doubt that had been where the mouse had disappeared. It was back there, in the wall somewhere, hiding.

I finished up for the night, and wondered if I'd seen a mouse all these years instead of imagining I was seeing something. I got down to the floor on my hands and knees and poked my finger in the baseboard crack, and I could barely get the tip of my index finger inside. How could an entire rodent fit through that?

"Hey, bubba," I spoke toward the hole. "Your days are numbered."

When I got home I found, to my anger and dismay, a battered blue GMC pickup in the driveway. The house was brightly lit from the inside, as if every light was on. It was maddeningly late on a Monday night. The lights were supposed to be off, the kids were supposed to be sleeping, and the driveway was supposed to be empty. Goddamn Tony, I thought. He and his buddies better not be keeping Annie up.

I slammed the car door, stormed into the back door, entered the house through the kitchen and found Annie at the kitchen table, an assortment of books piled on the table. She looked up at me the same time Cody Phillips did. He was seated alongside her at the table, a pencil in his right hand and his left arm upright, his hand propping up his head. I'm sure I looked beaten and weary. But I looked eager and fresh compared to Cody. It was hard to tell if he was more dejected or exhausted.

"Done for the night?" Annie asked me. She wore jeans and a Yellowstone National Park sweatshirt. Tony's old Yellowstone National Park sweatshirt, it looked like, and it was probably two sizes too big for her.

"What are you doing?" I demanded.

I detected movement from the living room, and saw Tony sprawled out on the couch. He had been sound asleep. He sat up, and I could see the lines of couch corduroy etched in his face. He stirred slowly, and for a second it looked as if he had no idea where he was. He had a large, ugly, green and purple bruise on his arm and elbow, and he grimaced briefly when he lifted his arms to stretch.

"He's been sleeping since about eight o'clock," Annie explained, and indicated Tony. "Cody's got an algebra and geography test tomorrow, so we've been studying."

"You," I pointed at Cody. "Out. Now."

He nodded, as if that was exactly what he had expected me to say, as if he'd heard it a hundred times before. He looked guiltily at Annie, then began gathering up the books and notebooks.

"We're almost done, Lance," Annie said, a tremor of alarm in her voice. "We have one more geography chapter to cover."

Cody continued to gather up the stuff on the table. His reputation was not good, his upbringing had been worse, and trouble – all types, all the time – seemed to constantly shadow him. But it was my daughter, not Cody, showing defiance. He actually looked halfway clean cut; hair trimmed, a fairly new western pearl button shirt. He had a blonde wispy mustache that made him younger, somehow, not older, than age sixteen or whatever he was. Life with the Franklins must be agreeing with him.

"Does Ed know where you're at?" I asked Cody.

He looked away from me and downward, toward the floor. The kid acted guilty by habit. "I called and said I'd be home an hour ago."

"So why aren't you?" I asked.

Another guilty look. "I'm failing algebra," he said softly. "I'm not too good in geography, either." He hesitated, started to speak, stopped, and started again. "I'm just not good at books."

"And Lance," Annie added, "if Cody fails algebra, it means he's ineligible for football."

"It's way after midnight," I told Annie, but my anger was dissipating. "There's a curfew, and he's breaking it. He's not supposed to be here. He's not supposed to be anywhere but home. With the Franklins."

"Twenty minutes?" Annie told me. "One more chapter. Twenty minutes. I promise."

I pointed at Cody again. "Call the Franklins. Tell them you're with us and will be home in fifteen minutes."

He nodded. He may have wanted to stop his academic struggles for the night, but like Tony and me, found disagreeing with Annie was pointless.

"Want me to call?" Annie asked him.

He shook his head morosely. "I'll do it."

"Let me talk to Ed when you're done," I told him.

I went into the bathroom to take a leak, and when I got out Cody was finishing up the conversation, and handed me the phone.

"Twelve minutes left," I told him. "Get to work." I held the phone. "Ed."

"It's Alice," said a feminine voice.

"Alice. Sorry." I gathered myself. I put a little distance between me and the kids. "Where's Ed?"

"Standing by, with his jacket on," she said. "He was ready to head out again and search for Cody, and when the phone rang he threw on his coat.

"Cody and Annie are here doing some schoolwork. He'll be home in eleven minutes. Is that all right?"

"That's what he said," she said. "He called about ten, and we told him to be home at eleven. We hoped he'd be home by now." She hesitated. "We'd like to avoid Officer Manfredini, if possible."

"I just got home from work," I said. I looked around, as if I had to visually confirm something. "I think everything's okay here. Want me to drive him home?"

"Cody's a little wild, Lance, but he has a good heart," Alice said. I could picture her, speaking from a dark and chilly house, Ed standing by, listening. "No, he'll come straight home."

"You never thought you'd have a teenager living with you again, did you?" I said.

She emitted a brief laugh. "I don't have the energy I used to have, that's for sure." She sighed. "I'm sure you know this wasn't my idea. Cody's a handful and he likes to bend the rules, but there's something there to work with, Lance. He's trying. Truly."

Truly. I was seeing it. "So it seems to be working out?" I asked.

"Annie's a gift from heaven to him, although their friendship has to make you uncomfortable," she said.

Friendship? Annie and Cody? "You could say that."

"I'd keep your eye on him, if I was you, like any father would, but Annie seems to bring out the best in him," Alice said.

"You can count on that first part," I said. "You better get to sleep, Alice. Cody'll be home in ten minutes."

"Tell him there's some cookies on the countertop for him," she said. "Night, Lance."

"I'll tell him," I said. "Goodnight."

"Tell him what?" Annie asked the instant I hung the phone up.

"Alice has got some cookies on the kitchen counter waiting for you," I said.

Cody allowed a trace of a smile. He looked like he deserved a reward.

Tony, disheveled and bleary eyed, more or less stumbled into the bathroom, and moments later the sound of a stream of urine hitting the toilet water was the only sound in the house. We heard Tony hawk up some phlegm and spit, and then flush the toilet.

"Lovely," Annie said with disgust.

Tony opened the door, scratched his belly, and said, with a bizarre British accent, that he was going to bed. He ambled down the hall into his room.

"British?" I asked Annie.

"Toad," she answered.

"What?" I asked.

"Never mind," she said.

"You almost done?"

She looked up at me, but kept her finger on a point of a map in a book. The map may have been of Central America. I was looking at it upside down, and I desperately wanted to go to bed. For everyone to go to bed.

"Have a glass of milk," she told me. "It will help you relax."

"When I'm done with the milk, Cody's gone and we're all going to bed," I said.

Which is exactly what happened.

About the same time Cody would have arrived at the Franklins, Annie came out of her room wearing a Ranger long sleeve tee-shirt and sweatpants, her version of pajamas.

"We're going to have to have a talk about curfews," I told her as sternly as I could muster.

"Sure," she told me, dismissing my demand. She stopped. "Has Mrs. Cullen talked to you yet?"

Martha Cullen, the elementary school principal. I shook my head. "No. Is she going to?"

Annie nodded.

"And what is Mrs. Cullen going to talk to me about?" I asked.

"Not curfews," she said, and slipped into her bathroom.

"You want me to bring in one of my cats?"

That was the response from Laura Joyce early Tuesday morning, after I'd warned her about the Ledger mouse I'd seen about seven hours earlier. If I'd expected Laura Joyce to be frightened of the rodent, I'd have expected wrong.

“No, I don’t think we need a cat around here,” I told her. “I’ll pick up a trap at the hardware store when I go over and pick up the mail.”

Amy had been terrified of mice. They were vile, dirty vermin. She saw one in our Butte garage and her scream was an unnatural piercing wail, and immediately afterward she had burst into tears.

“A cat’s way better,” Laura Joyce said, with her customary laugh. She wore a western shirt and tight western jeans that were not particularly flattering to her figure. Laura Joyce was cheerful, even bubbly, but when she was bubbly in tight clothes her whole body bubbled. “We’ve had mice in our place. Happens almost every year about this time. That’s why we got us some mean mouser cats. It gets a little colder outside and the mice start looking for warmth indoors. Cats know it, too. Tilly, our Siamese, caught a couple mice the other day. One in the basement, one in the pantry. She’ll get the little bugger here, too, if you give her a chance.”

I held up my index finger. “Let me try a trap, first.”

“Tilly’s free. She works for food.” Laura Joyce giggled, jiggled, and sat down at her desk.

Laura Joyce was right about it getting chilly, especially in the morning. I had to turn on the heater in the Ledger earlier in the morning, and although it wouldn’t need to stay on long – just a couple hours – because the sun warmed the building all afternoon, it definitely needed to be turned on this morning. It was early October; the days were getting shorter, the nights were getting colder and there was a sense of gathering winter power up in the mountains.

We had another twenty-four page paper this week, and by noon eight pages were already laid out. We were actually ahead of schedule; we were typically so far behind schedule that a schedule made no sense.

By mid-afternoon another three pages were done, and Laura Joyce was wrapping up the classified page about the same time as Rhonda Horst, with perfectly bad timing, came in with a change in her classified ad. Rhonda was slightly stooped, with a homely square chin and a head of wild gray hair. She always reminded me of something from a Brothers Grimm fairy tale, but that could have been a stereotype simply based on her accent. She had a bag full of groceries and set it down on the counter.

“Vinter’s in da hair,” she said as she entered. Laura Joyce exchanged a quick glance. She knew disruptions on Tuesdays were frustrating to me, but she also knew I had a soft spot of sorts for Rhonda Horst.

“Lots of the trees are already bare of leaves,” Laura Joyce said from her desk. “Especially up in the mountains. You get up a ways in the high country, and you can tell winter’s right around the corner.”

Rhonda, her mess of silver hair spouting outside of a scarf wrapped around her head and under her throat, agreed. “I vent to da doctor in Butte da odder day, and in Butte it alveady looks like vinter,” she said. “Sometimes I dink Butte not too far from da Nord Pole.”

Butte, situated at over five thousand feet elevation, was notorious for cold weather. Any night, even in July or August, the temperature could drop below freezing, and on a typical day Whitehall was ten degrees warmer and several shades brighter than Butte. Part of me missed living in Butte, but it was a very small piece.

"Something tells me you want to change your classified ad," I told Rhonda. I didn't mind chatting with her – sometimes I thought outside of her boarders she didn't have a lot of other people to visit with – but it was Tuesday and I still had a half a paper to lay out.

"Da vat?" she asked. Then she suddenly realized what I'd said. "Acht, no, not dat rontal." She shook her head. "Jost leave dat da vay it is. Shtill von room empty."

Laura Joyce and I exchanged a quick glance again. That meant she would not have to adjust the classified page to fit something else in.

"Da play at da high shhcool, you go see icht?"

Rhonda had no vehicle, and to my knowledge had never learned to drive. Every day, she walked the half mile or so to the IGA and bought the groceries she needed that day. Once, years ago during my Monday morning ad stops not long after we'd moved to Whitehall, I'd seen her walking in the rain, and stopped to offer her a ride. She accepted, and tried to give me a dollar when we got to her house, a large square block residence that squatted across half a block on First Street. I refused to accept the dollar, but whenever I saw her since she'd never refused my invitation to take her either to the store or back, depending where and when I saw her en route. A couple times she had instructed me to wait while I pulled up in front of her house, and she'd waddle up the three steps, across the porch and into her house. Moments later she'd emerge with a plate of cookies, a pie, some pastry or other treat. Tony especially appreciated her pies. He claims he never had better pie, and I believed him, because I wasn't sure I ever had.

From the occasional and accidental rides to or from the grocery store, I'd occasionally taken Rhonda – at her suggestion – to community benefit dinners and other events, since she knew I had to attend to take pictures – and it looked like I would be escorting her to the WHS production of *The Wind in the Willows*. I'd taken her to a spring school concert and a Christmas program at the school before, and it was cute almost, how we'd walk in together, and then once inside immediately go our separate ways. She knew I had to work – *verk* – and had to either move around to get pictures or plant myself in the front row or even in front of the front row. She always gravitated toward the right side, I noticed, and sometimes when I spoke she'd turn her head slightly to her left, as if her left ear worked better.

I nodded. "Yeah, I'm going Thursday night. I have to go to Ennis on Friday and might not get back on time, and Saturday night I'm going to the Chamber's fall banquet. You want me to pick you up on Thursday? Is that night okay with you?"

"Ya, Tursday fine. Vhat time?"

"A little after seven, I guess, seven-fifteen. The play starts at seven-thirty and I need to get there early to get a good seat."

“Ya. I be ready.” She retied her scarf under her chin, picked up her groceries and got ready to back out of the door.

“You want a ride home?” I asked.

She shook her head. “No, naught so far from here,” she said, and was gone.

By four o’clock Laura Joyce had completed her work, had offered to bring Tilly the mouser a couple more times, and was on her way home. I figured I’d be done by seven o’clock at the latest, which was the same as having a Tuesday night off. I called Annie and told her when Tony got home after practice to come down to the Ledger and we’d go next door for a pizza. My guess was I’d almost be done at that point, and could finish up after supper and be home in time to spend a few hours with the kids.

Martha Cullen called about four-thirty and asked me if I could stop by her office on Friday morning, and I told her I could but that it had to be early. Ennis had no lights at their field and played only day games, and Friday’s game started at two o’clock. I had to get out of town by eleven-thirty and had quite a bit to do before I left. Martha suggested nine o’clock and I agreed. I gave her a chance to give me some sort of indication what we were going to discuss, but she ignored my invitation.

At a little after six o’clock Annie called me at the Ledger. Tony had play rehearsal and only had time to grab some A&W between football practice and rehearsal. He wouldn’t be home for supper and wouldn’t be home until after ten o’clock. Annie told me she was going over to Natalie’s house to start planning junior high Homecoming activities, and I instructed her to be home by ten o’clock.

Home was messy and dark and cold and dreary, and whenever I was there I couldn’t help but observe all the work that needed to be done around the place, and the knowledge that I would continue to neglect that work was like a burden. Tonight, a Tuesday night of all things, I was done with work and there was no one home. I finished up at the Ledger, admired the two pages trumpeting the Ranger victory, and walked down to Borden’s for a burger and a beer.

Gage Duncan, the town man, was perched on a bar stool nursing a bottle of Budweiser, and to his left was Brandt Smith, a local contractor. I grabbed the stool to Gage’s right, ordered a draft Rainier and cheeseburger with fries. I tilted my head toward Gage and Brandt, and Sally, behind the bar, nodded once, and brought the three drinks. Then she reached down under the top of the bar and pulled up ketchup, mustard and a container of napkins, and went across the bar to the café to order the food. Sally was attractive in a vampire sort of way. Her raven black hair framed a face with a complexion as colorless as cream and smooth as marble. She had unnaturally slickened red lips and possibly not an ounce of fat on her body. Her fingernails were the color of blood, and she wore more necklaces, rings and bracelets than a gypsy. She had given up drinking years earlier, the story went, and seemed to survive on coffee and cigarettes.

Brandt held up his glass, a brandy water if I remembered correctly, and tilted it toward me; the universal barroom signal for thank you.

"Lance," was all Gage said, by way of thanks. He took two gulps to finish off one bottle of Bud, pushed it toward the inside of the bar, and brought the fresh bottle closer to him. It was as if he was guarding it. He hunched his back a little, so Brandt and I could see each other. "Ask Lance," Gage told Brandt. "Maybe he's heard of those folks you was talking about."

Brandt was maybe thirty years old, with a wife who taught in the elementary school. They had three kids, all boys, between the ages of about six and ten. He primarily did sheetrock, floors, kitchen cabinets and some finishing work on new houses in about a fifty mile radius around Whitehall. He was reportedly good at what he did. He told me once if you put your name on the side of your truck you'd better be good at what you do. He had a bushy dark mustache and a swarthy stubble beard that seemed to perpetually lag only a couple days behind the mustache. I could smell the sawdust on his shirt, or perhaps coat, a black and red plaid insulated garment with holes in the elbows and frayed cuffs around the wrists.

"You know anything about those folks in Cedar Hills, moved here from California?" he asked.

I shook my head. Someone moving here from California wasn't all that uncommon lately. Sometimes people who moved in bought a subscription to the Ledger, but some of them not only didn't get the local paper, they remained totally disconnected from Whitehall. If they didn't have kids in school or work in town, a lot of the people moving into the Jefferson Valley shopped or worked in Butte or Bozeman and had no connection to Whitehall.

"Their last name is Garcia," Brandt said. "They say they're retired, but they can't be older than forty. Hell, she's more like thirty. Maybe younger. His name is Rod, and he says he used to work for Warner Brothers. You know, the movie studio."

"He an actor?" I asked.

Brandt and Gage both smirked. "Lawyer," Brandt conceded.

"Asshole lawyers," Gage muttered.

Gage wasn't what you'd call an optimist. In his view, the percentage of human population classified as assholes was substantially upwards of fifty percent. On a bad day, my guess was closer to eighty percent.

Gage soldiered through life dourly but doggedly, and although he did a good job on his multitude of duties and assignments for the town, he always acted as if he was somehow treated unjustly, or perhaps underappreciated. I knew that because once on these very same barstools he had told me that very thing. He was unhappy and I was pretty sure his wife had something to do with that. Her name was Delores, and in close to a decade living in Whitehall

I'd seen her maybe a dozen times and each time she looked as happy as an ulcer. Her mood would have to lighten considerably to be elevated to grim.

"Anyway, Rod and Tiffany, his wife – and not his first wife, maybe not even his second – are building a three thousand square foot log cabin over in Cedar Hills, about two miles south of Highway 2," Brandt said. "Pretty country. Great views of the Tobacco Roots and Highlands."

"Brandt's building their deck," Gage added.

Brandt nodded. "Right. Two decks, actually. One in front, and a smaller one, off their bedroom. The deck in front is almost done, the one in back's going to have to wait until spring."

"Tell him about the deer," Gage said, as if it was an accusation.

"I'm getting to that," Brandt said. "So I'm out there working last week and Tiffany starts complaining about the deer. Rats with antlers, she calls them. They've eaten all her flowers, they've been eating her new shrubs and trees all summer, and she's had enough. She tells Rod to buy a gun and start shooting deer. So Rod goes out and gets himself a rifle, and I notice it's loaded, leaning upright on the deck by the door."

"Don't tell me he shot a bunch of deer," I said.

"I asked Rod about the gun, and he says it's there to shoot the deer," Brandt said. "I sort of told them that that's illegal."

"Sort of," I agreed.

"Right," Brandt said. "Rod kind of chuckles, looks at me like I'm an idiot, and tells me of course it is."

"Is what?" I asked.

"Legal, he said. "He gave me a lecture. He's got the right to protect his property. It's a constitutional right, he says. Tiffany says of course they got the right to protect their property. The deers – she called them deers – are eating everything in their yard."

"This ain't California, you assholes," Gage muttered.

"In California, they say, they have a right to protect private property," Brandt said.

"Do you think Rod's ever fired a rifle before?" I asked.

Brandt shook his head. "Not a chance. I told you, the rifle was loaded, just leaning against the wall. When they weren't looking I put the safety on and took it inside and set it down on the floor by the fireplace."

"So what do you think?" I asked. "Does he go blasting deer every dusk and dawn?"

Brandt shrugged. "I told him it was against the law. I gave him the talk about wildlife being owned by the public, and that Montana had legally defined hunting seasons and quotas. I made it pretty clear you couldn't shoot every deer that walked across your property."

"You shoulda told them that assholes from California weren't even allowed to own a gun in Montana," Gage said.

"I gotta admit, people like them are good for business – my business, anyway," said Brandt. "But there's getting to be more and more Californians in this country."

"It's our own damn fault," Gage asserted. "Like idiots, we're *inviting* them."

He was right about that. The Montana Office of Tourism was aggressively promoting Montana in national magazine ads, on TV and radio, and even through special tourism packets sent by the governor's office. And the marketing campaign was working. More and more tourists – millions of them each year – were not only visiting Montana, but a lot of them liked what they saw and were staying.

It was easy to see why. Outside of a handful of urbanized or industrialized areas, Montana was still unspoiled, still scenic, still mostly unpopulated and, compared to most other states, affordable if not downright cheap. An average home or acre in Montana cost less than half what a home or acre in other states costs. Montana wages weren't much to brag about, but if you brought your money with you, you could live pretty well for a long time on the cheap and still have a terrific view.

"I was in Bozeman a few weeks ago and they got a big billboard on the freeway saying *Welcome to Big Sky Country* right outside of town," Gage said. "I'd like to put a sign next to it that says *But You Ain't Welcome to Stay!* Montana's a big state but there's a limit how many Californians we should have to take."

Sally set another Rainier in front of me. Brandt must have thought it was his turn. Gage was seldom eager to pick up a round.

"Burger'll be up in a minute," she told me, and winked large black eyelashes.

"I'm not sure we can stop 'em," I told Gage. "Montana's the best place to live. We have what everyone wants. We've still got what everyone else lost."

"Shit," argued Gage.

"I'm serious," I said. "Look at the mountains, the rivers, the views, the clean air, the clean water, the wildlife, the fishing, the hunting, skiing, hiking, rafting, snowmobiling. We have the best of everything."

"What, you working for the Chamber of Commerce now?" asked Gage.

"Maybe our new slogan should be, *Spend Money and Leave*," said Brandt.

"How about this?" said Gage. "*Montana: It's Ours, Not Yours.*"

Brandt held up a hand like he was holding a headline. "*You Still Fricking Here? Go Home!*"

I smelled the cheeseburger before I saw it. I turned around and the waitress from the café was behind me, getting ready to slip the plate in front of me, from my right. I leaned back as she slid the plate across the bar, and as she left I reached for the ketchup.

"Damn, that smells good," Brandt said.

I gestured that he could have some of my fries.

He shook his head. "I better get home to momma and the boys," he said.

Gage had no such obligations. There was nothing more than a scowl waiting for him at home. "We need a slogan that keeps people out," he said.

"*Montana*," I said, "*Where the Rattlesnakes Roam.*"

"*Montana*," said Gage, "*Where Bear Shit Contains Humans*."

"*Montana*," said Brandt, "*Even Our Otters are Dangerous!*"

Brandt was referring to an infamous episode in which some floaters on the Jefferson River were allegedly attacked and bitten by an otter, of all things.

"I got it," I said. I waited until they both looked at me. "*Montana: If Our Wildlife Doesn't Kill You, Our Weather Will.*"

Brandt snapped his fingers. "Perfect."

Gage nodded, and smirked. "I like it."

It *was* perfect; tragically and accurately perfect. There were a lot of different ways to die in Montana, and every year someone discovered a new one. A grizzly bear mauling was an annual event. A mountain lion would occasionally plink a kid off a front porch. A hiker would take a tumble off a cliff. A whitewater rapid would knock a rafter in the water and he'd be found two days later. A climber would take one misstep. A rattler would take a nick out of someone's toe. A warm water swimmer would make it halfway across a cold water lake. An outfitter's horse would take a header off a mountain trail. A blizzard would strand a hiker, a climber or even a family bound home after seeing Grandma at Easter. People seemed to die each year in Glacier or Yellowstone, and sometimes it wasn't their fault. In Gage's mind, the problem was the Montana accidental deaths did not involve enough Californians. Or lawyers.

I pulled up in front of Rhonda's home on Thursday night and before I could run up her steps and knock on her door she was already outside and opening the passenger side door. I had looked down to undo the seat belt and suddenly she was climbing in the car. She had to have been waiting outside for me.

"You're fery kindt," she said. She wore a scarf over her head and in the dome light as the door opened I thought I spotted a bit of red rouge on her cheeks.

"No problem," I said. "You all buckled in?"

"Ya," she said. "We go."

We drove five blocks, pulled into the student parking lot off the varsity gym and after I opened the back door of the car to grab the camera I looked up and saw Rhonda was already twenty feet in front of me, walking toward the high school doors that led into the multi-purpose room. She'd find me after the play. I wasn't sure if she didn't want to slow me down, didn't want me to think she was my responsibility, or if she simply didn't want to be seen with me.

I grabbed a play program at the entrance from Tanner Walker's mom and found an empty seat in the front row, just left of middle. I noticed the names of at least three kids were spelled incorrectly in the play credits, although Tony's was spelled right. People who didn't produce information for the public had no idea how challenging it was to get facts straight and names correct.

Off to the outside of the section of metal folding chairs to my right sat Annie, Natalie, Trish and right behind them, it looked like, sat Cody Phillips, Dave Dickson and a couple other football players. The rest of the front row was filled with obviously proud parents and grandparents. Their kids or grandkids were theatrical stars – at least for three nights in Whitehall – and they'd earned the right to bask in that accomplishment.

The seats were nearly all filled. Some of the parents and family members would watch the play all three nights, but I suspected a fair amount of people had to attend on Thursday night because they had other things to do on Friday and Saturday nights. I put a telephoto lens on the camera, but would shoot pictures with no flash. I would probably take fifty photos during the play, and fifty flash pops would be extremely disruptive to the actors and intrusive for the audience. I had to open the lens aperture as wide as possible and shoot at a slow shutter speed despite using the fastest film I could get – 1600 ASA. Typically for a play I waited for opportunities when the actors were completely motionless. Any head movement blurred the photo, and any kind of body movement ruined the shot. But if I took fifty pictures, ten of them would be usable, and ten was plenty.

It was always hard for me to watch – I mean truly watch, like a normal person in the audience would watch – a game or a play through the camera. Too often I was focused away from the ball in the game or focused on a specific person in a play and a lot of times I missed the context in which someone scored in a game or what the play was actually about. I was focused on precise people at precise times doing precise things at the play and it was those exact production moments I cared about.

And the truth was, even though I watched *The Wind in the Willows* twice – Annie and I made it back Friday in time to watch it again and take another fifty pictures – I could honestly say the play made absolutely no sense to me.

There was a character named Toad, played by a grungy kid named Bonner Labuda, who also played guitar in a fledgling Whitehall rock band. Toad spoke with a British accent, seemed to be vain and compulsive, and in one scene he was racing around in a cardboard car, in one scene he was apparently in jail and at the end he routed a band of weasels out of his house, called Toad Hall, I was pretty sure. There were characters named Ratty and one named Mole, also British, and eventually I realized all the characters were wearing odd costumes and face paint, and were, in fact, intended to resemble animals; apparently British animals. Mr. Badger reminded me of Winston Churchill, and the kid playing him – Tanner Walker from the football team – wore a full length fur coat and had black stripes painted horizontally across his cheeks.

The only real people in the play were women – girls in the WHS version – and Aspen O'Toole wore a low cut blouse as, and I'm guessing, a jailer's daughter or granddaughter. A couple times Aspen leaned forward to the audience, and I avoided focusing my camera exactly where every pair of male eyes in the room were focused.

Tony was in only one scene, and I had no idea how or why the god Pan showed up in the play about English furry animals. Tony wore some kind of Olympian-looking wreath around his head, and wore what looked to me like drapes. One shoulder and half his chest was bare, and I have to admit, he struck an impressive pose up on the stage. He spoke more than recited his lines, and seemed confident and poised for his first real high school play.

As if I was objective. Parents were notoriously terrible judges of their children's performances, and I was no different. In any sport, in any play, in any endeavor, parents were not – and could not be – impartial. Parents weren't supposed to be objective. As a parent, you were supposed to think – obligated to think, actually – your little Johnny or Sally was the best player or best actor or best dancer or best student. That's what parents were for: to cheer on and bolster their kids. The problem was parents thought they were objective, and believed they actually objectively thought that little Johnny or Sally was the best.

The play ended with some sort of a battle that cleared out Toad Hall and then the stage lights went up and the actors were taking their bows. It was all very puzzling to me. There was one line from the play I liked and kept hearing in my head, although I had no idea which character or characters spoke it. The line was, *Oh, poop, poop*. It was sobering if not disturbing to watch a complete high school play twice in which the characters were costumed as British animals and fail to understand the plot or any message in the play, and after ninety minutes of essentially focusing on the characters through a telephoto lens to emerge as highlights a confused sense of mortality and the line with the words, *Oh, poop, poop*. I couldn't shake the thought that somehow more was expected of me.

I put the camera back in the case, chatted with a few parents and audience members, and found Tony outside the door of the multi-purpose room locker room, or in the case of the play, the dressing room. He had attempted to wipe off the makeup but traces were still visible on his neck and around his ears. Annie was also at the door, as was Trish, some of the football players and other cast members. The entire O'Toole family had Aspen surrounded, and they looked like they just stepped off the cover of *People* magazine.

"Well?" Tony asked me.

"You were fabulous," I told him. "I'm going to have to start calling you Pan from now on."

"He's right," agreed Annie. "You actually acted."

Trish put a hand over her mouth and giggled.

"What did you think, Trish?" asked Tony.

She brightened at the question. "I liked it. It was funny."

Tony nodded. “Bizarre, is more like it. It’s like whoever wrote it was on drugs.”

“Not really,” said Annie. “It’s more like a commentary on the class structure and hypocrisy within early twentieth century British society.”

“*Oh, poop, poop*,” said a voice behind me. It was Cody, with a few other football players.

So evidently Cody and I agreed on the play’s highlight.

About ten feet behind them stood Rhonda, waiting quietly and patiently, more or less looking down at the floor, her scarf already wrapped around her head and tied tight under her chin.

Tony saw her over my shoulder. He took a half step toward me, looked me squarely in the eye, less than a foot from each other. “You two on another date?” he asked, replete with a British accent.

The parking lot was mostly empty when Rhonda and I climbed back into the Escort. On the way home I asked her if she liked the play and she said she didn’t understand it.

“Join the club,” I told her. “Why were they all animals? What was Toad doing driving and crashing a racecar? Why were they all English? The whole thing was totally confusing.”

“Ya,” she admitted. “But vos funt.”

I pulled up to her amazingly large square home. Lights were on all over the place. The boarders must all have been awake and active.

“You vait,” she instructed. Up the steps she went, and a moment later down the steps she came. She held two pies.

“Rhonda,” I protested. “No. Not two.”

“Ya,” she said. She set them gently on the passenger side seat. “Vun for you. Vun for dat Pan.” She smiled. “He like my pies.”

Chapter 22

When I arrived at Martha Cullen's office on Friday morning I had to bring in my own chair from the office reception area because the three chairs in Martha's office were already in use. The woman from the University of Montana, Diane something, if I recalled, and the old lady from the Office of Public Instruction, whose name I forgot, were in the office and seated. So was Annie, wearing a ragged Ranger hooded sweatshirt that she'd selected for the game later that day in Ennis.

Annie's eyes were puffy, and her cheeks colorless. It had been another late night at our house, with Tony and Aspen and friends, energized by their public performances, rehashing the play over and over, all the while eating fresh homemade apple and peach pie piled with vanilla ice cream. It was almost midnight when I more or less booted them out of the house by reminding them they had a football game to play the following afternoon. Cody had not been present at the house, but around ten p.m. Annie had been on the telephone with him, and even as she seemed to patiently describe and amplify the benefits of the Louisiana Purchase to him I could see the fatigue in her posture and hear it in her voice. Seated in Martha's office, the early morning sun shining in through the eastside windows, Annie had what looked like lightly shaded smudges under her eyes. Her face seemed wan, and I could see in her appearance and attire the shortcuts she'd taken this morning to get herself up and out of the house to get to school. Her mother could never hide fatigue. Deep half moons, the gray color of mold, would sag cruelly under Amy's eyes and her posture would droop as if weighted by an unmanageable burden.

"Lance, you remember Nancy Toups from the Office of Public Instruction," said Martha, and the older woman smiled my direction. "And Diane Fordham from the University of Montana." The younger woman gave me a slight, warmless, nod.

"Morning," I said. I glanced, for some reason at the baseboard of the wall that ran parallel to my right. I had two traps set along a baseboard at the Ledger, a baseboard not unlike the one in Martha's office. My traps at the Ledger had caught nothing. On Wednesday night, before I left work, as I set the traps and stuck a glob of peanut butter on it, one trap rapped my knuckles on my left hand and left a welt that lasted most of the night. But the traps had been empty Thursday and Friday mornings.

"Well, Lance, I suppose you're wondering why we've called you here this morning," began Martha.

Initially, I thought it was a rhetorical question. But neither Martha nor anyone else spoke, so I figured I was expected to say something. "My guess is it has something to do with Annie."

Diane Fordham, the younger of the two education ladies, tensed her chin slightly, in either dismay or disgust. She had a structured look to her somehow, as if she thought someone, somewhere, was grading her posture.

"Are you familiar with an organization called Mensa?" asked Martha.

I was, vaguely. I had a hazy notion about it being, maybe, political. Actually, no, I was not familiar with it, and was surely the only person in the room who was not. "I might have heard about it, I'm not sure."

"It's a worldwide group of intellectuals," said Martha. "It's celebrating its fortieth anniversary this year."

"Worldwide group of intellectuals?" I asked. I said it out loud because, really, how many times in your life do you get to utter the phrase *worldwide group of intellectuals.* I looked at Martha, who offered a sympathetic smile. Her hair was firmly sprayed in place, and was an unearthly color of brown. "What's it cost to join?" I asked.

That prompted a weak cackle of disapproval from Miss Fordham. Miss Fordham was either single, I decided, or there was a most unfortunate Mr. Fordham in Missoula somewhere. But my guess was there was no Mr. Fordham. Miss Fordham, I was betting, probably lived alone in an apartment – an immaculate apartment – with a fat spoiled cat.

"It's a very prestigious and exclusive club, Mr. Joslyn," explained Nancy Toups. "Mensa International has perhaps fifty thousand members worldwide, and the only people eligible are those whose IQ is in the top two percent of the population."

"Let me guess," I said. "You want Annie to take the IQ test to see if she's eligible."

Martha shook her head.

"She's already taken the test," I guessed again, "and she *is* eligible."

Martha nodded.

"Congratulations," I told Annie, who looked too weary to receive congratulations. "So, what do you want from me?" I asked Martha.

She hesitated, and it was obvious I'd directed the question to the wrong person.

"Mr. Joslyn," said Miss Fordham, "we at the Montana Office of Public Instruction would like to help submit Annie's test scores to Mensa, if you wouldn't object. And to assist her in joining Mensa."

"Don't ask me," I answered. "Ask her." I turned toward Annie. "You wanna join?" Before she could answer, I turned back to Miss Fordham. "What does *join* actually mean?"

"There are not a lot of stipulations," said Mrs. Toups. "Mensa was created in England in 1946 to bring intelligent people together in part to create an upwelling of social consciousness and in part for simple companionship."

"So it's what, like a Rotary Club for geniuses?" I asked.

Miss Fordham sighed. "Hardly," she answered. "We are talking about the most intelligent people on earth, Mr. Joslyn." Something in the way she said my name was undoubtedly meant to alert me and everyone else in the room that I was most certainly not one of the most intelligent people on earth. I had to agree, I wasn't. I couldn't even trap a goddamn mouse.

"Lance, Mensa membership is quite an honor," Martha said. "I don't know a great deal about the organization, but Mensa members are the type of people who change the world."

"Indeed," said Miss Fordham. "Mensans are inventors. College professors. NASA scientists. Doctors. Astronomists. Government leaders. Pediatricians. Mensans really do change the world."

"Because they're in Mensa, or because they're smart?" I asked.

"Because they're smart," answered Annie. "Mensa is a club. It's like high school Honor Society except it's international and it's open to everyone who's got the test scores to qualify."

"What's *Mensa* mean?" I asked.

Annie's expression suggested she was not supportive of me asking too many questions.

"It means *table* in Latin," answered Miss Fordham.

"Table?" I asked. "No kidding. I would have got that wrong on a multiple choice test."

"Table as in a round table, as in a round table society," said Miss Fordham tersely. "People of all cultures, all nationalities, all skin colors, all religions, all incomes are eligible and welcomed."

I suddenly had a thought. "You're a Mensa, aren't you?"

Proudly, she nodded.

Annie, bless her, instinctively read my mind. I didn't want my daughter ending up some dried out prissy puckered intellectual who looked like she went home on Friday nights and read Proust or graded essays or did crossword puzzles until nine-thirty before wearing ankle-to-chin flannel pajamas to bed. Tony, Annie and I may be dysfunctional, but at least we lived life.

"Lance, truckers are in Mensa," Annie said. "Athletes are. Movie stars are. Kids are. Moms are. Dads are. Grandparents are. Poor people are. Rich people are. Middle class people are. There are a lot of geniuses who don't act like geniuses."

"Lance," said Martha, "I sense you're hesitating for some reason."

"I don't care if Annie joins a group, Martha," I said. "But these two," I meant Miss Fordham and Mrs. Toups, "wouldn't be here just for Annie to join some club. Something else is going on here. What do you want from me? What do you want from Annie?"

There was a lengthy pause, and it was clear Martha was not going to answer the questions. She expected the response to come from either Missoula or Helena. Instead, it came from eighth grade.

"They want to promote my Mensa membership," Annie said. "They want to use my Mensa membership to promote public education in Montana and the quality of education students in Montana receive."

"We'd like to bring the governor to Whitehall and present the Mensa certificate to Annie," said Miss Fordham. "Their joint appearance here means statewide recognition for Annie and her accomplishment."

"We'd schedule an all-school assembly for the award ceremony," said Martha.

I looked at Martha. "You think this school is responsible for Annie's intelligence?"

"Do you think you are?" Miss Fordham snapped.

"I told you," Annie told Martha.

"Told her what?" I asked Annie.

"That you weren't going to like the promotional part," she said.

"They're using you, Annie," I said.

"I'm sort of using them too, Lance," Annie assured me.

No one spoke. Martha looked like someone who realized they should have expected the worst.

Annie lowered her eyes straight at mine. "If someone other than me qualified for Mensa, you'd make a big deal about it in the Ledger, especially if the governor came here. It would be on the front page. And you'd think you were fulfilling two of your priority paper goals. You'd be recording history and you'd be filling scrapbooks."

She had me there. I surely would make a big deal about that, and for those two very reasons.

"Annie would be the youngest Mensa International member in Montana," Mrs. Toups said softly. She was a large woman but the weight was distributed evenly, and she looked like a kindly grandmother. "Your daughter has a special gift. She is a remarkable child, Mr. Joslyn. You can be extremely proud of her. She's a very impressive young woman. The Montana public education system can in no way claim credit for creating Annie's intellectual talents, but we can certainly recognize and celebrate them."

"Perhaps you and Annie would like to talk about this in private," suggested Martha.

"We really don't have anything to talk about," I said. "Annie's right. If we're talking about anyone else besides her, I'd be all for it. It's totally up to her. She's earned it, and whatever she wants is up to her."

"What about Tony?" Annie asked me.

"What about him?" I asked, but I knew what she meant.

"How will he handle it?" Annie asked.

"Are you kidding?" I answered. "The god Pan?" I looked at Miss Fordham. "The boyfriend of Aspen O'Toole?" I turned back toward Annie. "He'll be fine. You're a good sister, and a good daughter. But Mrs. Toups is right. This is something to recognize and celebrate."

Martha emitted a deep sigh of relief.

"Okay, so we're set?" I asked.

Martha nodded. She appeared on the verge of tears.

"You need to be at the Ledger at noon," I told Annie as I stood. I shook hands with Mrs. Toups and Miss Fordham. "Big game in Ennis this afternoon," I told them.

We – Annie, Trish, Slack and me – grabbed some A&W and got out of town a little later than I'd hoped. It was after twelve-thirty by the time we all gathered at the Ledger, made a stop for food and gas, and headed south for Ennis.

I slipped in the *Darkness on the Edge of Town* cassette, and Springsteen immediately burst into *Adam Raised a Cain*. I saw Annie's mouth moving quietly to the lyrics. Bruce was not singing softly. This was a road trip, this was supposed to be fun, and volume was required.

The Escort was packed; four people reaching for food and drinks at the same time cramped the interior. I had just exited town heading east on Highway 2, right at the barely noticeable bridge over Whitetail Creek when Slack spilled mayonnaise, lettuce and ketchup on the front of the seat and the floor.

"Whoops," he said, and dabbed with a napkin to rub the stain permanently into the fabric. "Sorry," he added sheepishly.

I waved him off. "It's not really a new car anymore," I said. I practically had to shout; I turned down the stereo a notch or two.

In the backseat, Annie was unwrapping Trish's fish fillet and setting out fries on the opened fish fillet wrapper in Trish's lap. Trish was sporting a yellow Ranger football jersey – Tony's, I realized after I had a chance to read the number in front – and a new pair of sunglasses. With the bright silky jersey and sunglasses, and her seated in the backseat alongside Annie downing fast food, you would have never known there was a wheelchair clogging the Escort trunk. Trish looked remarkably like a healthy and physically able high school girl. I wondered, briefly, if she ever aspired to that.

"How's the fish?" I asked her.

"Good," she said. "Annie got fish too. But she got onion rings."

"I hate onion rings," Slack stated.

"Why's that?" I asked.

Slack hesitated. "I just do."

"Have you ever tried onion rings?" I asked.

He hesitated again. "I don't like onions," he said.

We wound our way past Cardwell, over the Jefferson River and into Madison County, over the South Boulder River and eventually to the highway near Harrison that led straight south to Ennis. The weather was blustery and chilly, and spare coats and hats were stuffed in the backseat and in the trunk. A skiff of snow was visible to the west high on the Tobacco Root peaks, and a thicker coat of brilliant white covered the peaks of the Madison Range south and east of Ennis.

Ennis was a combination ranching/fishing village in a beautiful valley north of Yellowstone Park. The town's edge buttressed the fabled Madison River, one of the most famous trout rivers in the world. The Madison flowed off to our left, and beyond the water stood the mountains, rolling south all the way to Yellowstone National Park. With the sun off to our right, the mountains were bathed in a soft autumn glow, and this time of day, this time of year, the top of the pass was one of the most scenic places in the state.

I was going to comment on the view but Slack was sound asleep, his chin down and rested on his chest. He was getting fleshy around the jowls, and the combination of the double chin, whisker stubble and drips of greasy mayonnaise smeared across the corner of his lip was not a flattering portrait.

Annie's head was nodding to the music. Trish was looking out the window; as if deep in thought. I wondered if she was. If I suddenly asked her, could she tell me with precision what she was thinking about?

We raced down the hill to the valley bottom for the final leg of the trip into Ennis. Thanks to the late start we weren't going to get to the game as early as I liked. I preferred to get on the field during warm-ups, to get both my camera and me in position and prepared for taking pictures. I needed time to see which side of the field was best from a lighting standpoint, to make sure the flash was working right, to make a quick check of the game program and to see for sure which players were injured and possibly not playing. There would be no time for all that in Ennis; we weren't going to get there until just before kickoff.

Ennis was tied with Boulder for first place in the conference, and both teams were undefeated at 5-0 and both were in the top ten Class B rankings. The Montana Standard article on Friday morning suggested the Mustangs wouldn't have much trouble with the Rangers, especially since Colt Harrison was out of the game with an injured shoulder. Whitehall had one win all year, and had given up forty or more points three times. Ennis had scored forty points in four of its five games. The Mustangs had a senior All-Conference fullback named T.J. Wolf who had rushed for over two hundred yards against the Rangers in Whitehall the previous year. He was a strong, tough kid who was also a bruiser of a basketball player in the low post. He couldn't jump, but he had such a wide body and he boxed out so firmly he seemed to get every rebound.

The Ennis school colors were green and white, and by the time we parked the car and got Trish's wheelchair out and her in it, the green-shirted Ennis band was on the field getting ready to play the national anthem. Off to the side, in the south end zone by a small grove of trees, I spotted a handful of parked parade floats. It was Homecoming for Ennis.

At the booth I used my press pass for me, and was paying for Annie, Trish and Slack when the first notes of the National Anthem echoed across the field. The ticket-takers stopped, took off their hats, and stood at attention. I took the cowboy hat off Slack's head and handed it to him, and he held it at his chest. Together, the six of us stood as the band played an up-tempo version of the Star Spangled Banner.

One of the ticket-takers, an older guy with a silver beard, leaned toward the other ticket-taker, a taller man wearing a thick, insulated coat.

"Look at them Whitehall kids stand at attention," the older guy said in a hoarse whisper. "They ain't movin' a muscle."

The tall man nodded, standing at attention, his hand over his heart, facing the field, where the cheerleaders held the flags.

"Look at 'em," marveled the old guy. "They're still as statues."

The tall man continued to face the field.

"All of 'em," said the old guy.

The song wound down to a close.

"Those kids may not know how to play football, but they surely do know how to stand at attention," said the old guy as the song ended.

Annie, Slack and I – Annie pushing Trisha's wheelchair across the dirt path that led to the field – headed toward the Ranger sidelines as the band and Ennis cheerleaders marched away from us off the field.

Trish was so excited her face turned a hue of pink. I gave her a pat on the shoulder and left the three of them at the corner of the miniature four or five rows of visitor bleachers. The Ranger bench was directly in front of the bleachers – maybe ten feet away – and I slipped under a rope separating the fans from the sidelines. The sun was in the southwestern sky, and the light would be better if I stood on the Ennis sidelines, so I motioned to Annie to show her where I was going and crossed the field just out of the south end zone.

I stood on about the twenty yard line, well away from the Ennis bench, as little Dave Dickson prepared to kick off to the Mustangs. Across the sidelines Coach Pete stormed back and forth, pounding on shoulder pads or helmets. He wore purple Ranger shorts and a gold Ranger tee-shirt. I was wearing three layers and an old MSU stocking cap. Ennis was surrounded by mountains capped with snow, and you could smell – almost taste – the scent of snow on the wind. Jersey wore a black leather jacket and sunglasses shaped much like Trish's shades. His black hair had a shine to it, like a reflection almost.

"Time to ruin another Homecoming!" I hear Coach Pete yell all the way across the field.

Colt Harrison stood not far from Jersey, clipboard in his hand. He wore his Ranger letterman jacket. His arm wasn't in a sling or brace, and he could stand straight, both of which I took as an encouraging sign. I heard a couple of players on the sideline yelling encouragement, and every now and then I'd hear the faint but emotional cheer of Trish as she urged her Rangers to win.

Ennis handed the ball to T.J. Wolf five straight times before the quarterback threw an incomplete pass and the Mustangs had to punt. In the first quarter each team punted twice and neither team was even close to threatening to score. I couldn't say for sure, but I it looked like Logan Bradshaw tackled Wolf each time the Ennis fullback carried the ball.

And so for a while, the game settled into a contest between T.J. Wolf and Logan Bradshaw. Each kid was a bruising running back who lowered his head and ran straight ahead, and each kid got plenty of opportunities to carry the ball. They each led their team in rushing and tackles.

With the second quarter winding down, Dave rolled out to the wide side of the field – my side of the field – on an option play. He had faked the ball to

Logan up the middle, pulled the ball out when the defense converged, and took the ball to the outside. He was a magician with the ball. You could never be sure if he kept it or handed it off. He was five yards downfield when he pitched the ball to Nate. The pitch was not quite where it needed to be, and it bounced off Nate's outstretched fingertips. An Ennis defender caught the deflection off Nate's hands, and he raced sixty yards the other way for a touchdown.

The Ennis fans celebrated, but I sensed it was more a sigh of relief than outright joy. Ennis was gunning for a conference title and a trip to the playoffs, it was Homecoming against lowly Whitehall, and the score was not supposed to be tied at zero late in the first half. The extra point made it 7-0 and that was all the scoring before halftime. Even though offensive yardage and first downs were just about even, I had the feeling Whitehall had to play perfect to win, and perfection had already been lost with the fumble on the pitch.

I bought a cup of hot chocolate at halftime, and talked briefly with Annie and Trish. Slack was up in the bleachers with a handful of parents and siblings who'd made the trip from Whitehall. Day games cut down on attendance – as did a 1-4 record – and there were maybe thirty total fans on the Whitehall side of the field.

The halftime Homecoming celebration was mercifully brief – or at least it seemed brief compared to the marathon at Townsend – and instead of a production made of each royalty candidate the production centered upon the actual king and queen themselves. T.J. Wolf was the king and the queen was a girl who looked like she could have been his daughter. T.J. looked like a *man* standing there with a crown perched on his head.

And he played like a man in the second half. Up only 7-0 early in the fourth quarter, he carried the ball eight straight times, and the final carry was a nine-yard touchdown run through a weary and battered Ranger defense. The Ennis fans clapped and cheered, but the fan response was fairly subdued. The game wasn't supposed to be this close.

The Rangers put together their best drive of the game on their next possession. Dave completed a couple passes – one to Tony for a first down and one to Cale Bolling to get the ball inside the Ennis twenty yard line – and both Logan and Nate ripped off long gains on the ground. But a fourth down and goal pass in the end zone to Tony was overthrown, and Whitehall turned the ball over on downs.

On second down and ten, Ennis ran a simple looking screen pass to T.J. Wolf on the short side of the field, and when he caught the ball I was shocked to see there were no Rangers anywhere near him. Wolf had two blockers in front of him and eighty yards to the end zone, and it took him about ten seconds to get that far. The touchdown made it 21-0 and that's the way the game ended. Ennis was too big and too strong, and the Ranger offense, without Colt at quarterback, sputtered the entire game.

"Poop, poop," Colt muttered when the Rangers trudged despondently off the field.

The loss left Whitehall 1-5 overall and 1-2 in conference play with three games left. The loss guaranteed another losing season for the Rangers.

"Unless they make the playoffs," Annie told me as we walked to the car after the game.

"They'd have to win all three games to even have a chance at the playoffs," I said. She shook her head. "I don't much care. But this giving up under thirty points a game is wreaking havoc on my bet with Tony. I needed Ennis to score fifty-plus points today and they were lucky to score twenty-one. Unless Whitehall gets a lot worse, Tony's going to win the bet."

Cold, defeated, weary, we piled back into the Escort. All the jackets that had been wedged into open areas on the way to Ennis were kept on the way north to Whitehall. The sun was sinking behind the rose-tinted peaks in the west. Slack was asleep in the passenger seat before we even hit the hill leading up and out of sight of Ennis.

Since we made it back to Whitehall a little after six o'clock, I went to see the play a second time, and for a second time the various animals on stage moved around with seemingly no purpose and no direction until the stage lights were up and the actors took a curtain call.

Mary Kristofferson was in the audience, a row or two behind me, and I nodded a greeting to her when I sat down, and we chatted awhile during the intermission. She asked me about the newspaper business, I asked her how school was going. She told me what impressive kids I had, and I told her what a fine job I thought the play cast was doing. She seemed slightly nervous talking to me – her eyes cast furtive peeks at the people moving behind me – and when the lights flashed to warn the intermission was over I think we were both relieved.

I took fewer pictures, and I suppose I understood the play plot a little better, and I possibly understood the distinctions in the characters a little more clearly. Tanner was an excellent Mr. Badger. Tony again was impressive – as judged by his father, an impartial and objective parent – as the god Pan. He seemed to limp some, and he had a bruise the size of a grapefruit – and colored like a plum – on the area where his chest and shoulder connected. I thought he actually did a better job on Friday than Thursday, and my theory was the fatigue took an edge off some of the apprehension or tension. He had been beaten and battered by T.J. Wolf and the unbeaten Ennis Mustangs. How hard could wearing drapes and reciting a few lines be compared to that?

I went straight home after the play, and for about fifteen minutes I was the only person in the house. I figured I knew where Tony was, but Annie's whereabouts was a mystery. Friday nights at home alone were not uncommon occurrences for her. I sat in my recliner and turned on the TV. I might have dozed off for just a minute as I watched what might have been a talk show with someone who might have been Joan Rivers as host. Whatever it was, it was awful. If I'd had any energy I would have changed the channel. I had about fifteen minutes until the news came on, and my drowsy plan was to watch the TV sports and go to bed.

And that's pretty much what I did. But, for the first time in my life, far as I could recall, I went to sleep with both kids still awake – and both hosting guests – at home.

Annie, Natalie, Cody Phillips and Dave Dickson showed up close to ten o'clock, and had a board game – *Monopoly* – in tow. Ten minutes after that Tony and Aspen showed up. I lacked their energy, so I officially call it quits and went to bed.

I fell asleep to the pleasant sound of their voices. And after that, I dreamt of their voices.

Chapter 23

When the kids were little and we were a family of four living in Butte, Amy woke up early one frigid January Saturday morning to comfort Annie, who had been maybe three or four at the time. It was bitterly cold and dark, as bitter dark and cold as only winter in Butte could get. The old house we'd lived in creaked and cracked around us, as if we were aboard an old ship.

Annie had quickly graduated from *Sorry* and *Candyland* and *Chutes and Ladders* to games like *Stratego*, chess and *Othello*, and winter Saturday mornings were unofficially set aside by Annie for games.

Tony had his own room downstairs and on cold mornings could stay in his warm bed until noon. Not Annie. She had a bedroom across the hallway upstairs from ours, and she would wake up early, slip on a robe and read books while curled up on her bedroom floor in front of the furnace vent. Sometimes she'd be awake before six o'clock, a tiny light across the room on above her dresser, on her knees, actually, in front of the heat vent, reading books, magazines, catalogs, anything in the house that could be read. She would kneel there, on the floor, reading by dim and distant light, reading – sometimes to her herself, sometimes out loud – until she detected awakenings in the bedroom across the hall. Never did she deliberately wake us; never did she leave her room for the kitchen or a breakfast meal. Once in awhile she'd quietly slip down the hall to the bathroom, but she wouldn't even flush the toilet.

Amy left our bedroom the freezing January Saturday morning at about seven o'clock and I heard the door to Annie's room squeak slowly open and slowly shut. I heard the slight echo of Annie's childish voice and Amy's soothing murmured words as they selected a game to play. By the plastic clinks of game pieces, my guess was *Othello*. The games used to be kept downstairs, but eventually found a more natural home in Annie's room. I'd seen her play against herself in *Chutes and Ladders* and she would sometimes play a combination of chess and checkers, using rules I never understood even though I'd watched her play several times. I liked to play her in *Stratego* and *Battleship*, mostly because in those two games we talked back and forth, and the sound of her sweet young voice always made me smile, even when she beat me.

Othello was more silently strategic. I fell back asleep, and was jolted awake by a loud noise – a clash of some type – from Annie's room. Instantly, Amy was back in our bedroom. She jerked back the covers, hurled herself back into bed, buried her face into the pillow, and sobbed. She failed, or refused, to respond to my questions, which wasn't unprecedented, even then.

I got out of bed, and crossed the hallway into Annie's room; the wood hallway floor was like ice beneath my bare feet. I found Annie on hands and knees, crawling across her bedroom floor, picking up the scattered black and white coin-like pieces of the game.

She was nearly as unresponsive as Amy. I got on my knees and helped her, and when all the pieces were in the game board cylinders, without a word Annie stood and walked out of the room. I followed her as she went down the hall, through the living room and into the kitchen. The house seemed to groan with each step. We turned the heat down low at night to save money, and the temperature had dropped so much that frost formed on the inside of the windows. Annie's tiny hands opened the door to the garbage canister, stood up on her tiptoes, and stuffed the *Othello* game into the trash. She was without guile, remorse or resentment.

I woke up Saturday morning in Whitehall and found Annie already up and at the kitchen table reading the morning newspaper. For a child genius she could look astonishingly disheveled. Her hair was matted in the back and a wispy mess above her forehead. Her lips were dry, creased with tiny parched cracks.

"Reagan and Gorbachev are over in Reykjavik, but they can't seem to figure out a way to reduce the number of intermediate missiles in Europe," she said with dismay.

I was going to ask her what an intermediate missile was, but what I really wanted to know was the score of the Three Forks and Boulder football game from the previous night.

Beads of moisture dotted the outside of the kitchen window. I could hear a light smattering of rain hitting the portion of the metal rain gutter still attached to the house. I looked outside and was greeted by unmistakably dreary gray and damp weather. Leaves soggy with rain were stuck to the cement steps, and a few earthworms crawled with painfully slow difficulty across the sidewalk.

Inside it was drier, but just as disorderly. Remnants of the Friday night gathering were evident throughout the house. The *Monopoly* box – in two distinct pieces, the top and bottom – was on the kitchen counter, with the money and game pieces merely tossed messily into the top rather than properly placed in compartments in the bottom. Empty and crunched cans of pop were piled on the kitchen countertop and a smattering of potato chip crumbs littered the kitchen table. A container of tobacco chew rested flat on the table, as out of place as a hockey puck.

I thought about asking Annie why worms felt compelled to inch their way across pavement every time it rained, but the truth was I had no real desire to expand my knowledge of earthworms. So I asked her something else. "Who won the *Monopoly* game?"

She lifted her gaze, but not her head, from the newspaper, with a calculated *Who do you think won?* expression.

"I thought maybe you'd let Cody win," I said it as a joke. She did not find it humorous. Too early in the day, I figured.

"Cody played his first-ever game of *Monopoly* last night," Annie said. "Which is sort of sad, if you think about it."

Annie's world was filled with nuclear arms threats – assuming U.S. and Soviet intermediate missiles were nuclear, which was as much a guess as an assumption – regretful domestic conditions and fierce academic expectations, and I wondered just how big of a burden she could tote around.

"How'd Cody do on those tests you were studying for?"

She sighed. Perhaps I was interrupting her reading of the paper. "He did well enough to stay eligible, but he got C's on both tests." She turned the newspaper page. "He should have gotten A's. He knew the material."

"School's not easy for some kids," I said.

"Correct. But there are two issues here," she said. "I understand school can be a challenge for some people. But some kids have trouble learning or understanding the material. I thought that was Cody's problem, but it isn't. He reads it, he understands it and learns it. Somehow, though, that didn't translate well to the tests." She hesitated. "We'll have to work on that."

"That his?" I asked, and indicated the canister of chew.

She nodded.

"Get it out of here," I told her. "I don't want anyone chewing, drinking or smoking in this house. We're clear on that, right." It wasn't a question.

I received another sigh of resignation. "He lives by different rules than we do," she explained.

"When he's over here, when he's with you, he lives by your rules," I told her. "And you know what the rules are. If he can't follow him, I don't want him over here."

"Does Aspen have to follow the rules?" I detected the barest hint of a smirk.

"What's that supposed to mean?"

"You have a double standard," she said. "You're discriminating against Cody because of his lineage, his poverty and his struggles at school."

"Is that can of snoose his or Aspen's?" I asked.

Annie didn't answer.

"You're a smart kid, Annie, but you're still just a kid," I said. "Cody's seen more than his share of trouble. We both know that. He's seen and done things neither one of us want to know about. He's seen brutal and ugly things. You can see it just by looking at him. I'm not saying I don't want him over here. I think someone like you is probably good for a kid like him. But if he's going to be over here, he's got to leave the brutal and ugly things behind. He's going to follow our rules."

"Nicely done, Lance," she said, and nodded approvingly. "You were persuasive, logical and authoritative." She smiled. "I know you care, and I know you mean well. And I'll keep him in line. He wants me to keep him in line. He *expects* me to keep him in line. You know and I know I've been largely unsupervised so often and for so long that I know absolutely what the rules are, in part because I'm the one who made the rules. Don't take this the wrong way, but whatever rules exist around here will be enforced by me, not you, and they'll be enforced because I want them enforced, not because you want them enforced or because I know you want them enforced."

There was no wrong way to take it. I was absent so often I couldn't enforce anything. I had to trust her, and I did trust her. I had always trusted her.

"What age was it, Annie, when you became the authority figure?" I asked.

"I don't remember," she said. "But I don't remember a day when I *wasn't* the authority figure."

Neither did I, I realized. We may be a dysfunctional family, I thought, but we were a dysfunctional family with a genius, which gave us an advantage over the typical dysfunctional family.

I went to the refrigerator. Inside I found milk, pop, cheese, and a jar of peanut butter. I grabbed the milk, closed the door, and open the cabinet door and looked at the cereal options. Cheerios. That was it.

"I'm going grocery shopping this morning," Annie said.

"Looks like we need some cereal," I told the empty cabinet.

"We need some everything," Annie said. "Here," she told me, and slid the sports section to an empty spot across from her at the kitchen table, "you're going to want to read this. Three Forks beat Boulder last night."

The plan for this Saturday was to divide the day into two parts. Part one was getting the mail, catching up at the Ledger for the work I'd missed by attending the game in Ennis, then interviewing Jersey and writing the football article. Part two was attending the Whitehall Chamber of Commerce fall banquet at Borden's.

Getting the mail in Whitehall was often not as easy as it sounded. The physical task was simple enough, but the social and conversational responsibilities were sometimes demanding. Whitehall had rural mail delivery, but no in-town mail delivery. Everyone who lived in town had a box at the post office, and everyone got their mail pretty much every day, at pretty much the same time, which meant each day a few hundred people trekked to the post office. Somewhere between ten o'clock and noon were the busiest times, and there were days when it would take me up to an hour to simply walk the two blocks to the post office, open the box, remove the mail, and walk back to the Ledger. It was possible to conduct a dozen brief, and at times lengthy, conversations on the way to the post office, at the post office, and on the way from the post office back to the Ledger. There were some days I didn't have a half hour to spare, so I sent Laura Joyce to get the mail, and invariably she had the same problem I did.

I stopped at the post office after I finished the Cheerios and chatted about the weather, the Ennis football game, the Chamber evening banquet, a junior high student's appearance on the Honor Roll and the quality of the Friday clam chowder lunch at the senior's center.

It was quaint, I suppose – if anything can truly be quaint – this small town custom of socializing at the post office. But Whitehall was certainly a small town, and the truth was that if the U.S. Postal Service decided to venture into in-town mail delivery, it would create a sizeable and disheartening social gap each morning for hundreds of Whitehall residents. Maybe life is simpler in a small town, but the plain truth was a lot of people, including me, planned their day around the midmorning trip to the post office.

At the Ledger I had a couple hours to catch up on Friday's missed work and prepare for Monday's workload before Jersey showed up for the interview. It was his idea to come by the Ledger; I suspect he preferred to avoid his classroom during the weekend.

As I sat at my desk sorting mail I saw a tiny dark blur scoot across the floor. The mouse skirted the baseboard in a panic as if I'd surprised it, as if it knew it was a Saturday morning and expected no one to show up in the office. He scurried between the front counter and the wall and then made a break across the short open space to the crack in the wall. Three traps were still scattered around the Ledger and the mouse had again avoided all three of them. I had the feeling more traps wouldn't make much of a difference. The mouse barely slowed down as it seemed to dive through the narrow slit in the baseboard.

It was an odd feeling, but the mouse made it appear as if it was entirely comfortable and knowledgeable inside the Ledger, as if a trip through the office was wholly routine. So, the next option, I figured, was poison. The problem with poison was that the mouse ate it and died behind the wall somewhere and stunk up the place. I put down the mail and headed for the hardware store for some pellets.

Jersey knocked and entered exactly on time, to the minute, at two o'clock sharp. It was his first time at the Ledger.

"So this is the infamous Ledger newspaper office," Jersey said. He looked around. "It's smaller than I thought it'd be."

"Don't let the size fool you," I said. "We can be as ruthless as any big paper."

"Oh, I've seen it," he said, joking, I hoped.

There was a small round table – a dining table, actually – set up in the corner of the office, with four mismatched chairs around it. This is where interviews were conducted, and on Tuesdays it was where Laura Joyce sat to arrange the labels for the Wednesday mailing of the Ledger.

Jersey wore a dark gray Rockin' Rudy's sweatshirt that was spotted with black splotches from the rain outside. He hadn't shaved and had a thick, short black stubble on his chin, less so on his cheeks. He seemed taller close up, or perhaps taller seated, and he had to sit with his legs to the side because his legs didn't fit under the table.

We did the usual interview, with him more or less saying the usual things. He complimented Dave Dickson and Logan, and said Logan was emerging as one of the conference's best players. He was happy with the way the team tackled and pursued on defense, and thought special teams outplayed the Ennis special teams. He liked the intensity of the players and said he thought the team was showing improvement every week. He was hoping to get Colt back in a week or two and singled out Tony and Nate on defense. He said the offensive line – especially Cody and JeffScott – did a good job opening some holes for Logan.

Then he said something offhand, in a casual yet confident tone of voice that didn't fit in with his previous comments and struck me as odd for a team with one win and five losses. "We're going to win the rest of our games, and when we do we've got a good shot at the playoffs."

It seemed so unrealistic that I didn't even write it down. Jersey caught my omission, narrowed his eyes and told me to go ahead, put it in the paper.

I hesitated, and actually cleared my throat. "Don't you think," I started and didn't have the heart to finish.

"Do I think people will think I'm crazy?" He gave me a wry grin.

"Or foolish," I admitted.

"What do you think?" he asked.

"Well," I said. He was looking directly into my eyes. "I think you've won one game this year, and you've lost five. Your starting quarterback is out with a bad shoulder. You have to play Three Forks for our Homecoming next week, and Three Forks just beat Boulder, who previously beat Whitehall by four touchdowns. So, while I wouldn't say you're crazy or foolish, I would say you're maybe, just maybe, a wee bit optimistic."

He leaned back. He leaned his head at an angle, a *fair enough* gesture. "You have to be optimistic to be a coach. Every coach has to go into every game thinking he or she's going to win. If you don't you're already beat."

"All that's fine," I said, "but that doesn't mean every coach with one win and five losses tells the local newspaper they're going to win the rest of their games and make the playoffs. Not everybody is going to make the playoffs and a lot of those teams that won't make the playoffs already have more than one win right now."

He rubbed his chin, as if in thought. "Is that a mouse?"

I whirled around. Yes, it was. I half stood and stomped the floor, and the mouse froze as if pondering where the noise came from, then did an abrupt turn and scurried back into the hole.

"Apparently, it's a trained mouse," Jersey commented.

"It will soon be a dead mouse," I said. "Traps didn't work, but I went over to the hardware store and got something that will work. Guaranteed."

He seemed on the verge of saying something, then opted not to, then went ahead and spoke. "So the mouse has outsmarted you?"

"Temporarily," I asserted. "The mouse's days are numbered."

"That appeared to me to be a confident mouse," Jersey said.

"It's been a week now since I first saw him," I admitted, "and he's getting bolder. He's even coming out during the day now. Before it was only at night."

Jersey sat there, looking at me and behind me, where the mouse had disappeared. Jersey's eyes were so brown they were almost black, and his hair was so thick and so black it looked unnatural. He looked like he was trying to figure something out.

"Okay," I said, to get us back on track, "you really want me to write that you're going to win the rest of your games and go to the playoffs?"

He shook his head. "We can't control whether we make the playoffs or not, because there's going to have to be an upset or two along the way for us to get in. But we *are* going to win the rest of our games. If we play the rest of the way like we did the last two weeks, we'll beat Three Forks, Manhattan and Big Timber."

I nodded. "That's a better way to put it. *If* we play as well as we did, we'll win the rest of our games." I wrote it down in my notebook. I decided not to ask how he figured to beat Three Forks. Given the scores, Three Forks should be a six-touchdown favorite.

"We're not the same team we were when we played Boulder," Jersey said, as if I had, in fact, asked the question about how he figured to beat Three Fork. "We're stronger, we're more confident, we're more versatile and we've got the right people in the right positions. We're a far better team than we were two-three weeks ago."

"Will Colt be ready to play against Three Forks?" I asked.

"We'll see," was all he said.

"It's his senior Homecoming year," I said, "I hope he can play."

"Homecoming," Jersey muttered. "You know, Homecoming is great for the community, for the school, for the kids, for school spirit. It's a big festive day for everyone. But for the players, it's a huge distraction. The bonfire, the pep rallies, the parade, the royalty ceremony are all a lot of fun, but they also divert the focus of the players. This is a big game for us, and after we win we'll be in great shape the rest of the way."

"Last year we lost our Homecoming game 34-0," I said. "There wasn't much festive about that."

He stood up. The interview was over. "This year will be a different story." He walked toward the door. He looked down at the floor. "I have a hunch you haven't seen the last of that mouse."

"That mouse is history," I assured him.

I more or less followed him to the door. He turned around just as he reached for the doorknob. "Hey, congratulations to Annie on the Mensa membership. That's really impressive. It's a great thing for her, her family, the school, the community, everyone. I hope you're proud of her."

I found myself nodding, and looking up at him. "I am. She's an amazing kid."

And he was looking down at me. "You need to tell her that."

I was still nodding when he closed the door.

Sunday early evening I was back at the Ledger. I had taken pictures the night before at the Chamber of Commerce banquet, and between the play, the football game and banquet I had taken well over a hundred pictures on four rolls of thirty-six-exposure film. As I developed the film – two rolls at a time – I vacuumed the Ledger floor and emptied the trio of wastebaskets into the dumpster that sat in the parking lot behind the building.

When Amy and I first bought the Ledger, the office was cleaned each week. Since then, I vacuumed once a month at most, and took out the garbage whenever the wastebaskets got full.

The first rolls of film developed were from the Chamber banquet. I had good crisp pictures of the Whitehall business of the year – Patacini Tire owners Tim and Sue Patacini – both with wide grins holding the plaque handed to them by Chamber president Lyle O'Toole. Other photos from the event were of Chamber volunteers of the year, Mary and Ryan Jones of the IGA; of the newly elected Chamber board of directors; of the Chamber employee of the year, Wanda Freman, who worked at Whitehall Drug; of a special award given to Golden Sunlight Mine for its contributions to the Chamber and to the community and of Tim Mulligan of The Corner Store for his donations to the Whitehall Food Pantry, of little Bryce Grayling – the mayor's son, who was also in attendance – playing a few songs on the piano during the social hour. The plan was to put a couple banquet pictures on the front page, and fill an inside page – page eight, probably – with six or so banquet photos.

Some of pictures from the play didn't turn out sharp enough – I just could not master the lighting conditions without the use of a flash – but there were a handful good enough for a small town weekly newspaper. Since the football game had been played in Ennis during daylight hours I had several good actions shots including two good pictures of Logan, one on a tackle when he was driving the Ennis ball carrier backward and one on offense running over a tackler. I almost never put two photos of one kid in the same edition, and couldn't remember ever putting two pictures of a kid from one game, but Logan had earned it.

I had learned early in my tenure at Whitehall that it was essential to spread the pictures of students across as broad a spectrum as possible. Parents were extremely sensitive to anything even resembling a hint of favoritism. I got the impression parents didn't care how often their kids' picture was in the Ledger as long as it was as often as other kids' pictures. One week a few years earlier the same girl – a high school senior named Kelly Davis – had her picture in the paper five times in the graduation edition: She had placed third in the high jump at the state track meet, had won the VFW Voice of Democracy essay contest, was class salutatorian, had led a group of seniors who had raised money and donated a check to the Whitehall Head Start program and had earned an academic full-ride scholarship to Washington State University. In the Ledger's defense, I argued none of the photos were optional. It wasn't my fault one kid did them all. I had a hunch a few parents of football players would gripe about Logan being in the paper twice, but he led the team in carries and tackles. In a game where the Rangers were shut out and lost their fifth game of the year, Logan was the story, and even though some people wouldn't like it, Logan was getting some ink in his hometown newspaper because he deserved it.

The film had been developed and was drying in strips in the darkroom when I got twelve two-page sheets of paste-up paper started on the layout bank. I heard a faint scratching behind me, and turned to see the mouse crouched under the corner of the desk where Annie sat to do the paperwork and accounting.

Slowly, I took a couple steps to my right and silently reached for the rifle. I had intended to buy poison at the hardware store, but as I was looking for it on the shelves I spotted a Daisy BB gun, and knew immediately and instinctively that use of a gun was the best option to dispatch the mouse. Shooting it would avoid the possibility of the mouse dying and rotting in the wall or someplace where I couldn't reach it.

Like most American pre-teen males, I'd had a BB gun in junior high, and like all American pre-teen males, I had fancied myself a pretty good shot. The instant I spotted the BB gun in the hardware store I instantly knew it was the preferred weapon to address the newspaper's vermin problem.

I held the gun, and as quietly as possible, pumped the lever to get a BB in the chamber. The mouse stopped, motionless and listening, then stood up and sniffed. It leaned forward to return to all fours, and as it crept carefully out from under the desk drawer I had it lined up on the sight of the rifle barrel.

It moved a little away from me, toward the far wall, and I raised the rifle as I kept the mouse in the small v-shape of the rifle sight. The mouse turned slightly to its left, so its body was facing me lengthwise, which gave me the broadest target possible. I squeezed the trigger, felt the rifle jerk up slightly and heard the muffled *pop* as the BB fired from the gun. Next I heard a *ping* sound and then something whacked me above my right eye, on the flesh of my forehead right above my eyebrow.

I'd shot myself. The BB had gone high, above the mouse, and hit the wall hard enough to ricochet back and hit me in the forehead. Jesus Christ, I thought, I've been hit. The mouse scurried back to the hole in the baseboard before I could get a second shot off, but to be truthful, there was never an intention of a second shot. My forehead hurt. I put the gun down, and went into the bathroom to inspect the damage. I had an ugly red knot the size of a pea above my eyebrow. I bunched up a couple paper towels, ran them under cold water and then held them to my head.

I wasn't bleeding, but pretty quickly the knot sprouted to the size of a marble. I was holding the paper towels against my forehead when the distinctive knock of Jefferson County Commissioner Cal Walker sounded from the Ledger door. He opened the door just as I tossed the paper towels into the bathroom wastebasket.

"Anyone home?" Cal asked as he entered.

"Come on in," I said, and he practically gasped when he saw the bump on my forehead.

"What the hell is that?" he asked. He set the pop and bag of popcorn on the counter. "I don't know," I lied. "When I woke up this morning it was like this."

Clearly he didn't believe me. He put his hands on either side of my head, near my ears. He was close enough for me to smell the popcorn on his breath. He inspected my head, turning it slightly to see the welt from different angles.

"It looks like someone just hit you in the head with a hammer," he said.

"To be honest with you, it kind of hurts," I admitted. I didn't know what I would tell Cal, but I knew what I wouldn't tell him. I wouldn't tell him I missed a mouse and instead shot myself in the head with a BB gun. Give that story three days in a small town and see what happens.

"You woke up with this?" Cal asked with disbelief. The brim of his cowboy hat rubbed against the top of my head as he inspected the bump. Our eyes were about eight inches apart, and I could read his mind: *Lance is lying*.

"Maybe I got bit by a spider," I tried.

"Maybe, if the spider was the size of a bulldog," he said. He finally let go of my head and leaned back. "You might want to get that looked at. By a doctor, I mean."

I nodded, as if that was exactly what I might do.

He shook his head with incredulity. "That's the damnedest thing I've ever seen. I swear it looks like someone just took a ball peen hammer and thumped you a good one." He smiled. "You royally piss off someone recently?"

I laughed, as if Cal had actually said something humorous. On the floor, behind him to his left, just outside of the baseboard wall, stood the mouse. It was propped up on its hind legs, it's nose sniffing and whiskers twitching, and honest to God it looked as if it had crept from its hole out of curiosity, to see who I was talking to. It shifted its gaze from Cal and me as if it was a third member of the conversation.

"Outside of a mysterious giant welt, how is everything?" Cal asked. He'd emphasized the word *mysterious* as if he suspected it wasn't a mystery to me, and he wanted me to know that.

Cal saw where my eyes were aimed, and as he turned to look down at the floor his jacket rustled and the mouse dived back into the hole.

I dabbed at the knot on my head. It felt like the size of a golf ball, but I knew it couldn't possibly be that big. I did not invite Cal to sit down; we stood standing, and I hoped he'd take the hint and keep his visit short.

"Sounds like the kids played pretty well in Ennis," he said.

"They did okay," I said. "Ennis is big and strong, and we aren't."

"Did that Harrison kid not playing hurt the team much?" Cal asked.

I shook my head. That was the last time I'll do that tonight, I thought. The skin surrounding the welt was so tender I felt the chill of the air when my head moved. "We would have lost even if he had played. Ennis is just a better team."

"The Rangers played 'em tough, though," Cal said. "Not too many teams held Ennis to three touchdowns."

"Logan Bradshaw was all over the field," I said. "He made almost every tackle."

"I heard that," Cal said.

The mouse started to sneak out of its hole again. Tentatively, sniffing constantly, it eased out until its entire body was out of the hole and on the floor. It rose onto its haunches, sniffing, sniffing, and turned slightly, sniffing.

The popcorn. The little shit smelled the popcorn. The mouse was perched on its hind feet, sniffing, looking up at the counter top. I reached past Cal and grabbed the popcorn.

"Help yourself," he said, puzzled.

I stomped my foot and the mouse ducked and scurried back into the wall.

Cal was still in the entryway of the Ledger, the door not five feet behind him. He knew this was not a typical visit – where I invited him and he sat in Laura Joyce's chair and we chatted until the popcorn was gone – but typically my forehead wasn't sporting a bump the size of a plum.

"I think I'll clear out," he said, and I didn't say anything to suggest he stay. He pointed at my forehead. "I'm serious. You better get that thing checked out. I swear it's bigger now than when I first walked in here."

"Good idea," I said.

"Congratulations on Annie and that Mensa thing," he said. "That's the name, right? Mensa?"

"Yeah, smartest people in the world," I told him.

He shook his head. "I gotta admit, looking at you now," and he indicated the knot at my forehead, "it's hard to figure how your daughter's a genius."

"Tell me about it," I said.

Chapter 24

Homecoming, one of the grand Americana high school traditions, was celebrated in Whitehall in much the same way as every place else in the country: Pep rallies, talent show, parade, coronation, dance, football game, returning alumni, bonfire featuring abundant if artificially manufactured school spirit and, usually, an unwelcome and unnecessary amount of teenage angst and melodrama.

A few years earlier in Whitehall a traffic accident after the Homecoming night dance resulted in minor injuries and a totaled pickup south of town on the Waterloo Road. The next morning I took a picture of the truck, and it was astonishing anyone survived that kind of carnage. A couple years before that the Madison County Sheriff's office busted a Homecoming kegger near Bone Basin that resulted in 21 minor in possession citations that terminated the season of football players from three different high schools.

Butte, the nearest metropolitan area near Whitehall, was built on grit, courage and stupidity, and Whitehall – in both miles and attitude – is not far down the road. Butte's culture is based on hard rock mining and hard luck living, and its residents are proud of both. Whitehall mixed in railroads and agriculture with the hard rock mining, and while we're far from a mirror image of Butte, there is an element of lawlessness and menace in Whitehall. Kids like Logan Bradshaw and Cody Phillips, kids you know have broken the law and you know will break the law again, kids who understand and have experienced the dark side of life through violence, poverty and addiction, are an accepted part of Whitehall, perhaps even an embraced part of Whitehall. When you live in a small town, you have the nagging thought you're only one bad decision, car wreck, layoff or recession away from violence, poverty and addiction yourself. Still, the dichotomy was we never locked our car door or house door in Whitehall, even when Amy lived here. I had no idea where our house keys were, or if even we had any.

That's not to say crime is unheard of in Whitehall. Most of the basic crimes – shoplifting, spousal battery, drunk driving, poaching game, moving traffic violations, an occasional stolen vehicle, bar fights, domestic eruptions, child abuse – occur in Whitehall, but all our crimes are solved right away, and the guilty party is typically either an alcoholic, is chronically unemployed, mentally ill, or all three. I'd never heard of an unsolved major crime in Whitehall, and the only killings – a hit and run and the shooting of an abusive husband – saw the culprits captured moments after the crime. Manfred, the town marshal, a man so overweight he could lose his breath by merely getting out of a car, once told me he estimated that ninety-five percent of the crime in Whitehall was committed by maybe a dozen people – not the same dozen, but a revolving dozen comprised of about thirty people – who filtered in and out of town, in and out of jail or prison, in and out of rehab, in and out of work, in and out of sanity. He also told me he could walk into any Whitehall elementary grade classroom right then and point out the two or three kids who eventually would run into trouble with the law. Most kids talked about Manfred with hushed decorum, and more than once I'd show up to cover a court hearing to see the accused wearing a bump, discoloration or bandage, roughed up for resisting arrest.

Monday night of Homecoming week was reserved for the bonfire, and the Whitehall Volunteer Fire Department – led by Cale Bolling's dad, Kyle – oversaw the fire while Manfred sat off to the side, away from the fire, in darkness, watching the crowd parked inside the police cruiser. The WHS pep band played the school song, a song from the band Chicago, a Credence Clearwater Revival song and a few other songs I'd never heard.

It was a pleasant night for a fire. The temperature had dropped when the sun went down, and it was cold enough to see your breath if you drifted too far away from the fire. The wind had also lain down with dusk, so there wasn't much danger of the fire getting away into the shelterbelt of trees surrounding the football field, an unfortunate accident that had actually occurred one year after we'd moved to Whitehall.

Kyle, who worked at the Golden Sunlight Mine mill, had only lived in Whitehall for four or five years but had years of firefighting experience in Nevada. Cale was a younger, thinner version of Kyle, and as trumpet player in the band he was clearly silhouetted with the fire behind him.

I took a few pictures of him and the band as they played, then wandered over to the fire truck to visit with Kyle.

"What happened to your head?" he asked as I leaned against the front of the truck. "You get thumped by Manfred?"

"Nope," I said. Damn mouse. It was probably back at the Ledger that instant, sniffing around for popcorn and whatever else it could find.

"You didn't hit another cow, did you?" he asked.

"Shit," I told him, "you hit one cow and it follows you the rest of your life."

"That's a serious bump you got there," Kyle persisted.

"In Anaconda last week when we were printing the paper a lunk waffle flew off the press, bounced off the cement wall and caught me in the forehead."

"A *what* flew off?"

I waved him off. "Ah, never mind. Part of the press. I'll be fine."

In the flickering shadows of the fire I could see he was tempted to push his inquiry further, but opted to pursue a different topic. "Well, it sounds like we each have kids nominated for royalty this year."

We did? I couldn't hide my puzzled expression.

"That's what I was told," he said. "Tony was nominated. Let's see, who else? Logan Bradshaw. Dave Dickson. Colt, of course. Tanner Walker, I think. You didn't know?"

"When did all this happen?" I asked.

"Just today."

So I had no chance of knowing. It was a typical Monday at the Ledger, which meant every second of every minute of every hour had to be squeezed for maximum productivity. Tony had football practice after school and then maybe went home, I didn't know, or ate dinner at A&W or at O'Toole's with Aspen before the bonfire. I searched the bonfire crowd and spotted him off to the side, his arms wrapped around Aspen, who stood directly in front of him, her face lit in gold by the firelight. Annie was supposedly somewhere in the crowd of students around the fire, but it was so dark and she was so small compared to all the high school students I couldn't find her.

"I haven't had a chance to talk with Tony all day," I told Kyle.

"How many hours a week do you work?" Kyle asked. "You're at every community event I'm at, and I know you're at all the community meetings and activities I'm not at."

"Too many," I said. "The first forty hours a week aren't bad, but the next forty pretty much tucker me out."

He shook his head. "The only job worse than yours is owning a dairy," said Kyle, "and milking cows twice a day."

"According to Bill Powell, my job's worse," I said. The Powells owned a dairy east of Whitehall, in the South Boulder area.

"How's yours worse?"

"Bill says if you own a dairy you don't have to know how to spell."

Kyle laughed. He pointed to my forehead. "Or get whacked by flying chunks of printing presses."

Involuntarily I reached up and touched the knob on my forehead. It wasn't as prominent as it had been Sunday night, but the skin was still tender and was turning a dark shade of grayish purple. It had been quite a conversational piece during my Monday ad stops. "I better go take some more pictures. Congratulations to Cale. I hope he's ready to beat Three Forks on Friday night."

"He said he's tired of losing," Kyle said. He paused. "He says it like he means it."

I walked around the edge of the fire and came up on Tony and Aspen from behind. They were leaning into each other, her head laid back on his shoulder.

"So, were you both named royalty candidates?" I asked before they could see me.

If I thought I would startle them into discomfort or to at least shift their posture, I was wrong. Both turned their faces toward me, but outside of that neither one budged. "Hi," Aspen beamed. Her white teeth practically glowed in the dark. I couldn't help but think that she was one incredibly healthy young woman. Healthy in every way. Perfect appearance in every way.

"Yeah, both of us," Tony said.

"Congratulations," I said.

"I'm skipping school tomorrow to go with my mom to Bozeman to shop for a new dress," Aspen said.

That's a statement, I thought sadly, Annie would never be able to utter. Aspen was totally healthy and wholly lucky to be born into a perfect family, but such luck, health and family wholeness were foreign to my kids. I wondered, briefly, if Annie and I were going to have to take Tony shopping and buy him a new shirt or something. I'd have to ask Annie about that.

Aspen's Homecoming attire seemed to hold no interest for Tony. He leaned with contented affection against his girlfriend, the golden light of sparkling fingers of flame that highlighted the youth, softness and innocence of their faces. His long dark hair hung over the collar of his purple and gold letterman's jacket. He needed a haircut again. Or perhaps still needed a haircut. The kid was in perpetual need of a haircut.

I could have left without saying a word, and they would never have noticed. I was absolutely inconsequential to them at that moment; everything outside their embrace was insignificant.

"Well, I better get to work," I said and began to shuffle off.

"Lance, owww, what happened to your forehead?" Aspen asked with anguish, as if the bump broke her heart.

"He won't tell us," Tony told her. "He came home with it Sunday night, but won't say what happened."

"I told you what happened," I said. I looked at the lovely Aspen O'Toole. "I was developing film in the darkroom when a shelf collapsed and hit me in the head. It's pitch black in there, you know, total darkness, and at first I had no idea what hit me."

"Ohh, that sounds terrible," Aspen moaned.

"It also sounds like nonsense," Tony said.

"Nonsense?" I said. "Look at this knot and tell me it's nonsense. It was the main wood shelving that held paper and supplies above the enlarger, and I couldn't do anything about it until after I wrapped the film onto the spool and got it inside the canister."

"Well, I'm glad you're okay," Aspen said, and said it so there was no doubt I had been officially dismissed.

"See you kids later," I said. "Tony, you need to be home by eleven. And you need a haircut."

"Right," he said with indifference.

I circled the bonfire and took a few more pictures. A fire is a photogenic event, but only one or two photos at most of the bonfire would make it into the paper, so after ten minutes or so I put the camera away. I'd taken a picture of Trish, leaning awkwardly to her left in the wheelchair, gazing toward the fire. I looked again for Annie, but still didn't see her. I had to head back to the Ledger for a couple hours of basic Monday night work when Manfred waved me over to the police car. Like Kyle with the fire department, Manfred was there 'just in case' and sat in the parked police car – the driver's side door open – as a simple show of authority.

Manfred's face was glistening, and it seemed like it was continually sweating. I opened the passenger side of the car and climbed into the front seat. A short shotgun was propped up vertically in the area between the two front seats. Manfred reached over and turned down the dispatch radio. The car was parked just off the track east of the bleachers, facing the fire. Manfred was hatless, his forehead moist in the flickering light from the flames.

"How's the Ledger guy?" Manfred asked.

Manfred and I were friendly, mostly because we had to be. It was more of an unspoken truce than actual friendship. He couldn't afford to alienate his hometown press, and I needed him to answer official questions related to crimes, investigations and arrests. The relationship was somewhat tenuous, but Manfred had been genuinely grateful the way the paper had handled the Merle Stoviack suicide. The way I handled it had nothing to do with Manfred, but it seemed uncharitable to tell him that, so I let him think what he wanted to think.

"Fine," I said. "How's the police guy?"

Manfred simply nodded. He looked straight ahead, observing the fire, the crowd, the action. He turned to me. His face was so wide you'd have sworn the inside of his mouth held two helpings of mashed potatoes.

"Son of a bitch, what happened to your forehead?" he asked, startled.

"Nothing," I told him.

"Nothing, my ass," he said. He leaned toward me to get a better look at it. He furled his brow. "You look like you got hit in the head with a baseball bat." He paused. "You owe someone in Butte some money?" He chuckled.

I thought he'd drop his interrogation, but he didn't. He sat more or less glaring at me, as if silently demanding an answer. I supposed he wanted to make sure he wasn't missing some kind of a crime committed either by me – an unreported car accident – or to me – someone beat me up.

"It's nothing," I said. I thought about telling him the truth, but it was too embarrassing. Plus, I was uncertain about Whitehall's gun laws. For all I knew, it was illegal to shoot a BB gun inside the city limits. "I was hauling a couple bundle of papers into the IGA and couldn't really see where I was going. I caught the damn automatic door half open and it whacked my head."

Manfred kept glaring at me, and I resisted the urge to keep on talking. We sat there silently, not three feet apart, and his expression all but called me a liar. Manfred had a professional look of malevolence that suggested bad intent.

"That Phillips kid didn't do it, did he?" Manfred finally asked. It was not an offhand question.

"What?" I said. "Cody? Phillips? No," I was surprised at the question, but as I thought about it I understood Manfred's perverse and dogmatic logic. "For Christ's sake, Manfred. No. A high school sophomore did not do this to me. Trust me, I did it to myself."

"I've seen his rig parked in your driveway," Manfred said, as if we were conspirators. He meant to say it coyly, but not much about Manfred was coy. "Sometimes late at night." He squinted just a little. "Sometimes when you're still working."

"He and Annie are friends, I guess," I said. "She's helping him with his schoolwork. You think you know something different?" It was as much accusation as question.

Manfred shook his head, and I heard his neck whiskers brush against his shirt collar. He looked toward the fire a moment, then turned to face me. "Cody Phillips is nothing but trouble. Been that way since the day he was born." He looked me in the eye. "You're asking for trouble. You understand me, don't you?"

I did. But if I agreed with him I thought I'd somehow be betraying Annie. "I appreciate your concern, Manfred, but so far I haven't seen any problems." I didn't sound convincing. The town marshal, whose life's work dealt with trouble, knew Cody far better than I did or would ever want to or have to. I understood his comments, and I should have appreciated them. Should have. But there was malice and intolerance in his warning.

"I'd keep my eye open, I was you," Manfred said. "Annie may be smart, but Cody's got a bad attitude." He looked straight out the windshield. "Just want you to know that."

"Got it," I said. My right hand went to open the door; my left hand reached down to grab the camera case. I wanted to get out of there. "Thanks. I'll have a talk with Annie."

"You do that," Manfred said.

I closed the door, took two or three quick steps, and in my haste, bumped into someone, and that someone was Mary Kristofferson. Her back was toward me as she spoke to a group of junior high girls, whose eyes were wide with excitement at attending what may have been their first high school bonfire.

"Sorry," I apologized. I was fleeing Manfred with such force I had to hold one of her shoulders to steady us both.

She turned toward me with an initial fierce expression of educational authority that immediately relented to slight stunned confusion when she saw it was me.

"Sorry," I told her again. "I didn't see you there."

"I've only been standing here for twenty minutes," she answered cheerfully.

The junior high girls giggled, and Mary sort of shooed them away.

My back was to the fire, so my face was lit dimly by a couple of bleacher yard lights. I could see her eyeing the bump on my forehead.

"Go ahead," I said.

She shifted her gaze momentarily to my face, then involuntarily lifted her eyes toward my forehead. "Go ahead what?"

"Ask," I said.

"Ask what?" she asked.

"You know what."

"Looks like you ran into something besides me," she said. She crouched down a bit, for a better angle to view my forehead. I even turned so she had the best view possible. "Wow. That looks like it hurts."

"It does hurt," I told her. "I shot myself with a BB gun."

She hesitated. She leaned closer, to not be overheard. "You tried to commit suicide with a BB gun?" she asked softly. It was spoken with a hint of mischief.

"Actually, I was shooting at a mouse in the Ledger, and the BB ricocheted off the wall."

She winced. "You shot a mouse indoors?" she asked, puzzled.

"I had to," I explained. "I set traps but the mouse avoided them. So I bought the BB gun and the first shot I took missed and hit me in the head."

"You shot a mouse indoors?" she repeated.

"No, I shot *at* a mouse indoors," I corrected. "I *missed* a mouse. I think I aimed too high, but I don't know for sure. The only thing I actually hit was me, on a rebound off the wall."

She started laughing. It was the first time I'd heard her laugh. She laughed so hard I thought for a minute she was going to have to sit down.

"I'm not sure you've noticed," I said, "but this is a pretty big knot I got here on my forehead. And it was pretty painful. I mean, you shoot yourself in the head with a BB gun and see how it feels."

She kept on laughing. She was still laughing, truly enjoying herself, when I walked away, cut across the empty practice football field, cloaked in utter darkness, and walked the three blocks down Division Street back to the Ledger.

The mouse scurried across the floor into the baseboard crack when I opened the door and stayed in its hole for close to three full hours.

But at about eleven o'clock it carefully, slowly, snuck its nose, then head, then body outside the baseboard. It rocked back on its haunches, tilted its nose in the air, and sniffed as if searching for an odor. It crept away from the wall, sniffing at every step. It was headed for the crumbled up half of a Ritz cracker I had covertly and strategically set on the floor directly across from my desk. I had a clear shot across the room from me to the cracker, and I had the BB gun cocked and loaded, upright between my desk and the wall, not unlike the shotgun aimed at the roof in Manfred's police car. I also had added a safety precaution: wide plastic-rubber eyeglasses I had purchased at the hardware store during my morning ad stops. They were essentially high school shop safety glasses, and as the mouse silently sniffed its way toward the Ritz cracker I slipped the safety glasses strap behind my head and the glasses in front of my eyes.

I immediately realized – like an idiot – that thick rubbery plastic glasses screwed up my vision and depth perception. I had to lift the glasses away from my eye, sight the rifle on the mouse, lower the glasses for the shot, but then I couldn't see. I had to lift the glasses to sight, and lower the glasses if I wanted to shoot, as the mouse crept toward the cracker. Finally, the mouse reached the tiny pile of cracker crumbs, and I held the glasses away from my eye for one last sighting with the rifle. The mouse picked up a crumb, and shifted it delicately in its paws as he brought it to his mouth and began to nibble.

Looking through the eyeglasses, I held my breath, locked in on my target, and squeezed off a round. The BB must have hit the wall behind the mouse, bounced back toward me, missed me, bounced off the file cabinet behind me, and hit the glass window about two feet above the mouse and cracker.

To see clearly, I tipped the eyeglasses up on my forehead; which hurt, because of the welt from the BB the previous night. I had to raise the glasses so they were sitting almost squarely on top of my head. From across the room I spotted the chunk of glass the BB chipped from the window. The window wasn't broken or cracked, but it was chipped. Twice I'd tried to shoot a mouse. Once I shot myself, the other time I shot a window.

The mouse simply sat back and munched on the cracker. I'd missed by so much he didn't know he'd been shot at. He reached and picked up another piece of cracker, brought it to his mouth, and started to nibble.

I threw the rifle at him. The mouse instantly whirled and in a blur scurried back to its hole in the wall.

I was at the Ledger by seven the next morning, and noticed the pile of Ritz cracker crumbs had disappeared. I had intended to kill the mouse the night before, and instead all I'd managed to do was feed it. My goal was to have the paper done by seven o'clock that night so I could attend the WHS Homecoming talent show without having to return to finish laying out the paper afterward. To help facilitate that goal, I'd planned a twenty-page paper, knowing the following week the Ledger – with all the Homecoming photos – would be twenty-four pages or possibly even twenty-eight pages.

A twenty-page paper was also cheaper to print and mail than a twenty-four-page paper, and in a general terms took about six hours less work to produce. But the economics of printing and publishing could be surprising. One two-inch by three-column add – six inches total on a seventy-five inch sheet of newsprint (five columns of fifteen inches) – pretty much paid for the total costs of printing and mailing that page. So it didn't take many ads to transfer a twenty-page paper into a just as profitable and a better – more articles and photos and opportunities to be more creative with layout – twenty-four-page paper.

By Tuesday noon I had all the articles written, all the photos printed and cropped and twenty-pages framed in – the masthead on page one, page headings in place, column headings in place – and ready for layout. Provided Laura Joyce got pages eighteen and nineteen done before she left – the classified ad page and what we called the *Happy Ad* page – I had a chance of wrapping up layout before the talent show.

I was playing the radio, laying out the paper, humming a Tom Petty song, a can of Coke in hand, as I finished up page sixteen, the Ledger's farm and ranch page. It was about three o'clock when Rachel Brockton, the town clerk, showed up at the Ledger carrying a manila folder filled with papers. I looked at Rachel, looked at the clock, and again at Rachel. Laura Joyce's thoughts were similar to mine. Rachel was here to run a legal notice, which were mandated by precise and intractable deadlines. Legal notices could also be lengthy and complicated, and if she wanted to place a lengthy classified ad this week – a full day after the alleged deadline – we'd have to prepare and run the legal because the town was a good customer and it was the *town*, and you'd couldn't turn the *town* down. Plus, we were paid good money for legal ads, and we never turned down good money.

"Is that a legal notice you're carrying?" I asked Rachel.

She glanced at her folder. "As a matter of fact, it is," she said.

If it was a lengthy and complicated legal notice, my goal for wrapping up the paper by seven o'clock was obliterated. If it was a simple and short legal notice, it was only a minor – but a purchased – inconvenience. If it was a legal notice for next week's paper, it was money in the bank with plenty of time to do the job.

"When's it run?" asked Laura Joyce.

"Tomorrow," Rachel said.

Laura Joyce and I exchanged glances. I moved from the layout bank to the counter, where Rachel stood with her folder.

"We're seeking bids for painting the interior of the post house," she said.

That would put this legal notice into the simple and short category. It's possible I emitted an audible sigh of relief.

"I know it's late," Rachel apologized. "Luke just signed the papers during lunch. We need to run the notice three weeks. The work needs to start in November and for fiscal and budget reasons needs to finish by the end of the year."

That was the best thing about legal notices: They ran either two or three weeks straight, and made us money each time they ran.

"No problem," I told Rachel. "What do you got?"

It was a four-paragraph legal notice. Laura Joyce had it typeset, proofread, and laid out on page nineteen within a half hour.

"We're in pretty good shape this week," Laura Joyce announced triumphantly as she finished up her two pages. "You'll be home in time to eat dinner with the kids before the talent show," she said with a chuckle. As cheerful as she was, Tuesday mornings were naturally and consistently tense at the Ledger, caused by the volume of work and the possibility that something, anything, mechanical, procedural or journalistic, could still go wrong. By late afternoon, all the equipment had been in use, and if nothing had broken down by three o'clock, chances were nothing would.

A James Taylor song came on the radio, and Laura Joyce told me that the song had been sung at her wedding. She was writing her hours on her timesheet. She was done for the day.

"I picked out the music," she said, giggling, "and Bud picked out the beer."

"Seems fair," I said.

"I picked out the wedding colors," she said, laughing harder, "and Bud picked out the beer."

"How much beer did you have?" I asked.

"Enough to last until about seven the following morning," she said, laughing. "When Bud's family ran out of beer, they knocked on our motel room door to roust Bud to go get them some more." She found the memory hysterically amusing. "I told Bud if I ever got married again I wasn't telling anyone where I was staying."

"What did Bud say?"

"He told me I wasn't ever going to get married again," she hooted.

She put on her coat, looked over a couple of the laid out pages, and went in the backroom to retrieve her Tupperware lunch containers.

"I hear you're getting friendly with one of the new teachers," she said as she fished her car keys out of her purse. She wore a thick, long blue coat, and looked huge under it.

"What?" I heard her right, but it didn't sound right.

She laughed her way out the door.

I finished the can of pop, turned up the radio a bit, and settled into the final few hours of laying out the Ledger. I'd have the paper easily laid out by seven o'clock, but wouldn't have the final proofreading completed. It only took about twenty minutes to complete that, so I figured I could get up a little earlier on Wednesday morning and finish it. I'd be able to attend the talent show, and then go home with the kids, the same as every parent in every other family.

On an impulse, I called home. No answer. Tony was at football practice. Most Tuesdays Annie stopped by the Ledger after school, but not today. So where was she? With Trish? With Natalie or some of her friends? Working with a teacher after school? Not with Cody. Cody, the kid called *trouble* by the town marshal, was at football practice. If Cody was trying to corrupt Annie while Annie was trying to reform Cody, Cody didn't stand a chance. But Cody could resent the reformation, and if he did, the antagonism would be directed at Annie. I called home again. Again no answer. I then did what any rational parent would do. I slipped in the Springsteen cassette of *Born to Run*.

At ten minutes to seven o'clock I had the entire twenty pages laid out and four pages finalized and placed in the box for transport to Anaconda the next morning.

I grabbed the camera bag and just as I was closing the door on my way out I spotted the nose and whiskers probing the area just outside the baseboard.

The multi-purpose room lights were already off and the first talent show act – some kind of skit related to the movie *Top Gun* in which Tanner Walker in his best Tom Cruise imitation was shooting down enemies – was already in progress.

I moved through the darkness to the front row to have a good angle for pictures. There was no room in the front row for me, or in the second or third row, so I moved to the side – where Trish was usually parked – and sat on the floor.

Tanner ran across the stage – a small cardboard replica of a jet was fitted to his waist and jet engine noise was played through the sound system as he crossed the stage – and then the Kenny Loggins *Top Gun* theme song blared through the speakers. Tanner flew across the stage the other direction, this time chasing a poor imitation of a wolf – the Homecoming opponent was Three Forks and their team nickname was the Wolves – and sure enough, Tanner got the wolf in his sights and blasted it off the stage. Dave Dickson portrayed the wolf, and it died a noble death.

The Whitehall talent show was comprised of two elements: actual displays of talent and what could loosely be termed skits. The skits by the kids typically took a theme a little too far or were a little too crude, like a skit a few years earlier that involved an unsubtle suggestion of a Whitehall football player sexually molesting a sheep, an apparent mockery of the Big Timber Sheepherders. Outrage spurred by Daniel Purdy and Ginny Wilcox caused a predictable amount of community angst, and since then every school Homecoming skit had to be pre-approved by the high school principal.

One of the Davis girls – Melinda – did an Irish jig while her brother – Lanny – accompanied her on the tin whistle. Both were younger siblings of Kelly Davis, the girl who once had her picture in one edition of the Ledger five different times. These two Davis kids were a year apart in age and grade, with Lanny in his first year of high school. They were active in Whitehall's Catholic church, St. Teresa's, and played in some kind of Butte Irish music and dance troupe. We'd had a couple stories about them in the Ledger. They'd even been to Ireland. When I'd first arrived in Whitehall I'd attended a dinner at St. Teresa's and was seated and eating when the two of them – Melinda and Lanny – set their plates on the table and sat across from me. They looked like a boy and girl version of the same kid – strawberry blonde hair, blue eyes, slightly built – and were obvious siblings. They were both in early elementary school at the time.

"You look like a brother and a sister," I told them as they sat down.

Melinda, a year older, her silky long hair down to her shoulders, nodded agreement.

Lanny hesitated momentarily after my observation, then said helpfully, or perhaps for additional clarification, "I'm the brother."

Tony was in the next skit, and he portrayed Rambo, apparently. He was shirtless, in camouflage paint and a camouflage headband, Army pants and boots, and he was heavily armed with machine guns and some kind of a missile launcher. Speaking in guttural and mostly unintelligible Stallone-ese, he blew away red-shirted bad guys (Three Forks' colors were red and white) and saved a bunch of kids in cowboy hats – Cody Phillips was one of them – who represented Rangers. I may have been a nonobjective parent, but even then it was apparent Tony had something close to a stage presence. He prowled through the skit with confidence, and he looked formidable up there, sinewy and firm, with his blue and green makeup and plastic guns.

There were a couple more skits – one of them involving the television show *Dallas* and one of them a take-off on the movie *Back to the Future*. Brian Baxter played a song on the piano that sounded suspiciously like an Elton John tune, two freshman girls in colorful makeup sang a song from a Disney movie and the JeffScott twins did a labored comical 'magic' act that included "twin telepathy" jokes.

There's a group of kids in every Whitehall High School class who seem to be in everything – sports, music, drama, school government and academic clubs – and a smaller group of kids who, magically, amazingly, are in nothing. An average WHS class size might be fifty kids, and every spring, when the Ledger published its annual high school graduation section, there were two or three kids who had, to my astonishment, spent four years in Whitehall High School without once getting their name or picture in the paper. A lot of Whitehall kids had some type of mention or photo in the paper a few dozen times before they graduated from high school, and my viewpoint was the more the better. It was an annual revelation to me that some kids had managed to escape local newspaper coverage their entire four years of high school. It was a mystery to me how they did it. They couldn't have been actually trying to successfully avoid the paper, because the type of kids who weren't in the paper typically weren't successful at anything. It was just that they were totally and absolutely disengaged in the culture of high school. They weren't a member of any club, any team, any extracurricular activities or academic organizations. They went to school – most of the time – and that was it. Once in awhile Tom Wheeler, the WHS shop teacher, would give me a heads up about a couple kids who fixed something, built something or designed something unique, and it was these kind of kids who typically failed to get recognition. They were usually pleased to be in the paper once I was standing in front of them with the camera pointed their direction, but opportunities to point the camera at them were sometimes difficult to find or manufacture.

But suddenly up there on the stage during the Homecoming talent show were four kids I vaguely knew attended WHS but two of whom had never once had their photo in the paper. Where have these kids been, I wondered. They stood on stage, an imitation of Bruce Springsteen & The E Street Band, and they kicked off a decent version of *Born in the USA*. The singer and lead guitar player was a kid named Bonner Labuda who occasionally went to school during the day, had been in school dramatic plays before, and worked as a dishwasher at the Land of Magic Supper Club at night. He had long black hair – bound by a red headband – and dressed like a lumberjack. I took six pictures of him belting out the song, and noticed a respectable impression of Springsteen included the *Baawwwn!* as a substitute for *Born!* as he sang. Bonner's mom was a Hispanic woman who waitressed at the Land of Magic Supper Club and who likely wasn't Bonner's actual mother. I had no idea who the drummer was. He had to have been a student at Whitehall High School but I swore I'd never seen him before in my life. The bass player was a kid who went by the name Caddy, but I didn't know if that was his first name, last name, or a nickname. He had been arrested a couple times for stealing cigarettes at the Town Pump, and he'd probably get arrested a couple more times before he finally graduated, assuming he'd graduate. He and Bonner must have spent some time playing in a band because they knew how to play their instruments. The saxophone player was Carrie Lindstrom, a heavyset blonde WHS senior who, unlike the other kids in the band, came from a two-parent functional family. She looked out of place on stage with what had to be three juvenile delinquents; she was an Honor Roll student and the lead saxophone player in the WHS band, and she had always played the sax like she meant it. During halftime of basketball games or during more formal school concerts, she would clamp her eyes tight shut when she played, and she put so much force into the music her face color would transition from white to pink to crimson as she played. Her three band mates were dressed like a bum, a motorcycle rider and a lumberjack; Carrie wore the kind of flowery print dress my grandmother used to wear.

I noticed some movement to my left, and saw the kids in the front row nodding to the music, some of them even swaying to the music. And up on the stage, Carrie's face was contorted and earnest as her saxophone screamed out a solo that I thought was a brief keyboard solo in the recorded version of the song. You could make fun of Carrie if you wanted, with her size, her looks, her print dress and academic prowess, but she was the real deal when she had a saxophone in her hands.

The instant *Born in the USA* was finished Bonner began the count for a second song. The WHS kids sensed the moment and cheered and applauded as Bonner yelled out, *One, two, three, four* and the band – and at that point it could legitimately be called a band – blared the first few notes of *Born to Run*. Bonner closed his eyes as he sang, and the audience more or less bopped and shuffled in the aisle. During her saxophone solo, Carrie took a few steps toward the edge of the stage, hunched her shoulders up and then down, and shook her hips to the music. Maybe – maybe – Carrie Lindstrom had shaken her hips in public before, but it was doubtful. The kids hollered and sang along to the *tramps like us* and the *whoa whoa whoa* parts toward the end of the song.

Had Bonner and the band known a third song, they would have had to play it. Carrie bowed formally, the same way she rigidly stood and bowed after a song during the WHS spring music recital. The audience kept cheering and I could read Bonner's lips as he held his guitar in the air and mouthed the words, *We don't know any more songs*.

The curtain floated closed across the stage, and it took a few minutes for the audience to settle down. There was a lengthy pause before the next act, and if there was one trio that could follow a raucous Springsteen live set this was the one: the O'Toole girls, poised center stage, for a *Charlie's Angels* skit.

Charlie's Angels seemed to be an odd choice, in that the show was past its peak during the 1970s, but once the 'Angels' were on the stage it was obvious why it had been selected: the wardrobe. All three wore short, tight shorts, and various styles of revealing blouses or shirts.

The skit involved something about the Three Forks gangsters kidnapping Whitehall football players, and when the three Angels rescued Colt Harrison the crowd cheered and whistled when he and Holly embraced after he'd been freed. There was lots of posing by all three girls, but the biggest cheer occurred when the three of them were searching for 'Charlie.' Trish, wheelchair and all, was suddenly on stage, and with exaggeration motioned for the Angels to follow her. They did, and were somehow suddenly in the gangsters' hideout. Holly karate-chopped a bad guy (Cale), and Trish laid a different bad guy (Logan Bradshaw) low with a strategically placed kick to the groin. Peach actually flipped a bad guy (Nate Bolton) over her back and onto the floor. The girls then lifted high a large cardboard box up off the floor and under it, seated and bound, was Jersey. Aspen quickly untied him and he jumped to his feet and yelled, *Goooo Rangers!*

It was all so sudden and so shocking I failed to capture the moment on film.

The NEWSWEEK magazine was folded open and balanced perfectly on my chest during my Wednesday afternoon nap. I had read most of one article about President Reagan's weapons scandal, laid the magazine down, and within three seconds was asleep. Some men lusted for drugs, women or gold. I lusted for naps.

The telephone jarred me awake. For just a moment, I wasn't sure where I was; at first, I thought it was the alarm clock and I was in bed.

The thing about an afternoon nap is, once you're woken up, you're woken up for good. The magazine slipped off my chest when I stood to answer the phone. I thought it might be Laura Joyce with a problem or question at the Ledger.

"Is this Mr. Joslyn?" a perky female voice asked.

"Yeah." It sounded like a telemarketer.

"This is Mary Lou Ford, appointment secretary for Governor Ted Schwinden. How are you?"

"Me? Fine." I was groggy. "How are you?"

"I'm just great, thank you." Mary Lou Ford was clearly not waking up from an interrupted afternoon nap. She sounded as if she truly was just great.

She had more energy than she needed, I thought, possibly even more energy than I could tolerate.

I cleared my throat and spat into the sink. I was pretty sure I had the telephone mouthpiece covered, but I wasn't sure.

"The Governor is coming to Whitehall within the next couple weeks, and we wanted to schedule a time that was most convenient for you and your daughter, Annie," Mary Lou Ford said.

Governor Schwinden was coming to Whitehall? Right, I realized; we'd all talked about it in Martha's office. Automatically, my mind shifted to publisher mode. "A Thursday or Friday," I said.

"Pardon me? A Thursday or Friday?"

"Yeah, a Thursday or a Friday," I repeated. "Anytime on any Thursday or Friday works for us."

"Any Thursday or Friday?" She was enthusiastically puzzled.

"Yeah, Thursday, the day after Wednesday. And Friday, the day before Saturday. Either one of those two days. Anytime during school hours. Don't come on a Monday, Tuesday or Wednesday."

"Oh, I see," she exclaimed. "That certainly makes it easy."

"Right. Have you called Martha Cullen at the school?" I asked.

"Yes, yes," gushed Mary Lou Ford, and I could practically read her mind: *Of course I called the school.* "She told me to call the newspaper, and at the newspaper they told me to call you at this number."

Thanks, Laura Joyce, I thought. You ruined a perfectly good and badly needed nap. Not that I could blame Laura Joyce. It wasn't every day the governor's office called. I was sure Laura Joyce thought she was doing me a favor. It would have all been fine, or at least acceptable, had a more sedated Mary Lou Ford called twenty minutes later.

"Can I ask you a couple questions about Annie?" Mary Lou Ford asked with earnest sincerity. "You must be extremely proud of her. "

That's not a question, I almost said. Instead, I stifled a yawn and said, "Go ahead and ask."

"She's in eighth grade, is that correct?"

Oh, I thought, these are going to be difficult questions. But I remembered Annie was in her final year of middle school, and since high school started with ninth grade, she had to have been in eighth grade.

"Eighth grade, right," I said. But I opted to hedge my bet. "That's what Martha says, right?"

"Correct. Mrs. Cullen also said Annie is a straight-A student, a county spelling bee champion, the recipient of state and regional academic awards and is now the youngest Montana member of the International Mensa Society. Is all that correct?"

If you say so, I thought. "Sounds about right," I said.

"Your first name is Lance, correct?" Mary Lou Ford cheerfully asked.

"Yeah."

"And your wife's name?"

I thought about how to answer it, if I had to answer it.

"Mr. Joslyn?" prompted Mary Lou Ford.

Apparently I did.

"Amy," I said. "Annie's mom's name is Amy. But she doesn't live in Whitehall. Anymore. She won't be here on whichever Thursday or Friday the governor shows up."

The response was met with silence. I had the impression I'd ruined Mary Lou Ford's day.

"Annie has a brother named Tony, who's a sophomore," I offered. *A sophomore*? Yeah, a sophomore. "He'll be here on just about any Thursday or Friday."

"So," Mary Lou Ford ventured carefully, "it's just the three of you?"

I was perversely tempted, just for a moment, to tell Mary Lou Ford that I was getting friendly with a teacher. Just to re-brighten her day. "Right, Annie, Tony and me."

"And you work at the local newspaper?"

"I'm the publisher of the local newspaper," I pointed out. "I own the paper."

"Oh, good for you." She praised me like I was a puppy. I could practically see her beaming. "Well, I think that's all for now. Yes, yes, that's all for now. I'll give you a call when we have an exact date and time. On a Thursday or a Friday," she added, and giggled. "Thanks so much for everything. And congratulations again to your Annie. We're all so proud of her."

"Thanks for the call," I said out of habit, because I said that all the time at the Ledger.

Friday morning I dreamt it was raining, and when I opened my eyes I discovered I wasn't dreaming. The drumbeat of fat wet drops was as loud as small rocks banging on the roof. The sky was the gray swirl the color of cold water on soaked concrete. Friday was Homecoming parade day, game night, coronation night and dance night. Between the parade, the game and the coronation I usually took over a hundred pictures. The Ledger tradition the following Wednesday was six two-column pictures of each nominated royalty pair – twelve kids in all; one pair for each of the three undergrad classes and three pairs of seniors – and on the front page a three-column photo of the Homecoming king and queen, taken at halftime of the football game, right after they'd been crowned.

If the weather held, they'd be a soaked and miserable king and queen at halftime at a wet and miserable football game. A squall had moved in from the west overnight and had settled in the valley; sleet and tiny chunks of ice were pelting the bottomlands. Each slushy raindrop had enough heft to make what sounded like a dent in the roof. I looked outside through my wet-streaked bedroom window; to the south and west, in the mountains, the storm was turning trees and slopes white with snow at an elevation of about five thousand feet and up. The parade was at two o'clock in the afternoon. If the temperature dropped five degrees it was possible the floats would need snow tires.

Tony, Annie and I all got up at about the same time on Friday morning and when that happened – and it only happened on Thursdays or Fridays during the school year – the bathroom order was Annie first, me second, and Tony third. Because of the weather I knew I'd be driving them both to school, an embarrassment to Tony, who would likely again lecture me about my parental failure to sign him up for driver's education, which in his mind forced his pathetic dependence on his father occasionally taking him to school.

Annie was reading the newspaper when I emerged from the bathroom. I was dressed with a sweater over a long-sleeve shirt which was over a short-sleeve shirt. It was cold inside the house, but with a wet gray sky and the sleet pounding against the house, it even looked and sounded cold. Annie wore her Ranger hooded sweatshirt, and she had the hood over her wet hair as she ate what looked like a bowl of horse meal.

"It's not a good day for a parade when you wake up wondering what the wind chill is," she said, not even looking up from the newspaper.

"Good morning to you, too," I said.

"If you want a bowl a cereal you better get to it," she said, still not looking up from the newspaper. "There's only enough milk for one bowl."

"What's that in your bowl?"

"Granola."

"It looks like mush."

"It's all we got."

I sighed. Lousy weather. No milk. Mush. This was not a good start to a long day.

"Go for it, Lance," Tony said from behind me. "I'm going to have some pop tarts."

Tony looked like James Bond. He wore a deep maroon silky shirt, black slacks and a black vest. All of which were new. As were the shoes. As was the haircut. None of which I'd ever seen before.

"Well, look at you," Annie said, beholding him with admiration.

Tony was slightly embarrassed, and slightly boastful.

"What's all this?" I asked.

"We did a little shopping," Annie said. "Aspen, Tony and me. Look at this kid." She held both arms open his direction. "A star is born. He looks like Tom Cruise, only taller and less, I don't know, impish."

"Impish?" I asked. "Is that even a word?"

"Of course it is," Annie said. "Elfin. Puckish."

"What language is she speaking?" Tony asked.

"I have no idea," I admitted. "But you, you do look awesome."

"You're supposed to be dressed up if you're royalty," Tony said. "You oughta see Aspen."

Annie rolled her eyes. "She looks like a slutty Snow White."

"Yesterday you said she looked like Cinderella," Tony said.

"Disco Cinderella," Annie corrected. She put down the paper. "Look at this weather. Aspen can't be wearing the Sleeping Beauty dress in this. Bare shoulders? Cleavage? Clingy satin?" Annie shook her head. "I don't think so."

The weather did look horrible. Outside, on the bushes close to the house, the branches were encased in ice, like brown fingers inside a glass glove. The sky seemed to end abruptly with scudding clouds just above the treetops.

It was so cold in the house the smell of toasted warm pop tarts seemed pleasant.

We dashed outside to the car; Tony and I ran, but Annie walked at her normal pace, as if she refused to be hurried by something as commonplace as weather. The rain pelted the Escort roof with such force it sounded like a small animal was on top of the car banging with a wrench. Tony jumped in the front passenger seat and Annie sat in back.

"This is going to ruin everything," Tony complained. "The parade, the game, everything. Why can't it be nice out? It was nice yesterday."

"Ohhhh," Annie moaned sarcastically from the backseat. "Is that my big brother I hear whining up there? About the *weather*?"

Tony whirled in the seat to face her. "That's easy for you to say. You don't have to ride in the back of a pickup during the parade, stand out there at halftime or try to play football in this slop."

"Look on the bright side," Annie said. "Next year for Homecoming you'll be driving your own car to school. Unless Three Forks scores about seventy points, which seems unlikely for a multitude of reasons, one of which you guys are starting to actually play some semblance of football, I'm going to lose the football bet. Lucky you, you'll get a car."

"How's that work, exactly?" I asked Annie. "You lose a bet and I have to buy someone a car? I never agreed to that. How about if I make some stupid bet and I lose, so you have to clean the house every week for a year. Does that make sense to you?"

"Hey Lance, I do clean the house, thanks for noticing," Annie said. "And what is with my two boys? You've done nothing but whine all morning."

It didn't break my heart when the two of them exited the car and hurried into the school. Driving the three blocks south on Division Street, with the bulky gray Tobacco Roots straight ahead in the distance, it was almost impossible to discern where the ground left off and the sky began. The pavement glistened with moisture but not snow, but the top of the Patacini Tire sign, twenty feet above the street, held a couple of inches of snow on top of it.

The first thing I did at the Ledger was turn on the heat. Before I even turned on the lights the space heater kicked to life and you could smell the delicious heat before you felt it. Laura Joyce was fifteen minutes late, and said the road from Cactus Junction to the overpass just outside of town was coated with a shiny layer of slick ice.

"The back end of the pickup was sliding all over the place," she said, and laughed. "My back end hasn't wiggled like that in ten years."

I tried to focus at work, but the weather, the Homecoming festivities, the governor's pending visit, the mouse and the football game all conspired to weaken my concentration. I basically puttered around, and even tidied up the darkroom, a chore that served no tangible purpose.

Laura Joyce stood at the window mid-morning and said she thought the sky seemed a little brighter. The snow, or sleet, had diminished to a drizzle, and everything everywhere in town was soaked or frozen.

"What happened to the window?" Laura Joyce asked. She was running her fingers over the chip where the BB had hit.

"What do you mean?" I asked.

"There's a chunk of glass missing," she said. "Like it's chipped or something."

I shrugged. "I don't know." I added, "I didn't do it."

She fingered the window, then sort of craned her neck to look out toward and past Legion Avenue. "Yeah, I'd have to say the weather is definitely improving. I think I even see a hint of blue up there."

A little while later I slipped on my coat to fetch the mail. And while the sky overhead may have been a shade less dark, Laura Joyce had been seeing things if she saw any blue. To the west the sky above the Highlands was still a dark turbulent mass. Most of the ground ice and slush had melted, but water was everywhere. If you described Whitehall in one word the word would have been soggy.

Moisture, unfortunately, was not charitable to Whitehall. A couple of the streets were properly paved, but only one – Legion Avenue – had curbs and gutters. The result throughout town was that storm runoff collected at every corner and every low spot, and the low spots dominated the town's streets. Potholes filled with thick muddy water, and some of the potholes were the size of small ponds. The entire post office parking lot was underwater. A puddle on Main Street outside of Borden's could have hidden a U-boat. Whitehall, after the storm, essentially had three surfaces: puddles, ponds and mud.

The storm had wrecked all of the exterior Homecoming decorations on Legion Avenue and Main Street businesses. The purple and gold inspirational quotes or drawings were limp and soggy and some were totally unintelligible. The Whitehall Mint Bar had a rather elaborate – by Whitehall standards – drawing meant to be a cowboy (Ranger) shooting a wolf (Three Forks) that resulted in a gusher of blood spouting from the wolf's chest. But the Ranger was washed away and the wolf was faded and soaked and torn to be nearly unrecognizable.

The post office was abuzz with weather reports. Half a dozen people were gathered and some of them, I had the impression, had been there a while.

Boulder had reportedly received six inches of snow. The mountains received a foot or more. Ennis had so much snow the school declared a snow day – a first for October. I-90 west up Homestake Pass had been closed for a couple hours earlier in the morning when a semi-truck had jackknifed across both westbound lanes.

Some of the other weekly newspapers in the area – the Dillon Tribune, Boulder Monitor and Anaconda Leader – were in the mailbox, and I figured I could kill twenty minutes paging through them. Most of the time I simply scouted them for advertising ideas. On the walk from the post office to the Ledger I took a substantial detour – halfway across town (four blocks), actually – to check out the football field. That took another ten minutes. I had work to do, work that would have to be done later, but I'd learned over the years that when I got antsy I was literally incapable of concentration, and it was no use attempting to focus. Some people could fight through the diversions, but I never could. The football practice field was squishy wet where there was grass, and where there was bare ground there was mud. The track surrounding the football field was brown mush. I placed one foot on the track surface and left an almost perfect footprint impression in the mud. I didn't see standing water on the field, and the grass was snow free; the bleacher seats, however, held a good two inches of snow.

From a newspaper standpoint, I realized, the story of Homecoming would likely be about weather as much as it was about the game or the festivities.

Chapter 25

The parade music and cheering seemed muffled, quieter, as if the sounds were muted or hushed, and the colors even appeared washed out and dreary. Yet the event certainly wasn't joyless or lifeless. Everything that would have happened under perfect weather still happened, but it happened under the dark doom of atmospheric turbulence. It just wasn't as agreeable, perhaps, or as inspiring, and while the high school kids themselves soldiered through it, the crowd was sparse, wet, cold, and bundled up. The elementary school kids had stayed mostly over at Division Street, near the end of the parade route, close to the warmth of the school. By two p.m. the weather had warmed slightly, but the drizzle was steady and anyone outside had probably been soaked during parade lineup, before things had actually started moving.

The weather dampened the parade, but you couldn't really say it damaged the parade. The band marched down Whitehall Street to Legion Avenue to Division Street, and only the band members on the outside edges – closest to the Legion Avenue street gutters – had to walk through standing water. Each class had a float – the freshman float was the most creative, a wide hay wagon featuring someone in a Ranger football uniform drop-kicking stuffed wolves through the goal posts as two other kids operated a manual scoreboard and kept racking up Ranger points – and the E Street Band, complete with the mystery kid banging on the drums, Bonner Labuda on guitar, Caddy on bass, and Carrie Lindstrom on saxophone, had its own float with lettering across it that read: *Rangers Are Born to Win.* The cheerleaders did their best to project school spirit through the stark and soggy gloom, and the football players – on another hay wagon pulled by Brent Walker's half-ton Ford pickup – looked damp but semi jubilant in their game jerseys as the truck crawled by.

Each Homecoming royalty couple graced the parade, flowing in order from the freshmen to the seniors. One freshman couple, Randy Svenenson and Sherry Hankinson, were shivering as they rode standing up in the back of a dune buggy. Tony and Aspen rode in style; Lyle had outfitted his pickup with a loveseat in the truck box. The loveseat faced backward, so the very dashing Tony and the lovely Aspen waved when they were already past you. I took a handful of pictures of each couple; I'd been at enough school and community events that almost all the kids knew me and waved directly at my camera and me. Colt Harrison and Holly O'Toole rode inside the darkened cab of an old Model T-looking car, which meant I had to track them down immediately after the parade for their picture. From start to finish, the parade lasted about twenty minutes. Not a single person in Whitehall wished it had gone longer.

Immediately afterward, I went home. I wanted to take a hot shower to warm up, and the agenda after that called for a nap. It was going to be long weekend. The game started early, at six o'clock, because of the Homecoming festivities and dance, but it was still going to be a late night.

When I stepped out of the shower I heard voices – seemingly lots of voices – in the house. I got dressed and stepped timidly out of the bathroom to find at least a dozen kids in the kitchen and living room. Purple and gold WHS letterman jackets were everywhere. Three kids – Logan, Dave and Tanner – were on the couch and Annie was seated with superiority in the recliner. Bonner Labuda had his head in the refrigerator and emerged with a can of Pepsi in his hand. It appeared the whole E Street Band was seated around the kitchen table. Cody was on our telephone, and Trisha – a blanket across her legs – was in her wheelchair next to Carrie Lindstrom. They were indoors, a bank of massive angry clouds covered the sky, but for some reason both Carrie and Trisha wore sunglasses. The clothes they all wore were soaked, so wet that it smelled and felt humid inside the house.

"Lance," Tony called out above the other voices. I couldn't locate him at first, but then found him at the stereo. "Listen to this."

He fumbled a bit with a cassette box, then loaded the cassette player. I could see him move his right wrist and I knew what he was doing: turning the volume up.

It was Springsteen, it was loud, and it was a melodic piano version of *Thunder Road.* And it was a live recording; I'd never head this version of the song before. Tony saw the expression of confusion on my face.

"It's a bootleg," he explained. "From Jersey. This is Bruce Springsteen from one of his early concerts in New York."

"Awesome," grunted Bonner.

I have to admit, I looked around the house, just for an instant, to see what was laying around for Bonner to steal. I didn't see much. My wallet and car keys were still in the Escort.

"Hope you weren't planning on taking a nap," Annie said. She gave me a sly smile. She knew that was exactly what I'd been planning.

The music was so loud I declined to answer. I just shook my head.

I went into my bedroom to add another layer under my sweater and as the Springsteen bootleg cassette – whatever *bootleg* meant – blared a live version of *Hungry Heart* the volume of the kids grew louder above the music. The only voices I heard clearly talked about the looming football game against Three Forks. Cody complained about the Three Forks quarterback, and said something I didn't quite understand that made the other kids laugh. I heard Tony distinctly say if Three Forks played man to man coverage he'd be open deep for a touchdown. Dave said it was cold and wet and muddy, and then he said some words I couldn't make out, then finished with something about the weather being perfect for a hog like Logan.

It really wasn't a party the kids were having as much as it was a pre-game pep talk during a Springsteen concert.

There was a knock at my bedroom door.

I opened it and found the drummer in the E Street Band was standing with a Pepsi in his hand. He saw me and pointed behind himself with his thumb. "There's some old lady at your door."

I found Rhonda Horst standing on our doorstep, hunched and chilled. She was all bundled up in scarves and hats and mittens and jackets, and she held a plastic-covered pie pan out in front of her.

"Rhonda?" I asked, a little flustered. She'd never been to our house before. I stepped aside. "Rhonda, come on in."

She took one tentative step then stopped. She peeked around the corner at the group of kids, and they, collectively, returned the wary expression. Conversations ceased; only Bruce continued to perform.

"I bringt dis," she said, and extended the pie. The smell was distinctive; warm fresh, pumpkin pie.

I reached out for it. "Rhonda, you don't-" I started.

"Accht," she said, and shook her head. "Is not for you." She looked beyond me. "Is for him."

I looked behind me to find Tony already walking toward her. He was grinning, and when I looked back toward Rhonda, her pale skeletal face conveyed an expression of pride. Her entire head and the outer edges of her face were covered by a combination of hats and scarves, but I could see her eyes, and they lit up as Tony approached.

She held out the pie toward him. "Goot luck," she told him, reached up and patted his shoulder after he accepted the pie.

He inhaled deeply. "Oh man, does this smell good." He balanced the pie on one hand and took the other arm and wrapped it around her shoulders. "Rhonda, we're going to eat this right now for good luck. Thanks," he said and laughed, "thanks so much." He sort of leaned toward her, and pulled her toward him. The top of her head was even with his shoulder, and he was not particularly tall. "You want to come in and meet the team?"

She responded with short but firm shakes of her head.

"Well, you're going to the game tonight, right?" he asked her.

She looked up at me. I hesitated, unsure what was expected from me, but then caught on. "You bet," I said.

"Vhat time?" she asked.

"I have to get there early, you know," I said.

"I be ready," she vowed.

"She'll be ready," Tony assured me.

"Okay. Game starts at six." I thought about it. "I'll swing by about five-thirty."

She shook her head. "I be here at fife-tirty."

And she whirled and walked away at the same instant Tony went the opposite direction, as if on cue, as if they'd rehearsed it. Tony moved inside the house, with the pie aloft, and strode into the kitchen where he – and the pie – were greeted by cheers.

I stood at the door dumbfounded. The house was filled with kids. I didn't get a nap. Rhonda Horst brought a pie to my house but the pie wasn't for me. A *bootleg* Bruce Springsteen concert was blaring out of the stereo. Rhonda would be back at fife-tirty. Outside, it was cold, wet and already surprisingly dark.

I realized Annie was standing next to me. She looked outside, then down the sidewalk, then at me. "I don't think she's coming back real soon." Annie carefully nudged me out of the way so she could close the door. "Lance, it's getting cold in here." She closed the door then bumped it with her shoulder so it was shut tight. "Come on over here and have a piece of pie."

I followed her into the kitchen and had to maneuver around the drummer at the kitchen table. He had a chipped front tooth and about five hairs on his chin. "Cool place, Lance," he said.

"Who are you?" I asked him.

"Max Weinberg," he answered. He was three steps away before I realized he'd given me the name of the E Street Band's actual drummer.

"I *like* it here," Trish proclaimed to us all. "At my house everything is so clean and neat."

The crowd was meager and initially quiet for a Homecoming game. Part of the problem was the odd early evening starting time. Part of the problem was the weather; the lights were already on and the cloud cover was so thick it felt like it had been night all day. Part of the problem was the Rangers' lowly won-loss record and dismal play.

The bleachers were about a third full, only about half the WHS band showed up, and everyone was bundled in winter jackets, stocking caps or snowmobile suits. The band and high school kids had blankets spread out over their laps, and the older folks sat on thick blankets plus had blankets spread out over their laps.

Trisha, ever faithful, was parked in her usual spot on the track at the west end of the bleachers, her wheelchair standing on top of a sheet of plywood to keep it out of the mud. She was wrapped head-to-toe in a thick purple blanket and wore a hooded jersey that left only the middle of her face uncovered.

I spotted Rhonda up in the bleachers. We had parted ways at the ticket booth. She was buried under several layers of clothing and sat motionless. She reminded me of a bird in a tree on a bitter cold afternoon.

The field grass glistened a deep dark green under the lights, and when you looked up toward the lights you could see a gentle mist mixed with occasional tiny smatterings of snowflakes floating in isolation to the ground. The Rangers stood rock still while the WHS band played a hollow-sounding version of the national anthem; the only movement on the sidelines was the small puffs of breath fog from the players. Somehow, maybe because of the vapory moisture and dense sky, the Three Forks football team – and Slack and the chain gang – looked farther away than normal on the opposite side of the field.

Herbie waved to me from the press box, a cup of steaming coffee in his gloved hand. He wore a scarf, winter coat with the collar up, gloves and a Scotchman hat with the earflaps down. He looked dressed for Arctic survival.

Three Forks had only about thirty kids in red and white uniforms standing across the field, and they looked cold and forlorn. A handful of quiet parents in winter clothes stood behind the Wolves players, and hardly any Three Forks kids had made the trip to Whitehall. Three Forks and Whitehall were arguably two of the worst – if not certifiably the two worst – teams in the conference. Townsend had beaten Three Forks, and Whitehall had upset Townsend, so Three Forks represented Whitehall's best chance for its second win.

Colt Harrison was back in the lineup for the Rangers, and started at quarterback. His parents stood behind the fence on the west end of the field; each held a Styrofoam cup of steaming coffee. I wore a thick parka and a stocking cap pulled low over my ears. I had never learned to take pictures while wearing gloves, so for the first quarter the gloves stayed on and the camera stayed snug in the carrying case. I figured I only needed two or three pictures from the game itself, and could get that done during the second and third quarter, when the players would be soaked and muddy.

The first quarter ended in a scoreless tie. Neither offense could move the ball. The field was slick, the ball was slippery, and each team turned the ball over. A Three Forks punt returner muffed a punt on the Three Forks nineteen yard line, but after a seven-yard gain Colt fumbled the ball on a quarterback draw and Three Forks recovered.

No one scored in the second quarter, either. No one even came close. That meant six straight scoreless quarters for the Rangers and a scoreless tie at the half. Fans wearing gloves and mittens applauded softly when the teams trotted off the field, and my guess was a lot of fans applauded the fact that the game was half over.

The Homecoming halftime festivities were not all that festive. Herbie tried to muster some enthusiasm, but it was cold and wet and Homecoming was something we needed to simply get through. The damp and dismal nominated royalty paraded unsteadily in front of the Whitehall bleachers and bundled up parents took pictures of the mildly nervous girls and mildly embarrassed boys as they strode – arm in arm – under a small archway decorated with soggy and sagging purple and gold balloons. They lined up, freshmen through seniors, some of them shivering, furtive eyes searching for comfort, facing a bleak and largely empty Ranger bleachers. The four Ranger players stood in uniform, and all of them were water soaked and mud splattered. Tony's hair was sopping wet and a foggy mist rose from his head like smoke from a smoldering fire. Aspen's dress was black, and her waist looked about the width of a pool stick. She smiled and waved like a Rose Bowl queen. After a suitable dramatic delay, Colt was named Homecoming king and Holly O'Toole – Aspen's older sister who looked like a Swedish twenty-five-year-old international model – was announced as queen. They stood there, awkwardly, in the frigid night air and under the field light poles, as camera flashes – including mine – came at them from all directions. Holly was wearing a light blue shiny satin dress that exposed her shoulders, and she was doing her best to appear comfortable. She scrunched her shoulders just a little, to ward off the cold. Colt and Holly had been in the Ledger and read the Ledger enough to know what to do. They looked directly at me and smiled as I took one, two, three pictures of them. Only then did they shift their pose for their parents, school yearbook, other family members and community members, who were ganged up just behind me.

That was the highlight of Colt's night. Whitehall took the ball to start the second half, and after Tony returned the kickoff to about midfield, it was Dave Dickson – not Colt Harrison – who came from the sidelines to play quarterback. It was breathtakingly controversial, from a WHS standpoint, to replace at quarterback. It was as bold as it was puzzling. In the dark gloom of the sodden night I had a hard time figuring out if Dave handed off the ball or held on to it, and if he handed it off who he handed it off to. I apparently was not alone in that confusion; the Three Forks defense was as mystified as I was. On the fourth play from scrimmage he faked a handoff to Logan and skirted outside for twenty-two yards, the longest gain by either team all night. The next play Logan busted a run inside for eight yards, and then Dave cut off-tackle for another seven yards. Cale Bolling took a quick pitch and followed the block of Tanner Walker for another first down. Dave ran off-tackle to the short side of the field – where I was standing – and was tackled on the five yard line but because of the slick grass slid across the goal line and halfway into the end zone. He scored on the next play, and I took what I thought was a terrific photo of the JeffScott twins holding Dave aloft after he'd jumped into their arms. The Rangers had the lead.

Three Forks turned the ball over on the next possession, and Logan scored a couple plays later for the second Ranger touchdown in just over two minutes.

"That's what I'm talking about!" Herbie said in the press box. He said it away from the microphone, but his voice carried across the field.

Since the first play of the second half, one team picked up its passion and effort – the Rangers – and one team slid abjectly toward defeat. Having seen that imprint of defeat permeate the Rangers multiple times during recent years, it was easy to recognize when it happened to someone else. The final score was 24-0. The Rangers had scored four touchdowns – Logan had two of them – and no extra points. Although it had occurred on a wet, sloppy field and the players were soaked and muddy, and although the temperature was barely above freezing and only a handful of fans were still around by the end of the game, it was a win – better yet, a Homecoming win – that improved the Rangers to respectability, 2-2 in conference games.

I was absolutely freezing by the time the game was over. The temperature had to have dropped ten degrees between kickoff and the conclusion, between dusk and nightfall. My feet were numb; I had worn regular shoes when winter boots would have made a lot more sense; I was cold from bottom to top, and through to the core.

Colt had played some of the second half at wide receiver, but not a single play at quarterback. He didn't even take his helmet off when he walked alone off the field.

Tony wore a huge grin as he walked toward me. You could barely see the color of his uniform under the mud. By my calculation he played every play. Slack splashed through the field and reached Tony at the Whitehall sideline. He jumped up and patted Tony's shoulder pads, and Tony reached out and pumped Slack's hand, which prompted a wide childish grin from Slack. Tony gave Slack his helmet, and Slacked walked off the field with a black cowboy hat at his side and a Ranger purple football helmet on his head.

Whitehall won the game. Tony was happy. Slack was happy. Even Rhonda Horst, standing up on the bottom row waiting for me, wore a sly smile. It was Homecoming weekend. What could go wrong?

It took me two strides to find out.

"Either you talk to that son of a bitch, or I'm going to," Hank Harrison warned Ed Franklin as both stood in the narrow dark corridor between the bleachers. I had not seen them when I ventured into the corridor on the way to the Escort and more importantly, the warmth of the Escort heater.

Hank, tall and broad, wore a down winter jacket and a Denver Broncos cap. Ed was wearing an Elmer Fudd kind of hat with the earflaps down, and he looked more like a skinny Iowa corn grower than a Montana school superintendent. It looked a little bit like the class bully picking on the class brain.

I attempted to back up unseen, but failed. Both turned toward me; Hank looked away in disgust, but Ed pointed at me. "Stick around, I have something to ask you." He returned his attention to Hank.

There was no doubt what they were talking about, and it was one of most common dramas in high school sports: *My kid didn't play enough*. It was not a drama I needed to see or hear. I backed away so I was out of sight, but it was difficult to wander far enough to get out of listening range. Hank talked loudly, and he didn't care who heard him.

"You listen to me, and listen good, Franklin. That coach is a goddamned idiot and I'm not going to let him ruin my son's senior year of high school," Hank said. "Is that understood?"

"Hank, we have school policies on this, you know that," Ed said. Ed had immediately reverted to his rhythmic speech pattern inherent in school administrators that by tone alone demonstrated patience and understanding, and suggested the other party in the discussion should also be patient and understanding. "There are protocols to follow, and we'll follow them."

Hank would have none of that. "Don't give me that *let's just relax* bullshit. That Dickson kid isn't good enough to carry Colt's jockstrap and you and everyone in Whitehall knows it."

"I know the Rangers have won two of three games, and scored twenty-four points in the second half tonight, all with Dave Dickson at quarterback," answered Ed.

"Oh bullshit. Bullshit. That's bullshit and you know it," Hank sneered. "Dickson didn't throw a pass the whole game because you know, I know and everyone knows *he can't throw the ball.*"

"You don't have to pass when-"

"Ed, goddamnit, you're not listening," Hank interrupted. "Colt was All-Conference last year when Frank was coach, when we had a real coach. You remember that, when we had a real coach? Colt's the best quarterback in the conference, probably the best Class B quarterback in the state and one of the best quarterbacks in Montana at any level. Are you telling me he's not as good as some piss-ant freshman who can't even throw the ball? Is that what you're telling me? Ed? Is that what you're saying? Have you been taking the same idiot pills the coach has?"

The disease, in my mind, was called parental blindness. Every parent thought little Bobby or Johnny or Sally – or Colt – was a superstar and any coach who did not recognize that was blind and foolish. Hank, like most parents suffering from parental blindness, was way off base. Colt looked like a quarterback, but he didn't perform as well as he looked. Never had, really. Dave was the opposite; he looked like he should be playing chess somewhere, but his physical performance was inspiring. He was a magician handling the football. And despite his youth and what appeared to be a hyperactive personality, it seemed like the other players performed better with him in there.

"What I'm saying, Hank, is that we're going to follow the school policies," Ed said. "I'll set up an appointment for you to talk with Coach Jersey, and I'll sit in on the discussion. After that coach and I will talk. Then you and I will talk. If you're not happy, you can make your case to the school board."

"Do whatever bureaucratic bullshit you have to do," Hank said. "But all of it happens right away, because Colt's starting against Manhattan next week. You got that, Ed?" *Ed* sounded like a dirty word.

Hank stormed away and I could see Ed looking around for something. Me, was my guess. He emerged from the dark corridor and found me leaning against the bleachers. Rhonda was still standing out of the mud in the bleachers, waiting patiently for me, with no idea why she was waiting. As many layers of clothing as she was wearing, she still had to have been cold to the bone.

"Hey," Ed greeted me, "I got a little problem."

"Yeah," I muttered, "I heard."

Ed glanced to the side, where he and Hank had spoke. "No, not that," he said. He made a facing suggesting *You think that's a problem?* "Did you see the way the Dickson kid handles the ball? He's like a tiny Houdini out there. No, Hank's not a problem."

Rhonda looked uncertain if she should follow me or wait, and I motioned her to wait there.

"Actually, here's my problem," Ed said. "I need a chaperone for the dance tonight. And here's my solution." He did a magician's *ta-da* move with his hands. "You're it."

"Oh no you don't," I said. "I already had to chaperone a dance. I already fulfilled my obligations. No way I'm doing that again."

"Sure you are," Ed said. "Look, Mary Ann Kling was supposed to chaperone but she says she thinks she's sick or something from standing out here in the cold all night. She told me that ten minutes ago, and I'm desperate. Bring Annie if you want. Dance starts at eight-thirty."

"*She's* sick from standing out here all night? Shit, Ed, my spleen is covered in hoarfrost, I'm so cold." I drew a deep breath. "And I don't even know what a spleen is."

"Ask Annie," Ed said, "on the way to the dance."

"I'm not going to the dance," I told him.

Ed looked at me, his Elmer Fudd hat low on his head and his ears covered with flaps. "Of course you are," he said. "See you at eight-thirty."

And he walked away.

I was still cold at nine o'clock, when a handful of girls were out on the multi-purpose room floor dancing to a Madonna song. My toes were still chilled and my fingers felt as if the blood in them was congealed. Bonner Labuda and a couple other kids were serving as DJs for the dance, and Bonner wore a red kerchief headband not unlike Springsteen.

The boys wore slacks and dress shirts, except for the cowboys, who wore pressed jeans, shined boots and dress western shirts. Bonner undoubtedly wore his nicest lumberjack shirt. Bonner had virtually been invisible his entire life until the past week, then I saw him everywhere I went. That was pretty hard to explain in a town the size of Whitehall.

The girls were more fashionable, with evening gowns, curled hair and abundant makeup. Even Annie wore a dress, clingy and satiny with an uneven bottom, as if it had been hand-cut with a scissors by someone with very poor eyesight. I suspected the dress was new, and I suspected it wasn't a surprise to her she was – as an eighth-grader – invited to the high school Homecoming dance. She had, in fact, *expected* to attend the dance, when in fact she had no right to such an expectation.

Earlier, after I had dropped Rhonda off at her boarding house – and received a Tupperware bowl filled with warm and pungent cinnamon rolls – I got home and found Annie in her bedroom getting dressed for the dance, and in my bedroom I discovered a dress shirt and slacks laid out on the bed.

"Where have you been?" Annie told me when I got home. "Hurry up."

"Hurry up for what?"

"The dance," Annie said. "It starts at eight-thirty."

"How come you know you can go? Who invited you to the dance?"

"Interesting questions, I'm sure, Lance, for another time. Right now I need for you to slip on that shirt and those slacks or we're going to be late."

"I'm taking a hot shower first," I told her. "What makes you so sure you're going to the dance? What makes you sure *I'm* going to the dance? I just found out about it."

"Mr. Franklin invited me," Annie said.

"*When* did he invite you?"

She waved me away. "Hurry up. Take your shower. Make it a quick one."

I not only put on the dress shirt and slacks, but I also slipped on the same long underwear I wore to the game and dug through my closet until I found a sweater I had received a couple years earlier as a Christmas present.

"You're sure about the sweater?" Annie asked me when we left the house.

"I'm sure I need the warmth," I said. "Get in the car."

"Dig the sweater," Tanner Walker said as he walked past me, hand in hand with Maggie Bolton, a cheerleader and Nate Bolton's sister.

An Eddy Money song blared through the sound system. The dance went until midnight. I had three hours of duty ahead of me. Annie was soon stationary in a cluster of girls standing self-consciously off to the side of the bleachers. Jersey and Ed were conferring by the refreshment table, and by their relaxed posture and manner I doubted they were discussing the Harrison family ultimatum. Tony and Aspen were seated at a table with Dave Dickson, Logan Bradshaw, Cale Bolling and some girls who were so transformed in formal wear that I had no idea who they were. The girls were mostly listening; by their gestures, the boys were recounting the football game. There seemed to be a great deal more recounting after a win than after a loss. Holly was in attendance, but Colt was not. He may be boycotting the dance, but it would take a lot more than nasty weather and her boyfriend and Homecoming King getting benched for her to miss the dance. The *Everybody Have Fun Tonight* song came on, a tune I found absolutely worthless, if not patently offensive.

"Here, have some punch," said a female voice to my left. Mary Kristofferson handed me a squat plastic glass three-quarters full of blood-red punch.

"Thanks," I said.

She was almost exactly the same height as me, I realized; or maybe she seemed taller because her hair was pinned up. She wore a loose dark green blouse and black slacks.

"God, I hate this song," she muttered.

I sipped the punch and immediately detected alcohol. My eyes opened wide.

"Don't worry, the punch isn't spiked," she whispered. "This is just a little treat for us." She patted her purse.

I nodded. "Very clever, Ms. Kristofferson."

"And very stupid," she added. "I'm breaking about forty public school regulations. Teachers are *not* supposed to bring booze on school property. It's immediate grounds for dismissal."

"And then some," I said.

"Indeed," she said. Her cheeks were flushed red, either from the cold weather or the punch. "I nearly froze out there watching that game." She trembled, as if mention of the wet cold sidelines brought a shiver. "My dad used to like a toot when he got cold."

"I bet he never had a toot in a high school auditorium," I said.

"You'd be surprised," she told me. "He learned the hard way. The phrase *prosecuted to the fullest extent of the law* comes to mind." She took a sip of her punch, and then watched the kids dance. "Christmas present?"

"Pardon?"

"Your sweater?" she asked me. "Christmas present?"

"What the hell's wrong with my sweater?" I asked. "You're the second person to comment on it."

"Nothing's wrong with it," she said. "Who was the first? To comment on the sweater?"

"Tanner Walker had something smartass to say when he walked past me."

She chuckled. "Tanner's a hoot. He doesn't have a mean bone in his body."

We both watched Tanner for a moment; he caught us, and responded with a ceremonial bow, which drew a laugh from both Mary and me.

Some Latino-blend song came on the sound system and a collection of girls – including Holly and her sisters – jumped up to dance. They all gathered in the middle of the dance floor, raised their hands above their heads, wiggled their hips and shuffled their feet, laughing the entire time.

"When you're sixteen and beautiful, and your daddy owns the bank, do you have a care in the world?" Mary asked.

"Apparently not," I answered.

"Were you ever that carefree?" Mary asked me.

I thought for a moment. "No, actually."

Mary shook her head. "Me neither. Never. Not once." We watched the girls – lithe, graceful, brash – glide around the dance floor. "I wish I was once, just for a night or a song or a moment."

"Why don't I go get us another glass of punch," I said. Mary handed me her cup, and I made my way to the refreshment table. Ed and Jersey stood silently off to the side; chaperoning, I supposed. I spotted Annie, standing awkwardly in her satin dress, casting furtive glances toward a group of boys across the room. Cody was there, dressed like a rodeo rider.

Annie wasn't the carefree type. Perhaps she thought too much, or maybe for her the assimilation of information never ceased. She smiled, and I nodded her direction.

Ed wore a pressed white shirt, red tie, and dark brown slacks.

I filled the two glasses with punch, acknowledged Ed, who motioned for me to move over toward the two of them.

"I appreciate you filling in like this," Ed said. We were close enough to the music so he had to practically shout.

"You owe me," I told him.

He smiled and nodded. "Dutifully acknowledged."

Jersey stood on the other side of Ed, and was outside of earshot. "You tell him about Hank Harrison yet?"

Ed shook his head. "Let him enjoy victory for awhile." He hesitated. "I'll tell him tomorrow afternoon."

I nodded. "Okay. I have to interview him sometime on Sunday."

"Don't you bring it up," Ed cautioned. "This is all supposed to be between the coach, the parent, and the school."

"I'm not going to bring it up," I said. "I don't want to know anything about it."

Ed nodded; he put a hand on my shoulder to reassure me, then leaned back a bit. "Hey, nice sweater."

"Kiss my ass," I told him.

"What?" he asked, and too late I realized Ed had meant it as a sincere compliment. To Ed, it really was a nice sweater.

For two hours the kids danced and swirled to an unfortunate collection of totally forgettable songs. Every generation thinks music ceased to be worthwhile as soon as they reached adulthood, but the music of the late 1960s and early 1970s had to be – had to be – superior to the music of the 1980s. The songs I heard – despite attempting to not really listen – were vapid, mindless and heartless melodies that may have been harmless, but were also worthless.

Mary's small flask of whiskey was emptied; I wandered around and visited with Annie, who had eventually locked onto Cody for a few dances. But my sweater and I obviously bored Annie, and she chatted with Jersey and Mary longer and with more animation than she spoke with me. I made my way around the gym and talked to Tony and Aspen, who had danced with such frequency and intensity her hair at her temples was damp and she smelled like something exotic. I had talked football with Jersey, who assured me the win over Three Forks was no fluke and that if the kids stayed focused they'd beat Manhattan next week.

With a little less than an hour to go in the dance, Tony was somehow on stage and announcing the next songs were dedicated to the Ranger football team and Coach Jersey. Tony held up a cassette tape and proclaimed everyone had to come out and dance to the next two songs.

"Mr. Franklin, Lance, Coach, Miss Kristofferson, all of you," Tony said. "Just these two songs. They're both from a Springsteen bootleg concert and if you're here, you gotta dance to honor the victorious Rangers!"

Everyone cheered. Tony handed the cassette to Bonner, who loaded it up and judging by the first note, cranked the volume up loud. The kids crowded to the dance floor, and started dancing and singing to the first song, *Born to Run*. People have claimed that it's difficult to dance to Springsteen. It wasn't for these kids. Mostly, they were jumping and whirling in circles.

Annie crept up behind me and pushed me out to the dance floor, where she started to jump and clap and sing along to the lyrics. The song had integrity, I always thought, and had a core of rebellious truth and authenticity that drove straight to the heart. Perhaps the kids responded to that. They hopped and jumped and clapped and spun in circles. No way was I doing that. The littlest O'Toole, Peach, hauled Ed onto the dance floor and he looked – I hoped – more awkward than me. Jersey danced with Holly and seemed to be holding his own. Mary was with Tony, and she looked like she couldn't wait for the song to get over with.

Born to Run ended with thunderous applause from the real-life audience from the real-life concert, and without interruption the next song started with a Springsteen countdown.

Then boom, the unmistakable cords of *Devil With the Blue Dress* roared to life. Ed grinned; he knew this song, music from his era. The Little Richard song had been a dance favorite since I'd been a kid, and probably even before that. But here was Springsteen playing it, and the volume was louder than a jet engine.

"Get up now!" shouted Bruce. "Come on! Hit it!"

The kids all cheered, paired up, and began to shake like a 1960s sock hop. Holly slithered over to me and somehow, easily, somewhat theatrically, pulled the sweater off me and tossed it aside by the bleachers.

Springsteen shouted the lyrics as the band thundered into the song.

The music was so loud you could feel the base thumping as if the sound waves had physical heft behind them. The kids were jitterbugging as if they'd been doing it their entire lives.

I found myself paired with Mary; that had to have been accomplished with a little sleight of hand from Annie, who shook and shimmied with Jersey. Holly had danced toward Ed, and they were bopping, hand in hand, and suddenly Ed spun Holly like a top. The only reason I believed it was because I saw it. Tony twirled Aspen, and danced like he meant it. I looked around; everyone danced like they meant it.

Springsteen and the E Street Band transitioned into *Good Golly Miss Molly* and the entire dance floor picked up the tempo. Ed started to move with such velocity his hair flew in mussed little circles, and then to my surprise Holly reached over and with both her hands deliberately mussed his hair. Ed danced on, seemingly in another time and place.

Jersey and Annie bopped around in a tight circle, one of Jersey's hands holding one of Annie's hands while their other hands flew in the air, and spun so their backs were to each other before spinning back to face each other.

I always thought Springsteen and his band were good, but not until right then, listening to the old classic songs I'd heard dozens of bands play before, did I realize *how* good Bruce and the E Street Band were. The volume and quality of music was nothing like I'd ever heard before. A keyboard solo, backed by drums, led into the song *CC Rider*. The band belted out the chorus and then screamed back into *Jenny Jenny*.

A compact guitar solo served as a bridge for whatever happened next, and the kids started to shuffle to the outside in a circle, and clapped in rhythm as Ed and Annie danced together inside the circle. Annie was wiggling her hips an arm's length across from Ed Franklin, Superintendent of Schools for the Whitehall School District, and the two of them were holding hands, dipping shoulders and head bopping to the music, the two of them alone on the dance floor, surrounded by a raucous and applauding WHS Homecoming dance crowd. Arguably the two most intelligent people in Whitehall, reduced to rhythmic mayhem by guitars and drums.

A piano eased in to supplement the guitar, and Ed's hips twitched in time to the melody. The kids hooted. The drums kicked in and Ed did a little something with his shoulders to the background beat of the music. He looked like some insane mixture of an IBM accountant and Elvis Presley. I stood outside of the circle, watching my daughter shimmy and shake unlike anything I'd ever seen her do before, but it was Ed who had me clapping and laughing. I thought right then if commanded by police to cease, Ed would simply have been unable to stop dancing. He was possessed, astonishingly, with what I later learned Springsteen call his *Detroit Medley*. Ed's hair was a mess and strands fell loosely down over his forehead. His face glistened with sweat. He was oblivious to us. Oblivious to everything. He was literally lost in the music. Ed Franklin. Lost in the music. I leaned back, face skyward, and hooted toward the ceiling.

A saxophone crept into the song, and Ed added a head bop to his hip twitch and shoulder wiggle. He bent his knees and lowered himself to the floor, and Annie followed. Ed did a version of the twist with his rump barely above his heels, and Annie was down alongside him, just as low and just as energetic.

The music picked up intensity, and Springsteen sang, *Hold it*, several times, softer at first and louder and louder to the finish, stopped for one miracle pause, then bawled out lyrics starting with *Jenny! Jenny! Jenny!*

Ed jumped up from his crouch, punched toward the ceiling with both fists, one at a time, grabbed Annie at the waist and practically threw her as he spun her through the air. She landed flawlessly and shimmied right back at him, and they held hands at arm's length, their eyes locked on each other, their shoulders churning and their feet churning, their hips twisting violently from side to side. Everyone in the gym was hollering, clapping and cheering.

The song ended with Springsteen hoarsely saying, *Thank you* and it was impossible to tell which cheering was louder, the thousands of fans at the real concert where the song had been played or the sixty roaring and amazed people in the Whitehall multi-purpose room.

Ed, his face flushed red, placed his arms in front and behind at his waist, and bowed deeply. Annie followed a beat later, and her smile was something I'll never forget.

After the dance ended, after we'd finished off Rhonda's cinnamon rolls and the last drop of milk in the house, the half dozen people still gathered in the Joslyn family living room were Tony and Aspen, Annie and Cody, and Mary and me. As long as there had been food and harmless conversational topics, the awkwardness was held in abeyance, but immediately after the rolls were gone the self-consciousness asserted itself. We were an odd collection.

Mary wasn't a teacher to anyone in the house, but she was a teacher, a school authority figure, and it was possibly the first time Annie and Tony had ever helped entertain a school authority figure in our home. Never once had a woman been in our house since Amy had left. Not once. It was late, and it had been an emotional day – the weather, the game and the dance – and everyone, including the kids, were sleepy. I'd turned up the furnace, but dark and cold had descended with cruelty; it was suddenly chilly inside and the house stubbornly refused to warm up.

Aspen was half-asleep on the couch, curled up with her knees drawn toward her chest, her head on Tony's lap as he sat upright, his feet extended to the table. Aspen wore Tony's letterman jacket as a blanket.

Mary sat wearily in the recliner; wearing my sweater. She'd vowed to never return it, and I had threatened violence if she ever did. Cody was seated on the floor, his back braced by the table that held the only lamp in the room. Annie sat alongside me, on the floor, covered with a blanket. She was drifting in and out of sleep, her head on my shoulder. We'd all arrived home about an hour earlier, all revved up and all talking at once. The conversation jumped from Ed at the dance to Dave at the football game, to Jersey's halftime speech to the Homecoming coronation to a dozen other topics. But the energy didn't last. Milk, cinnamon rolls and fatigue had slowed us down to the point where we had exhausted not only real conversation but even feigned conversation. I thought we all could have fallen asleep right then and there in the exact positions we were in, but that was neither realistic nor acceptable.

I carefully leaned Annie's head away from me, stood and stretched, and only the weary eyes of Cody and Mary observed me. "Okay boys and girls," I said. Tony's eyes opened, but Aspen only groaned and slightly shifted her position on the couch. "We've got to break up this party before the cops show up and shut us down." Only Mary responded, with the barest hint of a smile.

Annie pulled the blanket completely over her head.

"How are we going to do this?" I asked no one in particular. Cody, Mary and Aspen had to get home. Cody's truck was in the driveway, but Mary's car was at the school parking lot and Aspen had arrived at the dance with her sisters, who could be anywhere. I looked at Annie to tell me how we were going to do this, but she was hidden, covered by the blanket.

"I could drive Aspen home," Tony suggested.

I shook my head. "You don't have a license, and you know Manfred's on the prowl tonight," I said. "It'd be just our luck he'd catch you."

He was too tired to scowl, although he offered a feeble attempt at one.

We had some *appearance* problems to address, and I wasn't the only one aware of them. Mary pensively watched me attempt to think it through. Cody, a high school junior, should not and could not drive an elementary school teacher home close to one o'clock in the morning after a dance. That would have to be my responsibility. Neither Cody nor Aspen could spend the night at our house; that was unthinkable, despite their individual and collective fatigue.

"Cody, you go ahead and scoot home, and tell Ed he was absolutely remarkable tonight," I said. "Straight home," I warned him. He nodded. "Ed was awesome," Annie mumbled from underneath the blanket.

Cody stood gingerly, sore from the football game. He reached out and shook my hand, and thanked me. I had no idea what he was thanking me for.

"You okay to drive?" I asked him. He was moving like an old man.

He nodded. "I'm tired, is all."

"Tell you what, you ride with us. I'll take everyone home. No sense you driving this late on slick roads."

Cody nodded agreement. Annie hadn't removed the blanket and she and Cody hadn't spoken a word of farewell.

"You," I pointed to Tony, "and you," I touched Annie's head, "clean this place up and get to bed. I want to see both of you in bed asleep when I get back."

Tony responded with a weak glare, but his heart wasn't it. He ran his hand through Aspen's hair and started to whisper to her. She groaned.

The windows of the Escort were glazed with ice. Mary sat in the passenger seat and Aspen and Cody crawled into the backseat. I turned the defrost on high and scraped the windows. The scraper slashed across the windshield and stars were cut sharp as diamonds above in the black sky. It was a silent trip to the Franklin place; the front step light was on, as was the kitchen light. The door opened and Cody slipped inside.

I brought Aspen home next. The O'Toole's lived up in what some folks called Snob Knob, a hill on the northwest side of Whitehall that crested above the town. They lived in a large two-story house with a wide paved driveway. The O'Toole porch light was on, and the driveway was a sheet of ice. Aspen was virtually somnolent and I was afraid she was going to slip and fall, so I walked her to the front door and rang the doorbell. Lyle was there in an instant, and greeted us with an expression of concern.

"She all right?" he asked.

I nodded. I more or less gently shoved Aspen into her dad's arms, "She's just tired. We were over at my place after that dance. We had milk and cinnamon buns. It's been a long day."

"Cinnamon buns?" Lyle asked. "Living the dream, eh Lance?"

"Yeah," I said.

Aspen murmured, "Is Holly home yet?"

"No," Lyle said. "I thought that might be her in the front seat." He crouched to get a better view, but it was dark and I had parked midway up the driveway. "Who is that in the front seat?"

"Ms. Kristofferson," Aspen answered.

Lyle looked at me. "Get a load of Lance," he beamed.

"Not now, Lyle," I said.

"Night, Lance," Aspen mumbled, and to my surprise, she reached out and pulled me closer, and kissed my cheek.

"Let him go, honey," Lyle said. "He's got some business to tend to."

"Grow up," I told Lyle. He just smiled.

I got back in the car, strapped on my seat belt, and put the car in reverse.

"This is how rumors start, isn't it?" Mary said, watching the house as I backed out into the dark street.

Chapter 26

By Monday morning pretty much everyone in Whitehall knew that Hank Harrison intended to get Jersey either demoted or fired, and that the school board had scheduled a special meeting for Tuesday night. Hank was lining up support – Daniel Purdy was one, a few other disgruntled parents were others – to back him up at the board meeting.

Tuesday night was the absolute worst meeting night for weekly newspapers that publish on Wednesdays. In my case, my weekly goal was to have the Ledger done by midnight on Tuesday. A meeting meant I wasn't laying out the paper because I was at a meeting, and it meant I had an article to write after the meeting. It meant probably three hours of extra work – two hours at the meeting, an hour to write the article – after seven o'clock on Tuesday night.

Lyle O'Toole told me about the special meeting when we met on Monday morning, and he said his guess was the meeting would be closed. Government bodies were allowed by state law to close a public meeting when the discussion related to personnel matters, such as student discipline, disciplining a teacher or relieving a coach of his duties.

"Don't worry, Jersey's not going anywhere," Lyle told me. He sighed, and adjusted his tie so it laid flat on his shirt.

"It takes a special closed school board meeting to change quarterbacks?" I asked.

Lyle shook his head. "Hank says Colt was benched not because of talent, but because of personal animosity. Hank alleges Jersey is punishing Colt because he – Jersey – dislikes Hank."

"Everybody dislikes Hank," I pointed out.

"True, but not everybody punishes Colt because of it."

"That's nonsense," I said. "Have you seen the way the kids play with Dave back there?"

Lyle held his hands chest level, as if to back me away. "Of course it's nonsense. But Hank's smart enough to know he can't get Jersey fired by benching his kid for a better player. Hank's read the rules. He knows a school board can dismiss a coach for malicious behavior, which is what Hank's asserting."

I shook my head with disbelief. Lyle selected one of the ad layouts and made one minor change in the ad copy. He stood up. He had work to do. So did I. I stood up. We walked together the dozen or so steps to the door of his office.

"The kids played a helluva second half against Three Forks," Lyle said.

"Pretty impressive, wasn't it?" I said.

"That little Dave Dickson," Lyle said, amused. "He's a peewee wizard back there. He gets me so mixed up I can't tell who's got the ball."

"Tell me about it," I said. "It's pretty hard to takes pictures of the guy with the ball when you don't know who has the ball." My back was to him as I moved toward the door.

"Heard you had a good time at the dance," he said, and I turned around to see he had more than a hint of mischief in his smile. "When I saw you pull up with Aspen I thought maybe she hit another deer."

"You hear about Ed Franklin at the dance?" I asked.

Lyle nodded. "Aspen said he looked like a Mormon elder on acid."

"You wouldn't believe how that guy can *move*," I said.

"Amazing," he said. "Ed Franklin. Who knew?"

I nodded a goodbye and was headed out his door but he followed me for another step.

"Hey," he said in a soft conspiratorial whisper. "What time did you finally get home Saturday morning?"

I just kept walking.

I had worked six hours on Sunday but was still behind schedule – as always – on Monday. I had plenty of good pictures to choose from, but I had to get into the darkroom and get them printed. I had a nice photo of Colt and Holly, WHS Homecoming king and queen, for the front page, and photos from the parade, bonfire, talent show and the game, plus other assorted photos, including a picture I took of a layer of about four inches of snow piled up on the railing in back of the WHS drummer during the football game. I could print about five pictures an hour, which meant for this week's paper I had a minimum of four hours in the darkroom. I enjoyed taking pictures, and developing film was routine and essentially mindless, but printing the actual halftone photos – with the stench of chemicals and the frustration of redoing and redoing an exposure in an attempt to get the print *just* right, *exactly* right – was painful for me. A halftone needed contrast, but not too much contrast, and it had to be dark enough, but not too dark, and light enough, but not too light. A halftone was actually a collection of dots – the darker the area the bigger the dots – and if the dots were too big the area would fill in completely with ink and turn into a dark glop. If the dots were too little you'd lose them during the transformation from layout page to negative to plate to newsprint page and end up with an area as blank white as the page edges. It took a true photographer and a true darkroom technician to produce a true top quality halftone, and I was neither.

By three o'clock Monday afternoon I still hadn't gotten into the darkroom. I hadn't even found a chance to eat lunch. The county treasurer in Boulder had faxed down a large legal notice about fall tax notices, the local electric cooperative ran its annual advertisement notifying customers of its yearly meeting and trustee election, and a feed store in Dillon wanted to advertise a big sale of livestock supplements. We had over five hundred total inches of ads, which was excellent financially and positive from a layout perspective, but it translated into a crushing amount of work for Laura Joyce and me.

I was just about ready to slip into the darkroom for a long shift of work when Annie came in the Ledger – after school already? I thought – followed, surprisingly, by Trisha. Outside the door Annie spun Trish's wheelchair around and rolled her in backward – up with a bounce over the four-inch ledge at the door – into the Ledger office.

"Hang on," Annie told me, and bolted back outside.

"Hi, Trish," Laura Joyce called out.

Trish looked toward where the voice came from, her eyes active but not quite focused. "Hi," she tentatively responded toward Laura Joyce, then located her.

Annie returned to the Ledger with a thirty-two ounce plastic Pepsi cup from The Corner Store. "Here," she told me. "I figured you'd be needing this."

She was right. I was needing that. She was always a step ahead of me.

"Thanks," I said. "I'm way behind schedule," I said, as if it was an apology. She knew what my tone and words meant: She was on her own for dinner, she was on her own all evening, and I wouldn't be home until well after she'd gone to bed.

"You heard about the school board meeting tomorrow?" Annie asked me.

"Yeah," Trish said. Seated, she looked up toward me, her neck twisted in a slightly unnatural angle. Her comment was directed at me, an affirmation to Annie's question.

I nodded. "About Jersey? Yeah. I think they'll close the meeting." I had a sudden sense of dread. I looked at Annie. "Don't tell me you're thinking of going."

She shook her head. "Some of the players might go, but I think that's it. We have this, though." She pulled a piece of paper out of her pocket. "Trish wrote it."

"Yeah," Trish said with authority.

My eyes scanned from Annie down to Trish. Annie returned my look of suspicion; Trish's eyes looked glazed. Whatever this document was, Annie wrote it, was my guess, and stuck Trish's name on it.

I took the sheet of paper and my expression told Annie I had misgivings about whatever it was I was about to read. The Pepsi, I realized, was a bribe, an apology, or a peace offering.

It was a letter to the editor, and it was in childish handwritten scrawl that had to have been Trish's. I looked up at Annie, who motioned with her hand: *Keep reading*.

"The deadline for letters is noon," Annie told Trish. "But I'm sure Lance will get this in."

I looked over at Trish. She smiled at me. I scanned the letter, and although some of the words were hard to decipher, the meaning was clear, and it was equally clear the thought behind the words belonged to Trish. Annie may have inspired the creation of the letter – maybe not – and Annie may have whispered some assistance during the actual writing – maybe not – but the words were pure Trish, as if she had spoken them rather than written them. I had to fix it up a little, but this would be the lead letter in the Ledger that Wednesday:

Dear Editor:

Where was everybody on Friday? Where were you? The WHS Rangers played a great game and hardly anybody was there to see it. Were you too cold? I wasn't cold! I was happy!

The Rangers played with a great heart and teamwork. I was so proud of them. Thanks Jersey and all the Rangers for trying so hard and winning that game! Too bad some people left during halftime. Too bad some people never showed up. The Rangers are a great team!

Go cheer on the Rangers! Show them your team spirit!

Trisha Ryan
WHS Student

Nearly ten hours later, after two o'clock in the morning, I was still in the darkroom printing pictures. I was so weary I was having difficulty clearly focusing my vision on the image through the enlarger, and I was tempted to take a short break and do something else – anything else – for awhile, but the pictures had to get done and I was the one who had to do them. I only had five pictures left and I was determined, and desperate, to finish them.

I was placing a new negative in the enlarger when I thought I heard something – a rustling of some kind – outside the darkroom in the Ledger office. I stood motionless and listened, but didn't hear anything else. I fitted the negative, adjusted the enlarger aperture and time setting for the exposure – the photo was of Carrie Lindstrom and her saxophone – and it was relatively easy to focus the image on the negative-reversed fingers on the sax.

I drowsily slid the photo paper into the processor and again heard something outside the darkroom door. It was a scratching sound. I heard it again. A slight scraping. I wondered if the mouse was trying to join me in the darkroom. There was no one else working in all of Whitehall except the graveyard crew at the Town Pump, the town marshal and on the mountain top northeast of Whitehall, the Golden Sunlight Mine night crew.

The door into the darkroom was light-tight with an old blanket folded and stuck into the crack between the floor and the bottom of the door. A slight seam of light filtered through the top right corner of the door as well, and I had to stick a piece of tape up there to prevent light from leaking in. To exit the darkroom I had to make sure the photo paper was safely back in the box, and then when I re-entered I had to re-tape the corner above and diligently stuff the blanket down below.

When I opened the door and stepped over the blanket, the mouse scurried away from the door, along the wall and behind a cabinet where we stored recent editions of the Ledger. I went to the backroom and grabbed the BB gun and safety glasses and cocked the rifle as I quickly returned to the middle of the room, with a perfect view of the area between the cabinet and the crack in the baseboard.

The mouse sniffed its way carefully along the wall, inching along on four feet, rising momentarily on its back legs, sniffing the air and the floor. It presented a better target when all four feet were on the floor, and I waited until it stopped. I had it in the BB gun sight and was just about to pull the trigger when something caught the corner of my eye.

First came a tiny nose, then a wispy head of another mouse, warily creeping out from the crack in the wall.

Multiple mice. Tandem mice. Mother and daughter mice? Husband and wife mice? I lowered the rifle, and the movement spooked the first mouse into a sprint. Both ducked inside the wall and disappeared.

I was in my usual seat at the Tuesday school board meeting, but it was an unusual crowd at an unusual meeting. A handful of parents were in attendance, including a grim Hank Harrison, who sat between his son and his wife. Colt looked as if he wished he were somewhere else. Kathleen seemed somehow regal, as if she intended to do her best to rise above the injustice done to her son.

About twenty high school kids were in attendance, including Trish and, to my surprise, Tony. I hadn't seen him since Sunday, and while I had worried about Annie and her attitude showing up at the meeting, it had never occurred to me that Tony – indifferent and passive Tony – would be seated in the center of a group of letter-jacketed football players in the back two rows. They must have gone from practice to dinner to the meeting; the odor of A&W burgers and onion rings seemed to hover around them. Trish was off the corner of the front row. Her mother was a school board member, and Molly was unsmiling and silent as she sat, her elbows on the table in front of her, waiting for the meeting to begin. To her left sat Daniel Purdy, perched on the front edge of his chair as if he was fully prepared to immediately respond to some real or imagined insult or challenge or inequality.

The A&W smelled incredibly good. I had twenty-four of twenty-eight pages of the paper done, and left about an eight-inch hole on the front page and about a six-inch hole on the back page for the jump. I would write the school board article to fit the exact space I had left. To get twenty-four pages laid out and proofed by the Tuesday seven o'clock meeting I'd worked until four o'clock Tuesday morning, began work three hours later, had grabbed a quick pizza lunch next door and skipped supper. I hadn't realized how hungry I was until I'd smelled the food.

It was obvious a school board meeting was foreign territory for the football players. They saw both school principals and the school superintendent in front of the room, observed a stoic and stern collection of school board members, and the kids were smart enough to sense and understand the decorum required during the expected official and solemn proceedings.

Lyle gaveled the meeting to order. The first thing he did was ask Ed if he thought the meeting should be open or closed, and Ed said closed. Lyle looked at the audience and said state law allowed the school district to close the meeting when the board dealt with a personnel or student matter, which this was, so everyone except those explicitly involved was required by law to exit the meeting room. Lyle explained that the board would invite individuals to comment one at a time during closed session, with only the board, petitioners and school administrators present.

So we stood, gathered at the door, and filed out the door into the hallway, which immediately smelled like A&W. I walked over to talk to Tony, and the feeling was like two friends who haven't seen each other for a while.

"You smell like A&W," I told him. He was surrounded by friends – Logan, Dave, a JeffScott, Cale, Nate.

"You smell like darkroom chemicals," Tony answered.

"No, I don't," I said. "I haven't been in the darkroom all day."

"Trust me," Tony said, "you smell like a darkroom."

There was no point in arguing with either one of my kids. "You want to do me a big favor?"

"Such as?" he asked.

"Head over to A&W and get me some food?"

"I don't drive, remember, because-" he started.

"Yeah, we can go get him some food," Logan told Tony.

"It'll only take a couple minutes," I said.

"How's this work?" Tony asked me, indicating the meeting behind the closed door to our left.

"You got time to run to A&W and back," I assured him. "First, the school board talks with the Harrison family, and after that then Ed will call in people individually to comment."

"You mean Fast Eddie?" joked Tony, and did an Elvis hip swivel.

"Cool it," I told them. "You're in school, remember." I decided to change the topic. "This'll take awhile. You've got time to make a food run and comment, if you want." I looked up at Tony. He was taller than I remembered. "Are you going to comment?"

"Yeah, I think I am," he answered with confidence.

"What are you going to say?" I asked.

"Why would I tell you? You're the press," he said. "It's a closed meeting, remember. You're not supposed to know what I say. You're probably breaking a law just by asking."

"Go get my food," I told him. It apparently took seven football players to fetch me dinner, because they all followed Tony down the hall and out the door. None of them, I realized, asked me what I wanted to eat.

I covertly surveyed the crowd in the hall to mentally add up the comments for and against Jersey. The Harrisons had forced the meeting based on the alleged improper disciplining of Colt, but the meeting was more accurately a referendum on Jersey. I was certain the kids, including Trish – or perhaps, especially Trish – would support Jersey. Daniel Purdy would comment and vote against Jersey specifically to antagonize Ed and Lyle.

It was all pretty much a charade. The school board was not going to wade into athletic team members' playing time, no matter how bitter and angry Hank Harrison was and no matter what he alleged or whom he accused. Jersey wasn't even present to defend himself. That may not have been wise, but it was understandable. It was a little awkward that Colt was dating Lyle's daughter, but everything and everybody is connected in a small town.

Outside of the Harrison family and Daniel Purdy, I saw no one in the hallway who I thought would comment or testify against Jersey.

I smelled the food before I saw it. Tony dumped it in my hands. The bag had some heft – it contained a double cheeseburger, a large order of fries and a large Pepsi. It would be my third large Pepsi of the day.

When you're a reporter and the meeting action takes place in a room you're excluded from, there's no tangible drama and barely even anything to take interest in. I sat on the hallway floor, my back against the lockers, and ate my dinner. My fries were gone before the meeting room door opened from the inside out, and Ed poked his head out to announce the public could now comment. There was still nothing for me to do, so I shoved the burger into my mouth and watched Trish get her wheelchair squared and roll into the meeting room. The door closed behind her. It was appropriate, I supposed, that Trish led off the comments. During the course of the next hour or so all the kids except Dave and JeffScott took a turn in the meeting room, with Tony's comment taking the longest. He spoke, by my calculation, for over ten minutes. By eight-thirty, there was no one in the hallway who wanted to testify, but it took twenty minutes after that for Ed to re-open the door and admit the fifteen or so people back into the meeting room. By then my food was gone, my pop was gone, my belly was full and I was having a hard time staying alert.

The first thing I saw when I re-entered the meeting room was that Hank was seething. I could see a blood vessel bulging along his temple. His chin was clamped tight shut and his breath whistled in brief gasps through his nose. His breath seemed pulled in and forced out through his nose in bursts, and his mouth was clamped angrily tense and shut tight.

Lyle casually explained the motion was not debatable, which meant there would be no discussion among the school board or anyone else about what had transpired during the closed session.

Lyle called for a motion.

Daniel Purdy made a motion to relieve the WHS varsity football coach, Jerry Conte, of his duties. The school board members shifted in their seats, but none spoke. Lyle asked for a second. No one spoke.

The motion dies, said Lyle, for lack of a second. He asked if there was a second motion. Silence. He pounded the gavel. The meeting was over. It was nine o'clock on a Tuesday night, and I had to fill a fourteen-inch news hole from a meeting that offered absolutely no public information outside of a motion that failed without discussion and without a second.

Tony and the football team filed out of the room first, careless and seemingly mindless. Trish waited for her mom, who was gathering up her meeting materials.

I waved goodbye to Lyle and Ed, and was already thinking about the filler material for the article – a little background on Jersey, the large number of high school students who commented, an update on the Ranger football team – to fill the fourteen inches.

"You going home?" I asked Tony as we walked down the hallway to exit the building.

"Eventually," he said.

"Eventually?" I asked. "What's that mean?"

"You're a journalist and all," he said, "you can figure out big words."

I was in no mood for Tony's antics. "What's Annie doing?"

"How would I know? I've been here the past two hours. Except when I had to fetch your food."

"What was she doing last time you saw her?" I asked.

"I don't know," he said. "She was at the bank this afternoon for something." He shrugged. "I think she said something about having to help Cody with some school stuff tonight." He hesitated. "Don't quote me on that, though." He smiled, pleased with his little joke.

"I'll call her when I get back to the Ledger," I said. "I want you home sooner than eventually. I want you home by eleven. It's a school night. I should be done by midnight, one at the latest."

We were going to part ways on the elementary school sidewalk.

"Hey," I asked him. "You were here to comment. It's not like Annie to stay out of a fight. What's your guess on why she wasn't here to let them know what she thought?"

"She didn't have to," Tony said. "Don't tell her I told you, but why do you think she was at the bank this afternoon?"

"You lobbied the chairman of the school board today at his place of business?" I asked Annie. "Is Cody over there?"

"Slow down, Lance," Annie told me. "One accusation at a time."

"What did you do?" I asked her. "Who did you talk to?"

While I was on the phone a mouse snuck out of the hole and stretched up on its back legs, its front legs placed softly on the lowest drawer of the filing cabinet, sniffing the air. From my desk and the phone, I threw a pen at the mouse and came closer to hitting it with the pen than I ever had with the BB gun.

"I didn't do anything," she said. "And I believe the school board did nothing. So it's settled."

"The school board voted to not discipline Jersey," I said. "So he's still coach."

"Actually, the school board technically didn't vote on anything," Annie pointed out. "Officially, it took no action of any kind. It only heard comments."

"Who told you? Is Tony home already?"

"No, I'm home by myself. No Cody," she said.

"So how'd you find out?" I asked.

She hesitated. "Well, I guess you already know that Lyle and I had a chat this afternoon. At the bank."

"Let me get this straight," I said. "The chairman of the Whitehall School Board told you – a middle school student – how a board vote was going to go later that evening? Are you telling me that's what happened? Because I'm pretty sure that's improper if not illegal."

"He didn't tell me, precisely," Annie said. "Mr. Franklin and I had a brief discussion previously, in study hall. I merely continued that conversation with Lyle at the bank."

"What?" I couldn't believe what I was hearing. "Do I have this right? You first talked to the school superintendent and then conferred with the school board chairman about the vote tonight, and after you shared your thoughts with them, and them with you, you were satisfied you knew what the vote was going to be. So you didn't have to show up tonight. Did you orchestrate this whole thing?"

"Lance," she said, in her *you should know better* tone of voice.

"What kind of answer is that?" I asked.

"What kind of question is that?" she said.

"What kind of question is what?" I asked.

"Lance, you're confused. Finish the paper, come home and get some sleep," she said. "It sounds like you need it."

"There's two mice down here now, did you know that?" I blurted.

"Down where?"

I just shook my head. "Never mind. You're sure Cody's not there?"

"Yeah, pretty sure," she assured me sarcastically.

"Tony told me he was there. You were helping him with homework."

"That was earlier this evening," she said. "Previously on this call, when you asked, you'll remember I informed you I was alone. Typically, when a person is alone, he or she is not with a person named Cody, or any person named anything."

"I'll be home in about an hour," I said. I had surrendered, and she knew it.

I hung up the phone. Jesus, I was tired. I spotted one of the mice as it crept out of the hole along the baseboard.

"I need some sleep," I told the mouse. It ignored me.

It only took me a few minutes to write the first half of the article, and it would have taken me only a few minutes to write the second half, but a distinct but soft knock came from outside the Ledger door. It wasn't Cal's knock, and it wasn't Sunday night. I called out to come in, thinking it was probably Lyle, but it wasn't. When the door opened, I saw Molly Ryan.

She sort of ducked when she entered. "Sorry," she said sheepishly. "Am I bothering you?"

"No, no, of course not. Come in." I stood up. I was so weary that when I popped to my feet I felt a little woozy.

"I'm sorry, to intrude like this, but I have a quick question to ask you," Molly said.

Molly Ryan, to my knowledge, had never before been in the Ledger. She looked around a little bit, as if sizing up the place. She was lean but not skinny, had short silver hair and tended to wear men's clothes – tee-shirts, sweatshirts, Ranger windbreakers. She had a firmness to her, probably from constantly negotiating her daughter's wheelchair. Her concession to fashion were earrings: She usually had some kind of elaborate hoops or something hanging from her ears. Tonight her ears featured little silver replicas of cowboy boots.

"Is Trisha's letter going to be in the paper tomorrow?" Molly asked.

"Yeah," I said. "Here, look." I found and lifted the paste-up of page four, the opinion-editorial page. Under the eighteen-point Helvetica type headline of *Go cheer on the Rangers!* rested Trisha's letter. It was a late night, Molly had been through a stressful school board meeting, but when she saw that letter, sitting prominently above the fold on page four, her eyes beamed, and she couldn't help but allow a smile of delight cross her face. And that made the hours and hours of Ledger effort worth it, to bring that kind of momentary joy and pride to the life of someone like Molly Ryan.

"Thank you, Lance, so very much." She looked at Trish's letter as if it contained magic. She continued to look at it as she spoke to me. "Trish wrote the letter, and told me she brought it down here. I never read it, or even saw it. She was so happy and hasn't stopped talking about it the past two days. But I wasn't sure if it was, you know, good enough to be in the paper. If it wasn't I was going to explain to her that not all letters submitted to the paper are printed in the paper."

"All of the letters she submits will be," I said.

"That's so nice of you," she said. "You, Tony, and of course, Annie, have always been so considerate and supportive of her. We are so grateful for you, especially Annie, who's a dear."

"She's something else," I admitted.

She stood there, gazing at the letter. "You have no idea how much this means to Trish."

Actually, I thought I did have an idea. This letter would mean a lot to Trish, and I was honored to play a small part in that accomplishment. Knowing the joy the Ledger would bring to Trish this week made the eighty hours of work worth it. The letter, perhaps insignificant to most everyone outside its author, was something Trish would treasure the rest of her life.

Molly turned absently and began walking toward the door.

"Quite a meeting tonight, huh?" I said.

"Oh, I guess," Molly said with distain. "A major waste of time, really."

"It's hard to feel sorry for Hank, especially since he brought all this on himself," I said. "But he was livid when the meeting was over. He's not used to humiliation, especially public humiliation."

"I'm not going to waste any pity on him," Molly said sternly. "He tried to corrupt the team, and he tried to corrupt the team for his own petty reasons."

She was almost to the door, but she wasn't quite ready to open it.

"High school sports in Montana are still pure and innocent," she said. "Is there anything more honest and uplifting than a high school kid who just scored the winning touchdown or made the winning basket? It's a clean and emotionally truthful joy, Lance. It's honest, it's valiant and it's inspiring all at once, wrapped in sincere and utter joy. It warms my heart to see these kids win a football game. Or excel in the play. Or win a spelling bee. Not just because of the happiness it brings Trish, although anything that brings joy to Trish warms my heart, but because of the heartfelt and wonderfully expressive thrill it brings to those kids. And you know what, Lance? That heartfelt and wonderful thrill is so genuine, so pure, that almost nothing can damage or diminish it. Coaches can't ruin high school sports. The kids themselves can't ruin high school sports. The media can't. School administrators can't ruin it, school boards can't, and neither can referees. Only one group can spoil high school sports. Parents. Parents, and only parents, can destroy the pure and innocent joy of high school sports. Parents like Hank and Kathleen. That's why they'll get no pity from me."

"Or from the rest of the board," I said.

"Except for that royal asshole, Daniel Purdy," Molly said.

I expected her to make an apology for her language, but she didn't.

"I probably shouldn't tell you this," she said. "Especially since you're the publisher and all." She hesitated. "Promise you won't say a word of this to anyone."

I nodded.

"I mean it," she told me. "It's against the law for a board member to talk about what happened during a closed meeting."

"Don't worry," I said. "I usually find out what happens at closed meetings. None of it ever makes the paper."

"Okay," she said. "This is just between you and me. All right? The main reason why Hank was so incensed was because Colt spoke during the meeting. Colt stood up, stood right next to Hank, and told the board Hank was wrong. Colt told the board Jersey showed no favoritism toward any players and harbored no resentment toward anyone. Colt stood up, Lance, and confronted his father, with his father sitting right there. My guess is Colt never before defied Hank, and here he stood up and did so in front of the school board and administration." She smiled weakly. "Talk about a pure heart."

No kidding, I thought. It took a pure heart bolstered by raw courage to get up in front of the school board and contradict someone like Hank Harrison, especially when someone like Hank Harrison was your father. I could just imagine the discussion going on right now in the Harrison household.

"Well, I better go," Molly said. "Sorry to take up so much of your time this late at night. Tell Annie thanks for her help tonight, and thanks so very much for publishing Trisha's letter." She shook her head in amusement. "I can't wait to see her face tomorrow afternoon when the paper comes out. Goodnight, Lance, and thanks again."

She had opened the door, and I could feel the cold night air coming inside the office.

"Good night," I said. But I had to ask. "Molly?"

She turned in the doorway to look back at me.

"You said a minute ago to thank Annie," I said. "Thank Annie for what?"

"She didn't tell you?" Molly looked at me quizzically. She hesitated, as if unsure what she should say. "She called most of the board members last night." Molly paused. Her eyes opened wide. "You really didn't know? Honestly?" She placed a hand in front of her mouth and laughed softly. "Annie more or less rallied the board members in support of Jersey. We were on his side anyway, of course. But it was nice to hear her perspective, and to get a heads up on Colt."

"Are you telling me she told you last night that Colt was going to speak in favor of Jersey?" I asked, incredulous.

Molly nodded. "Sure seemed that way." She laughed softly again. "Your daughter is a very special child, Lance. I admire that girl. I truly do."

Chapter 27

The legend of Special Ed Franklin's raucous dance moves had swept through Whitehall with more speed than a vicious inaccurate rumor.

In fact, the story was contrary to a rumor, the opposite of an exaggeration, the reverse of idle gossip. What people had started saying, and continued to say, about Ed was not only true but in reality a muted version of the truth. The high school kids buzzed about the dance for a solid week, and judging by the way Tony and his friends joked about Ed's performance, the kids voiced a strange newfound respect for him. He had been Special Ed, nerdy and prim school official, and his exuberant routine on the dance floor had transformed him into Fast Eddie, fanatical rocker and mystery man. It was Logan, I think, who essentially voiced a not unreasonable theory that if Mr. Franklin – Logan actually called Ed 'Mr. Franklin' – wasn't a dweeb like everyone thought, and had a hidden wild and uncontrolled dark side, the stark truth was Mr. Franklin may be further capable of behavior or actions no one had previously thought possible.

The new Ed still looked like a cross between Buddy Holly and a NASA physicist. He dressed much like the old Ed, but not exactly like the old Ed, and instead of looking like a bureaucratic dullard he took on a persona, somehow, of someone slightly mysterious, potentially rebellious and possibly even dangerous.

And Ed knew it. People perceived him differently; he perceived *himself* differently. Somehow, for a brief instant, Springsteen's thunderous *Detroit Medley* had resurrected youthful dance floor escapades Ed had forgotten decades earlier, or perhaps never previously even had. He had displayed something unknown and even unimaginable about himself for a shining moment in the Whitehall multi-purpose room, and he was going to enjoy whatever momentary celebrity and notoriety came his way.

He called me up to his office on Thursday to discuss the school's assembly to honor the governor's presence and salute Annie's intellectual accomplishments, and he volunteered that people seemed to be looking at him differently.

"Probably because you went psycho on the dance floor," I told him.

"The music moved me," he said with a grin.

Amy still received the Ledger. I wasn't sure she read it, or if she even saw it or if she saw it, understood it. I continued to send her the paper as a way for her to stay connected to her family, and her family – in an irregular way – to stay connected to her.

It was possible, I thought, a picture of Annie and Governor Ted Schwinden appearing in the Ledger would be viewed by her mother. I sometimes found myself distantly wondering about Amy; what she used to be and what she is, and without intending to, or even realizing I was, I always wonder if there had been some way to have avoided the unfortunate transformation.

Looking back, her slippage behind her veil of emotional and psychological desolation was signaled through abundant warning signs. At the time, neither one of us, regrettably, knew what they were. Midday seclusion. Imagined insults. Sudden despair. Isolation. Gloom. Inexplicable fury. Phantom enemies. Sullen apathy mixed with abject frustration. All for seemingly no reason. But God help us, there had been a reason. We just weren't aware of it.

I recalled one of my family jokes, when the kids were young, was an admission that when Annie was mad, Annie suffered; when Tony was mad, Tony suffered; when I was mad, I suffered; when Amy was mad, all four of us suffered. It seemed mildly comic at the time; later it seemed ironically tragic.

I thought about Amy at odd times in odd ways, and wondered if she thought about me. Could she think of me? Did she miss me? Did she remember our wedding, our honeymoon, the birth of her two irrepressible children? Did she remember how she and I danced, laughed and cuddled? She used to like that word, cuddle. She cuddled Tony as a child, and he would coo and snuggle into her arms in response. I didn't realize it at the time, but Amy was distant with Annie. I didn't see it, or if I saw it I didn't recognize it or understand it. In my naïve world of emotional health, mothers loved their children. All their children, all the time. It was automatic and unconditional.

Sometimes I saw the kids – whole and healthy – and I wondered what they think about their mother and their melancholy family situation. They essentially had an absentee father; a father who feared discussions about their mother. I should talk about Amy, I knew, and if I had any courage, I would. But courage has never been my strong point. And the truth was I was not ashamed of Amy; I was ashamed of my failure to protect her, to help her, to keep her safe.

Amy's drift into mental instability had been deceptively and terrifyingly gradual, and despite its distinct and potent influence, neither individually nor jointly did we do anything to stem the surge of insecurity and misery. And that was the worst: Amy's isolation and my helplessness. The year before she departed Whitehall she was consumed by bitterness and loneliness, and I didn't know why. And what haunts me is I didn't care enough to find out. She would drag herself through the work day – and oftentimes the work night – at the Ledger, gloomy, sullen and confrontational, only to go home and without cause rebuke the kids. Looking back, I should have known. Something was wrong. Her hostility was unnatural. Something was wrong and growing worse. But the business grew, the business dominated our lives – my life, anyway – and her lengthy bouts of petulance and dreariness were easier to escape or ignore than address. So I hid, basically. I fled. I pretended.

She was forced to address her dejection and animosity on her own, by packing what served as a suitcase and suddenly, firmly, forlornly, driving away from her community, her home and her family. Forever, as it turned out.

And I watched her leave, and did nothing. I had been a coward, and she paid – we paid, all of us, Tony and Annie included – for that cowardice. And all four of us kept paying that price every day.

On Thursday night – after a volunteer fire department meeting in which the board of directors voted to purchase a new fire truck; front page news in Whitehall – I arrived home about ten o'clock and as was the growing trend, had to park on the street because the driveway was full of cars and pickups. I recognized two pickups – Cody's orange quarter-ton GMC and Morgan's battered little Chevy Luv.

All the house lights were on – another trend – and I heard what sounded like an argument even before I opened the door. The doorknob turned – spun, actually – without purpose on the front door. Another household item broken. I pushed the door open with my shoulder.

It wasn't an argument, I discovered; everyone in the house was simply talking at once. Pepsi bottles and pizza boxes were spread around not just the kitchen but the whole living room as well. The kids were wound up about something; I could see it in their faces, flushed and animated. Springsteen sang softly on the stereo, *Racing in the Street*.

"Sorry about that doorknob," Morgan apologized to me. His beard was so long it was messy, like a mountain man's. "I can fix it."

"What happened to it?" I asked.

He shrugged. I thought he was going to say something, perhaps offer an explanation what could have happened to the doorknob, but all I got was the shrug.

Six kids were scattered around the house. Annie, Tony and Aspen, Cody, Dave Dickson and Morgan. The toilet flushed off to my left. Seven. Bonner Labuda, again, the hip little guitar player and singer in the Whitehall version of the E Street Band, walked past me.

"Lance," he mumbled, and nodded in greeting as he went by me.

But the conversation ceased when I entered. Their sudden discomfort and uncertainty were obvious. Whatever they had been talking about was something they clearly did not want to discuss with me present.

"What?" I said to the group.

"Nothing," said Cody.

Cody? I thought. *Answering to me*?

Tony and Aspen were close together on the couch. She wore a tight turtleneck blouse that was an absolutely unnatural color somewhere between yellow and orange. Tony wore a dress shirt that was mostly unbuttoned and when I looked a little closer Aspen's hand was hidden inside the shirt and was resting on his belly. It was innocent, mostly.

Annie was perched in my recliner, her lithe leg hanging lazily over the arm of the chair, and she wore socks but no shoes. Cody was on the other side of the room, seated on the floor alongside Dave, their backs against the stereo. Cody had a purplish discoloration under his left eye. His hair had dried after the after-practice shower and was a frizzy mess. Dave had a plate layered with two pieces of pizza in his lap, and his head gently moved in rhythm to the music as he ate. Nervously, he chewed; his eyes darted from me to Annie, back to me and back to Annie. My guess was Dave wasn't used to keeping secrets. Morgan took no chances; he ceased to make any eye contact with me. He looked toward the television, which offered a black empty screen, since it was not turned on, and continued to watch it, as if it was.

Bonner, faded orange pizza sauce dabbed on the left side of his mouth, sat on the couch, opposite Tony and Aspen. Bonner reminded me somehow of a nineteenth century Russian serf, despite the fact I had no real idea what a nineteenth century Russian serf actually looked like. He wore a stocking cap and a lumberjack shirt, and the shirt was two sizes too big, with holes in the elbows and frayed cuffs. I detected, somewhere, some Native American ancestry in his background; there was something about the eyebrows and forehead suggesting tribal blood.

"What's up?" I asked Tony.

"Not much," he said, with a gesture that backed up his words.

"Is it my imagination, or did you stop talking the instant I walked in?" I asked.

"Getting a little paranoid, aren't we, Lance?" asked Annie. I was standing directly above her and the chair. She lifted her face and vision straight up, looked at me and smiled. Whenever she made any reference about mental illness, a phrase like *a little paranoid*, she made sure she reassured me with an expression of comfort or attachment. It was as if she wanted to assure me she was confident and mature enough, given our family history, to offer humor within the realm of emotional distress, and further wanted to assure me that I, also, should be strong and confident enough to accept the category of humor.

I surveyed the group. The orange smear of pizza was a more natural color than Holly's shirt. Dave and Morgan refused to look my direction.

"Cody, what were you guys talking about?" I asked. I figured Annie would bail him out.

"Nothing," he blurted.

"We were discussing homosexuals," Tony said. He slanted his head. "There, you happy?"

Actually, no. Homosexuals? "What kind of a topic is that?"

Bonner pointed at Annie. "Not her, man," he said. "She was talking about math."

"Yeah, thanks for that," Annie deadpanned.

Cody looked my direction briefly, then his eyes instantly flitted away. Bonner looked up at me, and sort of nodded toward the kitchen. "Grab some pizza, man, and join us," he said. He indicated Annie. "She was giving us a lecture on homos."

"Oh God," sighed Aspen.

"I wasn't giving anyone a lecture," Annie said with authority. "I was just trying to explain how illogical your assumptions are."

"No," Tony said, "you weren't lecturing. You would never lecture."

I sat down between Bonner and Aspen, with two slices of sausage pizza resting on top of a plastic plate. I reached across Aspen, who smelled far better than Bonner, and patted Tony's knee. *Leave your sister alone*, the pat meant, and he knew it.

"Tell him your theory about homos," Bonner told Annie, and nodded my direction.

"They're not homos," Annie said. "They're homosexuals. They're just like everyone else, like all of us, except-"

"Do we have to talk about this?" Cody pleaded. There was a desperation in his voice, and for a moment, I had to admit, a strange thought crossed my mind.

"Don't even think it, Lance," Annie told me.

"Think what?" Cody said.

I wondered, *since when did Whitehall have homosexuals?*

"Lance, don't even think it," Annie said again, sternly this time. "And please, please, don't say it."

"Say what?" pleaded Cody.

Annie's eyes warned me to be quiet. Everyone was quiet. Annie had the floor.

"In sex ed today," she started, "some of the sophomores learned about gender confusion, transsexuals and homosexuals."

"Ooh please," whined Aspen.

"Relax, Aspen, this is a grownup conversation but it'll be over in a couple minutes," Annie said. If she had been within reach, I would have patted her knee. *Leave your brother's girlfriend alone.* "Cody is in Mr. Knight's class, so today Cody learned that roughly" – she glared at Cody, to keep him quiet – "roughly, ten percent of the people in America are homosexual."

"That sounds high to me," pondered Bonner, as if he'd previously given the matter a considerable amount of serious thought.

"It might be," Annie acknowledged. "Studies vary, and there's no doubt there is abundant research out there whose results are neither accurate nor valid. Frequently the studies themselves reflect biased and concealed political agendas."

Bonner nodded thoughtfully, as if after careful consideration of the statement, he was in complete agreement.

"But let's use ten percent as the example cited by Mr. Knight," Annie continued. "Let's assume the ten percent figure is accurate. That doesn't mean-"

"I didn't mean it was *for sure*," Cody pleaded. "I was just *figuring,* was all."

Annie held up a hand; *calm down*. Her eyes swept the room with an unmistakable message: keep your mouths shut and let me finish. Such was

Annie's power. Cody was a rough stock rider, frequently brutal to his classmates and possibly his teammates, a kid whose alcoholic and promiscuous mother was killed in a violent accident, a kid who had a fistfight with his grandfather, a kid who had visited the dark side of malevolence, but he was like the rest of us, cowering in response to Annie's direction and dominance. Bonner had seen the inside of a jail cell, had scoured around through a tough existence, yet he without hesitation deferred to the wishes of a slight junior high girl.

"Okay, ten percent of the people in America are homosexuals," Annie said. "For the sake of argument, let's agree on that." No one spoke; everyone, for the sake of argument, apparently had agreed on that. "That doesn't mean that one in every ten people is a homosexual. It doesn't mean that four of the forty kids in Mr. Knight's class are homosexuals. That's not how it works."

"See," Bonner told me, by way of enlightened instruction, "she's really talking about math. Percentages and stuff."

I detected the foul smell of cigarettes on him. There was more, and possibly worse, filtering out from him and his clothes, but I could not quite place the odors. I decided it was best to not try too hard.

"So you think four kids in your class are homosexuals?" I asked Cody.

"Not really," he said mournfully. "I was just *checking,*" he added.

"Checking what?" I asked.

"The yearbook," Annie explained. "After practice, while we were waiting for the pizzas, Cody sat on the floor paging through the Whitehall yearbook, examining his sophomore class, trying to figure which four of them were the homosexuals."

"It doesn't work that way," I told him.

"I *know*," he cried, his eyes wide with alarm. "I was just wondering *if* there was four, *which* four would it be."

"Who'd you come up with?" Bonner asked earnestly.

"He didn't *come up* with anybody," Annie blurted. "There is no number to come up with, okay. That's the point. That's my whole point. That's not a large enough sample size and there's no finite number you can determine based on a simple estimated percentage and a defined population number."

Bonner nodded his complete concurrence.

Annie looked at Cody. "So stop trying to figure it out," she ordered. "Nothing good will come from that thought process."

He nodded sheepishly.

"I mean it," Annie said, and she did. "You can't figure it out, because there's nothing *to* figure out. You won't figure it out, so just drop it."

Cody just kept nodding sheepishly. Tony and I knew that nod; we had employed it not infrequently ourselves.

Bonner himself nodded, as if in professorial contemplation. "I'm thinking," he said slowly, slyly, "that could you first figure out the ninety percent who aren't homosexuals, and once you know that, the ten percent who are left would have to be homosexuals, wouldn't they?"

Annie pointed to the front door. "Go home, Bonner. This instant."

To my utter surprise, he immediately and wordlessly obeyed. He hoisted himself to his feet, waved a faint friendly sign of departure, and meekly left through the self same door Annie had pointed at. When the door shut beyond him, Annie sighed deeply, looked my direction, and dared me to say something.

Instead I stood up myself, vanquished. I didn't need her to point out the door to my room.

A weariness settled in my mind and limbs. It happened that way; quickly, without me realizing it until I seemed suddenly exhausted. But there was one question I had to ask before I called it a night. "How'd you get the black eye?" I asked Cody.

He hesitated.

"A fight?" I asked.

He nodded.

"With who?" I asked. "At school?"

"Go to bed, Lance," Annie told me. "We'll talk about it later."

Annie had been a child, four years old maybe, maybe even younger, when I took her and Tony for a walk south of Whitehall along the Jefferson River, near the Kountz Bridge. Amy said she needed a break from the kids, one of the abundant early warning signs I'd failed to appreciate until it had been far too late.

Tony immediately took off his shoes and walked into the river. I told him he could stand on the north bank of the river, in Jefferson County, and throw a rock into the next county, in Madison County, whose border was on the south bank of the river. So that's what he did; he stood in knee-deep water and attempted to throw rocks across the river into the next county.

Annie, a slim little child with slightly curled hair in the damp summer air, quietly sat in my lap, in the shade along the river. We were already aware of her intelligence, and she sat there, each tiny hand resting on my thighs, and I thought I could actually see her intellectually absorbing the sounds and sights around her. Her brother was standing in the river, throwing rocks, and had already lost his balance and tumbled in once. It was a warm early summer afternoon, and the water was cold. He was oblivious to the cold, and to everything else except his search for rocks to throw.

"That's a meadowlark," Annie said, pointing to a yellow-breasted bird perched on a fencepost ten yards behind us, away from the water.

"I think it's the state bird," I said.

"Good for you, Daddy," she squealed. "It *is* the state bird." She rejoiced in my accuracy.

"Listen to it sing," I said.

"They sing in spring as part of the reproductive process," she told me. "There's another one singing over there." She lowered her voice to a soft whisper, to protect Tony from learning about a possibly uncomfortable subject. "They sing to find mates, to make babies."

We were four in the Escort – Annie, Trisha, Slack and me – headed up the Cardwell Hill east toward Manhattan to watch the Rangers and Tigers play a game that would mathematically eliminate the loser from any possible playoff contention. Ahead of us, the sky was purple dark, and behind us, it was orange bright.

We had started the trip with a warm fresh loaf of Rhonda Horst's pumpkin bread, and even before we descended the grade down toward Three Forks the bread had vanished, with a measurable amount of it scattered as crumbs in Slack's facial stubble. The car's interior seemed bathed in pumpkin.

Rhonda had shown up at the Ledger a few minutes before departure to Manhattan, and I was startled to see her. She wore a scarf tied tight under her chin and a warm winter coat that covered her from neck to toes, and initially I thought she expected a ride to the game with us; a problem, since the Escort was stuffed to hold four. There just wasn't room for five.

But no, she had no intention of traveling to Manhattan. She merely wanted to treat us to some of her baking, although even as she explained she made the bread with Tony in mind I knew he'd never see any of it. When she'd shown up on our doorstep he had already been long gone on the team bus for Manhattan, and with four of us in the Escort for forty-five miles I knew the bread had no chance of survival to kick-off.

It barely made it past the crest of the Cardwell Hill. Trisha had two thick slices – cut by Annie with Slack's pocketknife, and I resisted the temptation to wonder what else Slack's knife may have sliced through in recent weeks – and sort of groaned with pleasure as she ate them.

At breakfast earlier that morning – or what would have been breakfast if we'd have had milk – Annie told me the disheartening story of Cody's black eye. A high school senior had recently transferred from Butte to Whitehall after having been kicked out of Butte High. Annie said the kid, named Johnny Pep, was in foster care and had been in and out of juvenile detention facilities throughout the state. He had been convicted of crimes varying from drug possession to vandalism to burglary to assault, and was living with an aunt on Railroad Street who herself had moved to Whitehall recently from Butte. Annie said she knew all this because she read Johnny Pep's transcript when he enrolled at Whitehall. Court documents and a probation officer's report had been attached to the transcript.

It was inevitable the paths of Cody Phillips and Johnny Pep would cross in a small high school, and the inevitable happened shortly after lunch during Johnny Pep's second day in Whitehall. Like two hostile homeless tomcats that brawl on first scent at midnight in an alley, Cody and Johnny Pep barely exchanged a word before Johnny threw a lethal right hand at Cody's face. Cody was a country hellion and no stranger to belligerence and fists, but Johnny Pep had experienced an urban world of violence and brutality Cody could barely imagine, and Johnny Pep decked Cody before Cody saw the punch coming. Both Johnny and Cody were expelled from school for the rest of the day, which meant nothing to Johnny Pep but meant Cody was ineligible for the football game, a decision that had been made Friday morning. Cody attempted to argue he had not been in a fight, he had simply been punched. Someone without Cody's reputation may have gotten away with it. It seemed unfair, and the suspension had to have been a difficult decision for Ed to make, for many reasons.

As we crossed the bridge on I-90 over the Madison River I snuck a peak at Trish in the rearview mirror. Her gaze was directed, absently, out the side window, her mouth not quite open, not quite closed. It was impossible to tell what she was thinking, or if she was thinking. The four of us rode in silence, which was completely inappropriate as a prelude to a high school football game. I reached over into the glove box and pulled out the cassette tape of Springsteen's *The River*. The song *The Ties That Bind* blared through the stereo, and to make sure no one missed the point, I turned it up even louder. You cannot escape the ties that bind.

"Tonight the Rangers make it three wins in four games!" I shouted above the music.

"Yeah!" cheered Trisha.

"Last year Manhattan creamed us," Slack said.

"That was last year," Annie said. "Last year we didn't have Dave Dickson, last year we weren't good enough to win back-to-back games and last year we didn't have Jersey."

"And last year we didn't have the E Street Band!" I said, and turned the stereo another notch higher.

Trisha offered a baffled smile and clapped her hands over her ears.

Springsteen sang about wondering about who can quiet your pain.

Sometimes, you do wonder that.

It was a perfect night for football. Moths that had survived the previous week's mini blizzard were fluttering in thick scattered formations around the lights.

There's something about arrival at a high school football game, first hearing the band, the initial spotting of the players warming up under the lights, sensing the tension and anticipation, searching for your child – there he is, number twenty-three, coasting under a pass during pre-game drills – and the initial awareness that you don't get excited about much, but you are excited about this.

Slack drifted off the rope line behind the bench to stand with some of the Whitehall fans, and shook hands with Kyle Bolling and Brent Walker. Trisha, with Annie pushing the wheelchair, settled on the hard surface of the track, just off the corner of the bleachers.

In what seemed like a weekly rite for the Rangers, it was their opponents' Homecoming, and a large crowd dressed in Manhattan orange and black filled the bleachers. Tiger paw prints were everywhere; on hand-held signs, on the cheeks of cheerleaders, on the fifty-yard line, on the Manhattan helmets, on large banners taped to the fence and on floats parked outside the end zone over by the concession stand.

During the national anthem the Rangers stood as firm and stoic as stone; no one even blinked. I momentarily scouted the sparsely populated WHS side of the field and spotted Ed and Alice Franklin, bundled up in winter coats and blankets, as if a winter storm front was poised to hit at kickoff. Cody sat next to Alice; he wore a white cowboy hat and jeans jacket. As he stood for the national anthem, his bright white cowboy hat over his chest, he was motionless as a sculpture. I wondered how hard it must have been for him to watch his teammates from the bleachers. Hank and Kathleen Harrison sat in the absolute middle of a small visitor bleacher section, although there seemed to be some empty space surrounding them. JeffScott's mom sat next to Dave Dickson's mom, and behind them sat Morgan's mom, dad and grandparents. A group of a half dozen girls – including the O'Toole brood – sat and talked with animation in the front row of the bleachers. Maybe thirty Whitehall people total were scattered around the bleachers and behind the rope. They were going to watch two teams, each with two wins and two losses. One team would keep weak playoff hopes alive for a final conference game next week; one would be playing for pride the following week.

The Rangers had a chance with a victory tonight to win two in a row, three of four and improve to three wins and two losses in conference games. A win over Big Timber at home the following week would give the Rangers an outside shot at the playoffs. A win next week was eminently possible for Whitehall, since Big Timber hadn't won a game all year. A win in Manhattan, however, was considerably more difficult.

Whitehall kicked off to Manhattan to start the game, and the Tiger returner took the ball on about the ten yard line, cut to his left – toward the Whitehall bleachers – and ran to midfield before he was tackled. Three plays later the Tiger halfback ran untouched down the sideline for a sudden and instant Manhattan lead.

Coach Pete let loose with a loud and angry guttural growl and threw his baseball cap on the ground and stomped on it once, twice, between the touchdown and extra point. Jersey looked across the field, appeared to ponder the animated festivities from the Manhattan fans, then moved slowly toward the center of the sideline, where he quietly gathered the Ranger players. Coach Pete whacked Tony gently on the side of the helmet and slapped Logan's shoulder pads as he stood and listened to Jersey. Whatever Jersey was saying, he wasn't saying it loudly. The noise from the Manhattan bleachers carried boisterously across the field, but I heard clearly the plastic crunch of Logan's shoulder pads when Coach Pete smacked them. Jersey crouched inside the loose circle of players and despite being less than ten feet away I couldn't hear him. The players silently broke the huddle, Jersey stood and Coach Pete yelled at the kickoff receiving team to get their asses in gear.

"Hit somebody, Morgan!" Coach Pete yelled. "JeffScott! Knock someone down!"

The boisterous Manhattan crowd rose to a crescendo as the kicker booted the ball downfield to about the Ranger twenty yard line. Tony ran up under the ball, caught it cleanly in his midsection, and took off to his right. All eleven black-jersied Manhattan players, eager to make it two big plays in a row for Manhattan, turned as one like a heat-seeking missile to bury the ball carrier. But Tony flipped the ball across his body just as Nate Bolton crossed behind him. Nate caught the ball in stride and when I looked where he was looking – and where he was going – it looked like an empty green golf fairway with white lines across it. No one was even close. He sprinted down the sideline, a golden blur contrasted by the black Manhattan players on the bench, and the Manhattan side of the field seemed to realize what was happening all at the same time, groaned collectively, and it was so quiet when Nate scored I heard him from seventy yards away as he dropped the ball in the end zone and let go with a single solitary shout of joy.

I also heard, behind me, above the muffled cheer of the Whitehall fans, Trish's solitary voice of glee. "That's what I'm talking about!" she declared. The simple game of football, and the simple act of Whitehall scoring a touchdown, were indispensable joyous parts of her life.

So just like that – just like Jersey had apparently diagramed it sixty seconds beforehand – the Rangers were back in the game.

Logan made sure there would not be back-to-back kickoff returns for touchdowns. The Manhattan player caught the kickoff in stride, drifted to his right, and just as he thought he saw an opening and squared his shoulders to burst up field little Logan launched himself at the ball carrier. The ball and the runner separated, and both went tumbling out of bounds. The ball was put back in play, but the ball carrier wasn't. I spotted him later after the Homecoming festivities at halftime wearing his black jersey, jeans, and a huge wrap on his left shoulder.

Cale Bolling scored on an eight-yard run to put the Rangers up 14-7 midway through the second quarter, but the Tigers scored on a screen pass just before the half to regain momentum and tie the game at 14-14.

During halftime, the band played *Eye of the Tiger* three times: when the team left the field, during the Homecoming festivities, and when the team returned to the field for the second half.

"Is it a state law that every school we play has to celebrate its Homecoming?" Ed asked at halftime. He was standing next to Slack, along the restraining rope behind the team bench.

"Evidently," I said.

"Kids are playing pretty tough," Ed commented.

"You're Special Ed," Slack said, and grinned.

"He's Jerry Lee Lewis," I said, which confused Slack.

"I'm an authority figure the two of you are supposed to treat with respect," Ed said.

Slack merely continued to grin.

"How's Cody doing?" I asked.

Ed frowned. "This is pretty tough on him. He hasn't felt like he belonged to much in his life, but I get the sense he believes he belongs on this football team."

"Must have been a tough decision to suspend him," I offered.

He looked skyward a moment, "Not really. Just followed the rules." He sniffed. "To paraphrase Charles Dickens, sometimes the rules can be an ass."

Slack guffawed.

"He and Annie have sort of been hanging out together," I said, more or less to see what he'd say.

He nodded. "He's never adored anything in his life, but he adores Annie. Alice also adores Annie, and you know I always have."

"I gotta admit, having Cody over to the house kind of worries me."

He nodded again. "I don't blame you, but Cody knows what's at stake."

"How about those Rangers?" boomed a voice from behind me." It was Cal Walker.

"When Manhattan marched right into the end zone I thought it was going to be one of those nights," Ed said.

"Not for this bunch," said Cal. He held a cup of coffee in each hand, and was merely passing through. "These kids got a little fire in their bellies."

Slack snickered. I think he mentally pictured fire in a belly.

Cal wore a cowboy hat and a turquoise western jacket. I'm surprised I didn't spot him earlier. It wasn't like he was hard to find.

"What's this I hear about you turning into Elvis?" Cal asked Ed.

"Don't believe everything you hear," Ed told him.

"I just never pictured you as a rock and roll star," Cal said.

"The music moved him," I told Cal.

"That's what I heard," Cal said. "Moved him like Elvis."

"Let's say the music put a fire in his belly," I said, mostly to just watch Slack laugh again, which he did.

Cal tipped his head toward the field. "Any predictions?" he asked me.

"Anybody's game," I said. "I like our chances."

"That Dickson kid's a pistol," Cal said.

"We're gonna win," Slack said. "I can tell."

"How can you tell?" Ed asked.

"I can just tell," Slack said defiantly.

After Whitehall took the second half kickoff, ran two plays and got its initial first down of the second half, I could tell, too. There was something about the way the Manhattan fans quieted down, the way the shouting of the Manhattan coach grew more urgent and imploring, the way the Rangers comported themselves, the way the Manhattan players looked to the sidelines for help and the Whitehall players looked to the sidelines for affirmation.

Dave scored untouched, and almost unseen, on a sweep – following the blocks of Morgan and Logan – to make it 21-14, and just before the end of the third quarter Dave threw a sideline pass to wide receiver Colt Harrison that Colt turned into a touchdown for a 28-14 lead. Dave sprinted into the end zone and hugged Colt, who hugged him back and – probably six inches taller than Dave – patted Dave on the top of his helmet almost like you'd pet a dog. After the extra point they trotted to the sidelines toward Jersey, who shook Dave's hand and reached out and held Colt. Jersey's face was an inch away from the side of Colt's helmet when he said something which made Colt nod, then Jersey patted Colt on the rump as they separated.

When the teams changed ends of the field at the start of the fourth quarter the Manhattan cheering section was both muted and depleted. It was as if the Tiger fans had received word of a death in the family.

Manhattan's quarterback, under pressure from JeffScott, rushed a pass that was probably intended for the tight end. The ball sailed high, into Tony's upstretched hands. He whirled to avoid a tackle, burst toward the sidelines and outran a trio of Tigers into the end zone. Dave cruised down the field behind him and the two of them collided in celebration at the back of the end zone.

The final score was 42-14, with little Nick Lowery – a reserve freshman running back who had possibly never scored a touchdown before in his life – taking an inside handoff and rumbling into the end zone from twenty-six yards out. When Nick got to the sidelines, Dave hooted and cheered and tackled him.

The Rangers had their third, and most convincing, conference win of the season.

On the way home to Whitehall the Escort was filled with laughter and everyone talking at once. Slack told us all he knew the Rangers were going to win. Annie wanted to know if I got a picture of Coach Pete stomping on his hat. Trish, flushed red with emotion, said Jersey was the best coach in the world. I told them Dave Dickson was going to hurt someone celebrating in the end zone. Slack laughingly said the Rangers had fire in their bellies. Annie said no one was going to schedule Whitehall for an easy Homecoming win next year. Trish said the Rangers were the best team ever. Slack said the Rangers had fire in their bellies, just, I think, to hear the words again. And Annie officially gave up on her bet, and warned me I was going to have to buy Tony a car.

We arrived in Whitehall before we knew it. Buoyed by a silly high school win from a team that still had an overall losing record, in a ridiculously – in what truly mattered in life – unimportant child's game of football, we all but floated home in what amounted to, really, pure ecstasy, overjoyed with each other's company and overwhelmed by what we witnessed and experienced.

You could say it was a sad commentary on our existence, but we wouldn't have believed you.

Chapter 28

Jersey met me late Sunday afternoon at the Ledger, on a bright sunny autumn day with the temperature above sixty and a warm sun dipping low in the western sky. It was mid October and during the past three days we'd had three seasons, with Sunday turning into a picture-perfect summer day. Jersey showed up wearing his trademark sunglasses and a dark blue short-sleeve tee-shirt that bore a large black and white photo of Bruce Springsteen with his guitar and Clarence Clemens with his saxophone not quite identical to the cover of *Born to Run*.

That was entirely appropriate, because I was playing the cassette of *Born to Run* when Jersey arrived.

"We should be fishing or something like that on a day like this," Jersey said when he entered.

"You don't really strike me as a fisherman," I said. We both gravitated toward the round table in the corner where we did the weekly interview. The discussion was becoming a Sunday traditional, and after this interview we only had one more game and one more interview before the season ended.

"There's your mouse?" Jersey said, stopped where what would have been almost directly across from the crack in the wall.

"Which one?" I asked.

"How many do you have?"

I sat down in my usual place at the table. "Two of them, actually, running around here. I've sort of got used to having them. Sometimes I even find myself talking to them late at night when I'm down here."

"Do they talk back?" he asked. He pulled out a chair at the table.

I looked and saw the first mouse – darker than the other – cautiously creeping away from the baseboard. "I've tried several different methods to kill them, but the truth is I think they're smarter than me. So we've reach kind of an unspoken truce."

"As opposed to a *spoken* truce?"

"As opposed to me keeping on trying to kill them. We more or less have learned to tolerate each other."

Jersey sort of smiled. He looked back toward the crack in the wall, and his smile widened slightly. "Congratulations to all of you involved," Jersey said. "Tolerance is an admirable character trait."

"Yeah, well, that, and the fact they seem to be pretty much indestructible," I admitted. "I don't think I could kill them with a bazooka."

"I wouldn't advise you to try," Jersey said, and folded his hands on the table. That meant it was time to begin the interview.

"So," I began. I stopped myself. "Do you fish? I just don't see you as a typical fisherman."

"I'm probably not your typical anything," Jersey said. He stopped abruptly, as if closing the topic. I was supposed to begin the official Ledger interview with the football coach.

"You're three and two in conference play," I said, "and have a chance to end the season with three straight wins."

Jersey hesitated. "We have a chance to win three straight, and we have a chance to make the playoffs. We don't plan on ending our season on Friday."

I had to think that through. Ennis was unbeaten and Boulder lost to Ennis earlier in the year. Boulder lost to Townsend the same night Whitehall beat Manhattan. That meant Whitehall, Boulder and Townsend each had two losses, but Boulder thumped Whitehall earlier in the year and held the tiebreaker over the Rangers. Boulder played Manhattan the same time Whitehall played Big Timber, and a Boulder win over Manhattan put them in the playoffs. Boulder had beaten Whitehall badly, Whitehall had beaten Manhattan badly, and it was fairly obvious that Boulder – in Boulder – with a playoff spot on the line, was logically expected to crush Manhattan, a team that logically had nothing to play for.

"How do you figure that?" I asked, just to make sure I had it calculated right.

"We beat Big Timber, Manhattan beats Boulder," Jersey said.

"Manhattan beats Boulder?" I asked. The doubt in my voice couldn't be missed. "The game is in Boulder. Boulder is six and two on the year, with a close loss in Ennis, right, and a fluke upset in Townsend? Boulder beat us and we beat Manhattan pretty easily. I don't want to be a pessimist, but if I had to bet, I'd bet Boulder destroys Manhattan."

Jersey leaned back. "Don't put all your money on that bet." He rubbed his chin, and his black stubble sounded like sandpaper. "Boulder thinks they'll beat Manhattan. But Manhattan's not a bad team. We played our best football of the year on Friday, and we were lucky to come back the way we did in the second half. Boulder is thinking playoffs. Manhattan will dedicate themselves to one final game. Anything can happen."

"I wish the game was in Manhattan," I said.

"Won't matter." He leaned forward. "I think our kids have earned a break, and I think Manhattan's going to give us that break." He leaned even more forward, toward me. "I believe in our kids. They've come a long way, and they've given themselves a chance. I think their courage and hard work are going to be rewarded."

"In Boulder, by Manhattan?" I asked.

"Remember when Shawn Davis came over and talked to the kids about what it takes to be a champion?" Jersey said. "He said it takes three things to be a champion: preparation, determination and execution. That's the difference between average and excellent. Remember when he said that? You were there. We'd lost three straight games and it looked like we might not win a game all year. We didn't have what it took to be champions."

I nodded. I did remember. Shawn's pep talk seemed like years in the past; could that really have taken place a month ago?

"Look at what's happened since," Jersey said. "The kids have prepared to win. They've played with determination. And they've executed with confidence. You saw it all on Friday night."

"It looked to me like Manhattan more or less ran out of gas," I said.

Jersey shook his head. "No. We took the gas out of them. After their opening drive, we outplayed them almost every play. We tackled better. We ran harder. We blocked longer. We hit harder. Manhattan did not lose that game. We won it. We took the game from them. During their Homecoming, in Manhattan, after we were down by a touchdown."

"It was pretty impressive," I admitted.

"That was a playoff team you saw Friday night," Jersey said. "Look at our team now. Dave's provided a spark at quarterback. Colt's turning into a very good wide receiver. JeffScott shatters pass protection. Tony knows where the opposing quarterback is going to throw before the quarterback himself knows. Logan runs over tacklers. Cale is almost always the fastest kid on the field. Cody plays like he's out for revenge every play. These kids are something else, Lance, and their best football is still ahead of them. These kids now know what it takes to win, and they take the field prepared, determined and ready to execute. You watch. We're going to make the playoffs. And after that… watch out."

I didn't have the heart to contradict him. I took notes, and figured I'd write my story for the paper as if Whitehall had a chance – *a chance* – to qualify for the playoffs. The season would be a success with a winning conference record and three straight wins to close the season. I refused to set up a situation in which the season could end with disappointment even with a Ranger win.

When he left, Jersey turned and said he appreciated my viewpoint and understood my argument to not build up false hopes or unmet expectations. He held the door open, and the setting sun behind him turned him into a featureless black silhouette. He was more voice than physical presence.

"You write your article any way you want," the voice told me. "But our season *will not* end Friday."

"I hope you're right," I said. "The Rangers making the playoffs would be…" I searched for the right word. "Historical."

"You remember that word," Jersey said, and walked away.

I closed the door, turned, and there were both mice, just outside the baseboard. It was as if they ventured out to see who was there and what all the talking was about, or to bid farewell to our visitor.

"What are you looking at?" I asked them. I took a step and one mouse stood up on its hind legs, perhaps to get a better look at me. The other one sniffed the air. "You two are supposed to be scared of me."

They stood there, little front paws helplessly held in the air, tiny sharp noses fuzzily sniffing my direction.

"So what do you think?" I asked. "Are the Rangers going to make the playoffs?"

To my utter amazement, standing tentatively on its back legs, one mouse sniffed, blinked, and with calm assurance, I swear it, nodded its head.

It turned out that the governor appearing in Whitehall at the school was historical in its own right.

I showed up at the elementary school office on Thursday twenty minutes before the governor was scheduled to show up and found Doris Shaw, a ranch wife from Cardwell and one of the Whitehall and Cardwell school board members, stylish in an Indian-looking turquoise-colored dress accented with a turquoise necklace, earrings and bracelet. She might have had her hair freshly coiffured as well, and her face was flushed with agitation as she excitedly huddled in the hallway with Martha Cullen. Both women wore purple and gold lilies pinned to their dresses just below the collarbone, and I noticed Martha's finery – a sky blue satiny dress that unfortunately appeared to be a little clingy in the hips and waist – was prominent and, for her, trendy.

"Is he here?" Doris asked me breathlessly.

"Schwinden?" I asked. "Not that I know of."

My answer immediately rendered me worthless. What good was I, the local newspaper owner, without important news of the governor's arrival? Doris returned her attention to Martha, and placed a hand on Martha's arm as she carried on about the stage decorations and the sudden urgency in exploring the costs of new stage curtains.

Lyle O'Toole and Ed Franklin, both wearing suits with purple and gold lilies tucked in their coat lapels, turned the hallway corner at the same time and approached the elementary school main entryway and principal's office. Ed's suit appeared suspiciously new, a charcoal grayish color with contemporary pleated slacks.

"You take one turn on the dance floor and you think you're James Bond?" I asked him.

"Pat Boone called," Ed said. " He said he wants his sweater back."

The governor's first stop would be the elementary school office for a short conversation with school faculty, administrators and board members, and then a short introductory chat with Annie.

As it turned out, I knew the governor's schedule better than anyone in Whitehall, thanks to Mary Lou Ford, my exuberant young contact in the governor's office.

Mary Lou had called Monday, Tuesday, Wednesday and again on Thursday morning, all in anticipation of the governor's sixty-minute visit to the Whitehall school district.

Monday's call – a callback from her first call, which I'd missed when I was out doing morning ad stops – came just before two o'clock and interrupted my stint in the darkroom. I had just finished printing a picture I'd taken on Sunday of the local game warden crouching next to a dead moose calf that had been poached not more than two miles from Whitehall's town limits and only had a few pictures left to do when Laura Joyce knocked softly on the darkroom door – she knew how much I disliked being interrupted when in the darkroom – and in an apologetic voice told me the governor's office was calling. Mary Lou Ford was so cheerful I wanted to choke someone. I had to tell her five times in a ten-minute conversation that the governor coming on Thursday afternoon was fine with me if it was fine with the school and had to tell her five times in ten minutes that yes, I could, in fact, get an article in the Wednesday paper about the governor's school visit. She promised three times to fax me the governor's biography and three times I had to promise her I'd read it right away.

"I saw that mouse of yours this morning," Laura Joyce said after I'd hung up the phone.

"It's not my mouse."

"Whose ever it is, I saw it. It stood up on its hind legs and all but waved good morning to me when I got here."

"Yeah, they're pretty friendly."

"*They*?"

"There's two of them, you know," I told her. "Mice."

"They're multiplying?" she gasped.

"Apparently," I said.

"Are you ever going to get rid of them?"

"I'm thinking of charging them rent," I said. "Or maybe putting them to work. Maybe I could get them to write a column."

Laura Joyce snorted an unjovial laugh and I snuck back into the darkroom.

Tuesday's conversation with Mary Lou Ford was just as irritating as Monday's call, just as repetitive and just as lengthy. She called late morning as I began to lay out the twenty-four-page Ledger, and each minute on the phone with what I imagined to be a hyperactive, thorough and dedicated staffer – which is an exhausting and overwhelming combination for a weary listener – put me another minute later into the evening. Three times I confirmed I'd received the governor's faxed biography and four times I had to pledge there'd be an article in Wednesday's paper about the governor's visit, and at least twice I had to reassure Mary Lou that Annie *couldn't wait* to meet the governor. Four times I had to listen to Mary Lou exclaim how happy the governor was to meet an outstanding Montana student like Annie.

When I hung up the telephone on Tuesday, Laura Joyce looked at me and said, "That girl must wake up talking."

By Wednesday afternoon, Laura Joyce was no longer impressed by taking a call from the governor's office. I had made all my vendor deliveries and Annie was at the Ledger office working on the accounts receivables and billing when Mary Lou Ford called and with great enthusiasm asked me if there was an article about the governor's visit to the school. There was, on page three. It would have been on page one had the purpose of the visit been something other than to honor my daughter and if Mary Lou Ford hadn't turned into such an unrelenting pain in the ass.

Annie overheard my portion of the entire conversation, and from my comments she could clearly decipher Mary Lou Ford's merry remarks and clarifications. I had to reassure Mary Lou – and thus the governor – the entire town was thrilled at his appearance in Whitehall. I also had to again state with fraudulent conviction that Annie was absolutely excited to meet the governor and was honored to have an opportunity to visit with him. Annie's expression – *me? since when?* – almost made me chuckle. Three times, each time emphasizing the same details with the same energized inflections in her speech, Mary Lou Ford told me the governor would be driving to Whitehall with his education aide, a man named Clayton Brewer, and that if I or anyone at the school had any questions, concerns or comments they should bring them immediately to Clayton, who, by the power vested in him by his title, apparently, would magically and intuitively know exactly what to do or say. I had never met Clayton Brewer, but already I didn't like him. Three times I promised I would introduce myself to Clayton and receive any last-minute instructions or schedule modifications from him.

When I hung up the phone I was exhausted. I immediately stood up to go home and take a nap.

"If she calls back tell her I've left the country," I said. "Tell her I died. Tell her I've been kidnapped. Tell her anything you want. Just don't tell her where I am."

"Want me to talk to her?" Annie asked.

I thought about it, then shook my head. "Probably not a good idea. You're the star of the show here, and my guess is you're not supposed to sully yourself with things like planning or organizing the governor's trip."

"Is everything under control?" Annie asked.

"Absolutely," I answered. "We may not be child prodigies but I think between the full complement of the governor's staff and a fleet of school administrators we can handle a one-hour appearance by the governor. We're not completely incompetent."

Annie's look said volumes: *we'll see.*

But on Thursday – the big day – the governor's visit had genuinely generated a thrilling sense of anticipation throughout the school. Upon closer inspection, I noticed all faculty and administrators wore purple and gold lilies, and I was all but certain when Governor Ted Schwinden showed up he, too, would be wearing a Ranger-colored lily through his lapel. I had intended to make a routine check with Martha to see if everything was ready – to essentially make sure nothing about the governor's schedule had changed – but she was surrounded by school board members and teachers and I saw no need to add to her apprehension.

The governor's appearance would take place in the multi-purpose room, and as I made my way there I met a group of little elementary school students – probably the kindergarteners – who marched quietly down the hall with bright, energetic faces and who carried a large hand-made banner that read *Welcome, Governor*. Mary Kristofferson trailed behind them, with twin purple and gold lilies stuck, somehow, in her hair, one flower above each ear.

"Well," she said, "tell me why our local publisher and father of the academic honoree is not wearing a gubernatorial blossom."

"Well," I answered, "tell me why our elementary physical education teacher is wearing gubernatorial blossoms in her hair."

"Because she chooses to," she said mischievously. Mary stopped, and the children and other teachers continued their sojourn down the hall.

She reached up, took the gold flower from behind an ear, and placed its stem through a shirt button in the middle of my chest.

"Big day, apparently, the governor here and all," I said.

"Martha's in quite a tizzy," Mary answered, in a bit of a tizzy herself. It dawned on both of us we were standing a little too close together for a public school hallway; we both backed up a half step.

"I think Annie's the only person not nervous about all this," I said.

Mary smiled. "Why should she be worried? It's the governor who should be worried. Up there on the stage, he's going to be compared to Annie Joslyn."

And with that, she slipped past me down the wall, with a quick whirl and wave before she turned the corner toward the multi-purpose room.

The high school band spilled out in front of me from the music room, and the kids were dressed crisply in their black and white spring concert formalwear. They marched silently, instruments held tightly, held properly, and they wore stoic, serious expressions, as if they'd just been lectured about the importance of this occasion. Their couple of songs would almost certainly represent the only time in their lives the Governor of Montana would ever watch them do anything.

From the opposite direction – but toward the same destination – the WHS choir strode down the hallway, girls in their golden formal long dresses and boys in white dress shirts and skinny, shiny black ties. Dave Dickson, Brock Warren and Tanner Walker looked scrubbed and presentable; Dave's hair had been freshly trimmed, slicked and brushed. He looked twelve years old. I suspected his mother was already somewhere in a corner of the multi-purpose room, nervous and practically invisible, soundless and proud of her boy.

I entered the multi-purpose room immediately behind the choir, and instantly felt the hushed exhilaration in the room. Some kids were excited to see the governor, some were excited to perform for the governor, and some were excited just to get out of math class. The elementary school children – with teachers and aides shushing them along the way – perfectly filled up the bleachers child by child, row by row, class by class, and were simply excited to be this close to the older students.

The high school students who were not performing during the event were more disorganized and less energized. Assemblies were nothing new to them, and their indifference to an elected official was largely real, not feigned. Half the kids not only didn't know *who* the governor was, they probably didn't know *what* a governor was. I spotted Tony, dressed in a crimson short-sleeved dress shirt I didn't know he had, and I noticed – not the best time to do so – that he either still needed a haircut or again needed a haircut. He came down the aisle, saw me and nodded a greeting, then he and Cale, Nate and Logan settled into the bleachers stage-left. Tony knew who the governor was, and could do a fair imitation of Schwinden's slightly shocked facial expression, and could even contort his mouth to somehow mimic the governor's rodent-like incisors.

The stage was elegantly attired with bouquets of gold and purple lilies, purple bunting along the front of the stage and the podium. The deep purple velvet back curtain – slightly battered – was pulled across as a backdrop, and the black curtains on either wing of the stage were extended about five feet out, and blocked sightlines to either edge of the stage. The ceiling lights were lit and bright and trained on the podium and a handful of chairs in the middle of the stage, to the right of the podium. Someone had fairly elaborately – by Whitehall standards – set up and decorated the stage. Somehow, for some reason, I sensed Mary Lou Ford was complicit in the execution of the stage organizational details, and it was exhausting to even think of the number and length of calls it must have taken to arrange it.

I parked myself in the front row, just to the right of the center stage, between and below the podium and an arrangement of chairs. The room was full; the governor would be playing to a packed house. A handful of parents and community members were present. I looked around and saw Trisha; she and the wheelchair in their customary spot, just in front of the first row, on the right side of the stage. I also saw a kid who had to be Johnny Pep, a slender Hispanic youth who entered the room friendless and indifferent. He had short black hair and scraggly facial hair on his chin and upper lip that couldn't honestly be called a beard or mustache. He wore a Los Angeles Dodgers blue and white jersey that had a rip in the shoulder seam. He sauntered around the aisle momentarily, as if casing the place, then sat in an open area in front of the bleachers left of the stage, almost directly across from the front row on the main floor behind Trisha.

Jersey stood off to the side, directly across the room from Trish, and from his vantage point he could see the entire floor seating and the far wing of the stage. He seemed thinner, and his shirt hung loosely on him. I waved, and when he saw me he lifted his head then quickly walked my direction.

I stood up to greet him, and we shook hands.

"Good article in the paper," he said. "Thanks."

I had walked the tightrope between his unrelenting optimism and the potential hurdles the Rangers faced.

"And congratulations," he told me.

“For what?” I asked.

He looked around and gestured. “All this. It’s all for your daughter. And she deserves every bit of it.”

I nodded, because I couldn’t think of anything to say.

“We’re all very proud of her,” Jersey said. “We respect her, admire her, adore her, and we’re thrilled at this recognition for her, her family, this school and this community.”

I nodded again, because I still couldn’t think of anything to say. Jersey patted my arm in passing, went over to give Trish a hug, and backtracked to his spot in the front left corner of the room. As I watched him walk toward the side of the room I knew there was something I should say, but I still couldn’t think of what it was.

The main lights suddenly were turned off, which provoked a collective gasp of expectation from the audience. Only the stage lights were still on, and the rest of the room was darker, but not dark. From stage right, the assigned cast began to emerge and take predetermined seats close to the podium. Nancy Toups, the elderly staffer from the Montana Office of Public Instruction, and Diane Fordham, the pointed representative from the University of Montana, were among the first two to take center stage. It was fitting, I supposed, that the two bureaucrats – one from state government and one from the university system – who’d shone the official education spotlight on Annie should be present when that spotlight would be intensified brightly and directly. Ed Franklin, looking astonishingly sporty in a his new suit and slacks, stood alongside the chair closest to the edge of the stage, and nodded a greeting my direction. Lyle O’Toole led three other school board members who’d attended – Doris Shaw, Molly Ryan and Daniel Purdy – to the second row of the metal folding chairs on the stage. Both principals, Martha Cullen and Leonard McDougal, occupied seats closer to the podium. The dignitaries on stage received a polite round of applause from the kids and smattering of adults who’d shown up for the event.

Ed moved closer to the podium, tapped the microphone with his right index finger, looked out toward the crowd, and then opened the event by greeting everyone and introducing the authorities on stage.

In the stage wings, behind the curtain, Ted Schwinden materialized, whispering in the ear of a young man in a suit who had to be Clayton Brewer. He looked like a Clayton Brewer. Ed looked that direction, Ted nodded, and Ed seemed to lean slightly toward the audience, and boomed, “Let’s give a big Whitehall welcome to Montana’s governor, Ted Schwinden!”

And out walked the governor, a former grain farmer from Wolf Point, smiling and waving, saluting the audience, shaking hands with everyone on stage, all the while the WHS band serenading him with the state song, *Montana*. Elementary students cheered and applauded with genuine youthful and uncertain enthusiasm; the audience whistled and hollered, and the governor acknowledged the loud and boisterous applause with what he intended to suggest was heartfelt appreciation. I took several pictures of the governor; he saw my camera flash, looked my direction a few times, smiled and waved, as if he knew who I was. Which he didn't. But he was smart enough to know *what* I was – the local newspaper publisher – and because he was a politician and since one of the reasons he came to Whitehall was to get his picture in the paper, he made an effort to make it easy for that to happen.

The band finally finished with the state song and Ted motioned for the audience to quiet down, which it did. In fact, it quieted down to absolute silence.

The governor then talked about how delighted he was to be back in Whitehall, although I had no knowledge of him ever being here a first time, talked about his affection for small towns like Wolf Point and Whitehall, and made a joke about the towns in Montana starting with *White*: Whitehall, Whitefish, White Sulphur Springs, Whitewater. He briefly looked down on the podium, where he had a small piece of paper, and said he was going to momentarily turn the microphone over to the school board chairman, Lyle O'Toole.

Lyle received a nice round of applause, led, I suspected, by earnest young men seeking to impress anyone of Lyle's three daughters with visible support of their father. All three daughters were in the choir, all looked related, and all looked beautiful.

Lyle thanked the governor, welcomed him to Whitehall on what Lyle claimed was an *historic occasion*. Just then, I realized I hadn't seen Annie yet, and it was she who caused this historic occasion. And an instant after I realized I hadn't seen her, I saw her, standing in almost the exact same spot off stage the governor had stood moments earlier. Clayton Brewer, a doughy-looking lad whose favorite sport was probably chess, was giving Annie directions she was absolutely ignoring. If I had been standing next to him, I would have told him not to bother. You don't give Annie Joslyn, bless her heart, directions.

Lyle introduced the WHS band, and to my amazement and amusement, the band cranked up a not unworthy instrumental version of Springsteen's *No Surrender*, a song with the memorable lyric about learning more from a three-minute record than from anything in school, which was very likely untrue in the case of Annie or Mary Lou Ford. Carrie Lindstrom poured her soul into the saxophone.

How odd is this, I thought, that simply because Whitehall High School has a football coach from New Jersey – and of course the poignant quality of the music – Montana's hick Governor was in the cowboy town of Whitehall listening to a high school band version of a Bruce Springsteen song. My guess was Ted was more of a Merle Haggard or Willie Nelson fan. Ted sat on stage, a frozen smile on his face, while Ed – Bond, James Bond – bopped his head to the music. In the audience, Tony was bopping his head in an almost flattering imitation of Ed. The band stopped, and the governor led the audience in applause. Then the WHS choir performed, and again to my continued amazement and amusement, the selection was again Springsteen, this time

She's the One, a song far more appropriate in title for the event than for actual lyrical content.

After the applause, Lyle stood up, lowered his voice, and said he wanted to tell us a little about Annie Joslyn. The mention of her name drew a few cheers and a ripple of applause, and Trisha beamed like a proud mother.

Before he was done, Lyle actually told us quite a bit about Annie Joslyn, about her academic achievements, her lengthy list of scholastic accomplishments, her helpful nature around the school, her willingness to mentor and tutor other students, and not once but twice called her the *pride of Whitehall*. Lyle then urged the crowd to cheer on Annie, which is what happened when Annie cautiously stepped out onto the stage and gamely, perhaps gravely, waved to the audience.

The governor jumped up to his feet as he applauded. Then everyone else on stage jumped up while they applauded, then everyone else in the room jumped up and applauded and cheered.

Annie shyly nodded, averting her eyes away from the main body of people in the audience, although she spotted me and wanly smiled. Annie wore a tan blouse and gray slacks, and her blouse was decorated with purple and gold lilies, one each. Maybe her hair was just the way she wanted it; it looked to me like her hair was too long on one side of her face. She looked like she'd rather be someplace else, and if she could have spoken her mind at that moment, she would have instructed everyone to please sit down and stop that cheering and applauding. It dawned on me as well that this was perhaps a day when I should have helped select or at least been aware of what my daughter was going to wear to school. Annie motioned for the crowd to cease applauding. The governor would have none of that. He kept right on smiling, kept right on applauding, kept right on his feet.

Finally, the kids cheered and clapped themselves into weariness, and Annie gently sat down in a chair alongside the governor, who patted her knee and kept right on smiling. You had to hand it to him, Ted Schwinden was one happy governor.

Lyle introduced Ed, who on his way to the podium hugged Annie, and then talked about Annie's generosity and kindness, and how she made the Whitehall school system a better place to learn, teach and work. Next came Martha Cullen, who was so nervous addressing the Governor of Montana she was actually sweating – I was close enough to see the little bubbles of perspiration on her forehead – and she raced through her introduction of Nancy Toups of the Montana Office of Public Instruction so fast that not once did Martha mention Annie's name and skittered past Annie without an embrace. There was no hug from Nancy, but she more than mentioned Annie's name; she droned on with a glowing and – even for me – boringly detailed explanation of Annie's impressive ranking on certain national percentiles of this and certain national percentiles of that. No one knew what she was talking about and no one cared. Nancy turned it over to Diane Fordham from the University of Montana, who stood there like she was doing you a favor by letting you hear her speak. She pretty much gave a paid endorsement for Mensa International, and accidentally, I was sure, slipped in her credentials as a member of Mensa International. She touted the prestige, exclusiveness and international reputation of Mensa, and then touted Annie's 'remarkable accomplishment at such a remarkable young age.' She reintroduced Lyle, who reintroduced the governor, and I couldn't help wondering how many calls to the school it took Mary Lou Ford to conceive then confirm the complicated speaker schedule. Then I wondered how she had time to call me, given what I was certain was a large magnitude of calls to the school to ensure the speaking order and verify the speaking order and reconfirm the speaking order. I looked over and saw Clayton Brewer by himself in the wings off stage, and I wondered what exactly it was he did. He seemed pretty useless, but for all I knew he was the brains of the Schwinden Administration. It was obvious from his appearance that Clayton Brewer was not the brawn of the Schwinden Administration. Whitehall was filled with hardy ranch kids and rough miner kids, and whatever the opposite of a ranch kid and miner kid was, Clayton Brewer was that.

The governor took the podium to another rapturous round of applause. Ted had a streak of appropriate gray in his black hair, and had a loaf-shaped belly paunch above his belt. He wore a charcoal suit and a tie the exact color of the gray in his hair. His smile showcased his incisors, and his face held a faint rodent quality; it wasn't necessarily unpleasant, just slightly noticeable. Watching him, my mind momentarily drifted to the Ledger tandem of mice.

He raised his hands to quiet the crowd, and magically the kids simmered down. Ted turned and offered Annie a friendly, avuncular gaze, and then refocused his attention on the audience.

And Ted was magnificent. He did not get elected governor by accident. He praised the community of Whitehall for its nurturing and caring of children in general and Annie in particular. He expressed fondness – again – for small towns in general for their closeness, their neighborliness, their generosity and sense of community. Ted lavished acclaim on the Whitehall School District – teachers, administration and even classified staff – for their dedication and professionalism, and singled out teachers like Ken Kinzer and principals like Martha Cullen for their fierce devotion to the students and the community. Ted congratulated and applauded the Whitehall School Board, a loyal and committed group of volunteer trustees who made it possible for children like Annie Joslyn to excel and reach their full potential. Ted complimented Annie's family for its gallantry and affection that fostered an environment of learning that allowed and even stimulated her intellect and quest for knowledge.

"Finally," Ted intoned, muted for dramatic effect, "we come to this precious," he offered a large warm smile, "and precocious, eighth grader named Annie Joslyn."

The crowd applauded softly, and behind me in the crowd a couple kids – Tony, possibly – whooped their enthusiasm.

"My guess is everyone in this room has been proud of Annie's accomplishments for a long, long time," Ted said. "And for good reason. She is a genuine intellectual diamond, if you will, a young woman with a mind so advanced, so impressive, so inspiring, she is virtually in a class by herself. Yet look at her, as genuine and earnest and honest as any of us."

Annie was as uncomfortable as I've ever seen her. She usually looked you straight in the eye and dared you to return her glare. She had a fire burning inside her that pursued and demanded intellectual stimulation, fulfillment and satisfaction. But as the governor spoke – and spoke – the more uneasy she grew. Her eyes were directed to her left – my right – and she was apprehensive, even agitated about being singled out for such lavish and extended praise.

"So, Annie, I want to give you a token of our appreciation, and by *our* I mean everyone in this room, everyone in my administration, everyone in this state," Ted said. And he beckoned off stage, toward Clayton Brewer, who took a couple steps backward and disappeared behind the curtain. Seconds later he stepped back into my sightline, and then emerged from the wings onto the stage itself, carrying a large framed painting or certificate, its back to the audience.

The audience oooed and ahhhed and rustled in their seats to see what gift the governor was going to present Annie.

"Your dreams, your drive and your intellect can take you anywhere, Annie," Ted said soberly, shielding the frame from view. Annie wasn't even looking at it. "You have been endowed with a special gift, Annie, a gift that can, literally, change the world. You are a remarkable and extraordinary young woman, and your journey through life in many ways is just beginning. To help guide you, to provide you inspiration, to serve as a type of role model, I wanted you to have this special portrait" – and the governor turned the frame to show the audience – "of Montana's most influential woman, Jeanette Rankin."

The people who knew who Jeanette Rankin was – maybe a couple dozen people in the room – led the audience in applause. Rankin was the first woman elected to the U.S. Congress, and she was elected from Montana. She was an early and mid-twentieth century Montana legend, a Montana hero, a Montana icon, and she looked back at us intently in black and white from behind the glass protecting the photograph, her eyes wise and worldly and sad all at once, as if she'd seen things we should avoid.

"Please accept this gift from my administration and myself, from the State of Montana, the Montana Historical Society, the University of Montana, the Montana Office of Public Instruction and from the people of this great state," Ted said. "May she inspire you. May she pilot you. May she motivate you. May she provide you a source of emotional comfort and intellectual nourishment."

Then he grinned an *I know something you don't know* grin, cast another furtive glance off stage, and set down the photo against the side of the podium.

"And," the governor said, drawing the words out so it took five full seconds for him to say it, "there's this."

Again Clayton Brewer emerged from the wing and again he carried some framed object. He delicately and ceremoniously handed it to the governor, as if the document – I could see it was a document, not a photo – was some kind of precious international treaty. The governor held up the frame above his head for all to see. The audience roared approval without a clue what was inside the frame.

Ted offered us all a broad political smile. "I am proud to announce to you all that I have officially proclaimed this day to be Annie Joslyn Day in Montana," the governor practically shouted into the microphone.

The crowd cheered and hollered, and Ted basked in the applause.

"I formally proclaim today Annie Joslyn Day in Montana," the governor said again, in case, I supposed, we missed it the first time. "This is a state proclamation, signed by me in the capitol this morning, and I am honored to read to you right now."

There were lots of "whereases" and lots of repetitive compliments about Annie's intelligence and accomplishments, and all the while Ted read and the audience applauded and cheered, Annie sat uncomfortably, with a sincere attempt at grace and tolerance, but she couldn't fool me. I knew she was desperate to be off the stage and out of the spotlight. She maintained a stern expression off to my right, and I wondered if it was just a deliberate way to avoid eye contact with the audience.

Ted held out both the Rankin photo and certificate toward Annie, and obviously Annie was supposed to stand, approach the governor, accept and acknowledge the two gifts.

For just a moment – an awkward moment – it appeared as if Annie would do no such thing. Which would be just like her. *Get up, Annie,* my mind urged, pleaded, *get up and take the photo and proclamation from the governor. Please, Annie, now."*

Annie sighed with grim determination, stood, and stepped with reluctance toward the governor. It was as if someone invisible was pushing her his direction. I stood and snapped three or four photos of the governor handing her the photo and frame, as the crowd applauded and cheered wildly. Ted smiled, clapped, and after a minute or so stood off to the side of the podium, as if encouraging Annie to speak to the audience.

Okay, I thought. *Annie, please Annie, show some grace and appreciation.*

Annie looked again to my right, considered the invitation to speak, then handed the photo and framed proclamation back to the governor. She was barely taller than the podium and when she stood on her tiptoes and gripped the outside edge of the podium with both hands it produced a little laughter from the audience.

“Thank you all so much,” Annie said in a voice of full confidence and some impatience. She was slender and young, a child really, but she spoke with authority. “You have no idea how much this means to me, to Tony, to Lance,” she paused, “and to my mom.” She looked again to my right and her eyes suddenly locked on someone or something. Her expression turned into a scowl. “And you listen to me, Johnny Pep. If I ever – *EVER* – see you do that again, I’ll kick your sorry ass back to Butte myself.” She continued to glare, presumably toward Johnny Pep. “Trust me, you little shit,” she warned him, “I can do it.”

The governor was stunned and speechless for a moment, but just a moment, and there were low murmurs throughout the room. Unsure what to do next, the governor began a hesitant and confused final round of applause. Annie stormed off the stage empty-handed as the applause mounted, the governor chasing her, in his desperate attempt to re-bestow the gifts of Jeanette Rankin and a state Annie Joslyn Day proclamation to the pride of Whitehall.

Chapter 29

I woke up in complete darkness – an absolute, total absence of light – seated on Annie's bed, the back of my head against the wall. Annie's room was darker than the Ledger darkroom; she'd created her cocoon of blackness deliberately, years earlier. Initially, I was worried the aversion of illumination may have been connected – either emotionally or psychologically – to her mother, but Annie kept her room bright enough during the day, and read assisted by as bright of light as possible.

In her room, at night, it was black. Somehow, I think Annie felt safer in the dark.

I felt her warmth beside me. She was asleep; I could feel and hear her breathing, a gentle rhythmic expansion within the blankets. I had been sleeping seated, with my mouth open. My throat was dry. My neck was stiff. My left leg – folded under my right leg – was asleep. It was impossible to tell what time it was.

Slowly, softly, I felt for the edge of the bed, found it, and slid carefully and unsteadily onto the floor. Annie stirred, but didn't wake. I felt my way toward the door, patted the wood and found the doorknob. The door creaked as it opened, and Annie stirred again. I froze, waiting for her voice, but in silence she drifted back to sleep. I stepped out into the cold hallway, and closed the door behind me, enveloping Annie in the safety of utter darkness.

The cold floor creaked under my feet. I realized I was still wearing shoes. The interior light of the refrigerator seemed as bright as a searchlight. I reached in, grabbed a can of Rainier, slipped my shoes off, and in my stocking feet, padded quietly into the living room, where I sat in my La-Z-Boy recliner. The only interior light filtered in from the streetlight out front. I reached over toward the end of the couch and pulled off the blanket – a handmade quilt Annie had purchased at a Whitehall charity auction a few years earlier – wrapped it around my legs, and poured beer down my parched throat. It was just before three o'clock; I'd been asleep sitting up on Annie's bed for nearly three hours. The beer felt cold on my throat; it chilled me inside all the way down to the bottom of my belly.

The governor had successfully foisted the gift of Jeanette Rankin onto Annie, who grabbed it and ran backstage. When I exited the multi-purpose room, in a failed attempt to track down Annie in the hallway, the last thing I saw was Ed with a fist full of Johnny Pep's Dodger jersey. The governor and Clayton Brewer caucused covertly and briefly on the right side of the stage, and then the governor hurriedly shook hands with the confused and aghast collection of education officials still gathered anxiously on stage. Diane Fordham's expression suggested she'd seen a walking corpse. Martha may have been weeping; she was either overcome with emotion or vastly disappointed, or both. The elementary school teachers were escorting the kids out of the multi-purpose room in semi-organized style, looking back toward the stage as if it held menace. Tony had led a small group of football players toward the stage in the general vicinity of Johnny Pep but was intercepted by Jersey, who when I vacated the room was firmly shaking his head no and blocking the aisle as Tony shifted his weight from side to side in an attempt to move past him and get to the corner of the stage and Johnny Pep.

I drove home, looking for Annie, and couldn't find her. I returned to the school to continue the search, but she wasn't there. I found Ed, Lyle and Martha, all three still wearing their purple and gold lilies, and while they were sympathetic and supportive, they didn't know Annie's whereabouts. When I asked them if they'd seen her, the impression I got was that none of them had wondered where she might have gone. You could see in their eyes the thought never occurred to them to worry about Annie; none of them had ever had reason to worry about her before. I went down to Jersey's room, and there was a soft din of noise from the kids as they chattered about the assembly. Jersey immediately stood when he saw me standing in the hallway, and rushed toward me and the door.

"Where's Annie?" he asked.

"I don't know," I said. "I was hoping she was here."

He shook his head. "Have you looked at home?"

"She's not there."

Jersey frowned. He hesitated, then said with what sounded like confidence he didn't think she was at the school.

"Goddamnit. What did this Johnny Pep kid do that made her so mad?" I asked.

Jersey put an arm around my waist and escorted me a little further into the hallway, fully out of the classroom's listening range.

"He was mimicking Trisha," Jersey said with physical and emotional sorrow, as if uttering the words caused him actual pain.

"She's handicapped, for Christ's sake," I said.

Jersey nodded. "Trisha didn't see it, I don't think. Or, if she saw it, she didn't comprehend it. He was seated behind her, and her attention was largely focused on the stage, as you can imagine, and on Annie."

"But Annie saw it?" I said.

Jersey nodded. "She was looking out from the stage to the audience, probably watching Trisha. You know how Annie is."

Yes, I knew. I knew how she was, but now I needed to find out *where* she was.

"This Pep kid's trouble," I told Jersey.

"He was today," Jersey agreed.

"Could Annie be trying to track him down?" I asked. "Where's *he*?" I looked around the hallway, as if I could somehow see him. "She needs to stay away from him. She's doesn't know what kids like him can do."

He hesitated. "Check the Ledger. Annie feels safe there."

Laura Joyce was in tears when I arrived, but Annie sat silent, glaring straight ahead at nothing. The Jeanette Rankin photo was propped up against the wall, facing the wall. Annie's eyes were red and swollen, her face a pasty white. I hugged her, and she stood up.

"Let's go," she told me. "Thanks," she waved weakly to Laura Joyce, who waved weakly in response, and strode out the door.

At home, she wrapped herself in a blanket and almost immediately fell asleep on the couch. It was only four o'clock in the afternoon, and it was the two of us – strangely – together at home on a Thursday afternoon. I dozed off, woke up, saw Annie still sleeping, and fell asleep again.

It was dark when voices woke me – us – up. Tony was in the house with Dave and Cody, and between the time they opened the back door into the kitchen and the time they walked into the living room Annie had risen and disappeared into her room.

Her door closed just as all three of them got into the house. They must have caught a glimpse of Annie before she closed her door.

"She okay?" Tony asked me.

My thoughts were disorganized and sluggish. I had to slowly rewind the past few hours, put together where I was and what I'd been doing, and despite my best effort, I had no answer. It was after six o'clock. Annie and I had slept off and on for three hours. It was Thursday. A few hours earlier the governor had been in Whitehall honoring my daughter.

"You okay, Lance?" Tony asked.

I rubbed my eyes with a thumb and index finger, then ran my fingers through my hair. "I'm fine," I said. "Quite a day," I added, stupidly.

Cody opened our refrigerator door as if he was part of the family, and just like a member of the family, he scouted its contents with disappointment, and closed the door empty handed. We had some beer, milk, Velveeta, and some green leafy things on the bottom shelf no one ever touched.

"Scarce pickings," Cody said, as if disappointed but not surprised. "How's Annie?"

"I think she'll be okay," I said. "She's a little distraught." Even to me I sounded like an idiot.

"Johnny fucking Pep," Cody muttered.

"Let's hit A&W," Tony announced. Not only was there no food available here, it was obvious to Tony there was distress and discomfort in the Joslyn home, and it was just as obvious Tony wanted none of that.

"Pep was making fun of Trish," Cody declared, as if expecting me to defy him.

Tony, his WHS letterman jacket on and unbuttoned, his shirt buttoned and untucked, looked my direction. "You hungry?" he asked.

"Not really," I said, but I didn't know for sure.

Tony looked at Annie's closed door, and back toward me. "I'll bring you guys back something."

The instant the front door closed after Cody, Dave and Tony left the house, Annie's bedroom door opened. She was wearing what passed as her pajamas – long sleeve WHS shirt and some kind of black stretch pants – and she looked like a forlorn Irish waif, spectral almost, as she hobbled, more or less, into the bathroom. A few minutes later she emerged, headed directly to her room, and I got out the words, "Tony's going to bring-" when her door closed.

It wasn't until later, a little after eleven o'clock, after Tony was getting ready for bed, when I ventured into Annie's bedroom. The room was dark and warm and moist; and the first sound I heard was a sniffle. I sat on the edge of the bed; her little body was generating a great deal of heat.

The room was so dark I couldn't really see anything. I reached, felt with my fingertips, in front of me, and found her shoulders under the blanket, reached further and found her damp neck, cheek and hair. She sniffed again, and after a rustle under the covers I felt her hand search for mine, find it, clamp it with hers and hold it under her cheek. She was trembling.

"When I saw you up there on stage with the governor, I never thought this day would end like this," I whispered. With my other hand, I brushed away damp wisps of hair away from her ear.

She spoke into the covers, her voice was muffled, her voice tortured with emotion. She told me how she had a clear view of Trish, who was in her customary spot off the aisle in the front row. They had exchanged a brief excited wave, Annie said, and I had missed that. I must have been taking pictures then. Annie said Johnny sat behind Trish. Close to the end of the assembly, Annie said she saw Johnny slant his head awkwardly, at an unnatural angle, toward his shoulder, much like Trish. Then Johnny let his eyes absently drift up toward the ceiling and slackened his mouth in an anguished and near complete imitation of Trisha's merciless handicap. Disgusted, Annie saw it, watched it, and then, to Annie's ultimate horror, Trisha realized Annie wasn't looking at her, but past her, and began to turn – twist, actually, for Trisha, in her wheelchair – to her right for a glimpse of what Annie was looking at. That's when Annie issued the warning, she said, which redirected Trisha's confused expression back to Annie. Annie said she was unsure if Trisha saw the cruel imitation or not, and if she did, if she actually understood the mockery at her expense. Annie sobbed as she finished, her body wracked by heaves of torment and fury.

She needed comfort, but I wasn't of much help. One of my hands was pinned under her wet cheek and the other stroked her soft and moist clumps of hair.

"I'm glad you said what you said," I reassured her. "I think your brother wanted to fight Johnny Pep right after the assembly."

Annie said Johnny Pep carried a knife, and she was pretty sure he knew how to use it. She said she wanted Tony to stay away from him. She made me promise to order Tony to stay away from Johnny Pep, and I promised. As if I could order anyone to do anything. It was not the proper time, but I knew later I would have to encourage Annie to order Tony to stay away from Johnny Pep. He might actually listen to her.

We sat that way for several minutes; I stroked her hair, and she sobbed, sniffed, trembled. I gently attempted to pull my hand away to exit and retrieve the Kleenex box from the bathroom, but she held on tight.

Gradually, she grew quiet, and I thought she had fallen asleep. But then she shifted her weight, adjusted her position, and she was motionless, face toward the dark ceiling, her hand still clamped on mine, held against her cheek.

She moaned, misery and hostility perceptible in her weary voice, that it wasn't fair that she was a so-called child prodigy while Trisha would be handicapped her entire life. The words flew in a torrent. The phrase *child prodigy* was spoken with absolute contempt. She was a genius because of one miniscule aberration in one microscopic segment of one invisible slice of genetic material. And Trish was handicapped because of another miniscule aberration in one microscopic segment of one invisible slice of genetic material. She said her intellect was as abnormal and exceptional as Trisha's disability, and it wasn't fair that Annie was rewarded with honors and gifts while Trisha was saddled by severe physical hardship, or that a bully like Johnny Pep ridiculed Trisha's adversity. None of it was fair, none of it made sense, and none of it was acceptable.

When she was young, I told Annie she would have to accept certain things she couldn't control. Back then she'd resisted and resented my suggestion, which she perceived as a failing, a weakness.

She was silent for several minutes, talked out perhaps, emptied of her frustration and rage, discouraged possibly by my reluctance to debate or dispute her.

Then, in a soft voice barely above a whisper, she asked if her mom still received the Ledger. Annie knew the answer, and knew I knew she knew the answer. Annie was no stranger to our subscription list and regularly presented me statistics and percentages of our circulation growth and income from subscriptions.

I told Annie we sent a Ledger each week to the hospital where her mom lived.

There was a pause, and I knew Annie was intellectually asserting her mother's mental illness was unfair and undeserved. We had been through that argument many times before. After the hesitation, Annie asked in a voice barely louder than a breath if her mother would see the Ledger article about the governor presenting her the gift and designating the day in her honor.

I answered, my voice no louder than hers, that there would be a photo to accompany the article and that anyone and everyone who saw the Ledger would know about the governor's visit to Whitehall.

She hesitated again; she shifted her weight and rolled to her side. She did not release my hand. She sighed, choked back a sob. She commanded, not asked, the Ledger to avoid any mention of the assembly's regrettable conclusion. Softer, she said her mother needed to be proud of something. Moments later, I heard her slow rhythmic breathing.

I eased my hand away from her clutch, and Annie stirred but did not wake. So that was why she allowed the governor and the school to make such a fuss. It was a gift to her absent, mentally and emotionally stricken mother.

I was on my way back to the Ledger after taking a picture at the Mormon church Friday afternoon, and as I passed the elementary school on Division Street I discovered Manfred, the town marshal, had pulled over a driver in the opposite lane who looked regrettably like Cody Phillips, seated in a GMC pickup that looked problematically like Cody's.

I slowed down, saw Cody, aggravated, glaring dead ahead with a silent and simmering hostility. The brim of his white cowboy hat was pushed high on his forehead, and his hands dangled at twelve o'clock on the steering wheel, his fingers clenching and unclenching a fist. I had just taken pictures of a kid named Ryan Walker, Tanner's younger brother, who had recently been promoted to Eagle Scout.

Ryan had been gleaming with pride when moments earlier I had taken his photo. He wore sashes, badges, kerchiefs and an aura of respect and reverence. Cody, in contrast, sat slumped in his seat, seething with an expression of unabashed contempt.

I drove past the two vehicles – Manfred's police car's lights were flashing as he sat inside in the driver's seat, his head down, obviously writing something – and for reasons that will never be fully clear, even to me, I pulled over and stopped. I saw Manfred lift his head, look in the rear view mirror back in my direction, then resume writing. I opened my car door and closed it, which prompted another glance from Manfred, and as I approached from behind them I could see both Cody and Manfred looking back at me. Manfred was watching me from the rearview mirror, and Cody followed me through the side mirror, next to his elbow just outside the driver's side window. Neither looked particularly happy to see me.

Manfred hoisted his massive heft out of the car, and stood alongside it, the car door open, the dispatch radio bursting with clipped conversation from other law enforcement officers somewhere around Jefferson County.

"What happened?" I asked Manfred.

He shook his head. "No sir, mister editor," he said with a deliberate warning in his voice. "This don't concern you."

He stood, large and defiant, sweat trickling down his temples.

"What happened?" I asked. I indicated Cody. "Is he all right?"

"Depends," Manfred said, "on what you mean by *all right*. He's not injured, but he is in a fair amount of trouble."

"What'd he do?"

"Not sure that's any of your business," Manfred said smugly. "Why don't you just walk back there, get in your little Ford, drive home like a good boy and let me do my job."

It was probably good advice, and I probably should have taken it. Instead, I sighed, looked over at Cody, sighed again, and strolled Cody's direction. He saw me coming through his side mirror, and turned toward me as I approached and watched me from the driver's side window.

"What do you think you're doing?" Manfred demanded from behind me.

Walking ahead, eyes ahead toward Cody, I reached behind my back and waved once to Manfred, a gesture that I intended to convey my wish that he, Manfred, relax. Because to answer his question, I had no idea what I thought I was doing.

I reached Cody's truck, and stood opposite him; he lowered his eyes, a look I interpreted as implied guilt. I put both my hands on the door, on the ledge at the bottom of the rolled down window. A car went by, slowed, but kept going.

"What happened?" I asked Cody in what was intended to be a friendly question.

Cody shook his head. At that moment, there was nothing friendly about him. His fingers held dirt in the creases; he had a large half-healed scab on a wrist, probably a football injury. He was a tough kid, and while most kids his age either feared or respected the law, Cody did neither. This was not his first brush with Manfred or other more professional law enforcement officers.

"Manfred's been out to get me all year," he said tersely. "He got me speedin', he says, but I wasn't." He jabbed the steering wheel with his palms, and looked in the rearview mirror. I heard the crunch of footsteps on grit and pavement, and turned to see Manfred approaching. He didn't look pleased.

"How fast were you going?" I asked Cody.

"You best be moving along, Lance," Manfred ordered from right next to me. He was breathing heavy; it could have been prompted by his anger or the fifteen-stride walk from his car to Cody's truck. Manfred was too fat for his heart. He was too fat to be a cop. He was too fat, period.

"How fast was he goin'?" I asked him.

"Too fast," was the response. "You got no business being here. Now git."

"How fast?" I asked again.

"Goddamnit," Manfred howled. He used his stubby arms and hands to nervously hitch up his pants, adjust his hat, and pat the sidearm on his holster. "I'm ordering you to leave. Now, damnit."

"Just tell me how fast," I said.

"I wasn't speeding," Cody interjected.

"You shut your mouth," demanded Manfred. "You're in enough trouble already."

A pickup drove by slowly, then kept going. I could hear the stories already, the initial wonderment, followed by quick and inaccurate guesses, followed by embellishment, followed by individual and personal agendas. Manfred was right. I should get out of there, for a lot of reasons.

"How fast were you going?" I asked Cody.

"I wasn't speeding," he complained.

I turned toward Manfred. “How fast, Manfred?”

“Not everyone’s as impressed with you and your kids as you think they are,” Manfred said with bitterness. “The governor may kiss your ass but that don’t mean I have to.”

“What are you talking about?” I asked.

“You tryin’ to obstruct justice?” Manfred demanded.

I just wanted an answer. “It’s a simple question, Manfred. How fast was he going?”

“Fast enough,” he declared. “Twenty-two in a fifteen-mile-an-hour zone.”

“Twenty-two?” I asked. “Shit, Manfred, everybody goes twenty-two through here.”

He shook his head. “It’s posted for fifteen. Always has been. Twenty-two is speeding.”

“School’s been out for an hour,” I said. “Christ, Manfred, how many tickets have you written during the past year for someone here going under twenty-five miles an hour?”

Manfred’s face was a study in rage and sweat. “It’s posted for fifteen. Twenty-four hours a day, not just during school hours.” His eyes glared my direction. “And Mr. Phillips here can’t produce his driver’s license. That’s another violation, on top of the speeding.”

“Where’s your license?” I asked Cody.

“Home, I think,” he said with dismay. “Maybe in my locker.”

“You got a license, right?” I asked.

He nodded eagerly. “Yeah.”

“But he can’t produce it, which is a violation,” Manfred said. “I’m running a check now, on priors.” He smirked. “You never know want might turn up. We’ll soon see if Mr. Hot Shot here gets a ticket or something a little more serious.” Manfred turned to me. “Hope that won’t mess your kid’s love life up much.”

Cody leaned back harshly in the seat, and he smacked a palm against the cab ceiling.

“That’ll be enough of that,” warned Manfred.

“Feel good about this, do you Manfred?” I asked, even though I knew I shouldn’t. It was as if I heard myself talking and couldn’t believe what I was saying. Something, some juvenile sense of justice and outrage at injustice, some masochistic need to root out and expose discrimination and unreasonable and immoral actions, had flared up. It had been an emotional twenty-four hours, and Manfred should not have brought my family into his animosity. So I wasn’t just asking for trouble; I was expecting trouble. I knew it. And still I didn’t stop. “This make you feel important? Make you feel like a real cop?”

Manfred immediately reached out, grabbed my shirt at the shoulder, and spun me away from the pickup. “Get your ass-” he started, but stopped. I looked at his face, and followed his eyes, which were pointed in alarm and dismay toward an El Camino, the only El Camino in town, owned by, and driven by, Pete Duffy. Coach Pete.

Manfred let go of my shirt the same time Pete cruised by, an expression of confused outrage directed toward us from Pete's whiskery white face. He stopped the El Camino so abruptly the tires skidded with an abbreviated squeal. Pete had probably been going twenty-five-miles-an-hour, but of the four of us now semi-gathered I was likely the only person who noticed. He stepped out of the El Camino, wearing his Ranger purple shorts and windbreaker, a purple shoelace around his neck holding a silver whistle, and I realized we were only a couple hours from kickoff. The Rangers had a game with a possible playoff spot on the line, and Pete had been on his way to the locker room for final game preparations.

All three of us – Cody, Manfred and me – immediately internalized the situation and suspected we were either individually or collectively in trouble. Which, truthfully, we all were. Pete had been a Montana Highway Patrol officer for years, and he still carried an aura of instant and unchallenged authority. Bad leg and all, he jumped out of the car, and he hobbled excitedly our direction. He was not happy. My first fear was that he was not happy with me.

"Jesus Christ, Manfred," he said, "what the hell do you think you're doing." It was not a question.

I felt as if I dodged a bullet. Manfred was not as lucky.

"I'm doing my job," he said defensively, but his bluster was already diluted. Pete was a real cop, and Manfred knew it.

"You okay?" Pete asked me.

Me? I thought. *Me?* Sure, I'm okay. I nodded.

Pete looked at Cody. "What's going on?"

"He says I was speeding, but I wasn't," charged Cody.

"He was going twenty-two," I told Pete.

Pete glared at Manfred. "Twenty-two? Twenty-two? Shit, Manfred. The whole world goes twenty-two through here." He looked skyward momentarily, as if in a brief attempt to control himself. Then he leveled his attention toward Manfred. "Why were you roughing up Lance?"

Manfred's eyes went wide. "What? I wasn't." Manfred's uncertain scowl went back and forth from Pete to me to Pete. "He was resisting arrest."

"Him? What's he under arrest for?" Pete asked Manfred.

"I didn't. He's not," Manfred stammered.

"Manfred, did you arrest Lance or not?"

"Not yet," Manfred admitted.

"Then how the hell could he resist arrest?" Coach Pete leaned on his bad leg, so Manfred had to look down at him.

"He was interfering with *his* arrest." Manfred pointed at Cody.

Pete also pointed at Cody. "Him? He's under arrest?"

Manfred hesitated. "Well-"

"Well, my ass," Pete shouted.

It was as if without Jersey within earshot Pete was letting loose with a reservoir of pent-up curse words.

"I'm checking on priors," Manfred ventured.

Pete glared at me. "He shoved you, didn't he? I saw him." He turned to Manfred. "Manfred, I saw you grab him. I saw it right when I turned the corner. I'd have to say that in court. Lance here could charge you with police brutality if he wanted, and I'd have to back him up based on what I saw."

Manfred's horrified eyes burned with an expression that looked a lot like panicked hatred, and I thought it was possible he was going to have a coronary on the spot. "He harassed me," Manfred said without real conviction.

"Oh bullshit," Pete said. "Lance has never harassed anyone in his life."

"He was interfering with the duties of a law enforcement officer," Manfred asserted.

Pete glared at Manfred. "Do you expect me to believe that happy horseshit? Do you expect anyone to?" Pete let out a loud breath of air, then turned to Cody. "You sit here and keep your mouth shut." He looked at me. "Get back in your car, Lance, and wait for me there. I'll only be a couple minutes." He looked at Manfred. "Manfred, we're going to have a little chat back in the squad car."

Pete put a meaty arm around Manfred's shoulder and led him back to the police car. Manfred weakly protested, but Pete physically and firmly insisted. I retreated past the squad car to my Escort, slid in, and waited. I could see inside the police car, two large men arguing, arms waving, hands punctuating assertions, and even with the windows up I could hear muffled angry voices. At most they were in the car three minutes. Pete opened the police car door, got out, and shut the door. Then the police car revved up and sped away. Manfred didn't even look back my direction as the car charged down the street. Pete held up one index finger my direction – *give me one minute* – and limped toward Cody's truck. Pete stuck his head inside the cab of the truck, and thirty seconds later Cody and the truck crawled away and turned the corner east on Yellowstone Drive. Pete ambled down Division Street and I rolled down my window as he approached.

"Well, that was interesting." Pete said. He looked around, as if checking to see if anyone was watching. "After additional consideration, Town Marshal Manfredini opted to give Cody a warning this time. I promised Manfred you wouldn't bring charges against him provided he back off this hard-on he's got against Cody." Pete hesitated. "Manfred wasn't exactly enthusiastic about it all, but he saw it my way."

I let out a deep breath of relief. "I was lucky you came along, Pete."

"Be damned careful around Manfred," Pete advised. "He's pissed off and he carries a badge."

"And a gun," I added.

Pete grunted. "And he don't know how to use either." He tapped his palms on the roof of the Escort. "Get out of here," he suggested. "Congratulations on Annie's awards and recognition. It's pretty impressive, the governor and all."

"Yeah, thanks."

"Hey," he said. "My language got a little rough with Manfred." He smiled sheepishly. "Promise me you won't say anything about it to Jersey, okay?" He shrugged. "You know he don't like my cussing."

"Don't worry," I told him. "Go Rangers," I added.

Was it really possible, I wondered as Pete hobbled back to his El Camino, as I eased the Escort into the traffic lane, that Annie Joslyn's father almost got himself arrested the day after the official Annie Joslyn Day in Montana?

The American flag waved softly during the Star-Spangled Banner before the Friday night football game against Big Timber. The breeze blew gently from the west, behind the backs of the Rangers, who stood so motionless they appeared sculptured. Three separate semi-truck horn bleats signaled camaraderie from the interstate.

There was an above average crowd for the final game of the year – Senior Night – as the Ranger players paraded out with parents in a brief pre-game ceremony. The Rangers had a chance to win three straight games and give themselves an opportunity to qualify for the Class B football playoffs. Despite that, as I stood on the sidelines, attaching the flash to the camera and absorbing the atmosphere, I detected no drama, no tension in the air. The crowd, some of whom probably hadn't been to a football game all year, seemed unaware or unimpressed by the importance of the game. There seemed to be a general appreciation or acquiescence that this was the final game of the year, and no one seemed aggrieved by that fact.

I was still troubled about my run-in with Manfred. Never before had I argued with a law officer. The previous most serious encounter with a policeman in my life was in Butte, years earlier, when someone had broken into my car at the mall parking lot.

The student section was relatively quiet, seated close together, Ranger jackets interspersed with thick flannel shirts. Johnny Pep was there, sitting next to a kid I hadn't seen before, both indifferent to the other students. Jersey and Ed had both assured me there would be no trouble between Johnny Pep and other WHS students, and apparently they'd been successful.

Annie sat in the corner, above Trisha, whose wheelchair was positioned in the customary spot just below the front row of the bleachers. Above Trisha, alongside Annie, sat Bonner Labuda and Caddy, a pair of kids as opposite from Annie in every way possible. The visitors – a Big Timber team that hadn't won a game all year – were introduced and the dozen, at most, Big Timber fans cheered as each player's name was introduced. I saw Slack across the field, not far from the Big Timber bench, his right hand holding a yard marker and a lopsided grin visible from fifty yards. He anticipated a Ranger victory.

"And now," boomed Herbie from the press box, "the starting offense for the Whitehall Rangers."

In the bleachers, up popped Ed Franklin, and he led what amounted to a standing ovation. Everyone stood, and everyone cheered and applauded. Johnny Pep looked around casually, then stood.

"Starting at wide receiver, number seven, senior Colt Harrison!" Herbie thundered.

Colt had been standing across the field, the Ranger closest to the Big Timber sideline. He turned and sprinted across the line of Rangers standing at the twenty yard line, and slapped hands with each player as he crossed the field and then was expected to sprint to midfield to await the introduction of the next starter. But when Colt reached the end of the lineup of Rangers he didn't run up the field. Instead, he continued rapidly past the players, off the field, past the sideline, onto the track toward the bleachers. He surprisingly crossed the sideline not far from where I stood. I saw the eye black smudged under his eyes, the towel tucked inside his belt, the high white socks and thick white wristbands, and was close enough to even feel a hint of air movement when he ran past me.

He stopped in front of Trisha and held both hands palms up at his waist. Trisha didn't hesitate for a moment. She awkwardly lifted her two arms and swatted her hands across Colt's hands, and he cheered, whirled, and dashed back onto the field. The Ranger fans were cheering loudly when the next Ranger was introduced, quarterback Dave Dickson, who followed Colt's lead, and gave Trisha a double hand slap before rushing midfield to exchange high fives with Colt.

I saw a bemused look on Jersey's face as Dave and Colt celebrated and waited for their teammates to join them at midfield. The look on Jersey's face suggested he was not aware of Colt's plan to reward and recognize Trisha, but accepted the gesture, and even approved. All eleven Ranger starters eventually slapped hands with Trish, and before the rest of the team whooped it up at midfield they all hustled over to the bleachers and surrounded Trisha, cheering, patting her on the shoulder, slapping hands, while the Ranger fans stood and applauded. Trisha positively glowed, and I snapped a picture of her broad uneven smile before the last of the Rangers departed from her for the sideline.

Coach Pete shuffled over after the players left and – like an old fashioned cop – shook Trisha's hand. Jersey followed, and he gave Trish a brief hug. It was as if the entire Whitehall High School football team had just told Johnny Pep he meant nothing to them.

Big Timber never had a chance. They kicked off to Whitehall and Tony returned the kickoff into Big Timber territory.

"Tramps! Tramps! Tramps!" called out Jersey as White offense took the field for the first play from scrimmage.

I later found out what 'Tramps' meant. It was from Springsteen's anthem *Born to Run,* and tramps were born to run. 'Tramps' was a new Ranger power formation in the offensive backfield, with Morgan, an offensive lineman, in the backfield as an extra blocker. Logan Bradshaw carried the ball five straight times for forty-six yards, three first downs, and a nine-yard touchdown run.

By halftime the Whitehall Rangers had tramped their way to a 28-0 lead. Tony had even scored on a wide receiver reverse. Whitehall had more touchdowns than Big Timber had first downs. The Ranger game was no longer in doubt; interestingly, the Boulder game was. Late in the second quarter, Herbie announced a score: Boulder led Manhattan 14-13 at the half, which spawned a groan from the fans who understood its significance.

Annie brought a bottle of pop to me along the sidelines. She looked better, slightly more alert, but still wan, and somber.

"Thanks," I said.

"Is it true you punched Manfred this afternoon?" she asked me.

"What? Me? No," I said. "Who told you that? I never punched anybody."

"What happened then," asked Annie, "over on Division in front of the elementary school office? Word is you and Manfred got into it. Hey, don't deny it if it's true. If it is true, you're a hero."

"I'm not a hero," I said. "It's not true. I didn't punch him. We had a," I chose the next word carefully, "misunderstanding. We had a misunderstanding."

"A misunderstanding?" asked Annie. "What are you, a mafia lawyer? You don't have misunderstandings with law enforcement officers. You're either arrested or you're not."

She hesitated, so I answered. "I wasn't arrested."

"Why did Manfred stop you?" Annie asked.

"He didn't. No one stopped me. I stopped myself."

She looked at me puzzled, and I could see the wonder behind her eyes, the possibility of a brief unfortunate stop at Borden's.

"You stopped yourself?" she asked.

"From doing what?" a voice asked behind me. It was Cal Walker, wearing a big white cowboy hat and sheepskin jeans jacket.

"Nothing?" I said.

"You get arrested?" Cal asked me, with a smirk.

"You're going to get a suspiciously firm denial," Annie told him.

"Denial of what?" he asked her.

"That he punched Manfred," Annie said.

"You punched Manfred? The town marshal?" Cal wondered.

"No, I'm denying I punched Manfred," I said. "Weren't you listening to her?"

"Why would you punch Manfred?" Cal asked. "You can get in trouble for that."

"Big trouble," added Annie.

"I didn't punch anybody," I protested. "Not Manfred, not anyone."

The three of us had to move aside to let the Rangers stream through an opening in the bleachers.

"Go get 'em," Cal said.

"Touchdown Tony!" Annie called out when Tony jogged past us.

"Manfred's a big mean chunk of man," Cal told me.

"My hero," said a voice, a Ranger, Cody, as he ran past us toward the field.

Annie looked at me with disbelief. "Did Cody just call you a hero?"

"Why are you a hero?" Cal asked.

"I'm not a hero," I said. "Now leave me alone so I can get back to work," I said, and headed to the sideline.

The highlight of the second half was when Morgan, a stocky and hairy number sixty-three lined up in the backfield, and bulled his way into the end zone for a third-quarter touchdown. It was his first carry of the year, and the Ledger noted he scored touchdowns on one hundred percent of his runs. He intended to spike the ball, but when he lifted the ball up to slam it down it slipped out of his hand, and it flew out of the back of the end zone.

"The Mighty Mite!" yelled Dave Dickson after Morgan had scored. They hugged and shouted in the end zone.

The Rangers were ahead 42-0 late in the fourth quarter when the Whitehall student section, buoyed by the euphoric glee of victory mixed with an unpleasant retaliatory zeal from previous losses, began singing the chorus of the "*Na na na na, na na na na, goodbye*," song. At its core, it was a song sung in spite, as an insult, to offend and disgrace a fallen foe. It had been sung repeatedly in previous years in places like Three Forks, Townsend and Boulder, sung to serenade an abysmal and inept Ranger football team. This Ranger team had already heard it abundantly this year, but Big Timber would only hear it for an instant.

Jersey turned away from the field, turned away from his players and away from the game, and took about ten strides toward the students, gently waving his arms in front, urging by voice and actions for the kids to quiet down. Some of the WHS fans ceased singing as he approached, and everyone stopped when Jersey started talking.

"No, no, no. We don't do that here," he said. He spoke firmly, but he didn't shout. "These players, on both teams, have played with pride here tonight. We respect all of them for their commitment, their teamwork, their effort and their passion," Jersey told them. It was absolutely quiet. You could hear the footsteps of the players on the grass on the field.

It was utterly silent after he spoke. So when Herbie broadcast the Boulder-Manhattan score, everyone, even the players, heard the announcement.

"We have a final score from Boulder," Herbie's voice blared through the silence. "Boulder twenty-seven," and the crowd groaned as one, "Manhattan twenty-eight."

It took a moment, but then the crowd understood Herbie's little trick and roared as one. The Rangers were in the playoffs.

The Rangers were in the playoffs?

The Rangers were in the playoffs.

Dave Dickson, on the field, in the huddle, had heard the score, and immediately grasped its meaning. In a burst of unscripted and unrestrained joy, he took off his helmet and tossed it thirty feet in the air. The picture of him, helmetless, hair matted with sweat, facing the Ranger bench, his arms outstretched in absolute joy, wearing a grin that could be measured in yards, appeared on the front page of the Ledger. He received a fifteen-yard penalty for his burst, and Jersey quietly removed him from the game for the final minute or so in a 49-7 Ranger win.

And to add a touch of irony to a bittersweet season, Colt Harrison filled in as backup quarterback and took a knee for the final two snaps of the 1986 regular season for the Rangers. In an emotional moment that oddly symbolized the entire season, Colt took the final snap, dropped to a knee, and as the final seconds ticked off the clock he jogged to the sidelines, through a group of dancing and euphoric Ranger players and outside of the track toward the bleachers where, mobbed by cheerleaders and fans, he placed the ball firmly in the lap of Trisha Ryan, who clutched it to her chest as if it were a lost treasure.

Chapter 30

Success is an intoxicating elixir, and unexpected success particularly sweetens everything it touches. Slack's smile glowed from forty yards away, and he and his father crossed the field from the opposite sidelines with grins that couldn't have been muted under threat of death. Slack jumped into my arms and squeezed me so tight I worried about damage to my camera. He smelled of dirt and tobacco and sweat and staleness, and he reeked of glee. His Rangers were in the playoffs.

Mary's embrace was a little softer, and smelled considerably better. Annie's hug was so earnest and blatant I never wanted it to end. Tony's embrace was soaked with sweat and every part of him was either damp or slippery or both, and though he would never admit it, tears leaked from the corners of his eyes as he accepted praise and congratulations from the dozens of kids and fans who simply refused to abandon their celebration on the football field.

In a conservative rural community where an embrace typically equates with death or long absences, the hugs on the football field were contagious and universal and unprecedented within the world of Whitehall. I either initiated or responded to hugs from Molly Ryan; Lyle O'Toole and, fortunately for me, all the O'Toole women; Rhonda Horst gave me a brief weak hug and whispered hoarsely something close to *Got bless you*; big and burley Coach Pete, tears streaming down both cheeks, almost squeezed the wind out of me; frail little Sara Dickson, standing by herself with her tiny hands clasped as if in prayer at her throat, couldn't escape the frenzy and accepted hugs from Coach Duffy, me, Slack, Ed Franklin and finally, warmly, her still frenetic son; Ed and Alice Franklin, clad in bright Ranger purple and gold, laughing and cheering exchanged hugs with me and with half the student body; Cody Phillips and I shook hands, paused, and embraced. It is possible that every parent of a Ranger football player hugged each other parent. Jersey crossed the field, after consoling the Big Timber team and coaches, and he alone among the Ranger Nation was stoic and steadfast. He seemed detached somehow, separate from what he himself had created. And as I made my way to congratulate him, he slipped through the crowd and disappeared somehow. I was intercepted by Brent Walker, Tanner's dad, and when he saw me he lifted his cowboy hat high in the air and hollered. We shook hands thirty yards from the end zone where a couple months earlier we had jointly spied the midnight gang doing up-down drills and watched several Rangers empty their insides of KFC original chicken until the field was littered with enough throw-up to attract multiple and unnatural species of birds for the vomited pickings.

I spotted timid and hushed Sara Dickson again, and again I couldn't help myself and she could neither avoid nor reject my embrace. Trish was close to the sideline, clutching her football as if it were a lost-but-found infant, and her unfocused, dreamy eyes emitted sheer exhilaration. Hank and Kathleen

Harrison, just a little too dressed up, were present but hadn't really joined in the festivities. While an embrace was perhaps too much sentiment toward them, I reached out and shook hands with them both, and both of them offered praise for the team and my son.

The spontaneous football field celebration was silly. Ridiculous, really. It was only a high school football game, the Rangers still had a losing season, and qualifying for the playoffs meant, simply, one more football game, at a location far away against a far better team. But if it was only a high school football game, how can you explain the sense of hope, of pride, of accomplishment, of unity, of an unshakable bond that joined us at least temporarily as a community, tighter and more affectionate than even a family?

The Sunday night telltale knock came at about nine o'clock, when I was three hours into

a four-hour shift at the Ledger. I had been developing film, and as Ledger publisher I was having a difficult decision to make for the Ledger's front page. I had a good picture of Annie receiving the certificate from the governor, I had a very good picture of Colt Harrison and Trish, the football clutched firmly in her lap and I had the shot of Dave Dickson's beaming smile on the football field.

"Anyone home?" Cal called, as he opened the door. Popcorn.

I was only an instant ahead of the mice. First one, then the other, sniffed their way out of the hole in the wall. To prevent Cal from seeing them – and worse, seeing them and then telling everyone he saw them – I stood and stomped my foot once on the floor, which sent them scurrying back into the wall.

Cal entered, a large bag of popcorn in one hand and a plastic cup of pop in the other.

"How was the movie?" I asked him. His fleece-lined jeans jacket was speckled with tiny bits of white popcorn.

"Oh, okay I guess, if you like dumb movies about stupid Australians," he answered. The movie was *Crocodile Dundee*. "It was so dumb I think I'm going to punch the next Australian I see, just to punish them for a movie that bad."

I had already dug into the popcorn. At some point, I wondered, was I expected to pay Cal for all the Sunday night treats? I hope he wasn't expecting me to, because it wasn't going to happen.

"See Tony?" I asked.

Cal nodded. "He was surrounded by boys wearing Ranger jackets and girls wearing perfume. Lovely girls, I should add. After the show, when I was getting popcorn, he and the gang walked past me and Tony was talking exactly – I mean *exactly* – like the Aussie in the movie. Kid's got a gift."

"Yeah, he's had that gift, if that's what you want to call it, since he was born. He can imitate teachers, friends, police officers. The governor. Actors. He heard Mick Jagger talk on television once and for a week Tony went around talking with a goofy cockney accent."

"Locals?" asked Cal. He settled his girth into Laura Joyce's chair and spun it to face me.

"I heard him imitate me once," I said. "He was probably about ten years old. He had made a mess in the kitchen and when I got home and saw it I called him in from outside and told him to clean up the kitchen. A half hour later he was back outside, playing with his little buddies, and from inside the house I heard me – it was my voice – yelling at him to *clean up the goddamn kitchen* and to be honest, it was not a flattering impersonation. It was accurate, but it's sobering to hear yourself through the voice of a ten-year-old."

"You're lucky you have such good kids," Cal said. He offered a sly smile. "Does he do me?"

I shrugged. "I don't know. I've never seen it, if he does. I'm sure he could, if you want him to."

Cal laughed. "No thanks. I was just wondering."

"Did you see that movie about the kid in Chicago, *Ferris Bueller's Day Off*?" I asked.

Cal shook his head. "Looked like a movie for kids."

"It was," I said. "I never saw it either. But Tony loves that movie – he's quite a movie fan – and I saw him doing about five voices from that movie, and he could imitate mannerisms and everything. I assume from the reaction of his friends the imitations were accurate. They were all howling with laughter."

"Like I said, it's a gift," he said. "He does like to make people laugh, doesn't he?

I had never thought of it that way. But I guess that was true, he did.

"I always think of Tony as trying to bring a little more sunshine into this world," Cal said.

There were worse thing to bring into the world. "Sometimes he tries a little too hard," I said.

Cal frowned in disagreement. "You have two wonderful kids, and you know it. I know it. Everyone knows it. Consider yourself lucky, my friend." He reached back and cupped his hands behind his head. "Annie was at the movie."

"Who with? Cody?" I asked.

Cal shook his head. "Not tonight. Some kid I don't know. Hippie-looking kid. A definite step down from the last guy I saw her with. The governor."

"Sounds like Bonner Labuda," I said.

"Labuda?" Cal winced. "What's she hanging out with a Labuda for?"

"Couldn't tell you," I said. "The child continues to mystify me."

Cal's expression suggested uncertainty. "She trying to reform him?"

"Who knows. Could be, I suppose. When she's with kids like Cody and Bonner, they bow to her pressure, not her to theirs."

Cal just grunted. "Good luck on that. Cody's rough around the edges, but he's just a bad boy in a barroom brawl kind of way. These Labuda kids are bad boys in a drug trafficking kind of way."

What do you want me to do? I thought. I work seventy hours a week. My kids have to supervise themselves, and I have to have some confidence in them to do that. Annie especially knows her way around. Bonner Labuda is not going to corrupt Annie Joslyn.

"She was something else at that ceremony the other day, there with the governor," Cal said. "She really is wise beyond her years, isn't she? I mean, she's smart, we all know that. But she's way more than just book smart. She conducts herself like an intelligent young woman."

"She's been an intelligent young woman since she was four years old."

"Did you see her handle the governor?" Cal asked. "A lot of kids – hell, a lot of people; I mean almost anyone and everyone – would have been in awe of a big deal like that. I'll be honest, Lance, *I* would have been in awe of a big deal like that. But Annie," he chuckled, "Annie handled it like it was just another Thursday. She stood there, on stage, looking out over the crowd, like she was in a grocery store aisle looking out over canned goods."

She wasn't in awe, I almost told Cal, because she was unimpressed and indifferent. The person who cared the least that Thursday had been declared Annie Joslyn Day in Montana was Annie Joslyn herself.

"I heard about what that Johnny Pep kid did," Cal said darkly. "I didn't see him doing it, but I heard about it right afterward. You wanna talk about trouble, Johnny Pep is trouble."

"Kid kind of gives me the creeps," I said.

"It's too bad kids like him end up in places like ours," Cal said.

"The sooner he's gone from here, the better." The popcorn was finished; I slurped the final few gulps of pop. I still had at least an hour of work to get done. Both kids were probably arriving home from the movie. I needed to call them.

"I talked to Ed Franklin," Cal said, "and I talked to the guys at the mine about a team dinner on Thursday night. Sort of a community barbeque to salute the team. Ed said we could use the multi-purpose room, Golden Sunlight'll buy the beef and Lyle said the bank'll take care of pop and chips, and stuff like that. All we need is for people to bring desserts."

"Great idea," I said. "I'll get an article in the paper."

"Stick in an ad, too," Cal said. "Everyone's invited. Send me the bill. Make it about yea big." He held his hands apart about quarter-page size. Cal knew how much I liked to get advertising, and I knew he knew.

"We'll charge people three bucks for the meal, and the money will help pay for the team to spend Friday night out at Baker someplace," Cal said.

The Rangers would meet the Baker Trojans in the first round of the playoffs. Baker was undefeated, ranked number two in Montana Class B football and had been the state runner-up the year before. Welcome to the playoffs, Whitehall.

"Turns out the school budget didn't figure on paying for an 800-mile roundtrip overnight football playoff game in Baker," Cal explained. "The kids need to spend Friday night in Baker. No sense stretching the school budget when we can raise the money through a community barbeque."

Cal was right. I hadn't thought that through. It was impossible for the team to get up ungodly early on Saturday, drive all day, step off a bus, and play football. I wondered if it was possible for me to get up Saturday morning and make it to Baker for a two o'clock football game. It didn't seem possible.

Cal stood up. Not a bad visit; popcorn, pop and a quarter-page ad. I also stood, and stomped my foot again to make sure the mice weren't too inquisitive.

"You might want to be careful around Manfred," Cal said as I followed him out.

"I was never under arrest, and I didn't do anything wrong," I told Cal's back.

"Never said you had," he answered.

The sun shone in Whitehall that week. Monday, Laura Joyce and I shared a pizza for lunch. We were behind schedule because people kept coming into the Ledger office to place Happy Ads for football players, to find out for sure who the opponent was and where and when the Rangers played, to check if we knew anything about a school pep bus, to find out more about the Thursday night community barbeque and to simply come in and talk about the game.

It took me almost an hour on Monday to go to the post office and back. Some of the people I talked with at the Ledger asked me the same questions an hour later at the post office. My Monday morning ad stops took over an hour longer than normal, but that was not a problem; victory had lifted spirits and opened checkbooks. Everyone placed an ad, signed on the *Good Luck, Rangers* business signature full-page ad, placed a business ad or added a *Go get 'em, Rangers* message to their ad, which made their ad bigger, which increased Ledger revenue. I didn't want to be mercenary about it, but Ranger winning was good business. Lyle placed a normal bank ad with a *Go Rangers* message, a Happy Ad, signed onto the signature ad and doubled the size of the community barbecue ad. The typical ten to fifteen-minute ad stop conversations lasted thirty minutes, and while I dodged questions about my run-in with Manfred there was no way to abbreviate my discussions with a supportive Whitehall business community flushed with the pride of playoff football.

Three times during lunch Laura Joyce and I were interrupted by customers who wanted to buy an ad, including Rhonda Horst, who placed two Happy Ads and delivered some banana bread for Tony. Not for me; for Tony.

"I bring more foodt for dat trip to Baker," Rhonda told me. "Such a vunderfull day," she marveled as she tied the scarf under her chin.

It was a wonderful day. The sun was bright and warm, the sky a limitless blue, the fall colors were usually muted in our dusty dry valley, but vibrant oranges and yellows were visible as close as the trees in the park across the street on Legion Avenue.

Annie stopped by the Ledger after school and so many people had paid for Happy Ads with cash and checks she decided to make a Monday deposit. At the bank, two of the football players' moms – Morgan's and Cale's – stopped her and in the bank lobby placed Happy Ads in the Ledger.

The Happy Ad page was full, we had over seven hundred inches of advertising and would have to go twenty-eight pages. Between the governor's visit, the Ranger trip to Baker and a full-page signature ad, we had plenty of material to fill all twenty-eight pages.

The only question was which picture went on the front page. I was in the darkroom when Annie got back from the bank, and I was still in the darkroom when Laura Joyce left at six o'clock and still in the darkroom at eight o'clock when I heard noises from outside the darkroom. Since the Ledger was closed I knew it was the kids. I figured the mice wouldn't venture out amidst the kids.

"Lance," I heard Tony call out to me. "Pizza. Here. Now."

I had spread out several photos on the layout board. Inside the darkroom I still had only the rest of the football photos to print. Pictures from the Eagle Scout ceremony, of the 4-H fashion show, a quartet from the governor's visit, various other pictures and the football pre-game photos including the picture of Colt and Trisha were printed, dried and ready to be waxed and cut. Among the photos from the governor's visit was a large three-column picture of Annie accepting the certificate and print from a beaming Governor Ted Schwinden.

"I'll be right there," I said from inside the darkroom.

I could hear the muffled voices of Tony and Annie as they browsed through the photos scattered across the layout table.

"You look like a dwarf alongside him," I heard Tony say, and I knew exactly which picture he was talking about.

"Wow, he looks a lot happier than you do," a voice – Bonner Labuda's – said and I knew they all were talking about the same picture.

"He's a politician," Annie said. "He can smile on cue. Just a like monkey or a dog."

"Once on TV I saw a monkey shoot pool," Bonner said.

"I saw a monkey water ski once," said a voice. Cody Phillips was my guess.

"There's over one-hundred and twenty-five different species of monkeys," Annie said. "They can live almost anywhere, in almost every kind of climate.

In rain forests, islands, steppes, scrublands, savanna, mountains, even in snow. Know what the pygmy marmoset weighs?"

"The what?" asked Bonner.

"Less than five ounces," Annie said.

"I saw a movie about apes once," said Bonner.

"*Planet of the Apes*?" asked Tony.

"I dunno," answered Bonner. "The apes talked and shot guns and rode horses. It was wild, man."

I heard Charlton Heston say something about *damn dirty ape*, but I was pretty sure it was only Tony.

As I opened the door to escape the darkroom I found Annie waiting. "This one," she greeted me, and pointed to the picture of Colt and Trish, "goes on the front page."

It was not a recommendation or a piece of advice. There was no indecision in her voice, no room for a differing opinion. She was giving me a directive.

"How about this one?" I showed her the one of she and the governor.

Annie shook her head. "You got four pictures. Fill a page inside."

I thought about it. "Page nine. This one," she and the governor, "top right." Anyone looking at the paper, anyone at all, would see the photo. Other photos from the ceremony included the governor and Lyle, a horizontal five-column picture of the dignitaries onstage and a picture of Carrie Lindstrom performing in the pep band.

Five blue plastic cups of Pepsi surrounded what looked like a half sausage, half pepperoni pizza. Tony liked sausage; I liked pepperoni; Annie found both acceptable and my guess was Bonner's and Cody's thoughts were neither solicited nor offered. Bonner sat, black stocking cap pulled low on his forehead, a too-large ratty blue and gray flannel shirt hanging on his thin frame; his black high top tennis shoes shuffled nervously under the table. He looked like he'd been working under the hood of a car all afternoon. He needed a bath the way a ranch dog needed a bath. Cody was presentable, a mandate, I suspected, when residing with the Franklins. The inner hostility he carried with him seemed muted, or possibly merely temporarily cloaked. He seemed at ease with the five of us. I wasn't sure if I was happy about that or not.

When Cody had first started hanging around with Annie I had been worried about what every father worries about when his junior high daughter appears to be dating a troubled and aggressive high school boy. But in reality they were not dating, and weren't much more than friends. Bonner had been added to the mix, three kids without moms, three kids without much parental guidance or instruction. They were a trio bonded by apparent parental neglect.

Even though it was my second pizza of the day, the pizza smelled terrific. The melted cheese on the first slice I picked up started to slide off as I lifted it from the box toward my plate so I brought it instead straight to my mouth, where it instantly burned a large patch of my tongue. I gasped and let out a couple fast huffs of air as I quickly moved the pizza to the plate and reached for the cup of pop.

"Lance, it's melted cheese," Annie informed me levelly. "Listen," she said, as if speaking to a child, "it's still sizzling. Do you think maybe it could be hot?"

To my right, a panicked Bonner was gasping and huffing and yanking the pizza out of his mouth and dropping it on his plate.

"Monkey see, monkey do," said Annie. She still hadn't reached for the pizza. "You both might get Aphthous stomatitis."

"Whath that?" asked Bonner. He was actually dunking his tongue down into the glass of pop.

"A mouth sore," answered Annie.

To our amazement, Bonner picked up the same piece of pizza, slid it into his mouth, again gasped and huffed again and again dropped it on his plate.

I couldn't help it. I burst out laughing. So did Cody and Tony.

"I gotta tell you," said Tony, still laughing, "I don't even think a monkey does that twice."

"In case you were wondering, that makes a monkey smarter than you," said Annie.

Bonner picked up the same piece of pizza for the third time, held it in front of his mouth, and blew on it like it was on fire. He blew on it like it was a flame that wouldn't go out.

"I owe you a big thanks for helping me with Manfred the other day," offered Cody. "You really bailed me out."

Annie's glance shifted from Cody to me. She opted to reach for the pizza instead of speaking.

"How fast did you say you were going?" asked Tony.

"I dunno," Cody said. "No faster than I always go. No faster than everyone else goes."

"Manfred's a prick," said Bonner. It sounded suspiciously like the voice of experience. Bonner had a glob of tomato sauce on his cheek. Annie handed him an A&W napkin from the stash we kept on the windowsill near the table. He accepted it, then appeared at a loss what to do with it.

"Aspen's dad said if you guys were smart, you'd stay away from Manfred," Tony said. *You guys* meant Cody, Bonner and me.

"That might be easier said than done," I said.

"Yeah," agreed Cody. "How do you avoid a cop who stays on your ass?"

"Manfred follows you?" I asked.

Cody nodded. "Or he waits for me. He knows my truck and he knows where I live."

"I'm not sure he's supposed to do that," I said.

"Of course he's not," Annie said. She was tempted to say something else, but stopped.

"Manfred's a prick," Bonner repeated.

"He's the town marshal," I pointed out.

"That doesn't mean he's not a prick," Bonner said. He still hadn't wiped the tomato sauce off his face.

"Maybe I should talk to Luke Grayling," I said.

"Or Rachel Brockton," Annie offered.

"Who are they?" asked Cody.

"Brockton's the witch at town hall," Bonner said.

"The town clerk," I corrected. If Bonner knew he'd been corrected, he didn't show it.

"She's the power behind the throne," Annie explained.

Neither Cody nor Bonner understood the expression. You could almost see Bonner trying to remember if there was an actual throne somewhere in town hall.

"The mayor is the governmental leader of Whitehall," Annie said. "But Rachel is the actual leader of Whitehall's government."

"She knows where all the bodies are buried," I explained.

"Manfred's the one who put them there," Bonner said.

The multipurpose room on Thursday night was flush with purple and gold. *R-A-N-G-E-R-S* was spelled out in massive purple letters against a gold background. Large purple cutouts of football helmets were taped to the top of each table, sort of like a large placemat. Glittery gold string – like you'd see at New Year's Eve parties – spiraled down from the ceiling. The cheerleaders were dressed in purple skirts and gold shirts. The Ranger players themselves wore their purple jerseys.

Annie paid twenty bucks for the two of us and told Brock Warren's mom, Lacy – who sat at a table inside the doorway to collect the money – to keep the entire twenty dollars. Lacy was a frequent ticket-taker and money-taker at community events, with sufficient experience to ignore me when we entered and look with expectation for Annie to pay for our meals. Lacy also knew Annie would likely not expect any change back.

"Wow, look at this crowd," I said to Lacy as we entered and looked around. Food and beverages were to our left, desserts to our right. The tables were more than three-quarters full with people relaxed and casual, eating and talking. No one looked in a hurry to finish doing either.

"We've served over a hundred and fifty people so far," Lacy said, with a hint of a boast.

Annie had three bags of Old Dutch potato chips to contribute; it was strictly a token gesture, but the twenty bucks more or less made everything okay.

"There any food left?" I joked.

"Plenty," she assured me. Lacy had been born and raised in Whitehall, married young and had a baby daughter in her first year of marriage. Brock had been born close to twenty years after that. His sister's name was Belinda, and I had written an article about her. She was an airline stewardess and traveled the world. She had been in over thirty different countries, and the article showed her posing at places like the Eiffel Tower and the Great Wall of China. Her mom had rarely ventured out of the Jefferson Valley. "Look at those desserts!" Lacy encouraged.

Three long folding tables were lined up end-to-end against the wall, filled with pies, bars, cake, brownies and cookies.

Hank Harrison, surprisingly, manned the sloppy joes, and gleefully, it appeared, slopped a metal spoonful of meat onto my hamburger bun.

"Want some more?" he asked cheerfully. "We got plenty."

"No thanks," I said. I was so stunned by his good spirits I couldn't think of anything to say.

"And here's some for our young scholar," Hank said to Annie. His dark hair was combed just perfect, and he wore a blue dress shirt under the apron. "Congratulations on that award from the governor," Hank told her. "That was a nice picture of Colt and Trisha Ryan on the front page," Hank said. For some reason he had waited until I was four steps past him before he commented on the photo. Was he embarrassed or ashamed of his past behavior? Perhaps a compliment was his version of an apology.

It *was* a good picture. It printed perfectly in the paper, the two faces with detailed and sharp facial features and skin tones. The black background of darkness focused attention on their faces. The three-column photo dominated the front page, above a caption that read: *Ranger Spirit Playoff Bound*. Trish's facial expression – eyes wide in surprised and raw joy – lifted the photo from technically good to emotionally moving.

Kathleen offered a wan smile and placed a scoopful of potato salad on my plate. She had probably been pretty in her youth, but looked now like someone trying far too hard to retain that youthful beauty. It looked as if she wore a mask of makeup.

With a plateful of food and plastic cup of lemonade, I stood momentarily scouting the tables for a place to sit. I knew practically everyone in the room, but none of my regular gang –Slack, Cal, Ed or Lyle – were around just then. There were a couple seats open next to Jodi and Tucker Collins, the parents of the JeffScott twins.

"How's the paper guy?" Tucker asked when I sat down.

"How's the plumber guy?" I asked in response.

Tucker was owner and the sole employee of Collins Plumbing. He had a big walrus-like mustache and shaved about once a week, so the rest of his face was about seven days of hair growth behind the mustache. He perpetually wore bib overalls, a battered gray baseball cap with *Collins Plumbing* in script stitched in the front, and no matter what the weather – the torrid dry heat of August or the frigid dark cold of January – he wore a tattered thermal underwear shirt under the bib overalls. And he never seemed too hot or too cold.

"Do you believe this collection of knuckleheads made the playoffs?" Tucker asked whimsically.

"I have to admit," I said, "I never saw it coming."

Annie had spotted a group of friends and abandoned me. She sat across the room at a table that held a flock of junior high girls who appeared to be entertained by Dave Dickson's mere presence.

For dessert, Tucker had selected three brownies, each about the size of brick. He was a large man, with large fingers, a large head, and large nose. One of the brownies disappeared in three bites. He didn't seem to have chewed them; they went into his mouth and vanished after he swallowed. It was like a magician's trick; now you see it, now you don't.

"First Stockett kicks the bucket, then Wally Hope quits without even coaching a game," Tucker said. "Then no one wants the job." He shook his shaggy head in astonished dismay. "No one." It was as if he found it all amusing.

"And it's not like we were defending state champions," I said.

"Oh hell, we were crappy last year," Tucker said. "You know, most people don't know this, but really, when you think about it, there was a lot more talent on last year's team than this one."

"Yeah," I agreed, "they kind of underperformed last year."

"And now look at them!" Tucker exclaimed. "I still don't believe it."

"I do," Jodi said quietly.

Only one brownie remained on Tucker's plate. I not only didn't see him chew the second one, I didn't even see him reach for it or stick it in his mouth. Maybe he could will food into his mouth.

"You were the only one then," I said, nicely, I hoped.

She shook her head. "Jersey believed." She hesitated, as if anticipating a contrary opinion. None came. "He believed from the start," she said with quiet defiance.

Jodi had been in the newspaper a couple times through her work at the Jefferson Valley Baptist Church summer bible school program, and judging from her letters to the editor she was militantly against abortion. She had long gray hair and just a hint of a faint downy mustache, but was friendly and adored her twin boys, her only children.

"From the start?" I asked.

"From the start," she confirmed. "Jersey called one day back last summer and then came over to our house to visit with the boys. He talked to them about playing football, and he told them then they would have a chance to play in the championship game."

Tucker groaned. "Come on, honey. All coaches say that." The tone suggested they'd had this debate before.

"He's not *all coaches*. He's a different kind of coach," she said.

Both Tucker and I nodded in agreement. The third brownie was gone. That was impossible. He hadn't even moved.

"The *state* championship game?" I asked Jodi incredulously.

She nodded with certainty. "He's honest, God-fearing and compassionate," Jodi said. "He's a saint, if you ask me."

"I don't know how he saw two football players in those two hellions of ours," Tucker said. "No one else ever did."

"Tucker," Jodi chastised.

"You ever hear him cuss?" Tucker asked me. "Jersey. You ever hear him curse or swear?"

I hadn't. "I don't think so," I said.

"He even got Coach Pete to quit swearing," Jodi said.

"Tell me you saw that coming," Tucker said.

"Yeah, I never saw that coming," I said.

"He comes over to the house every Monday and Wednesday night and helps the boys with their schoolwork," Jodi volunteered.

"Who does?" I asked.

"Coach Pete," she affirmed. "Shows up at seven o'clock each night and works with each boy for an hour each night."

"Really?" I asked. I wasn't sure which surprised me most: Pete serving as a tutor, or me not knowing anything about it.

"He pounds the books into their heads, and even if they mess up he watches his language," marveled Tucker.

"The boys struggle in school a bit, especially in spelling and writing and such," Jodi said.

"Take after their old man," grunted Tucker. "That's why I'm a plumber."

"So Pete works with their English reports and reading and writing, bless his heart," Jodi said. "The boys may not be 'A' students, but they're passing all their classes."

"And staying academically eligible for football," I added, and Tucker nodded, knowingly.

I looked at Pete, who sat across the room, across from Sara Dickson, Dave's tiny, timid mother. He was doing all the talking and gesturing and she all the listening; it was actually unthinkable to have those two roles reversed.

"So Lance, you said you've never heard Jersey cuss?" Tucker asked again.

I returned my attention to Tucker. "Right. Not once."

"You ever see him angry? I mean really mad, like all coaches get."

"Well, there was the late night session in the end zone," I pointed out.

"Yeah, but did he yell and scream and cuss? You heard it and saw it, right?"

"And smelled it," I added. "But no, there was no screaming or cussing."

"You ever see him really yell at a kid?" Tucker asked. "Just pick a kid out and give him holy hell?"

"Not really," I said.

"Think about that," Tucker said. "A coach who don't yell or cuss." He hesitated, to give me a moment to think about it. "I played me some football, and every coach I ever had cursed like a drunk sailor, was always mad about something and was always yelling at someone, usually me. Not Jersey. The boys say he talks so soft they got to strain to hear him."

"And look how hard the boys play for him," Jodi said, practically in awe. She waved an arm. "All of them. Goodness, they work hard. They respect him. That's his secret. That's why they made the playoffs."

"But how could he have known all this before the season even started?" I asked. "No one thought the Rangers were going to win more than a game or two. He's never coached before. How could a coach with no experience, coaching a losing team no one else wanted to touch, say they were going to the title game?"

"He just knew," Jodi said. "He had faith."

"It's not that simple," I told her.

"Sometimes," she said, with the voice of a true believer, "it is."

The Rangers were scheduled to depart for Baker Friday morning about 10:00 o'clock. The cheerleaders had decorated the windows of the bus with the finger-purple painted names of each player with several large *#1* insignias scattered around the bus. The school day had opened with announcements about the game, and after homeroom the entire school – elementary students included – headed to the elementary school gym for an assembly that served as a pep rally to send the team east across Montana.

The band played the school song and the state song, the cheerleaders lined up in front of the bleachers and all five hundred or so kids from kindergarten through high school senior screamed the spelled version of *R-A-N-G-E-R-S* multiple times and raucously participated in thunderous applause.

I had never seen such euphoria inside any Whitehall building. Ever.

The community and student body glee was encouraging, but the Rangers were prohibitive underdogs. Baker entered the game as a conference champion with nine wins, and the Rangers had backed into the playoffs thanks to a Boulder loss. The Rangers had a losing four win, five loss record, and given up more points in their first two games than Baker had surrendered all year. The Great Falls Tribune, in its Thursday article promoting the Class B playoffs, wrote, 'Baker hosts the Whitehall Rangers on Saturday and will then host the winner of the Cut Bank – Frenchtown game the following week.' The Tribune sports writer made that first Baker win a given; an absolute, a fact.

The Ledger article was much more positive of a possible Ranger win, but in truth, the Ledger editor privately agreed with the Tribune sports writer. The Rangers beat only one team with a winning record all year, and that was the miracle victory in Townsend that cost them – the Bulldogs – a trip to the playoffs. My unarticulated hope was the Rangers were neither punished nor embarrassed in Baker. If the Rangers avoided the Mercy Rule – kept the game within thirty-five points – embarrassment could be avoided. The Rangers were in the playoffs, but there was some debate whether they *belonged* in the playoffs. My covert hope was the game in Baker wouldn't prove the Rangers didn't belong.

The elementary school kids were especially fired up. Some of them had siblings on the football team and shared in their glory and accomplishment, and others who didn't follow sports were simply revved up by all the excitement and enthusiasm.

Jersey, however, was calm. He looked like a guy standing in line at the post office as he stood and listened to a boisterous Ed Franklin thank the band, salute the cheerleaders and elicit still louder cheers by yelling questions like *Are we proud of our Rangers?*

Standing on the gym floor, in the middle of the tip-ball basketball circle at half court, Jersey accepted the microphone and for some reason, without being encouraged to do so, the crowd quieted down. Perhaps they were unsure if Jersey would chastise them again, as he had after the *Na na na na, na na na na, goodbye* episode at the end of the Big Timber game a week earlier. He wore all black; turtleneck and dress slacks.

He thanked the fans, the faculty, the administration. He thanked the students, the band, the cheerleaders. He thanked Coach Pete, who received a large ovation, which he acknowledged sheepishly. He thanked his players, and then he introduced them, one by one, and each received a nice round of applause. Dave Dickson, the smallest Ranger, received the largest cheer.

To close the assembly, the band played *Born to Run,* with Bonner on lead guitar and vocals, and everyone cheered and clapped. But immediately afterward Ed, taking a hint from Jersey's wardrobe and wearing a black dress shirt and black jeans, took the microphone and announced the pep rally wasn't quite over. There was going to be a final skit, he said, then the band would play the school song, and after that the students and faculty would form a human tunnel from the elementary gym to the bus to send the Rangers with as much school spirit as they could manufacture.

There was a momentary buzzing from the smaller kids in the stands because skits were fun, skits were unpredictable and skits meant you weren't in the classroom. Many of the elementary school kids may not have understood the Ranger football team, may not have understood the significance or stunning reality of the Rangers qualifying for the playoffs, may not have understood where Baker, Montana, was or that the team would be boarding a bus in fifteen minutes or so for the epic trip east down I-90 and I-94 to Montana oil and coal and cattle country, but they did understand something unusual, something special and something exciting was in the air.

The cheerleaders, led by Holly and the O'Toole girls, their purple and gold pompoms flying, led the boisterous, even silly, grade school kids in a raucous cheer that ended with the demand that everyone stand up and holler. And everyone did.

Ed motioned for the kids to sit, and amidst chatter and youthful energy, out from the doors leading to the locker rooms, strolled a somber handful of Ranger football players, all still wearing their jerseys. Logan, Colt, Morgan, Nate, JeffScott, Cale, Brock, Chance, Corey, and Cody. They were attempting to imitate a group of serious football players, but there was too much energy and emotion for them to actually appear serious. They stopped about midway toward the gym floor, near what would be the scorer's table at a basketball game. They sat down in a loosely formed circle, and Colt said something no one could hear above the din of noise from the audience.

A flurry of *shushes* quieted the crowd, and Corey said something about how the Rangers had no chance to win the game, how they – the Rangers – should feel lucky just to get in the playoffs. People in the bleachers responded with a half-hearted chorus of playful boos. Behind the circle of players, Jersey and Ed stood near the microphone stand, watching with bemusement. In a phony actor's voice, Nate whimpered about the quality of Baker's team, how they'd won nearly all their games and had earned their way into the playoffs. Brock allowed that he wasn't sure we – the Rangers – deserved to make the playoffs. That resulted in a few more good-natured boos.

The group of Rangers sat dejectedly, shoulders slumped, lamenting their downtrodden status and their losing record.

Then a figure emerged from beneath the bleachers. It was Tony. It was Jersey.

It was Tony as Jersey.

Tony even managed a fair imitation of Jersey's slow, long stride. He wore sunglasses, a black dress shirt, black slacks, and his hair was wet and dark and sculpted as much like Christopher Reeves' Superman as Jersey's. The crowd slowly, gradually, understood what was happening, and the cheers built into a roar as Tony strolled toward Jersey and Ed. Tony extended his hand and shook Ed's hand, and just like Jersey, Tony reached with his left hand and held Ed's shoulder briefly. Ed, I swear, never looked happier in his life. Tony stepped to the left and did the same with an amused and perplexed Jersey. They didn't look like twins, but they could have been brothers. When the two shook hands – both with a reassuring and brief grasp of the shoulder – the intensity of the roar from the crowd was deafening. Tony calmly reached for the microphone, expertly slipped it off the microphone stand, flipped the cord to avoid the stand, and turned – in the same sort of dipped-shoulder way Jersey would have – and faced the audience. He raised his hands to quiet the crowd, just as Jersey had a week earlier at the end of the Big Timber game. It was an eerie physical imitation.

"You'll cheer when I tell you to cheer!" Tony said, with *cheer* clipped into *cheeia* in Jersey's Jersey accent.

Jersey silently laughed, lowered his chin, and shook his head. Ed absolutely beamed. Ed had been a school administrator over three decades, and somehow, I sensed, this was a highlight of his public, professional and personal life. He had known about, and approved this skit. My guess was only Ed, Tony and the seated Rangers knew what was happening and what would happen next. Coach Pete's face was flushed red with joy and his eyes beamed an exuberant *Do you believe this?* expression.

The crowd quieted down as Tony solemnly approached the Rangers, then entered the circle of players and stood in the middle. The kids in the audience fell virtually silent, as if they truly wanted to hear what Tony as Jersey would say next. *I* wanted to hear what Tony said next. I also wondered how he'd looted Jersey's wardrobe. I tried to find Annie in the bleachers, to see what she thought of all this, but I couldn't find her in the sea of faces. I saw Mary, who held her hands clasped under her chin, enthralled with the performance.

"Lift your heads," Tony ordered. The seated Rangers immediately obeyed. "Lift your spirits. Lift your hearts." *Hearts* was *hahrts*. "We are (*ahh*) a team, and we've had a great year!" *Year* was *yeeah* and Tony nailed the inflection and rhythm of Jersey's voice.

The Ranger players nodded on cue, but unconvincingly.

Tony looked around the circle, face to face, at each of the players.

"Take pride," Tony said. "Take pride not in yourselves, but in your accomplishments, your accomplishments as a team. Individually you cannot achieve success on a football field, but together, together as a team, you can rise to glory!"

The players nodded with a little more enthusiasm, and the crowd applauded and cheered.

"Remember in August, when we first began this journey together," Tony began. His shoulders, under the silky black shirt, were somehow even broader than normal, nearly as broad as Jersey's. "We learned from Shawn Davis that the difference between average and excellence is embodied in three simple traits. Preparation, determination and execution. We were average when this campaign began. We are now excellent!"

More cheering, more applause.

"Where's my jacket?" Tony called out.

On cue, Dave Dickson rushed out from the locker room, carrying a black leather jacket. It probably was Jersey's actual jacket, because it looked two sizes too big for Tony. Tony turned and from the back Dave slipped on the black leather coat as the crowd cheered. Oh, it was great theater.

"Champions prepare, champions exude determination, and champions execute with precision, poise and excellence," Tony said. "Gentlemen, we are prepared. We are *righteously* prepared! Practice after practice, we prepared as champions, to be champions. Game after game, our diligence and dedication proved we could play like champions! Gentleman, there are sixteen Class B teams still playing football in Montana and *none of them* is more prepared to be a champion than the Whitehall Rangers!" Tony thundered.

Mary lifted her head and cheered toward the sky.

"And you ask about determination?" Tony said, as if someone had actually asked about determination. He spoke a slower, more conversational tone of voice. "We lost our first four football games. We lost those four games by over a total of one hundred points. Had there not been a mercy rule, it would have been over two hundred points."

A few high school students booed, and Tony lifted his head from the seated Rangers up toward the bleachers, and the booing stopped instantly.

"But remember the west end zone in Whitehall after a bus ride from Cascade," Tony told the Rangers. "Remember the pain, the sweat, the anger. Remember the vomit. Remember the smell. Remember the determination to never again fail to give our best effort. Remember our collective determination that night to never, ever, ever, ever fail to give it our best effort as a team. Remember the win the next week, remember the determination in Townsend, remember the heart and strength and purpose we displayed to rally for victory, and remember the sheer force and conviction we showed in winning our final three conference games. And above all, remember this. I say to you, carry this – all of you – in your hearts." He hesitated. He and the sunglasses surveyed the gym. "To those who suggest Whitehall doesn't deserve to be in the playoffs, let me say this. *No one* deserves to be in the playoffs more than the Rangers!" Crowd roar. "No team is more determined than the Whitehall Rangers!" Crowd roar. "We *are* Whitehall and we *will* be champions!"

Kids and teachers jumped to their feet as one and cheered. Ed had both hands above his head as he cheered.

The seated Rangers jumped up and huddled in a unified embrace as the WHS pep band improbably launched into an impossibly loud encore version of Springsteen's *Born to Run*, with Bonner Labuda blasting away on the guitar and Carrie Lindstrom – interestingly wearing a black leather jacket and sunglasses – wailing on the saxophone.

The students and faculty cheered and kind of stomped and danced as they moved en masse from the bleachers toward the gym floor. Surprisingly fast, the entire student body started to form two parallel human lines from the middle of the gym, up the aisle, out the west door of the gym, into the parking lot to the decorated WHS bus that awaited to transport the Ranger team to Baker. It was the first human tunnel I'd seen from Whitehall fans, yet there they were, a few feet apart from each another, arms raised up and over the space across from each other. Hundreds of kids of all ages lined up, with teachers and parents and school administrators intermixed, every face regardless of age flushed with joy and passion and simple unrestrained thrill as the Ranger players lined up and spaced about twenty feet apart made their way through the tunnel, slapping outstretched hands, some of the players yelling as they went, accepting embraces, shoulder squeezes and at times even a quick kiss from a sibling or girlfriend or mother. Slowly, one by one, they made their way through the tunnel and into the Ranger bus. Then I spotted Annie, just outside the bus, standing alongside Trisha and her wheelchair. They must have been positioned near a gym door, to make a quick exit to reach the bus in time to terminate the tunnel. The players each acknowledged Annie and then Trish, who wore Colt Harrison's home number seven jersey. Some players hugged her, some patted her head, some slapped her hands, but the final action for each player before boarding the bus and leaving town was some gesture of affection toward Trisha, and some hazy gesture of affection from her to them. Tony, still dressed as Jersey, and Annie embraced before he climbed on the bus. Then Tony and Aspen embraced for another twenty seconds.

Then, to our amazement, the team was on board, the doors swung closed, the wheels started to turn and the highly decaled and decorated bus began to crawl away from the curb. We cheered as the Rangers departed; then we found ourselves waving toward the back end of a bus. And for a moment, oddly, as the bus turned the corner out of the parking lot north onto Whitehall Street, toward the I-90 onramp and out of sight, it was like something incredibly important had just vacated our now suddenly silent and empty lives.

Chapter 31

We were four in the Escort, part of a loose and informal caravan from Whitehall to Baker, 425 miles east down the Yellowstone River to the South Dakota border. Annie rode shotgun and in the backseat was the remarkably mismatched tandem of Rhonda Horst and Bonner Labuda, two people who had absolutely nothing in common outside of Ranger football.

A handful of WHS family and friends were heading to Baker. Lyle and the O'Toole girls filled their Suburban, Slack and his parents were making a weekend of it and planned to do some upland bird hunting after the game on Sunday on the way home. Trish joined her mother, Molly, who drove the pep bus. The pep bus, carrying cheerleaders, some band members together with a few parents and siblings of players, was scheduled to pull out of the WHS high school parking lot at three o'clock Saturday morning, the day of the game. Annie demanded an earlier departure – Friday at three o'clock in the afternoon – with the intention of spending the night in Miles City, a place Rhonda, Bonner and Annie had never seen before. I'd been there twice, once for a power company conference during my days with MPC, and later, still with MPC, to attend the infamous Miles City Bucking Horse Sale, part of a media junket with some east coast reporters. The first trip was uneventful. The second trip was eventful, thanks to an staggering overindulgence of alcohol.

Annie mouthed the words to *Darkness on the Edge of Town* as we sped east on I-90 away from the setting sun and into the edge of darkness. She looked like a waif inside Tony's purple football jersey. Her hair had been cut, I realized, and seemed not just shorter but thicker, perhaps even a shade darker. A downy twist of wispy blonde just below her hairline on the back of her neck – running vertically along her spine – reflected the dimming light behind her.

She was so small, in both height and weight, that I wondered when, and if, she would mature into a more substantial physical presence. I also wondered how it was possible for so much intelligence, so much passion and so much strength to be packaged inside such an insubstantial frame.

As the Escort chugged up the pass east of Bozeman, while golden yellow trees absorbed the dying light on a ridge to our right, I wondered absently how we were going to do the motel check-in in Miles City. It wasn't practical for all four of us to share one room. I didn't want to split up with Annie and it was unlikely Bonner and Rhonda would share a room, so it was possible we'd need three rooms, and I had a hunch I was going to end up paying for all three of them. It was possible we weren't going to get to Miles City until close to midnight, and my guess was you could count on one hand during the past ten years the number of times Rhonda had been still awake at midnight. The plan was to eat a quick supper in Billings; Rhonda's banana muffins would tide us over until then.

Bonner had shown up at the Ledger precisely when we were leaving town. I had given final instructions to Laura Joyce about closing up early and walked with Rhonda and Annie to the car when Bonner – wearing his black stocking cap and a sooty black winter jacket – strolled up to the car as if we'd been waiting for him. Annie looked as surprised as me when he asked if we had room. He carried not a single possession with him; not a toothbrush, not a change of clothes, not a bar of soap, not a thing. And not a cent, I was sure. I asked him if he knew Baker was over an 800-mile round trip from Whitehall, if he knew the game was played the following afternoon and if he knew we had to spend at least one night in a motel. He uttered something that sounded like a grunt as he slid into the backseat. I couldn't tell him no; it would have been like kicking a stray dog off your doorstep.

Before I started the car in Whitehall I told Annie to get in back and let Rhonda sit in the front, but Rhonda protested, and started to butter four banana muffins.

Two hours out of town headlights were on but essentially useless as a soft gray twilight filtered light through the Yellowstone Valley. Thirty minutes later we passed a government sign announcing a prairie dog town, and it was too dark to see any animals off the road.

"Everybody thinks Lewis and Clark named them," Annie said. "But French trappers named them first. The prairie dog." She paused. "Just think if they'd been named prairie rats. I doubt they'd still be around."

"They look sort of like a rat," I said. "More like a rat than a dog."

Annie said, "Actually, their genus, *Cynomys*, derives from the Greek for *mouse dog*. They bark like a dog, but they also squeal or shriek almost like a whistle."

"I've never seen a single prairie dog my whole life," admitted Bonner. "I wouldn't know one if it jumped in my lap and read me a comic book."

"Ahht," said Rhonda whimsically from behind me, in the darkness of the backseat. "Dey kant reat."

"It's impressive they can even survive," Annie offered. "Anything that eats meat on the North American prairie eats them. Hawks, eagles, wolves, coyotes, foxes, badgers, snakes, ferrets. Prairie dogs defend their village with vigilance, but up on the ground they're basically a furry meal. Their tunnels are engineered wonders with a sophisticated network of escape hatches, so to speak. You have to admire them. They found a way to exist."

"That's the longest I've ever heard anyone talk about prairie dogs," Bonner said. There was a hint of awe in his voice.

"She con do dat about anytink," Rhonda said, also with a hint of accented awe.

We gassed up in Laurel and voted for Burger King for dinner. We surrounded a white plastic table and I browsed through the Billings Gazette as I ate my Whopper. I have always – even before owning the Ledger – enjoyed paging through newspapers. I like the feel, the smell, the look of a broadsheet newspaper. Newspapers provide a vast amount of information; the articles, the headlines, the reporting, the layout or placement of the article, the photos, even the advertising. A newspaper is like a window into a community, and a reflection of the people who live there. The editorial page – especially letters to the editor – is always my favorite section of a newspaper. The Gazette at Burger King had been paged through all day by dozens of ketchup-stained fingers, but the editorial section was less battered than the others. The editorial, a brief piece supporting the U.S. House of Representatives vote rejecting the Reagan administration's 'Star Wars' policy, had no real relevance to the people of Laurel, Billings or Yellowstone County. That was why the editorial section had largely been ignored by diners all day at the Burger King.

"Get a load of this," said Bonner. He held up a battered sports page. Annie was reading the front page and Rhonda was pretending to read the rules of some contest on the side of a plastic Pepsi cup. We all looked up at Bonner. "Says here Baker's gonna cream Whitehall." We all looked up at him, and his dark brown eyes panicked briefly under the brim of his stocking cap when he realized we were waiting for him to read the article out loud. He quickly shifted the paper to Annie. She started mentally reading the article, scowled, and moments later lowered the paper.

"It's an overall article about the Class B playoffs, and the Baker coach is quoted as saying his team will have a tough game on the road next week in Fairfield," Annie said. She lifted her eyes to the heavens "When will they learn?"

"Baker plays Whitehall," I said. I had a fleeting terrifying thought that we were on the way to Baker when Whitehall actually played somewhere else.

"*Next week* against Fairfield," Annie stressed. "Listen. Here's how the article goes. *Whitehall backed into the playoffs with a 4-5 record after Manhattan upset Boulder, and travels to 8-1 Baker on Saturday. In other action, Fairfield hosts Superior, undefeated Fort Benton hosts Plentywood and undefeated Ennis hosts Troy. Superior is the only other playoff team with a losing record, also at 4-5, but beat Stevensville for a playoff spot. Whitehall is led by junior running back Logan Bradshaw and is making its first playoff appearance in several years. The Rangers lost to Columbus 56-6, while Baker easily handled Columbus 41-0 later in the year, which may make the game in Baker on Saturday a lopsided affair.* Okay, here's what the Baker coach says." Annie looked up at us, then back at the paper. *"We'd like to rest a couple kids in the second half to make sure we're healthy next week in Fairfield,' said Frolich. "Fairfield is loaded with talent, but we match up with them pretty well."* Annie looked up again. "*Frolich and the Spartans are 6-0 in home playoff games the past five years. "Western Montana teams especially have a tough time crossing the eastern Montana badlands and playing on our field," said Frolich. "Our kids are always ready to play, and some of the less disciplined teams are a little intimidated by us."*

"I wonder if we even have a chance," I said.

"Sure, we have a chance," Annie said. "The Baker coach says less disciplined teams are intimidated. If there's one thing the Rangers got going for them, it's discipline."

Rhonda held up a thin little tab she'd pulled off her cup. "I yust von free foot."

There was no real need for a discussion about room or sleeping arrangements. We arrived in Miles City before eleven o'clock and immediately understood – as evidenced by the Blue Pony team bus parked lengthwise on the edge of a motel parking lot and an abundance of number 12 license plates – that Havre High School was in town for a Saturday game against the Miles City High Cowboys football team. Just like the Class AA, Class B, eight man and six man football playoffs, Class A playoffs were under way and Miles City was full of Havre High fans.

Montana's license plates designate a county by number. License plates starting with *51* were from Jefferson County. We were the only fifty-one license plate I saw in the parking lot. Nearly all the vehicles had 12 license plates, and many of them had soap-lettered words of support on the back windows, things like *Go, Blue Ponies*, *Jeff #21*, *Blue Ponies Ride to Victory* and *Honk for Havre*.

The four of us tentatively approached the motel lobby. Annie looked half asleep and Bonner, with his stocking cap pulled low, looked like a convict. Rhonda, her scarf tied tight under her chin and her flesh tone somehow bluish under the motel's fluorescent lights, was a couple strides behind me when I approached the registration desk. A doughy looking college kid staffed the front desk and an older guy, a horseshoe of curly black hair around a bald head, was on the telephone off to the kid's right.

"Do you have a reservation?" the kid asked hopefully when I asked if a room was available.

I grimaced and shook my head.

"Sorry," the kid said, as if he meant it, "we're full up."

"Football game?" I asked.

"Yeah," the kid said, nodding. He wore a shirt buttoned at the neck with a collar that was so loose it barely touched his skin. A two-tone brown tie that had to be older than the kid, possibly older than the motel itself, hung crooked from the collar. The kid's grandpa, I thought, maybe wore that tie.

"Is there a room available anywhere in town?" I asked, knowing the answer.

The kid shook his head. "I doubt it. We're full. I'm pretty sure everything's full. I think the whole town of Havre's here tonight."

The bald guy on the phone was half listening to our conversation and half listening to whoever was talking on the phone. His dark brown eyes snuck furtive glances at Rhonda, who absently looked around the lobby as if she was lost or worried. The harsh lobby lights played games with her color; her facial skin was tinted blue, but her lips were more yellow or an unnatural orange. She wasn't listening to my conversation with the hotel clerk. She wasn't listening to anyone or anything. She was simply waiting for whatever happened next, however long it took, whatever it turned out to be.

"Where's the nearest place we can stay?" I asked the clerk.

The kid sort of shrugged. "Glendive?" he asked.

"Glendive?" said Annie dreamily from behind me. The lights were so bright and she was so sleepy she was squinting. I had to get her to bed. "We're not going to Glendive. That's that way." She pointed. "We have to go that way." She pointed a different direction.

"There's no rooms in Miles City," I told Annie.

"All full up," the clerk confirmed. "Sorry."

The dark bald guy had hung up the telephone behind the registration desk and in what seemed like slow motion, approached Rhonda, and to my absolute amazement carefully reached out, held both her hands in his hands, and started talking to her in a foreign language.

She responded in what was probably the same language, whatever language it was, and he cooed to her as if she were his fiancé. She shyly lowered her eyes and smiled, and he patted her hands as she patted his.

"I think they're talking Polish," Annie whispered to me.

My eyes questioned the desk clerk. "He's the owner," he told me softly as the owner and Rhonda spoke quietly to each other. "Gustov Zamoyski. We all call him Gus."

"He's Polish, right?" Annie said.

The clerk nodded. "His whole family is."

Annie looked like she was about to add something, something possibly sarcastic, but resisted the temptation.

Moments later he suddenly broke away from Rhonda, eyed me fiercely, glared at me as if he doubted I was acceptable, then gave me one firm nod, man to man. Sternly, he grabbed a key from a drawer to his left, and pressed the key firmly in Rhonda's hands. He leaned across the counter and kissed her softly on the forehead, just below the edge of her scarf.

"Go," Gus said, and waved me away. "Room two-two-two. Is under renovation. Smell like paint. But clean. Very clean. You go." He waved us away again. "Go now."

We obeyed. I had a sense we had just been extremely fortunate in a remarkably unique way, but with Annie leading the way, Bonner right behind her and Rhonda and me together bringing up the rear, we found room two-two-two, which when we opened the door we discovered had been freshly painted. The instant I noticed the bed had no pillows and no blankets, the doughy desk clerk showed up at the door with an armful of pillows and blankets.

"We don't have any more rollaways, sorry," the kid said. "There's just the one bed. Here's some sheets and a blanket for the bed, and here's some extra pillows and extra blankets."

The kid stood there for a second, and Annie slipped him a couple dollar bills before I realized his hesitation in departing.

Annie opened up the window a crack; the outside air would help diminish the paint smell. I went down to the car to fetch our luggage – Annie's backpack and an old green suitcase I had from college – and when I returned Annie and Rhonda had the bed made and fluffed up, crisp pillows propped up against the wall. The room had no television, no headboard for the bed and no hangers in the open closet. But it was a room, and it was ours. It was also, apparently, free. We had a bathroom, with running water. Rhonda was not present, and I heard her in the bathroom.

"My guess is the roof leaked or something and caused water damage," said Bonner. "This wall's new," he laid the flat of his hand on the wall to his right, "but the other walls are old. You can smell the wood here. And you can see the old floor grooves and baseboard of the other walls."

It was the longest statement I had ever heard Bonner utter in my life, and it was the first statement I ever heard from him that suggested he possessed knowledge about something. I looked blankly at him; fatigue had settled in and confused blankness was the best I could muster.

"Same thing happened to our trailer," Bonner said, as if he felt a need to explain. "My brother and me patched the roof and had to put in a new sidewall."

"I have to sleep," was my response.

"You got the floor, Lance," Annie said. "Rhonda and I get the bed. You two'll have to figure out how you'll configure yourselves."

"How we'll what?" asked Bonner.

Half an hour later we had completed our turns in the bathroom, the lights were off, the window open a narrow slit, the two females in bed and Bonner and me on the floor, sleeping horizontally two feet apart at the foot of the bed. I was drowsy, but I couldn't sleep. It wasn't that I was uncomfortable; the blankets and pillow made the floor more tolerable.

"Go to sleep, Lance," Annie told me from above. It was pitch black in the room. A scant sliver of light from the parking lot sliced along one edge of a thick window curtain, but the light dissipated before it actually illuminated anything.

"How do you know I'm awake?" I asked.

"I can tell."

"Ya, schleep," Rhonda told me. "You neet it."

"How come that guy gave us a free room?" I asked her. "Because you're both Polish?"

"No," Rhonda said. She had worn a thick wool robe to bed, with her hair under a different scarf than the one she'd worn all day. Without her glasses on she looked one hundred and twenty years old. "Jewish."

"You're Jewish?" I asked the darkness.

"So what if she is?" asked Annie.

"I guess I just never knew," I said defensively. I was not up for a debate with Annie. It was nearly one a.m. and I was sleeping on a carpetless wood floor in Miles City after driving an Escort for over seven hours. "I guess I really never thought about it."

"Jewish?" asked Bonner. "Like the Bible?"

The pause from Annie meant one of two things. She was either controlling her zeal to verbally tear Bonner apart, or she was hesitating to make her correction and tutorial more relaxed and understood.

"Yeah," Annie said, and simply sighed a weak little laugh, "like the Bible." She was, thankfully, letting Bonner slide.

"So Rhonda," I asked. "How'd a sweet Polish Jewish girl like you get all the way to Whitehall, Montana?"

"Da hart vay," she answered, and those were the final words spoken in room two-two-two that night.

The shower in the room next to me, possibly room two-two-three – with the water hitting the other side of the wall a couple feet from my head – woke me up a little after seven o'clock, but the next thing I knew it was eight-thirty and someone in our bathroom was running what sounded like bathwater. Bonner was to my left, on his back, his stocking cap pulled low over his eyes, his hands crossed over his chest as if resting in a coffin.

I sat up and saw the bed was empty. I figured it was Rhonda taking the bath. The bed was empty. It was hard to guess where Annie was.

Continuous consumption of Pepsi during the drive the night before necessitated a definite and prompt need for me to use a bathroom, but of the many things Rhonda and I couldn't share, a bathroom topped the list. I had worn my clothes – shoes and all – to bed, and sixty seconds after I awoke I was walking down the hall to the motel lobby area where there had to be a bathroom. On the way down the hall I saw a door was cracked open and lights on, and I got the feeling its occupants had already checked out. I stopped and peeked in; the room was empty. I stepped inside and took a leisurely and lengthy leak, and as I emerged from the room I nearly bumped into Annie, who was carrying a cup of coffee in one hand and a bag filled with bakery pastries in the other.

She looked past me into the room, heard the toilet finish its flush, offered just a barest and briefest puzzled expression, but said nothing. She held up the bag as if to say, *Follow me.*

The door was locked, and I had failed to take a key. Annie had not failed, and let us in. We found Bonner, stocking cap on, face up, still sound asleep, this time on the bed. His mouth was open, as if uttering the word *who* and his breath flowed evenly with a rattled murmur. It was the same rattled murmur I had heard all night.

"Game day, Bonner," Annie proclaimed. She leaned over the bed. "Breakfast is served." She took a donut hole and placed it daintily inside Bonner's mouth, then pressed down. He gagged, coughed, choked and awoke.

He realized his mouth was filled with food, so he chewed, wiped his mouth with the back of his hand, swallowed, and took another donut hole. The coffee was for him, not Rhonda.

"Are these homemade?" I asked.

"Yep," said Annie. "Rhonda's got a grocery bag filled with eats and treats. There's even a pan of brownies for later, after the game."

The game. We had four hours to get to Baker. We had plenty of time, but I had a sudden urge to get rolling. It struck me as exciting, suddenly, that we were halfway across Montana to watch our family, our high school kids, our friends and neighbors, play in a high school playoff football game.

The bathroom reeked of something – some kind of pungent flower – after Rhonda exited. I jumped in for a quick shower. Annie followed with a shower and Bonner maybe – maybe not – washed his face. I'm pretty certain the stocking cap was never removed.

The Escort, to my surprise, had large soaped lettering across the back window. Annie's sly grin told me who was responsible. The top line of the lettering read *Whitehall Rangers* and the bottom line, in a little larger writing, read *Born to Win*.

"Tramps like us," I told Annie.

"Baby, we were born to win," she sang.

"Perfect," I told her. "Absolutely perfect."

"Let's go kick some badland Baker butt." Annie said it as if she meant it.

A ninety-minute straight shot on a flat prairie Highway 12 east brought us toward Baker. Bruce was cranked up so loud the speakers cackled and hissed between songs. Between songs I asked Rhonda if I should turn the music down and she shook her head. "Lout is goot today."

Springsteen's songs of urban angst were diametrically out of place among the dry, dusty and isolated prairies of eastern Montana. The country was much like Whitehall, except more sparse, more dry and more barren. Cows, sagebrush, petroleum derricks, dilapidated fences and old, desolate and abandoned homesteads dotted a yellow and brittle landscape.

A large maroon sign proclaiming Baker was *Home of the Spartans*, greeted us as we eased from the flatlands onto pavement and the dwellings of town. Baker was a classic Montana water tower town – a handful of western-themed bars, a couple churches gussied up with oil money, paved main streets without curbs or gutters and dusty dirt roads on the other streets, a three-block commercial district with one vacant building on each block. We headed straight to the football field – found by looking for the light poles – and got there over an hour before game time. Rhonda and Annie produced homemade whole wheat bread from the Escort's trunk and some kind of honey butter or something as a spread.

I spotted Tony right away, number twenty-three, loping under a punt, catching it, and sprinting about ten yards upfield.

Bonner ate half the bread loaf himself. He held up a piece of bread lathered with butter. "This is without doubt the best bread and the best butter I have had in my whole life." He looked directly at me, as if I had doubted him. "I'm serious," he assured me. "The best ever. I had no idea bread and butter could taste so good."

"Accht," said Rhonda, smiling. She dismissed him with a wave.

"I'll tell you what," he told her. "If you were a hundred years younger I'd marry you."

Rhonda laughed. "Not wid dat hat," she said, pointing to his head.

The weather was cool and cloudy, but the wind was gentle without a hint of moisture in the air. Both teams were on the field warming up, and both of the sidelines began filling with fans. Everyone in Baker wore the maroon and gold colors of the Spartans. Maroon and gold cheerleaders bounced around the sidelines. The home bleachers were painted maroon, the announcer's booth was painted gold, one end zone was maroon and one was gold, and the concession stand was maroon with a large silhouette of a classic Greek Spartan. It was all first class. Everything about the field broadcast success, quality and confidence.

You could see it in the eyes of the Baker fans, especially the men wearing the maroon and gold windbreakers and clean going-to-town cowboy hats. Baker was a traditional ranch community with a flourish of recent oil money mixed in. Even the handful of what looked like bankers and oil executives wore cowboy hats.

Most of them offered us a look of sympathy, or perhaps mild resignation. Everyone in Baker seemed to offer silent condolences to us, this ragtag handful of purple people from Whitehall, a place with no tradition and a team without even a winning record. The somber glances were all but spoken and tangible: *You came a long way, you Whitehall folks did, to end the season with a miserable lopsided loss in a game more than likely decided by the middle of the first quarter. We know you're excited, we know you're optimistic, but we've seen it before, we know how it ends, and sorry, but it doesn't end good for you.*

The Baker people were friendly enough; friendly in the same way you're friendly with a guy who just got laid off his job.

The *Whitehall Rangers, Born to Win* lettering on the back of the Escort got a fair amount of scoffs by Baker kids as they walked past us to their side of the field.

"Born to be beat," one bulky Baker kid said from under a large black Stetson as he walked by. He looked directly at Bonner when he said it.

"Oh the boys try to look so hard," Bonner said, licking honey butter off his fingers.

"Brusch," acknowledged Rhonda.

The WHS pep bus delivered about forty groggy and subdued Whitehall adults to the field about twenty minutes before kickoff. Ed and Alice Franklin were the first to exit. Hank and Kathleen Harrison followed, then Martha Cullen, Slack and Sue Henkel. The mayor, Luke Grayling, stretched as he stepped out of the bus, and Rachel Brockton, to my surprise, stern and straight, emerged next. And then, to my complete surprise, stepped out mangy Young Tom Langston followed by spindly and unsteady Old Tom Langston. Cal Walker stepped out wearing a large white cowboy hat, followed by Mary Kristofferson, wearing a new shiny purple Ranger windbreaker. A clutch of parents were next, most of them wearing purple, including Dave Dickson's diminutive mother, Sara, Nate Bolton's mom and dad, Tanner Walker's dad and stepmom, JeffScott's parents and siblings, a few other parents and then, from the back of the bus, came the kids. The WHS students emerged with substantially more energy than the older folks, and immediately moved toward the sidelines where the Rangers were warming up. All told, there were probably fifty to sixty WHS fans on our side of the field. That was a pretty good turnout, since it was substantially larger than the crowd at the first home game two months earlier.

The back of the school bus opened and the ramp for Trisha slid down. Molly assisted with the wheelchair down the ramp, and Trish and Molly both were resplendent in their Ranger purple. Gold and purple pom-poms were affixed to the handles of Trish's wheelchair. The spokes of her wheelchair held some sort of kaleidoscope of twisting and shimmering purple and gold.

Baker's assessment of impending Ranger doom had not yet sunk in. Whitehall didn't look like or act like losers. Possibly it stemmed from youthful excitement, or maybe from community enthusiasm, or more likely from pure athletic ignorance, but looking at us, you'd have thought we had a chance to win.

I took my camera out, walked across the field, and positioned myself on the Baker sidelines, the sun at my back, the Ranger bench across the field. The time of day and weather were perfect for football. I could use my big lens without a flash and shoot at high speed. Photos would be no problem.

Coach Pete prowled the Whitehall sidelines with his distinctive limp but with such aggressive intensity he shook and trembled as if in a violent rage. He kept adjusting his hat and twitching his shoulders as if something was crawling on him. He huddled the defense in front of the bench and kept screaming – *Respect! Respect! Respect!*

Jersey stood motionless from the sidelines as he privately addressed Dave Dickson. Jersey looked as if they could have been discussing the relative merits of properly inflated truck tires. But Dave couldn't stand still. His helmeted head nodded a couple times, he clapped his hands, and he said something that made Jersey laugh and tenderly pat Dave on the top of the helmet. I noticed Dave wore white wristbands. I didn't remember him wearing wristbands all year.

I felt more like Coach Pete – wound tight and short of breath – than I would have thought. Caught up in the moment, some people called it. My body tingled. I could feel my heart race. I checked the camera shutter speed six times in five minutes. Then I checked it again.

The Baker High School band lined up across the field at the thirty yard line and the players of both teams stood motionless throughout the national anthem. The Baker crowd sang the words in a loud and deliberate chorus and collectively whooped as the final note drifted with the slight breeze east toward South Dakota. There was an exuberant confidence from the Baker side of the field. They couldn't wait for the game to start, for the rout to get under way. In a way, I was dreading the start of the game. We still had a chance as long as the score was tied at zero.

But that didn't last long. Baker won the toss and took the ball. Eight plays later – all running plays – the Spartans were in the end zone and took a seven to nothing lead. Baker had a pair of lean, strong running backs and they each had about thirty yards on four carries. There were no long runs on the drive, just five to ten yards a carry, almost every carry. Tony made half the tackles ten yards downfield. If Baker had a script, I imagined it went something like winning the toss and marching easily downfield for a quick and demoralizing touchdown. It took us twenty hours from the time we left Whitehall to the time we arrived in Baker. It took four minutes for the Rangers to fall behind during the game.

Tony returned the kickoff about ten yards to the Whitehall twenty-five yard line. Dave faked a handoff to Logan and was about to give the ball to Nate when a Baker defensive lineman leveled Dave from behind. On second down a screen pass floated over Nate's head and on third and long Dave was sacked for a ten-yard loss.

It was exactly what the Baker players and fans thought would happen. They'd seen it over and over; teams with playoff dreams come to Baker where the dream dies. It was also, unfortunately, the way I anticipated the game would start. But even if you think it's going to happen, it's still painful to watch it happen. The Whitehall sidelines were already quiet. Annie sat stoically with her elbows on her knees and her chin in her hands. To her left sat Trish, in her bright purple and gold wheelchair, cheering and applauding as if she by herself could will the Rangers to victory.

Baker took over at its own forty yard line and three plays later was on the Whitehall forty yard line. The Baker fullback lowered his head for six yards. The Spartan halfback slashed off tackle for nine more yards and a first down. But on first and goal from the eight yard line the Spartan halfback spun around Cale Bolling's tackle into the arms of Colt Harrison, who pulled the ball away from the Baker ball carrier. When the two of them – Colt and the Baker halfback – fell to the ground Colt somehow had possession of the ball. It was first time all year any Ranger defender had actually stripped the ball from an opponent.

The Rangers got a first down on a quarterback sweep to the short side of the field, but Dave took a shot from a linebacker that sent him flying out of bounds. The Baker fans applauded the hit, and Dave even got a smattering of recognition when he bounced to his feet and ran back to the huddle. Dave faked a handoff to Logan on the next play and followed Logan off tackle for five yards. I had trouble finding the ball – as usual – with Dave's fakes in the backfield, and I realized the wristbands were part of the trickery. The white on his wrists mirrored the white stripes on each end of the ball, with tan arms and hands matching the brown ends and center of the ball. The announcer in the broadcasting booth also had difficulty at times finding the ball. Three times in the first two drives he had to correct himself and change the name of the Whitehall ball carrier.

The Whitehall drive stalled at midfield, and Colt's punt pinned Baker inside its own ten yard line. It took Baker thirteen plays to cover the ninety yards and score a touchdown midway through the second quarter that put the Spartans up by two touchdowns.

Across the field, the Ranger faithful looked like they were losing faith. Coach Pete stood in front of both JeffScott twins and screamed at them so loud I heard him – *You GOT TO penetrate! They're beating you off the ball EVERY time!* – all the way across the field. I spotted Rhonda, seated next to Sara Dickson, all four of their legs under a blanket, both wearing scarves tied neatly under their chins. They sat like thin birds on a railing somehow anticipating bad news.

Whitehall – with Logan pounding the middle for short yardage – got a couple more first downs, including one on a twelve-yard completion from Dave to Tony. Just on the Baker side of the field, the Spartans held on third and short and with a little over three minutes left in the half Jersey called a timeout. He talked quietly to Dave while Coach Pete verbally abused the offensive line. Dave and Jersey opted to go for it on fourth down and a little over two yards to go. Dave first tried to draw the Spartan defensive line offside, but Baker was too disciplined for that. Dave took the snap, whirled to his left, and faked a handoff to Logan. Dave then took two steps back and lobbed a pass to a wide open Tony. But a defensive lineman had forced Dave to rush the pass so the ball sailed high and behind Tony, incomplete. The right play had been called, and the right play was executed perfectly. One Baker defender had ruined the play.

The Baker fans cheered and the Spartan crowd, as one, looked at the clock to see how much time was left with one collective thought: Do we have time to score?

Plenty of time. A screen pass gained fifteen yards. A short out pattern gained another eight yards and stopped the clock. A sweep gained about ten yards and again stopped the clock. It took Baker under a minute to move the ball to the Whitehall twenty yard line. Two plays and thirty seconds later the ball was just inside the Whitehall ten yard line. Baker called time out with fifty-five seconds left in the half. A weary Ranger defense knelt around Coach Pete after he'd briskly hobbled his way onto the field.

Baker ran another screen pass but Tony saw this one coming and tackled the receiver for a four-yard loss. Another sweep gained eight yards and Baker called another time out. This time both Jersey and Coach Pete gathered the defense. Coach Pete yelled excitable warnings about a corner pattern and about a draw. Jersey spoke softly to Cody Phillips, who nodded the entire one-way conversation.

With thirty-four seconds left on the clock, Baker had one final time out, and had the ball third and six yards at the Whitehall eight yard line. The play Baker opted to run looked like an off tackle run by their fullback. But at the snap the running back's right foot slipped out from under him as he bolted toward the line to accept the handoff. He slid to a knee. He recovered quickly, but not quite quick enough. The quarterback turned to his right to either hand off or fake a handoff, but when he looked and saw the fullback momentarily on a knee, he tucked the ball and spun forward toward the line. Cody had shed his blocker and when the quarterback spun he hit the back end of the guard, who'd been shoved into the backfield by Cody. The ball hit the guard's hip or rump, I couldn't tell, and bounced out of the quarterback's hands. It hung there, in the air, neither spinning nor rotating, suspended at a jaunty forty-five degree angle. Just as the quarterback reached for it the long arm of Colt Harrison slapped at the ball with one hand, tipped it to himself away from the fullback who had just gained his footing, and gathered it to his chest in nearly a full sprint. A stunned Baker sideline and crowd watched the lanky Ranger senior run an absolutely straight line down the hash marks into the Ranger end zone to cut the lead in half, 14-7.

It was an utterly shocking play, and an utterly stunning swing not only on the scoreboard but also of emotion and momentum. The Whitehall players mobbed each other on the sideline and the Whitehall crowd mobbed each other in the bleachers.

Colt squib-kicked the ball to the Spartans, who covered the ball at their own thirty-five yard line. With time for only two or three plays left, Baker took a knee and ran out the clock. Jersey said he knew right then Whitehall would win. When teams, he told me that following Sunday during our interview, who feast on intimidation of the opposition, take a knee with any kind of a chance to score, they essentially transfer that confidence to the opposition. Baker's confidence was shaken, Jersey said, and confidence was a big part of their success. Whitehall, he said, was suddenly the opposite of intimidated.

The Rangers – with about one-third the crowd size of the home team – received nearly the same volume of applause as the Spartans when the two teams took the field for the second half. The Whitehall fans – all of them – were on their feet to loudly greet the Rangers when they emerged from the locker room.

Whitehall got the ball first in the third quarter. Tony returned the kickoff past midfield but got blindsided by a Baker tackler who knocked the ball loose. Morgan pounced on the ball and just to make sure Corey Walker pounced on Morgan.

Dave handed off to Logan, who burst through the line on the first play from scrimmage in the second half and when he and a Baker safety collided ten yards downfield it was the safety who tumbled backward and Logan stumbled forward for another seven yards before he went down. The woozy safety was helped off the field. On third down and less than a yard from inside the Baker twenty yard line, Dave faked a dive to Logan and drifted back in the pocket to pass. Colt came around and took the ball on a wide receiver reverse and one Baker defender – an outside linebacker – had read the play perfectly. Colt improvised and pumped a fake pass, which drew the linebacker off his feet with his arms and hands in the air. With the linebacker airborne and helpless, Colt scrambled past him and romped in the end zone for a touchdown. One second after he got there, Dave tackled him in a joyous collision.

"Badlands!" Dave sang to the heavens as he spun circles while dancing off the field, surrounded by his teammates. "Whoa whoa whoa whoa, Badlands!"

The Rangers, or at least Dave, had evidently seen the Gazette article.

The game entered the fourth quarter tied 14-14. Colt Harrison had scored all fourteen points for Whitehall.

Still tied, Baker got the ball on its own twenty yard line with a little over three minutes left in the game. A dive got four yards, another dive got five yards, and on third and short another dive picked up a first down. There were ninety seconds left to go in the game and the Baker coach called time out. It was so quiet from the Baker side of the field that I heard distinctly the coach call the time out. It was as if the Baker fans had retreated into silence. Hope had replaced confidence. Our defense had outplayed their offense, and their offense and their fans knew it.

Jersey and Coach Pete gathered the Ranger defense on the field, near the sideline, not far from the Ranger bench. Both teams had gathered in huddles along the sidelines, and on both sides of the field, the fans were hushed. Trish was the exception. She raised her frail arms and shook her purple and gold pompoms. Across the field I could hear her voice but not quite her exact words. Then I realized she had started a chant, *Rang-ers! Rang-ers! Rang-ers*! and within a couple heartbeats everyone on the Whitehall side of the field – even the players on the bench – joined the chant.

The chant grew louder and even though the Baker fans started their own cheer, the Ranger fans were louder, with Trisha Ryan, parked by the bleachers stairway in her wheelchair, the catalyst for all the noise at the Baker football stadium.

Baker went from the sideline to the middle of the field and quickly lined up in formation. If it was supposed to surprise the Rangers, it didn't work. The Baker quarterback took the snap and retreated back in the pocket to pass, but Cody Phillips squeezed through a gap in the line and got pressure up the middle. The quarterback drifted to his right and cocked his arm to throw a pass to a wide receiver who had run a ten-yard out pattern near the sidelines. The receiver was open, and the quarterback got the ball off just before Cody dragged him down from behind. But JeffScott had jumped at the line of scrimmage and deflected the pass, and the ball twisted and floated crazily high in the air, and hung there for what seemed like forever. Nate Bolton and a Baker receiver both went up for the ball, but it was Nate who jumped higher, reached higher, snatched the ball, and came down with it.

Bedlam erupted on the Ranger sidelines. Coach Pete leaped so high and landed so awkwardly on his bad hip he toppled clumsily to the ground. I saw him fall and feared he'd had a stroke. Then I saw him lift his arms and legs, his back on the ground, and shake his body with agitated excitement. It made for a Ledger photo that was talked about for weeks after the paper came out.

Jersey calmly called time out and slowly walked toward the middle of the field to the jubilant Rangers. Coach Pete stayed on his back along the sideline, shaking his arms and legs in the air. The offense was Jersey's responsibility.

There was dead silence from the Baker side of the field. The Whitehall fans chanted *Rang-ers* until Jersey motioned them to quiet down as he left the huddle and approach the sideline.

The Rangers scored on the second play after the interception. On the first play, Dave handed off to Logan, who banged his way into the line for four yards. On the next play Dave faked a handoff to Logan and then pitched the ball outside to Cale Bolling. Except Dave didn't pitch the ball to Cale Bolling. Dave had kept the ball, dodged one tackler and scored on a twenty-seven yard run to put Whitehall up 20-14. Colt's extra point made it 21-14.

Baker tried three long desperation passes and Tony picked off the third one on what turned out to be the final play of the game.

Whitehall won. I watched the celebration in stunned disbelief. Whitehall went across the eastern Montana badlands and beat Baker.

Rang-ers! Rang-ers! Rang-ers! The Whitehall fans shouted in pure and total euphoria. Everyone dressed in purple and gold was hugging everyone else in purple and gold. Annie and Bonner gave Trish a wild ride along the track in front of the bleachers – the wheelchair tilted back with Trish screaming wildly – and ended up on the sideline near the players.

Whitehall won. Young Tom, scrawny and bristled wearing a beat-up Budweiser cap and reeking of cigarettes, and Old Tom, leaning on a cane, seemed vaguely confused about his surroundings and presence, came up and congratulated me, as if I had something to do with the win.

"Best game I ever seen," proclaimed Young Tom.

"One play," Old Tom shouted, and held up one index finger. "That fumble there," and he pointed toward the end zone where the Baker quarterback fumbled late in the first half, "turned the whole game around."

Old Tom, whose insights and judgments were oftentimes questionable, unintentionally hilarious or even unrelated to anything connected to realty, was exactly right. *That fumble there* had turned the whole game around.

"You're right," I yelled to Old Tom.

"Goddamn right I am," he answered.

"Where and who do they play next?" Young Tom asked, lighting up a cigarette.

I had no idea. I had never even thought to have that idea. I didn't think I had to. I did know Baker wasn't playing anyone next.

"I'll have to find out," I said.

"What about my bucket?" Old Tom asked.

I looked at Young Tom; he had smoke streaming from both nostrils.

"What bucket?" I asked Old Tom.

Old Tom hooted a laugh and placed a wrinkled and withered hand on my shoulder. The hand was wizened like a withered talon. "You'll see," he said, laughing.

My attention, and puzzlement, were directed to Mary, who was half running, half skipping my direction. When she got close enough she practically jumped into my arms and wrapped her arms around me, to the amazement of Young Tom, Old Tom, and me.

"That was incredible!" she announced to us all, to everyone and anyone.

"That play there, that fumble," Old Tom told her, "turned the whole game around."

"Oh yeah," Mary agreed, "it sure did."

"Goddamn right it did," Old Tom told her. He peered into Mary's face. "You that smart one?"

I shook my head. "She's a teacher," I told Old Tom.

"The hell," Old Tom muttered.

Mary's glee drew a crowd. Cal Walker, Lyle O'Toole and his wife and daughters – except for Aspen – joined us in what essentially grew into a group embrace.

"You tell Tony we're all proud of him," Cal told me, his face six inches from my ear. We were surrounded and compressed together. Our group embrace added a couple more outside layers of parents and even some kids. Rachel Brockton and Luke Grayling joined, and even, to my left, Sara Dickson and Rhonda Horst. "Tell them all we're proud of them," Cal instructed. "You tell them that."

"I will," I assured him.

"You tell everyone how proud we are of them," he demanded. His voice held so much emotion I thought he might start weeping.

"I will," I again assured him.

"They played like champions today," Cal said.

"Goddamn right they did," Old Tom said.

"Incredible!" Mary kept saying. "Incredible! This is so incredible!"

Old Tom peered at her. "You don't look all that smart to me."

We were such a large group now, with Mary and me in the center, and so tightly pushed together that it was actually a little difficult to breathe. What air I was able to get confirmed what I already knew: the O'Toole family smelled a lot better than the combination of Old and Young Tom.

The group embrace began to disburse on our right side, and it was clear why. The players had finished the handshakes with the Baker players and had completed a brief huddle in the end zone to hear from Jersey. The Rangers were moving toward the sideline, whooping and hollering, pumping their helmets in the air. Annie and Aspen reached Tony nearly simultaneously, and he hugged them both. His eye black had smeared across his cheek and nose, his hair was wet and matted to his scalp, and his uniform was grass and dirt stained. One sock was up nearly to his knee, and one was loose down closer to his ankle.

"What's your headline, Lance?" he asked with a grin as I approached him.

I gave him a brief half hug; Aspen held on to the other half of him.

"How about *Rangers cross badlands to victory*?" volunteered Annie. She had some of Tony's eye black smeared across the bridge of her nose.

"How about *Rangers rule badlands*?" Tony said.

"What a game," I told Tony. Headlines could come later. "You stood up to them and just plain outplayed them."

"We didn't come here to lose," Tony said. "And we didn't. We came here to prove something." He hugged Aspen tight, but he looked at me. "Prove something to their coach, and prove something to ourselves." His voice lifted a note in tone. "And we did." He paused and in his normal tone of voice added, "Colt, man. Colt was the man today."

I nodded. "He was. You all were. You came to Baker and outplayed Baker in Baker." I could hear the awe in my own voice. I patted Tony's shoulder pads. "We're proud of you, Tony. I am. They are." I waved my arm indicating the euphoric and giddy Whitehall crowd. "We all are. Whitehall is."

Tony nodded. A couple of his classmates – kids wearing unabashed wild-eyed glee – sprinted up and hugged him, then hugged the next Ranger they saw. Then more kids and parents – Lyle and Rose each gave Tony a long embrace – mingled and hugged and cheered and, in cases, wept.

The football players slowly phased out of the celebration and began wandering toward the team bus. They took off their shoulder pads and helmets and carried them up to and into the bus, and each player – even the little young freshmen with slender bodies and clean uniforms – yipped and yelped with joy inside the bus as they moved to an open seat.

"Do you believe this?" asked a voice from behind us. I was standing alongside Mary.

It was Ed Franklin. He wore the broad grin.

"Do you believe this?" he asked again.

"It's still sinking in," I answered.

"Amazing," Ed said. "Absolutely amazing." He shook his head in wonderment. "This is the biggest upset in Whitehall history. We're talking close to a hundred years here. Whitehall was incorporated as a town in 1889."

"It's like I'm in shock," I told Ed.

"This was the best football game in Whitehall High School history," Ed said. "Think about it. Think about where this team started."

I nodded.

"I'm serious," he told me. "That needs to be your article. This was the best game in Whitehall High School history."

"Goddamn right it was," Old Tom said as he hobbled past us with his cane.

"Too bad you can't put that in your paper," Ed said.

"Who says I can't?" I said.

The pep bus was slowly filling for the long ride west to Whitehall. The team bus was also nearly full. It was full; no Ranger players were on the field or the sidelines.

Annie and Bonner were with a group of kids gathering near the pep bus, and off closer to the back of the bleachers Rhonda stood silently and patiently, her mouth pursed tight and her face held firm with a scarf tied tightly under her chin. She held a long silver pan of what I remembered were brownies for the team, or, more specifically, for Tony.

I took a step away from Mary toward Rhonda. "Those are for the team, right? Do you want to go into the bus and give them to the boys?"

She didn't answer. She merely extended the pan to me.

"You want me to do it?"

She didn't say anything. She more or less forced me to take the pan of brownies and motioned with a backhanded wave for me to go inside the bus. I hesitated just an instant, and she motioned with a second, more resolute, backhanded wave. I understood the assignment.

I did as commanded. I heard a dull sound, a faint roar, really, that grew louder the closer I got to the bus. I glanced down at the brownies and saw white frosted writing. The words were upside down. I had to turn the pan the opposite direction to read the writing: Whitehall 21, Baker 14, and the outline of a football.

I froze. *No way. No way could this have been a prediction.* I looked back to Rhonda, who shooed me with both hands, toward the bus. I looked at the writing. *Oh come on. This was impossible. Did Rhonda predict the score? Rhonda? This score? Of this game?* I looked back again. She put both hands on her hips, disgusted by my delay.

The faint roar was no longer faint. It was thunderous, a collective outpouring of noise from inside the team bus. It was a loud chant, or singing, and I could see the bus, still stationary as I approached, rocking back and forth on its springs.

The bus door opened, and a rush – a pulsating wall – of raucous sound hit me as firm as a burst of breeze. I stepped up the bus stairs, turned and looked down the length of the bus. Somewhere in the back a boom box was playing Springsteen's *Badlands*, and the Whitehall Ranger football team was singing at the top of its high school lungs. Jersey, sitting in the front row, smiled at me wistfully. Coach Pete, seated next to him, was as red as a beet, with sweat still running down his temples. Still, I saw him eye the brownies.

Together, as one, the Rangers sang. Tony stood in the aisle, in the middle of the bus, howling toward the roof, leading them in the *Whoa, whoa, whoa, whoa* chorus of the song.

They were shouting. Shrieking. Their eyes closed, their faces taut and streaked with dirt and sweat and fatigue. They lifted their faces and sang to the roof, to the heavens, or looked at each other and screamed into each other's faces.

And impossibly, it grew louder. It was deafening. It was near frightening. It was a terrifying and remarkable spectacle of raw emotion, brute power and sheer joy.

I didn't quite complete my assignment; I merely handed the brownies to Coach Pete and escaped down the steps and off the bus. Any further intrusion into the celebration was improper.

Have you ever seen a group of thirty high school football players raise their voices with ecstatic naked emotion, as unified and powerful in voice and spirit as anything on earth?

If you haven't, let me tell you something. It is amazing. It is extraordinary. And it is unforgettable.

Chapter 32

"Do you believe they won?" I asked. It was a little before two o'clock in the morning on Tuesday. I was taking a break from the darkroom. I was on my second – and final – thirty-two ounce Pepsi of the day, but I could feel my eyelids droop and I was seeing dull specks of blurred movement from the corner of my eye.

All day long, wherever I went, the question was constantly and amusingly asked: *Do you believe they won?* It was almost as if the question was, *Did they really win?* As if word of victory had been a rumor, an exaggeration or a fabrication.

But, yeah, I believed it. I was there. I took pictures of it. Eight pictures, including one on the front page, would be featured in the Ledger. The barrage of questions about the game – from people who were there and from people who weren't – significantly slowed my progress throughout the day, and the large number of pictures slowed me in the darkroom. And I still had another hour of darkroom work before I could head home. Before the Ledger had officially even opened at eight-thirty that Monday morning the phone started ringing. Did the Rangers really win? Who do they play next?

My clothes stunk of darkroom chemicals and my vision was getting blurry, so I was a little disappointed with the lack of response. So I asked the question again. "Do you believe they won?"

The mouse peered nervously up at me as if for a moment attempting to decipher my presence, then continued to titter and sniff. There was only one mouse tonight.

"Where's your buddy or wife or whatever?" I asked. Again, no response.

It was possible had the mouse been able to speak, it would have expressed a desire for me to shut up, turn off the boom box, turn out the lights, and go home.

"You should have been there," I told the mouse. "Incredible win. The Rangers beat Baker in Baker. *In Baker*. I know, I know. Impossible, right? No one beats Baker in Baker." The mouse ignored me; it crouched on all fours, turned its back to me, and sniffed its way anxiously across the floor. "I gotta tell you, though, it's been great for business."

The mouse made its way fretfully across the floor until it slipped itself back into the hole along the baseboard. It had enough of me.

"Where you going?" I said loudly. Behind me, Springsteen was singing *Glory Days*. "I thought mice were nocturnal."

We had arrived home in Whitehall well past midnight, early Sunday morning, after the game, staggering into town emotionally and physically drained. We had floated, it seemed, to Forsyth or so, filled with energy and exhilaration, but Annie conked out first, and Bonner was snoring by the time we reached Hysham. Rhonda insisted on buying dinner – at the same Burger King in Laurel – about nine o'clock, and forty miles later by the time we reached Columbus I was the only person in the car awake.

It had only been – astonishingly – a little over two months since we had hauled ourselves home exhausted and dejected from Columbus after a 56-6 drubbing in the season's opener. The Rangers had then looked small, weak, inexperienced, slow, sloppy and indifferent. At times during that game you would have thought the team in purple and gold had never practiced before, were complete strangers to each other and had possibly never seen a football before in their lives. And as bad as they played, as disorganized as they were, as bad as they got beat, it wasn't that big of a deal, because we had all more or less expected it. Somehow during the course of the season, the performance of the Rangers got better and the expectations got higher. Not impossibly high – not expectations of a win in Baker – but expectations the team would play with enthusiasm and some semblance of ability to be if not victorious then at least competitive.

Driving home that night two months earlier, just barely within the swath of headlights, a herd of as many as a hundred deer stood motionless in a field, a stone's throw away from the pavement. Their eyes glowed eerily in the reflected light. The Yellowstone River shimmered in the moonlight. It had been the second game of the season, during the playing of the national anthem, when I noticed with a sense of awe, almost, the demonstrated power of standing motionless, together, in a unified and rigid formation. The Rangers showed unexpected but impressive discipline somehow by simply lining up and standing as one, frozen, respectful. They wanted to move, they wanted to loosen shoulders, swivel their neck, but willed themselves to resist any urge and to prevent any movement. A group of kids who could do that had some potential.

But no one predicted this. From Baker, the Escort was pointed dead west toward Bozeman, and after the improbable and some could say historic win we followed the Yellowstone until it turned south toward its source inside the park, south of the Paradise Valley. The wind had picked up and buffeted the car from the southwest. Springsteen sang playfully about the *Cadillac Ranch* on the car stereo. Annie's head rested against the passenger window. Bonner's head was straight back against the backseat, his mouth open. Rhonda's chin was down on her chest, the scarf slightly off kilter, her head weaving gently as the car bounced in the winds. Could there be, I wondered, a more mismatched quartet currently traveling on I-90?

The Ranger team bus hadn't arrived in Whitehall until close to three o'clock in the morning on Sunday, and when I woke up Sunday mid-morning Annie was still asleep in her room, Tony was still asleep in his room, while in the living room Bonner was snoring on the couch, Cody Phillips had a blanket wrapped around his shoulders and chest while sleeping in my recliner and a kid was asleep on the floor, lying on his shoulder in the corner, his nose seemingly pressed against the wall, his back aimed my direction. I couldn't tell who it was, and whoever he was, he wasn't moving. He couldn't have been closer to the wall had he been stapled to it.

I spent three hours at the Ledger – developing film, opening mail (doing both tasks at the same time in the darkroom), reading notes from Laura Joyce about telephone calls and other items she needed me to know about. We signed up three new subscribers on Friday, and an auctioneering firm placed a half-page ad and a lengthy classified ad. There had been no Ledger emergencies or catastrophes, and no Whitehall emergencies or catastrophes that I'd missed by being out of town. The first few years we'd had the Ledger, I'd never leave town, afraid town hall would burn down or something sensational would happen and I'd not only miss it, but I'd never live it down.

By early Sunday afternoon my first shift was over and I was home, with a bag lunch of A&W on my lap as I seated myself in the recliner, with the Denver Broncos playing on TV. Not only was the recliner empty, the whole house was empty. I was so tired I actually fell asleep with unchewed food in my mouth. Somebody scored a touchdown and the television crowd woke me; I chewed, swallowed, and drifted back to sleep. When I woke up about an hour later the house was full of kids, none of whom had made a sound. The TV sound was turned off, a different football game was on, kids were seated on the living room couch, kids were seated on the floor, and kids were at the kitchen table. I smelled pizza, and noticed pop cans and paper plates and pizza slices.

I rubbed my eyes with the knuckles of my index fingers and tried to get my mind in gear, but the weariness had settled deep inside of me. I could catch fleeting glances of the kids – Carrie Lindstrom, the saxophone player, who offered me what I interpreted to be an awkward expression of sympathy – and Jordan Kling – the *f-word* speller – were seated together on the couch. I had never seen them together before, and had never before seen Jordan in my house. Some of the regulars – Cody, Aspen, Bonner, Cale and Morgan – seemed to essentially ignore me as I struggled to wake up. From behind, so I didn't see her coming, Annie sat herself on the arm of the chair, tousled my hair, and set a cold can of Coke in my hands. Tony was in the kitchen slicing up the pizza.

"You want some pizza?" she asked.

"Yeah, I suppose," I said.

Natalie, Dave Dickson's little sister, slid me a paper plate with two pieces of sausage pizza.

As my mind worked itself into a little sharper focus, I realized there were high school kids and junior high kids in the house, athletes and musicians, student academic achievers bound for college and faltering students bound for trouble, rich kids and poor kids, teacher pets and juvenile delinquents. It was like our house was a Whitehall High School ark, carrying one or two of every kind of kid in town.

"We were all at the park hanging out," Annie explained, "and got hungry." She shrugged. "Tony and I got some pizzas and everyone followed us here."

I nodded, as if I understood completely. Something about Carrie struck me as odd. She was not an attractive girl. She was big and shapeless, with a complexion problem and a face that was almost square in shape. It was her jacket. Dark green corduroy. The kid sleeping against the wall this morning before I'd left for the Ledger had been wearing that jacket. Had Carrie Lindstrom spent the night on the floor of my house, in the same room as Bonner and Cody? What, I wondered, had they all been doing here?

"Carrie's parents are in Great Falls at the state bowling tournament," Annie said, as if I'd actually asked a question. Perhaps I had. I was still disoriented in the twilight between sleep and awake.

Again, I nodded. I had drifted into a sound sleep in an empty house with a bag of A&W in my lap and woke up to a house filled with a disconnected gang of kids stuffing pizza into their mouths. I was having difficulty comprehending it all. I decided I didn't want to comprehend it. I needed more sleep. A lot more sleep.

During the interview with Jersey on Sunday night, he told me where, when and who Whitehall played next: the Fort Benton Longhorns, with an 8-2 record and a 27-7 home playoff win over Plentywood. Fort Benton, along the Missouri River about an hour north of Great Falls, was the birthplace of Montana, and if I recalled correctly, was the place where wounded soldiers from the Battle of the Little Bighorn were put on steamships for the trip downriver to civilization.

Jersey said Fort Benton was led by two impressive linemen and a tight end/linebacker named Troy Johanssen who was supposedly going to be offered a football scholarship to play for the University of Montana Grizzlies.

"They start almost all seniors, are really well coached and will be the biggest team we've played all year," Jersey had told me during the Sunday interview. "They only lost to Malta by one point and to Cut Bank on the road by a touchdown. They're big and strong and experienced and have a great tradition."

Only eight teams remained, and – amazingly – Whitehall was one of them. Whitehall was the opposite of Fort Benton: No size, no strength, no experience and no tradition.

Malta, Roundup, Fairfield, Cut Bank, Ennis and Frenchtown were also still in the playoff hunt. They had as many combined losses – five – as the Rangers had during the season. Both Malta and Frenchtown were undefeated, and Malta had beaten Forsyth by fifty points – 57-7 – to advance. I learned all that information from a Great Falls Tribune article. The story was a wrap-up of the high school football playoffs and all it reported about Whitehall was that *senior Colt Harrison was the difference in a stunning upset of Baker. The young Rangers, who with the win now have won as many games as they've lost, will travel to Fort Benton to take on Troy Johanssen and an experienced and talented Longhorn squad.*

Jersey hadn't shaved Sunday, and he yawned a couple times during our interview. I yawned in return. Exhaustion prompted tears to leak from the corners of my eyes. A dull ache tapped away at the inside of my right temple, and my belly seemed to leach dank fumes up into my throat, as if all the pop and pizza were churning and bubbling in my gut.

I had arrived at the town council meeting just as they finished the Pledge of Allegiance, and just before Brandon Grant made a point of order about the agenda. Town attorney Chance Dawson scowled and shook his head as Daniel Purdy jumped to his feet and threatened to sue the town if it either did something or didn't do something, I initially couldn't tell which, and at that point I couldn't really have cared less. It was a Monday night, I was already drag-ass tired, and the last thing I needed was a drawn out and bitter town council meeting. I had a minimum of three hours of work waiting for me at the Ledger. Every minute at the town council meeting meant another minute delay of sleep.

There were only four people in the audience. Daniel Purdy was one of them. Old Tom, a month removed from the council, apparently couldn't break the first Monday of the month habit of attending town council meetings. He was so skinny he didn't even look human; he resembled a scarecrow wearing a baggy sweater and shapeless slacks. He sat in the back, his walker parked alongside his chair. His loose sweater was purple with the numbers *21* sewn on a pocket. It was an old WHS sweater, and if Old Tom graduated in 1921, I figured he would have been born in about 1903, which made him about eighty-six years old. Sitting there, he didn't look a day over ninety-five. A couple other people were in attendance; a lady named Lucy who was there to apply for a business permit to open a hair salon, and I knew that because she had been in the Ledger that afternoon to place four weeks of advertising for Lucy's Hair Salon. Scott Wilson, a worker at the mine who owned a home east of the school, was there to apply for a building setback variance, and I knew that because it was there in the agenda, the very same agenda Daniel Purdy and Brandon Grant were challenging.

"Tell you what, Dan," Mayor Luke Grayling told Daniel Purdy, "why don't you sit down for now and when it's time for you to speak we'll let you know."

Rachel Brockton made a weak attempt to disguise her smile.

"You can't do that," Daniel Purdy asserted. "I'm an American, this is America, and I got rights."

"But you are not a member of this council, and right now you are out of order," Luke explained patiently. "The council determines the agenda, so we, as a council, are going to do that. You, as a member of the public, are going to sit down and behave yourself."

Daniel Purdy emitted one of his dramatic sighs, a public appeal – his *Do you believe it?* sigh – lifted up his arms as if beseeching some higher authority, and sat down exasperated as if he'd tried *everything* to reason with these people.

"Thank you," Luke said. He turned to the town attorney. "Chance?"

"Yes, mayor, if I understand Mr. Grant properly," said Chance, "he suggests the town lacks statutory authority to proceed with a grant application seeking state funds to study the condition of the town's municipal water delivery system. Is that correct, Mr. Grant?"

Brandon, who owned the RV park and motel on the east end of town, didn't want to look at Daniel Purdy for guidance, but he had to, so he did, and Daniel Purdy nodded.

"Mayor, state statute clearly grants local government legal authority to seek study grants for municipal infrastructure projects, including drinking water system projects," Chance said.

Daniel Purdy jumped to his feet and pointed at Chance. "You didn't notice it. You gotta publish a legal notice three weeks. You gotta seek public comment. You gotta give us a chance to oppose it."

"A grant application?" Chance asked incredulously. "A *study* grant application? That's what we're talking about here."

"You wanna build fancy new waterlines, put in water meters, and raise all our water rates," charged Daniel Purdy. "You can't do that without proper public notice, and you know it."

"Yes, we know that," said Luke. "And if we do decide to propose new waterlines, if we do decide to improve the water system, if we do decide to propose installation of water meters, and if we do decide to propose increased water rates, we will publish proper legal notices and Lance there at the Ledger will write story after story about the proposal, but right now there is no proposal. There is no proposal to even make a proposal. There is nothing."

"There's the grant!" Daniel Purdy demanded.

"There is that," confessed Luke, who rolled his eyes.

"Yes, there is the grant," Chance told Daniel Purdy. "A study grant from the Montana Department of Commerce is just that, a study grant. The grant itself is just a check from the State of Montana to the Town of Whitehall, for the Town of Whitehall to hire an engineering firm. To conduct a study. That's it. That's all. Just to hire an engineering firm. Just to study our drinking water delivery system. The study will contain recommendations-"

"Recommendations!" crowed Daniel Purdy.

"Recommendations," Chance continued, as if speaking to a child, "that may or may not indicate new waterlines are needed, which may or may not be advanced by this council. The report and any recommendations will be made public, I assure you, through public notices and articles in the Ledger, and will be thoroughly discussed by this council before any actual proposals surface, if any proposals surface at all."

"The Ledger?" Daniel Purdy guffawed. "That's reassuring."

It was a sour, sarcastic comment, and I was in no mood for sour sarcasm from Daniel Purdy.

"Sit down and shut up," I said before I realized I'd spoke.

The remark was met with palpable shock. Never before, not once in a decade, had I said anything like it in public before. My body was so exhausted and my mind so dim my mouth blurted words before my sluggish brain could check them. Everyone was surprised; no one more so than me.

Daniel Purdy glared at me, his eyes opened wide in anger. Just as his mouth formed an ugly snarl in advance of an ugly comment a creaky voice from behind me spoke up.

"It's a goddamned grant, Daniel," Old Tom blurted. "What part of that don't you understand?"

Three remarkable things had happened virtually simultaneously. One, the Ledger publisher uttered a caustic insult. Two, Old Tom had uttered a coherent and salient comment. Three, with that comment Old Tom had directly and publicly chastised his mentor, Daniel Purdy.

Rachel Brockton cocked her head and offered a *Well, good for you, Old Tom,* smile. Daniel Purdy stood silently, looking beyond me toward Old Tom. Daniel Purdy wore a look of stupefying confusion, combined with utter distress.

Mayor Grayling recognized an opportunity when he saw it. "So, we're agreed, then. What we're talking about here is a grant application, not a proposed expenditure toward a proposed project. So it can be part of the agenda and acted on. Everyone's okay with that?"

Up at the council members' table, heads nodded. Daniel Purdy didn't even bother to sit back down. He whirled and stormed out of the council chambers, and slammed the door behind him as he exited. I snuck a peek behind me, at Old Tom sitting in the back row. His eyes were aimed straight ahead, and he shook his head in dismay. For years, even before my arrival in Whitehall, Old Tom had carried Daniel Purdy's bidding on the council. It was bizarre to think at whatever actual age Old Tom was that he'd begun thinking for himself. I wrote down the quote, *It's a goddamned grant, Daniel. What part of that don't you understand?* At that moment I was angry enough to put it in the paper. But only at that moment. I knew, even as I wrote it down in my notebook, that I would never put the quote in the Ledger article. I wouldn't do that to Whitehall, to the council, to Old Tom, or even to Daniel Purdy.

The council completed its agenda in a little under two hours. The water system study grant application was approved by unanimous vote. The traditional item on the council agenda was an open-ended opportunity for public comment, and very seldom did anyone ever hang around long enough to comment on something not previously discussed as part of the agenda. Scott Wilson had left happily immediately after his building permit had been approved and Lucy Lombardi had left pleased with her business license approved. Outside of the council, it was only me and Old Tom left, and I had no comments. I thought about apologizing to the council for my earlier uncalled for remarks, but I didn't feel like apologizing, especially an apology that involved Daniel Purdy or delayed my final shift at the Ledger that night.

"Any public comments?" Luke asked. Members of the council were folding up their briefing books for departure. I did the same. But I saw Luke's eyes focus on something behind me, and then I noticed the council members stopped putting away their meeting information. I had already stood. I turned behind me and saw Old Tom in the final stages of a creaky effort to rise, his walker squarely in front, pulling himself to his unsteady legs.

"Tom?" asked Luke.

Old Tom clawed at his cheek briefly, as if pondering his first words. "I went all the way to Baker on Saturday and saw something pretty special," he said. is limbs were so thin they were barely wider than the slender legs of his walker. "This football team of ours did something we all should be proud of."

I sat down and began to take notes. It was the first time in my memory a WHS athletic team had ever been discussed at a Whitehall Town Council meeting. A couple of the council members looked curious about *why* a WHS athletic team was being discussed at this Whitehall Town Council meeting.

"Those kids played their hearts out," Old Tom continued. "They weren't the biggest team on the field that day. They weren't the fastest or even maybe even the best. But they won." He said *they won* as if he was still surprised by that fact. "I played me a little football for Whitehall back in the old days and we never did anything as glorious as these kids. For years I've been waitin' for the Rangers to do something special, and here they did. They won themselves a playoff football game." You could see the pride and wonder in his eyes. He shook his head, briefly, in admiration, just thinking about it. "So I'd like to see the council pass a resolution honoring these boys, this team. A resolution that tells them how proud the whole town is of 'em."

Luke nodded gravely, as if considering the proposal. "I agree, Tom, that it was a pretty remarkable football game. And that we should be proud of the team and the coaches."

Old Tom continued to stand unsteadily. His WHS purple sweater was draped over his shoulders like a blanket over a skeleton.

"And I'll be glad to call the school tomorrow and as mayor, you know, congratulate the school and the players," Luke said. "But I wonder if we shouldn't also hold off on the official resolution and public displays until the season is over."

Old Tom nodded. "Until they win the championship?"

Luke cleared his throat. "Well, or until the season is over. They have to win, what, three more games, to win the title?" Luke looked at me, and I nodded. It would take three more improbable, or impossible, wins, for the Rangers to win a state title. "So they've had a great year by making the playoffs and winning a playoff game, but maybe we should see how they do next week."

Old Tom pursed his lips. "I know what you're saying, mayor. You doubt our Rangers. But I don't. Whitehall's gonna win the state championship this year. And when they do, this council needs to give those kids a huge pat on the back."

Luke simply smiled. "You bet, Tom. We will, I promise."

"Good," Old Tom said. He grinned, just thinking about it.

The best thing about the dim and dirty pressroom in Anaconda was that it was the only place I knew that made my home tidy by comparison. Dust and grit that may have existed since shortly after Montana statehood formed a lower layer in the areas not regularly trafficked in the pressroom, with layer upon layer of dust on top, not unlike the sedimentary rock formations throughout Montana. In a forest, you could look at a ponderosa pine tree and think to yourself that the tree had been a sapling during the Revolutionary War. At the pressroom, you could have swept up dirt from a corner or under the collating machine with knowledge you disturbed dust created during Prohibition. Of course, no one ever swept up dirt in the pressroom.

My routine in Anaconda was to enter through the alley in the back door, and set the pages on the layout table just outside the darkroom. Larry had the darkroom prepared and, in the winter, warmed up, to shoot the Ledger pages. The Ledger and I were customers – customers who paid in full and on time – but Larry always treated me as an employee of his. Part of that was my own fault. I willingly assisted in the production of the paper, primarily to monitor print quality but also to speed up my time in the pressroom. The less time in Anaconda, the sooner I got back to Whitehall, and the sooner I got back to Whitehall and got the papers delivered the sooner I could begin my nap.

This Wednesday began as almost every other Wednesday in Anaconda. The late October weather was cold in Whitehall but colder in Anaconda with a brisk wind that zipped through the alley. The wind held a threat of snow. The tallest peaks in the Pintlers south and west of Anaconda were covered with fresh white powder and the crisp chill of the snow felt closer than it looked.

I brought a twenty-eight-page Ledger into the backdoor of the pressroom and set the box of paste-up pages on the layout table. I could hear Larry in the darkroom, could smell the sharp acrid odor of new developer and fix chemicals in the trays, and could even smell the pale musty scent of heat; he must have switched on the old furnace when he arrived.

"How many pages you got?" Larry asked. He stood in the doorway, half in, half out, of the darkroom. He wore a loose black sweatshirt, and long black hairs curled at his throat out and over the shirt. The hair from his head ran down the back of his neck like a carpet and I figured his back was a carpet of thick mad Russian bomber hair.

He asked me how many pages I had every Wednesday morning, and every Wednesday morning I got the impression no matter what my answer was, it was the wrong answer. "Twenty-eight," I told him.

He more or less grunted some kind of response, took the box of Ledger pages, and ducked back inside the darkroom. I blew some warmth onto my cupped hands, and continued my routine. It would take Larry a few minutes to shoot and process the first page, so I spent five minutes or so getting myself organized. The inserts – flyers for three Butte grocery stores and a Butte drug store – were stacked into piles, each group of twenty-five reversed for balance and to assist with the count. I brought about half of them about twenty feet across the room to what essentially was my Wednesday morning work station, a bleak metal table wedged in the corner directly under the furnace blower. I arranged them in stacks for insertion into papers destined for the vendors; each stack was earmarked for a vendor, and the count was made then to help with orderly bundling later, after the inserts and actual Ledger had been merged into one unit.

I heard the darkroom door creak open, which was my Wednesday cue to head back to the darkroom to start to pull negatives and begin the tedious job of opaquing the pages. Larry always looked at the first two-page set of negatives to gauge the quality of the negative. If the print portion of the negative – the reversed white portion – was too dense, extensive opaquing would be necessary and once transferred from negative to plate to press the print on the newsprint page would be too dense and would draw excess ink which smeared and blotched. If the print portion was too fine, or thin, the ink on the newsprint page would be faded black, closer to dark gray and white instead of black and white. Larry held the damp negative up toward the ceiling light, looked at the tones of both the black and white, looked at all four corners and the center for consistency, judged it acceptable and affixed it to a clothesline with two clothespins to allow the negative to dry. It offended him to see me then inspect the same negative and make my own judgment. He resented my attempts at quality control, but I knew sometimes the first negative was more of a test than an absolute and frequently he made an adjustment after the first negative was processed. The truth is the quality of the negatives was far more important to me than to him. Had I been shooting the pages, I would have thrown the first one away and made them all the exact same density and same quality. But Larry didn't like to admit mistakes, and he didn't like to throw things away. For that reason, I always stacked the paste-up pages in the box with page two and page twenty-three (shot together on a twenty-four-page tab) on top; the two pages seldom held important photos, and it was less problematical if they were inconsistent with the remaining eleven negatives.

Larry went back into the darkroom to finish shooting the pages. I brought the first negative – pages two and twenty-seven – to the light table to begin to opaque the pages. Because the pages were negatives, whatever was light would later print as black on the newsprint. So I took a red grease pen and filled in any and all unwanted and unintentional light specks, lines, type shadows or other imperfections. For all the other publications printed in Anaconda, Dan, Bryce or Mike – the press crew – pulled negatives and opaqued pages. But I pulled Ledger negatives to ensure consistent quality and opaqued myself because I had to do something and I could help make sure the job was completed properly.

I stood over the light table with the opaque pen when Dan, an older guy who seemed absolutely immune to cold temperatures, arrived and as he did every Wednesday morning, got the coffee machine turned on and placed his lunch in the refrigerator behind the stairwell.

"Whitehall beat Baker, is that what I heard?" he asked.

I nodded. "Pretty amazing."

"Baker," he said, "wow." He looked over my shoulder and saw me working on pages fourteen and fifteen. "Twenty-eight? Who's up next for you guys?"

"Fort Benton," I answered. The aroma of coffee drifted from the stairwell.

Dan shook his head. "They're tough at home. They got that Johanssen kid."

"Yeah, I think he's headed to Missoula to play for the Griz."

"Kid's a beast," Dan said. "I saw him play basketball last year at a tournament here. He plays basketball like a football player, that's for sure. He's a bruiser."

Bryce showed up next, which was typical. Dan and Bryce worked the press during the printing of the paper; Dan typically wore a sleeveless tee-shirt and Bryce wore three layers, usually a flannel shirt over a sweatshirt and tee-shirt. Dan arrived this morning wearing a tee-shirt and an unbuttoned vest. Bryce wore a winter jacket, stocking cap and gloves. The fourth member of the Anaconda backroom crew, Mike, a dour little man with bad breath, bad teeth, bad habits and a bad attitude, showed up just as the final negatives were rolling out of the processor.

He simply nodded when he arrived and immediately paired up the twin paste-up pages into a quartet of pages, which he sliced at the top edge and taped together. The image of the quartet of negatives was again reversed to resemble the paste-up pages except they'd been burned onto thin metal plates. During the press run I stood at the end of a brief conveyer belt that took the printed and folded papers to Mike, who gathered and stacked them for the mailer, a machine that placed the labels on the paper for mailing. I pulled one paper about every hundred papers or so that hit the conveyer belt and quickly browsed through it, checking on the print quality. The Ledger was about three-hundred papers into its run when I spotted a two-inch band of light – the black was a dark gray – ink along the bottom of pages sixteen and seventeen, two of the three pages that featured the Ranger win in Baker.

I held up the pages and showed them to Mike, who as he gathered a stack of papers, turned to look behind toward Dan, who was somewhere working the press. The press itself was so loud you really couldn't converse; you either shouted or used hand and body signals to converse. Mike shrugged, as if to say, *I tried*, when in reality he hadn't done anything. So I walked around Mike's workstation and held up the paper to Dan, who was working on an interior portion of the press – turning dials and peering over his head as the paper zipped along its route toward the folder. Dan looked up and saw me holding up the paper outstretched in front of me, and his shoulders sagged just a bit, *Now what?*

"Sixteen," I yelled and showed him the bottom of the page.

Later in the press run, a slight paper crease developed in the middle two pages, pages fourteen and fifteen. The crease formed a kind of lip, or flap, across the sheet and prevented ink from reaching the flat center portion of the page. I caught it and showed it to Mike, who looked absently toward the counter on the press that counted the individual papers, or impressions, that had come off the press during the press run. He did that to see if enough papers were still to come off the press to make a correction worth the effort.

There were still five hundred papers left, so there was plenty of time to fix the problem. But Mike stood there as if nothing happened, gathering the papers.

I stepped quickly around him and spotted Bryce, and showed him the creased papers. He frowned, and made a motion like he intended to do something, but he didn't actually move. By this time there were still well over four hundred papers left in the press run, but by the time I got Dan's attention there were closer to three hundred papers left, and by the time Dan got the problem fixed the press run was nearly over. I had put a week of my life into these twenty-eight pages, and in ten minutes the press crew had, in my mind, ruined much of that work. The middle two pages were the Ledger's community pages and the bottom left corner of a picture of John and Mary Lee Smith, celebrating their fiftieth wedding anniversary, had a crease through it.

What the press crew should do, I had always maintained, was stop the counter, pull all the imperfect papers, and start the counter again after the problem had been corrected. Anaconda insisted on fixing the problem as the papers were printed and the count continued, which meant the problem was part of the press run and part of the papers I mailed and delivered, and that people read.

After the press was slowed down and turned off, I opened a Ledger to pages fourteen and fifteen and held it open on the conveyor belt for all three of them – Dan, Bryce and Mike – to see. Mike and Bryce ignored it, and me, and had no time for my petty complaints. But Larry more or less glared at me.

"You got a problem?" he demanded. He knew the answer. We'd gone through this far too often.

"What do you want me to tell them and their kids when they ask me what happened to the picture?" I said. I pointed firmly at the photo. "These are the Smiths and they've never been in the Ledger together before. Look at them, they're in their seventies. This is the only fiftieth anniversary they're ever going to have in their hometown newspaper. Look at this. Look at it. What do I tell them when they ask me what happened?"

"The picture's fine," Larry argued. "The faces are clear. Outside of the bottom corner there there's nothing wrong." He looked at me, at the photo, and back to me.

I shook my head. "I'm going to apologize. I'm going to tell them I'm sorry. I'm going to tell them I'm sorry about the way the picture turned out. I'm going to tell them I'm sorry I let them down."

Larry trembled, balled his hands into fists, and stormed away.

The Wednesday weather turned pleasant in the afternoon and the living room was perfectly warm when I stretched out on the couch with an intention of briefly pretending to read before falling asleep. I felt the dull ache of exhaustion behind my eyes. I knew from experience it could be cured only by sleep.

There was a blanket – maybe it was ours, maybe it had been left by someone who'd stayed here – balled up on an end of the couch and despite the warmth I spread it out to cover my legs and feet. I kept my shoes on when I napped. Above my head, between the ceiling and a wall, a loose strand of a silky spider web floated lazily on the air. The living room was dirty and gritty and messy, but the kitchen was worse. The kitchen smelled bad. The bathroom also smelled bad, but the kitchen smelled worse. The last thing I thought before I fell asleep was that we had all – Tony, Annie and me – been so busy none of us had done any cleaning, or done anything even close to resembling cleaning. I'd have to have Annie at least muck out the kitchen and bathroom before we left Saturday morning for Fort Benton.

A perfect Wednesday nap lasted twenty minutes. Shorter than that and I woke up still in need of sleep, longer than that and it was like I woke up after an overdose, lazy and slow. I viewed a nap as God's tip of the hat to my incessant and oppressive duties and obligations, a tiny concession to make life slightly more bearable. When I earned a nap, and took a nap, it was like a promise fulfilled. The kids used to make fun of my napping but by now they understood, by both my words and action, how much I valued them – the naps – and in fact how much I needed them. I could almost always feel my mood improve after a nap, and kids could also see an immediate upgrade in my attitude.

I woke up to a shuffling of some type in the kitchen. I had slept just under thirty minutes. It was about four o'clock in the afternoon. I could get back to the Ledger for an hour or so to take apart the paper, start the advertising run sheet, get thoughts and assignments arranged for the following edition, and close up the shop.

I stretched, rubbed my face with both hands, and stretched again. Annie was in the kitchen, and I smelled – before I saw – the tangy sharp smell of Mr. Clean floor cleaner. A plastic garbage bag was half full and set on the living room carpet just off the linoleum kitchen floor. I could see the steam from scalding hot water rising from the sink. The refrigerator door was open and emptier than I'd seen it last.

"Morning," she said flatly.

“Howdy,” I said. I sat up; rubbed my face again. “Thanks for doing that.”

“It reeked,” she said. “It’s reeked for two days and no one else will do anything about it, so I have to.”

There was nothing I could say. She was right.

The backdoor slammed shut, which meant additional people, or an additional person, was in the house. She, he or they would need to take about five strides further into the kitchen before I saw them. I’m not sure who I expected to see. Bonner? Natalie? Not Tony and not Cody; they’d still be at practice.

Who I saw was Johnny Pep, the Mexican hoodlum, and he carried a refrigerator tray that still dripped wet; he had apparently washed it at the backyard faucet, most likely after verbal direction from Annie.

“You remember Johnny?” Annie asked me.

I was too stunned to respond. Johnny, skinny and brown with eyes that held me in something like indifference, stood awkwardly for maybe two heartbeats, then offered me a faint and passing single nod before he turned to slide the cleaned tray back in the fridge. I was sure he’d interpreted my stunned expression with the accuracy of a survivor; *What are you doing here with my daughter?* He’d no doubt seen that look before, probably seen it his entire life. My eyes had conveyed my thoughts perfectly, without any intention of that conveyance.

Finding Johnny Pep in my house helping my daughter clean the kitchen was not a surprise. Finding the Lipizzaner Stallions grazing the front yard would have been a surprise. Seeing Johnny Pep in my house was shocking.

“I was helping Johnny with some algebra after school,” Annie said, handing Johnny a mop and using her foot to slide the bucket his direction. “We went down to the Ledger so I could show him some practical math applications, and then I figured he might as well help me swamp out the kitchen and bathroom.

He took the mop handle with one hand and with the other hand pointed at Annie. “She’s very smart, yes.” He looked straight into my eyes, and I could see he wanted a truce of sorts, that he wanted me to understand that he and I had no quarrel. But we did. Had I not been here, he would have been alone with my junior high school daughter. He had been alone with her between school and the Ledger, and between the Ledger and here. Someone like him was not supposed to be alone with someone like her.

“Tony, Cody, Dave and a bunch of the team are coming over here for A&W after practice and I figured we’d better get the place tidied up before they got here,” Annie said.

Johnny lightly widened his eyes and nodded as if to assure me she was telling the truth. He lifted the mop out of the bucket and swished it across the floor under the table. He wielded a mop with a level of experience and competency. Reform school, I figured.

“What are you going to do?” Annie asked.

“Me?” I asked.

"Yes, you. Are you going to help clean up the living room, or are you going to go down and close down the Ledger?"

There was no way I was going to leave her alone with him in this house. "I can close up later."

"Then get the vacuum," she told me. "Pick up all that first," she meant the newspapers, magazines, shoes, clothes, dishes and the baseball cap that were scattered across the floor. "Put it away or throw it out, and then vacuum. They're going to be here about five-thirty."

Johnny lifted up the half-full plastic garbage bag and handed it to me. He had a tattoo of a dagger lengthwise down his slender brown hairless forearm. *What's a kid with a dagger tattoo on his arm have in common with my intellectual child prodigy?*

Annie lifted two old oranges out of the fridge that resembled mottled prunes. I had a vague recollection of buying some fruit at the IGA in a momentarily optimistic attempt at improving my diet and providing some healthy food to the kids, but my thinking was that had been during summer and it was now, what, nearly November? Could oranges really have been in our fruit container for almost six months? She dropped the two rotten orbs into the garbage.

She caught me looking at her. "Why aren't you doing what you were told?"

Johnny looked up briefly, then continued mopping the floor. He was doing what he was told.

I began gathering debris from the floor.

"Do you believe they won?" Bev Mightward asked me Thursday night at the second community barbeque. She had dyed black hair with steel-colored roots and years earlier, before her weight had roughly doubled, she had probably been considered attractive.

"I was there," I told her, "and I still don't believe it."

"Can they beat Fort Benton?" she asked.

We were in line at the potluck, filling plastic plates with spaghetti and meatballs and thick white buns. The multi-purpose room was packed, and loud. Large hand-painted Ranger signs adorned the walls. Annie was somewhere in the room, but I couldn't find her. I had been waved through the line by Martha Cullen, who was collecting money, which meant Annie had paid for me and had also arranged to bring or purchase whatever part of the meal I had been responsible for.

"I don't see why they can't," I told her. She had a barest hint of chin whiskers; you could see the dark pores in her skin where she plucked the hairs. I wondered if Morgan's unique ability to grow facial hair in junior high was inherited, oddly, from his mother.

She grabbed a serving spoon. "At the start of the year I didn't think they could beat anybody." She plopped two large metal spoonfuls of spaghetti onto her plate. It was roughly twice the amount I took.

"That about sizes up their year," I said. "First, they couldn't beat anybody. Now, they can beat anybody."

She took a stack of chocolate chip cookies. We parted ways after we each filled a plastic cup with lemonade, and I drifted toward a seat at a table that held an unlikely combination of Loren Shaw, the local Fish, Wildlife & Parks warden and his prim and proper wife Laurie, and Sally McCrae, a chatty Corner Store clerk who gleefully told most anybody she had shot and killed her abusive husband a few years before I'd moved to Whitehall.

Trisha's wheelchair was anchored slightly into the aisle, and Annie and a group of junior high girls surrounded Trish and the table opposite ours. Trish clutched a fork unnaturally, between her index finger and middle finger, and leaned forward toward the table to keep the distance between the plate and her mouth to a minimum. She looked bulky under a purple Ranger windbreaker. Whenever I saw Trish I couldn't help but assess her appearance compared to the previous time I saw her, as if to judge the depressing and debilitating pace of her deterioration. She wearily raised her head when I walked by her and her face lit up. "Great spaghetti, Lance!" she exclaimed. Her unfocused eyes gazed about six inches to my left, and I was tempted to shift my presence slightly that direction, but I knew that wouldn't help.

"Good," I told her. I steadied my plate with one hand and patted her shoulder with the other. "You going to Fort Benton, Trish?"

She answered with an exaggerated nod. "With mom. On the bus."

"Good," I said.

"I never been to Fort Benton," she exclaimed.

"Me either," I said and moved down the aisle.

Sue and Walt Henkel, along with Slack, sat shoulder to shoulder to shoulder on the same side of a table, and had there been any room at the table I would have joined them. But the place was packed, and loud.

"Did you ever think the Rangers would be a couple wins away from the Class B title game?" I asked Walt.

He shook his head. "Not in my lifetime," he admitted. He had long black sideburns and I always suspected he fancied himself bearing a resemblance to Johnny Cash. With a little imagination, you could see it.

"I still can't believe they beat Baker!" Slack said.

"Neither can Baker," I said.

"But we did," said Walt. "We outplayed 'em. We out hit 'em. We flat out beat 'em."

"Yeah," said Slack. Sitting there, an empty plate on the table, his elbows propped up much like his father, his cowboy hat on straight and his eyes slightly narrowed, Slack looked as a solid as any other rancher in the room.

"You going to Fort Benton?" I asked.

Slack was nodding before I even finished the question. "We're going to see Uncle Kyle in Great Falls first," he announced.

"I have family in Great Falls," explained Sue. "We're going to spend Friday night up there."

"We're going to get a steak at Eddie's!" Slack announced.

Walt nodded. "Best steaks in the state."

"Yeah!" Slack said.

"Enjoy your steak," I told them all. "We'll see you in Fort Benton."

"We're going to get a steak at Eddie's!" Slack announced again.

Sue patted his hand, and smiled my direction as I moved down the aisle.

"Thanks for the spaghetti, Lance," Loren Shaw said as I sat down in an open space at the table.

"What spaghetti?" I asked.

"That spaghetti." Loren pointed at my plate. "I thought you made it."

"Me?" I shook my head. "Not a chance."

"They just announced it a minute ago, before you got here," said Laurie. "They said the spaghetti was courtesy of Lance Joslyn and the Ledger."

"No kidding," I told them. That was news to me. "Annie's usually in charge of that kind of stuff."

Laurie had plain dull brown hair, a plain pale face, a plain shapeless body and a plain and achingly uninteresting personality. She had nervous plain hands that always seemed to be fingering a locket – a plain locket – she wore on a necklace at her throat. A couple years after we'd bought the Ledger she had marched in the office and angrily canceled her subscription and demanded her money back because of something I'd written against the school board's decision to change the school's tardy policy or some other petty matter, but since she'd originated the proposed policy change she intended to punish me personally and the paper financially by canceling her subscription. They had never renewed the paper in all the years since, although Loren had always been friendly and supportive of the paper. He wrote an occasional hunting column and once in awhile gave me a heads up about a kid shooting his first bull elk or mule deer buck.

"Belated congratulations on Annie's awards and honors and all that stuff," Loren said. Laurie looked the other direction.

Loren and Laurie had maybe six kids; I lost track of the precise number. One was a freshman on the football team who didn't get a chance to play much but had caught a pass in the win over Big Timber. His name was Lee and he was the oldest kid, probably. The youngest, unless they had a younger one at home, was an infant still in diapers crawling his way up Loren's plain chest.

"Yeah," said Sally, the Corner Store clerk. "Annie comes in the store all the time, and she's always so polite and shy. You'd never know she was a child genius or whatever."

Sally was anything but plain. She was a large blonde with a large voice and a large laugh, and she was the only person I knew who actually shot and killed someone. I'm told her alcoholic husband, Ricky, had a mean streak fueled by whiskey. People told me about it when I first arrived in Whitehall, but it wasn't much of a discussion item anymore. No one thought Sally was guilty of anything. Coach Pete had told me once he was the first officer to arrive on the scene, and he said Sally, blood smeared across her forehead and shirt, met him at the trailer house door and greeted him with, "Well, I done it. He's dead." Coach Pete, Officer Duffy at the time, said he found Ricky on the floor, blood soaking into the cheap and dirty dark green carpet. Pete said as he knelt down beside the body he silently hoped Ricky was truly dead and not merely wounded. This hadn't been Officer Duffy's first trip to the McCrae trailer home. Ricky's hand gripped a three-foot shaft of a hockey stick. But Sally was right. Ricky was dead, all right. The gun, a pistol, was lying on the kitchen table. Sally had a three-inch cut just above her right eyebrow.

No one pressed charges. Pete said there wasn't even a real investigation. The general thought around town wasn't why Sally did it, but why Sally waited so long to do it.

Still, there's something wickedly intriguing about a woman who actually aimed a gun at a guy, pulled the trigger, and boom, killed him. She still lived in the same trailer home in the southwest corner of town south off Highway 2. She'd been a beaten and battered wife, had killed her husband, had never had a child, never got married again, never worked anywhere besides The Corner Store, but she was arguably among the most visibly happy people I'd ever met. She bowled in at least two different leagues at Roper's Lanes in Whitehall. Every now and then on my nocturnal drifting through the town bars I'd bump into Sally and we'd have a beer or two, and even though I enjoyed our usually drunken and muddled conversation, no matter what my level of consumption had been that night, I possessed enough sense to part ways immediately after the second beer.

"Pete still one of the football coaches?" Sally asked me. Under the bright lights of the multi-purpose room, she looked a little more aged than I'd remembered. Dark barrooms hid her age and what had to be a rough life. Maybe she wasn't used to the bright lights and was squinting.

"Yeah," I answered. "He more or less coaches the defense."

Sally laughed. "Is he still as excitable as he used to be?"

Even Loren laughed at the question.

"You could say that," I answered. "Last week he collapsed on the sidelines and rolled around like he was putting out an imaginary fire or something."

Loren nodded. He'd seen it.

"Coach Pete was so happy I guess he just couldn't contain himself," I said.

"Was it his idea to have them kids out there puking their guts out that night?" Sally asked.

I twirled a fork-full of spaghetti as I thought about the answer. "You know, I don't know who came up with that. Whoever it was wanted to teach the team a lesson."

Sally waved a hand. "I can't imagine what lesson that would be." But she thought about it a moment. "But now look at all this. Winning all those games." She waved both arms, as if showing off the room full of families, fans and purple-jerseyed players.

"Lee came home that night and smelled like a sewer," Laurie complained. "He reeked of vomit."

"Tell me about it, darlin'," said Sally. "I went to work that morning at seven with a hangover sent from hell, and I couldn't get rid of this odor of puke. I thought it was on my clothes or in my hair, but I couldn't figure out how. Then I realized it was in the air, and I figured that out when every time someone opened the door I got another whiff of it. And then I looked, and the football field over there was covered with a bunch of goddamn birds. Must have been a hundred of them. It was like that movie, where the birds attack everyone."

"They were eating upchucked Kentucky Fried Chicken," I explained.

"Lovely," said Laurie, and looked away.

"Better they eat puke than attack everyone," reasoned Sally.

Loren handed whatever kid it was crawling on him to his wife, and asked me if I would print a picture of a dead moose calf someone poached on Golden Sunlight Mine property near the North Boulder River.

"Why would someone shoot a moose calf?" I asked.

"Some people are idiots," he said. "They got a gun, something moves, they shoot it." He hesitated, checked to make sure no one else was listening to him, and leaned toward me. "Heard you had a little run-in with Manfred."

I also hesitated. It wasn't news Loren knew what happened; in a small town everyone finds out about those kinds of events. They usually don't hear the truth, but what they hear is at least connected to the truth. What was disconcerting was that Loren, a law enforcement officer of sorts, did not want to be seen or heard discussing it. "Yeah," I said softly. "We had a bit of a disagreement."

Loren leaned closer. "You'd best be careful." He arched his eyebrows. "Use your blinkers. Drive the speed limit. Full stop at stop signs."

If I did those three things, I'd be the only person in Whitehall who did. But it was obvious Loren was trying to help. He was offering sincere advice. As a law officer he was closer than most to Manfred. I got a sense Loren was warning me. I nodded my agreement.

I told him we'd be glad to run the photo. "You'll need to give me some details about what day and what time you think it happened."

He nodded. "I got all that in my notebook out in the truck. I'll swing by tomorrow."

A couple years earlier Loren had picked me up in his truck to show me a streambank restoration project state agencies and a landowner were doing on a tributary to the South Boulder. They fenced off the streambank, drilled a well to fill a stock tank for the cattle about two hundred yards away from the moving water. Vegetation was re-established with the cattle out of the stream and the water was clear with fish returning to it. Off in the distance we heard a cry, or more like a wail, and at first Loren ignored it and kept explaining about the importance of the project. But the cry or wail persisted, and finally Loren and I jumped in his truck and he drove up out of the creek bottom and above the road on a bench dotted with quaking aspen trees. The wail was louder, and when we walked into the copse of trees we saw a whitetail fawn kneeling, her feet under her, as a coyote gnawed on her ribs. The deer was watching itself get eaten.

"They hamstring them," Loren had whispered. He grabbed the back of his leg. "Right here. The deer can't run then, and they don't defend themselves."

The deer looked at us with a sense of panic, but the coyote stood calmly, defiant. Loren then retreated to the back of his truck, and I was sure he intended to get a gun to shoot the coyote. Instead he returned with a small hatchet. He walked past me toward the prone deer, further into the trees, and the coyote reluctantly skirted away, not far away, still visibly circling in the brush. Loren approached the deer from behind, held up the deer's head gently under the chin, so the deer was looking level with the ground the opposite direction of him. Loren raised the blunt end of the hatchet a foot or so above the deer's forehead, carefully aimed a strike, and with one firm tap of the hatchet the deer's head fell limp on the side of its neck. He'd killed it with one expertly placed blow. The coyote stood and watched it all.

"Mother Nature can be a bitch," Loren said as he walked toward the truck.

Every time I saw Loren I recalled the hollow thud of that tap, and the cold calculating look of the coyote as I turned back toward the truck.

Laurie suddenly looked at something behind me, and I turned around to see Mary Kristofferson, Annie and Rhonda Horst, each carrying plates of spaghetti, walking toward our table.

Sally saw them and grinned. "Well, I better get going." She was simply making room for others to sit down. Sally winked at me as she stood and began to move away from the table. "Annie," Sally said, "you get more beautiful every time I see you."

Sally reached and placed a hand on Annie's head. And Annie, to my surprise, didn't seem to mind. Annie's short fine hair contained some static electricity; strands of it seemed to rise toward Sally's hand.

"Lance," Sally said, "this is a very special child you have here. I look forward to seeing her each and every time she comes into the store."

"And the only reason I ever come into the store," Annie said, "is to see you."

"Ohhhh," said Sally, proudly.

Rhonda untied her scarf and tucked it into her coat pocket. She had just come in from outside; her face was red and her nostrils glistened with snot.

"Are you going to eat all that?" I asked Rhonda. She and Mary sat across the table from me. Annie sat to my left. Rhonda had taken as much food as I had. I took my finger and thumb and wiped my nose, hoping Rhonda would take the hint. She didn't.

"Too mooch foodt," she said. One of the nostrils looked like it was about to drip.

I looked away, at Mary, who smiled warmly. Loren and Laurie exchanged a glance, and I knew the look meant that they just discovered it was true, Lance at the newspaper was friendly with one of the schoolteachers. Great. More gossip, more rumors.

Let them. I didn't care anymore.

"Blow your nose, Rhonda," encouraged Annie.

Rhonda immediately set her fork down, pulled out a balled-up hanky, and blew her nose with a forceful snort.

"Lance," Annie said, "the four of us are riding together to Fort Benton on Saturday. We're leaving about seven-thirty."

"Which four?" I asked.

Annie motioned to me, Mary, Rhonda and herself.

Rhonda blew out the other nostril with a second burst. "Ya, more Brusch Schpringsteen."

Chapter 33

The sun was just starting to peek above the Elkhorns as the Escort wove through the Boulder Valley north to Great Falls and beyond. The sweet aroma of sugar glazed homemade cinnamon rolls filled the car's interior as the dark dawn surrendered its gray for amber. From the back seat, Rhonda kept feeding me freshly cut sections of cinnamon roll so that my mouth was essentially filled with food for the entire length of the Boulder Valley. There had barely been a word spoken since we'd left Whitehall. By the time we actually crossed the Boulder River and slowed down for the town of Boulder, the pastry tray was empty and wiped clean and my mouth was so dry I decided to stop at the Town Pump to buy a pint of milk. Mary, in the front passenger seat, had marveled at the beauty of the landscape – fresh snow in the mountains, the river fluid and black in the shadows, the draws still holding remnants of autumn reds and oranges – but dozed off shortly before we reached Boulder.

She may not have been a morning person. As she slept, her curly brown hair framed the edges of her face, and her complexion and features were naturally striking without any artificial adornment. She wasn't petite like Annie; Mary was proportioned in a slightly unfeminine manner, with a rigid posture and substantial shoulders and thighs. She wore a dark green turtleneck sweater and had brought a thick bandana to cover her ears during the football game.

She stirred awake the instant the car slowed down at the outskirts of Boulder. She yawned, her mouth uncovered. Boulder itself was barely moving; a hobo-looking guy rode an old bicycle and glared our direction as we passed, an obese woman wearing gray sweatpants waddled out of the post office and an older woman in a waitress uniform, a cigarette dangling from her mouth, closed her car door and stared at us as we drove on past. Those were the only three people moving in Boulder early on a Saturday morning.

At the Town Pump I bought a carton of whole milk, Mary bought a cup of coffee and used the restroom, Annie bought copies of the Great Falls Tribune and the Helena Independent Record, and Rhonda stayed firmly in the car as if on guard duty.

"Is there a more depressing town in Montana than Boulder?" I asked as we rattled over the cattle guard at the on-ramp to I-15.

"Yeah, there is," Mary assured us. "Have you ever seen Browning on a cold dark winter morning? Or places like Poplar, Chinook, or Lodge Grass? Some of the reservation towns are so desperate and depressing they make you cry."

There was a lot left unsaid in those comments, I figured, about her experiences on the reservations, and it was better they stayed unsaid. Mary had been a teacher for close to ten years, at least three of them, I knew from previous conversations, at reservation schools. During those years one of her students, high after sniffing some kind of fumes, had frozen to death walking three blocks to school, and another student had been killed in a car accident caused by his drunken father.

"Too quiet," Rhonda offered during the silence that followed Mary's comment.

"Our bellies are full and our mouths are dry from those rolls of yours," I said.

"Dat's not vat I mean," she said. She jabbed a finger toward the dashboard, toward the cassette deck. "No Brusch?"

"Should I play some music?" I asked her, surprised.

"Ya. Tunes," she said from behind me, and sort of giggled.

"Here," Annie said from the backseat. She handed me a cassette tape. "Tony got this the other day from Jersey. It's a bunch of new Springsteen live stuff."

"Another bootleg tape?" I asked, slipping it in the cassette player.

"Yeah," Annie said. "I don't know where Jersey gets them."

The first song was *Thunder Road*, and Springsteen sang it as a ballad, accompanied only by the piano. Judging from the volume of the applause, there couldn't have been more than fifty people in the audience. He had filled stadiums for years.

"Is this from one of his first concerts or something?" I asked.

Annie had been hidden by the front section of the Tribune. She lowered her arms and shrugged. "How would I know?" she said. She listened. "Sounds plausible. No one's there." She disappeared again behind the paper.

I pressed the eject button and the cassette popped out. I took it, held it, and looked it over. It was a plain TDK tape with no writing on it anywhere. "Where do these things come from?" I asked. "How do people living in the Montana wilderness end up with Springsteen bootleg tapes?"

No one answered me.

I slid the tape back in. The next song offered a rollicking intro to *Rosalita* and drew a boisterous cheer from a large and loud live audience.

"That's not the same crowd," I said. "It's a lot bigger."

"Well, obviously," Annie said.

"But it's two different songs from two different periods in his career sung in front of two different audiences," I said. "On the same tape. Where do these tapes come from? Who makes them? How do they get the songs?"

"Mysteries all, Lance," Annie said from behind the paper.

"I don't understand," I said. "These tapes don't just magically appear."

"But they are magic," Annie said. "Someday we have *got to* see Bruce live. All of us who are part of this ridiculous football season. Anyone who has ever been in this Escort should go with us to see Bruce."

Rhonda gazed up from her lap toward me, and through the rearview mirror I saw one firm nod of her head. "Ya, coundt me in," she announced.

Rhonda was in. I couldn't help it; I had to laugh. She did Rhonda.

I had seen a couple concerts during my late teens, to see a band called Rare Earth, and then a group of us ventured to Denver to see a Grateful Dead concert. Neither had been particularly inspiring or memorable. But before we reached Helena on our way north I knew with a clarity and a certainty that Annie was right about seeing a Springsteen concert. I not only enjoyed his music, I respected and admired it. There was no doubt in my mind he and the E Street band would be not only entertaining but inspirational and memorable. There was an integrity to his music that you felt in your heart, your soul and your bones.

"Remember the first time we were here?" Annie asked as we skirted the east side of Helena along I-15. "The Kentucky Fried Chicken caper?"

I remembered. It had manufactured a team meal based on an impossibility and later in Whitehall, an early morning team communion of sorts that some believed spurred the astonishing run – *this ridiculous season*, as Annie called it – of the Ranger football team.

"Was that only two months ago?" I asked. "Eight games or so, a game a week," I thought out loud, "so yeah, it was only a couple months ago. It seems like it happened years ago."

"Or just yesterday," Annie said softly.

"I still don't see how a half-bucket of chicken filled a whole high school football team," I said.

Annie groaned. "Give it up, Lance." My constant bewilderment about the chicken had most definitely outlived its usefulness.

North we went, past the Sleeping Giant rock formation, along Prickly Pear Creek, through the canyon section between Helena and Great Falls and one of the most beautiful and underappreciated drives in all of Montana. Massive rock outcroppings first buttressed a small creek then the Missouri River on either side, raptors glided up and along the cliffs, and a sharp blue sky framed by green conifers and rock spires greeted us at every wide curve in the road. A couple Whitehall vehicles – one of them carrying the O'Toole clan – zipped by us, with a friendly horn honk and much excitable waving. Lyle had a hard time figuring out Rhonda Horst's sudden affection for Whitehall Ranger football, and as he sped past I could see the bemused look in his eye at Rhonda stoically hunched in the backseat. Truth was, I also had a hard time figuring out Rhonda's sudden affection for Whitehall Ranger football. She simply kept showing up when it was time to leave for the game.

"You've heard of companies named Sperry Rand and Burroughs, right?" Annie asked from the backseat. I heard the rustle of the newspaper, and I was hoping she didn't intend to quiz us about the world's business or finance dealings.

"Sperry Rand sells business equipment," Mary said. "They supply the school district with supplies and things like that. Why?"

"They just merged to form Unisys, the world's second largest computer company," Annie said.

"Computers," Mary said with contempt.

Rhonda perked up, and lifted her chin. She probably wondered what a computer was, and why a nice lady like Mary would hate one.

"Daily newspapers are all going to computers," I said. "There was just a big article about it in the Montana Press Association newsletter.

"I got news for the both of you," said Annie. "The whole world's going to be using computers."

"You think so?" asked Mary.

"No doubt about it," Annie said. She was using her tone of voice that suggested a confidence that only a fool would challenge. "Eventually everyone will have their own computer."

Mary apparently was unfamiliar with Annie's confidence. "Their own computer?" she asked. "Why? Nothing is more frustrating than a computer. They're always breaking down."

"Let's think this through," Annie said. Thus, I knew, began the lesson. "Take this car, for example. Ford created mass manufacturing of automobiles in what, about 1908 or so. Vehicles were unreliable and unsafe then, came in only one color with no real accessories."

Experience taught me that whenever Annie said *Let's think this through* she wanted to enlighten me about something. We were just north of Cascade. It was possible we would be enlightened all the way to Great Falls.

"Ya," Rhonda said. "Ve hadt an oldt Fordt." She waved a hand dismissively. "Idt barely verkt at all."

"But now look," said Annie. "Can you imagine life without cars, trucks, motorcycles? A couple human generations after their invention, life without a car is unimaginable. It's unthinkable. And think of the automobile's technological and practical advancements and improvements. Think of the revolutionary design enhancements and comfort upgrades. Automatic transmissions. Air conditioning. Power steering. Disc brakes. Cassette decks. Think of the shapes and sizes and colors and models. The list of improvements is endless. All in, what, two lifetimes."

I remembered our family's first car. It was a heavy block of moving metal.

"Think how fast things change now," Annie said. "Look at television from its debut to now. Look at medical advances. Think of airline travel. The manual typewriter will be gone – I mean *gone* – before I graduate from high school. My kid, if I ever have a kid, may never hear the words *manual typewriter* spoken in his or her entire life."

She went on like that, responding to Mary's comments and challenges, verbally tapping Mary's thoughts into place, until we stopped for an early lunch in Great Falls. Bruce was singing a somber live version of *Racing in the Streets* when I turned off the engine at a Wendy's on Eleventh Avenue.

"And in your lifetime, Lance," Annie told me in the silence after the engine quit running and the stereo quit playing, "you'll be reading newspapers, watching movies and playing music on a computer. A tiny computer, no bigger than a watch."

Rhonda guffawed and waved a hand as if to say, *such foolishness*.

A computer no bigger than a watch? That seemed farfetched. But I knew better than to argue.

After lunch we still drove north, through central Montana flatlands; winter wheat fields, telephone and power lines on either side of the two-lane highway, with Mary nodding off to my right, and Bruce soberly in concert singing about the human frailty, brutal violence and tragic heartache in a live and stark version of *Nebraska*. The bleak and barren and withered landscape seemed a perfect match to the solemn and disheartening music.

In the backseat, Rhonda sat slumped and asleep; she reminded me of a vulture's posture in a tree. Annie continued to read the newspapers. I asked her if there was anything in either paper about the Whitehall – Fort Benton football game, but she said the Tribune only had the time and location of the game.

"Sorry," she said, "no artificial emotional or psychological incentives for the Rangers this week."

"Speaking of emotion," I asked, "tell me again about Johnny Pep. What was he doing over at our house?"

"I told you," she said. "He apologized. He said where he was from that's what they did, make fun of handicapped people."

In truth, she hadn't told me. I had asked, and she had responded in terse and tiny phrases but she hadn't explained how she had gone from emotional devastation in her bedroom to 'Here, Johnny, clean our fridge.' She was reluctant to talk about it, and when she was reluctant to talk about something it made me nervous.

"Johnny's part Salish and Kootenai," Mary said. "He's experienced things no child should ever have to experience."

"So has Trish," I argued.

I gave Mary and Annie a chance to speak but neither one did.

"When did the Johnny Pep Whitehall Fan Club officially start?" I asked.

Neither one of them took the bait.

"I don't want that kid at our house again, and I don't want you alone with him," I told Annie. "We're clear on that, right Annie? I mean, come on. First Cody, then Bonner Labuda for Christ's sake, and now Johnny Pep."

She did not respond. That meant I might as well not even bothered.

In silence, we passed great empty fields, sections of cropland of bare dirt. They were summer fallow fields, the ground rested on a rotating basis, with fields of winter wheat stubble laid low touching all four corners of the fallow land.

"See all that dirt?" Mary asked me. "All that bare ground?"

"Yeah?" I answered, as if it was a guess.

I could see the mischief in her eyes. "Know what causes that? It happens when the farmer makes a mistake and plants the wheat upside down."

"I can see that happening," Annie deadpanned.

"Seriously," Mary said. "When you plant a seed, it has a top and a bottom. You have to make sure the top is pointed up, toward the top of the ground and the sky. If you plant it upside down, the plant just grows down, deeper into the ground, and dies."

"I'm surprised so many farmers make that mistake," I said. "You'd think they'd be smarter than that."

"And they do it so perfectly," Annie said. "I mean, look at those fields, those are some perfectly exact lines."

"The whole field was planted upside down," Mary said, and laughed. "You have no idea," she told us, "how little kids on the reservation take extreme delight in the mistakes of the dumb white farmers." But then she stopped laughing, and simply looked out the window.

There were virtually no trees; power lines ran along the highway; a railroad track that seemed to run straight through grain elevators paralleled the highway to the east. The only wildlife we saw was one lonely coyote in the distance. It loped away from us with indifference.

And then, a little after noon, we turned off the highway down the hill into the Missouri River valley bottom and entered Fort Benton. You could see the school and football field from the flatland rims above, and you could hear the high school band from almost anywhere in town. We drove to the school and field looking for a place to park and ended up three blocks away in front of a row of houses. The Fort Benton bleachers were already filled and kickoff was still over a half-hour away. The town didn't look big enough to have that many people at a football game.

Both teams were on the field warming up, and my eyes searched for – and found – Tony, reaching down and stretching his legs, head down, holding his ankles. Rhonda insisted on paying for Annie and Mary at the gate, and I used my press pass. There wasn't much sun through a scudding layer of slate-colored clouds, and the wind had a bite to it. I wore my winter jacket, and stuffed a stocking cap and gloves into the pocket.

The WHS pep bus – with purple soap Ranger scribbling all across the windows – pulled up and dropped off purple and gold clad Ranger fans. Old Tom led the troops off the bus. He wore his ancient WHS purple sweater and an odd cap that reminded me of a turtle's shell; I looked closer and saw it was an old leather football helmet. It looked so historic, I thought you'd need carbon dating to determine its age. Young Tom was next off the bus, and before he had taken two steps he'd lit a cigarette. He looked like he slept under a bridge the night before. Morgan's mom was next, followed by other parents including Sara Dickson, and Laurie and Loren Shaw; school officials including Martha Cullen and Ed Franklin. Ed wore sunglasses and a black leather jacket that was an uncanny replica of Jersey's coat. Jersey had his on, so I knew it wasn't the original. All in all, forty or so Whitehall fans emerged from the bus, paused to get their bearings and stretch their legs, then made their way toward the field. Old Tom drew some stares and amused glances as he made his way across the field to the portable bathrooms at the far end of the north end zone. I went a little out of my way to cross paths with him as I got into position to take pictures.

"Do you believe the size of this crowd?" I asked him when we were virtually side-by-side.

He wagged a finger at me. "I gotta piss like a racehorse," he answered.

I sort of pointed toward his headgear. "Where'd that come from?"

"From the past," he told me.

My estimations of crowd size had always been poor, but my guess was there were over five hundred people in the bleachers and behind the plastic orange snow fence along the Fort Benton sideline.

I walked all the way down the Fort Benton sideline behind the players and in front of the fence to get to the far end of the field, the south end zone. The goal posts were painted maroon and a large and colorful Texas longhorn emblem was painted in the middle of the field. The grass in each end zone was painted maroon, and almost every person I passed along the fence wore a maroon Longhorn windbreaker or Longhorn hooded sweatshirt. Every now and then I spotted a farm supply or national implement dealer logo, and while a bright green John Deere logo was appropriate for a place like Fort Benton, it was out of place along the Longhorn sidelines.

Both teams were finishing their warm-ups. Tony jogged to block an imaginary defender as Dave pitched the ball to Logan on a sweep. I opened the game program to find the number of the All-Star Longhorn linebacker, Troy Johanssen. Number eighty-one. Six feet, three inches tall. Two hundred and nineteen pounds. Senior. I stuck the program in my coat pocket and looked up the other end of the field to find Johanssen, and spotted him immediately. You could tell he was an athlete by the way he moved. I saw him before I even saw the number on his jersey. He stood out just standing.

After a stirring version of the National Anthem sung by an Air Force choir from Malmstrom Air Force Base in Great Falls – with the Rangers locked in unflinching position for every note – and after the relatively scant number of Whitehall fans cheered introduction of the Rangers, it was time for introductions of the home team. The Rangers – outside of Dave Dickson who sprinted and screamed with exaggerated glee – trotted out of the end zone when introduced and perfunctorily slapped hands as the starting offense gathered one-by-one at midfield. The Longhorn players rumbled down the field, as their fans stomped and cheered, as the band played and as the cheerleaders jumped and twirled and danced. One at a time, the Longhorn players dashed from the end zone to midfield, each time with boisterous and emotional accompaniment, and when the Longhorn players met at midfield they banged heads, pounded shoulder pads and leaped into the air. It was all an impressive display of school and community spirit, of team camaraderie and individual enthusiasm.

The first Longhorn offensive drive was impressive as well. They took possession at their own thirty yard line and ten plays later were in the end zone for a 7-0 lead. Johanssen played tight end, and they ran to his side of the field almost every play. He caught one pass for about seven yards and it took three Rangers to bring him down. When the Longhorns scored, the cheer from the Fort Benton fans was deafening. They cheered as one, with one voice, as if they'd been practicing it all season.

Whitehall ran the ball three times for two yards and had to punt. Johanssen made two of the tackles and on the third play, a sweep where Dave pitched the ball to Nate Bolton, Johanssen drilled Dave right after he'd pitched the ball.

A couple penalties helped stall the next Fort Benton drive. Whitehall had to punt after two short running plays and after Dave was sacked for a loss on third down. The truth was apparent: Fort Benton had big strong players, including the best player on the field.

The Longhorns scored again to make it 14-0, and late in the second quarter a Fort Benton punt returner went sixty yards for a touchdown to make the score 21-0 at the half. The Longhorns left the field to a standing ovation from what I was sure were now close to a thousand fans. A few Longhorns pumped their fists in the air as they trotted to the locker room. The Whitehall players, heads down, battered and bruised, wearily hiked toward the bus, and gathered in a loose group between the bus and the sideline. Dave, helmet in his hand, was the only Whitehall player showing any animation. He patted players on the rump when he jogged alongside them; he patted other teammates on the shoulder pads and seemed to have an encouraging word for each Ranger. I saw he was wearing a big bandage on his chin, probably from the early collision with Johanssen, who had continued to whack Dave on virtually every play. Tony's posture suggested seething frustration. Even Coach Pete trudged across the field dejectedly, his head down. Jersey seemed to be pondering one of life's vast and complex uncertainties as he strode toward the end zone for the halftime team meeting.

I headed to the concession stand for some hot chocolate. I couldn't wear gloves to operate the camera, and the combination of the cold air and cold metal of the camera always chilled my entire body via entry through my hands.

"I don't care if we win," said Annie, "I just hope all our players get out of here alive." She was carrying two cups of hot chocolate. "Do you need some money?" she asked.

Actually, I did need some money. I hadn't even thought of that. She gave me two one-dollar bills.

"Poor Dave," Annie said. "Have you seen what they're doing to him?"

I nodded. I even had a few pictures of him getting hit or flying through the air. "It's legal," I said, "to hit the quarterback when he doesn't have the ball."

"I know, because sometimes he does have it," Annie said. "But he's like a child out there. It's like a boy playing against men."

"A noisy child," I added. "You notice how he's always talking?"

Ed Franklin saw us and stopped. "Our poor Rangers," he said.

"We're getting our ass whipped," Cal Walker said. "That number eight-one is brutal."

Ed agreed. "He'll be a star playing college ball for the Griz, and we have what, a fifteen-year-old at quarterback who maybe weighs one-thirty with his belly full and his helmet on? Tell me who has the advantage there."

On Whitehall's first possession in the second half, on a third down and eight yards to go pass play, Dave threw a pass over the middle to Tony. Whitehall had made back-to-back first downs and a completion would have made it three straight first downs. Tony made a sharp cut toward the ball and was stretching, reaching his hands out for the catch, when a maroon blur stepped in front and launched himself just as the ball touched Tony's fingertips. It was perfectly timed and violently executed; a ferocious and vicious collision. Johanssen's helmet hit Tony between his chin and throat, and Tony was probably unconscious before he hit the ground. The Longhorn players on the field and on the bench had cheered every hit on every play, but after an initial burst of exhilaration as Tony collapsed helplessly to the ground there was a stunned silence. The only noise was from Johanssen himself, who stood above the fallen Ranger; he pounded his own chest once, twice, and waved his arms over Tony, the international boxing *you're out* sign.

Tony had landed on his side, his neck twisted at an angle on the ground. One of the referees quickly crouched, then dropped to his knees to look at Tony's face. One second later the referee frantically waived at the Fort Benton bench for the trainer to come out and immediately a young woman was scurrying from the sidelines to the field, where Tony still hadn't moved. On his own, I later found out, a doctor from Fort Benton climbed over the snow fence and jogged to the field toward Tony.

I didn't know what to do. I resisted the natural inclination to snap some pictures of the trainer and doctor on their knees alongside Tony's motionless body. I saw Annie across the field, her hands up near her chin, covering her mouth, Mary standing to her side with an arm around her. I started to walk from the sidelines onto the field, but stopped when Jersey departed the sideline and trotted toward Tony's prone body. He stopped and gathered the other ten Rangers on the field into a circle, had them take a knee, and then approached Tony. By then, somehow, the thin and distant wail of an ambulance filtered in my consciousness. I found out later the announcer in the booth called the Fort Benton ambulance crew as soon as he saw the doctor kneel next to Tony's damaged body. The siren sound grew louder, and as I stood there, dazed and in a way, numb, the red lights swirled in the somber gray sky as the ambulance drove right onto the field and stopped not ten feet from Tony.

The next thing I knew Annie was sprinting across the field as two ambulance attendants – dressed in cowboy clothes and wearing baseball caps – took out a stretcher. I began running from my side of the field and to my surprise no one – not the referees or school officials – stopped either Annie or me as we converged on Tony's body from opposite sides of the field. I could see the terror in Annie's eyes, and I could tell from her expression she saw the same thing in mine.

"Is he going to be okay?" Annie cried out in a voice that startled me.

Jersey held Annie by the shoulders. "He's still unconscious."

I could see Tony's eyes were closed; his arm bent oddly under his body. His legs were split apart in an angle that had to be uncomfortable. He hadn't moved since he'd hit the ground.

"Is he breathing?" Annie moaned.

"Miss, we gotta get him to Great Falls," one of the ambulance attendants said.

"As a precaution," the doctor said.

Tony coughed. No one moved. Tony coughed again and by himself rolled flat onto his back, face to the sky. Annie plopped on the ground, behind Tony, her knees on either side of his head. I moved over and stood a foot or two from Annie. The doctor, on his knees, leaned forward above Tony's face with his nose about six inches from Tony's.

"Do I know you?" Tony asked the doctor.

I couldn't help it. I burst out laughing. Just a short burst of relief.

The doctor lifted Tony's arm and asked him something I didn't quite hear.

"Did we win the game?" Tony asked.

"Do you know where you are?" she asked him.

"You just came out of coma," I said.

"Not a coma, actually," Annie corrected.

"Lance?" Tony made an attempt to sit up but the doctor held him down. All around me, from both sides of the field, a smattering of fans clapped and cheered weakly at Tony's movement.

"Don't move, young man," the doctor said. "Okay, stay put for a minute."

"Is he going to be okay?" Annie asked again, a little more courage in her voice this time.

"Annie?" Tony asked.

"I'm here, Tony. Right here," she said from just behind the doctor.

"Annie?" Tony asked. "Did we win the game?"

"Not yet," said a determined voice. It was Dave Dickson, who had ventured toward Tony from the kneeling circle of Rangers.

"Get him out of here," ordered the doctor. One look from Jersey sent Dave back to his teammates.

The doctor asked Tony a series of questions – his name, where he lived, where he was – and Tony struggled with the answers. He said he was thirsty. Then he neatly looked to his left and vomited.

The doctor moved some of Tony limbs and had him shift his head to the side and up and down, but the doctor still had the ambulance attendants lift and slide Tony onto a stretcher. Fans from both teams erupted into amazingly loud applause and Tony drew a cheer when he lifted one hand and waved. It was not a *I'm okay* hand sign. It was a *goodbye* wave. The kid knew how to play to a crowd. They slid the stretcher into the back of the ambulance; one attendant jumped in the back, and closed the doors. The ambulance drove away lights flashing without the siren on. It departed the field with a visible bump-bump when it went over the curb and hit the street.

“Are you his dad?” the doctor asked me. “He’s got a concussion for sure. If he’s lucky, and I think he is, that’s all that’s wrong with him. Nothing seemed broken or torn, no sign of any internal injuries. He’s on his way to Deaconess in Great Falls. I want him there for observation overnight at least. Okay?” He paused. “Jesus H. Christ, Johanssen about broke your poor boy in two. You have no idea how happy I was to hear that kid cough.”

I nodded. “Thank you,” I told him.

“I’m going with Tony,” Annie said. She was already starting to move away from me. “I’ll get someone to take me.” She was further away. “You stay. I’ll see you in Great Falls after the game. He’ll be fine. Come get me in Great Falls.” She turned and ran off the field.

Lyle and a horrified Aspen O’Toole met her at the sidelines and all three of them took off in a trot.

The game resumed in what seemed like slow motion. The crowd on both sidelines was muted, almost tentative, and the players themselves were initially less vocal, less emotional and less enthusiastic. Except for one kid. Dave Dickson couldn’t stand still and wouldn’t keep his mouth quiet.

There were eight minutes left in the third quarter when Whitehall got the ball back, and Dave stormed onto the field toward Troy Johanssen and pointed an index finger up toward Johanssen’s face. The top of Dave’s helmet was about halfway to the top of the *8* in Johanssen’s number eighty-one. Johanssen was nearly a foot taller and seventy pounds heavier than Dave. Dave did, in fact, look like a child.

Dave did not, however, sound like a child. “We’re going to run this ball right up your ass,” Dave told him. I heard the words clear as I’d ever heard anything in my life.

Johanssen shoved Dave out of the way, toward the Whitehall players, and Dave put his mouthguard back in and marched into the WHS huddle.

On the first play Dave kept the ball and gained four yards on an off-tackle run. He and Johanssen collided and Dave went straight down. He also popped right back to his feet, mouthed off to Johanssen – with his mouthguard in he was harder to understand, but it sounded like he called Johanssen a pussy – and got back to the huddle. The next play Dave carried the ball on a sweep and gained another three yards before being tossed out of bounds by Johanssen almost at my feet. It was like a lion tossing a gazelle.

“That all you got?” Dave yelled, still on his back. He got to a knee and stayed there a second and grimaced as he attempted to stand. Johanssen stalked back to the Fort Benton huddle. “That all you got?” Dave yelled. “That all you got?”

He looked up, and saw me standing there, watching him, camera in hand. “Hey Lance,” he said. “We’re going to win this son of a bitch for Tony.”

Logan carried the ball up the middle for no gain, and Whitehall had to punt. It was a low snap, Colt bobbled the ball for just an instant, and he got the punt off just before two Longhorns collided with him. Fort Benton was flagged for roughing the punter, and Whitehall suddenly had the ball in Fort Benton territory.

"Coming your way, eighty-one," Dave said as he walked from the huddle to the line of scrimmage. "Right down your throat, bad ass."

"Shut up, you mouthy little shit," Johanssen shot back.

The referee told them both to shut up and play football.

Dave turned and handed the ball to Logan, who broke free for a fourteen-yard gain. Morgan and one of the JeffScott twins double-teamed Johanssen and he wasn't in on the tackle.

"Where were you, eight-one?" Dave taunted him. "We missed you. You take a little break? We're going to sweep left this time, and we're going to pick up another ten yards."

Johanssen growled like a caged animal, and took a step toward the line of scrimmage. Dave pitched the ball to Nate, who turned the corner on the sweep and gained eleven yards. Johanssen drilled Dave and drove him backward five yards. Johanssen got up while Dave struggled to his feet. He towered above Dave. "What?" Johanssen said in a voice of mock surprise. "I can't hear you."

Dave wasn't all mouth, but he certainly wasn't shy. He had shouted and cheered and cajoled his teammates, the officials and the opponents all year, but he had never done anything like this. First, though, he had to catch his breath. He got up, bent over, and made his way to the WHS huddle. The Rangers were now inside the Fort Benton twenty yard line.

"We're coming to get you, eighty-one," Dave said.

"Bring it, you little shit."

Dave stood over the center. He looked up at Johanssen. "Who you calling little? You trying to hurt my feelings?"

"Oh, I'm going to hurt you," Johanssen answered. "Count on it."

Logan busted up the left side for fourteen yards and another first down. Two plays later – both inside power runs by Logan – Whitehall was on the Fort Benton four yard line, third and goal.

Whitehall broke the huddle and lined up. "Okay, here's what happens next, eighty-one," Dave said from behind the center. "I'm going to turn and fake a handoff to him" – he pointed to Logan – "and he's going to tear a hole through you into the end zone. Then I'm going to step over your sorry ass and celebrate a touchdown." He put his mouthguard back in. Then he quickly took it out. "On two. Okay. We're going to run right here" – he motioned just off the center – "on two."

Amazingly, a Fort Benton lineman jumped offside; the referee moved the ball a couple feet, half the distance to the goal line.

"You think I was lying?" Dave yelled at the Fort Benton players. "I said on two. It's on two. Not on one. Two."

It was on two. And Dave did fake a handoff to Logan, who lowered his head and collided with Johanssen at the goal line in a thunderous and brutal clash of pads, muscle and determination. Both fell sideways, and Dave leaped over them for the touchdown.

The Whitehall sideline and bleachers erupted into cheers.

"There's six, baby! There's six." Dave screamed as he jumped in circles. "See you next drive, eighty-one."

I had spent the whole game on the Fort Benton sidelines and there was a palpable change when Whitehall scored to make the score 21-7. And while all the other Whitehall fans watched the jubilant Rangers trot off the field, from the Longhorn sidelines I watched number eighty-one leave the field, jogging slowly, his shoulders oddly sloped, his left shoulder lower than the right and his left arm hung loosely down the side.

He was greeted by the Fort Benton trainer, who took him back to the bench and sat him down, and although I was twenty yards away from him, I could see him grimacing in pain. His breath came in rapid gusts through his nose. Helmet off, he put his head back and aimed his face straight up toward the darkening sky, which he seemed to be beseeching for relief.

Johanssen stayed on the bench, two trainers working on an obviously injured shoulder, when the Longhorns got the ball. Fort Benton lost two yards on two running plays and a third down pass was incomplete. After the punt Whitehall had the ball on its own forty yard line. Although Johanssen hadn't taken the field as tight end on offense, Dave acted as if he was just noticing then the Longhorn linebacker was absent from the field.

"Where's eighty-one?" Dave called out as WHS broke the huddle. "Here eight-one, come on," Dave said, as if he was calling a dog." He got behind center and looked at the defense. "Oh, oh. He's not out here. He got an owie? What you boys gonna do without the big man, huh?"

Dave took the snap and the play flowed left, a sweep to the short side of the field. He pitched the ball to Nate, who was tackled the instant he got the ball. But the ball hadn't actually reached Nate. Cale Bolling had gone the other way, against the flow, and caught the pitch – intercepted the pitch, really – for a reverse. Outside of Cale, not a single player from either team was still on the right side of the field. Cale was a track sprinter and no one even touched him until the Rangers mobbed him in the end zone. In what seemed like a heartbeat, Cale had scored a touchdown on a play Whitehall hadn't ever run before. The Longhorn fans were silent as a stone while the WHS fans cheered and yelled. My mind surely had split loyalties. I tried to focus on the game but couldn't keep my mind off Tony.

The score was 21-14 when the third quarter ended and the two teams switched ends of the field. I walked behind the Fort Benton bench and Troy Johanssen sat with his shoulder pads off and a large ice bag on his left shoulder. His elbows were on his knees and his head, covered in a towel, was bowed. He was physically and emotionally done.

Logan and Corey Walker tackled the Fort Benton running back for no gain on the first play of the fourth quarter. Logan and Cody Phillips tackled the runner for a loss on the next play, and Cody and one of the JeffScott twins forced the quarterback to throw the ball out of bounds on the next play. Fort Benton punted again, and again Whitehall had excellent field position.

Across the field from me, Coach Pete's face was bright and glistening and he and the reserves stood as one single agitated line along the sideline. Jersey, in his black jacket, was an island of calm. The sky had darkened enough to require me to put my flash on the camera, and Jersey's sunglasses were perched high on his head. He stood, arms folded, quiet, studious. Coach Pete couldn't stand still; Jersey almost looked indifferent.

"Here's what we're gonna do," Dave lectured the Longhorn defense. "We're gonna march down the field and score a touchdown, and do you know what?" Dave paused, as if waiting for a response. "There's not a goddamn thing you can do to stop us."

The Rangers were in the Tramps formation, with Morgan in the backfield. Logan became what turned into a human battering ram. He carried the ball three straight times for a first down, and opened the hole with a block for a seven-yard gain by Dave. From the sidelines I saw Logan's right elbow covered in blood and the right side of his jersey and pants soaked with blood. He had a gimpy stride when he walked, but he still ran as hard as he had on the first play of the game. Dave may have been the vocal leader of the team, but Logan was the commander. He was just an ornery and tough kid, and brought that toughness to everything he did. The Rangers ran the reverse pitch to Cale again, and although Fort Benton had defenders in position to stop the play, Whitehall still picked up fourteen yards.

On first down, Dave faked to Logan and threw a sideline pass to Colt for another first down. Dave threw a wide receiver screen to Colt for another twelve yards. A couple plays later Morgan opened a hole, Logan followed, and scored standing up, with a Longhorn safety draped over him. The photo of Logan standing, ball firmly in the crook of his arm, a Fort Benton player hanging off him almost like a monkey from a tree trunk, was on the front page of the Ledger that week. The extra point from Colt made it 21-21 with six minutes left in the game. Johanssen lifted his head when Whitehall scored, then dropped it again, alone and silent on the bench.

Fort Benton bobbled the kickoff and simply fell on the ball at their own eighteen yard line. Logan snuffed a run up the middle and on a sweep Nate tripped up the ball carrier. On third and four the Fort Benton quarterback dropped back to pass and Tanner Walker sacked him for an eleven-yard loss. Tanner had defeated his blocker so quickly he almost beat the quarterback back to the pocket.

A shaky punt – that produced an audible collective groan from the Longhorn fans – gave Whitehall the ball close to midfield with just over three minutes left to go in the game.

The Rangers broke their offensive huddle with a clap and a quick step while the Fort Benton defenders sauntered into their positions.

"See the scoreboard?" Dave asked the Longhorn players. "See it back there, behind you?" Dave repeated, and a couple Fort Benton players actually turned to look. "Pretty soon the visitors are gonna have 28. I know it and deep down, you know it. Admit it." He got behind the center to accept the snap. "You can't stop us, and we can't be stopped."

"That's enough," Logan told Dave.

Logan pounded the middle for six yards. He needed a helping hand from Morgan to get to his feet. On the next play he ran for two yards and for the first time all game fell backwards.

Under center, Dave sniffed once, sniffed twice. "I smell the stink of defeat. And it's coming from you," he told the Longhorns.

On third down and two yards to go the Rangers ran the reverse pitch again, and this time the Longhorns were ready. Cale got the ball and saw two Fort Benton defenders waiting for him. The Rangers had run the play once too often.

But Cale pulled up and stopped, lifted his arm, and threw a high floating pass twenty-five yards downfield to a wide open Colt Harrison, who hauled in the ball at about the twelve yard line. Had it been a better pass, he would have scored easily, but the ball hung in the air long enough for two players in the Fort Benton secondary to tackle him just as the ball arrived.

On first down Logan ran off tackle for three yards, and on second down Dave tucked in the ball and skirted off-tackle for seven yards, down to the Fort Benton two yard line. Jersey called time out and with a bottle of water in each hand walked across and down the field to join his players. Logan took his helmet off and dropped to a knee, with his hand on the facemask, the helmet pinned to the ground. The rest of the Rangers, except for Dave, did the same thing. All the Longhorns trudged wearily to their sideline. They reminded me of a boxer who was one punch away from going down. Despite the relative quiet along the Fort Benton sideline, I couldn't hear what Jersey was telling the Rangers. I saw him talking, saw the players listening, and heard the sound of his voice and a random word, but I couldn't hear what he was saying. It was odd, I thought, that I could hear a one-hundred-thirty-pound quarterback over the roar of the crowd, but couldn't hear the head coach twenty yards from me when the crowd was essentially silent.

It was third and goal at the two yard line with just over one minute left in regulation, and the Rangers lined up in their Tramps formation.

"You know what happens next?" Dave asked the Longhorn players.

"Shut up," Logan ordered from behind. I heard the words clearly, with the buzz of the crowd directly behind me. "Just give me the goddamn football."

Dave put his mouthguard in and wordlessly stood behind the center. He took the snap, whirled to hand the ball off to Logan, who crashed through a Longhorn tackler. He scored standing up and lifted the ball aloft when he strode into the end zone. Later that night, he gave Tony that ball in a Great Falls hospital room.

The Longhorns had sixty seconds and three timeouts, but they never mounted anything resembling a drive. Four straight passes went incomplete, and the game ended with Dave quietly taking a knee and jubilantly absconding with the football.

Old Tom, gout and limp and all, was the first Whitehall fan on the field, and he ambled directly to Logan and gave him a long hug. Logan seemed a bit surprised to find himself in the arms of an old guy he had maybe seen around town a couple times – an old guy wearing an ancient helmet and a baggy purple sweater – but Logan, bloody arm and all, allowed and tolerated the embrace.

The Whitehall sidelines were chaos and exhilaration, cries of happiness, wild expressions of raw pride and sheer elation. The Whitehall kids and parents cheered and jumped on each other and on the players, but their demonstrations of joy hushed when I showed up. It was because of Tony. I needed to see and talk to him as soon as possible, and my aim was to head immediately toward Great Falls after the game. I shook hands quickly with an ebullient Coach Pete, who asked me if I knew how Tony was doing. I told him I intended to find out. I found Jersey, who quietly assured me Tony was fine. He couldn't know any more than I did, and I had no such assurances. I quickly congratulated him and a few of the players – Colt and Cale – came to me and asked about Tony. I needed to find Mary and Rhonda and make hurried arrangements for them to get rides to Whitehall and instead found Trish, who sat all bundled up, her glistening cheeks wet with tears. She opened her arms and I bent forward for a surprising firm hug. She hung on to me longer than I expected she would.

"We did it," she said into my ear.

"We sure did," I said.

"Tell Tony I love him," she said.

"I'll tell him," I assured her.

She let me go and I turned around to see Slack, his cowboy hat crooked on his head, a broad smile crooked on his face.

"Yeee-hawww!" he yelled far too loud. I was only a foot from him. His shrill cry echoed in my ears. He practically jumped into my arms, although my arms hadn't been necessarily held open. Holding on to me, he kept jumping and jumping. And jumping. And yelling like a cowboy herding cattle.

Finally I spotted Mary, standing five yards away, talking with Ed Franklin and some other schoolteachers. Except for Mary they wore muted grins. She kept stealing anxious glances my way because she knew I'd want to get out of Fort Benton and on the road to Great Falls.

I pried myself away from Slack and headed toward Mary, who immediately headed toward me. I held her arm and asked her where Rhonda was, and Mary told me to follow her. I must have had a quizzical expression on my face.

"Just follow me," she told me again.

I did, and she led me to the Escort. There in the dark backseat, alone, rigid as a statue, sat Rhonda. I opened the door but she didn't look my direction.

"Rhonda, you should ride home with someone else," I said. "We've got to get to Great Falls and see Tony."

She shook her head.

"Rhonda," I pleaded. "You don't want to get stuck in Great Falls for God knows how long."

She nodded tersely. "I go."

Mary and I looked at each other, as if seeking help. I was tempted to yank Rhonda from the car and escort her to the bus.

"Wouldn't you rather ride home on the bus, or with the Franklins or with," I hesitated, "anyone going to Whitehall? I don't know how long we're going to be in Great Falls

Rhonda looked up to me from the dark car's interior. "Drive," she told me.

When we – the three of us – entered Deaconess Medical Center after our frenetic drive to Great Falls we found the reception room completely empty. Not a soul was there to greet us or help us or commiserate with us or do whatever someone is supposed to do when three anxious people enter a strange hospital for the first time.

Rhonda hadn't uttered a word the entire drive to Great Falls, and still hadn't spoken when she exited the car in the hospital parking lot and followed a few steps behind Mary and me into the hospital.

"Where would he be?" I asked Mary in the hospital reception area.

She didn't know.

"We have to find Annie," I said. Because, of course, Annie would know.

I caught a glimpse of a nurse walking down a hallway to our right, but she turned a corner and vanished from our view. I took off running after her, and after I turned the corner into a different hallway I saw three or four nurses going different directions. One saw me suddenly stop running and hurried my direction.

"Can I help you?" she asked.

"My son is here somewhere," I said. "He's got a concussion."

"The football player?" the nurse asked.

"Right," I said. "From Whitehall."

"He's over here," she said. She took two steps in front of us, stopped, and looked back at me. "Did you guys win the game?"

It was not the question I expected her to ask. "Yeah."

She laughed. "You have no idea how happy he'll be to hear that. Follow me."

I followed her. Mary, with Rhonda in tow, couldn't quite keep up, and followed about ten yards behind me.

"So Annie's your daughter?" the nurse said.

"Right." I was tempted to ask what prompted her question.

"Delightful child," the nurse said coldly.

"Where is she?" I asked.

"Wherever she wants to be," the nurse said. "Here we are." She opened a door and there, in a mostly dark room, in a mostly unwrinkled bed, was Tony, lying neatly and serenely on his back, resting.

"Hey Lance," Tony said slowly when he saw me. He made a motion to raise an arm to wave, but thought better of it.

"I'll send for Doctor Cooney," the nurse told me, and disappeared.

I got alongside the bed. "How you feeling?" Mary and Rhonda stepped into the room, and Rhonda went over and gently patted Tony's shoulder. Mary hung closer to the wall.

"Okay, I guess," he said dreamily. "I can hardly move my neck. My head hurts."

"But you can move everything? Arms and legs and all that?" I asked.

He ignored my question. "Did we win the game?" he asked.

"Oh ya," Rhonda answered. "Viteholl von."

Tony never took his eyes off me, even when someone else spoke.

"You were knocked out for a long time," I said. "Jesus, you had me worried."

"Did we win the game?" Tony asked again.

"Yeah," I said. "28-21. Logan was a monster. Cale and Colt worked some magic on a reverse pitch play, and Dave never shut up the whole game."

Tony's expression suggested he wasn't sure of the response. "Did we win the game?" he asked.

I nodded. I figured he'd understand what a nod meant. "They won the game for you," I said. "Dave told me that. Dave told me that *during* the game. While Whitehall was still losing he told me that."

Tony closed his eyes and clamped his mouth closed as if something painful streaked through his head. His eyes fluttered open. Only a tiny light was on, a single tiny bulb that cast a dim beam of light straight down, off to the side of the room. Despite the shadows and murky light it was obvious Tony didn't look quite right. His skin tone was pale or bleached, toneless and bloodless. His eyes seemed not fully open or alert. And he looked skinny somehow, and weak, almost frail under the blanket. I thought about turning on a light but something told me the lights were not off by accident.

"It's called perseverating," Annie said from behind me. She had just entered the room.

"What is?" I asked. She moved toward the bed and stood next to Tony, within reach. His eyes didn't follow her. She looked like a waif, I thought, slender, young and innocent. But she was already in charge.

"Did we win the game?" Tony asked.

"That is," Annie said.

"What is?" I asked.

"He's asked me fifty times if we won the game," Annie said. "I keep telling him that yeah, we won, by a touchdown. But he keeps asking. That's called perseverating…asking the same question over and over."

"How do you know we won the game?" I asked.

"Wouldn't a more proper question be, *How do you know what perseverating is?"* Annie asked. She didn't wait for an answer. "Lyle called somebody," she added. "He found out right away."

"Lyle?" I said. That's right, I realized, Lyle and Aspen brought Annie to the hospital. "Where's Lyle now?"

Annie shrugged. "Aspen started crying every time Tony asked her if we won the game, and Doctor Cooney thought it was best for everyone if she left the room for awhile. They might be down in the cafeteria, I don't know."

"Where were you?" I asked.

"Doctor Cooney's office," she said. "I was looking through some textbooks about concussions." She flipped her thumb the direction of Tony. "Hot shot there's got a doozey."

"Doozey of a concussion?" I asked.

"Right," Annie said. "That Johanssen kid really rang Tony's bell" – she looked at Rhonda – "sports jargon for head trauma." She looked back to me. "He's got every classic concussion symptom. He's confused. His responses and reactions are delayed. He's got blurred vision. Sensitive to light. He keeps asking the same question over and over and simply does not understand or comprehend the answer to that question. He hasn't thrown up again but my guess is he will if he eats anything. He's got a headache, which is understandable since he got absolutely creamed by that kid. And you'll love this. He doesn't remember anything about the game or the bus ride to Fort Benton. He remembers leaving school and getting on the bus, but that's it."

"Jesus," I said.

Rhonda shook her head with slow, sincere sorrow.

"Is he going to be okay?" I asked.

"Should be," Annie said. "We're going to have to keep him here overnight. For observation."

We? I wondered.

"Did we win the game?" Tony asked.

It was astonishing how quickly you could ignore someone who asks the same question over and over, even when that someone is your injured son.

"He can go home tomorrow?" I asked.

"Not sure," Annie said. "We'll have to see how he feels in the morning."

We? Shit, who's we? I wondered.

Sadly, I regret to admit I also allowed the selfish thought of how far Tony's injury would put me behind at work. No matter how injured he was, or how long he was in the hospital, I still had to get a paper out on Wednesday. I was falling further behind by the minute. Work was piling up just by standing in a Great Falls hospital room.

"You'll be fine, Lance," Annie said. "I can help with the paper. Laura Joyce can pick up the slack. There's nothing you can do but wait, so you might as well relax."

"Did we win the game?" asked Tony.

"I think I'm going hit him myself the next time he asks that," Annie said, and smiled.

A tall gray-haired man in a white smock walked in.

"Dr. Cooney," said Annie, "this is Lance, my dad." We shook hands. "That's Mary, a friend of ours, and that's Rhonda, who makes the best cinnamon rolls in the whole world."

"Nice to meet you," Dr. Cooney said. "Did Annie here fill you in on Tony's condition?"

What the hell, I thought, *how does Annie fill us in on Tony's condition?* "He's got a concussion," I offered.

"Exactly," agreed Dr. Cooney. "With any head trauma we want to err on the side of caution and keep him here overnight. We'll monitor his condition, and provided his mental faculties start to return in the morning he should be able to go home tomorrow."

"Can he play football next week?" I asked. The instant I asked the question I knew I shouldn't have.

"I wouldn't advise it," Dr. Cooney said directly. "But legally I can't prevent it." The tone of his voice suggested he wished he legally could prevent it.

"Did we win the game?" Tony asked. Everyone ignored him.

"He's not playing next week," Annie said, shaking her head. "No way." She kept shaking her head. "Absolutely not."

"I agree with Annie," Dr. Cooney said.

I agree with Annie? I thought. *She's a kid and you're a doctor. You can agree with her on who was the tenth U.S. president or what the capital of Norway is but shouldn't you take the lead on medical diagnosis?*

"Once you have a concussion you're more susceptible to another one," the doctor continued. "We're talking head trauma, which is a serious injury. His brain, essentially, has been temporarily damaged. It will need time to heal. How many chances do you want to take with his brain?"

Tony closed his eyes.

"You okay?" Annie asked.

He just sort of hummed in response.

"You need some rest," she advised.

"Is he allowed to sleep?" Mary asked. "I thought if someone has a concussion you're supposed to keep them awake."

"Lots of people think that, but it's not true," Annie said.

I looked at Dr. Cooney for confirmation. "She's correct," he said. "Let him get some sleep. We'll keep an eye on him."

"Maybe we should get something to eat," I said. "Can we come back later?"

Dr. Cooney nodded. "Come back in an hour or so. If he's awake you can stay for a minute or two. He really needs to rest."

“Got it,” I said. “Tony, buddy, get some sleep. We’re going to grab some food but we’ll stop back after a while. Is there anything you need? Anything we can bring you?”

The questions baffled him. “Did we win the game?” he asked. There was a tone of sorrow in his voice, of fear perhaps.

“Get some rest,” I told him.

We filed out of the room, Annie last, with Dr. Cooney lingering behind, for a final check on Tony’s condition.

Lyle and Aspen were upstairs in the hospital cafeteria, seated closely at a table along a window that reflected the light from within and allowed no view through the darkness outside. A tray rested on the table in front of each of them. Lyle had eaten whatever had been on his tray; Aspen barely touched some kind of salad. Her makeup had run in streaks down her cheek, and her eyes were red and wet and mournful. Lyle was considerably more upbeat, in part because he had to buoy his daughter and in part because he was amazed and awed by the Ranger win over Fort Benton.

“They really won that game?” Lyle asked me when I approached the table. Aspen barely looked up.

“Thumped them,” I answered. “Thanks for taking Annie and for watching out for us. I mean, thanks for everything. But you should have seen those Rangers. Logan and Cale, Colt and Dave, all of them. My God, they played some serious football.”

“Did you see Tony?” Aspen asked. Distraught, heartbroken, pale and pouty, she was still a beauty.

“He’ll be fine,” Annie answered.

Clearly, Aspen wasn’t so sure. “He’s so…” but she couldn’t finish. She leaned her forehead on her father’s shoulder.

He held her gently by the back of the neck and rubbed her hair softly. “She’s not sure he recognized her when she first walked in the hospital room,” Lyle said.

“He has delayed brain functions,” Annie said in her lecturing voice. “I told her that. Several times, I told her that. He recognized her when she walked in, but it took a little while for that recognition to register externally as awareness.”

A tale of two viewpoints, not the first example of the disparity between Aspen and Annie. Aspen’s reaction was personal and emotional, and Annie’s was impersonal and clinical. Whatever the cause of Aspen’s concerns and sorrow, Annie wasn’t helping.

“Do me a favor, okay Annie,” I asked. “Get me a cheeseburger or something. Take Mary and Rhonda with you and get them whatever they want. All right?” She hesitated. She wasn’t used to taking orders from me, or from anyone, actually. "Thanks," I told her. I looked at Mary. "Go ahead, go with Annie. I'll be there in a minute."

Haltingly, Mary led Annie and Rhonda toward the food service entry point to obtain a tray, silverware and food. Rhonda held onto her purse as if some mysterious and invisible stranger was just around the corner, prepared to pounce and snatch.

"You okay?" Lyle asked me when it was just the three of us at the table.

I nodded. "I'm fine. I wanted to say thanks again. Really. Thanks."

Lyle's expression told me to stop thanking him.

"I gotta spend the night here with Tony," I said. "But you can head out anytime you'd like."

Lyle's expression told me not to worry, as if to assure me he was in no hurry.

"Could you take Mary and Rhonda home with you?" I asked. "I got a hunch Annie's going to insist on spending the night here with me."

"You couldn't march Annie out of here at gunpoint," Lyle said.

"She's a bit headstrong," I admitted.

"A bit," agreed Lyle. "You should have seen her at check-in." He resisted an urge to smile. "She kicked some hospital ass." It was possible Aspen intended to speak; Lyle pressed her head softly against his shoulder.

"What did she do?" I asked. No matter what the answer to that question was going to be, it was not going to surprise me.

"Well," Lyle said, "there was some initial static about his insurance coverage or something, and Whitehall was not in the Deaconess service area. Something like that. I don't know. I didn't catch it all. Apparently the school doesn't have a relationship or contractual arrangement with Deaconess. I didn't catch it all."

"They weren't going to admit him?" I asked, amazed. "Jesus Christ, he came here in an ambulance."

"I know, I know," Lyle said. "They were going to admit him, I'm sure, but no one knew his name, the name of his parents, his insurance provider or that kind of thing. That's when we showed up. I tried to help, but Annie took over."

I didn't need to be told what had happened then. I'd seen it and lived it in other venues, in past years, in other conditions.

"She's only a kid, Lance, she's a child, and she essentially commandeered the place," Lyle said, marveling at the recollection. "She's what, four and a-half feet tall? She insisted she was his official guardian, that she had legal authority, and that she was capable of making any and all decisions related to Tony's condition or medical decisions."

I shrugged. "She more or less is."

"Lance, she's just a kid."

"She's not just any kid," I said. "You know that."

"Yeah, but *they* didn't," he pointed at a table of dining nurses when he said *they*. He shook his head in wonderment. "It was them against her. Them and all their decades of hospital regulations and laws and procedures and protocols and administrative orders and red tape against one single, what, thirteen-year-old, girl." There was amazement in his voice. "And the thirteen-year-old girl won. She stood up to them, defied them, and conquered them."

Like they had a chance, I thought. "She might be twelve," I said. "I lose track."

Lyle waved away my objection. "Her actual age doesn't matter. The point is she took charge. Of a hospital admission! Of an emergency room metropolitan hospital admission! She could have easily told them I was chairman of the school board and could handle or confirm whatever needed to happen, but she refused to do that. Even when I tried to help she would have none of it. She insisted that this was between them and her, and she won. Christ, Lance, she is one determined little girl. She would not back down. She would not relent. They may not have known what they were dealing with when they started, but they sure as hell did by the time it was over."

"She can get that way," I admitted.

"She told them to call the governor's office," Lyle said. "She even gave them the telephone number of the governor's office off the top of her head. She even handed a nurse the telephone receiver and gave her the governor's personal phone number." Lyle was terrifically impressed.

"She probably had to call it once when he came to Whitehall to give her that award," I said. If she saw the number she'd remember it. It wasn't all that long ago, anyway. It wasn't that impressive for her, I thought. He'd been to Whitehall only a couple weeks earlier.

Annie, Mary and Rhonda took seats at a table nearer to the cafeteria entrance. Annie probably knew it was best she maintain a little separation from Aspen. Annie waved me over.

I stood up and was about to thank Lyle again. He shook his head. *Quit thanking me*. "You guys go ahead and eat. We'll be glad to take Mary and Rhonda back to Whitehall. Whenever they're ready, we can head out."

"The strange thing about all this," I told Lyle, "was that even had I been here when Tony was brought in, the same thing would have happened the same way. The sad truth, Lyle, is that she really is his guardian. She probably does have legal authority. I don't know, to be honest. I don't know about our insurance coverage. I don't know about any of that stuff. She takes care of all of it. She takes care of everything. She has to, Lyle. She has to, because I don't."

Later that night, close to nine o'clock, just before Annie and I were saying a final goodnight to Tony – to my utter amazement – Jersey, Coach Pete, Cody, Colt, Dave and Logan showed up sheepishly outside Tony's doorway. The team had showered in Fort Benton, took the bus to Great Falls, dined together, and despite receiving no encouragement from hospital officials decided to make a quick stop to see Tony.

"I called from Fort Benton and asked if we could stop and visit Tony and some jerkoff at the hospital said no," Coach Pete said. His face had a sheen to it. "So I thought, Crap, we can't stop. But the more I thought about it, the more I decided Crap, we're going to stop. And here we are."

"We worried about hauling in the whole team, so we elected to send some emissaries," Jersey said meekly. "We won't stay long. We promise. How is he?" Jersey calmly looked as if he'd just left a library meeting. You'd have never known he had engineered one of the biggest upsets in Montana Class B football through nothing short of a miraculous comeback victory.

"He's sore and…" I wasn't sure what to say.

"And disorientated," Annie chimed in. "He's confused. And he's got a bad headache. He suffered some serious head trauma."

"Tell me about it," Dave said. "You could measure that collision on the Richter Scale."

"Yeah, that was ugly," I said. "Legal, but ugly."

Jersey nodded his understanding. Coach Pete understood; he'd been at the scene of dozens of accidents in his law enforcement career.

The four boys, in their Ranger jackets and slacks, were timid and respectful, shy and uncertain about the formal and sterile surroundings of a hospital.

"Can we give him this?" asked Logan. He winced as he held up a beat-up football, filled with scribbled signatures.

"Is that the game ball?" I asked.

Colt nodded. "We all signed it."

There was no doctor or nurse in the hallway, and no one knew if six more people should be allowed in Tony's little hospital room. Instinctively, we all looked at Annie, who nodded. "I think he's still awake. You can't stay long, though."

The same group of boys who had stormed down the football field in Fort Benton were unsure how to enter a dim and quiet hospital room. With short, tentative steps and worried, anxious expressions, they opened the door and crept in. Tony managed a weak smile, but the friendly banter only lasted a few minutes. The four boys knew precious little about hospitals and brain trauma, but they recognized pain when they saw it, and they saw it in Tony. Logan quietly slipped the football toward Tony, but instead set it on the bed. Logan would say later he wasn't sure Tony even saw the football.

Tony, to my relief, did not ask them who won the game. He either didn't or couldn't say anything.

"Logan took care of the kid who hit you," Colt said.

"He laid him *out*," added Cody, whose forehead was rubbed practically raw from repeated collisions using his helmet.

"You'd have been proud of us," Colt told Tony. "We out-hit them, we out-worked them and we out-fought them. We did exactly what you told us at halftime."

Something about what Colt had said registered a hint of recognition within Tony's mind, and you could literally see his brain struggling – and failing – to retrieve the fullness of that recognition. It was an awful thing to see.

"Okay," said Annie, taking a protective step toward Tony, "we need to let him get some sleep."

No one needed to be told twice. The boys filed out immediately; the football remained, resting on the bed. Jersey was last to leave.

Tony's eyes were already closed before the players and Coach Pete had vacated the room. Jersey held up a hand toward Annie, a gesture meaning *give me just a minute*.

He stood at the head of the bed and lightly held one of Tony's hands. Tony's eyes never opened. Jersey put his other hand somewhere behind Tony's head and leaned forward. "We're going to win next Saturday, with you on the sidelines next to me," Jersey whispered, but whispered loud enough for Annie and me to hear. "And you're going to score a touchdown in the state championship game. I promise."

Chapter 34

Tony dozed softly in the passenger seat and Annie scoured the Sunday Great Falls Tribune as we somberly drove south from Great Falls. Annie was worried about me falling asleep so bought me a sixty-four ounce cup – more like a barrel – of pop for the drive home. Annie and I had spent the night in the hospital waiting room. We slept a little, but not enough. My head felt filled with a dull ache and my eyes were dry and bleary; my eyelids seemed to crackle when I blinked.

Springsteen's album *Nebraska*, volume turned low, with its stoic narration and mournful stories, was an unfortunate yet appropriate match for our weariness. It had been less than twenty-four hours since WHS had won arguably its biggest football game in the school's existence, but we were so emotionally and mentally drained it seemed almost personally and athletically insignificant. The weather wasn't helping. A cold gray metal sky spit faint flurries of halfhearted sleet, and intermittent gusts of wind howled from the west.

"It says here the Rangers got standout performances from Logan Bradshaw, Colt Harrison, Cale Bolling and Dave Dickson in an impressive come from behind win over a talented Fort Benton team," Annie said from behind the newspaper. She was quiet a moment as she read the article. "It's actually pretty well written," she said. "Not only does the article have the right players and the right players' names spelled correctly, the article is also quite complimentary of the Rangers and Jersey. It calls the Rangers a gutsy and gritty collection of over-achieving players that showed the heart of a champion." She paused again. "They make a pretty big deal of Cale's pass to Colt."

I looked over at Tony. His eyes were open.

"Had you guys ever run that play this year?" I asked him.

"Maybe a couple times in practice," he said morosely. He had demonstrated enough mental and emotional progress to be released from the hospital shortly before noon on Sunday. His cerebral faculties were returning, but not yet fully returned. He was aware the Rangers had won, and he was aware he had been injured in a football game, but he remembered nothing about warm-ups, taking the field, playing the first half, or even ever being in Fort Benton. He seemed dejected, in part because he was still in pain, in part because he had no true connection to the startling win and in part because his analytical powers had progressed to the point he understood he would not get to play for the Rangers in their next game. "The pass is supposed to go from Colt to me," he added sullenly.

"I wondered about that," Annie said. "I wondered why Cale threw it and Colt caught it, when Colt is the former quarterback and knows how to throw. Cale's a pretty good receiver. Not as good as you," she added quickly, and kindly.

“Next time Colt’ll throw it,” Tony said. It sounded like each word cut a painful path from his mind through his mouth. “Then sometime I’ll throw it. Jersey says if we rotate the positions no one’ll see it coming. It’s like a new play every time.”

“Seems a little simplistic,” Annie observed.

“It’s football,” Tony said, “how complicated can it be?” He would have shrugged, I think, if it hadn’t hurt to shrug.

Ahead, a dismal gray sky darkened to an angry black, and I noticed oncoming traffic had fresh snow pelted into the grilles and on license plates, almost like plaster or frosting. Beyond the swirling darkness you could see more faded gray, but the upcoming squall was bringing a nasty swath of sudden and early winter weather.

“If I drink all this pop I’m going to have to water a tree every ten miles,” I complained. The thought of exiting the car in that weather was not appealing.

“Better that than falling asleep, Lance,” Annie said. “You looked awful this morning, if you must know. You don’t look too good now, in fact. You resemble a bum, actually.”

“Jesus Christ, Annie, I spent the night on a saggy hospital couch, bright lights everywhere, in a reception room,” I complained. I looked at myself in the rear view mirror. It was not a pleasant sight. “I slept in my clothes, haven’t showered or shaved, or even brushed my teeth. How am I supposed to look?”

“Little testy, are we?” Annie asked.

“Stop it,” Tony said wearily.

The storm hit as suddenly as a collision. I immediately eased my foot off the gas. The driving lane was still clear, but snow had quickly accumulated in the passing lane, on the shoulder and across the landscape. For five minutes we were buried, nearly blinded, in a blizzard, then just as suddenly, almost violently, released into a dry pale sky. No snow anywhere. It was as if we emerged into a different time or place. You could have stood on the highway and pointed exactly where the squall started and stopped. The abrupt changes in weather never ceased to impress and astonish me. The kids were used it. Driving in and out of the snowstorm drew no comment from either of them.

We stopped in Helena for a bathroom break, and we stopped in Boulder for a bathroom break. When I got back in the car there was a sixteen-ounce bottle of Pepsi on my seat.

“I’m going to be able to float home,” I said.

Tony had never left the car, but an unopened bottle of Gatorade was in his lap.

“Regrettably, you need the caffeine,” Annie told me. “Not only do you have to get us home safely, something tells me you’re going to be up half the night at the Ledger.”

She was right, I would be. It was only the middle of the afternoon and I was already bone weary.

We drove in and through and out of Boulder on a Sunday afternoon and saw not a soul outside of the Town Pump.

"Where is everyone?" I asked Tony.

He was already sleeping. Sixty seconds from the Town Pump and his chin was on his chest and he was asleep. He reminded me, slightly, in his posture there in the Escort passenger seat and his modest mental dysfunction, of Slack. I looked in the rearview mirror and Annie was reading the Helena newspaper.

"Eyes open and eyes on the road," she told me.

"I'll have to take a leak before we get to the Elkhorn turnoff," I complained.

"Thank you for that fascinating announcement," she told me.

The Boulder Valley offered us a blaze blue autumn sky and golden and maroon colors along the river bottom. Tony slept the entire journey.

I was home for less than twenty minutes that afternoon, and during that time the telephone rang three different times so three different people could ask the same question: *How's Tony?*

It was a good question. He had gingerly parked himself on the living room couch and turned on the TV to watch a pro football game, and I had Annie sit next to the telephone so the noise of the phone ring would only happen once. He watched TV with the sound completely off and I was a little worried about his lingering painful sensitivity to light and sound. I took another piss before I left the house and to make sure Annie got the message, I left the bathroom door open.

"I could float a battleship in here," I called out to her.

"Very mature," she said, not even looking my direction.

Before I left the house for the Ledger, Tony's eyes were closed and his mouth was open, a soft hoarse rasp wheezing from his throat. I wished I could stay home with him, but that was impossible. The amount of work facing me was staggering and depressing.

I had been at the Ledger an hour and the telephone rang four different times so four different people could ask me the same question: *How's Tony?* I finally stopped answering the phone. I had too much work to do. An hour later I called Annie, though, to make sure she stayed home and make sure none of Tony's friends came over to the house.

Before I spoke, Annie said, "He's fine. He's got a headache. He's sore but he's home and sleeping right now."

"Annie, it's me," I said.

"Oh," she said. "Are you calling to tell me you urinated again?"

"You're not going anywhere, right?" I asked.

"No," she said. "I'm Tony's answering service."

"How is he?"

"Sound asleep," she said. "He was awake for a few minutes. He wants the light off and the TV sound off."

"Is that normal?" I asked.

"Sort of," she said. "I called Doctor Cooney and he said it may be a result more from the headache and collision than the actual concussion. If he's like this still tomorrow we're supposed to bring him to Butte for a checkup."

"You called Doctor Cooney?" I asked.

"He said I could," she said. "I have four phone numbers for him. He was at home, I think, because I heard a football game in the background."

"He never gave me a phone number," I said.

"You want to call him?" Annie asked.

"No," I said. "Are you sure he wants you to call him? I heard you got a little testy when Tony was admitted."

"From who?" she asked. "Lyle," she said, answering her own question. "Yes, I had to get somewhat firm with a nurse," she confessed. "She wasn't what I would call cooperative, so I sought someone who would be, oh, let's say, just a little more responsive. Doctor Cooney showed up and we got along right away."

I tried to think of something to say, but nothing came to mind.

"Mary called," Annie said. "I said you were at work but probably wouldn't be answering the phone."

Right, as always. "I should probably call her."

"Probably," Annie agreed.

"Okay," I said. "You stay home. Call me if you or Tony need anything."

"I will. I might as well tell you right now that Tony is not going to school tomorrow, and I'm going to stay home with him."

"Sure," I said. Like I was going to argue with her. "I'll call the school first thing in the morning."

"Actually," she said, "you'll *intend* to call the school. You know what Mondays are like. *I'll* call the school. I'll ask them to make an announcement over the intercom so we won't get every tenth grader at Whitehall High School coming over here tomorrow."

As usual, she was several steps ahead of me.

"What would I do without you?" I asked her.

"That is not a question we want to contemplate right now," she said. "Get to work. I mean it. You can't spend all night there. You looked ghastly when you left here. You need to get home and sleep."

She was right about that.

Jersey showed up about six o'clock. Unshaven, in his black leather coat, a black sweatshirt underneath, he looked almost as tired as I felt. He sat down slumped at the table and rubbed his eyes harshly with the palms of his hands.

"How's Tony?" he asked.

I explained about the headache, drowsiness, sensitivity to light and sound, and slowly recovering cognitive abilities.

"Cognitive abilities?" he asked. "You got that from Annie, didn't you?"

"Not necessarily," I said. "I know some big words myself. I'm a newspaper publisher, remember."

"So what's a cognitive ability?" asked Jersey. He smiled. "I'm kidding. It sounds like Tony's getting better, which is wonderful. He took a wicked shot," Jersey said. "Clean, but wicked. That Johanssen kid can hit."

"Yeah, but he also ended up on the bench wearing an icepack," I said.

"Indeed he did," Jersey agreed. "That was a brutal collision with Logan in the end zone. It was the kind of hit that can cause thunder."

"I don't suppose I can use that for the paper."

Jersey shook his head. "It's not an appropriate comment. We should commemorate the team's accomplishment, not one violent collision."

Which, I realized, is more or less what I expected him to say.

We talked about the future: About Whitehall hosting a playoff game on Saturday afternoon against Fairfield. Fairfield was unbeaten and had been ranked as high as number two in the state, but the way the playoff schedule worked, our conference held the right to host a game, and Whitehall was the only conference team still alive. The Fairfield Eagles were annually a powerful playoff team and had thumped Cut Bank 41-0 to become one the four final Class B football teams contending for the title, along with Whitehall, Roundup and Frenchtown. Not a single team that had beaten Whitehall earlier in the year was still playing football.

We talked about the past: About the first half, about the talent of Fort Benton, about the large and supportive crowd, about the electric atmosphere in the stadium, and then he told me about halftime in the Ranger locker room.

"We were down 21-0, right, and although we weren't necessarily playing bad, we weren't playing the way we'd played the previous couple weeks," said Jersey. He sat up a little straighter, as if he was going to enjoy telling this story. "So we get into the locker room, and Coach Pete is throwing a fit. I mean *a fit*."

"None of this is for the paper, is it?"

He smiled and shook his head. "Not a chance."

I put down my pen and leaned back in the chair.

"I'm not kidding, *a fit*," Jersey continued. "I'm surprised you didn't hear him out by the concession stand. Pete slapped a wall with his clipboard, and screamed so loud no one could understand him. I sure didn't understand him. He was virtually unintelligible. Anyway, in the locker room, against the far wall, across the room from me, Tony stands up. Stands up straight and strong, you know, like he can do. Stands up defiant. Stands up like a man. Coach Pete stops in mid-sentence. In mid-word. Just stops talking. I was going to scheme up a defensive adjustment and reassign some blocking assignments on our Tramps formation sweeps but Coach Pete and I both see Tony is just standing there. He looks angry. Hostile. It's like there's a simmering fury inside him."

I nodded. I'd seen the look before.

"But Tony's quiet," Jersey continued. "You can hear him breathing through his nose. It's the only sound in the locker room. Everyone is looking at him, and we're all wondering what happens next. Because we're pretty sure something's going to happen. You know what I mean?"

I nodded again.

"Except for Tony," said Jersey, "it's utterly and absolutely silent. And Tony just stands there, not saying a word. We're all waiting for him to speak, but he just stands there."

"He was probably waiting for permission," I offered.

"That's exactly what he was waiting for," Jersey said quickly. "I nod to him once, a *go ahead* nod, and he nods once back, a *got it* nod. So he climbs up on the bench and stands taller, far above everyone else. His head is up toward the ceiling. His teammates are all seated on the bench or on the floor, and he's standing on top of the bench."

"Did he imitate you?"

"No," Jersey said, surprised at the question.

"Or Coach Pete? He does a mean Coach Pete, never when Pete's around, of course."

Jersey shook his head. "This was all Tony. Pure Tony. There's a bit of theatre in him, you know."

"A bit," I agreed.

"I don't remember his exact words, but they went something like this. 'We don't need to be screamed at by Coach Pete and we don't need new plays from Jersey. We don't need anything new. We don't need anything special. All we need to do is be *us*. All we need to do is play like the team that beat Baker. All we need to do is play like the team that won its last four games. All we need to do is play like the team we know we are. We need to quit playing like cowards. What are we afraid of? Of losing? Of Fort Benton? Of Johanssen?'" Jersey smiled and grunted a small chuckle. "Little irony there, I admit. Anyway, then he takes his helmet and bashes it against a metal locker. I mean, *bang*! Then he keeps going. '*We* didn't come to Fort Benton to play afraid. *Bang!* 'We came up here to win.' *Bang!* 'We came up here to win.' *Bang!* 'To win.' *Bang!* 'And we do that by out-hitting them.' *Bang!* 'Out-playing them.' *Bang!* 'Out-hustling them.' *Bang!* 'Out-fighting them. They're over there right now, in their locker room, laughing.' *Bang!* 'We need to shut them up and shut them down.' *Bang!* 'We're going to dominate the second half.' Bang. 'Dominate!' *Bang!* 'Dominate!' *Bang!* 'Dominate!' *Bang!* 'Dominate!' *Bang*!"

Jersey leaned back in his chair and looked at me like I was supposed to say something.

"What?" I asked.

"You didn't hear any of this? No one out there near the concession stand heard all this? The shouting or the banging?"

I shook my head. "I didn't. No one's ever said anything about it."

Jersey seemed amused at that. "That's surprising, because we were really making a racket in there. Everyone in the room, Coach Pete included, *especially* Coach Pete, is yelling 'Dominate!' and whacking their helmet against a locker, the bench, a wall or the floor or something. Coach Pete was pounding his clipboard against the wall. Sheets of paper were flying everywhere." He hesitated. "And that was our entire halftime chalk talk. We made no adjustments. We made no personnel changes. I never said a word. Not a single word. And look what happened. And do you know what the most amazing aspect of all this is?"

I shook my head. It was too much to comprehend at one time.

"The guy who made this inspirational speech, the guy who was yelling to dominate and smashing his helmet into a locker, the guy who made himself at that moment the emotional leader of his football team, the guy everyone is looking at for leadership, the guy who said he wasn't afraid of anyone or anything…that guy goes out and early in the third quarter gets himself knocked out," Jersey said. "Just like that." He snapped his fingers. "Out like a light. Knocked out and nearly seriously injured." Jersey was looking at me; *don't you get it?* I didn't. His voice picked up an octave. "The underdog team is down by three touchdowns on the road, and then the leader goes down with an injury, and what normally happens? Come on, Lance, what normally happens when the team leader is gone?"

I opted to not guess.

"*The team folds!*" Jersey nearly shouted. "The team quits. The team invariably becomes unsteady and unsure, even unwilling." His eyes opened wide, and he held up his right index finger and tapped it on the tabletop. "But not *this* team. Not *this* team, Lance. This team watches their leader collapse, taken off the field on a stretcher and hauled to the hospital in an ambulance, and how do they react? You saw it. They immediately rally around him. They use the injury as inspiration. And they simply take over the game. They dominate. They dominate almost every position on almost every play." He ended, amazed, in awe.

"Dave never stopped chattering the whole second half," I offered. "You guys were losing by two or three touchdowns and during the second half, just after he got tackled by the sidelines, he looked in my eyes and all but guaranteed me the Rangers were going to win the game for Tony."

"In some ways, the mantle of leadership was passed from a sophomore to a freshman, although Dave's mouth sometimes goes inexplicably into overdrive," Jersey admitted. "But the way that team responded to Tony's injury is the most impressive thing I've ever seen take place on a football field. There," he said, "that's something you can put in your newspaper."

I winced.

"I don't care whose kid he is," Jersey told me. "You write that down and you put that in the newspaper."

Truth was, I had to write something about Tony, about his injury, his overnight stay in Great Falls and his inability to play in the next game.

"And here's the most ironic aspect of all this," said Jersey, his eyes wide with delight. "Tony gave the most spontaneous, most passionate, most electrifying and most inspiring halftime speech I've ever heard." Jersey leaned toward me. "And he doesn't remember a word of it. Not a word."

He was right. Much of that day, halftime certainly included, was completely blank in Tony's mind.

"Will he ever remember it?" I asked.

"I doubt it," Jersey said. "His brain took quite a jolt. In a few days he'll seem pretty close to normal, but he'll probably never recall what happened before or after the actual injury. And in some ways that's tragic. Because he'll never know what he said, and no one else in that locker room will ever forget what he said."

The Ledger phone rang four different times while I wrote the article about the Ranger win in Fort Benton. Ed Franklin called, had also called the house, and had also stopped by the house while I was at the Ledger, determined to check on Tony. Each caller asked about Tony, and each caller asked if there was anything they could do to help. *Like what?* I felt like asking. What could anyone do to help? Rhonda stopped by the house with a pan of chocolate brownies, Mary stopped by with some kind of hot dish and Molly and Trish Ryan stopped by with lasagna. The O'Toole family sent over a bouquet of flowers from Cottage Floral. Annie said Cody and some of the football players stopped by; Tony was sleeping so she wouldn't let them in. A bunch of girls in Tony's class brought by a cake from the IGA, and even though Tony was awake at that point she wouldn't let them in either.

All the while I was at the Ledger. I developed film, wrote the football article and re-wrote a couple press releases – about a federal PILT payment to the county and a new agriculture program for ranchers – to make them more specific to Whitehall. I opened and sorted the Saturday mail – which included a couple large checks – and got Laura Joyce's Monday morning work organized.

The mouse tentatively ventured out a couple times, cautiously probing the scant distance between the wall and the entryway counter for crumbs, but scurried back into the wall every time the phone rang and I reached over to answer it.

A little after nine o'clock the telltale county commission knock meant the movie was over and also meant popcorn and another dousing of pop. I saw his cowboy hat first, then Cal poked his head inside the doorway. The mouse must have smelled the popcorn the same time I did. It stuck its sniffing, pointy little nose out of the hole, but when Cal closed the door behind him the tiny nose disappeared.

"Shouldn't you be home with your boy?" asked Cal.

How does popcorn do it? How does it trigger an urgent and insatiable compulsion by a simple scent? I was no better or smarter than Pavlov's dogs. And is there anything better than that first mouthful of movie theater popcorn? Not to me, there wasn't. I eagerly and gratefully accepted the bag of popcorn and cup of pop.

"What was the movie?" I asked.

"Another Star Trek show," he said. He smiled. "The crew of the Starship Enterprise is getting to be a bunch of old geezers."

"As long as people like you keep seeing their movies they'll keep making them," I said.

"And as long as they keep making them, I'll go see them," Cal said. "How's Tony?"

It took me a moment to respond; my mouth was full of popcorn.

"He's not himself yet," I said. "His head hurts, he's slow to pick up words, you know, slow to respond."

Cal's face reflected worry.

"They say he'll be fine," I said. "Annie's home with him," I said, to reassure him; to reassure us both.

He smiled. "Doctor Joslyn?"

"So you heard about that," I said. It shouldn't have been a surprise. Cal heard about everything. "She helped him get admitted at the hospital, yeah."

"Helped?" Cal said. "I heard she assumed command, almost like a coup." He said it kindly.

"Sounds about right," I said.

"Does he remember anything about the collision?" Cal asked.

I shook my head.

"Just as well, I suppose," Cal said. He shook his head with dismay. "He never saw that kid coming. He was concentrating on the ball and was as vulnerable and exposed as you can be on a football field."

"You're not supposed to be vulnerable on a football field," I said.

"Yeah, well, he was. And God Almighty, he paid a price." He hesitated. "For awhile there, with him laying on the ground, I have to admit, I was scared."

"*You* were?" I asked. "What do you think was going through my mind?"

"I can imagine," Cal said.

But he couldn't imagine, actually. What was going through my mind should not have been going through my mind. And what should have, wasn't. I should have been totally absorbed by grave concern about the health of my son. Instead I was worried about losing light for the photos, about the delay in my arrival back to Whitehall, about the work waiting for me while I stood there, about the complexity of his injury and a possible doctor's visit on a busy Monday or Tuesday.

"For a long time he didn't even move," Cal said. "Then the doctors are out there next to him, and the ambulance shows up. I never really noticed before, but the hushed anxiety of a thousand people is unnerving, spooky."

I nodded. My mouth was full of popcorn. I had spilled some tiny white kernels to the floor, and I could see the mouse's nose – just the nose – in the wall crack.

"You guys spent the night in Great Falls?" Cal asked.

I swallowed and sipped some pop. I wondered briefly what the world record was for consumption of Pepsi in one twenty-four hour period. "In the hospital reception room. On a saggy soft couch. Annie slept in a chair. When I went to sleep she was reading a magazine. When I woke up she was reading a magazine. She told me she slept, but I have no actual proof of that."

Cal shook his head in amusement. "She's an amazing young woman, Lance," Cal said. "You're a very lucky man to have her as a daughter."

"I think that exact thought every day," I said.

"No you don't," Cal said. "But you should."

He was right.

"You tell her that?" Cal asked. "You tell her how lucky you are?"

"Not enough," I admitted.

"You have two special kids," Cal told me. "You're buried in work here day after day after day and night after night, and I appreciate that, but every now and then you have to tell those two kids of yours how grateful you are for their behavior, attitude and discipline. I mean it."

"I know you do," I said. "And I know you're right."

"Some people would argue you have better kids than you deserve," Cal said.

"Some people would be right," I said.

Cal stretched, always a precursor to his departure. "You gonna put in an article about the Thursday night dinner?" he asked. "A breakfast meal this time. Pancakes, sausages and hash browns. The vets at the Legion Hall are cooking, and paying for everything. Sort of a Veterans Day – Ranger Football community dinner."

"At the school?"

"Same place, same time." He stood up. "That didn't last long."

The popcorn was gone. "Must have been hungry."

"Tell Tony we wish him well," Cal said as he walked to the door. "I heard his halftime speech is what turned the tide."

"He doesn't remember a word of it," I said.

"Too bad. I heard it was a dandy. Slamming the helmet into the locker and all that." He opened the door. "Go home. And tell both kids how much you appreciate them."

"Promise," I said.

Cal shut the door behind him. Both mice emerged carefully from the hole and crept in tiny spurts toward the white popcorn scattered across the dark carpet. When I walked toward the bathroom to toss the empty bag and cup one mouse crouched a moment, but that was it. We passed each other, more or less, as they skittered toward the spilled popcorn.

It was about two-thirty that morning when I made the deserted drive back home from the Ledger. I had always been intrigued by my isolated and lonely late night drives when I was seemingly the last person alive in the world. Except on this dreary night I spotted a police car parked across the street from the Ledger, south of Legion Avenue by the railroad tracks. I drove home slowly and carefully.

The dim kitchen light above the sink was the only illumination in the house. I assumed it had been deliberately left on; the kitchen had been tidied and the sink was empty, so I had Annie to thank for her thoughtfulness that evening. The scant light barely reached the living room, but it looked empty and picked up, further evidence of Annie's diligence and Tony's likely early departure to his room.

I went into the bathroom; beheld my reflected ashen, whiskered and exhausted face in the stark light in the mirror, urinated half a quart of Pepsi, splashed cold water on my face and brushed my teeth for what seemed like the first time in a week.

I had to be up in four hours. I had to work eighteen hours the next day, and another eighteen hours the day after that. I didn't know if I could do it, knowing I would, because I had to.

I took off my shirt and socks and threw them in the hamper. It was empty; apparently Annie had even done the laundry. Cal was right. I had to tell her how much I appreciated her, how lucky I was to have her as a daughter, how much I loved her.

And when I emerged from the bathroom, there stood Tony, hair askew and eyes squinty from the bathroom light. "I'm pretty sure that piss lasted ninety seconds," he told me.

"So would yours if you drank two gallons of Pepsi," I said. "How come you're awake?"

He breathed deeply, and opened the refrigerator door. He winced as he peered in the fridge, then shut it. He opened a cupboard door, reached up carefully for a glass, and started running tap water. "What time is it?" he asked.

"Going on three," I told him.

"In the morning?" he asked.

"Yeah," I said.

"That would explain the darkness." He hesitated. "Which morning?"

"Monday morning. Sunday night," I said. "Are you okay?"

"I'm better, I think," he said. He gulped the water. "I'm going to sit down," he said. He refilled his glass and shuffled through the relative darkness into the living room chair and the La-Z-Boy chair.

I followed him. I sat on the couch and wrapped myself up in the blanket. Tony was fully clothed, I noticed; shirt, pants and socks.

"You going somewhere?" I asked him.

He cast a glance down, at his chest and lap. He seemed somewhat amused. "Not that I know of. A few hours ago I didn't know what time it was, but I thought I should get dressed. So I did. A little while later I went back to bed still dressed." He looked up at me. "Goofy, huh?"

"You had quite a shock to your system." I said. "It's going to take a while to recover."

He nodded. "I might be slept out, though." He rubbed his eyes. "I'm not really sleepy now. That's probably a good sign, right?"

"I hope so," I said. "How's your head feel?"

"A little better," he said. "You know what hurts the most is right here," he said, and pressed his fingers near his temples, just below the outside corner of his eyes. "Right here, at the top of the jaw."

"You took quite a shot," I told him.

"Yeah, that's what everyone tells me." He sighed. "I don't remember it. I don't remember being in Fort Benton. I think I remember climbing into the bus in Whitehall, but I can't remember anything after that. I was in an ambulance, right? I don't remember that. I know I was in the hospital in Great Falls but I don't remember how I got there."

"You were knocked out on the football field," I said. "Out like a light."

He nodded slowly. "That's what I hear."

"Did you hear about your halftime speech?" I asked.

"Yeah. I banged my helmet on a wall, or something."

"Do you remember doing that?"

His answer was slow. "No. I don't. I try, but I can't remember."

"Your teammates remember it."

He was silent, motionless, for nearly a minute. "You know what I remember?" In the scant light, I could see him sort of smile. He paused, and slid his tongue over his dry lips. "Mom."

It wasn't what I had expected him to say.

He was silent for another minute. "I remember her eyes. Her hands. Her hair. Her touch. Her voice."

There wasn't anything to say to that. We sat in silence. The furnace kicked on, and a padded little purr pounded from the basement. It was a miracle the furnace worked. It had never once been cleaned or inspected or repaired, unless Annie had someone come in and maintain it without me knowing it, which was entirely possible.

"Do you remember Mom's smile?" he asked softly.

"Sure." She once had a smile that lifted your spirits by simply observing it. It had lit her entire countenance. But she'd lost her smile, and then she was gone.

Tony gulped some water; I could hear a gurgle sound from his throat. "I thought of her when I was in the hospital."

That was probably unfortunate, I thought. She was in her own institution, with her own kind of condition, facing her own kind of trauma.

He sighed. "Nothing was ever good enough for her, was it?"

"Tony, she was ill," I said. "Do you really want to talk about this now?"

He waited a moment to answer. "We've never really talked about it before." He sighed again. "I hardly ever think about her anymore."

He was right. We never really had talked about it. When they were younger, they were told their mother loved them, and were told she sadly had to leave us. There had been more to tell them since, but I never had the courage to truly do so. They generally knew of her illness, and also generally knew it was uncomfortable for me to talk about it. “You miss her,” I asked, gently, “your mom?”

He shook his head. He gulped a breath through his nose. “That’s the sad part. I don’t. When I remember her, I remember her scolding me about something. Nothing I did was ever good enough. I was just a kid then. Just a kid. Everything I did should have been good enough.”

I remembered once arriving home when Amy had been pregnant with Annie and Tony was just a toddler. I stepped into the house and Tony immediately and enthusiastically and frantically crawled toward me, a straight frenetic shot directly into my legs. He hadn’t stopped until the top of his head had banged into my shins. I found it comically amusing at the time, but I also noticed he’d looked back at her once, as if he was afraid she was chasing after him. When I’d looked up from Tony to Amy, her back was turned and she was walking away, out of the room. He’d been fleeing.

“But while I was in the hospital, I remembered her smile and how her hair smelled nice.” He gulped. “I remembered good things. Nice things. For the first time in a long time.”

“You’re a good kid, Tony,” I said. “I don’t tell you that often enough, and I’m sorry. But you are. I’m proud of you. I hope you know that.”

“Yeah, I know,” he said. He turned and looked directly at me. “I do know.” He sat motionless, a little slouched. “You don’t have to tell us. I can see it. We both do, Annie and me. You should see the look on your face when I do an impression of someone you know or make kids laugh or when I was on stage in a school play or in a skit.” He tilted his head. “You beam, Lance. You have this glow in your eyes and a dumb grin on your face and I know it’s because of me. Did you know you did that, Lance, make that face?”

I shook my head.

“It’s the same thing with Annie,” he said softly. “She’s a genius and a prodigy and all that stuff, but what makes her happiest is just talking with you. About anything. And seeing you smile. Mom never smiled. I know it wasn’t her fault, but she didn’t.”

“She couldn’t,” I said.

He hesitated. “We see how hard you work. How you pour yourself into the paper. How you live.” He hesitated again. “How you struggle. But we know you love us and you’d do anything for us. Anything.”

I couldn’t speak.

He yawned. “I guess I need to go to bed,” he said. “All of a sudden I’m really sleepy.”

He stood. “Tony,” I asked weakly as he rose from the couch. “Are you going to remember this conversation tomorrow?”

He looked at me. “I’m going to remember this conversation for the rest of my life.”

Chapter 35

Wednesday afternoon I slept for two full hours. Paper printed – with barely an unfriendly word exchanged in Anaconda – and paper delivered and distributed, I told Laura Joyce I was heading home for a nap and she told me not to come back. She laughed at my surprised reaction and said she was tired just looking at me. I opened a Newsweek and dozed off before I finished the second paragraph of the first article, something about President Reagan trading arms for hostages.

I woke up alone in a cold and dark home; a blanket had been spread across my shoulders. I stood up from the couch and felt as groggy and stiff as if rising from bed after a full night of sleep. So I went through a morning routine to wake myself up: shower, shampoo, teeth brushed.

When I got to the school board meeting I was actually feeling pretty good. The only troubling note was Manfred, who seemed to have been parked across the street in front of our house when I got in the Escort for the drive to the school.

"How's Tony doing?" Molly Ryan asked me when I got to the school board meeting. It was the same question I heard Monday morning at my ad stops, Monday at the post office, Tuesday at the Ledger and now Wednesday at the school board meeting.

Everyone within earshot had heard the question; they all ceased speaking to hear the answer. "Better," I said. "He's got a headache up here, at his temples, but he went to school today and seems to be doing okay."

"He took a helluva shot," said Craig Hanson, a board member. Craig had a couple kids in junior high.

I nodded. "I know it. He knows it too. He doesn't remember it, but he's heard enough about it."

The Ledger football article contained a paragraph on the jump page about Tony's injury. It did not seem to have obviated the need for people to converse about it.

"Trish said you spent the night in Great Falls with him," said Molly.

"Yeah, Annie and I both did. We slept in the reception room." I pretended to smile. "We had better nights."

"Trish was worried sick," Molly said. "It was nice of Annie to call Sunday morning from Great Falls."

"Yeah," I said. I had no idea Annie called someone from Great Falls, but if she called anyone, I was glad it was Trisha.

It was only a slight exaggeration that between Saturday afternoon – when the injury occurred – to Wednesday night at the school board meeting, I had told one hundred different people about Tony's mental and physical condition. There had been wild rumors and speculation – Tony's teeth had been knocked out, he suffered complete memory loss, he had numbness in his legs – and some people seemed surprised he was largely recovered and in school.

“How’s that boy of yours?” a hoarse voice asked from behind me. It was Old Tom, who’d snuck in late, after I’d sat down. He was wearing that odd old leather football helmet again, slightly askew, and it made him looked crooked, or standing at an angle. He wore an ancient football jersey, knitted, kind of, like a sweater.

“Better,” I answered. “He’s back in school and doing fine.”

He nodded his approval.

Lyle stopped in mid sentence and gave me a look suggesting I rise, and I knew he wanted to get the medical update over with so the meeting could begin without disruption.

I stood up. “Tony’s doing okay,” I said, addressing the board, and talking loud enough for even Old Tom to hear. “He spent Saturday night in Great Falls for observation but the doctor and Annie thought he was good enough to come home on Sunday. He had a bad headache for a few days but he’s feeling better now. He was in school today, but he can’t play in Saturday’s game. Thanks to all of you for your calls and concerns.” I sat back down.

Stern looks from Ginny Wilcox and Lorna Baxter, who’d led the charge against *The Confessions of Nat Turner* during a previous board meeting, showed displeasure with the deviation from the printed and distributed meeting agenda. My medical update was not on the agenda. Daniel Purdy must have come to the meeting straight from work; he wore his dark green lumberyard work shirt and his comb-over was slightly askew, a bit fluffed up on the side of his head where the hair came from, as if he’d taken a cap off in his truck right before the meeting.

“You’re a sourpuss, ain’t you,” Old Tom said directly to Ginny. Appalled, she turned with alarm to Lyle, who called the meeting to order, stood, and began the Pledge of Allegiance.

Old Tom stood, scrawny wrinkled hand placed softly on his sagging jersey, over his concave and emaciated chest.

Ed Franklin, wearing a sporty blue and green striped shirt, raced through the first few items on the agenda – an update on the school boiler, enrollment updates, a resolution from the Montana School Board Association, and then read a letter from the governor, who wrote in glowing terms about his visit to Whitehall and the Whitehall School District and his opportunity to recognize the special gifts of Annie Joslyn. Nothing in the governor’s letter or the short board discussion that followed mentioned the assembly’s sudden termination. During the discussion, Daniel Purdy seemed disinterested and Ginny and Lorna exchanged glances of annoyance. Then Ed held up the *Annie Joslyn Day* certificate and the Jeanette Rankin print the governor had given Annie, and said they had been donated to the school and deserved to be displayed somewhere prominent.

Lyle looked at me as if searching for agreement, but the best I could do was shrug. I had no idea where they’d gone or what Annie had done with them. The last I had seen them, best I could recall, had been a week earlier – maybe two weeks or maybe even three weeks earlier, I’d lost track of time –

in Annie's room, on the floor, leaning against the wall. She had made it pretty clear she had no interest in them, and while it wasn't surprising she didn't want them, it was surprising she would suggest they be placed on display at the school.

"Is this okay with you, Lance?" asked Ed. "We could make a little display of them here in the library, or even in the main entrance, outside the office."

"Anywhere would be fine," I said.

"Tell Annie thank you on behalf of the school board," Lyle said. He assigned Ed the task of finding a suitable place for them, and quickly moved on with the agenda.

The meeting topics veered into the math curriculum, a new special education ruling from a federal court, a special Thursday night pep assembly for the community and a proposal that the senior class take Friday afternoon off to help prepare the field and bleachers for the football game on Saturday.

Daniel Purdy shook his head, and Ginny raised her hand to comment.

"We'll take board member comments first," Lyle said.

Molly Ryan shot her hand in the air.

"Molly," Lyle said, to Daniel Purdy's disgust.

"I'd like to support the administration's efforts to involve the community to rally school spirit and salute these kids and these coaches," she said. "I bet we'll have a couple hundred people from Fairfield here on Saturday and I'd like to show them this community and this school supports its student athletes and recognizes their achievement."

"Is this a social club or a school?" asked Daniel Purdy. Technically, he hadn't been recognized. It didn't matter. "I thought these kids were here to learn."

"We're talking about taking two hours off Friday afternoon," Ed said stoically. "Same thing we do on Friday afternoon every Homecoming."

"It's another two hours, on top of Homecoming," Daniel Purdy complained. "We've had pep assemblies and pep buses and the team leaving early on Fridays for away games, and now we have a home game and you want the kids to get out of school early on Friday afternoon?" Daniel Purdy shook his head. "Is there going to be an assembly Friday morning?"

Ed nodded. "School wide assembly Friday morning, a spirit lunch at noon, and then the seniors – only the seniors – will be dismissed early to decorate the field."

Daniel Purdy shook his head with authority. "No, no, no. I object."

Lyle shook his head in dismay. "You mean you're not proud of these kids? You don't think we as a school and community should help celebrate what these kids are accomplishing?"

Ginny raised her hand, and Lyle nodded grimly her direction.

"Ginny Wilcox," she said formally, as if no one knew her name. "I would simply like to point out what the purpose of this institution is." She held in front of her the school district's official manual or guidebook. She found the provision she intended to read. "School policy Nine-H, approved by this school board, clearly states, and I quote-"

"*KEE-RIST,"* lady," Old Tom grumbled.

Ginny, stunned, stopped abruptly. The smelly old man behind her was not only out of order, he had taken the Lord's name in vain. Her expression beseeched Lyle for decorum; but in a willful violation of Robert's Rules of Order, Lyle did nothing, which essentially allowed Old Tom to continue.

"Learnin' ain't just in books, lady," Old Tom declared. He was spread out over three chairs; one leg was propped up straight ahead on the chair seat in front of him, one arm was around the backrest of another chair that his walker was parked in front of, and his scrawny body was slouched in a third chair. For a guy who weighed maybe ninety pounds and looked a little like a ventriloquist's lanky dummy, his raspy old throat implied something that sounded like authority. "Learnin's about life, about sorrow and tribulations and bein' somethin' you can be proud of. And these kids are learnin' more on a football field than you or anybody else ever learned by crackin' open some goddamned book."

Ed nonchalantly put a hand over his mouth to hide the smile, but I saw the twinkle in his eye.

Ginny opted to sit. Not only had she been deprived of her speaking privileges, she was being made an object lesson, neither of which she appreciated. She appeared deeply offended, and she intended to appear deeply offended.

Old Tom more or less glared at Daniel Purdy, who more or less glared back. My mind couldn't comprehend it: *When did Old Tom quit being deaf? And when had he started to make sense?* I scribbled notes furiously.

"Think about what these kids are learnin'," Old Tom continued. "They're learning about teamwork, and courage, and dedication and trust. You think you can learn that stuff in that book of yours, lady? You think you can learn how to work as a team, how to be a champion, by paging through the pages of some book?"

What the hell, I thought, *has happened to Old Tom?* The guy makes more sense than a college professor.

"And you," Old Tom, said, pointing at Daniel Purdy, "I've known you your whole life, and you always was a mean and contrary little shit."

"Tom," immediately cautioned Lyle.

Old Tom held up his right hand, an acquiescence he needed to watch his language. "Sorry, your honor," Old Tom said. "I'll sit down in a minute. I just want to say, though, that when these kids win the championship, I hope you have the biggest goddamn pep rally" – he held up a hand, he knew he'd said a bad word, and he was sorry – "the biggest pep rally in Whitehall history. They're doin' something special here, these kids," he looked directly at Daniel Purdy, "and only a fool can't see that."

Molly talked a little more in favor of what she called the school spirit recommendation, but no one else addressed the subject. The board voted unanimously – with Daniel Purdy maintaining a stern silence – to approve the assemblies and senior class early Friday dismissal.

"Thanks, Tom," Ed as the meeting adjourned.

"For what?" Old Tom asked.

Ed spoke up. "For your comments."

Old Tom stretched himself to his feet, hands firmly grasping the walker. His chin and lips moved as if gumming something inside his mouth. He surveyed the dapper man in the colorful shirt in front of him. "Didn't you used to be Special Ed?"

I arrived at Borden's two minutes ahead of Ed and three minutes before Lyle. Sally, the barmaid, wore a starched white blouse and a black lace vest. I doubted she weighed in triple digits, and I doubted she'd seen more than sixty minutes of sun the past year. You never saw her anywhere during daylight. She slid a bottle of Rainier in front of me before I'd even said a word.

"Where you been hiding?" she asked me.

"Working, mostly," I said.

"You've been at all the football games, I see," she said. A copy of that day's Ledger was open on the bar. She kept her cigarettes and a glass of water, along with – on Wednesdays – the Ledger, at the north end of the bar.

I nodded. "I've seen every one of them."

She indicated the paper. "Says your boy's okay?"

"Yeah, he's fine."

"I heard Annie helped doctor him in Great Falls," Sally said.

"Oh, I don't know about that," I told her.

"Sally, darlin'," Lyle announced when he entered, "whiskey ditch, please, and put it on Lance's tab."

"Lance is all paid up," Sally said. She winked at me. "Annie stopped by a week or so ago, paid up, and told me to stop smoking."

Ed walked in next. He asked for a draft Budweiser and motioned for us to join him at a table. My preference was to belly up to the bar, but Ed liked the relative seclusion of a table. A couple of cowboys hunched over drinks near Sally's section of the bar, and a couple younger guys were shooting pool. Wednesday nights were typically quiet for the Borden; Wednesday bowling league at Roper's occupied most of the bar crowd.

"Just a heads up, boys," Ed said. "Manfred's parked across the street in the park." He looked right at me when he said it.

"He more or less followed me here from school," I said. "Before that I think he was parked in front of my house."

"Because of that Cody thing?" Lyle asked me.

I shrugged.

"You should file a complaint with someone," Ed told me.

"With who?" I asked. "Based on what? He's a cop. He's just doing his job."

"What job? He's stalking you," Lyle said. "Like he's got a vendetta."

"That's the point," Ed said, "He does have a vendetta."

"Maybe I should go out right now and talk to him," I said.

"Bad idea," said Ed. "Very bad idea."

"Agreed," Lyle said. "You should avoid him, not confront him."

"I can't avoid him. He knows my schedule. Sunday night late, when I left the Ledger, he was parked over on Legion by the fishpond. Monday night when I was getting out of the car at my house he cruised by the driveway."

"Tell Rachel," Ed said.

"What's she going to do?" I asked.

"I don't know, but if you tell her she'd at least know," Ed said.

Lyle nodded. "Manfred hasn't earned his reputation by accident. He can be a real prick when he wants to be, and it looks like in your case he wants to be. You better tell somebody, either Rachel or the county sheriff or someone."

Sally stopped by with a tray of drinks. Lyle asked her where those came from as she placed them on the table. "Ed Franklin, you are one devilishly handsome man," Sally said.

"You ought to see him dance," I told her.

"Love to," Sally said. "Drinks are compliments of the gentlemen at the pool table."

In unison, all three of us looked toward the pool table. One of the guys held up his bottle of beer, as if in a salute. "Ledger guy," he called, "thanks for putting our wedding picture in the paper."

"You bet," I called back.

We'd had a wedding picture of one of the Kountz boys with his lovely dark-haired South Boulder Valley bride in the Ledger. A one-column photo was too small, and although a two-column photo seemed too big, I went with the two-column version. Apparently that decision was rewarded with a round of drinks.

"That's a good sign," Ed deadpanned. "You're drinking in the bar with your buddies the day your wedding picture is in the paper."

"He married one of the Simon girls," Lyle said. "I'm sure she's over at Roper's bowling."

"Hey, I have a question," I asked. "Do you guys think Sally's a vampire?"

"A what?" asked Ed.

"Vampire. You know, up all night, sleep all day. Drink blood, live forever, all that stuff."

"Sally?" Lyle asked. "She's worked here for twenty years."

"Maybe one hundred and twenty years, who knows," I said. "Have you ever seen her during the day?"

"How could someone like you have a genius for a daughter?" Lyle asked.

"I think Sally's a Lutheran," Ed said helpfully.

"Never mind." I told them. I could feel the energy draining from my body. The nap had given me a reprieve, but it was going on ten o'clock and I yawned before I could even cover my mouth.

"We keeping you up?" asked Ed.

"It's been a tough week," I acknowledged. I yawned again. "Shit. I think it's catching up to me."

"Is Tony really okay?" Ed asked. "You've said he is, and he says he is, but he took quite a wallop in Fort Benton."

"He'll be fine," I said. "I haven't seen him much the last couple days, but he went to school today. Last time I talked to him he said it still hurts right here." I put my index fingers on either side of my head, next to the temples.

Lyle nodded. "I heard him tell Aspen that. You know when he got hit, he got smashed from the front, in the gut and chest. He never saw it coming because he was watching the ball, and when he got whacked, his head when down so forcefully – with such velocity – his chin hit his chest. I bet that's what knocked him out, and that's why it still hurts up there by his temples. That's actually the top of your jawbone. When your chin gets hit, it jars the jawbone."

"Thank you Doctor O'Toole," said Ed.

"Guy gets a compliment from Sally and now he thinks he's better than us," I said.

Lyle ignored Ed and me. "Tony seems alert and he moves like he's okay. He was over to our place last night with Aspen and he seemed the same as always."

I had just started on the second beer when a third Rainier showed up.

"I bought one, then I'm heading home," Ed said.

"I liked you more when you were a nerd," Lyle told Ed. "Remember that," Lyle asked me, "when Ed looked like a job applicant at the IBM slide rule factory? Now look at him. Trendy corduroy pants. Longer hair. Some snazzy colored shirt like James Bond would wear. I saw those shades you wore up in Fort Benton." Lyle pointed at Ed. "Now that I think about it, you've been getting hip ever since Cody moved in with you and Alice."

"It's not Cody," I said. They both looked at me. "It's Springsteen. It's the Homecoming dance. That was a life-changing experience for Ed here. That dancing."

Ed grinned. "Tell me you didn't have fun that night."

I yawned instead. "Sorry. I'm pretty tired." I needed to get home and get to bed.

There were some female and male yips behind us. Bowling must have ended; one of the Simon girls jumped in the arms of the Kountz boy.

"Whooo! Ledger guy!" she called out, and held up her beer. I held up mine in response. Their actions stemmed from more than the wedding photo. I had taken Ledger photos of these kids for years; playing sports, in school plays, in the band or choir or rodeo or 4H or whatever else they'd done or accomplished. The Kountz boy and the Simon girl had probably each been in the paper five times over the years before they got married. The wedding was simply their first appearance as adults.

Sally showed up and slid another round of drinks on the table.

"Christ, Sally, now what?" asked Ed.

"The gentlemen and their ladies," she said.

We looked over, and about five people, led by the Simon girl and Kountz boy, hoisted their beers and cheered. We lifelessly and silently held up ours.

A tiny tear leaked from the corner of my eye. It was a tear of exhaustion. Next I would start seeing things out of the corner of my eye. Again, for a moment, just a moment, I realized I should get home. I was considering my exit options when someone was standing behind me with two big hands on my shoulders. It was Slack, a big lopsided grin on his whisker-stubbled face and a big gray cowboy hat on his head.

"I thought that was your Escort out there," Slack said.

"Have a seat, Slack," Lyle said, and with his feet pushed out the fourth chair at the table.

Slack nodded a formal greeting to Ed. To Slack, Ed was still Special Ed, the formidable school superintendent.

"Nice shirt," Slack told Ed.

"Slack, nice to see you," Ed answered. "Please don't take this personally, okay, but it's time for me to hit the road." Ed stood up and left some money on the table. He patted Slack on the shoulder. "Good luck with these two troublemakers."

"I better get going myself," I said, but no one listened.

Another round of drinks – a can of Squirt for Slack – showed up, and Sally said it was on Slack's parents, Walt and Sue. We looked over and waved. They had a brief friendly conversation with Ed, and then Ed was gone.

"Mom bowled a two-ten tonight," Slack said, giggling. "She beat Dad."

"A two-ten?" asked Lyle, amazed. "No kidding? A two-ten?" He looked back toward Sue. "A two-ten?" he called out to her.

"Yeah," yelled Walt. "A five-eighty series."

"Nicely done," called out Lyle.

I realized I was more than just tired; I was having difficulty following the conversation and starting to have a hard time staying awake. If I closed my eyes, I could easily and swiftly slip into sleep.

"You don't look good," Slack told me.

"I can hardly keep my eyes open," I admitted.

"You can't sleep here," Slack giggled.

Wearily, truthfully, I answered, "I might have to."

"You should go home," Slack told me.

He was right. "What time is it?" I asked Lyle. The words spilled from my mouth in slow motion.

"Time to get you home," he told me. I had a little trouble focusing, but I could see him peering at me critically. "Come on, Lance, let's go."

Lyle helped me to my feet, and guided me toward the door, past Sally's corner of the bar and not far from the pool table, where they all hollered a friendly parting to me.

"I'm parked over here," I told Lyle when we stepped out of the bar. It was cold and dark and windy.

"Right, like I'm going to let you drive with Manfred sitting there watching us," Lyle said.

I squinted down the street, across Legion Avenue, toward the fishpond where Manfred had been parked, but I couldn't tell if I saw anything or not. "Are you going to drive me home?" I asked, amazed.

"What have you had?" Lyle asked. "Two beers? Three?" He opened the passenger side of his pickup and helped me in. "Are you okay?"

The truck was only a couple months old, the replacement for the truck Aspen had wrecked with the collision with a Boulder Valley mule deer. I inhaled deeply. "The smell of new car," I said.

"What?" Lyle asked. He started the truck and head north on Main Street, away from Legion Avenue.

"I said, it still smells new," I repeated.

"Jesus Christ, Lance, I have no idea what you just said."

What seemed like a moment later I was being lifted out of the truck by Tony and Annie and Lyle, then helped inside the house and placed in the recliner.

"We each had two or three beers, that was it," I heard Lyle say. It sounded like an apology. "I don't know what happened to him. He literally passed out in the bar. I had to wake him up again when we pulled up to the house."

I could hear the alarm in Lyle's voice. No one wanted to displease Annie. I intended to defend myself. I knew what this looked like. I wasn't drunk. I was just sleepy. I wanted to tell them that. I wanted to tell Annie the lack of sleep, the stress in Great Falls, the late nights at the paper, the anxious nights with Tony, finally caught up to me. My body had surrendered to fatigue. I heard Lyle say goodbye to me and I heard the door close.

I woke up to daylight, with Annie seated cross-legged on my bed, wearing her pajamas, reading the newspaper.

I blinked once; it was like a windshield wiper on dry glass. My mouth and throat were so dry the first swallow got caught in my throat. Annie saw me and let the paper settle in her lap. My mind struggled to reconstruct what had led to me opening my eyes to morning light with Annie seated on my bed. I allowed myself a cautious, slow, deep breath, and swallowed again, but there was absolutely no saliva to swallow.

"Yeah," Annie told me, "your mouth has been open for about six straight hours."

Was it Thursday? I was sure it was Thursday. There was sunlight coming in through the windows. I swallowed again and brought my hands to my face and rubbed my eyes.

"It's going on ten," Annie said. "Don't worry. I called Laura Joyce and told her you wouldn't be in until after lunch. Tony and Cody got your car back here already this morning, before school. I think Tony took a loop down Legion Avenue into the A&W parking lot before he brought it back, but it's sitting right where it's supposed to be, there in the driveway."

My mind took inventory. I knew how I got home. I didn't feel good, but I didn't feel sick. I was wearing my usual nighttime attire – long-sleeve tee-shirt and underpants – and my pants were on the chair next to the bed.

"Tony undressed you," Annie told me. "You fell asleep in the chair. You staggered to the bed and were snoring before your head even hit the pillow. I'm not exaggerating, Lance. You were on your feet sound asleep, snoring."

Annie was missing school to nurse me. She had missed Monday and Tuesday, or maybe just Monday, I wasn't sure, to sit with Tony, and was now missing Thursday to sit with me. My hands were open and on my face; the fingertips were pressed into my eyes and palms on my cheeks. My voice was dry and scratchy. "I wasn't drunk."

"Of course you were," Annie assured me.

Hands over my face, I shook my head.

"Lance, you're exhausted," Annie said. "Even a little amount of alcohol and exhaustion is a dangerous combination. My guess is you should be hospitalized. That's how exhausted you are. That's why you needed to sleep in. You need to sleep in for a month. You should hire someone at the Ledger. You can afford it now."

The bed springs creaked when she stood. She folded up the newspaper. I knew she was still looking at me, but I kept my face hidden.

"No matter how hard you work, she's not coming back. It's not your fault, but she'll never come home." A floorboard groaned; she must have taken another step closer to me. "There's nothing you can do about it, Lance. There never was."

Chapter 36

When she was a child, during the years when we knew Annie was smart but before we knew exactly how smart, her mother and I thought she was destined to become a teacher. Annie, maybe three or four years old, would play alone in the basement of our old home in Butte and line up her dolls and stuffed animals as if they were students in a classroom, despite the fact she herself had never yet stepped foot inside an actual classroom.

She would teach them, one by one, and speak in different tones of voice for each one. She would play a game – that as far as I know she invented – in which she would roll dice to somehow select a letter of the alphabet, and then roll the dice again to select a number. If she picked a *d* and rolled a nine, for example, the student, a stuffed panda bear or a plastic doll, would have to name nine animals or cities or countries or people or whatever category Annie had picked whose name started with the letter *d*. And then she would stand there, using her version of an imitated voice of a stuffed lion or baby plastic doll, and name nine cities that start with *d* in rapid succession without any hesitation or apparent thought at all: *Denver, Detroit, Da Nang, Dover, Dallas, Dayton, Dillon, Duluth, Dublin*. She had never visited any of those cities. They simply existed in books or on maps.

Then in another voice, after another roll of the dice, she recited eleven animals starting with the letter *s*. *Salmon, sloth, sparrow, salamander, spotted owl, seal, shark, skunk, snow goose, spider, sheep*.

Her teacher voice then expressed divine pleasure in her students' abilities.

When she was young enough to still be strapped into a car seat, during long car trips Annie and Tony would play a game called Connect Four. The game requires the players to drop either red or black pieces into chutes to form a connection of four pieces vertically, horizontally or directionally at an angle. Tony grew disgusted with repeated losses to a child young enough to still have her baby teeth. He soon refused to play.

On a trip to visit Amy's family, while Amy drove I sat in back with Annie and set up the game between us. Annie won the first game, which everyone in the car found amusing. She won six or seven straight games, and began coaching me simply to prolong the game.

I would hold my red piece above a chute, look at her, and she'd shake her head. I moved it over another chute, and again she'd shake her head. Finally I'd find the right chute, and she'd nod. She still won. Without even seeming to pay attention, she won. Later on in the trip, right before I gave up, she shook her head when it looked to me to be the right move. I studied it closer and it still appeared to be the proper move. I questioned why I shouldn't move there. In a childishly patient but confident voice she explained how the next five or so moves would play out if I placed my piece in that chute, with her winning after the fifth move. She was in a car seat drinking from a plastic spill-proof Sesame Street cup, but she saw a half-dozen tactical moves in advance, through a vision of complex strategy.

“Play her in checkers sometime,” Tony muttered.

“Not a chance,” I told him.

Another time, when Annie was in first grade, she came home and plopped her books on the kitchen table. If I have one vision of Annie as a child in elementary school, it is of a tiny, slender, silky-haired kid toting a pile of books. On this afternoon she dumped her books on the table with obvious frustration.

“What’s wrong?” Amy asked her.

“We had a substitute teacher today,” Annie answered, and in a firm adult-like cadence added, “and she was not…prepared…to teach.”

In Annie’s indomitable youth, a day without learning meant she had been inherently deprived of something. But she was also as perceptive as she was intelligent, and witnessed and understood her mother’s decline more readily than her brother. In Tony’s cheerful little world, everyone was happy, healthy and whole. Annie, even as an infant, knew better. Even in diapers she knew there was a darkness in this world, layers of pain and guilt and sorrow that could neither be avoided nor shaken nor ignored.

I woke up later that Thursday – a mandated half-day vacation, as I rationalized it, and alone in the house, bleary-eyed and sluggish, found a note from Annie on the kitchen table. *Why are you reading this? Go back to bed.* It was almost noon. It was my first non-Thanksgiving Thursday off since owning the Ledger. I felt alien, like a thief in my own home. Like I was in hiding. Like I was doing something wrong.

I called Laura Joyce, who laughed as if nothing was wrong, told me it was a quiet day and that she was glad I was, in her words, ‘taking a breather.’ I was waiting for her to comment on the mice, but she never brought it up. I had a can of Chunky Soup for lunch, watched television for a few minutes, but soon drifted off to sleep again.

For a few years, when the kids were younger, I had harbored a hope one or both of them would want to own and manage the Ledger when they were older. That hope, if hope was the right word, went from doubtful to nonexistent as they grew older. Annie was clearly headed for destinations far beyond Whitehall’s and Montana’s borders, and Tony’s personality and talents would take him away from the isolation of rural Montana. There was something honorable and noble about publishing a newspaper in a small town, and it wasn’t as if Annie or Tony were above the job. They simply possessed talents that were not suited for rural publishing or community journalism.

When Amy departed the thought had occurred to me more than once that I should hire someone, a reporter perhaps, to help produce the paper each week. But I used to think the newspaper did not generate the income to support a full-time staffer. But now the Ledger had air conditioning and I had a portfolio, and as I curled up again on the couch I wondered if maybe Annie was right and I should consider maybe hiring an employee.

Annie got home about five o'clock, to a dark house, and found me asleep on the couch, a blanket wrapped around me, still wearing sweatpants and a long-sleeve tee-shirt.

She flipped on the light, and it was like the sun was just a mile above me. I put the pillow over my face.

"Excellent, Lance," she called out brightly. "Exactly what you needed."

I pulled the blanket up toward my shoulders. I couldn't shake the feeling I was guilty of something. I had not worked all day. I had failed, somehow. And punishment would follow.

"You better get up and jump in the shower," she said. "Some kids are coming over here pretty soon, and quite frankly you look a little frightening. Oh, and some good news. Despite your slothful behavior today I deposited nearly fourteen hundred dollars in the bank. We received a nine hundred dollar check from the county. Not bad, huh, for a Thursday? Maybe you should take more days off." She turned on the bathroom light. "I'm serious," she said, "get in there. You look like an Eastern European vagrant. Half a dozen kids are going to be here in a minute, and then we're all going over to the team dinner. You can take some pictures then. That way you won't feel guilty about taking the whole day off."

She took a quick tour of the house and picked up what she could. I was in the shower when she opened the bathroom door and brought in some clothes. She picked up my sweatpants and tee-shirt and stuffed them in the hamper. I heard a door close, and assumed it was the door to my room. The less her friends saw of our house, the better.

I let the steaming hot water run off my back and head, and heard voices and music – Springsteen – coming from the living room. The shower washed away much of my sleepiness and grit, and when I stepped out – pink, clean and refreshed – I saw Annie had laid out a blue denim shirt she liked and a pair of green khaki slacks. That was pretty dressed up for me.

When I emerged from the bathroom I was completely ignored. The kitchen was full of kids, all of them wearing Ranger purple. Natalie Dickson, Dave's little sister, had a purple *WHS* written on her cheek. Brian Baxter, the prim little spelling bee champ, and Jordan Kling, the f-word erstwhile speller, conferred with Annie near the kitchen table. Caddy and Bonner from the Whitehall E Street Band sat on the living room couch watching television as if they did so every day. Carrie Lindstrom, the saxophone player, sat on the floor, reading the album cover to *The River*, nodding her head to the music. Cody Phillips was looking in the refrigerator for something to eat. I did not see Johnny Pep.

Annie finally looked up and smiled and nodded once, a *looking good* kind of reaction.

As the lone adult in the room, I felt out of place, even if I was in my own home. I wasn't sure where to sit, what to do or what to say. Carrie scooted over on the couch, creating a place for me to sit.

"Ask him," Bonner said, as I sat. I looked up and saw he had spoken to Carrie. Bonner wore his black stocking cap and I noticed the emblem or whatever it was – a skull and crossbones – was off to the side, above his ear.

I looked from Bonner to Caddy, and from Caddy to Carrie.

She was a little too large, and tending toward chubby. She had broader shoulders than Bonner or Caddy, something of a weak chin, and a squareish, fleshy body. But she was, in her way, striking. I could see she was struggling with the dilemma of whether or not to ask me. Ask me what, I had no idea.

She looked from Caddy to Bonner, and then back toward me. She launched her question as if expecting the worst. "What's your favorite Springsteen song?"

"*My* favorite?" I asked.

"Mine's *Born to Run*," Caddy volunteered. He wore a battered jeans jacket that appeared to have some chains dangling out of a pocket. "Best song of all time, period, end of discussion."

I looked at Bonner, and gestured it was his turn. "*Darkness on the Edge of Town*. Man, that song gets me every time."

I looked at Carrie. "Oh, I don't know," she said breathlessly. "There's so many of them. *Thunder Road. Dancing in the Dark. Hungry Heart. Born in the U.S.A*. I love the sax in *Jungleland*. They're all so good. I can't pick just one."

"You have to," I said lightly. "That's what you asked me do. You have to pick just one. Your favorite Springsteen song. Your very favorite."

"Oh, all right," she said. Concentration did not improve her appearance. "*The River*. It's such a sad song, it breaks my heart."

"Why does *that* make it your favorite?" demanded Bonner.

"Yeah," added Caddy. "The guy in that song gets screwed."

Interesting selection of words, I thought. But I doubted a discussion about the perils of pre-marital sex would be appropriate or productive with this set of kids.

"It's art," I told them. "Music is art. You appreciate music the way you appreciate a painting or a book or a movie. *The River* is a great song, and it's okay if it's Carrie's favorite song. It's okay if it's not yours. Sometimes you can appreciate art without really knowing it."

Bonner nodded, as if he had thought that the whole time.

"So, Lance," Caddy said, "what's your favorite? Which Springsteen song do you *appreciate* the most?"

"Springsteen is a genius, you know," I started. "He's a once in a generation kind of writer and performer, and I admire all his music. I admire the integrity of his music. I see something magical in every one of his songs."

Carrie held up one index finger. "But you can only pick just one," she said in the same friendly tone of voice I'd used with her.

"*Badlands*," I said. "*Born to Run* is the best rock and roll song of all time." I looked at Caddy. "You're right, end of discussion." I looked at Carrie. "And I really like *Jungleland*."

"That saxophone solo," Carrie said dreamily.

I nodded. "But *Badlands* is something special. It's an anthem of youth. It's an anthem of love. Of passion, of determination, of *living*. It reaffirms the value of life and faith and hope and beauty and pride. And it does it in four minutes. Tell me that isn't amazing."

I looked up and saw Annie. "Lance," she said cheerfully when I got done talking, "get a load of you."

We all walked – the kids and me – to the community dinner at the school multi-purpose room. When we turned the corner to depart First Street onto Main Street a police car drove slowly past and Manfred stared straight ahead as he cruised by.

"Bite me," Bonner told the back end of the police car.

"He's awfully creepy for a good guy," Natalie said.

"Just because he's a cop doesn't make him a good guy," Annie observed.

"He's psycho," added Caddy.

My expression directed Caddy to watch his mouth. His expression suggested he really didn't care what I thought.

It cost me thirty dollars – or, it cost Annie thirty dollars since she had the money – to feed our assemblage. The instant they got their food the kids all but ditched me, and I spotted Mary Kristofferson at a table seated with five guys including Jack Dawson, a rancher in the Boulder valley, and Brad Knight, the bearded and burley English teacher who oversaw the Whitehall spelling bee. Also seated were Drew Erickson, wearing a trendy yellow fleece vest and Cullen Garrity and his wife, Lisa. Cullen was the pastor of Zion Lutheran Church in Whitehall, and was never seen without Lisa at his side.

I had my plate filled with scrambled eggs, pancakes and sausage. Brad scooted over and made room for me to sit next to Mary, who gave my arm a squeeze as I sat.

"Tony seems to have recovered nicely," Brad said. Brad was apparently into Ranger Pride in a major way; his bushy beard and mop of hair had been spray-painted purple, and he wore a purple Ranger sweatshirt. He nodded over my shoulder, and seated two tables away were Tony and Aspen, with Tony holding court, telling a story or a joke that involved feminine hand gestures.

"He'll be fine," I said.

"I heard he got walloped a good one last week," Jack said.

I nodded. "He was hurting for a couple days."

Mary offered a wan smile. Tony's injury had been a frightening experience.

"What have you killed lately?" I asked Brad, mostly to change the subject. I stuffed a spoonful of eggs in my mouth. It was November, and hunting season was either over, hadn't started, or was in progress, depending on which species you wanted to shoot. I was never a hunter. We ran all the season openings and closings in the Ledger, but there were so many – bow, rifle, upland bird, waterfowl, big game – that I forgot them or mixed them up the instant the paper was printed.

"I got a freezer full of elk meat," he boasted. "Got it up on Tom Carey's place. Huge bull." He shook his head in admiration. "Boone and Crockett rack."

"Did you notice Brad school's spirit?" asked Mary.

"Like I could miss it," I said.

"He looks like Grover," Drew said.

"He reminds me of a hairy grape," said Jack. Jack Dawson was a tough, thin cowboy and a contemporary of Shawn Davis. Jack played hard, rodeoed hard, worked hard and drank hard, but in conversation with him he was gentle and humble. You didn't want to rile him, though.

"He could be starting a fashion trend," said Cullen.

"Let's hope not," Jack offered.

A couple years after I'd arrived in Whitehall, I had taken a picture of Cullen and Lisa's high school daughter, Darla, a star on the girls basketball team. Darla was a classic Scandinavian blonde, same as her parents. She had injured her knee in the district tournament and her status for the divisional tournament was uncertain. She was fitted with a large metal brace, and during practice one afternoon I went up and took a picture of her more or less modeling her new knee brace. I positioned her with her injured leg up on the bottom bleacher, facing the camera. I took the picture. I developed the film. I spent twenty minutes in the darkroom printing and reprinting the picture to get it perfect. It probably took me ten tries to get the exposure just right. I cut the picture, waxed the picture, and put the picture on the paste-up page. But it wasn't until the paper started coming off the press – all twelve hundred or so copies back then – that I noticed her shorts were a little baggy and hung a little loose, and that the way her injured leg was propped up, to my utter horror, you could look right up the baggy shorts into her crotch area. You couldn't really *see* anything, but you knew you could see the vicinity of a young woman's body that should never be revealed in a community newspaper.

How I never noticed that visual misfortune before the paper was rolling off the press mystified me forever afterward. I had a cold hard feeling in my belly the instant I saw what I'd done, and the Anaconda printing crew leering and nodding enthusiastic *nice job* nods my way didn't help a bit.

So it wasn't a surprise when within an hour of the paper being distributed Cullen came storming in the Ledger with a wadded-up paper in his tense fist.

It would not surprise me, I realized as he stood there that afternoon, if despite his connections to God, he punched my lights out. I wouldn't have blamed him if he had.

"How could you do this!" he shouted.

"I didn't see it," I said. It sounded lame even to me.

"Nonsense!" He took a step toward me and I braced for a right hand to my jaw. But he didn't. He simply stood there and glared at me, an internal wrestling match going on between preacher and parent.

"Honest," I moaned, "I didn't notice it until it was too late."

"Then you're the only swinging dick in two counties that didn't," he yelled. He threw the balled up Ledger in the air and the pages fell apart and drifted harmlessly to the floor. Then he was gone, slamming the door behind him. I stood motionless for two full minutes. And while part of me was coming to grips with the realization I hadn't been harmed, another part of me wondered if I was the only person on earth who had ever heard Reverend Garrity use the phrase 'swinging dick.'

Cullen and Lisa failed to renew their Ledger subscription when it came due, but a couple months later spotted me at a church potluck and wrote a check to restart their subscription. I also heard – but never told her parents – what Darla had told me, which was that she liked the picture.

Darla had long since graduated from WHS, gone to college and moved out of state. I wondered where she lived and how she was doing. I knew better than to ask Cullen.

"I also shot a whitetail doe on the Mulligan place, an antelope over on Hanson's and I even drew me a moose permit for the Big Hole," said Brad.

"Not bad for a hairy grape," said Mary.

Willie Zankowski, a large man who never quite appeared to be clean, or clean shaven, joined our table, and set down a plate heaping with syrup-soaked pancakes. He was wearing ragged and dirty Carhartt bib overalls over a ripped and grimy winter jacket, and he always wore a blue and white train engineer cap.

"I resemble a Nordic God far more than a furry fruit," asserted Brad.

Willie slowly shook his head. "First time I ever heard talk from a hairy grape."

Willie had made a painful appearance in the Ledger about a year earlier, during a late summer trip up toward Homestake Pass to cut some firewood. He apparently got a little careless and somehow a chainsaw ripped through his thigh, with exposed muscle and sinew and blood everywhere. According to his brother, who took him to the hospital in Butte, Willie yelped, wrapped a shirt around his thigh as a tourniquet and hobbled to the truck. On the way to the hospital Willie reportedly sipped a can of Budweiser, looked at the gore above his knee and mournfully said, "Goddamn, these were a new pair of dungarees."

He was treated and released at St. James, missed at most two days of work up at the mine, and I never once noticed an observable limp.

"That was something, Lance, the governor coming here and bragging up Annie like that," said Drew Erickson, a Montana Power employee who lived north of Whitehall in the Whitetail. Drew was a former Montana State University basketball player who had been born and raised in Butte. He was in his late twenties, single, and was some sort of junior executive at MPC. I was gone from the power company before he'd started work there.

"She doesn't seem to think so," Mary said. "She's got nothing against the governor, she just doesn't think she herself deserves so much recognition."

"She thinks she's an accident of nature," I added.

Drew shook his head. "No, believe me, she deserves it. I remember I had to give a presentation to a bunch of schools about hydropower a few years ago, when Annie was in, I don't know, fourth grade, maybe fifth. Something like that."

I knew what was coming: another story about Annie's brilliance. Most people in Whitehall had their own personal encounter with Annie's intelligence. Fortunately, they seldom used it against her.

"These were elementary school kids, right, little kids," continued Drew, telling the story to everyone at the table. "So I gave them a very cursory and simplistic explanation about how dams store water and how the water flows and how the turbine works to generate power. I bragged a bit how hydropower is renewable, unlike power produced by coal and gas. I looked up and there's this skinny little girl with wispy brown hair kind of frowning at me. I asked if there were any questions, expecting something like, *how fast does the water flow?* Instead this little girl with the shiny brown hair asks me if I was aware of dams throughout the northwest blocking fish migration, preventing fish spawning, causing water degradation – that was the word she used, degradation – ruining entire fisheries, causing silt and sediment damage to gravel beds and water temperature problems for salmon, trout and sturgeon."

"Sturgeon?" asked Brad.

Drew nodded. "Yeah, sturgeon. It was emerging science at the time. And I'll never forget what she said after class. She came up to me and with supreme confidence told me she hoped that even though the Jefferson River was over-appropriated and chronically dewatered – she used those words, 'over-appropriated and chronically dewatered' – no one ever built a dam on the river." He chuckled at the memory. "She gave us a directive, a mandate. You better not build a dam on the Jefferson River. There was force in that child's voice of hers and it was not accidental."

Drew told a good story. He *was* a good story. He had nearly made the newspaper in a dangerous and entertaining fashion, but there was a sensitivity involved, with personal decorum intertwined, and even though the events would have made fascinating and scintillating reading, nothing was ever published. Which is not the same thing as saying no one knew what happened.

The way I heard it was Benny Andretti had unexpectedly come home sick after midnight one October morning. Benny was a graveyard shift truck driver at the mine, but after a couple hours of work thought he'd come down with the flu and checked out of work. Benny and his wife, Peggy, lived near Point of Rocks on a slight bluff above the Jefferson River. He found Drew's pickup in his driveway, which he found unsettling, and found Peggy in the kitchen, buck naked, which was downright troubling. He instantly figured it out. He threw his lunch bucket down and ran across the kitchen floor to the living room. Peggy instantly figured what he wanted in the living room: the gun cabinet. She screamed and Drew, also buck naked, emerged from the bedroom to find Peggy shrieking hysterically. Drew instantly figured what was wrong. Benny was home.

The first shot from a .22 pistol hit the wall just above Drew's shoulder. He dove back into the bedroom as a second shot grazed his rump. A third bullet, as fate would have it, went through a framed photo of Benny and Peggy on their wedding day. Drew jumped through the window and took off running into the darkness. Benny fired three or four more shots from the window.

Drew, barefoot and naked, hobbled painfully through a small copse of juniper brush and prickly pear behind the house and got a sore and terrifying quarter mile down a gravel road before he saw the headlights on the road behind him. He scuttled off the road, hopped a barbed-wire fence and ran through a pasture. He scraped his forehead and chest when he tumbled in an irrigation ditch, and crossed another county road closer to the river. Just as he climbed another fence he again spotted headlights, this time coming directly at him. He jumped the fence on the other side of the road and ran through the cover along a river slough and actually swam across a frigid river channel in October. He emerged on the Jefferson County side of the river, wet, cold and exhausted, the skin on the bottom of his feet split and shredded, found a road somewhere near the Renova juncture and figured he'd limp to the highway between Twin Bridges and Whitehall and flag down a car into town. He gimped his way a slow mile off the road along a fenceline until he came across a county road grader. He was shaking, numb, in pain and desperate, and he'd been a heavy equipment operator during college, so he hot-wired the road grader and climbed in, planning to leave it at the county shop just outside of town. As he drove toward town a pair of headlights approached him, passed him, then abruptly swerved, changed direction and closed in quickly from behind. Bullets ripped through the glass cab of the road grader as Benny shot from the driver's side window. Drew tried to lie flat on the cab floor and with his arm reach up and steer. He couldn't do both, and with bullets whizzing all around him and glass flying in the grader's cab he opted to lie flat. The grader drifted off the road, through the borrow pit, across a front yard, through a horse corral and smashed into a shed. The owners heard the crash and called the police, and Manfred arrived five minutes later to find Drew on the cab floor, bleeding from a bullet wound in the thigh and shivering uncontrollably.

In the end, no one pressed charges, and nothing was ever written in the Ledger. Drew paid for the shed, the corral and damages to the road grader, and did not want Benny prosecuted for shooting at him. Drew also had to pay for repairs to his pickup. At some point during the night Benny had shot up the windows, headlights and taillights, slashed the tires and beat the hood and quarter panels in with a baseball bat. Benny was gone for good after he understood he wouldn't be going to jail. Peggy, a teacher at the Cardwell School, kept her job but not her husband, and while risqué rumors still swirled around Drew, none of them seem to involve Peggy.

But I knew all about the incident, and Drew knew I knew, and Drew knew I could have published the whole unseemly affair in the paper, but didn't. I didn't because when you're part of a community, sometimes the community comes first. Nothing good would have happened to anyone if that story were published. But Drew didn't know what I thought. We had never talked about it. He only knew I knew. Maybe that was why he sat there bragging up Annie.

"What do you think Annie's going to be when she grows up?" asked Mary.

"Annie?" Drew said, and grinned. "Whatever she wants to be."

"And more power to her," added Cullen. His blond hair had thinned and turned a hint of gray, but he still looked Scandinavian enough to be the mayor of Stockholm. "She's a delightful young woman."

Lisa, a bit overweight with a wide center of gravity just above her thighs, nodded in agreement. If she had ever disagreed with her husband she had never done so in public.

"She is," Mary agreed. After a moment of thought, she added, "For a genius, for all the attention and recognition she receives, she's amazingly stable and well grounded."

"You haven't had it easy," Cullen told me gently. Not long after we moved to Whitehall, and before the photo of Darla, he had attempted to counsel Amy and me in our marriage

"Some ways I have, some ways I haven't," I said in response.

Cullen and Lisa hadn't had it easy, either. They had three children in addition to Darla. Sam was a teacher in a Christian high school in Idaho. Jacob was a minister in North Dakota. Both were Ledger subscribers. But Martha had gone from mischievous as a child to rebellious as a teenager to scandalous and unlawful as a young adult. She had a drug and alcohol problem and had twice written a series of bad checks in Whitehall and Butte. Cullen conceded they had prayed for Martha, sought therapy for Martha, prayed for Martha some more, and funded expensive and extensive rehabilitation treatment for Martha. Somehow Cullen and Lisa covered all of Martha's bad checks and financial woes, and in talking to the Jefferson County Attorney he told me charges had been dropped, restitution made, and there would be no fines or penalties against Martha. I asked if he thought there should be an article in the paper, and he said it was up to me. Cullen and Lisa Garrity had never broken a law in their lives, and had raised three model children. They would have been mortified and devastated if their community newspaper had published stories about their daughter's failings and afflictions. Martha, Annie would have said, was an aberration, a freak of nature. It made no sense to break the hearts of Cullen and Lisa Garrity for something completely out of their control. Martha's criminal adventures had been published in the Ledger.

"Martha's working for an accountant in Helena," Cullen told me, a hint of pride evident in his voice and expression. "She's taking some night classes at the vo-tech."

"We pray she's finally found her way," Lisa said.

"Pray for all of us," said Jack Dawson.

"Amen," added Drew.

Friday morning the elementary school gym was stuffed with the entire Whitehall student body and while it was possible the school song had been sung better it had certainly never been sung louder. The little kids, especially, absolutely screamed out the words as Carrie and the rest of the WHS band belted out the music.

The band launched into a raucous version of Kenny Loggins' *Danger Zone* with the cheerleaders – wearing sunglasses and something resembling pilot jumpsuits – doing some kind of coordinated movement to the music, then came a piped in live version of *Born to Run*, with Jersey and the Ranger football players – on cue, apparently – emerging from the stands in ones, twos and small groups, to cheers from the assembled students. They wore their home purple jerseys and slowly and haphazardly joined Colt and JeffScott in walking along the first row of the bleachers and slapping hands with all the elementary school kids.

The music stopped but the cheering did not. Ed, looking astonishingly sharp in a gray sport coat, black shirt and black dress slacks, had to gesture three or four times to quiet down before the kids turned it down a notch.

"I'm not sure if any of you kids know," Ed said mischievously, "but we have a football game here tomorrow."

Wild cheering resumed, and during the cheers Tony came around behind Ed. Tony took off his sunglasses and slipped them on Ed. For some reason the kids found that hysterical, and an amused Ed kept the sunglasses on.

"The Whitehall Rangers – these Whitehall Rangers," Ed said, his arm with a sweeping gesture toward the assembled football players, "are one of the four best Class B football teams in Montana and one game away from playing for the state title."

More wild cheers.

Annie sat in the first row of the high school section of bleachers, wearing Tony's gold away jersey. Trish was in front of her, wearing what looked like a purple pom-pom on her head and Colt's gold jersey. Mary was surrounded by tiny children in the elementary school section, and she ventured a timid wave my way when I spotted her. Brad Knight's beard was still purple, but the color had faded somewhat to the color of a bruise. He now resembled a bruised hairy grape.

Over the din of cheering and raucous noise Ed told the students to attend the game and cheer for the Rangers and encouraged them to bring their parents and neighbors. He gave a brief summary of the Rangers' sensational season and then to a deafening uproar of cheers introduced the "best high school football coach in Montana."

Jersey wore a black long-sleeved tee-shirt and black leather vest, black jeans and black athletic shoes. He took the microphone, turned to the players and applauded their direction, and the players returned the applause, facing Jersey.

Jersey started to speak, and the loud cheers and applause began to fade.

"I'm not the best high school football coach in Montana," Jersey started, to a chorus of boos and *nooos*. "But I am the luckiest high school football coach in Montana."

More wild cheers.

"I'm lucky to have the honor and the pleasure of working with this outstanding group of young men. I'm lucky to have the opportunity to begin a journey with these young athletes that has taken us – all of us – to this precipice," Jersey said. "I'm proud of what they have accomplished. More importantly, I'm proud of the way they have accomplished it."

The crowd cheered, but it was obvious Jersey was not seeking a response or approval. There were some things he wanted these people to know.

"You should be proud of what this team has accomplished. As a team. As a *team*," Jersey repeated. There was only a smattering of applause. "Think about this team when the season began. Think about the adversity this team has encountered and conquered. Think about what was said and written about this group of young men a few short months ago. Think of the bond these young men have forged. An unshakeable bond built on trust and pride and faith and sweat and courage and an absolute refusal to lose, to surrender, to accept anything short of their best."

Jersey had been in the middle of the gym floor. He took a couple steps closer to the bleachers. It was so quiet you could hear his footsteps. He reminded me of a preacher almost, in front of a reverent crowd during a Sunday service.

"It's true, we are one win from playing in the state championship game," he said, "but if our season ends tomorrow, these young men, this *team*, can exit the field with their heads held high, proud of their collective accomplishment. And I have a secret for you all. This is something I haven't even told them." He indicated the silent, slightly nervous, group of boys wearing purple jerseys. "Tomorrow, we'll be playing the best Class B football team in Montana." There was a murmuring from the stands. "Fairfield is bigger and stronger and faster than we are, they are better coached than we are and have more experience and talent than we do."

More murmurings from the stands. Even I wondered what kind of pep talk this was. In a traditional pep talk, the team was uplifted and bestowed with confidence. I detected no uplift in Jersey's words or behavior. I found myself wondering: What do you call the opposite of a pep talk?

"Believe me, I've studied them on film, I've talked to opposing coaches, and I've looked at their lineup over and over, and I have to be honest, they don't have a weakness." He paused. He looked up at the faces in the bleachers. "Except for one," he said softly. "Their one weakness is they have to come *here*, to play us on *our* field, in *our* town, in front of *our* fans. They cannot win and they will not win in Whitehall. We will not allow that happen. *You* will not allow that happen. Tomorrow we will depend on you, and you will not allow us to fail."

There was an uncomfortable and uncertain smattering of applause, as if people were unsure of what Jersey had just said. *Did he say we were going to win?* Dave suddenly bellowed a wail of joy and started jumping up and down. A live version of the song *Badlands* magically burst through the PA system. The Ranger players all began jumping up and down and soon everyone in the bleachers was jumping up and down. Ed started jumping up and down and to my amazement, I found myself jumping up and down. Everyone in the building jumped up and down during the full song, and then the cheerleaders led us in the school song and teachers attempted to restore some kind of order to the festivities.

"Your little friend left a little present in my desk drawer," Laura Joyce told me that afternoon after the school assembly.

"Amazing," I said. "How'd he get in and out of a closed desk drawer?"

"That was not the response I was hoping for," she said. "I still think I should bring in one of our mousers from the ranch."

"I'll take care of it," I said, knowing I wouldn't.

"Right," she said, knowing she wasn't.

It was Friday afternoon at four o'clock the eve of the semi-final Class B football game, and it was no use even attempting to concentrate. Laura Joyce had done an unexpectedly good job of compensating for my day of hooky a day earlier, and was caught up enough to leave work early, at four o'clock. I did a couple basic, mindless tasks – the advertising run sheet, rewriting a couple press releases – when the office door opened and Annie walked in, followed by Mary.

"Lance, you leaper you," Annie said. "You should have seen yourself jumping."

"Everyone was jumping," I said lamely.

Mary hesitated at the door, by the counter, while Annie took off her stocking cap and walked toward my desk.

"Come on in," I told Mary. I pulled out Laura Joyce's chair. "Have a seat."

Annie sat down at what essentially was her desk. She looked at the income sheet for the day and started to make up a deposit. She typically made a deposit every Friday. "Two things, Lance," she said. "Let's handle the more unpleasant one first."

Her voice was all business. That tone in combination with the word *unpleasant* was meant to be a warning. Annie walked over to the little round table where I typically conducted my interviews, grabbed the Montana Standard newspaper, opened to an inside news page and handed it to me. She tapped her index finger on a short article under the headline *Youths arrested in parking lot clash.* The article briefly outlined what sounded like a gang fight in an uptown vacant lot. A half dozen of the combatants had needed hospital treatment and another half dozen were in police custody. When I'd completed the article I looked at Annie.

"You sent a wire transfer to a bail bondsman in Butte and bailed out one of the participants in that fight," she said.

"Why'd I do that?" I asked. *How'd I do that*, I wondered. I'd never sent a wire transfer or talked to a bail bondsman in my life. I didn't even know what a wire transfer was or what a bail bondsman did.

"Because it was the right thing to do," Annie answered. "Johnny Pep transferred from Whitehall back to Butte last week, and he's one of the kids in the Butte jail. Who *was* in the Butte jail. He posted bond, thanks to you."

"Doesn't Johnny Pep belong in jail?" I asked. What does *posted bond* even mean, I thought. Did it mean I was a crook?

Annie shook her head. "He needs a chance. You gave him one. Let's see what he does with it."

"Maybe he needs a year behind bars," I suggested.

"Maybe eventually, but not yet," Annie told me.

"Can I get in trouble for bailing a hoodlum out of jail?" I asked. "Am I responsible for him now?"

Annie shook her head. "No, and I can get the money back later, if you want."

Her tone suggested I didn't want her to do that.

"Next topic." Annie said.

"Is this one unpleasant too?" I asked.

"Depends on you," Annie said. "What are you doing tonight?"

I looked from Annie to Mary, back to Annie. "Why?" I asked, then added, "Does this involve Johnny Pep?"

"See," Annie told Mary, "I told you. He is socially dysfunctional. Lance," Annie asked me, "when was the last time you actually had Friday night social plans?"

"Why are you asking me that?" I asked in a defensive, evasive measure. "What do you want?"

Mary had kept her coat on, but unwrapped a scarf from her shoulders and neck.

"Well, I'm glad you asked," Annie said brightly. She started to stamp the endorsement of a handful of checks. "Our house is going to get somewhat cluttered tonight and I was thinking it was best if you were, say, elsewhere for awhile."

"Cluttered?" I asked. I looked at Mary for help but she averted her eyes.

"Totally," Annie answered. "Tony and Aspen and the cheerleaders are going to use our kitchen and living room to make football banners and signs, and Trish and a couple of my friends are going to assist. You know, help with spelling and grammar, that kind of thing."

Mary suppressed a laugh.

Annie shrugged. "I'm serious," she said. "Tryouts for cheerleaders do not include a spelling test. I've seen Aspen spell the word *victory* wrong."

"You just made that up," I said.

Annie smiled. I'd caught her. She *had* just made that up. "Anyway, there's going to be boxes of pizza, cases of pop and a gang of hyper kids with oodles of purple and yellow paint. You really don't want to be part of all that, Lance."

She had a point. "What have you got to do with all this?" I asked Mary.

"Unless I'm mistaken, I'm your date," she said. "I've apparently been chosen to serve as a diversion for the evening."

"That may be a bit mercenary," Annie said, "but technically correct. You need to stay out of the house until about eleven or so," Annie told me. "Miss Kristofferson has indicated a willingness to keep you company this evening, perhaps out of pity, perhaps out of a sense of duty, I'm not sure. But she's probably better than you deserve, obviously better than any other option you have, and seems to accept the task with an intriguing combination of cheerfulness and zeal."

"What did you have in mind?" I asked Mary.

Annie answered. "I was thinking maybe you should head over to LaHood for dinner, perhaps take in the movie next door, and then come home. No Borden's. No bars of any kind. I want you home at eleven and in bed by midnight."

"What's the movie?" I asked.

Annie simply shook his head. She looked at Mary. "Have you seen a more backward sense of social behavior?" Annie turned to me. "The name of the movie is inconsequential. Do us all a favor, okay, and just go to the movie."

I looked at Mary. "Is all this okay with you?"

She nodded. "Sure."

"Perfect," Annie said. "Let me go to the bank and make a deposit." She looked at Mary. "I'll get some money for the evening. He's a child about finances."

"I have money," I declared.

"You've got money?" challenged Annie. "Show me. Let's see it."

"Well, not on me," I conceded.

Mary couldn't quite muffle a snicker.

The movie turned out to be a pool hustler movie with Paul Newman and Tom Cruise. When Mary and I entered the movie theater, the owners, Karen, stationed to sell tickets, and Kerry, at the concession stand, looked past me, expecting to see Annie and the money. They didn't see Annie and looked from me to Mary back to me in confusion until I took out a five dollar bill and paid.

Instead of a stop at Borden's after the show we went over to Mary's house, the left side of a duplex on Second Street, not far from St. Teresa's Catholic Church, and watched the ten o'clock news from Butte. The second story of the broadcast featured a gang fight in uptown Butte. Mary's place was simple and sparingly furnished. A Charlie Russell print of Native Americans watching a paddleboat on the Missouri River was hung above the couch and a wood carving of a slender blonde horse stood on an end table. Her place was far tidier than mine, but not much more contemporarily or richly appointed. The news transitioned in the weather, and thankfully there was no story about Johnny Pep being mysteriously bailed of out jail.

At the end of the sports segment they did a short preview of the Whitehall game, which featured brief interviews with Jersey and Colt. Jersey's east coast accent somehow seemed more pronounced on television. He said the team had had a wonderful year, and said he expected a 'super' amount of fan support in Whitehall. Colt, wearing his purple home number seven jersey, looked surprising comfortable on camera. He said the team had earned a home game by beating Baker and Fort Benton on the road and although Fairfield was a great team with great players, the Rangers had an advantage by playing in Whitehall.

"Can the Rangers win tomorrow?" Mary asked me.

"A month ago anyone and everyone would have said Fairfield was five touchdowns better than Whitehall," I said. "But a month ago seems like an eternity. It looks to me like Jersey's got these kids dreaming the impossible and accomplishing the unthinkable. I think they honestly think they're going to win."

At eleven o'clock Mary and I turned off Johnny Carson and headed over to see the banner-spellers and poster-makers in action. We had to park across the street because the driveway and the side of the street in front of the house were packed with cars. The lights were all on inside the house and I heard the beat of *Born in the U.S.A.* pounding through the walls before we even got to the outside steps.

Just as I reached to open the door from the outside, the door opened from the inside, and there was Rhonda Horst, exiting.

"Goot Got!" she said, surprised by meeting someone in the doorway.

"Rhonda," I said, laughing. "You're helping make signs?"

"I brout rolls," she told me.

I looked more closely at her scarf; it was tie-dyed purple and gold. It was tied tight against her hair and under her chin, but looked like something from a Grateful Dead concert.

"Nice scarf," I said as she scooted past us on the steps.

She brought a hand to the side of her head. "Ya, day gifted to me."

"You need someone to walk you home?" I asked as the open door passed from her hand to mine.

"Oft course nut," she answered firmly, then headed down the sidewalk into the darkness.

Mary followed me into the house, and the pulse of the music was so loud it was like rhythmic wind striking your skin. I must have scowled, or perhaps winced, and Carrie – also wearing a purple and gold tie-dyed scarf – turned the stereo down a few notches.

"Lance, man, come on in," called Bonner, waving me in, as if he lived here and I didn't. "Want some pizza?"

"How about a cinnamon roll?" asked Aspen, who wore her purple scarf around her head like a bandana. "Miss Kristofferson?"

We both shook our heads.

There were probably fifteen kids in the house. There was a mix of junior high kids and high schoolers, of honor students and inept students, of stunning cheerleaders and homely rabble, of the wealthy and the poor, of kids headed for college and headed for poverty, of the school elite and school disadvantaged.

Johnny Pep, fresh from the Silver Bow County slammer, held down the corners of a broad scroll of paper, aided by Brian Baxter, as if the two of them had something in common. Johnny Pep apparently got bailed out of jail, evidently by me, and then showed up at my house. I wondered absently if Manfred could arrest me for that.

Caddy was painting a banner featuring a large purple Ranger football helmet with a large gold number *1* in the middle. A long banner with the words *Rangers are Born to Win* was taped to the living room wall and wrapped along a corner behind the couch. Aspen seemed to be manufacturing pom-poms from silvery threads of purple material.

"Where's Tony?" I asked Annie.

"At Cody's," she said. "He's spending the night. Didn't he tell you?"

I shook my head. "That's a bad idea." It was a terrible idea. "He's not sleeping over there the night before a game."

"Settle," Annie told me. "Go ahead and call. Ed's probably still awake. Three or four of the players are spending the night there. They were going to watch film or something." I was shaking my head. "I'm serious," she said. She motioned toward the phone. "Call Ed. It has been set up for a few days. Tony's not playing anyway, so it's no big deal."

I did call Ed, and he said the boys were already asleep. Cody, Tony, Logan and Colt had turned in early, he said. He asked me if I was at Borden's, because of the racket, and I told him I was home with the sign-making contingent.

"It sounds like you're at a Springsteen concert," he said, then told me he'd see me Saturday at the game.

I answered but Ed had already hung up. It was possible, I realized, he'd been in bed himself.

Trish sat in her wheelchair at the kitchen table, with a scissors and sheets of purple and gold paper, cutting out numbers and letters to be affixed, it appeared, on the backs of large purple cutouts of Ranger uniforms. Her hair was purple.

A pile of pizza boxes was crookedly stacked on the kitchen counter, and cans of Pepsi stood on every surface of the house.

"When are you going to be done?" I asked Annie. She wore a purple scarf around her neck like a western outlaw.

She shrugged. "I'd leave, if I was you. I bet we have two hours – at least – of work to do."

I shook my head. "You're done by midnight."

She shook her head. "Not going to happen. We still have a lot to do, and let me ask you this, Lance. Does this look like a crew that's going to get up early in the morning and finish the job?"

"Midnight," I insisted.

"Miss Kristofferson, please take him somewhere and talk some sense into him," Annie said. She looked at me. "Lance, this is a big deal for us. We have a home football playoff game, so let us get all squirrelly for it, okay. See you later. Stay out as late as you want." And I was dismissed. She picked up some of Trish's cutout purple numbers and everyone resumed work. Aspen waved goodbye, although I hadn't yet taken a step toward the door.

"Come on," Mary said, and gently nudged me to the door.

"Wait, wait!" yelled Bonner. "Lance, hold it!" Bonner jumped from the couch toward the stereo and a moment later *Badlands* blared from the stereo. "It's an anthem of passion, of determination, of *living!*" he shouted. And then he started jumping. When I exited the door everyone else in the house was jumping except for Trish, who pounded the table with the palms of both her hands.

I got home about eight o'clock Saturday morning. The house was remarkably picked up, remarkably empty, remarkably quiet. I had called at twelve-thirty and was told by Annie that only Trish and a couple other girls were still working, and they were finishing up. She assured me Johnny Pep, Bonner and Caddy were gone. I told Annie I'd be home within thirty minutes, but it didn't work out that way.

I surveyed the living room and found nothing broken, no sleeping bodies and no evidence of trouble. The house was actually clean, for our house. I looked through the kitchen window and saw behind the fence in the backyard, atop the garbage can in the alley, sat two fat black garbage bags stuffed with cans and pizza boxes and discarded remnants of everything purple or gold purchased in Whitehall. A fuzzy coat of white frost covered the top of the wood fence but not the bags. They hadn't been out there that long. Annie knew the festivities would last late into the night at our house. She'd planned for both Tony and me to be elsewhere to ensure we got some sleep.

A low sun squatted in the eastern sky. The temperature had dropped – cold enough to see your breath – but held a promise of what passed for early November warmth. I opened the refrigerator door; nothing seemed amiss. A corner of the living room held neat stacks of rolled up banners and cutout figures and helmets and pom-poms and more banners and signs. I could smell the moisture of the paint and even the faint scent of glue.

Five hours until game time. I needed a shower and something to eat, then a few hours at the Ledger to compensate for my absence on Thursday. I couldn't resist a peek into Annie's room just to make sure she was safe and healthy and at home with me.

"Ummm," she said dreamily at a faint click of the doorknob. She squinted an eye open.

I entered her room and sat on the edge of her bed. I put my hand on her forehead. There was a hint of dampness. I wondered again, as I'd done so many times in the past, how such a slight little frame of a body could generate so much heat.

"Lance, you little rascal," she said to me softly, still partially asleep. "You had a sleepover, didn't you?"

Chapter 37

Fresh snow capped the Highlands to the west and the Tobacco Roots to the south, but the Bull Mountains – lower in elevation – were damp and brown to the north. A gentle biting wind blew down the valley floor and across a Whitehall High School football field that had large swaths of yellow dead grass and a chewed-up brown dirt patch down the middle. It had been a long time since our football field had had to withstand football practices in November.

Ranger colors were everywhere. Purple streamers waved from the goal posts. The wind was mild for Whitehall but stiff enough to make the streamers bluster horizontally, flowing eastward. A large purple *WHS* was chalked at midfield, the end zones were outlined in purple and yellow, and a few long banners were suspended with rope at either end of the field. I recognized some of the banners from the previous night.

The stadium seats were packed, and fans stood two and three rows deep along the sideline. Fairfield brought an army of blue-clad fans, the largest crowd of visiting fans I'd ever seen in Whitehall. And by game time the Whitehall stands were filled – first time in a long time – and the parking lot overflowed and people continued to file their way toward the field. People were parking up and down Whitehall Street and in a dirt field across from the Town Pump.

The cheerleaders were resplendent in shiny new purple windbreakers, purple wool ear warmers – courtesy of Lyle and the bank, I'd been told – and glittering gold wind pants with the word *Whitehall* down the outside of one leg and the word *Rangers* down the other. They waved and shimmied pom-poms that, if I was not mistaken, had been assembled by Trish and company in the Joslyn house the night before.

The WHS pep band mixed in *Smoke on the Water* and *Joy to the World* with *Born in the U.S.A.* and *Born to Run* while the teams warmed up. The Fairfield Eagles looked more like the Fairfield Oxen; there were about forty of them – compared to less than twenty-five Rangers – and each Fairfield kid looked like a tackle or linebacker. I watched them stretch out and an unscientific survey indicated an average Fairfield player was substantially bigger than our largest player.

The wind was stiff enough to warrant multiple layers of warm clothes. I wore an old pair of long underwear, thick wool socks, my winter boots, four layers including a sweatshirt on my upper body and a Dallas Cowboys stocking cap of Tony's that fully covered my ears and the back of my neck. Tony, conversely, in street clothes on the sideline, was hatless and wore his WHS letterman jacket unbuttoned over an untucked flannel shirt. I wondered how he had accepted his inability to play in his school's biggest football game of the year and possibly the biggest game in his school's history. Our paths hadn't crossed much in the previous couple days. I really hadn't had a chance to talk to him about his injury, his mental and emotional state of mind, or his attitude about being forced to stand helplessly along the sidelines.

Off to the north, on I-90, a truck beeped its horn in tribute to the game.

"What do they feed those Fairfield kids? Raw meat?" asked Annie. Good daughter that she was, she had fetched me a cup of hot chocolate. I was hovering just off the field, down at about the twenty yard line, just taking in the atmosphere, energy and tension surrounding me.

"They're big boys, aren't they," I said. "Thanks for this. It's downright chilly out here."

"I'd like to check the birth certificates on a couple of those guys," Annie said. She was wearing a hooded sweatshirt under an old winter coat that I believed had been her mother's. I opted to not ask. "Look at number seventy-two," said Annie. "He's as big as a dump truck."

"What about sixty-eight?" I said. "Look at the size of him. You don't block a kid that size. You harpoon him."

Annie scoured the game program. "Anderson," she said. "Sixty-eight is Hunter Anderson. He's won the state heavyweight wrestling title as a sophomore and junior and will win it again as a senior. He's going to the University of Minnesota on a wrestling scholarship."

I sipped my hot chocolate. "It says that in the program?"

"No, there was a big article about him in the Tribune on Wednesday," she said. "He's been all-conference in football all four years. He's the state shot put champion, too." She paused. "I'd say Hunter Anderson is so talented he deserves the governor declaring a Hunter Anderson Day in Montana."

"Let's just hope it's not today," I said.

"Let's hope a lot of things," Annie added.

I watched the Fairfield players warm up. They went through their drills smooth and confident, and on our end of the field slender Dave Dickson looked like an elementary school student compared to them. "How are our poor kids going to compete with kids like these?"

"Quickness and deception from tiny Dave Dickson and speed from kids like Colt and Nate, and then get lucky," said Annie.

"Was that in the Tribune too?" I asked.

"No, that's what Jersey told me yesterday." Annie scouted the Fairfield players. "They had a senior quarterback who was pretty good. But that's him over there, on the sidelines, leaning on the crutches. He hurt his knee last week. The second string quarterback is okay, but Jersey said Whitehall is going to have nine guys on the line of scrimmage to stop the run. If Fairfield's going to win, Jersey told me, their quarterback is going to have to throw the ball downfield."

"What, all of a sudden you're Howard Cosell?" I asked.

"Howard Cosell's a jerk," she said.

"So they have a player banged up and out of the game, just like us," I said. We both looked over at Tony. "How's he doing?"

"Surprisingly well, actually," Annie said. "But he's going to freeze his butt off if he doesn't get some more clothes on."

"He's recovering from his injury, I know, but how's he handling the not playing thing?" I asked. "You know he'd love to be out there on the field."

"Yeah, well, he can't," Annie said. "I've got a scarf and hat in my locker," she added. "I think I'll go and grab them for him. I think there's a pair of mittens in the back seat of the Escort."

"Those are Mary's mittens," I protested. "He'll never wear a woman's mittens or your scarf and hat."

"He will if he gets cold enough," Annie said. She turned to depart, off to her locker, was my guess, to retrieve a hat and scarf.

"See you at halftime," I said. "Bring me another one of these, okay?" I held up the hot chocolate.

And she disappeared in the crowd, a little girl swallowed up by a growing mass of purple and gold humanity.

Two trucks, twenty seconds apart, tooted their horns over on the freeway.

The teams were mostly done with warm-ups and stood along the respective sidelines, popping shoulder pads and exchanging high-fives. Upon closer inspection, the Fairfield players didn't get smaller. Their team manager was bigger and stronger than our quarterback.

Another indication this was not just another game was the media present: A couple TV crews were standing by to shoot some quick early-game footage then head to some other assignment and I spotted sports reporters from the Montana Standard and Great Falls Tribune across the field.

On the Whitehall sidelines, Dave Dickson whacked each Ranger on the front of the helmet, shouting instructions and encouragement or just plain shouting. He looked like a purple child compared to the chunks of humanity in the blue and white uniforms. Colt paced the sidelines, head down, like someone waiting to be summoned for an important task. Nate Bolton jumped in place, bringing his knees nearly chest-level. JeffScott stood side by side, both looking the same direction, standing the exact same way, leaning to the right with the right knee bent slightly. Dave walked in front of them and gave each one an open hand slap on the helmet, and each accepted it identically. Dave gave Logan a pop on the helmet and Logan popped Dave back, which wobbled Dave momentarily. Tracy Lonigan, Tony's replacement, a tall and slender junior who was better at basketball than football, walked over and slapped Tony's hands.

Jersey stood, arms crossed, head bowed, listening to Coach Pete, who was gesturing with both hands, one of them holding a clipboard. Jersey wore his customary black. Coach Pete wore a Minnesota Vikings baseball cap and Carroll College sweatshirt. Both teams were purple and gold, like the Rangers. The two coaches appeared, as they spoke on the sidelines, as if they had absolutely nothing in common.

I wandered through the west end zone and across the corner of the field to the visitor's side of the field, to check on Slack and the chain gang. They would have to hold cold metal sticks all game, and were dressed for a North Pole crossing. Slack wore what I assumed were his ranch winter Carhartt overalls, since the knees were covered in muck and mire of what I assumed was calving guts and blood. He wore a hooded sweatshirt under the Carhartts and only a small eight-inch or so hole opened in the middle so he could breathe and see. I could detect his eyes and nose, but his chin and mouth were covered by the bottom slope of the hood.

"Is that Admiral Peary in there?" I asked.

"No, it's me, Slack," he assured me.

"What's your prediction?" I asked him.

"Ummm," he said, thinking. Already, before kickoff, there was a slick coating of snot below his nose, above his upper lip. "What's yours?" he asked slyly.

"You see the size of some of those kids?" I asked.

"Yeah," said Slack's dad, Hank. "Who're we playing, Fairfield or the New York Giants?"

"That sixty-eight is as big as a bear," Slack said.

"Mean as one, too," added Hank.

"But we got quickness and speed on our side," I declared. "I predict we win twenty-one to twenty."

Slack cheered, as if my prediction was fact, would indeed be the outcome of the game.

"I wish Tony could play," Hank said.

I saw a hint of sorrow, or distress, in Slack's face. I wondered if Slack knew that he and Tony were both relegated to the sidelines because of brain trauma. The distinction was Tony's was mild and temporary.

"He'll be back next week," I told them. I looked over across the field and found him applauding as the Rangers went through final warm-ups along the sideline. To my surprise and amusement, he wore Mary's orange knitted mittens, Annie's white and black striped stocking cap, and Annie's white scarf was wrapped around his neck like he was a German movie director. He no longer looked like an injured football player. He more closely resembled a statistician who was also in the drama club.

The flags flapped and snapped in the breeze during the presentation of the colors by the cheerleaders. The band played a cold and hollow version of the national anthem. I attempted to mirror the stone-like trance of the Rangers, and noticed Whitehall fans did their best to stand firmly and respectfully. I was facing across the field, the flags between me and the Rangers, and not a Ranger so much as blinked while the music played.

Whitehall won the toss and took the ball, but would have the wind in their face. The Fairfield kicker was a stocky big kid and with the wind at his back put the ball in the end zone.

The Rangers gained a couple yards on two handoffs to Logan and then Dave took off on a wide sweep. Just as he turned the corner and headed upfield a linebacker probably twice Dave's weight whacked him with such velocity Dave actually flew through the air out of bounds and landed at Coach Pete's feet. Dave stood unsteadily, and Jersey lifted him to his feet and helped him stay upright.

Fairfield got the ball close to midfield and picked up six, nine and seven yards on three successive carries. On the second play, a run off tackle, the Fairfield runner carried Whitehall's best tackler – Logan – for three yards after initial contact.

A couple plays later the Eagles were on the Whitehall fifteen yard line. On first down the runner barely got back to the line of scrimmage. I took a picture of the Ranger defense; ten purple jerseys and gold helmets were visible on or near the tackle. The next run only gained three yards. There were too many Rangers at the line of scrimmage for Fairfield to block. On third down the Fairfield quarterback overthrew an open receiver and on fourth down the Fairfield holder botched the snap on an attempted field goal and the game remained scoreless.

The game stayed a scoreless tie until midway through the second quarter when Fairfield got a touchdown on an impressive run up the middle by the fullback. The ball carrier was squat and stocky and ran right through Colt's attempt at a tackle.

On the next possession the Rangers mounted their best drive of the half. A screen pass to Nate went for fourteen yards and Logan busted outside on the next play for twelve yards. Colt caught a pass on a short curl pattern for another first down and with a couple minutes left to go in the half the Rangers were inside the Fairfield twenty yard line. On the next play Dave faked the dive to Logan and faked a pitch to Nate before ducking inside for a gain to the eleven yard line. On the next play Dave ran a sweep and had an opening and cut to his left. He was just about in the end zone when a defender hit him from the side. Dave didn't go down, but the ball flew loose, and after a mad scramble involving three or four players from each team the ball squirted out of the end zone for a touchback.

The combination of sorrowful groan, plaintive wail and anguished sigh of absolute desolation from the Whitehall stands conveyed the torment connected to the play. Dave took his hands and slapped each side of his helmet twice. The touchback gave Fairfield the ball on its twenty yard line and Whitehall was still scoreless.

"Shit, shit, shit," Coach Pete mumbled not quite under his breath.

Tony's gaze went skyward, as if beseeching a higher power for an explanation of what had just happened. I looked up as well, but didn't see many answers.

The half ended with Whitehall down 7-0, and looking at the stats, it could have been and probably should have been worse. Fairfield had over one hundred and thirty rushing yards in the first half, compared to forty-seven for Whitehall.

Annie mercifully brought me a cup of hot chocolate. She had been seated on the bottom row of seats, directly above Trish, who was parked at her usual spot next to the west corner of the bleachers. Annie and I walked over toward the crowd and the bleachers, to get a little protection from the breeze.

"Trish, tell Dave to hang on to the ball next time he's at the goal line," I said.

"I will," she answered sternly. The combination of emotional dismay, her normal slurred diction and cold weather made her voice sluggish and her words difficult to understand. She was wrapped in a thick purple blanket with a second blanket folded across her lap.

Sara Dickson, still tiny despite being bundled up in a snowmobile suit, appeared more stoic and more grim than usual. Her typical expression of someone who feared the worst was appropriate. Cal Walker walked past, steaming cup of coffee in each hand, and merely shook his head solemnly. Molly Ryan stopped by to tuck the blanket around Trish's legs and make sure the hat was snug.

"We're playing the most enormous collection of high school boys I've ever seen in my life," she said angrily, as if there was something unfair or improper about it.

"We'd be tied if we'd have hung on to the ball there on the goal line," I said.

"How come they got the ball after that?" asked Mary, who had suddenly appeared at my side. "They didn't recover the fumble."

"By rule, it's their ball," Annie said.

Mary looked at me for confirmation. I nodded.

"It's a stupid rule," she asserted. "We fumbled and they never recovered. It should have still been our ball."

Mary's cold face was splotched red in areas and a pale, ghastly white in others. She didn't look like someone you wanted to argue with.

Old Tom hobbled my direction, the leather helmet awkwardly and crookedly perched atop a stocking cap on Old Tom's scrawny head. He wore an old battered ski jacket that smelled so bad it had to have been on temporary loan from Young Tom.

"The goddamn flats have been open all day," he groused. His thin lips were so blue they were almost black. His grizzled white and gray whisker stubble glowed translucent as the sun settled low in the southwest.

"The what?" Mary asked, concerned.

If you didn't know him, you'd have thought Old Tom was peculiarly filled with rage and nonsense. Actually, you thought the same thing most of the time if you did know him. I was sure Mary had no idea what *flats open all day* meant.

"The what?" she asked again.

"I said the goddamn flats have been open all goddamn day," Old Tom claimed. He poked a crooked finger into my chest. "You tell that Johnny Cash-looking guy that." It was an order.

"Okay," I agreed quietly.

“Goddamn right,” Old Tom asserted. Neither the stocking cap nor helmet covered his ears, and his neck and throat area were uncovered. He reminded me of one of those ancient tortoises crawling slowly and without apparent direction or reason in cement cages at zoos.

A soft rumble of throaty cheering from the Whitehall fans – combined with the muffled sound of applause with gloves and mittens – indicated the Rangers were taking the field for the second half. They trotted out as a group, stern and silent, and started warming up at midfield. Annie gave me the rest of her hot chocolate, and Cal Walker passed me going the other direction, still with a somber scowl and a shake of his head.

“Are you warm enough?” Mary asked me.

“Yeah,” I said. “Are you?”

“I think so. It’s getting colder out here.”

She was right. The wind had picked up a notch, and its bite was worse.

“Tell him!” someone growled from the bleachers. I looked up and saw Old Tom, who was angrily jabbing the air toward Jersey. I hesitated. Jersey had his hands full without unsolicited advice from old men with questionable sanity. “Go! Tell him!” Old Tom commanded, again jabbing a scrawny arm in Jersey’s direction.

I turned from Old Tom and saw Jersey looking from Old Tom to me, and figured I had to say something about the geriatric guy under the lopsided leather helmet. Jersey watched me the whole time as I approached. When I got close, he put his arm around me and bent down to hear me better.

“I’m supposed to tell you the flats are open,” I said with some embarrassment. “The old guy up there in the leather helmet says the flats are wide open. I’m sorry. He wanted to make sure I told you that.”

“Fine, thanks, we’ll look at that,” Jersey said. “How are you feeling, Lance? I heard you fainted on Wednesday.”

“What? No,” I told him. “Well,” I added, under his gaze, “sort of. But I’m fine. Fine.”

“Good,” Jersey said. “You take it easy. We need you healthy.” He looked up into the crowd. He nodded toward Old Tom. “What’s with the helmet?” he asked me.

“I have no idea,” I said.

“You know the story of David and Goliath?” Jersey asked.

I nodded.

“David wore a helmet just like that.”

The first Ranger possession did not have the opportunity to exploit the allegedly open flats. On the second play Dave overthrew Colt on an inside slant, and the pass was intercepted.

“What the hell is that!” demanded Old Tom from the bleachers.

It was a mistake. Six running plays later the Eagles were in the end zone with a 14-0 lead. The Rangers were only down by two touchdowns, but because of the way Fairfield had controlled the line of scrimmage it seemed much worse. Dave’s tricks in the offensive backfield weren’t fooling anyone in part because he was under steady pressure and plays failed to develop on time or in the proper sequence. Once he wanted to pitch the ball to Logan but Logan had already been tackled, and there were times when Dave intended to hand the ball off but was hit as he pulled away from the center.

Fairfield got the ball back and moved the ball into Whitehall territory, and two sweeps made it first and ten at the Ranger nineteen yard line. The Fairfield fullback powered up the middle and collided with Logan – the explosive crash produced a fumble that was the featured photo in the Ledger – and then spindly Tracy Lonigan dived to the ground and covered the loose ball.

On first down Dave backpedaled in the pocket and looked downfield, then turned abruptly and flipped the ball to Nate in the flats. He got a full ten yards down the field before a tackler missed him, and then he suddenly cut across the field and was in full flight down the sideline – the opposite sideline, in front of the Fairfield bench – in a total sprint that ended with a collision at about the Fairfield twenty yard line. What happened then was clearly visible to everyone except those few men wearing the striped white and black referee's uniforms.

I saw it plain as day. What happened was the Fairfield defender launched himself broadside at Nate and the two of them went flying to their right, out of bounds. Nate hit the ground out of bounds and the ball bounded up in the air, hit the ground once, and fell into the hands of the defender, who had rolled onto his back, five yards out of bounds. The ball fell on his belly, and he immediately sat up and held the ball in the air and hollered. The referee, who was neither young nor slender nor nimble, trailed Nate downfield and showed up late. When he got there he found a jubilant Fairfield kid holding up the ball. The referee hesitated for just a heartbeat, which allowed the Fairfield coaches, bench players and fans to start yelling *White ball! White ball! White ball!*

The referee didn't know any better. He hadn't seen what happened. He couldn't have. He had been chugging his way upfield when the players tumbled out of bounds. He whirled and pointed downfield the opposite direction. Fairfield ball. The dull cheer forty yards away from the Fairfield side of the field was met instantly by groans and boos and angry shouts from the Whitehall side of the field. We all saw Nate with the ball tucked firmly under his arm when he went flying out bounds. It was impossible that anyone who actually saw the play would call it a fumble. Colt confronted the referee and I could see him pointing to the sidelines, to out of bounds and at the referee. Then I saw the referee reach his right hand to his back pocket and throw a penalty flag. Behind Colt, Dave jumped up and down and eventually took off his helmet and threw it to the ground. A referee behind him threw another flag. All the while the Whitehall fans were throwing a kind of collective community tantrum, and individual fans were screaming insults and allegations at the refs.

Coach Pete threw his hat to the ground and stepped on it, and with his body coiled into an absolute rage and his face contorted in fury he screamed at another ref on our side of the field who had nothing to do with the fumble call or the two penalty flags. The ref pretended to ignore Coach Pete, which was an impressive feat, considering Pete's outburst was less than an arm's length away. It was entirely possible the foam from Pete's fury sprayed the ref's clothes.

Fairfield broke the huddle and lined up to run a play, but the Whitehall booing and caustic shouts were so loud the players stood there, as if waiting for permission to proceed.

"Time out," Jersey called out. That triggered another layer of boos and hostility from the Whitehall fans. Jersey turned from the field and looked into the stands, and immediately the volume of noise diminished. He stood there, facing the Whitehall bleachers, silent, simply standing there, neither speaking nor moving. His expression was firm but he didn't appear particularly angry, and he offered no gestures of comfort or calm or commands. Despite the lack of an overt message, his intentions were unmistakable, and the chorus of disgust muted itself to a dull grumble.

Jersey slowly turned from the crowd toward the field, and with both hands held high, waved the players toward him and to the sideline. A furious and dejected group of Whitehall kids gathered angrily on the side of the field, not ten yards from where I stood. I heard every word they and Jersey said.

But first I heard what Slack shouted. He was fifty yards away, on the opposite side of the field, and I could hear him scream the word "Cheaters!" at the Fairfield players. "Cheaters!" he yelled again, and yelled it twice more before his father calmed him down.

"It should be our ball!" yelled Morgan at the sideline. He hawked up a wad of phlegm and spat out toward the field.

"This is shit!" Cody complained.

"Fumble my ass!" Dave yelled.

"Enough," Jersey told them. He looked at each one of them. "So it wasn't a fumble. We know it. And those Fairfield kids know it. They know what they did, and they know right from wrong."

"But they got the ball!" whined Dave.

"Yeah, I know it's their ball," Jersey said. It was as firm as I'd ever heard him talk.

The chubby referee – the same one who called it a fumble – trotted over and clapped his hands twice. "Let's get 'em going, Coach."

Jersey hesitated. "Time out." He paused. "Again."

"You already got a timeout, Coach," the ref said.

"I want to call another one," said Jersey.

"You want to use your second timeout? Now?" the referee asked, puzzled.

"Yeah, now leave us alone," he said, and the referee returned to the middle of the field where he signaled Whitehall's second timeout had been called.

"Chickenshit refs," Cody complained again.

"I said that's enough," Jersey ordered. "Now listen to me. Bad breaks are part of football. We got a bad break. So what. Bad breaks are part of life. You want to cry and give up? Call the refs names? You think that will help win the game? We got a bad break. All right. So deal with it. Meet it. Face it. Overcome it. This is life, boys, and life can be unfair. Life can be rough and cruel and unfair but never give up. Not here, not now, not ever."

"We're still gonna win this game," Colt said, and pounded Dave on the shoulder pads.

"Yes we are," added Jersey, "We will win this football game. You know why? Because we're better than they are. Because we can handle adversity. Because we don't give up. Because *nothing* can stop us."

A Ranger whooped, and a couple more players joined in.

The ref appeared behind the players, facing Jersey. He clapped his hands. "Let's go, Coach. Let's play some football."

Jersey shook his head in dismay. "Time out," he said.

The ref was visibly surprised. "That's your last timeout," he said, as if it was a question.

"I realize that." He stood motionless, eyes directed at the ref until the ref trotted again to the center of the field and let it be known that Whitehall had called its third and final timeout. There were a few groans from the bleachers.

"Did we just burn all three timeouts?" asked Dave.

"It's fine," Colt answered. "We won't need them."

"We just used all three timeouts at once," Dave marveled. "Pretty sure that's never happened before."

"Pretty sure that's never happened before, either," Colt said, and pointed to where the alleged fumble took place.

"I think in the history of football we're the first team to ever use all three timeouts at once," Dave marveled again.

"Come on, come on," Jersey said. "Bring it in." And the players all crowded in front of their coach. "We have an advantage now, and we know it and they," he gestured toward Fairfield, "know it. We can play the rest of the game with pride, and they can't. We will honor our community, our school, our team, this sport, this game and the spirit of competition, and because we will conduct ourselves with pride and dignity, we will not leave this football field defeated. And they will. I guarantee you, no matter what the score of this game is, we are going to leave this field as winners and we will be the only team to do so. Do you believe me?"

A few Ranger players shouted some kind of affirmative answer. Then a few players started clapping and yelling. Dave started jumping up and down. So did Tony. He looked preposterous in his mittens, hat and scarf, the scarf waving up and down as he jumped.

There were still scattered boos from the Whitehall crowd when Fairfield finally lined up to run a play, but something – the tone of the game, maybe, the emotions of the players or something perhaps intangible and unexplainable – had changed during the trio of timeouts. The Whitehall players had left the field before the timeouts as a demoralized and vanquished group, but stood in position now with a fervor and resolve that was palpable in their postures. They couldn't wait for Fairfield to snap the ball. Even the majority of Whitehall fans, a surly bunch before the time out, stood as one in vocal hopeful anticipation of the next play.

The play itself was nothing substantial. The Fairfield quarterback whirled and handed the ball off to the fullback who was tackled for no gain by Brock Warren. Fairfield tried a sweep the other direction and Logan and Cale combined on a fierce tackle for a two-yard loss. On third down the Fairfield quarterback barely avoided a sack by Cody and attempted a tentative pass that fell incomplete. Everyone in purple celebrated.

The third quarter ended with Whitehall down 14-0 on its own forty-two yard line. Cale skirted the end on a sweep for twelve yards before he was bounced out of bounds. There was no fumble.

Logan pounded up the middle for no gain. Dave faked a pitch to Nate and ducked inside for eight yards, and on third and short Dave hit Colt on a short sideline pass for a first down.

Nate caught a pass in the flats and ran untouched for sixteen yards and another first down. Another dive by Logan went for short yardage but on the next play Dave pulled the ball away from Logan on a fake dive and scurried for another nine yards before getting thumped at about the eight yard line.

Whitehall broke the huddle with a background din of cheering. The Whitehall volume of noise muted slightly as the Rangers lined up in formation.

"Hang on to the ball this time, Davy!" cried the unmistakably slurred voice of Trish. There was a moment of silence and then a gentle amused murmur from the crowd in response, and I snuck a peek at Tony, who pointed a finger of appreciation toward Trish.

Dave rolled out to his right looking to pass. He continued to look as he drifted toward the sideline, looked and waited a couple beats more, then tucked the ball under his arm and took off straight ahead for the end zone. He was met at about the two yard line by a linebacker who had a hundred pounds on the tiny Whitehall quarterback. But Dave lowered a shoulder and bulled his way through the defender, who flopped backward in the end zone with Dave on top of him. Dave jumped up into the arms of JeffScott, who lifted Dave upward like a trophy. Colt's extra point made it 14-7 with eight minutes left in regulation.

Fairfield had the lead and the ball, but Whitehall had something else. There was a singular pulse of excitement – an invisible force, a dominant energy generated from our side of the field – that fused WHS fans with the Rangers. It was as tangible as the wind. The cold air stifled something as ordinary as crowd noise, but under the muffled and routine sounds of cheers and shouts and applause was something else, like a current of electricity, something silent but alive and physical, almost like an invisible presence exerting command. You could feel it and sense it. You could almost see it, and you could certainly not deny it.

Tony felt it. I could tell by looking at him. He crept down the sideline and was whispering something to the Fairfield player on the kickoff receiving team, and the Fairfield player was pretending to ignore him. Coach Pete felt it. He was pounding the clipboard on the top of Cody's helmet. Jersey felt it. He had an arm around Dave and the two of them were sharing, of all things, a laugh.

Fairfield took over at their own thirty yard line. Logan stuffed the ball carrier for no gain on the first play, and a trio of Rangers – led by Brock and Cody – stopped the runner for a one-yard gain on second down. On third down the Eagles played conservative and attempted a sweep that picked up four yards but fell short of a first down.

With a little under six minutes in regulation Whitehall took over on their own thirty-six yard line. Dave ran for five yards. Logan busted through the middle for nine yards and a first down. Cale took a sweep for six yards, Nate caught a short pass for eight yards and Cale ran another sweep for four yards. I started to imagine the score tied at 14-14, and I wasn't the only one imaging that. The Rangers were tearing off big chunks of yardage on virtually every snap.

On first and goal, with under a minute left, Dave floated a short pass to Nate in the left flats – the Ranger side of the field – and at about the three yard line he bounced off one tackler, spun to pick up an extra yard and reached the ball toward the goal line. Just as he did, a defender dived and knocked the ball loose. It bounced once, twice, and Colt pounced on the ball in the end zone for a Ranger touchdown.

But then between the chaos and joy of the touchdown, and with Nate injured -- standing on the sideline holding his ribs -- and not in formation for the extra point, and with his substitute running onto the field late, Whitehall couldn't get the extra point kicked before the play clock expired. If they would have had a timeout, Whitehall would have used it. But they had no timeouts left, so after the delay of game penalty the ball was brought out to the eight yard line. The Rangers, with little Tracy Lonigan on the wing to block, lined up for the extra point. If Colt and Whitehall converted, the game was headed for overtime. If Colt and Whitehall missed the kick, Whitehall would lose 14-13 with Fairfield advancing to the title game.

The anxious and tangible pulse still reverberated through the stands and on the field as Whitehall lined up. Fairfield players on either end dug in to get a strong push off the line on Tracy's side to block the kick. As Whitehall lined up the thought struck me that this was the most important extra point in Whitehall High School history.

"Ohhh," Trish mourned when she saw the Whitehall players line up to kick. "Go for two!" she urged plaintively.

Logan lined up at an angle behind and just off the shoulder of the linemen, JeffScott, on the other side of the line. I wondered how high those tall beefy Fairfield kids could jump.

The extra point snap from Cody sailed high, far over Dave's head, directly to Colt, who caught it, whirled to his left and burst outside and untouched into the end zone for two points and a breathtaking and shocking and impossible 15-14 Whitehall lead.

Colt hopped into the arms of the Ranger offensive line as the anxious and tangible pulse pounded loose with audible power with shouts and even screams from the Whitehall sidelines and the Whitehall bleachers. It had been a designed play – an obvious direct snap to Colt – and had it failed the Ranger season would have been over. It was an illogical and perhaps irrational gamble, but it had worked flawlessly and brilliantly. Had it failed, Jersey would have had the impossible task of defending the call. The Rangers clearly and defiantly had possessed the momentum, had Fairfield backpedaling with a loss of confidence, and Whitehall was firmly in control of the game. It was risky, even reckless, to jeopardize all that flow of momentum on one trick play that hadn't been run once all year.

But despite the rowdy ruckus from the Whitehall side of the field, the game wasn't over. Fairfield would receive the kickoff with nearly a minute to play, and unlike the Rangers, Fairfield still had all three of its timeouts left.

A decent kick return brought the ball to the Fairfield forty yard line. On the first snap the unsteady Fairfield quarterback tossed a pass on an inside slant that needed to be delivered one beat sooner and with considerably more velocity. Tracy timed his tackle at the ball's arrival and separated the ball from the receiver. Colt swooped up the deflected pass and sprinted untouched and unpursued straight down the field for a touchdown. His extra point kick made the score 22-14 but the game still wasn't over. A touchdown and two-point conversion could tie the game. But Fairfield threw four straight incompletions. You had the feeling watching them that if they threw twenty passes they'd all be incomplete.

Whitehall won 22-14, and impossibly Whitehall would travel somewhere in seven days to play for a state title.

The Whitehall fans spilled euphorically out of the bleachers and triumphantly fanned out from behind the fence and swarmed the players. During the melee I watched Jersey as he took the game ball and slowly but purposefully moved alone against the swirling crowd toward the corner of the stands. For some reason I followed a ways behind him, moving with difficulty against the force of the people streaming toward the field, and saw him approach Trish, bundled up in her wheelchair, with Annie standing and cheering alongside her. Jersey navigated a path directly to the front of the wheelchair. He handed Trish the football, which she held in her lap. Jersey leaned forward, said something into Trish's ear, then kissed her on the forehead, just below the hood and stocking cap. Then he turned and flowed the other direction, toward his team.

I watched Trish, her dreamy, unfocused expression, her unbalanced posture in the wheelchair as she accepted the accolades of the people momentarily stopping and congratulating her and anyone else they saw. Annie beamed beside her, and accepted a hug from Molly Ryan when she showed up to join her daughter. I more or less fought my way to Annie's side.

"Unreal," she shouted above the racket.

"What did he say?" I shouted in response.

"Who?" asked Annie.

"Jersey."

She offered a puzzled expression. "He told her to honor the gift."

I wasn't sure I heard her right. "Honor what?"

"The gift," Annie said.

I looked from Trish to Annie. "What gift?"

Annie shrugged.

"The football?" I shouted. "Is that a gift?"

Annie shrugged again. "He told her to honor the gift. That's all he said."

Chapter 38

Fueled by a playoff victory and a strong sense of camaraderie, downtown Whitehall was hopping on Saturday night. Rules were broken, curfews were lifted, grudges were forgotten, debts were paid, promises were made. Excitement bled into early exhaustion for me, and I was home and asleep by eleven, and to my delight both kids were home together and watching TV when I rolled pleasantly into bed.

The Saturday wind had stripped most of the leaves from Jefferson Valley trees, but Sunday broke clear and crisp, and what foliage remained reflected light as sharp as blades of colored glass. I woke up early Sunday morning to get the majority of my Ledger duties out of the way as soon as possible. While at work, another Sunday in Whitehall played itself out. The Kountz family, wearing their best cowboy hats and kerchiefs, arrived in mud-splattered pickups at St. Teresa's for Mass. A couple ladies – Thelma Arkell and Brenda Cogdill – took their Sunday morning brisk walk through town. Ilen Stoll did some pre-winter garden maintenance. Erv Hedegaard, all bundled up in ski pants and stocking cap, walked his tiny dogs on long blue leashes down Division Street and around the empty track that circled the lonely football field.

Most of the stores were closed. Out by the freeway, Town Pump was open, as always. The Borden's Café was open as was the bar, primarily for the Sunday afternoon dance polka and waltz tradition. Cars with license plates from Helena, Butte, Dillon, Bozeman and Ennis – towns in five counties surrounding Whitehall – were parked on Legion Avenue or Main Street before the music even started. High thin clouds scudded across the southern sky, blown by a steady westerly breeze that sent dry and crackling leaves scurrying along the pavement. A few skiffs of dirty snow hid in the shade.

The little Whitehall depot stood empty and desolate, essentially abandoned since the passenger and mail trains had ceased running through southern Montana. Across Legion Avenue, the pizza parlor was open and four guys in winter coats and baseball caps sat around a pizza, watching an NFL game on TV. The Whitehall A&W was open, with its dull orange lights flickering a warm invitation. A handful of cars were scattered in the IGA parking lot; a few people planned a quick trip inside the store for an item or two, and left the engine running.

The Corner Store sold a case of Schlitz Beer to the burley Zankowski boys, who were headed up to Homestake Pass for another load of firewood.

The bars – the Mint, Borden's, Two-Bit and Roper's – were all open, and a few bar stools held cowboys or miners or truckers or others who had nothing better to do on a Sunday besides drink. Already, a few snowbird license plates from Alberta were flowing south through Whitehall to warmer climates in Arizona.

The valley floor was dull and chilled. It was the mountains – in all directions – that lit up bright white under the sun, early snow that would feed the valley streams and rivers into spring and throughout summer.

In a lot of ways it was a Sunday like every other November Sunday in Whitehall.

But in other ways it was a Sunday unlike any other November Sunday in Whitehall.

At St. Teresa's Mass that morning, Father Frank McCormick uttered a brief mention of those 'brave Ranger lads playing next Saturday.' Kelly Lonigan wore her older brother Tracey's purple number twenty-seven WHS Ranger football jersey when she stopped in the IGA. The Town Pump sold out of Butte newspapers before nine o'clock that morning. The Standard had carried a Sunday paper sports section featuring an article about the improbable run of the Whitehall Rangers football team. The article praised the 'gutsy call' of Whitehall head coach Jerry Conte to fake the extra point kick and go for the two-point conversion and the win over Fairfield. The Standard had also sent a photographer over: A three-column photo of Colt holding the ball aloft after he scored the two-point conversion dominated the front page of the Standard sports section, a sharp contrasty picture so clear behind the facemask you could see the expression of joy in Colt's eyes. None of my pictures would be as large or as professional.

In the pizza parlor, as the four guys pried apart the pizza slices, they talked about the Rangers traveling to Roundup on Saturday and pondered the possibility of a road trip to watch the game. At the Whitehall A&W, all the employees wore Ranger purple, and would do so all week. The Corner Store larger exterior sign on the corner of Legion Avenue and Whitehall Street, high above the stop sign on Whitehall Street, read *Congratulations Rangers! Good luck!*

The cowboys and miners and truckers in the bars argued about the weather and property taxes and the price of diesel fuel and whether or not the Rangers had a chance to win a state football title.

There was a sense of unprecedented expectation mixed with the awe of unanticipated accomplishment, and if you looked close, or listened close, you saw and heard it everywhere in town.

Jersey showed up at the Ledger at one o'clock, and as I grabbed my notebook and notes from the Fairfield game he skimmed the Standard and the article about the Rangers.

He shook his head. "If only they knew."

"It's a great photo of Colt," I said.

Jersey agreed. "That's one of the beautiful things about sports, and you know this better than anyone. That photo is something Colt will have the rest of his life. He's probably going to put on a football uniform one more time in his life, and then that's it. He's a good high school athlete, but probably not destined for collegiate athletics. But every time he looks at that picture, it will remind him of this game, this play, this accomplishment." He paused. "This whole team will have your series of articles and pictures, Lance, taking them from virtual incompetence to a state football championship. And that's important, in lots of ways, for lots of reasons."

I felt a responsibility to point out they hadn't won a championship yet. "You still have one more game you've got to win."

He dismissed my concern. "We will. Nothing can stop these boys now." He put down the paper. "There's an error of fact in this article you might not know about." He pointed at the newspaper. "It says there that I took a gamble and won when I called for the two point conversion."

"You don't think that was a gamble?" I asked incredulously.

He shook his head.

"Come on," I implored, "you had scored twice late, and Fairfield was looking pretty demoralized. They knew they were getting beat. The Rangers had all the momentum. That gave Whitehall a major advantage in overtime. But you risked all that on a fake extra point?" I nodded, as if to confirm my statements. "That seems like a pretty big gamble to me."

"That's all true," Jersey said, "which is why I didn't call the fake."

He let that sink in. I looked at him with a mixture of confusion and disbelief. He looked back, a slight grin on his face.

"This would be an opportunity for you to ask me who did call the fake," Jersey said.

"You didn't call it?" I asked.

"I just told you I didn't," he said. "We lined up to kick the extra point, tie the game, play some defense, perhaps force a turnover or – like you said – take our momentum into overtime."

"What happened?" I asked.

"Colt called it," Jersey said. "He saw the defensive end digging in to rush the kick, and just outside the end's shoulder the corner was digging in to get to the ball. Between you and me, Colt wasn't sure we'd stop them. We were a little undermanned at that point. We were asking Tracy to block a kid twice his size. Colt figured they'd sell out pinching inside to block the kick and if he could get outside he'd waltz into the end zone. Which is exactly what happened."

"Can he do that?" I asked. "With the season riding on a fake extra point, can he make that call?"

Jersey shrugged. "He made it." He ran his hand across a two-day stubble. "I can't fault his logic. Or the result." He put down the Standard. "I saw him call it after we lined up. Colt yelled a live color at the line, and then tugged at his face mask a couple times, which was the signal for Cody to direct snap to the kicker." He smiled. "The snap was perfect. The outside was wide open." He hesitated. "Whitehall wins."

"Can I put all that in the paper?" I asked.

"You better put all that in the paper," Jersey said. He laughed. "Cody and Colt conspired on their own." He laughed again. "I don't want people thinking I was crazy enough to call that play."

“Can I ask you this?” I said. “Had you tried the extra point, would they have blocked it?”

Jersey sighed. “I don’t know that, but I do know this. Colt’s a smart kid and a smart player, and those Fairfield kids were big and strong. Colt Harrison is our MVP this year, but not just because of his play on the field. He got hurt, remember, and Dave came in and lit a fire under the kids. We were a better team with Dave at quarterback, even though Colt is a better athlete and probably a better quarterback. At first there was some bitterness, remember?”

I remembered. Cody and Colt fighting, Colt’s parents seeking Jersey’s dismissal.

“But Colt stood up,” Jersey continued. “He stood strong. He opposed his father – possibly for the first time in his life – for the good of this team. Think about that, Lance. The hot shot star senior quarterback accepted his ‘demotion’ – if you want to call it that – to wide receiver and not only that, but went out of his way to help bond the team to Dave. Colt could have torn the Rangers apart. Instead he built them up, and built them into a state championship team.”

And, I thought, the two previous warriors – Colt and Cody – teamed up on the two-point play to beat Fairfield. Quite a turnaround.

“Here’s the best part of all this,” added Jersey. “The lessons and experiences these kids are going through this year will make them better people. I guarantee that. But Colt’s individual shift in attitude and commitment will elevate him later in life. You keep your eye on Colt Harrison. He’s going to accomplish some very impressive things in his life.”

Two hours later, the football article written and film developed, I locked up the Ledger and as I walked to the Escort a car engine started across the street, in the parking lot by the old depot. It was a police car, with Manfred behind the wheel. I stood and watched him as he turned from Division Street onto Legion Avenue and cruised past me, pretending I didn’t exist.

After the Monday ad stops and after a quick lunch at A&W, I swung by the town hall and found Rachel Brockton primly at her desk, municipal water and sewer bills spitting out of a printer.

She could have been a nun, I thought, or a women’s prison warden, and I did not think that in an unflattering manner. It was hard to imagine her laughing at a joke, let alone telling one. She had short dyed brown hair primly brushed back, and I had never seen a hair out of place. It was as if not a hair dared.

Behind her, hung on the wall, were certificates or civic awards or honors framed and arranged and displayed. Rachel had never been to college, but she had taken courses, seminars and classes through state offerings and from the

Montana League of Cities and Towns and was evidently proud of her intellectual advancement.

"Lance Joslyn, on a Monday?" she greeted me.

You didn't just drop by to see Rachel. At least I didn't. It was fairly obvious she did not like surprises or interruptions. So usually I scheduled my appointments with Rachel, and usually they were scheduled on a Thursday or a Friday and the discussion centered on the town budget, a proposed town council ordinance, the town water project or some other municipal issue or proposal. Rachel knew the state or local program or spending authority behind every dollar, the program behind every ordinance and the basis for every regulation. She had answered, when I thought about it, every single question I had ever asked her, factually and promptly.

"I came by to pick up my water bill, save you a stamp," I joked.

Not even a smile. Not even the hint of a smile. Not even a hint that she realized I'd been joking.

"Tony's fine?" she asked, instead.

"Right," I nodded.

"Excellent," she said with absolutely no emotion. "Those Rangers will need all the healthy bodies they can get."

"You got that right," I said.

"And Annie?" Rachel asked. "How's she doing?"

"Fine," I answered.

"Such a bright child," Rachel more or less whispered. "We all were so impressed when Governor Schwinden came down here and presented that award to her. I've lived here almost my entire life and that was the first time I remember that any governor ever gave anyone in Whitehall an award, and for it to be Annie, a child, really, for her outstanding intelligence," she marveled. "It was all very impressive. She's quite a young woman, isn't she?"

"She is," I agreed. It impressed me that Rachel was impressed by Annie. No one else I knew had ever impressed Rachel.

Rachel cleared her throat. She wore a gray turtleneck under a blue pantsuit and I had the feeling she had work to do that was more important than anything I had to say. I was sure she intended for me to have that feeling. The small talk was done. What did I want?

"I have a question about Manfred," I said, as if we were conspirators.

"Manfred?" she asked, then said, officially, "You mean town marshal Henry Manfredini."

"Yeah," I said, nodding. It was awkward, but I had to find a way to verbalize my purpose for interrupting her day. "Has he told you anything about me? Like he's out to get me, or something?"

Rachel frowned, which I did not take as a good sign. "Do you wish to file a complaint against the town marshal?" she asked.

"No, no," I said quickly. I held out my hands. "No, I don't."

"Has the town marshal threatened you in any way?" she asked.

"Threatened me? No, not threatened me, not really," I said. This wasn't going the way I had thought it would. "He's kind of following me around, though, watching me, which is kind of creepy."

"Has he physically threatened or intimidated you?" she asked.

I shook my head. "I was just wondering if you think I should be nervous, you know. Has he said anything to you? Is he still mad about the thing with Cody a few weeks ago?"

"Has he threatened you or your family, Lance?" she asked again.

"No," I admitted, again. "Not really. Some people have warned me about him. And he seems to be keeping his eye on me, for some reason. I was just wondering if you knew anything about any of that. If you had any advice."

"Not officially, no," she said officially. "If you were under criminal suspicion, of course, I wouldn't know anything about it, or be able to comment on it if I did. And if you were, it would be natural for the town marshal, in the course of his duty, to monitor your behavior. The town marshal is responsible for law enforcement in the town of Whitehall, and as such has clear statutory authority beyond the realm of this office."

"I'm not under criminal suspicion, Rachel," I told her. I added, "Am I?"

"Marshal Manfredini can be, shall we say, overcommitted, at times," she said, as detached as if reading a grocery list. "I am unofficially aware of some of the same things you apparently have heard, both related and unrelated to you. But I haven't heard anything directly from the marshal himself. Standard personnel procedures require some kind of actionable offence, and thus far I haven't heard you express or articulate one. He hasn't stalked you, threatened you or intimidated you, according to your own responses to my questions. Unless you want to file a complaint?"

I stood up. "No." What did I have to complain about, really? That I saw him around town? That rumor had it he was out to get me? I was looking for information, not wanting to start trouble. "Do me a favor, will you? Maybe privately mention our talk to the mayor. Just let him know I stopped by."

She looked up at me. "I had already decided to do that."

The printing crew at Anaconda was impressed with the Rangers beating Fairfield and with the oatmeal raisin cookies I brought to the print shop on Wednesday. The cookies had been a gift from Rhonda, who was unaware of Tony's absolute distaste for raisins. As a kid he had picked them out of his food and fed them to Annie like you'd feed a dog. Annie wouldn't eat coconut, but had always liked raisins and had eaten three or four of Rhonda's cookies; I could tell she snuck a few of them from the way the package had been neatly opened and how few cookies had been removed. I figured that without Tony devouring them they might get stale before they disappeared, which would have been an injustice to Rhonda's exceptional cooking. The cookies had apparently showed up Tuesday night while I was at the Ledger, and early Wednesday morning when I left the house with the paste-up pages I grabbed them, and even had a couple of them on the road to Anaconda.

"These are good," admired Larry. He had hold of the pages and was heading to the darkroom when I offered him the box of cookies. "Your daughter make these?"

"No," I said. "An old Jewish lady from Europe made them. She lives a couple blocks down the street and it seems lately about every other day she stops by with bars, pies, brownies, bread or cakes or something."

"I wish an old Jewish lady like that lived a couple blocks down from me," Larry said. He took another cookie and vanished behind the darkroom door. It was the most pleasant initial exchange we'd had in a decade of printing the Ledger in Anaconda. I decided to bring cookies more often.

We had a twenty-eight page paper. Of the forty-eight hours on Monday and Tuesday, I had worked thirty-five of them. We had nearly three hundred inches of advertising devoted to wishing the Rangers well in Roundup at the state championship game. The bank ran a full-page ad, and the IGA ran a half-page ad. The Corner Store's quarter-page ad simply read *Go Get 'Em, Rangers.* Parents of Ranger players filled a full page of *Congratulations* and *Good Luck* and *We're Proud of You* ads. I had two full pages of pictures from the Fairfield game, and a large photo on the front page of Colt and some teammates celebrating in the end zone after the two-point conversion. I had one hundred and fifty extra papers printed to make sure anyone who wanted to buy one had one to buy, and to make sure this slice of Whitehall history would never, ever be lost or forgotten.

"Do some baking, did you?" Dan asked when I offered him the cookies.

"Not me," I said. "A neighbor brought them by. She's always bringing food over, mostly for Tony. He loves her cooking and she loves cooking for him."

"She single and my age?" Dan asked.

"Are you about ninety years old?" I asked.

Dan was maybe thirty-five. "Not yet," he answered.

"Then you're out of luck," I said.

"Story of my life," he said.

Mike knew good cooking when he saw it; he took two cookies at once and bit into both of them at once.

"Good?" I asked.

"Taste like heaven," Mike said. "Who made them?"

"My future wife," Dan answered.

"How can a blind woman make such tasty cookies?" asked Mike.

Amazing, I thought, everyone's in a good mood because of a dozen cookies. I should have thought about bringing treats years earlier.

"How's Tony?" asked Dan.

"Back to normal," I said. "He'll play in Roundup on Saturday."

"I never thought of Tony as normal," said Mike.

"Whitehall's playing for a state title," Dan said, a hint of awe in his voice. "Did you see that coming?"

"No one did," I said. "If anyone says they did, they're lying."

Annie woke me up after a twenty-minute nap, taken quietly on the couch at home with a magazine placed strategically on my chest to make it appear I had been reading it before I dozed. It was as if I couldn't nap Wednesday afternoons without a magazine on my chest.

"You know how in *Top Gun* when Tom Cruise says he feels the need, the need for speed?" Annie asked me. "You're kind of like that, except that you feel the need, the need for sleep."

"Are you saying I have a lot in common with Tom Cruise?" I asked, on the couch, rubbing my eyes and stretching my arms.

"I'm saying you have nothing in common with Tom Cruise," she said. "You need to pay closer attention when I'm talking to you."

"What time is it?" I asked.

"Time to rise and shine. You have a date tonight."

I yawned and groaned at the same time.

"That was pleasant," Annie told me. "Refresh yourself, Lance. Get down to the paper and finish up whatever you need to finish up and be home by six."

"Who is this date with, and what am I doing on this date?"

"Miss Kristofferson, as if you didn't know, and I have no idea. I can't do everything for you."

"Since when?" I asked.

She tensed her chin. "Well, actually, I probably could," she admitted. "But I refuse. You have to take at least a modicum of initiative."

"How much is a modicum? What is a modicum? I just woke up. Don't use such big words."

"A modicum is just a tiny amount, just an inkling, a hint, a scrap, a miniscule amount."

"What do I have to finish up at the Ledger?" I asked.

"How would I know?" Annie asked. "I'm not the publisher. I'm just the accountant."

"Did you make a deposit?" We took in a lot of cash on Tuesday, and I always fretted whenever we had large amounts of money overnight at the paper.

"Get off the couch, Lance. I mean it." She stood with her hands on her hips. "Yes, I made a deposit. A rather large one, actually. You need to invest some money soon or you're going to get whacked by the IRS. That's why you're buying additional property in Gallatin County.

"Whacked?" I asked. "Is that an professional accounting term?"

“Don’t be contrary,” she scolded me. “A moment ago you told me to restrain my vocabulary. Now get up. Do something.”

“Do what? Quit bossing me around.”

“Do you want to know how large the deposit was?” she asked.

“The Rangers have been very, very good to the Ledger,” I said. It was true. The unexpected and unprecedented success of the WHS football team had a significantly positive impact on Ledger income. It also had a heavy impact on the Ledger publisher’s workload, which was why I had trouble waking up.

“Where’d those cookies go?” she asked.

“Wait a minute. Did you say *additional* property in Gallatin County?” I asked.

“Did you eat all those cookies?” She thought about it. “You couldn’t have.”

“Do I already own land in Gallatin County?” I asked.

“Around Three Forks. In Bozeman. And on the South Boulder. You know that, you dunce. You signed the papers. You brought them to Anaconda, didn’t you?”

“Brought what? The papers?”

“No, the cookies,” she said. “Come on, Lance, try to keep up.”

“I am trying,” I said, and sat up. “And I’m not a dunce. I have a portfolio.”

“You also own some property on the Jefferson,” she said.

“You’d think that’d be something I’d remember,” I said. “Owning property.” Although I did vaguely recall some purchases of vacant property – land, with no buildings – over the past year or so. I just hadn’t cared. I still didn’t, truthfully. The transactions had been done so quickly and simply, they seemed virtually inconsequential, and I had to immediately return to Ledger business.

“Why do we live in such a dump if I have a portfolio and own property all over the place?” I asked.

“Good question, Lance,” Annie said. “You can afford a better home, a larger home, and could even build a new home if you wanted to. Should I look into that?”

I stood up and stretched again. “No,” I told her, “there’s nothing wrong with this place.”

It held some of the only memories of Amy I still had.

“Why do you live in that ramshackle old place?” Mary asked me. We were in the Escort, heading south out of town, on a leisurely country drive toward Point of Rocks on the Jefferson River.

“It wasn’t ramshackle when we first bought it,” I confessed.

We had eaten at the Borden's Café, and during dinner Mary told me a little about her years teaching on the Blackfeet Indian Reservation up north and at the Northern Cheyenne Indian Reservation by Billings. She discussed some of the tribal customs, myths, legends and history, and talked quite a while about the Indian heritage and cultures in Montana. I mentioned at Point of Rocks, probably the most identifiable geographical spot in the entire Jefferson Valley, you could see some pictographs painted by people who'd lived thousands of years ago. I told her about the stories – rumor and fable mixed with glimmers of truth – about Point of Rocks, some of which I'd heard from the Kountz family and some of which I'd heard from Slack and his parents.

According to one story, years earlier, when a power company was first digging holes for electrical power poles, the rear wheels of a large truck loaded with equipment and poles had crashed through the surface of the dirt road into a large underground cavern. The walls of the cavern, it was said, had been painted with pictures of bison, an animal that looked like a camel, large mountain lions and other wildlife, natural scenes like the moon and stars, and human activity like hunting. The power pole holes had been dug, the poles placed, and the cavern had been sealed and forgotten, and no one today knew where the cavern was, what might have happened to it or why no one could find it.

Another story suggested that a cave at Point of Rocks had been discovered by early Jefferson Valley settlers, and that the cave not only contained pictographs but a treasure of prehistoric bones and skulls of animals, including the skull of a saber tooth tiger. All of it had been looted by some famously rich family – Mellon, Rockefeller, Morgan, or Carnegie, depending on the version of the story – and hauled back east to a private and secret museum somewhere. There were certainly caves at Point of Rocks, but no one had ever found another saber tooth tiger skull.

"Once upon a time, this entire valley floor was a lake," I said. "Prehistoric man patrolled the shores, and Point of Rocks is the most identifiable spot in the area, which made it a natural rendezvous spot."

"Let me ask one more question about your house," she said as we drove along the Jefferson River. "You're a successful business owner. Why not sell your place and get something more modern?"

"Because no matter where I live, as soon as I move in the place is gonna start looking a little beat up," I said. The river was to our right now, the mountains to our left. "I don't have time for yard work or painting the garage or raking leaves. The house we live in now was clean and sturdy when we moved in. It gets a little worse every year because I don't do anything to maintain it. Why do the same thing to a newer and better place?"

"Well," she said, "I suppose you could make an effort to maintain a house. It can be done. Millions of people do it."

"Not with my schedule, they don't," I said. "I work. I sleep. I see my two kids every now and then. That's it. There's no time for anything else."

"Doesn't sound like much of a life," she said.

"Sometimes," I said, "it isn't. I'm thinking of getting some part-time staff maybe to help me. That's it, up there. Point of Rocks."

The sun had sunk below the Highland Mountains to the west, but the valley floor held just enough light to pick out shades of gray and darkness.

"I can see how it got its name," she said.

Up ahead, the Point of Rocks formation jutted northwest across the valley to the edge of the river. The place was aptly named; a rock outcropping actually formed a sharp point near the riverbank. To the south and north the valley bottom was mostly rolling hills and across the river the valley opened up wide and flat. A stout mule deer buck spooked in our headlights and leapt gracefully over the top strand of barbed wire, clearing it by a full foot, and then immediately vanished in the settling darkness. Another critter, a skunk or raccoon, skittered under the brush down along the bank of the river.

"It got dark quick, didn't it?" I said, slowing the car and pulling off the road onto a wide spot on the shoulder.

"Like a curtain came down," Mary said.

The Escort stopped with the headlights slanted to the right, up and across the river.

"Where's the cave you told me about?" she asked.

"Up there somewhere," I said, and pointed up the dark slope to our left.

"Can we walk to it?"

"Better not," I said. "Too dark. One wrong step up there and it could be a long drop."

"Have you been up there?"

"To the cave? Yeah, once, a long time ago," I said.

"But you don't know where it is?"

"Not anymore, no."

"But you're sure it exists?" she asked.

"Yeah," I said.

"Someday I'd like to explore that cave," she said.

"Someday you can do that," I said. "But not tonight."

We sat close, shoulder to shoulder, both looking out the driver's side window.

"But I know what you can do tonight," I said.

"What would that be?"

"You can warm your toes in the Jefferson River," I said.

She laughed. "Right."

It was mid-November and the temperature outside was in the mid twenties. The water temperature in the Jefferson River was numbing-cold, the sky was a patchy black, and a frosty breeze blew from the west, across the cold water and the shaded pockets of dirty gray snow.

"I'm serious," I said. "Let's go stick our feet in the water."

"Not in that water," Mary objected.

"You'd be surprised," I said, and opened the door. "Come on."

I waited for her to reluctantly climb out of the car. I took her gloved hand and we carefully picked our way in the dark along a path of sorts on a short slope to the water. It had been a few years since I'd been there – with Tony and some of his friends after they'd floated a stretch of the Jefferson in inner-tubes – but it wasn't hard to find. The winter river flow was almost a perfect depth over the small row of rocks hand-placed along the bank inside the water. A neatly formed circle of stones extended from the shore; some of the stones were several inches above the water, some were under water and some were at the exact water's surface.

"Go ahead," I said, "take off your shoes." I sat on a rock on the bank and slipped off my boots.

"You're serious?" she said doubtfully, with a mixture of alarm in her voice.

"Here," I said. "Reach over and touch the water."

She crouched, and gingerly touched the water with the tip of a finger, then cupped her hand and ran it through the water. "It's warm," she said.

"There's a natural thermal hot springs here within the circle of rocks," I said. "If you look close you can see the bubbles coming up from the bottom." My boots and socks were off. To prevent a slip on the wet rocks I used the top of a rock – cold as frozen metal – to steady myself as I waded a few strides through ankle deep water into the river. I sat on a flat stone, leaned slightly forward, and let the water run past my legs and through my fingers.

"Now I can smell the sulfur," Mary said. She sat and began to unlace her shoes.

"There are hot springs all over this area," I told her. The water covering my stark white feet was bathtub warm. "Bozeman's got hot springs, Fairmont's got hot springs, Chico, Norris, over by Pipestone and there are some I think somewhere around Pony."

Mary waded in and sat directly across from me. "Oh," she said, "this is delicious."

"People say hot springs like these have restorative powers of health," I said.

"Ummmmmm," she said, cupping water in her hands and wrists. "I believe it." She stopped. "Have these hot springs always been here?"

"Sure," I said. It probably sounded like a guess.

"Just think," she said, and I could hear the awe in her voice, "years ago – thousands of years ago – prehistoric people probably sat right here on rocks warming themselves on cold November nights."

"They probably did," I admitted. "Then they spent the night in the cave up there drawing pictures on the walls."

"And maybe Lewis & Clark too," she said hurriedly. "They floated right through here, I think, on their way west."

"Yeah," I said. "They camped here in the Jefferson Valley. Maybe close to where we're sitting."

"Amazing," she said. "Think of it. Think of the history of this exact spot. Think if you could have had a camera here every day since the warm water bubbled up. Think of what you could see."

Right then, though, what I saw was a pair of headlights bouncing slowly down the gravel Point of Rocks Road, downshifting when the headlights found the Escort and then a squeak of brakes when the truck stopped. It was a white Ford F-150 with running lights atop the cab, and my guess was it was John Kountz's rig. A door opened. Mary stopped talking, and in the scant light I saw apprehension on her face. I should have tried to hide or camouflage the Escort or something. I had never expected company at the springs.

"Lance?" John's voice called out. "That you down there?"

"Yeah," I said.

"Everything okay?" John asked, and I heard him working his way carefully through the strip of brush between the road and the hot springs.

"Fine, John," I said. "Everything's fine."

"You ain't run over one of my cows, have you?" he asked.

"The cow jokes are getting kind of old, John."

He slipped once on a skiff of snow and we saw his white cowboy hat before we could make out his body or facial features.

"Who you got with you there, Lance?" John asked. "Is that Annie?"

"Ah, no, John," I answered. I had to tell him. "It's Mary Kristofferson."

"The new teacher?" John asked.

"Yes," Mary said, a little bashfully. "Good evening to you, Mr. Kountz."

"Good evening to you, too," he said. He seemed to ponder something for a moment. "Hang on a second, I'll be right back." And he turned and headed back up the short slope, through the strip of brush, back to his truck.

"Where's he going?" Mary whispered.

I had an idea, but wasn't sure. "We'll soon find out."

We heard two truck doors close, heard John's trip through the brush, and he returned a few minutes later. "Here," he said, "this'll hit the spot." And he leaned toward me and with an arm outstretched, handed me a half-full bottle of Jim Beam whiskey.

"I had a hunch that was coming," I said. "Take off your boots and join us, if you want."

"No," he said, "I better not." But he was already starting to remove a cowboy boot.

I took off the bottle cap and took a tiny swig. It burned a path to the very bottom of my belly. "Maybe you could educate Ms. Kristofferson here about some of the legend and history associated with Point of Rocks," I said.

John's favorite topic was Jefferson Valley history. He hopped on one foot and slid off the other boot, then nearly fell over when he hopped on his bare foot and took off the other boot. "Pretty nifty, John," I said.

"I'm a nifty guy," he said, and stepped carefully through the water and, being a country gentleman, sat next to me on the opposite side of Mary.

"Thanks for getting the picture of Cord's wedding in the paper a few weeks ago," he said. "That sure was a nice picture."

"You bet," I said.

"We bought about twenty extra copies that week," John said. He knew how much I liked to sell papers.

"That a boy," I told him.

"Where'd that bottle go?" he asked, and I handed him the Jim Beam.

In the shadows you could see his throat glug twice and two bubbles of whiskey make their way up the upside down bottle. He sort of gasped, a short inhale of breath through his teeth, then passed the bottle back to me. I could see a soft glisten in John's eyes and his general features, but it was too dark to see clearly or make out details.

"What is it she wants to know?" he asked.

"Well, you know Mary's the new elementary school physical education teacher," I began. "This is her first year in Whitehall and her first trip to Point of Rocks and the hot springs. I told her about the power company truck and the Carnegie's or whoever it was who took all the fossils and paintings and whatever back east."

"You told her all that?" John asked. "How long you been sittin' here?"

"Not that long," I said. "I gave her pretty much the Reader's Digest version."

"You tell her about the saber tooth tiger?" John asked.

"Yeah," Mary said. "Amazing."

"You didn't leave me much to tell," John said, a little disappointed. "You tell her about the smoke signals and arrowheads?"

"No," Mary said. "Smoke signals?"

"Oh yeah," John said. "Here." I thought he intended to show us something or say something about smoke signals and arrowheads, but when I looked I saw he had his hand out for the Jim Beam. I handed him the bottle. He took another sip. "This place right here – the Point of Rocks – has been heavily used since the first people got to this valley." He handed Mary the bottle. "Isn't this water great?" he asked, and laughed. "Look at how white our feet are. We have ghost feet," he said, and laughed again.

Our feet did look a pale and pallid white against the dark bottom of the river. I rustled up the muck at my feet and saw little dark flecks float at my toes.

"It was the most identifiable location in the valley, sort of a rendezvous spot," John said.

"For all the hunting and gathering," I said. "That's exactly what I told her."

"I'm trying to give the lady a little history lesson here," John said.

John was serious about his water rights, his family, his religion, his ranch, his cows and his history.

"Anyway," he continued, "there was a lot of traffic through here, right between the rocks up there and the river. Now, the riverbank wasn't always exactly there, but it flowed somewhere close, and this is where they all gathered. We've found arrowheads – points, they're called – on our place way up there on the bench. Sharpened flint or hard black obsidian for arrowheads and spearheads and weapons." The pace of his cadence picked up as he spoke. "And there's a spot up on Point of Rocks where you can see the entire valley, north and south and all the way across west, up toward Pipestone. And there's some dark rocks – burnt, you know, from fire – where they sent smoke signals. And then up by Pipestone, sort of at the base of Homestake Pass, just over on the north side of I-90, there's a round rock outcrop and years ago when the freeway was going in they found the same burned kind of rocks. So there had to be some Indians or whatever early man was called when he got here right up there on Point of Rocks, and some other Indians all the way across the valley by that other rock outcrop, and they'd send smoke signals back and forth to communicate where the bison were and stuff like that."

"Incredible," Mary said, which made John beam, even in the darkness.

"It is, isn't it?" John said, grinning. "When the first white people or first Europeans or whatever you want to call them got here to settle the valley they found paintings in the caves, arrowheads all over the place and fossils of animals that don't exist here anymore. I got a bunch of arrowheads displayed in cases up at the house, and so do lots of other ranchers. This summer out by our corral I found a huge chunk of obsidian, big as your fist. You can't find obsidian here in the Jefferson Valley naturally. It was brought here – that chunk I'd found had been brought here maybe a few thousand years ago – probably from those obsidian cliffs at Yellowstone Park."

"I've seen those cliffs," Mary said.

"Yeah," John said. "Every year the earth gives up more and more arrowheads and rocks and artifacts. You can still see teepee rings down the road here toward Waterloo."

"You can?" Mary asked.

"Well not right now, because of the snow, but in the spring and summer, when there's grass, yeah, you can see them."

I could see another set of headlights coming our direction, bouncing down the road.

"Who do you suppose that is?" asked John. The headlights slowed, and stopped, disappearing behind John's pickup. "Some party crasher."

"This place isn't all that secret, is it?" Mary asked.

John chuckled. "Well, it has been around awhile."

A car door opened. "Lance, that you down there?" It was, unmistakably, Slack. Two more car doors squawked open; Walt and Sue, Slack's parents, undoubtedly.

"John? Everybody okay down there?" Walt called out.

"We're fine," John answered.

"Whose *we*?" asked Sue.

"Come on down, if you want," John said.

"It's you and Lance?" called out Sue, puzzled.

"And Lance's friend, Mary Kristofferson," John called out. "The teacher."

Someone bumbled their way through the brush, and just as we saw Slack's cowboy hat through the brush we saw it vanish. He'd slipped on some snow or ice and fell back first along the slope.

"You okay?" John asked.

"I fell," Slack announced.

Above him, just above the brush, barely lit by the diffuse and muted headlights, Walt and Sue stood in front of John's truck. Sue had bowling league on Wednesday night, and they were on their way home. They'd probably suspected an accident – a car slipping off the road into the river – with John there to help and me there to take pictures.

"Slack, are you okay?" Sue asked.

"My butt's kind of wet, from the snow," he answered.

"He looks fine," John said. "You want to come in and warm up your toes, Slack?"

"Yeah," Slack said. We could hardly see him but he had already sat down and begun grunting as he tugged at his boots.

"No, Slack, you come up here," Sue called out.

"Oh, he's fine," John assured her. "We won't be long. You two go ahead and head home, if you want, and I'll bring Slack home in a bit."

"You sure?" asked Walt. "No one's hit a cow or anything?"

"Not yet," I called out, "but the night's young."

No one laughed.

"We're all safe," John called out. "We're talking prehistoric history down here and soaking our toes. I just told them about the chunk of obsidian I found outside the corral this spring."

"Big as his fist," Walt told us. "I've seen it."

"See," John told us. "Told you."

In front of the headlights I could see the outlines of Walt's and Sue's bodies turn toward each other to confer about what I was certain was the relative safety of leaving their son behind with the trio in the hot springs. Had I made the offer of taking Slack home, Slack would be riding home with his mom and dad. John had significantly more stature than I did.

"You'll drop Slack off at our place?" Sue asked.

"Sure," John called up to them. "You two go home and relax, nothing's going to happen. I promise."

"Slack?" Walt called out.

"Yeah, goodbye," Slack said abruptly, as in, *go home and leave me alone*. Slack was in the brush and just outside the headlights, and even though we couldn't see him we clearly understood his message.

So, apparently, did Walt and Sue. Without a further word, they climbed back in their truck and headed home, their taillights disappearing and the soft rumble of their diesel truck slowly fading into silence.

Moments later Slack emerged from the brush, wearing only his white boxer underpants. His skin glowed pale like white marble, like a spirit in the darkness.

"Slack," John asked, "where's your clothes?"

He stopped, and for the first time, obviously, looked to see what we were wearing, which was everything except our shoes and socks. Slack squealed, held both hands at his crotch, and John laughed so hard the water splashed at his feet. Slack tiptoed back behind the brush, and John told him it was fine, to come out and warm his feet in the water. Slack would have none of that. Behind the junipers there was mumbling and rustling and a few minutes later he stepped barefoot into view wearing his pants and shirt and even his jacket and hat.

"I figured you was skinny dipping," he said, as he carefully stepped through the rocks and into the hot springs.

"They were," John said, "until I showed up."

"Don't believe him," said Mary. "We've been sitting here, bathing our feet, chatting."

Slack settled down on a rock between John and me. John had put the bottle away.

"Look how pasty white our feet are," I said.

Slack peered into the water at his toes, then Mary's, then mine, and mine were invisible, buried in a thin layer of dirt I had absently and carelessly spread over them.

"Lance," said Slack, "your feet are gone!"

"The hell?" asked John. "Where'd they go?"

I uncovered my feet, and lifted them above the disturbed water.

Then it was strange; for a full comfortable five minutes, no one spoke. We merely sat in silence, surrounded by the night, the cold, the stars. It was winter, but we were settled low, mostly protected from the wind, and the water was pleasantly warm. I thought about Slack, his ability to comprehend bits and pieces of the world around him, but seldom completely and never consistently. It came to him in doses, parceled out unpredictably and frustratingly, and failed to provide a full picture of his own life.

Finally, John said, "Nice night, huh Slack."

"You bet," Slack answered, his hat tilted back high on his head.

"Do you come here much, Slack, here at the hot springs?" asked Mary.

"No," he said, with what sounded like a hint of regret.

"Every now and then you'll see some kids here, drinking and carrying on," John said. "Some Butte riffraff'll show up from time to time. Loud and drunk."

I'd noticed what appeared to be a used condom when I'd taken off my shoes. If we looked close, we'd have found empty beer cans and liquor bottles.

“When I was a kid I’d come down here at night sometimes and think about the old days, about people first finding these springs,” John said. “I’d wonder what they did, how they lived, what they looked like.”

“Then think about the challenges, the depravations, the early European settlers faced,” Mary said.

“Winter, isolation, cholera, drought, poverty,” John said. “A cough could kill you or your child or your spouse. No doctors. People watched out for each other back then. They had to. There wasn’t any government or welfare. People were on their own. They lived and worked and died. For a dream and a few acres. It was always a dream that brought people out west.”

“Still is,” Slack said, with remarkable clarity.

There really wasn’t much to say after that. It was growing late, and an elementary school teacher spending time in the Jefferson hot springs with three men was the kind of thing that caused talk around town. Mary emitted an audible yawn, and I knew it was time to get back to town.

“We better get you home, Slack,” John said. “Hell, look at that. My toes are starting to wrinkle.”

“There’s a sight you don’t want to miss,” I said.

“I have a question I always wanted to ask you,” John said. I looked up and saw the question was directed at Mary.

“What would that be?” she asked.

John sat off to the side, nonchalantly slipping on his boots. “What happens to the nude pictures Lance takes of all you schoolteachers?”

Mary gasped. Even in the shadowy darkness I could see her blush.

John almost fell over he was laughing so hard.

Chapter 39

Even after my Thursday morning shower my feet smelled like fish. I went home to a chilly empty house for lunch and a quick nap, and when I rustled awake for the second time in five hours I woke up again to the faint scent of fish. I thought about changing socks, but the smell didn't bother me enough to actually do something about it.

Laura Joyce was close to caught up with everything that had come in – the state championship game ads, a report from a group interested in creating a museum in Whitehall, the Jefferson-Madison 4-H fashion revue article and an article from Tene Brooke about her trip to Seattle to visit her granddaughter – and while I had work to do, it made little difference if I did it or not. Next week's major article – the state Class B championship football game – would, regardless of the outcome, serve as the focal front page story and with proper historical reporting through pictures and words the Ledger would chronicle every exacting detail of the game. But it was just Thursday and the game wouldn't occur until Saturday, so the bulk of my weekly work was severely back-loaded – again – until Sunday, Monday and Tuesday, three days in which I would easily work fifty hours. So on Thursday, I made sure Laura Joyce could work until closing, then escaped the office and drove over to the school to watch the end of the Rangers' football practice.

The team was working on kickoff returns when I showed up, kids in purple vests sprinting down the field to bang into kids in white jerseys. Jersey stood in the middle of the field, a tall black figure, his posture suggesting weary disappointment. The sun was low in the southwestern sky, but for November, the weather was acceptable. Coach Pete wore shorts and a tee-shirt, and the shirt was stained dark gray under the armpits and down a slender patch on his back.

"Start up the middle, then veer right, straight up the hash mark," Jersey told Tony, who had apparently drifted too far toward the sideline. "On film they stay wide to keep everything inside and try to force the ball carrier to the middle, and then they stack the middle. There's a gap there, right at the hash, between the outside and the middle, okay, between the outside and middle, where we might be able to pop one. But you have to start up the middle first, then snap it quick to the right… but not too far to the right."

Tony nodded, and flipped the ball back to Colt, who jogged back to the tee to kick off again.

"When you take it out wide like that you're running right into their strength," Jersey said. "Do it again. Middle first. Look for an opening – any kind of opening – there on the right and break straight up the hash marks."

It looked like chaos to me. The ball drifted far to the left, close to the sidelines, and Tony caught it, ran straight ahead, then ran smack into the back of a blocker – Cody Phillips – and then both fell down.

"Get your head out of your ass!" Coach Pete yelled. It was unclear who the comment was directed at. It was clear, however, that Jersey's expression suggested the comment should not be repeated.

"Let's try it again," Jersey told Tony. "Kick it in the middle of the field," Jersey told Colt. "They kick to the middle every time."

It still looked like chaos. I watched another half dozen kickoffs and if there was a plan or purpose to any of it I couldn't detect what it might have been. It looked to me like twenty-two kids running aimlessly around on a football field.

"Extra points," Jersey finally said, despondence in his voice.

"He's nothing if not persistent," Coach Pete said, meaning Jersey. I had walked down the sideline and he'd walked from the end zone toward me. The shirt was baggy and battered, and exposed a ball of gray fur at his throat. He was barely tall enough to not be short, but he was a barrel of a man through his chest.

"Remember when these same kids showed up back in August for two-a-days?" I said. "If you would have given me three wins during the year right then, I would have taken it."

Coach Pete cleared his throat and spat a wad of phlegm to the brittle yellow grass. "I'd have taken two," he grumbled so only I heard. "The team was a piss-poor joke to begin with. No core, you know." He grimaced. "No leadership. No purpose. No nothing."

"What changed?" I asked. "How'd *that* team turn into *this* team and get to the state title game?"

Coach Pete looked at Jersey. "That guy, right there. Don't ask me how, because I don't know. Actually," he said, "I do know. I'm not sure I can explain it. Hell, I *know* I can't explain it. He believed in them the whole time, right from the start, before they even believed in themselves."

"It can't be that easy," I said. On the field, Colt kicked an extra point through the heart of the goal posts.

"I didn't say it was easy," Coach Pete stated firmly. "Shit, I just said I couldn't explain it. But I do know that night when we got back here from Shelby, and he hauled their asses off the bus to this end zone right here and had them do up-downs in their own puke, I know that night and those up-downs have something to do with it. Something that night sunk in with these kids."

"Something besides the puke," I said.

"Something right here." I watched Colt kick another extra point, and I expected to turn and see Coach Pete pointing to his temple, as if the kids figured out something that night. But Coach Pete was pointing to his chest, his heart. "He's a smart guy, a good coach, and a good man. I admire him and I learned a lot from him."

"You even cleaned up your act a little," I pointed out.

"Had to, a little," he admitted. "He's got heart, and now these kids got heart. So we got a shot to be state champs, and it's all because of that guy, the skinny guy there in black with the whistle. I gotta call it like I see it, Lance. It's a fucking miracle. A total fucking miracle."

"I see you haven't fully cleaned up your act," I told him.

"Sometimes colorful language is needed to underscore a point," he said.

"Can we beat Roundup?" I asked.

"Hell no," he said, then chuckled. He shook his head; the answer to my question was, definitely, no. "Not a chance." He cleared his throat and spat again. "But we never had a chance against Baker, Fort Benton or Fairfield, either."

"But we won all three of them," I said.

Coach Pete shook his head. "Hell, I was there and I still don't believe it." He gestured toward the players. "I know they'll give it their best shot on Saturday, but I don't know. They got a wide receiver who's so fast he's just a blur on film. Kid's a track star or something like that. And they got fifteen seniors. It doesn't look like we can move the ball much against the Roundup defense. They're just too solid. That probably means no long drives. So we gotta shorten the field with kickoff returns. Jersey's worked on that the past hour and he's gonna work on it for an hour again tomorrow."

"Is that realistic?" I asked. "It seems desperate. Shortening the field with kickoff returns?"

"Is it realistic we're even having this conversation?" asked Coach Pete. "You and me, standing on the sidelines in Whitehall, talking about the Rangers playing in the state title game?" He shook his head. "I figure we dumped reality back in a ditch somewhere about the time we beat Manhattan. We're living a dream right now." He pointed at Jersey. "What's his buddy, Springsteen, say? Something about a runaway American dream? That's what we're living right now, right here in Whitehall, Montana. A bona fide goddamn real life runaway American dream."

The Thursday evening community potluck barbecue ran out of food about eight o'clock, and people were still seated on the hard cafeteria table benches an hour later. The meal offered chili, cornbread and chocolate chip cookies. First the portions shrunk, then the cornbread ran out, then the chili, then the number of cookies dropped from two to one, and then you noticed the cooks and servers suddenly were cleaning up. They had enough food, I was told, for five hundred people, and cut portions so they served over seven hundred people, said Hannah Bolling, Nate's mom, who more or less supervised this final community football potluck.

It was possibly the biggest crowd ever served in Whitehall, I figured, and reported that in the Ledger. And despite the lack of food, no one appeared in a hurry to leave. Most of the folks were wearing purple. Kids played out of the way, in the back of the room. A few of them tossed a soft spongy football around. If you were a Whitehall football player, your grandparents, parents, siblings, aunts and uncles and cousins, neighbors, friends, teachers and classmates were there to support you and your team. There was a sense of community, of being united, of sharing something important we all could take pride in. It was spoken – the pride and something important – but it was also unspoken or understated. It was communicated not so much in words as it was in deed and thought and attitude.

I left Annie and the school a little after eight o'clock. She and a group of her purple-attired classmates were all talking at the same time about the game and the pep assembly and the pep bus to Roundup and she barely acknowledged my departure.

The cold night air held a hint of winter in it. The parking lot was still mostly full of cars – pickups, mostly, to be accurate – and after I turned left onto Whitehall Street the first car I saw parked on the opposite shoulder of the road was the town police car, with Manfred behind the wheel. I saw the flashing police lights behind me almost the instant I turned onto First Street, and when I stopped, maybe twenty yards after I'd first seen the lights, the police car was flush behind me, practically touching the Escort's back bumper.

It was hard to see with the lights behind me, flashing in my side view and rear view mirrors, but I saw a shadow between me and the lights and then – it was sudden and confusing – the driver's side door of the Escort flew open, a fist was clenching my shirt at the chest and I was getting hauled out of the car. I still had my seatbelt on so at first I couldn't be moved.

"Get your ass-," grunted Manfred.

And then somehow I was pulled out of the seatbelt, out of the seat, out of the car and tossed down to the pavement. Manfred stood above me, a flashlight the size of a club raised high in his right hand. I knew what would happen next. Seated on the street, I raised my hands to defend against the blow. I held them there, but no one hit me. I looked up and saw Manfred, right in front and above me, looking to his right, down the street. Headlights approached. And from the other way, from down the street, headlights were also approaching; two cars, from opposite directions, converging toward the police car. The two vehicles met and stopped abruptly not ten feet from where I sat on the pavement. Their headlights lit up everything around me. Manfred stood stiffly above me, the flashlight still above me and above him. I could see the look in his face, his eyes, shift from hatred and violence to recognition or resignation or maybe even submission.

"Manfred, you drop that flashlight," ordered a voice. I couldn't see anything or anyone out beyond the headlights, but I recognized the voice. It was Luke Grayling, the mayor of Whitehall.

"Now! Drop it!" said another voice, from the other direction. I held my hand above my eyes, to shield them from the headlights. It was another cop. The car was a Montana Highway Patrol vehicle.

"He was resisting arrest," Manfred shouted.

“Manfred, it’s Lance,” pleaded Luke, as if Lance couldn’t possibly resist arrest.

“He’s drunk,” Manfred said. “Drunk driving.”

Later, I thought that was decently quick thinking on Manfred’s part. Lance may not resist arrest, but it was not farfetched that Lance could drink and drive. But Manfred either didn’t know where I’d been the past five hours – at football practice then a community barbecue – or was panicked enough to venture desperate wild guesses.

“He was just eating chili and cookies at the school for Christ sakes,” said Luke. He bent down to help me up. “He hit you?” he asked. I could see him looking me over. “I don’t see any blood.”

“I’m fine,” I said. I gathered my wits. “I think you might have got here just in time.”

“Looks that way,” Luke said.

Two troopers walked Manfred away from Luke and me, to the other side of their police car, and I could barely see their shapes over in the darkness. I wanted to keep my eye on Manfred. He still had a gun, and the malevolent expression of rage he’d flashed seemed capable of anything. But then I saw one of the troopers take a belt loaded with gear and set it on the floor of the passenger’s side front seat floor of the highway patrol car. And then I saw them walk Manfred more or less across the street. Manfred ducked and slipped into the backseat of his own patrol car.

Luke introduced himself to the trooper, and they shook hands. The trooper’s name was Lowery, he said, and he wanted statements from both of us. He told us the county sheriff, the county attorney, and highway patrol captain would soon be notified.

Something wasn’t right. “Wait a minute,” I said. “You two just met?”

“That’s right, sir,” said Officer Lowery.

“You arrived here together by accident?” I asked, incredulous. “The same place at the same time?”

“We got a call about a disturbance just off Whitehall Street,” said Officer Lowery.

I looked at Luke. He said he was heading home after the barbeque.

“You live the other direction,” I told him. I indicated Rocky Mountain Drive. “That way.”

“Yeah, I know where I live,” Luke said. “I was just swinging by here to see if our crew patched that pothole on Stanley Street. Then I saw the flashing lights and your Escort.”

A few cars crept past, and people gawked at the scene; two police cars with flashing lights, two cars headed the same direction and both with their driver’s door open, and Manfred alone in the back of the Whitehall town police car.

“Okay, we’re going to need statements from you two, independently,” Officer Lowery said. Luke nodded.

"Who called you?" I asked Officer Lowery. "Manfred stopped me fifteen seconds before you showed up. How could you possibly respond that fast?"

Officer Lowery looked at Luke. "Tell you what, Mr. Mayor, we'll take his statement first. Is that okay with you, sir?"

Luke agreed.

Two more Montana Highway Patrol cars showed up. One of the troopers kept what had become a slow flow of traffic moving, and two others parked themselves in the front seat of Manfred's patrol car. Manfred's head was down, as if reading something in his lap.

Officer Lowery sat in the driver's side of his MHP car, and I sat in the passenger seat. A bright dome light lit the interior of the car.

"Who reported the disturbance?" I asked him.

"Sorry, sir, but the purpose of this conversation is to get your statement." Officer Lowery produced a clipboard and a stack of forms.

"How do you know I'm not actually guilty of something?" I asked. "How do you know I didn't cause the disturbance?"

"Sir, I want you to know you are not under arrest," the officer told me. "There will be a full investigation into this incident, and you may want to contact an attorney."

I nodded. I figured I'd just talk to Annie.

Across the street, in the back of his own police car, Manfred looked up at me for just an instant, an expression of defeat or failure in his gaze, then lowered his head again. His belt, with the gun holster, handcuffs, radio and wad of keys, and a black bulky metal flashlight, formed a circular pile on the floor at my feet.

Baker. Fort Benton. Fairfield. Now Roundup. For four straight Fridays there had been WHS pep assemblies to commemorate and salute the Rangers before a playoff game they were expected to lose. After four straight Fridays the routine was getting predictable and perhaps even slightly manufactured, as if the kids had poured out as much emotion and support as they could, each time thinking – rightfully so – this was likely the final Friday assembly before the final game of the year for an astonishing bunch of overachieving classmates who had exceeded all expectations. The finality of this assembly was unassailable; this was the final Friday assembly before the final high school football Saturday of the year.

The gym was filled with an energetic and boisterous student body, purple and gold banners and pompoms, bouncing cheerleaders with big smiles, a raucous pep band clad in Ranger purple, and a stoic collection of Ranger football players again looking slightly uncomfortable as the center of attention under circumstances in which they were called upon to do nothing. We'd been through all this – almost exactly this – every Friday for a month and rolling through it again with an absolute certainty it was the final time lent a certain loss of wonderment or bereavement because of the certainty there was no background thrill or anticipation about earning the opportunity to play again. Win or lose on Saturday, there would be no playing again. The final chapter would end the drama in slightly more than twenty-four hours and there was a sadness, somehow, in that finality.

There had also been the drama of the previous night. Everyone knew, or thought they knew, about the altercation between Manfred and me, and I could see curious glances cast my direction from students and faculty members.

Jersey, wearing a silky black shirt with a high collar and a black leather vest, took the microphone from Ed, just as the microphone had been passed the previous three Fridays. The crowd hushed like it had the previous three weeks, and Jersey approached the bleachers just like he had each week.

But this week, this final Friday, Jersey not only approached the bleachers, he found a narrow opening among the elementary students in the front row and sat down, his knees together, his back straight, as he faced out toward the basketball floor, where the Ranger team had gathered. Jersey towered above the small children that surrounded him, some of them nervously shifting in their seats, giggling, even blushing, shy about their closeness to what they viewed as a foreign authority or some kind of mysterious power.

"What a journey," Jersey told them quietly. Those first three words announced emphatically that this was not going to be some standard ebullient, enthusiastic pep talk.

Jersey was not talking to the audience behind him. He was talking to his team in front of him.

"It started back in August, during those torturous and hot two-a-day conditioning practices, through a series of four standard but disappointing losses," Jersey said. Not another person made a noise. "Then you found your voice, found your strength, and after a disappointing loss – your fifth of the year – you've rallied for six straight wins and put yourselves in the state title game."

One isolated voice let loose a shrill *Whoooo!* that seemed shockingly out of place.

"I marvel at your accomplishments, at your collective sacrifice and your individual achievements, at your dedication to excellence and more importantly, your dedication to each other. You are not a team of individuals. You are an individual team. You have shared your success, honored your shared success, and shared that success honorably. You're going to beat Roundup tomorrow. You know it. You can feel it, sense it. No one can beat the Rangers, and no one will."

There was a smattering of applause.

For a team that stood solid as marble before games straight along the sideline during the national anthem, the Rangers scattered more or less haphazardly across the gym floor twitched shoulders, clenched and unclenched fists and shifted eyes toward each other, to Jersey and into the crowd. This was not the pep assembly or speech they had expected.

"So you'll be state champions, and that is something no one will ever, ever, be able to take away from you," Jersey said. He was the one rigid, straight, seated, but unmoving and unyielding. "But what I want to talk about with you right now is what you will forever take with you from this season, from your championship, from your success and from your sacrifice. This magical season has taught us about ourselves, about life, about faith, about commitment, about determination. And this entire season will provide you a reservoir of examples and ideals for you to draw upon throughout your life. That's the value of this season, that's what will be important as you move on in life."

There was a pause of nearly a minute. During the silence Jersey looked directly into the eyes of each of the thirty or so football players in front of him.

"You'll have to confront hardship as you mature and grow," Jersey said. "You'll be faced with personal and professional adversity. You'll be treated unfairly. You'll suffer setbacks. You'll fail, at times, and at times, be miserable. You'll experience tragedy. Life is that way, and you can neither avoid that nor conquer that. But you'll know when the game ends tomorrow, and know with certainty, that whatever happens in your life, you can summon the strength and character inside you to overcome that adversity and those hardships and that tragedy. You'll know that inside you rests the fortitude, the conviction, the devotion to overcome those challenges. You'll have faith in your abilities and your commitment because you have seen – you have lived – the results of what you can accomplish and what you can overcome. You are special kids individually, and you are even more special collectively, but it is your faith in your teammates and your sheer unified trust and belief in your abilities to succeed that will stand you in good stead your entire lives. Yes, for a fleeting moment, for a defined period, you are high school football champions. For that we all honor and congratulate you. But another team will be crowned champion a year from now. So when you leave that football field tomorrow as state champions, relish the moment. Enjoy the accomplishment. Bask, momentarily, in the glory of your efforts. And remember that feeling forever. Forever. Never forget that moment. But more than that," he paused, "remember what made that moment possible. What you went through – each and every one of you – to *earn* that championship. And apply that to the remainder of your life and to your family, and proceed firm in the faith that you – all of you – have demonstrated the living proof of power and spirit within you to overcome whatever hardships you face."

Jersey stood up. You could hear his footsteps as he crossed the floor to the center, where his team stood. He turned around, surrounded by Rangers, to face an absolutely silent and motionless audience.

"I'm pretty proud of these kids," Jersey told us. "I'm proud of what they've done, how they've done it, how they've conducted themselves, and how they've responded to adversity. Tomorrow, these kids will be champions. But more important, they'll be champions their entire lives. And all of you in this room helped make that possible. Parents and teachers, siblings and community members, local businesses and school classmates. Thank you to each and every one of you for your contribution to this remarkable season."

And that was how the final pep assembly ended. There was some applause, but not much; there was some halfhearted cheering and a pedestrian performance of the school song, and then as if they'd been told, as if on cue, the collected student body of the Whitehall school system quietly stood and in orderly fashion filed from the bleachers into the hallway and off to class.

After a Wednesday night at the Jefferson River hot springs and a Thursday night in a patrol car, my goal was to spend a dull Friday night out of sight and at home. We'd need an early start to Roundup on Saturday. Plus, after the drama of Thursday night, all day Friday I felt uncomfortable in public, the recipient of seemingly constant secretive or averted eyes or blatant gazes of – it was hard to tell – curiosity, mourning maybe, or regret, and possibly even some expressions of admiration.

Occasionally, though, you could read the thoughts behind the mix of expressions as clearly as if they'd been spoken. An old grizzled rancher named Boyd Carver stared me down at the Post Office, visually declaring me guilty of something, certain Manfred wouldn't have pulled me over if I hadn't committed a crime. Alice Franklin, Ed's wife, passed me along the sidewalk in front of the drug store and said hello while offering me a meek glance of sympathy. At the school assembly kids like Bonner and Caddy had beamed my direction. Jersey's sturdy observation essentially studied me, to determine my mental and emotional condition, and must have found it acceptable.

Mary's expression was less certain, more concerned and more obvious. We spoke briefly after the assembly, and she had reported a wild array of rumors. Manfred had threatened to shoot me. I had punched Manfred. The MHP troopers had to forcibly restrain Manfred and draw their weapons. Tony was somehow involved, as were drugs. Manfred had been hauled to the county jail in Boulder and was still behind bars. The county attorney was requiring Manfred to undergo psychiatric observation. Luke had punched Manfred. Luke was actually an undercover officer. I deliberately created the incident to sell newspapers. There was a full mixture of stories and fables tainted by agendas and histories, but some were also tinged with just a glimmer of truth.

I was uncertain how to address it all in the newspaper. How could I write an article when the subject of the article was me, and could I explain in print Manfred's puzzling and disturbing behavior? Friday night, alone at home, I had an opportunity to reflect on the incident and still couldn't make sense of it. I turned on the TV, then turned it off, and instead turned the stereo on softly, Springsteen's *The River,* and opened a can of Rainier. Manfred had never been friendly, but he hadn't turned outright hostile until after the run-in at the school with Cody and Coach Pete. I heard a slight noise, a timid knock at the door, and I would have ignored it had it not been obvious someone was home and just as obvious that that someone was ignoring the knock. I opened the door and saw Rhonda, purple tie-dyed Ranger scarf tight on her head, and without a word she extended a pan of brownies toward my midsection. Had I not taken immediate hold of the tray, it would have fallen to the steps. I could see her sneak a peek behind me, searching for someone, most likely Tony. I could see her sizing me up as well, looking for an injury perhaps, a bandage, a bruise, a cut, maybe even an indication if I was criminal or not.

"Come on in," I said. "What you got here?"

"Foot," she told me. She made no attempt to enter.

"Come on in," I said again, and backed up a step.

She looked on either side of me, and since no one else was home, she saw no one.

"He's not home," I told her. "He and some of the football players are watching TV or football films or something. He won't be home until ten."

She stood there, motionless, looking up at me, her thin, wrinkled, pointed jaw protruding outward. She blinked once, but didn't move or speak. We stood that way, me with the door open, her looking up at me and expecting me to say something.

Finally I understood. "Do you want a ride to the game tomorrow?"

"Ya, to Roundout," she said immediately. "Vat time you leaf?"

"We'll pick you up about eight," I said.

"No," she said, as I knew she would. "I be here."

"Thanks for the brownies," I told her back. She was already down the steps and halfway down the sidewalk. She flicked her right hand in acknowledgement without slowing down or turning around.

The pan was still warm, and once inside with the door closed the sweet smell of melted chocolate filled the house. I cut the pan of brownies into four large squares, cut the four squares

in half, and took two of them on a plate back to the couch. Perfect; the brownies were perfect. I had the second one mostly gone when there was another knock at the door.

I swung open the door and there stood Old Tom, rail thin, bundled up in what looked like four layers of rags, topped with his foolish ancient leather football helmet. He moved his arms abruptly, as if stunned that someone opened the door. Young Tom's beat-up little Toyota pickup sat in my driveway, with Young Tom in it, behind the wheel.

"What's that on your face," Old Tom said, in statement form. "Is that from Manfred?"

I wiped the back of my hand across my mouth and it came away with a slight smear of melted chocolate. "It's melted chocolate," I said. "I was eating a brownie."

"Yeah, I can smell them." He sniffed. "You eat them all?"

Old Tom was not coy or shy. "You want a brownie?" I asked. I looked out toward the pickup and Young Tom offered a timid wave.

Old Tom walked right in the house. "You bet." He walked straight into the kitchen toward the counter and looked down into the brownie pan. "Jesus H. Christ, I can't eat a piece that big."

I took the knife out of the sink and had to sort of elbow Old Tom out of the way to get to the brownies. He moved about a half-inch to the side.

"They smell like heaven," he said. "He's crazy you know."

I wasn't sure I'd heard him right. I looked at him, at the ratty flannel shirt over the ratty sweatshirt, the ridiculous helmet. He smelled like an ashtray. "Who is?"

"Manfred," he said, peering down into the pan of brownies. I paused to take in Old Tom's assertion, the knife held still, poised to cut the brownie. He jabbed an impatient finger toward the knife, and I cut one of the brownie squares in half. "Got a helluva mean streak in him, too."

I turned to open a cupboard door and reached for a plate, and when I turned back Old Tom already had scooped a brownie from the pan by hand. A bite already out of it and his mouth was full.

"Taste like heaven too," he mumbled, his mouth full, his eyes closed. "Who made these? Not you?"

I shook my head. "No, not me. Rhonda Horst."

"The lady from the old railroad home?" Old Tom said. "She's foreign or something."

"Or something," I agreed. "What makes you think Manfred's crazy?"

"What?" he said. He'd taken another bite; his mouth was so full it was more a sound than a word.

"What makes you think Manfred's crazy?" I repeated.

Old Tom gulped, and you could practically see the wad of brownie slide down his throat. "What makes you think he ain't?" he asked, his eyes bugged out, incredulous. "He's an asshole, too. Good riddance, I say."

"I knew he was an asshole," I said. "I didn't know about the crazy part."

"You do now, don't you?" Old Tom said. "Heard he beat the snot out of you with a flashlight." Old Tom furled his brow, leaned forward and inspected my face. "You must be a quick healer."

I shook my head. "He didn't hit me."

"What's he in jail for then?" Old Tom asked. "He must of hit someone. A cop doesn't end up in jail just for being an asshole. You got another one of these?" He displayed an empty hand, where a brownie had just disappeared. "All we ever get at home is store bought."

"These are better than store bought," I told him.

"You got that right," he asserted.

He waited for me to cut a brownie square in half and before I could hoist it off the tray with the fork he reached down with his fingers and grabbed it. "What time you leavin' for Roundup tomorrow?" he asked.

"Aren't you going on the pep bus?" I asked, hopefully.

He shook his head; the side straps of the leather helmet spun and rustled softly on his cheeks. "Too damn loud, all them kids. I'm thinking we better be on the road by seven, eight at the latest."

"We?" I asked dismally.

"I heard you got room for me," Old Tom stated. "The boy is on the team and the girl'll take the pep bus. I saw her at the chili feed last night and she said you had room for me."

"Annie said that?"

"Yeah, the brainy one," Old Tom said.

"What about Young Tom?" I asked.

"He's goin' elk huntin'." Old Tom took a bite of brownie. He said something else, but I couldn't understand him.

"Be here at quarter to eight," I told him.

"See you then," Old Tom beamed. "Bring the rest of those with you," he told me. He meant the brownies.

And he left, jaws working, chewing a brownie, out the door, down the steps, toward the pickup and Young Tom.

"People say you're lucky to be alive," Tony told me the instant he entered the house.

I put the magazine down on my lap. It was about nine-thirty.

"Where's your sister?" I asked him.

"I'm serious," he said. He wore his WHS Ranger letterman jacket and a shirt that was untucked and lower than the cut of the coat. His hair was too long, and sort of slopped over his ears and down low on his forehead. I noticed a wisp of peach fuzz on his chin.

"You need a haircut," I said. "And you need to get some sleep."

"Lance, did Manfred really pull a gun on you?" Tony was at the fridge; he opened up a milk carton, sniffed it, hesitated, sniffed it again, then poured himself a glass of milk. "Rhonda, you doll you," he said when he spotted the brownies.

I had given both Annie and Tony a condensed, toned down version of the incident Thursday night before we'd all gone to bed. I didn't want to trouble them so I might have underplayed the story a little too much; it was inevitable that what actually had happened would get blown out of proportion.

"Is that what you heard, that Manfred tried to shoot me?" I asked.

"Jesus, Lance, how many brownies did you eat?" Tony asked suddenly.

With a glass of milk in one hand and a chunk of brownie in the other he balanced himself momentarily then fell back rump first, perfectly centered into the recliner. It was the kind of simple graceful gesture only a young athlete could pull off.

"Do you really not know where Annie is?" Tony asked.

I attempted to recall if I knew or was supposed to know. I had a vague recollection about a sleepover somewhere.

"Natalie's," Tony said. "Remember? Half the middle school girls are over there. They had pizzas, went to the movie, and are all taking the pep bus to Roundup. I heard Annie tell you all that yesterday morning. Hey," he said, "I had brain trauma and I've got a better memory than you."

"Right," I said. I had listened to bits and pieces of it. Annie always offered far too many details to remember.

Tony was a striking kid, I noticed as he sat there, with his pale blue eyes, flawless complexion, square jaw and engaging hint of mischief in his eyes. He was a leader, not by design or choice but by unintended sheer presence, by his apparent distain for what anyone else thought about anything. He knew right from wrong, good from bad, excellent from good, success from near miss. He had an involuntary and implicit confidence in himself and he didn't need anyone to substantiate that confidence. I could see him giving an impassioned halftime speech, and I could see his teammates responding.

"What's it like having a cop point a gun at you?" he asked, amused.

"What part of that question could you possibly find humorous?" I asked. "If a cop, if anyone, waved a gun at me, what makes you think I would find that comical or enjoyable?"

"Well, Lance," he said, "I'm not saying you should find that amusing. I'm saying that *I* find it amusing, and I'm allowed to find it amusing because you survived intact. If you'd gotten shot, it'd be a different story. But look at you, you're fine. No bullet holes. No tragedy. Thus, it's amusing."

"*Thus*?" I asked. "What, you're suddenly from Harvard?"

He winced after a gulp of milk. "I wouldn't drink this milk tomorrow if I was you." His body had a brief shiver. "Okay," he said, "can we agree a tragedy was avoided last night?"

"For me it was," I agreed. "Maybe not for Manfred. I think he's in some trouble."

"He should be," Tony said, and bit into the brownie. "Does Rhonda make the best brownies in the world, or what?" he asked suddenly. "I'm serious. How could a brownie taste any better than this?"

I had to admit, they were pretty good. "Old Tom stopped by and said they tasted like heaven."

Tony contemplated the remark. "Old Tom? You guys buds now?"

"He told me he thought Manfred is crazy," I said.

"Manfred is crazy, but Old Tom wouldn't recognize crazy if it ran over him driving a Corvette," said Tony.

"Why does everyone keep saying Manfred's crazy?" I asked. Was I the only person in Whitehall unaware of Manfred's unhealthy mental status?

Tony leaned forward in the chair. "Come on, what happened last night? I've heard like ten versions of it."

"I already told you," I said.

He shook his head. "Not really. Tell me all of it. From the beginning."

"There's not that much to tell. I left the potluck dinner at the school, turned from Whitehall Street to First Street and behind me I saw flashing lights."

"Manfred?"

"Manfred," I said. "He pulled up right behind the Escort, I mean like right on the back bumper. He got out of the police car, opened my door, yanked me out, grabbed the flashlight like he was going to whack me, and then two cars came, from opposite directions. One was Luke Grayling the mayor and the other was two MHP troopers." I sort of shrugged. "That's it. The troopers asked me what happened, I told them, and then they hauled Manfred away. Ever since then just about everyone I've talked to has told me Manfred's crazy."

"He never tried to shoot you?" Tony asked.

I shook my head. "I never saw a gun."

Tony sighed. "The best versions of the story all have Manfred pulling his gun."

"Yeah, well, those are all wrong versions because there was no gun," I said. "Just a flashlight."

"Oh, I believe that," Tony said. "He liked banging heads with the flashlight." He hesitated. "You're a legend at the school now, for standing up to Manfred. My stock rose, because of you. So thanks, man."

"I wasn't standing up to Manfred, believe me," I said. "I wasn't standing at all, in fact. I was on the pavement, on my rump, and if those headlights hadn't come out of nowhere I was going to take a beating."

"Maybe you would have gotten a concussion," Tony said. "Lose your memory. Keep saying the same thing over and over. A family bond kind of thing."

"Most people don't view concussions in a family bond light," I said.

"Probably not," Tony said, "but I have to admit, it was scary this morning. Last night you made it seem like it had been no big deal, and then when I got to school this morning everybody was asking me how my dad was. I said you were fine, and people couldn't believe it."

I held my hands up. "I am fine. Not a mark on me."

"It was lucky those cars showed up," Tony said.

Amazingly lucky. I still couldn't figure out how the highway patrol could respond to a call in fifteen seconds, or how there could have even been a call. Nor did it make sense that the mayor would go out of his way to check out potholes at night.

"You better get some sleep," I said. "What time's the bus leave?"

"Seven," he said. "I'll get up a little after six."

"How's it feel on the eve of the biggest football game of your life?" I asked.

He cocked his head. "It's hard to say. I'm not nervous. I'm not worried. I'm anxious, you know, in part because I couldn't play last week. But it's a calm anxious, if that makes sense."

It made sense. He appeared calm.

"I think as a team, we're ready," Tony said. "For a month, longer really, we've ridden this high, you know, these incredible games. It's really been wild. Really wild. It's been exciting and it's been a lot of fun. But we know the ride ends tomorrow. And we're ready for it to end."

"Jersey sounded pretty confident at the assembly today," I said.

"He's been that way all week," Tony said. "Coach Pete's a walking heart attack, but Jersey walks around like he's killing time waiting at the dentist's office. Still, Jersey keeps talking in past tense." He imitated Jersey. "After *(aftah)* you win the championship, I expect you to conduct yourself as champions."

"To me that sounds over confident," I said.

Tony shrugged. "Roundup's a great team. We've watched two of their games on film the past two nights and they're really good. They play smart, they hardly ever get out of position, they always got all eleven guys on defense flowing toward the ball and their offense had only one turnover the two games we saw. But when we went to Baker, we were scared. And when we played Fort Benton and Fairfield, I mean, come on, deep down we were petrified. But maybe because we've been through all this, because we beat Baker, Fort Benton and Fairfield, we're ready for Roundup." He stood up. "Not that I remember beating Fort Benton. But all this week – we're pretty sure we can take on anything or anybody. Thus," he said, feigning what sounded like an elitist Ivy League accent, "our rather superior confidence, old boy."

Tony was up at six sharp. The distinctive splash of urine in the toilet water was followed by the sound of the shower. The water pipes hummed and rattled then banged, a trio of worsening vibrations that would eventually need to be fixed, either before or after what inevitably would be some type of soggy catastrophe.

My bed was warm; the house was cold and dark and it should have been tempting to remain under the covers. But this was a remarkably special day for Whitehall, for Tony Joslyn, for his teammates, for his family, for an entire community. It would be a historical day, regardless of the outcome. It would be an unforgettable day, irrespective of the outcome.

The cold wood floor creaked underfoot as I stepped barefoot lightly to the front door to fetch the morning paper. The cement steps outside were only slightly colder than the wood floor inside. It was mid November, completely dark at six o'clock in the morning, cold enough to see your breath outdoors and cold enough to encase the Escort in a layer of overnight fuzzy frost. The Standard carried a large article on the front page of the sports section about the final weekend of Montana high school football, with the various classes – Class AA, Class A, Class B, Class C and even eight-man football – all holding their championship games today. The Whitehall Rangers got a nice write-up with individual praise for Colt, Dave and Logan, and while the article outlined the talents of the Ranger players, the article focused – rightly, to be truthful – on the surprising success of the Rangers and the unlikeliness of their appearance in the Class B title game. In the bathroom, the shower stopped and the vibrating water pipes hummed, then clanked, then quieted. Tony emerged from the steam-filled bathroom drying his hair with a towel, wearing just a pair of underpants.

He had somehow, without me really noticing, become something of an impressive physical specimen. His waist was trim, his belly flat, and his shoulders broad and firm. As his arms worked the towel around his head I could see the muscles in his biceps and forearms flex and bulge, and I was pretty certain the last time I'd seen him dry his hair they hadn't done that. Either that, or I just hadn't noticed.

"I don't think we have anything to eat," Tony said from the hallway.

"Brownies," I answered. "I don't think we finished them last night, did we?"

"I might need something with a little more heft, if you know what I mean."

"What did you have in mind?" I asked.

"Real food. Eggs. Toast. Sausage. Bacon."

I thought about what we had in the house. Brownies. Cereal. Bread. Questionable milk. "I think we got everything you need except the eggs, sausage, and bacon."

Tony kept walking into his bedroom, toweling his hair dry. I should have thought about a healthy, nutritional breakfast for him. I should have thought about a lot of things.

"Play some Bruce," he called out from his bedroom. "Crank it up. Let's get this thing started right."

I figured the selection had to be *Born in the U.S.A.,* which I played so loud the rattle of the water pipes had sounded weak by comparison. I could hear Tony dimly singing from his bedroom.

"Want me to go to the grocery store and pick up some hefty food?" I called out.

Tony emerged at his doorway, still shirtless but wearing pants and shoes. "Grocery store's closed, but The Corner Store and Town Pump are open. Do you even know how to cook eggs and bacon and real food?"

It was a fair question. For years, the average breakfast in the Joslyn household had been cold cereal, store-bought rolls or donuts on a good day. But this was better than a good day, and demanded better than an average breakfast. I realized right then, for the first time, that I had never once in my entire life cooked eggs or bacon. But I'd seen it done often enough to have the general principles down. "How hard can it be?"

"That answer does not exactly inspire confidence," he said.

"You think about it," I said. "I'll jump in the shower and we'll figure it out when I get out. Maybe we'll take a quick trip to Borden's for breakfast."

The water hissed and spurted but I could still hear Springsteen's *Darlington County* above the spray. Somewhere in the walls the pipes rumbled. When I got out of the shower the first thing I noticed was that I smelled food – hot food, real food – and muffled voices under the music. I put on the sweatpants I wore as pajamas and emerged still wet from the misty bathroom to see Tony seated at the table, one hand holding a fork filled with something yellow, and behind him, barely taller standing than he was seated, stood Rhonda Horst, purple scarf tied tight under her chin, a slim smile creasing her thin lips. The aroma of the food seemed to fill the entire house.

"Scrambled eggs," Tony said, holding up the fork, "with chunks of bacon and peas in it. You gotta try some, Lance." He sort of chuckled. "Ask and ye shall receive."

Rhonda beamed. "Goot," and she thought for a moment, "foot. Heft foot."

Tony pointed the empty fork her direction. "How about this, Lance? Tell me you saw that coming."

I didn't, but should have. How could she not insist on sending Tony off to Roundup with a homemade breakfast in his belly? I went into the bedroom and threw on a flannel shirt and a pair of jeans and barefoot, approached the table.

"Eat," Rhonda told me, and pointed to an empty plate, next to a fork, set on the table. They weren't even our plates or silverware. She not only brought the food, she also brought the utensils. I thought, *she must think we're totally helpless*.

She hoisted a spatula and set a square of the firm, golden eggs on my plate. The eggs melted in my mouth, and at the same time burst with flavor. I chuckled the exact same way Tony had.

Rhonda put a hand on Tony's shoulder. "Such ah goot boy."

Tony wound up having three helpings of the eggs but I was stuffed after two. Logan swung by in a Ford pickup with *WHS Rangers Rule* soaped across the passenger window, with Cody already inside. I saw Cody reach over and honk the horn, and laugh. Tony grabbed his duffle bag with his gear, gave Rhonda a big hug, and – denoting the significance of the day – gave me a firm hug.

"Goot luck," Rhonda told him.

"Go get 'em," I said.

"You see the article in the Standard?" Tony asked. "Mostly says we're lucky just to get this far."

He waited for me to say something. "Well, you kind of are."

"Yeah, well, you can say that, and I can say that, but they can't," he said. "We've earned our way into this game. We belong in this game."

He bounced out of the house, greeted by the toot-toot of the Ford's horn as he pounded the truck's hood twice with his fist. He jumped up into the cab as

Cody slid over, and as the truck backed up out of the driveway, Tony said something that made all three of them erupt into laughter.

That left me alone with Rhonda, with a half hour or so until Old Tom showed up, before we picked up Mary and headed out of town.

"Brusch," Rhonda said, and I realized the house was silent. I went over to the turntable and flipped over the record as Rhonda moved toward the sink, to wash dishes.

"You don't have to do that, Rhonda," I said.

She ignored me. She had to have heard me, but didn't acknowledge me, didn't even flit her eyes my direction. So as Bruce sang about *no retreat, no surrender,* I went into my bedroom to get dressed for the game. I added more layers – sweatshirt and hooded sweatshirt on top and jeans over sweatpants on my legs – and when I came out of the bedroom Rhonda sat so carefully, so stiffly, her back firm as sheetrock, on the couch it was as if she believed if she moved she'd break something. I wanted to tell her to relax, to sit back and rest, but knew she wouldn't, no matter what I said or did. *At least take off the scarf,* I thought.

"As soon as Old Tom shows up we'll go pick up Mary and head to Roundup," I told her.

She cocked her head slightly. "Oldt Tom? Vit da helmat?"

"Right," I said.

She dismissed my comment with a wave of her hand.

The phone rang, and it was Annie. I could hear the animated chorus of young female voices in the background. She practically had to shout to be heard.

"Lance? Can you hear me?" she asked.

"Yeah," I shouted. "Where are you?"

"At Dicksons. We're getting ready to head to school."

"The kids sound pretty fired up," I said.

"They are," she said. "Are you and Tony up? Did he get to the school?" A shrill cheer erupted somewhere behind her.

"Yeah. Cody and Logan picked him up. Everything's fine."

"Do you have enough money for gas and food and whatever?"

"I'm not a kid, Annie."

"Do you or don't you?" she demanded.

"I've got money," I said, which had a fifty-percent chance of being the truth. I either did or I didn't. I'd have to check right after I hung up the phone. "Did you get any sleep last night?"

"Some," she said. "A few of these girls are a little squirrelly. Hey Lance, you're the talk of the town. How you beat up Manfred. I had no idea you were such a tough guy."

"I didn't beat up anyone," I said.

"I better get going," she said. "We're ready to pull out."

There was a sharp double-knock at the door, and Old Tom walked in, saw me, stepped back out on the steps and waved to Young Tom, a *Yeah, he's here, you can go* wave. "Hold on," I told Annie.

"Good Lord, it smells like a cafeteria in here," he called out. He was so anxious to be fed he was practically bug-eyed. He wore the leather helmet over a stocking cap that fully covered his ears, and the helmet didn't quite fit right above the stocking cap and was perched oddly high atop his head. He wore a knee-length army coat over his ancient WHS purple sweater, and his feet were covered by rubber irrigation boots that went up past his knees. He didn't look as much dressed as he did assembled by a mad scientist. "I smell it," he exclaimed, "but I don't see it!"

Still on the phone, I opened the refrigerator door and pointed to the pan of the egg and bacon dish.

"Sounds like Old Tom just showed up," said Annie. Old Tom reached into the fridge and hauled out the pan, and I quick gave him a fork and a plate before he decided to just reach in the pan and grab the food with his hands. "Okay, Lance, see you at the game. This is pretty cool, isn't it, Tony playing in the championship game."

"Very cool," I agreed. Old Tom took the fork and ate the food right out of the pan. He either didn't see the plate, didn't care, or didn't know what it was for. From the corner of my eye I saw Rhonda shaking her head in disgust. "Thanks for calling. See you in Roundup."

"Don't punch out any cops on your way there." Before I could respond she'd hung up the phone.

"Annie?" Rhonda said, making it sound like *Ahh-nee.*

"Yeah, she's riding on the pep bus."

Rhonda's eyes kind of crinkled. "You gat such nice kits," she said. "Goot kits."

Watching Old Tom eat was not a sight for women and children, but since there was no way I or anyone else was going to touch the food in that dish again, I let him keep eating. I turned off the stereo, grabbed the camera and set it by the door, put on my coat and gave every hint possible to Old Tom that it was time to leave and go pick up Mary. Five minutes later, the pan was almost empty. There was one corner of eggs left. He turned to me, greasy flecks of egg on his lips and chin, chunks of sausage in his teeth, the helmet perched even higher and odder on his head. He presented the pan toward me and asked, "You want to finish this?"

Chapter 40

East we went, bitter brown pastures and stubble fields on either side of the road, pods of gray snow tucked down in the gullies and amid the brush. The sun ahead was a low dull glow in the eastern horizon, weakly penetrating a chilly mist that seemed to hover below the mountains. We drove past the Highway 69 turnoff, where the Rangers had lost earlier in the season – and either past turnoffs or through Three Forks, Townsend, Manhattan and Big Timber – all conference teams expected to be better than Whitehall, and all of them with disappointing seasons long over.

Instead it was Whitehall Ranger fans, driving pickups, vans, big ranch Buicks and Fords, beat-up trucks and even a tiny Escort, with soaped windows bearing messages like *Go Rangers!* and *Whitehall Pride* who were on their way across I-90 to play in the state Class B title football game. Between Whitehall and Big Timber we saw – as they passed us – some 51-license-plated Whitehall-based vehicles, propelling themselves straight-shot along the freeway toward the rising sun. Some of the people, like the O'Tooles and the Walkers, honked and waved, and others – like the Harrisons – merely offered stately nods of recognition. As they passed on the left, people in the other vehicle spotted me and waved, looked to see who else was in the car – expecting maybe Annie or Trish or Slack – and instead found Mary in the front and Old Tom and Rhonda in the back, and gazed at them with brief expressions of bewilderment.

I should have been thinking about the game, about how Whitehall would stop Roundup's star wide receiver, a lanky kid named Rhett Blasdell – nicknamed Jett Blaze – fast enough to be the state Class B hurdle state record holder and defending 100-meter and 200-meter state champion. Roundup had seven kids retuning from the 1985 All-Conference team, had lost only once all year, to Fort Benton on the road by a single point, and had lost only one game the year before, a playoff game to the eventual state champion. But Whitehall had beaten Fort Benton in Fort Benton, and although Roundup was loaded with talent, Whitehall was loaded with confidence. And we in the Escort were also loaded with Rhonda's pumpkin bread.

But at that moment I wasn't thinking about the game. Without realizing it, I was thinking about Montana. The Yellowstone River, with small patches of snow and ice in the shadows along the streambank, flowed calmly and gracefully the same direction we were headed. Mountain ranges cut jagged skylines in virtually every direction, and I again couldn't shake the sense I always had when driving across Montana how lucky I was to live here. I didn't pursue a single outdoor recreational activity, I couldn't tell a golden eagle from a hawk or a ponderosa pine from a Douglas fir or a glacier lily from an Indian paintbrush, but my ignorance in no way detracted from the enjoyment I got from seeing Montana through a windshield. I couldn't tell a cutthroat trout from a rainbow trout or an otter from a fisher, or a mallard from a drake, but I still marveled at the beauty of the Yellowstone River as it flowed through canyons, slid over rocks, rolled past trees and cows and horses and wildlife. It was inspiring and humbling all at once. I sometimes felt guilty about living in Montana. How was I lucky enough to live here when so many people had to suffer through the misfortune of living somewhere else? Montana was so consistently spectacular that the temptation was to take it for granted. Only fools did so.

Perhaps Mary had read my mind, or parts of it.

"Is there a more beautiful place than Montana?" she asked.

"How could there be?" I said.

"Dis landt," Rhonda marveled from the backseat. "Got bless dis landt."

Mary's hair was frizzier than normal, longer, and outside of a wedge in front her hair covered her entire neck; she was wearing a turtleneck under some kind of Nordic-looking sweater. Between the turtleneck and the sweater was another thick shirt, and she had a scarf, stocking cap and winter coat on the floor at her feet. Just because Montana was a wonderful place to live didn't mean it didn't get cold outside.

Mary had a sparkle in her eye, as if she possessed a true spark of inner excitement. I thought about that – the inner excitement – and figured I had probably had it too. My guess was everyone in Whitehall had it. I snuck a peek in the backseat. Old Tom's eyes appeared agitated, which I figured for him was close to an inner excitement. Rhonda gazed out the window, and her head moved in subdued, almost dreamy rhythm to a ballad from Springsteen's *The River*, which I viewed as definite inner excitement.

The people in Big Timber had no such excitement. We stopped for a break at the Town Pump and for everyone except us it was just a dreary Saturday morning in November. We exited off I-90 and headed north on Highway 191, and just out of town I had to slow down for a small herd of deer wandering on both sides of the highway. As we headed north the sun floated higher in the sky and the deer thinned then disappeared by late morning.

I sipped a plastic bottle of orange juice that tasted worse than the plastic it came in. I should have known better. How is it we can put a man on the moon but we cannot manufacture a decent tasting bottle of convenience store orange juice? Behind me Rhonda sat stiff-backed as if rooted to a courthouse wood bench, waiting a call to testify inside a courtroom. Old Tom had drifted asleep, a hoarse throaty rasp nearly keeping time with the music. His chin rested flatly on his chest, and he had drooled or bubbled up some yellowish phlegm – remnants of the orange pumpkin bread was a good guess – through a corner of his mouth, down his chin, and onto the collar of his coat. His ridiculous helmet was tilted forward at a ridiculous angle. Rhonda was as far away as she could be from him in the scant space the Escort's backseat allotted. Had the trunk been an option, I think she would have crawled back there.

A curtain of snow, mixed with sleet and ice, swept past us on an upslope east of Harlowton on Highway 12 near Rygate, and just as I grew worried about the road conditions the squall was behind us, the sky brightened, and the road was merely wet.

Old Tom snorted himself awake as we slowed to enter Roundup, a town that upon first appearance had a lot in common with Whitehall. The sky darkened and we encountered a wet mist – not rain and not snow – but simple moisture, as if the clouds were sweating. We had an hour until kickoff but the first task was always to find the football field. Guided by the stadium light poles, we located the field on the west edge of town. The football field abutted the slope of hills to the west, and within the smattering of snow textured into the low and shaded areas were some bedded antelope, as if they were settling in to watch the game.

"I gotta piss like a son of a bitch," Old Tom announced.

"You also might want to wipe your chin," Mary told him.

The Ranger team bus was in the parking lot but only a few players – quarterbacks and receivers, it looked like – were in uniform and warming up. The pep bus hadn't arrived yet and only a few cars were in the parking lot.

"I ain't kiddin," Old Tom warned me. "I gotta go *now*."

"Can you make it to that café on main street?" I asked him.

"I can't make it another ten feet," he yelped.

To our left was what looked like the back of a storage shed, and I pulled over and stopped so abruptly Rhonda's forehead almost hit the back of the front seat. The building turned out to be a utility shack or small bus barn or something, because Old Tom disappeared toward the front of the building and came around the other end, looked around, turned toward the back of the building, unzipped his pants and let loose right through what I desperately hoped was a wide enough slit in his coat. You couldn't see the urine actually hitting the building, but you could see the foamy skinny stream running between his legs on the pavement in front and then behind him.

"I tink dat's against da law," Rhonda pondered.

"If it's not, it should be," said Mary.

"Remind me on the way home to take more bathroom breaks," I told them.

"Every chance we get," Mary said slowly.

It wasn't like we were at a deserted roadside late at night. It was midday and vehicles, both moving and parked, were spread out on all sides of Old Tom, and people were scattered on and around the field in virtually all directions.

"Did he go in Big Timber?" I asked absently.

"You expect Rhonda or me to know the answer to that question?" Mary said.

Finally, Old Tom finished. It should not have come as a surprise – but it did – that he turned around to face the car as he tucked in, re-zipped, hitched up the pants, and strode clumsily toward us.

"Had to drain the hose," he grinned as he approached the car.

"Let's get out of here," Mary told me.

"Should we leave without him?" I asked quietly.

Rhonda issued a gleeful snort.

Old Tom opened the door and folded himself into the backseat, then allowed himself a contented sigh. As we pulled away I could see clearly the splashed base of the wall and a small pool forming up in a slight depression ten feet or so from the wall. The urine was still flowing away from the building; by the time it was done, it was going to be an impressive little puddle.

Roundup reminded me a lot of Whitehall, a kind of cowboy town mixed with ranchers, small businesses and miners. Whitehall had gold, and Roundup had coal. Both had sagebrush, blustery winds, and scattered buildings and dwellings around town that could have been neglectfully occupied or successfully abandoned; looking at them, you could make a case either way.

We drove a few blocks to a café and when we walked in we found four or five tables filled with purple and gold Ranger fans. Drew Erickson and Brad Knight – his beard still purple – were in one booth along the wall, mugs of steaming coffee on the table, held by cupped hands. The Henkels – Sue, Walt and Slack – crowded around a small table, each with a frosted cinnamon roll, the frosting white and thick as caulking. Hannah Bolling sat with her mother and sister, and off in a corner I spotted tiny Sara Dickson, who sat with a large group of undersized people who more or less looked just like her. I figured Dave must have a large family contingent watching him today.

I waved to Sara, and she returned a timid little waggle of her fingers. As I walked past Slack I put both hands on his shoulders and asked him if he was ready for the biggest football game in Whitehall High School history, and he nodded with such vigor his cowboy hat nearly fell off.

A few of the Whitehall folks offered my oddly assembled quartet sly smiles or expressions of uncertainty as we made our way to a table. When the waitress came to get our order, though, my guess was she figured us as two couples, with Old Tom and Rhonda the parents of either Mary or me.

"You folks from Whitehall?" she asked as she wiped the plastic table covering with a wet rag. She was chubby, with fleshy arms and a bulging middle. "Here for the big game?"

It was a good guess, considering Old Tom's purple sweater and leather helmet. "Right on both counts," I said, because no one else at the table seemed inclined to speak.

"Well, good luck," the waitress said cheerfully. "I got a nephew playing for Roundup."

"Well, good luck to you too," Mary said.

"He's a good kid," the waitress said. "Sweet as can be. Too sweet for football, you ask me. What'll it be, folks?"

We ordered three coffees and a Coke. I was relieved Old Tom didn't order food. Seeing him eat was not something I wanted to experience again soon and definitely not something I wanted to share with the public.

I leaned back to get a better look at Brad. "I figured you'd be out hunting today. There's some antelope just off the field. You could shoot one at halftime."

"Might just do that," he said. He put his coffee cup down and wiped at his beard with the back of his hand. "We're spending the night here. Rifle's in the truck."

"That's a hell of a beard," commented Old Tom. "It's purple, you know."

Brad nodded. "Love the helmet."

Old Tom placed one scrawny paw on top of his head to settle the helmet, to arrange it more firmly on his head, as if talking about it made it crooked, or possibly more valuable, somehow. "It's older'n you are."

"Looks like it might be older than you are," Drew said.

"Ever carbon date that thing?" asked Brad.

Old Tom simply scowled at them and gripped his coffee cup as it arrived.

Slack moved over to our table, as I figured he would. He had that lopsided, contagious grin and the childish and unmitigated look of exhilaration shining through his eyes that made you smile just to see him.

"I never been to Roundup before," he announced to the world.

"It sort of reminds me of Whitehall," I said.

Slack's face twisted slightly in thought, trying to place my comment in context.

"You ready for this, Slack?" I asked. I put a hand on his shoulder. "The Whitehall Rangers are less than an hour away from taking the field for the Montana Class B state high school football championship game. Do you believe it?"

No person in the history of the world ever smiled bigger than Slack smiled right then. It was absolute and total joy. He couldn't find words to answer the question. His mind was reeling, his eyes were wildly expressive, his mouth was attempting to form words. But he was simply too happy, too excited, to actually speak. He made a guttural noise and reached out and hugged me so tight I thought he might pull me off the chair.

Both teams were in full warm-up mode when we got back to the field. I deliberately avoided parking anywhere near the shed drenched by Old Tom. I spotted Tony first, the Rangers in their road golden jerseys, lined up in neat square rows stretching out their legs. Old Tom dug out his wallet and sprung for his, Rhonda's and Mary's entry to the game, and my press pass got me through the gate and onto the field. The three of them wandered toward the small section of bleachers for visitors near the middle of the field. The pep bus had arrived, and all the kids were standing in a couple large groups in front of the cheerleaders. I found Annie by first finding Trish in the wheelchair. I waved to Annie, and she began moving my direction. She wore a purple stocking cap pulled low over her ears, Tony's home purple football jersey over a winter coat, making her nearly as wide as she was tall. We met at a plastic orange waist-high snow fence that surrounded the field, me on the inside, she on the outside. There was a dull pounding noise from fans on either side of the field, an undercurrent of energy and sheer mass, like a throbbing surge of electricity.

"Morning," she told me.

"Isn't this something?" I asked, gesturing to indicate all *this*; the field, the players, the game, the anticipation.

"You should have seen us on the pep bus," she said. "We were obnoxious. For four straight hours, we were obnoxious. I think we might be all cheered out."

"I hope not."

"Where were you?" she asked. "I looked for you when we arrived but couldn't find you."

"We found the field, then went uptown for some coffee," I said.

"I knew you got here before us," she said. "I got a cup of hot chocolate from the concession stand and they were talking about some old guy from Whitehall wearing a beat-up leather football helmet who peed all over the equipment shed."

"That was Old Tom," I admitted.

"Yeah, I pretty much had that figured," she said. "Lucky Manfred's not around." She turned toward the bleachers and waved, and Mary, Rhonda and Old Tom all waved back. "This is a big chapter in our lives, isn't it, Lance?"

I thought about that a moment. "Yeah, I suppose it is."

"This whole football championship thing," she said. "We'll remember this our whole lives, won't we?"

"Jersey made it seem like we're supposed to," I agreed.

"This game is historic, like you wrote in the paper, and like you said, it's an important part of Whitehall history. But it's an important part of the history of the families here, too," Annie said. "A lot of people will measure their lives by this game, won't they? By this season. Maybe by just a moment in this game. Or a previous game. Like when Tony got the concussion."

I turned to see Tony and the offense running plays at midfield against an invisible defense. Jersey stood stoically behind them, arms folded, sunglasses on, wearing his black leather jacket. Coach Pete wore a plaid Elmer Fudd-looking cap and a purple Carroll College windbreaker, clutched a clipboard around the goal line and seemed to be looking for someone, maybe anyone, to yell at.

"For some of the people in the stands and on the field, this game right here right now is going to be the high point in their lives," Annie said. There was no doubt and no editorial comment in her voice. "After this game, win or lose, they'll never again experience anything else like it." She looked away from me, then smiled wanly my direction.

I thought of Slack's burst of a smile at the café, of Old Tom in his helmet, of Dave's meek little mother. "Some people will carry this moment with them forever," I said. "They'll never lose it or forget it. They'll always have it, and hold onto it, no matter what happens. They'll experience it forever. Win or lose, Annie, this day will give them a precious treasure to carry with them the rest of their lives. There's nothing wrong with that."

She nodded thoughtfully. "You know what happened when we got here today?"

No, I didn't.

"There was a problem with Trisha's wheelchair when we all had to get off the bus," Annie said. "One of the wheels locked up or something. Bonner lifted her from her wheelchair, and someone else folded up the chair and took it down the ramp. Bonner carried her a few steps, but then she told him to put her down." Annie sort of closed one eye, and gave me a sly smile. Her pause was deliberately dramatic. "Then Trish walked off the bus."

I turned toward where Trish sat at the base of the bleachers, alertly, but firmly, in her wheelchair. She looked the same as she always did; like she couldn't walk.

"Oh, it wasn't pretty," Annie acknowledged. "She was unsteady and weak, and had to hold on tight to the handrails. We stood in front of and behind her, to catch her or hold her if we had to, but Lance, she shuffled on her feet down the steps and off the bus. First time she's walked in two years. Bonner unfolded the wheelchair and fixed the wheel, and we pushed her to the track there, and she's sat there ever since. But something's going on, Lance."

"Something like what?" I asked.

"Something," she started, and smiled at me, "precious, Lance. Something we'll carry with us the rest of our lives."

The wet football field glittered and glimmered and the lights had been turned on to illuminate the gray and dimming murky conditions. The maroon letters *P-A-N-T-H-E-R-S* painted at midfield looked soaked and black, the edges bled into the glistening yellow grass. When you looked up at the lights you could see a thin sheet of rain or sleet or snow or whatever combination of dampness was falling from the sky, but the actual moisture on your clothes or hands seemed scant to the point of simple humidity. Windbreakers and ski jackets looked slickened, but wool and cotton coats showed no wetness. Little moisture drops formed on my camera so I only took a few pictures before the start of the game then put the camera away until kickoff. I took a picture of Aspen O'Toole and two other cheerleaders in front of a purple *Rangers Rule* banner; of Colt and Logan, as Ranger captains, walking out for the coin toss; of Old Tom under his leather helmet; of Coach Pete and Morgan, one hand on Morgan's shoulder, the other hand – holding the clipboard – on top of Morgan's helmet, the clipboard flat as a mortarboard.

The Roundup High School band played an up tempo version of the national anthem, with a trio of Roundup female students nicely harmonizing the vocals. During the performance the Rangers were, as they'd been all season, rigid as stone, tense, absolutely stock-still, every player, every moment. Jersey stood passive but motionless, his sunglasses still on despite the dreary clouds and rain. Coach Pete stood as if at attention, his cap held over his chest, and was immobile except the clipboard, which trembled in his left hand at his thigh. Tony's hair was black and damp, his eyeblack already smeared and his towel tucked in his belt hung limp and motionless at his side.

Both sides of the field – fans and players alike – burst in loud spontaneous cheers and applause just before the final note of the national anthem drifted off into nonexistence.

This is it, I thought; the final game, the end of the season, the conclusion of a magical experience, the termination of something unforgettable. Let's go Rangers: Four quarters of football to make history, to claim a title, to achieve the impossible, to accomplish something you may never duplicate again in your entire life. All that was true. It was also arguably true that this was only a high school football game, and its outcome was totally inconsequential to anything remotely considered important in the grand reckoning of a life lived. But I knew, even then standing along the sidelines in Roundup, Montana, that years into the future people here on this day may not be able to recall with certainty events of lives in 1985 or 1987 or other years, but the year 1986 would be fixed permanently in their minds and hearts.

Whitehall kicked off, and Roundup took over at its own thirty yard line. I never did, and never could, figure out football strategy or schemes, but even I could tell the Rangers devoted two players – Tony and Colt – to the Roundup receiver, Jett Blaze. Wherever Jett went, Tony and Colt went, Tony in front of him and Colt behind him. If Jett lined up out wide, so did Tony and Colt. If Jett went in motion, on the opposite side of the ball Tony and Colt went as well, almost like a double reflection in a pond. And yet the Roundup quarterback threw to him twice. A sideline pass was wide, and a deeper ball was overthrown.

Still, Roundup moved the ball downfield on its first possession. They tossed a screen pass to the opposite side of the field from Jett, and picked up nineteen yards and a first down. On third and long, the quarterback – a stocky kid who looked more like a linebacker than a quarterback – scrambled for fourteen yards and more or less ran over Colt before Tony made the tackle. It was his first real contact since the concussion in Fort Benton, but he bounced to his feet and angrily slapped his hands – *fourteen yards on third and ten* – and showed no lingering effects from the collision two weeks earlier.

Logan and Nate tackled the Roundup runner for a loss on second down, and on third and long Cody sacked the quarterback for another loss. Roundup's punt sailed over Tony's head and bounced into the end zone.

On Whitehall's first play from scrimmage Dave dropped back in the pocket for a pass, except he didn't have the ball. It had been snuck into Logan's belly on a handoff and Logan lumbered up the middle for nine yards. On second and short Dave handed the ball to Logan, except Logan never got the ball. Dave turned and handed the ball to Colt on an end around, except Colt didn't have the ball. Dave drifted a few steps to the right and fired the ball to Nate, who was wide open. One Panther had a shot at him at about the fifteen yard line but Nate ran straight through the tackle to score the game's first touchdown. I got a good picture of Dave throwing the pass and in the photo you could see Cody, JeffScott and Brock Warren looking for someone to block. Part of the defense had hauled down Logan, and the other part had chased Colt. No one was coming after Dave and no one was near Nate.

The Whitehall fans were practically still cheering the Ranger touchdown when Roundup tied up the game. The Roundup quarterback faked a pass to Jett, then threw what seemed like a harmless short pass to a tight end who may have been the biggest kid on the field. A couple Rangers were in good position to make a tackle, but one Ranger hit him too low and simply missed, and another one hit him too high and simply bounced off. The Panther receiver rumbled in the end zone for a sixty-five yard touchdown and a tie game. The Roundup side of the field erupted in a cheer with such volume that it caused some restless and worried movement from the antelope up on the hillside.

Whitehall had the ball twice more and gained large chunks of yardage each time, but one drive was stalled by a clipping penalty and the other ended deep inside Panther territory when Dave was hit as he pitched the ball. The ball bounced off Cale's shoulder pad and was recovered by Roundup.

"David Randall Dickson!" Dave shouted at himself as he walked off the field. He took his palm and gave himself a good rap on the side of his helmet.

"Hang on to the ball!" Coach Pete yelled at him.

Dave whacked himself on the side of the helmet a second time.

The score was tied at 7-7 until midway through the second quarter when Roundup completed its first pass to Jett, a post pattern that gained twenty-four yards and moved them into Whitehall territory. Four plays later they were in the end zone on a quarterback sneak with a 14-7 lead.

Tony had a nice kickoff return to midfield and on the drive's first play Dave kept the ball on an option play for a first down. Logan banged the middle for a couple yards, Nate ran a sweep for another six yards and Dave ran off tackle for another first down. Dave faked a handoff to Logan on the next play and handed the ball to Colt for an end around, except Colt pulled up to throw a pass.

My eyes drifted downfield when Colt raised his arm to throw and just as I saw Tony wide open I heard a painful groan from the Roundup side of the field. There wasn't a single Roundup player on that side of the field. Cale was downfield covered by two Panthers, but Tony was uncovered. Tony slowed down and caught the ball against his belly for a touchdown and a 14-14 tie.

Roundup had a couple minutes left in the half to get a go-ahead score, and the quarterback completed back-to-back passes to the tight end. On the second completion Cale tripped him up from behind or he might have scored. On the last play of the half Roundup lofted a deep pass toward Jett, but Colt easily batted the ball down in the end zone.

During the halftime break I put the camera away in a mostly worthless attempt to keep it dry, but its hard surface was as damp and beaded with moisture as every other hard surface in the town of Roundup. The rain wasn't heavy; it wasn't even rain. Yet when I walked along the sidelines, my shoes were so wet they squeaked. High school kids from either school too stylish for hats pranced around with wet hair that sparkled under the lights.

I checked some of my notes and saw the statistics were as close as the score. Both teams had comparable rushing yards and passing yards, Roundup had a couple more first downs but Whitehall had more return yards. The drizzle was smearing the ink, so I folded the paper and put it away in the camera bag. As I walked around the turn on the track to the concession stand Ed Franklin approached from the other direction, each hand carrying a steaming Styrofoam cup of either coffee or hot chocolate.

"Here, figured you could use this," Ed said, and handed me one of the cups.

I looked into it and saw the creamy brown of hot chocolate.

"Don't worry, it's hot chocolate," he assured me. "You have to be the only newspaper publisher in Montana who doesn't drink coffee."

"Thanks," I said. The warmth felt good just hanging on to it.

"The first half didn't settle much did it?" Ed said.

"Nope," I said.

Ed was wearing some kind of a stylish yet rugged long dark green coat, thick gray woolen pants and light brown work boots. The days of him looking like a geeky church elder were gone. His sideburns were sharp and narrow along his ears and widened slightly at the bottom, a personal grooming tactic that would have never even occurred to Ed six months earlier let alone to actually invest the time to implement what really was a facial fashion statement. When the school year started Ed looked like an elderly benchwarmer from the movie *Hoosiers*. Now he looked more like a Las Vegas enforcer. The transformation was intriguing – from aging dweeb to his new cultivated and physical presence – yet somehow it seemed genuine, as if *this* was the true Ed Franklin. I knew the personality and appearance upgrade had something to do with Jersey and Cody and the Ranger wins and the Homecoming dance, but I couldn't figure out exactly how they all conspired to turn Ed into the elegant and masculine persona who stood before me on the track in Roundup.

"Tony's got a touchdown in the state title game," Ed said. "You have to feel good about that."

"How'd he get so open?" I asked.

“My guess is Roundup saw the TD pass to Colt last week but had nothing on Tony,” Ed said. “Tony wasn’t even in the line-up last week. They double-covered Nate but forgot about Tony.”

“So you expected him to be that open?” I asked.

“No, I’m saying Jersey drew up the play so Tony’d get that open,” Ed said.

We were standing more or less in the Whitehall traffic flow to the concession stand, and half a dozen people patted my shoulder or waved and complimented me on Tony’s touchdown. For an instant, maybe half an instant, there was an expression in Ed’s eyes that suggested something like pride or pleasure or success, and the thought occurred to me that he’d deliberately stopped me in the path of traffic to the concessions so I could receive the salutes and congratulations about Tony.

“Great to have your kid back in the line-up,” Cal Walker said as he passed me.

“Hope you got a picture or two of Tony in the end zone,” said Lyle.

“Hey, it’s Touchdown Tony’s dad,” Carrie Lindstrom called out.

“Rock on, Lance,” said Bonner.

An expanding roar behind us announced Roundup’s return to the field, and moments later the Roundup band let loose with their school song. A slightly more modest cheer erupted when the Rangers came back to the field, and the WHS pep band responded with a spirited version of *Born to Run* that had the student section head-bopping and singing along.

I wandered back to my spot along the sidelines but decided to leave the camera in the pack. Then I decided bullshit, it was the state championship game and the camera was going to have to get wet. If it suffered water damage, it suffered *state championship game* water damage, and that was acceptable. I checked on Mary, and saw her between Old Tom and Rhonda in the bleachers, Old Tom standing looking out to the field as if on a desert island looking out to sea for a rescue vessel and Rhonda gently stamping a foot and clapping her hands in rhythm, although at the time no music was playing. Down and to their left, Annie stood in the first row, above Trish. Annie held a blanket wrapped around her, and Trish had a blanket in her lap. There was a glow, a buzz, in the Whitehall crowd. They were nervous, they were excited, and they were hopeful. It was as if they couldn’t wait to see what happened next.

Jersey’s sunglasses were off and the black leather jacket was zipped up to the chest. Coach Pete’s Elmer Fudd hat was low on his head and in three quick successive motions he cleared his throat and spat, cleared his throat and spat and cleared his throat and spat. Above, up at the lights, the mist was visible as individual droplets, tiny crystals of water, drifting aimlessly from the sky.

Jersey huddled with Dave, and put an arm around his scant ninth grade quarterback. Dave said something that made Jersey laugh, a laugh so loud everyone on the sideline heard it. Jersey gave Dave an affectionate couple pats on the top of the helmet and Dave stood out on the field just off the sidelines and turned to face his teammates.

"What are we!" he screamed.

"Rangers!" the team yelled back.

"What are we!" Dave screamed again.

"Rangers!" the team responded.

"What *are* we!" Dave yelled.

"Rangers!" the team hollered.

Tony stepped out on the field and whirled back toward the sideline. "What are we!" he yelled.

"Champions!" came the response.

"What are we!"

"Champions!"

Tony's body grew taut, his neck seemed extended and his fists were clenched at his side. "What are we!" he screamed.

"Champions!" the team screamed back.

The players and WHS fans cheered and applauded and whistled and yelled in response to what had to have been a planned and possibly even a rehearsed act. Moments later, the Whitehall kickoff return team jogged out onto the field as the Roundup kickoff team lined up across the forty yard line. As the Panthers stretched their legs, jumped up and down and ran in place, the Roundup band played a rousing version of a song I think was from *Top Gun*.

The ball fluttered high in the mist and came down end over end into the waiting arms of Tony, who cut to the right then straight as a razor up the field and ran absolutely untouched into the end zone for a touchdown. He was like a streak of golden smudge dashing up the field and he ran full speed into and out of the end zone. It happened so fast there was no anticipation, no real upwelling of excitement or gradual building of drama or hope or expectation. The ball was kicked, caught, and then in what seemed like a heartbeat was in the end zone. Suddenly, abruptly as a rifle shot, Whitehall led 21-14.

They never lost that lead. Whatever the Panthers had talked about at halftime, whatever strategy or emotion they had planned and depended upon, had not been based upon a kickoff return for a touchdown and an immediate 21-14 deficit. The stunned silence from the maroon Panther team sidelines and tightly bunched fans in the bleachers was in reality a desperate roar of despair and panic.

On their next possession Roundup attempted a deep pass to Jett, but he was blanketed by three Rangers and Colt came down with an interception. Whitehall took over at midfield and pounded the ball with Logan up the middle, Dave outside the tackles and Nate and Cale outside on sweeps. Dave's ball-handling was both mystifying and magical and the way Logan, Dave, Nate and Cale carried out the fakes on the shadowy wet field you never knew who actually had the ball. Neither could the Roundup defense. When Cale skirted around the left side for a nine-yard touchdown run the Rangers were up 28-14.

The Rangers put together another nice drive early in the fourth quarter and took a 35-14 lead when Dave slipped into the end zone on a quarterback sneak.

"We got this one!" Dave yelled after he popped to his feet into Tony's embrace. "We got this one!" He leaned back, lifted his head and howled up toward the drizzling heavens.

On the next Panther possession the JeffScott twins combined to hit the quarterback at the same exact instant. The quarterback made the mistake of trying to grip a slippery ball with one hand. Tanner Walker fell on the fumble, Morgan fell on Tanner and Chance Nelson fell on Morgan. Five soggy grass-stained and muddy gold-shirted WHS defensemen were in on the play. In the photo of the fumble that was published in the Ledger, only one Roundup player – a helpless quarterback – was in the frame.

The Rangers tacked on another touchdown when two defenders lunged and hauled down Logan, and another two grabbed Dave and tossed him to the ground. Cale, however, had the ball, and the one tackler who had a chance missed him completely. WHS led 42-14 and after another interception by Colt, Jersey sent in the reserves for the final minutes of the fourth quarter.

Ranger fans were on their feet. They were applauding, watching the clock tick toward the end of the game, and there were embraces and handshakes and in the section where the kids sat there was unbridled glee and outright giddiness.

Mary stood, both gloved hands held to her mouth, in the classic posture of someone not believing what they're seeing. Rhonda had inexplicably moved to the student section, was standing directly behind Annie, and had her hands on Annie's shoulders. Ed and Alice Franklin stood side by side, leaning against each other. Hank and Kathleen Harrison were grinning, grinning and applauding. Rose O'Toole was standing directly in front of Lyle, who had his arms around her and had his head on her shoulder. Cal Walker had his black cowboy hat in the air, waving it like a rodeo star. The kids in the bleachers were so excited they couldn't stand still. They were cheering and singing and clapping and laughing and jumping and pounding each other. Rachel Brockton stood and simply nodded her approval. Brad Knight's purple beard held a greenish hue somehow, and he seemed to be dancing to an imaginary song or to tunes only he heard in his head. The WHS band was on their feet, high-fiving each other in every direction. The cheerleaders, bundled up in their sweatpants and purple windbreakers, were clustered, in tears. Sue and Walt Hinkel stood tense, hands clenched, as if anticipating some kind of disaster that could snatch away the victory. Slack knew better. His cowboy hat cast a deep shadow across his face, but a satellite passing in the heavens above could have spotted his grin. His arms were held up and his hands were clinched into fists that seemed to be pounding an invisible door above his head, his head nodding imperceptibly as each second wound down from the clock. Dave Dickson's mother stood stoically, shyly accepting the congratulations of all the family members around her. Annie stood between

Rhonda and Trish. She had a bemused little smile on her face, a look of approval, of accomplishment. Up behind her, I noticed for the first time, was Lila Stockett, widow of former coach Frank Stockett. She and the elementary school principal Martha Cullen were each crying without restraint. *Frank, wherever you are*, I thought, *you better be enjoying this*.

Trisha sat, blankets wrapped around her legs and shoulders, her head down, looking at her lap, her arms up and outstretched in a V-shape, her hands inside purple mittens.

Then I spotted Old Tom, his leather helmet soaked a darker color, hobbling down the aisle of the bleachers onto the track. I was afraid he was going to attempt to reach the sidelines and the players or the coaches but instead he stopped, and carefully on the slick and muddy track, he moved his feet in tiny, choppy strides until he angled his scrawny body to face the WHS fans in the bleachers.

"What are we!" his creaky voice called out.

"Rangers," came a muted response from the bleachers.

"What are we!" he squawked again.

"Rangers!" the crowd yelled back with more authority.

"What are we!" he yelled.

"Rangers!" we all yelled.

Jersey turned around, a soft expression of contentment on his face. There was no attempt to humiliate or disgrace the opponent. This was a uniform cry of pride, of respect, of achievement. Of praise. Of thanks. Of awe.

"What are we!" yelled Old Tom

"Champions!" came the response.

"What are we!" Old Tom yelled.

"Champions!" we all yelled.

"What are we!" Old Tom croaked.

"Champions!" we screamed.

Moments later it was true, we were champions. The clock ticked down to zeroes. A horn sounded. The game was over. The WHS fans roared as one and bound out of the bleachers, across the track and onto the field. Kids hopped over steel bleacher railings and the orange plastic snow fence and raced out on the field and into the arms of wet and weary Ranger football players. Dave took off his helmet and held his face firmly to the sky, as if to soak in everything he could possibly soak in. He held the helmet toward the patch of bleachers that held the extended Dickson family. The Rangers formed a loose line and both teams congratulated each other with handshakes, nods of acknowledgement and earnest pats on the back. The Roundup fans filed stoically out of their bleachers as well, and merged into a sea of maroon with the Panther players.

After the respectful exchange between the two teams Tony loped toward the Whitehall fans and ran into the waiting arms of Aspen, who was practically hysterical. Colt hugged his parents, then with his helmet off, hung low at his side, he walked over to Trish.

“We did it, Colt!” she called out to him.

“We did it, Trish,” he agreed softly, and crouched in front of her, kneeled, and buried his face into the blankets on her lap, and she placed her hands on his head. The picture I took was too personal, too intrusive, for the Ledger, but a glossy reproduction of the photo was given to both Colt and Trish.

Colt wandered away to the cheers of fans and students and I happened to be closest to Trisha. “Lance,” she said, with just a hint of a lisp, *Lanch.* She smiled, and she made no attempt to hide her tears, and put an arm around my waist.

“Trish, something very special happened here today,” I told her.

“Something precious,” Trisha assured me. “Something we’ll carry with us the rest of our lives.” She offered me a whimsical smile, a nod of recognition and finality.

Molly Ryan stepped down from the bleacher steps and stepped into an embrace from her daughter.

In the misty shadows along the sidelines, down toward the end zone, Annie and Tony were locked in an embrace, and as I approached them Annie broke my direction and after a short sprint jumped into my waiting arms.

“It’s just a stupid game, Lance,” she gushed into my neck, her feet high off the ground. “Why am I so happy?”

She had her arms wrapped around me, and I held her tight. “You know why,” I told her.

Tony had his helmet upraised in his right hand and pumped it up toward the falling rain. He was smeared and soaked, mud stains mixed with sweat. He put an arm around me. Aspen edged away, and joined in a group embrace of the other weepy cheerleaders.

“Do you believe it?” Tony shouted at me.

“Do you?” I asked back, and he cackled with delight.

Our eyes met, and his laughter ceased. He shook his head, and his expression changed into something more somber. He pulled my head close to his.

“Mom’d be proud,” I said.

He seemed to attempt to respond, but couldn’t. I held his forehead against mine.

He nodded in silent brief vigorous agreement, then raised his helmet again, and was gone.

Jersey had found Trish. His leather jacket glistened with raindrops and to me, somehow, he looked weary, exhausted, even older. When I joined him he was thanking Annie and Trish.

“You never doubted us, not for a second,” Jersey told Trish. “You’re a big part of this team and this achievement.”

“You,” Trish started, but couldn’t finish. Overcome, she hid her face behind her mittens. Jersey leaned over, gently patted her back, then leaned forward and gave her a kiss squarely on the top of her head.

“Lance,” he said when he stood and saw me. “I’m glad to see you. Thanks for all you did to make this possible.” He gave me no time to respond. “Think we should get a team picture?” he asked.

“Now?” I asked. I had taken a couple pictures of Colt and some of the seniors holding up the state championship trophy, but a photo in the darkness and the rain of thirty cold and wet kids seemed like a difficult assignment.

“No better time,” Jersey said.

The six-column team photo taken that afternoon ran on the front page of the Ledger. It was not a work of art. The outside of the frame, on either side, was slightly out of focus and darker – thanks to the camera flash – than the center. Morgan’s eyes were closed. You couldn’t really see a couple kids in the back row. Coach Pete couldn’t stand still, and because of the film speed, was a bit blurry. But there was something intensely personal about the picture, the sloppy expressions of unmitigated joy on the faces of Dave and Tony and JeffScott, the bold and confident accomplishment on the faces of Colt and Logan, who knelt in the front center, on either side of Trish and her wheelchair, as she held up the trophy slanted slightly toward the camera. Jersey stood in the middle of the second row, his eyes directed not at the camera but at Trisha and the trophy, and that’s what makes the photo so special. By looking at Trish and the trophy, he directs your eyes – every time you look at the picture – away from himself and at what he wants you to see.

Chapter 41

It began to sink in – to truly grasp the accomplishment – somewhere between Big Timber and Livingston, sometime around midnight, on the drive home to Whitehall. The Rangers, impossibly, were state champs. The remarkable achievement meant many things, among them it meant a big Ledger with a special section devoted to the new state champs. I'd essentially work three days straight, and on Wednesday I'd print an extra 500 papers. On the drive home from Roundup, anticipating the workload, I couldn't wait to get at it. It would be a tribute. It would be widely anticipated. It would be read word-for-word, front to back. It would be widely appreciated. It would be profitable. It would be historical.

To my right, in the passenger seat, Mary had drifted into a gentle sleep. Behind me, Old Tom snorted and snored, his lanky body upright, the back of his head on the headrest, his face pointed up through the back window toward the stars. Rhonda managed to curl up on the seat, her head against the door, her legs angled across the seat toward the middle, then slid down and away to the floor. At no time did any part of her body touch Old Tom's seating area. She had fallen asleep immediately, on the first leg of the journey from Roundup to Billings, where the WHS entourage held a rendezvous at a Pizza Hut for a quick, impromptu and soggy celebratory dinner.

Rocky Mountain Bank, Golden Sunlight Mine and the Ledger chipped in to fund a team, family, and fan dinner. Annie had arranged for the dinner and its sponsors, but I didn't find out about that until later. During the dinner, I sold the bank and the mine the concept of sponsoring a special section of the Ledger to honor the Rangers. Lyle at the bank and Rick from the mine immediately and enthusiastically okayed their sponsorship.

The dinner overall was buoyant but oddly, in some quarters, somewhat subdued. Jersey, his features drawn, his angular body slightly stooped, appeared exhausted, as if each movement was challenging or difficult. Coach Pete's face was a bright fleshy red, his plaid hat tipped back on his head.

There were no speeches, no grand eloquent statements, no wild ovations or excessive celebrations. It was somehow all more personal than that; speeches weren't necessary. The kids were happy, relieved, weary, overwhelmed. Some of the kids were giddy, some were stunned, some were stiff and sore. Dave, the feisty and combative warrior, sat drowsy and quiet with his mom and family, and before we left the Pizza Hut I'd caught him yawning three different times. Most of the players had a limp or an ache or pain somewhere, and the pain was just settling in. Colt hobbled with a sore knee. Tony's neck was bothering him; he had to turn his entire body to simply look either left or right. Logan's shoulder and rib cage ached. Both JeffScotts favored their left leg. Cody's chin had a deep gash that had bled through a bandage. Two fingers on Nate's left hand were swollen like sausages and stuck together with bright white adhesive tape. The skin from Morgan's left forearm was scraped raw and purple.

But they were together, these Rangers, they were joyful, and they knew what they'd achieved. And perhaps some of them were just then realizing that this was the final time this group of boys would ever be together as a team. When they stepped off the bus in Whitehall, the season was over and this team would abruptly and permanently no longer exist.

It was after ten o'clock in Billings before we rounded up everyone, headed out of the restaurant, and began, in cars, trucks and buses, to drift west to Whitehall. There was no attempt to caravan home, form a parade, to honk horns at passing cars, to boast to strangers in the night. We were too many, we were too scattered and we were too tired. The pep bus and team bus pulled onto the freeway just before us, and I passed them right away. Inside, the bus was dark, and I saw no movement.

On the way out of Billings I pulled into a convenience store and bought Pepsi to help keep me awake. Rhonda shooed Old Tom out of the car and into the bathroom. Before we even got as far west as Columbus, I was the only person in the car awake. I had the stereo turned low, and Springsteen was singing softly about driving alone in a stolen car through the dead of night.

The Yellowstone River was on our right side now, a shining sliver of fluid silver, running the opposite direction we were headed. The sky had opened up, and the moon glowed through scattered backlit clouds. The road surface here was dry, the air was cold and clear and crisp.

Alone with my thoughts, my daughter on the pep bus and son on the championship team bus, I wondered: *Was this one of the best moments of my life?* I had a couple hours to ponder the question, if I chose. Tony had scored two touchdowns and helped lead his team to an improbable if not impossible state title. Annie had a limitless future, and everything she did and said proved that. I was escorting home a lovely schoolteacher who understood me, my newspaper and my family better, probably, than I myself did. In the backseat was a mismatched duo of Whitehall aged citizens that represented, in their own way, Whitehall's heritage and traditions, and did so in their own indisputable individual manner. The Ledger, thanks in part to the Rangers, would have its best year ever, and the paper published in four days would likely be the single biggest edition of the Ledger ever produced. I didn't need caffeine to keep me awake. My thoughts alone were plenty stimulating.

"Where you figure we're at?" It was Old Tom. His voice was dry and creaky.

"East of Livingston," I answered. "How are you doing?"

I heard the mushy, pasty sound of him moving his mouth. "Pretty damn fine, actually."

"Glad to hear it," I told him. I wondered if he needed a bathroom. We'd been on the road nearly two hours. "Do you need to stop?"

"No, I'm doing okay." He cleared his throat. I felt what was intended to be a reassuring hand on my shoulder. "I can't tell you how grateful I am," he said. "I mean that."

He did mean it. I could hear the sincerity through the darkness.

"I'm glad we were able to take you," I told him.

"That's bullshit," he said, matter-of-factly. "I invited myself on this trip. You got stuck with me. You were too nice of a person to say no. I was counting on that, you know. You being too nice to tell me know. Hell, when I heard that loony Manfred almost shot you, my first thought was, 'Oh no, there goes my ride to the game,'" Old Tom chortled.

"He didn't almost-"

"Yeah, yeah," Old Tom interrupted, to shut me up. "I just need to tell you how much this team and these games have meant to me." He paused, and I heard him working his parched and pasty mouth. "I got cancer or something, some goddamned thing, in my liver and pancreas or someplace. It's killing me from the inside out, whatever it is. But I don't give a shit anymore. I've lived long enough. Maybe too long. But then this team came along and these boys carried me along with them, and it's been quite a ride, you gotta admit."

"Yes, it has," I admitted.

"And I got quite a kick out of all this," Old Tom said, almost invisible in the darkness of the backseat. "If I was you, I'd pull over somewhere in Livingston. Anyway, look at me, with my old helmet and my baggy old Whitehall sweater. For a while, Lance, just a little while, I got to be a kid again." He chortled, which prompted a brief coughing fit. "Goddamn cancer, Lance. Where was I?"

I ventured a guess. "You were a kid again?"

"That's right, I was," he quickly agreed. "I was a kid again. I got to be a part of this team, a part of something special, before I die. To enjoy it. To feel it. To really experience it. That's no small thing. No sir, no small thing. My mind's going, either from being old or being sick or the pills I take, I don't know and to tell the truth, my thinking is, who gives a shit? You thought I was crazy, didn't you? Senile or crazy or gone in the head? Didn't you?"

He stopped but didn't give me time to respond.

"Well, you was right," he continued. "But then I dug around in the basement and put on my old sweater and my old helmet, and I felt a little life in these sick old bones. And so I had to latch onto you, because no one else would take a crazy old hoot like me and I figured you were too nice of a guy to tell me to bugger off. And you were."

"We weren't-"

"You're too nice of a guy," Old Tom blurted. "Sometimes I thought you was even a little wimpy. I still can't figure why Manfred wanted to shoot you."

"He-" I tried.

"So anyway," Old Tom told me, "I'm gonna die pretty soon. Sure as that moon up there is shining, I'm gonna die soon. But I'll be goddamned if I won't die a happy man, because of these Rangers and this past couple months." He paused. "Hell of a thing, actually, what gets to be important."

I was tempted to comment, but I didn't think he wanted me to.

"I ain't afraid to die now," Old Tom said. "I ain't afraid of nothing. You tell Coach Jersey that."

There was a rustling in the backseat and then I sensed some fumbling directly above me, above my head, and then I felt what I instinctively knew was the old battered leather football helmet placed on my head, like a crown.

"I want you to have this," Old Tom said. "Give it to your boy, later, if you want."

"I can't-"

"Yeah, you can. I want you to take it. It would mean" – and I heard him sniffle – "a lot to me if you took this." Old Tom sniffed, and I heard him sit back into the seat.

"Thanks," I told him. "It means a lot to me, too."

It was almost two o'clock in the morning when we pulled into Whitehall. My mind was still alert, still racing with a thousand thoughts – I had decided the special section would be divided into three main sections; the regular season, the playoffs, and then the championship game – and as we approached town from the east on I-90 I spotted a Whitehall Volunteer Fire Department truck more or less blocking the incoming lanes of the off ramp. My first fear was that while in Roundup some catastrophic calamity had struck the town, and that the Ledger and I had missed it. I slowed down as we approached the truck, and in the darkness my headlights found a few cars parked at odd angles around and behind the truck.

The firetruck lights flashed and Brandon Bradshaw opened the door as the Escort slowed on the approach. He stepped down and stood outside, and lit by my headlights, he waved with both hands low, the international *slow down* signal.

I stopped and rolled down the window, and Brandon crouched and looked inside the car. I hoped he'd pretend to ignore the helmet; he gave Mary an appreciative nod, glanced with amusement at the helmet, and scanned Rhonda and Old Tom in back with a curious smile. He nodded then, as if regarding it all as normal, as if I usually drove into town at two o'clock wearing a wet old lopsided leather football helmet.

"What's up?" I asked.

"Great game, huh?" Brandon said.

"State champs," I said. "Whitehall. State champs." It felt good to say it.

"You ain't gonna shoot him, are you?" called out Old Tom from behind me.

"Not unless I have to," Brandon said, and grinned. "We're here to welcome the team home. Show a little support for them. You know where the team bus is?"

Excellent idea, I thought. Perfect. "Somewhere behind me," I said. "That's nice of you to do that for the kids."

Brandon nodded. "Coach Pete called us and said we ought to do something, and we should, for sure."

"What should we do?" I asked. "Hang around here, or wait over at the school? What's the plan?

"The plan?" repeated Brandon. "Don't know, really. Intercept the bus, I guess, then drive around town for a bit. Coach Pete'll have an idea. Other folks are at the school, and you can wait over there with them."

"What will happen when the bus shows up?" Mary asked.

"Oh, I'm sure there'll be a more official ceremony later," Brandon said. "For now we just want to raise a little ruckus for the kids."

"Let's raise a *big* ruckus," Old Tom said.

I maneuvered around the truck and checked with my passengers to see what they wanted to do. Mary's eyes held an anticipatory twinkle, and I knew she was good for the duration. Old Tom had found a second wind but I figured I'd take Rhonda home and then get to the school to meet up with the bus.

"Dun't you dare," she said flatly. "I vouldn't miss dis fer da verlt."

"Sir," Old Tom said lordly from the back seat. "I believe I'll need that helmet for a little while longer."

The exchange of the helmet backward to Old Tom was as formal as a British coronation. He gently, even tenderly, placed the helmet atop his head. He looked across the backseat at Rhonda, who sized up its placement and nodded her approval.

Another fire truck was parked back at the school, and the school parking lot held about fifteen vehicles, some with lights on and motors running, anticipating a late night roll through town. I pulled up across from the O'Toole pickup, and Rose, in the front passenger seat, buzzed down the window.

"We're going to have a parade!" she exclaimed. Her blonde hair was slightly mussed but by looking at her you'd never known it was the middle of the night and she'd just had a four-hour ride home after standing in the rain for three hours.

"I'm not sure this is going to be what I'd call a parade," I said.

"When's the last time Whitehall held a parade at two-thirty in the morning?" Lyle called out from the other side of the pickup, ignoring my comment. I could smell the warmth and scent of coffee sifting out the window.

"Not sure," I said.

"I thought you knew everything about Whitehall," Rose said cheerfully.

"I doubt that," I said. "But I doubt there's ever been a Whitehall parade at two-thirty in the morning."

"We're making history!" Old Tom announced from behind me.

"You bet we are," Lyle answered him.

Mary and Ryan Jones, owners of the IGA, pulled up on the other side of the O'Toole's. Mary emerged under a hooded coat, carrying a box of pastries, and went from vehicle to vehicle, knocking on windows and offering donuts. A couple additional vehicles pulled into the lot, including the Hinkel truck. Slack jumped out as soon as they stopped and ran in front of the Escort, pounded playfully, like thunder, on the hood, and yelled and pumped his cowboy hat in the air. I honked the horn in response, and throughout the lot a wave of scattered honks answered. Slack more or less skipped around the car and stood between Rose in her truck and me in the Escort, and he was so happy to be right where he was standing he couldn't think of anything to say. He looked my direction, eyes wide and filled and seemingly bursting with energy, then to Rose, then to me, and although his mouth struggled to form words the only sounds that emerged were grunts.

"We're state champs," I said, to help. "Whitehall Rangers. State champs."

"We did it!" Slack proclaimed.

Mary arrived at our car with the donuts – the box now about three-fourths empty – and Slack reached in and grabbed two. I shook my head no when Mary offered them toward me, but the scrawny claw of Old Tom reached from behind me and took a maple bar.

Perhaps it was Rose's beauty, or her calmness, or just Slack's need to release energy, but he simply bolted away and danced – danced is the only word for it – around the parking lot, to a smattering of honks that served as applause.

"This ain't bad," Old Tom said, his mouth half full of maple bar. "Nowhere near as good as your cooking," he told Rhonda.

The first bus – the pep bus – pulled in behind us into the parking lot, and car honks and headlight flashes greeted it as it coasted to a stop in front of the main school doors. It was dark, but enough lights were on to see as the puzzled, weary kids began filing out, surprised at the racket upon their arrival. Siblings and parents in vehicles greeted the kids with embraces and even though I couldn't hear the conversations, it was obvious the sleepy high school kid or kids asked what was going on, found out, and immediately perked up. Ed jumped onto the bus to talk with the driver as the kids continued to exit, and moments later he stepped off the bus with an arm around Annie, and they conversed as she walked toward the Escort.

"My goodness," Annie said, and opened her arms toward the parking lot, when I rolled down the window.

"You're that smart one, ain't you," Old Tom called out from the backseat.

"You're the one with the helmet, ain't you," Annie said. Old Tom found her comment wildly amusing.

Annie seemed so thin and pale, sleepy to the point of sluggish. Her hair on the right side – the side she'd obviously put against the window as she slept or tried to sleep – was flat, and a tuft of hair in back kind of stood up. "Look at all this racket in the middle of the night. It's a good thing you got Manfred out of the picture."

"We're makin' history!" Old Tom announced again.

“Yes we are,” Annie said, and she meant it. “Good for us. All of us.” She crouched and looked inside the car. “Can you guys fit me in there somehow?”

“You bet,” Mary said, and quickly opened the door. “I’ll climb in back so you can sit up front with your dad.”

“No, I can get in back,” Annie said. There was a rustling behind me, as Rhonda slid into the middle and in one motion Mary bailed out of the car and climbed into the passenger side backseat.

“Ya, plenty uf vroom,” Rhonda said.

“Thanks,” Annie said, and got into the front passenger seat. She looked at Old Tom, looked at me for a moment, then back at Old Tom. “You know, on a lot of people that helmet would look strange, but on you, it looks good.”

In the rearview mirror, Old Tom straightened, as if a noble.

“You’ll have a big paper on Wednesday, won’t you,” Annie told me.

“The biggest ever,” I answered.

People were wandering around in the parking lot, going from the bus to vehicles, standing outside of cars and trucks simply talking in small gathered groups, and more and more headlights were showing up behind us. Some of the kids and fans in the pep bus climbed into their own cars and trucks, and sat waiting, lights on, with an occasional gleeful honk.

Molly had helped Trish into their Blazer and was stowing the wheelchair in the back.

“The bus!” Slack screamed. He was laughing, pointing, and running as the Ranger team bus pulled into the parking lot. Slack, waving his black cowboy hat, ran alongside the slow moving bus, jumping and dancing and cheering. Lights flashed to bright and the night sky filled with honks. We all jumped out of our vehicles and greeted the weary Rangers – their squinty eyes adjusting to the bright headlights, their minds slow to awaken and bodies locked in stiffness and pain – with hugs and handshakes and pats on the back.

Both firetrucks crawled into the parking lot, lights on top flashing, and one of them let loose with just a hint of a siren’s wail.

“That’s what I’m talking about!” Coach Pete announced from the top of the bus steps as he surveyed the people and vehicles.

Coach Pete’s face still flushed red, his portly body awkwardly animated, he hobbled from the bus to the bigger of the two firetrucks, talked with the driver for a minute, then limped quickly – one hip and thigh straight as a board with an unbendable stride, the other leg in catch-up mode with quicker steps – to the other truck, and then back to the Ranger bus for a brief conversation with the driver.

“Okay!” he called out from the bottom step of the bus. He whirled his hand once in the air. “Let’s saddle up.”

“Let’s raise the biggest ruckus this town has ever seen,” Old Tom called out.

The town marshal police car pulled in the parking lot, and for a moment, just a brief moment, my belly went cold inside. But then I saw the cruiser was driven by Mayor Luke Grayling, with Rachel Brockton in the passenger seat.

Luke and Rachel both jumped out of the car, and tracked down Coach Pete as he tried to organize an unorganizable collection of people and vehicles. People were moving rapidly back and forth to and from vehicles, and as Coach Pete gathered players back into the bus, Luke shook Coach Pete's hand as Coach Pete nodded, said something, listened, and nodded again.

Luke and Rachel both climbed up the steps into the pep bus, followed by Coach Pete, and all three of them disappeared inside the bus. Cars and trucks were more or less lining up behind the firetrucks, or waiting in place to get in line, and as I looked around the parking lot I was surprised to see no one – not a single person – was left outside a vehicle.

Then Coach Pete materialized out of the bus, with Jersey in tow, Coach Pete's right hand holding a fistful of Jersey's leather jacket, and it looked for all the world as if Coach Pete was hauling Jersey to the squad car like in the old days, when Officer Pete hauled criminals to squad cars.

"I have to admit," Annie said to no one in particular, "I didn't see that coming."

"He ain't gonna shoot him, is he?" asked Old Tom.

Coach Pete jumped into the squad car driver's seat, and Jersey eased himself into the passenger seat. Suddenly, Slack crossed the parking lot at a dead sprint, and just as he reached the police car, Coach Pete got out and opened the back door, and Slack all but dived in. On went the police lights, the siren made a couple loud whoop-whoop-whoop blasts and Coach Pete sped the car to the parking lot exit, onto Whitehall Street. The firetrucks were next, lights flashing, horns honking, followed by the Ranger bus then the pep bus, then a string of maybe twenty cars, one by one, inched out of the lot onto the street.

"Unbelievable," I muttered, as we left the parking lot.

"Believe it," Annie assured me.

"This is nothing short of spectacular," Tom said, a trace of awe in his voice.

And for about thirty minutes, Coach Pete in the squad car led us on a tour of Whitehall, street by street, past most every house in town. Lights blinked on inside homes as the boisterous procession cruised by, and every now and then people – in pajamas and winter coats – jumped in their vehicles to join the parade, honk their horns and flash their headlights on bright. The kids in the buses had the windows rolled down and shouted as they went by – gleefully calling out the accomplishment, the score, the title of state champions – and people in late November, wakened and out on their steps or on their lawns at three in the morning – raised hands in cheer or pumped fists or applauded or saluted or turned their porch lights on and off quickly almost like fireworks, and the celebration touched almost every part of Whitehall.

One omission was the Purdy house. The procession stopped, honked, yelled, cheered and flashed lights. You could see Daniel Purdy inside, in the dark, but he didn't step out of the house, didn't acknowledge the parade, and was soon left alone, in his dark house.

The celebration turned out to last a full week. There was a school assembly on Monday afternoon that featured a state championship banner hoisted in the school gym and a state championship plaque and game ball officially placed in the school trophy case. A team meeting was held after school on Tuesday in which the players turned in equipment, watched the title game on film, congratulated each other and each received individual praise from Jersey. On Wednesday the Ledger came out, featuring a special tribute section to the Rangers, and also that day the Montana High School Association announced that five Whitehall players – Dave Dickson, Colt Harrison, Logan Bradshaw, Cody Phillips and Tony Joslyn – were named first team All-Conference and were named to the All-State Class B team. A community celebratory BBQ packed the multi-purpose room on Thursday. Jersey spoke during the BBQ and thanked each player, each student, each school board member and each community member for the gift of teaching and coaching in Whitehall. It was nothing short of spectacular.

On Friday, while Annie was working in the high school office, she absently looked through the stack of congratulatory phone call messages that flooded the school that week. The messages were written on thin little pink slips, and they came from all over – other schools, other coaches, our county commissioners, local businesses and others – and some of the messages were directed to the school district or the team as a whole, while others were directed specifically to Jersey. As she looked through the pile of slips, the phone rang, and she answered it.

The caller – a man – asked for Jerry Conte, and Annie told me she said he was in class and asked if she could take a message.

The caller sort of giggled, and said yeah, she could. Tell him we're proud of him back here in Jersey.

Okay, Annie said she told him as she wrote down the message on the little pink slip. She asked who the message was from.

The caller sort of giggled again. Tell him it's from the Boss.

Annie said she thought, The Boss? Not a boss, but the Boss? As in Bruce Springsteen?

Annie said the caller asked who she was, and she said she gave him her name.

Annie? the caller giggled. Annie the rock and roll dancer? Annie who's smarter than the governor? That Annie? The caller giggled again.

Annie said she asked, Who is this really?

Annie, Annie, Annie, the caller said. Jersey thinks the world of you. Not just 'cause you're smart, but because you're loyal to your family, you know, to your friends, and to your community.

Annie told the caller that Jersey was unlike anyone she'd ever met.

She said the caller said goodbye. Then he said, tell Jersey we had this talk. Tell all the Rangers congratulations. And Annie, the caller said, Jersey's unlike anyone any of us have ever met.

Afterward

As you might expect, I've measured the rest of my life by that fall, the autumn of 1986, when Tony was a sophomore, Annie was an eighth grader and the Rangers won their only football title in school history. Two decades later, in 2005, the world is a changed place and I'm a changed man. I no longer live in Whitehall, but I haven't drifted far, either physically or spiritually. I reside now just outside of Bozeman, and when I sold the Ledger part of the deal guaranteed me a free lifetime subscription to the Ledger. So I am still, and always will be, rooted to Whitehall.

It has been tough to track some of the people so prominent in that magical season, but throughout the years, either deliberately or accidentally, I've kept pretty close tabs on most of them.

Jersey taught the rest of the school year in Whitehall, accepted the football coaching position for the following season, then left Whitehall after school was out in spring of 1987 and was never seen again. He had been named Montana Class B football coach of the year, had given no indication he was unhappy or was contemplating leaving, but after the spring of 1987 he simply vanished.

He never submitted a letter of resignation, so we never knew why he left or where he went, but the assumption was he had accepted a better coaching position at a larger school. But if he did, that school was not in Montana. Once, in about 1995 or so, Annie gave me an urgent telephone call and with great excitement told me to turn on the television and watch a college game – Oregon State against UCLA or something like that – and instructed me to look for Jersey as a coach on one of the sidelines. She said she was sure she saw him. I watched the rest of the game but didn't see him or anyone who looked like him. Annie didn't leave it there, though. She searched on the Internet, which was still fairly new in 1995, and even called the athletic department of both schools searching for a Jerry Conte or anyone nicknamed Jersey. She came up empty.

She has conducted regular Internet searches since, and has never come across him. It is as if he vanished from the face of the earth.

Coach Pete, like Jersey, coached that single year in Whitehall, the magical championship year of 1986. Coach Pete had always resembled a walking heart attack, and in December 1986 – a month after the title game – the inevitable stroke finally caught up to him. It didn't kill him, but at times I think he wished it had. He was airlifted to Billings where they opened him up and put a new valve into his heart. He lost weight, strength, and finally, interest. The intense vigor that always characterized him was gone when he returned with that long straight chest scar. His hip caused him increasing pain. He aged ten years in ten months, and in 1990 – at age sixty-one – he gave up. Pallbearers at his service were all members of the 1986 WHS Ranger football team.

Ed Franklin retired in 1998 and in the five years after his retirement he fished in Iceland, hiked in New Zealand, snorkeled off South America, golfed in Hawaii, bungee-jumped in California, caroused in Ireland and toured Russia by train. In late 2002 he was at a Springsteen concert in Sweden and called me from the show, holding up his cell phone as Springsteen launched into *Badlands*, and I will go to my grave absolutely mystified and overwhelmed by the transformation that took place within Ed Franklin during the fall of 1986. Housing a young and bedeviled Cody Phillips may have had something to do with it, but that absurdly complete conversion from educational and administrative and technological nerd to cultivated and stylish and worldly sophisticate could have only occurred – like the creation of life itself – in the most exacting and complex environment conceivable. I remain convinced that the introduction of Bruce Springsteen's music, combined with Ed's appreciation for Jersey's persona and the stunning achievement of the Rangers, conspired to free an inner Ed or an alter ego Ed that once unleashed did nothing but expand and flourish. During Ed's retirement assembly, held in the Whitehall multi-purpose room on a gray spring afternoon, he was close to seventy years old and was surrounded by the current faculty, school board members and community leaders. Ed was the oldest guy in the room, and without question, Ed was the coolest guy in the room, and everyone in the room – including Ed, or maybe especially Ed – knew it.

In early winter 1986, after many objections from Laura Joyce, ***the Ledger mice*** had overstayed their welcome and one afternoon were liberated from the shop and released into the wilds of the parking lot behind the pizza parlor. Annie simply placed a popcorn bag on its side on the floor, and the two mice dutifully sniffed their way inside. Annie took them behind the Ledger in an alley and, as she put it, released them into the wild. They were only mice, but after they were gone, alone at the Ledger, late at night, I sort of missed them.

Old Tom passed away late on a Wednesday night in February 1987. Young Tom brought the cherished old football helmet to the Ledger, as Old Tom had instructed in a note. Jersey, Rhonda, Annie and Tony, the mayor and Rachel, and the entire town council attended the service. In honor of Old Tom, I wore the helmet to the service.

Johnny Pep never attended school in Whitehall again, but every now and then we in Whitehall would read about him. The Montana Standard, in its daily reporting of crime, frequently mentioned Johnny Pep throughout his teenage years, mostly in connection with drug transactions. But after a stint at a youth correctional facility in Miles City, Johnny straightened his life out and wound up employing his sales skills for a better purpose, and became one of Montana Broom and Brush's best salesmen.

Cal Walker finished his term as county commissioner, then ran for the state legislature, and won. One of his most prized possessions was a purple windbreaker with the words *1986 Whitehall State Champions* stitched in gold inside the outline of a football, and he regularly wore that jacket on the campaign trail and used that team as an example of the teamwork necessary to achieve great things. The Ledger endorsed his legislative candidacy, and as a state representative he still took in Sunday movies at the Star Theatre and still brought me popcorn and pop Sunday evenings. When the Legislature was in session from January to April during the odd years, he submitted a column on a weekly basis and once each session I'd travel to Helena to interview him and take a picture or two. After I'd sold the Ledger he said he'd continue to stop by the paper on Sunday nights with popcorn and a chat with the new publisher, but he stopped after a couple visits. He said it just wasn't the same.

Slack wore his purple state championship windbreaker almost every day. By 1990 he'd worn the jacket out. Slack and his dad served as two-thirds of the chain gang during home football games well into the 1990s, and each season Slack believed another state title was coming. It has never happened. He approached each game and each season with childlike enthusiasm and hope, and every season he was distantly disappointed. But the disappointment didn't last long. He was, and is, forever an optimist, forever prepared to celebrate a WHS win. He never did understand why Jersey left or where he went to, and I couldn't explain it to him because I never understood it myself. I still run into him when I visit Whitehall. He's still on the ranch, still living with his parents, but every now and then he'll flash that smile, the youthful innocent smile, the starkly stunning smile of happiness and pride, and you grin, you can't help it, just seeing him.

Rhonda died early in 1991. I wept as I wrote her obituary, alone in the Ledger on a bitterly cold Monday night. As I typed, I played *Brusch* in her honor. Annie and Tony both came home for her funeral service, held at St. Teresa's, which was as close to a synagogue, I guessed, as anything else was in Whitehall. I was afraid no one but the three of us might show up at her service, but the pews were largely filled with a diffuse collection of Whitehall residents, plus some people I'd never seen in town before. I struck up a conversation with some of them, and mostly they were former Whitehall residents who had rented one of the apartments in her old railroad house, and they all told stories of her kindness and generosity, and mostly, of her cooking. She had somehow made it to Whitehall on her own as a young woman sometime after World War II, worked at Borden's and saved enough to buy the railroad house, but she'd never had any real family with her in Whitehall or anywhere else in Montana. But in reality all of us were her family, and we all missed her deeply after she was gone. To this day, when I smell fresh pastry, I think of Rhonda Horst, and I always will.

Daniel Purdy sold his lumberyard in fall of 1987, left Whitehall without so much as a change of address form at the post office, and to my knowledge, never returned and never kept in touch with anyone from the community. When the Ranger celebration joyously passed the Purdy home that cold and historical early morning in November 1986, and when Daniel Purdy purposefully stayed in his unlit house, partially cloaked in the darkness, separated from the event, the community and the accomplishment, the separation was complete and irrevocable.

Henry "Manfred" Manfredini retired from Montana law enforcement shortly after the incident in Whitehall. I heard from someone that he was a 'mall cop' in Denver.

Nate Bolton, the lanky running back and wide receiver who was also a star high school sprinter and hurdler from Cardwell, earned a track scholarship to a small school in Oregon. Every now and then the school would send a press release about Nate's presence on the Dean's List or an athletic triumph. In his final year in college, Nate's times in the 200-meters qualified him as an All-American. He was one of the featured athletes in the school's athletic promotional materials. When asked about his favorite moment in sports, he wrote, *Beating Baker in Baker in the football playoffs*. When asked about the person he admired most, he wrote, *Jersey*. When asked why, he wrote, *He knows*.

Cale Bolling went to Concordia College in Minnesota and became a Lutheran minister. He grew a thick waist and a bushy blond beard, married a solid Minnesota Swede named Lana and they had five kids who looked like they just came off a boat from Scandinavia. Cale made a trip back to Whitehall every couple years or so, and even officiated his little sister's wedding at Whitehall's Zion Lutheran Church. Cale never failed to ask me about Annie and Tony, and at the reception at his sister's wedding he talked about the 1986 season and told me he used the lessons learned that year – lessons about sacrifice and determination, about knowing what you can summon when you need it to overcome adversity – on a daily basis. He said in counseling young couples, he would often find himself virtually repeating word for word some of the things he'd heard from Jersey a decade or more earlier.

Bonner Labuda did not become a minister. He more or less dropped out of school his senior year, despite my attempts to convince him to graduate. He lived in Butte for a while, and then I lost track of him. In late 1998 or 1999, I brought my car for repairs to a shop in Bozeman and it was Bonner – a fairly clean-cut Bonner – who emerged from the garage into the office to wait on me. To my surprise I discovered he owned the repair shop, and he sort of winked at me, and then I realized the name of the shop was *Boss Car Repair*.

He specialized in installation of high end car stereo systems, and found a perfect location in a college town like Bozeman. He still wore a black stocking cap, still toyed around with a guitar, and he and a band of part-time musicians played dances and frat parties. He mixed in Springsteen, he said, every chance he got.

Cody Phillips graduated from WHS and joined the Marines. Twenty years later, he's still a Marine, an officer now, and he still stays in loose touch with Tony and Annie. Cody's married to a Korean woman and they have three kids, all girls. Cody has been stationed across the world – Europe, Asia, Africa, the Middle East and at several military bases in the U.S. – a stunning turnaround for a kid who as a high school sophomore was always one mistake away from serious trouble and a diminished future. In conversations, he readily acknowledges the difference Ed and Alice Franklin made in his life, and gives them almost total credit for his military career. The portion of credit not specifically reserved for the Franklins he gives to Jersey, who Cody says helped him understand the distinction between right from wrong.

Morgan Mightward ranches up in the Whitetail Creek area north of town, married a girl he met while attending Montana State University, and the only time he ever left Whitehall was for the four years of college less than an hour from home. He's a man now, big, always wearing Carhartt and cowboy hats. He's active with the WHS Booster Club and with a local watershed group, and with his family he's active in local 4-H and community activities. During a Frontier Days street dance a couple years ago he told me most of his life has been a dull blur, but he can remember bits and pieces of 1986 as if they happened yesterday. He said he could remember every detail imaginable – the angle of the block, the elbow pad on his left arm, the sweat in his eyes, the length of the grass, Coach Pete's posture – when he made a block that sprung Logan for a touchdown in the win over Fairfield. He asked me if that was wrong, to remember the details of that year with such absolute clarity, when nothing else in the past really mattered to him. I told him no, it wasn't wrong, and he should hang on to those memories as clearly and as long as possible. I told him I did.

Logan Bradshaw tried college football at Western Montana College and it didn't work out for him. He tried football at a couple other colleges, in fact, and it didn't work out at any of them. He worked up at Golden Sunlight Mine for a few years, but he wasn't much of an employee, and was let go. He was let go from a handful of other jobs, and found himself, he said, drifting out west, living in his old pickup by a beach in California, essentially homeless and jobless. He was arrested for vagrancy in northern California and sentenced to community service, and ended up assistant coach for a playground little league football team. Three years later he was an assistant foreman at a local lumber mill and coach of the local high school's freshman football team. Two years later he was head coach of the Rio Dell varsity football team, and a year later he was named California High School Coach of the Year when his team won a state title. He came back to Whitehall in 2000 for Colt's wedding, and during the reception he told me late in the state championship game, after his team had just scored the clinching touchdown, for a reason he still can't explain, he looked up in the stands, way up in the top row of the bleachers, and he swears he saw Jersey standing up there, in that nonchalant way of his, wearing the same black leather coat and sunglasses, and applauding. Logan said he enjoys coaching, and he joyfully admitted he bases everything he does as a coach on Jersey's actions, words and philosophy. He said if he had one unfulfilled wish in his life, it was to find Jersey and thank him, thank him for everything.

Dave Dickson started at quarterback all four years at Carroll College where he and the Fighting Saints won back-to-back national championships. In almost every college game he played, Dave was the smallest and shortest player on the field, and he was also the smartest, loudest and most driven player on the field. He was an accurate thrower, but what made him great – and his teams great – was his leadership and relentless pursuit of victory. Dave went on to play professional football in Canada, and although he had a couple good years, a serious knee injury ended his playing career. He then went to law school in Washington state, and he became an assistant prosecutor for the Washington Attorney General. He apparently transferred all his grit and competitiveness from the football to the courtroom. It was harder to keep up with him before the Internet, but now online I check up on Dave the prosecutor all the time and in newspaper stories he is described as a 'bulldog' and 'relentless' and 'fierce' and 'confrontational' and after he'd won a major case a newspaper article reported he had a ninety-eight percent conviction rate. He was the grand marshal of the 2006 Whitehall Frontier Days Parade and he looked fit and healthy, eager as always and vocal as always. He and his wife have two boys, Bruce and Jerry.

Colt Harrison received an academic scholarship to attend Boise State and graduated with a degree in engineering. He moved to San Francisco and started at a junior level in a large company, and a few years later, Tony told me, Colt was on the verge of securing a management position as a project supervisor on a major downtown industrial complex when he abruptly resigned. Back in Whitehall, Colt's father, Hank, had passed away, and his mother, Kathleen, suffered from Alzheimer's and lived in a treatment center in Butte. Depressed by his father's death and mother's illness, he spent a night in a rundown Butte motel and when he woke up there was a message on his cell phone. The male caller didn't identify himself. The voice, Colt said, was Jersey's. There is no doubt in Colt's mind it was Jersey. The voice told him to call a phone number, but when Colt called it, it wasn't Jersey who answered the phone.

It was ***Trisha Ryan*** who answered the phone. Less than a year later Trisha Ryan and Colt were married in Whitehall. Trisha's story is pretty well known. By the end of her senior year in high school she walked with enough confidence and authority to cross the stage to receive her high school diploma. Her body grew in strength to free her from the shackles of her wheelchair, and she blossomed into a healthy, vibrant and enthusiastic young woman who attended Western Montana College and graduated with a degree in elementary education. She accepted a job in eastern Montana to begin her career – she taught special education – but a couple years later she was uniformly embraced as Whitehall's new elementary school resource room teacher. When she and Colt married she was a stunningly beautiful bride. Tony, Annie and I all attended the wedding – with Tony as a groomsman – and it was the most emotional wedding we'd ever attended. Colt now owns and operates a successful landscaping business that serves a territory from Bozeman to Butte and Helena to Ennis, and he calls his company *Ranger Landscaping*. Trish remains a respected and popular Whitehall teacher. The only true disagreement Colt and Trisha Harrison have ever had as a married couple is what Jersey's cryptic *honor the gift* meant. Trisha maintains Jersey meant the gift as her relationship with Colt, and Colt argues the gift refers to her escape from the bonds of physical and mental illness and her role in enriching the lives of her students.

Mary Kristofferson stayed in Whitehall for two more years, and then accepted a teaching position at CMR High School in Great Falls. Within a year after arriving in Great Falls she married a hardware store owner – I attended the wedding and even danced with the bride – but two years later her husband died in a traffic accident. Mary still lives in Great Falls, and we stay in close touch. A couple times we've hit the road together – once to Denver and once to Vancouver – to attend Springsteen concerts. Before she accepted the job in Great Falls, she told me there was something distant about me, something disconnected in my relationship with her. I knew I was supposed to reject her argument, dispute her assertion, but didn't, couldn't, knowing by my inability to contest her allegation I was in fact confirming it. Perhaps Amy took something from me when she left, or perhaps she left because she needed something I could never give. Mary and I will grow old together, apart.

Tony attended the University of Montana and majored in mass communications with the stated intention of being a sportscaster. It didn't work out that way. He did some acting in college, and after graduation made his way to California determined to become a movie star. That didn't work out, either. He worked in some commercials and every now and then had a small role in a TV series – he was in a police show, a hospital show and a lawyer show, but I never watched much TV and don't recall the names of the programs – and then he was a part-time or fill-in college theatrical director at a small school in or around Los Angeles. From there he obtained a masters degree in theatrical arts and went on to work as the full-time director of the theater department at the University of Colorado, and he's been there now for over five years. Their relationship went through several interruptions, but Tony and ***Aspen O'Toole*** eventually did marry, and they have four kids down in Boulder; girls named Annie and Amy, and boys named Lance and Bruce. When you walk into their home not far from campus, the first thing you see is a trophy case and in the case is an old and beat-up leather football helmet. Tony and Aspen's kids are absolute hellions, every one of them, and live life to the fullest. When they show up at my house in Bozeman they run around half dressed and reckless, and always break something – a garage window, a piece of furniture, one of their own arms. But I enjoy every minute with them, and they stuff an astonishing amount of fun and activity into an average day.

Annie graduated from WHS at age fifteen and graduated from Stanford University at age nineteen, and has traveled across the world studying, researching and lecturing on the subject of genetics. She has spent her entire life, it seems to me, wondering and worrying about the seemingly invisible sliver of life that makes each of us on this planet distinctive. I've come across her name and her research or her opinions in national magazines, she has been a guest on several different news shows, she has testified in court, she has appeared before Congress, talked with President Clinton and received some major prizes that come with – apparently – funding and other stipends. She has lived in Seattle, Toronto, St. Louis and Baltimore in the U.S., and has also lived in Europe for a couple years and in Japan for a year. She's married to a Spanish geneticist named Silvo Pena, and he's almost as famous in Europe as she is here in the states. It's not an average marriage, but they aren't average people. Annie is lithe, like her mother, and wears her hair short, not much longer than a crew cut, really. She is incredibly harried and busy, but she calls me all the time, at odd hours of the day or night, sometimes any time of night. Every now and then I can hear the fatigue in her voice, and I think sometimes she calls me to slow down and hear about my dull everyday existence in dull everyday Montana. She gets to Montana every couple years, usually passing through between coasts or countries or continents, and when she's here we always take a run into Whitehall. When I take her back to the Bozeman airport for a connecting flight to her real world, she always gives me a tight tender little hug that lasts pleasantly long, and it always feels like she's hanging on to me like a person clings to something lost or past.

To my eternal surprise, ***Lance Joslyn*** is rather wealthy, apparently. The portfolio Annie built for me when she was in junior high and high school matured robustly over the years, and before she went to Stanford she turned over my financial health to a guy at D.A. Davidson in Great Falls. His look of astonishment upon seeing a child walk in his office makes me laugh every time I think about it. So does he. He keeps track of Annie through the Internet, and is always sending me information about her. My portfolio must have been properly diversified and properly handled by Annie, then by D.A. Davidson and when I sold the Ledger in 2001 it turned out I never had to work again. The value of my land holdings alone in the Gallatin and Jefferson valleys were astonishing to me. I still forget my wallet, forget to carry money and forget the checkbook. I moved to Bozeman after I sold the Ledger because it didn't make sense to live there without a family, without a job and without anything to do. But no matter what happens to me, Whitehall will always be home. I take excellent care of my Bozeman home and landscaped property. And I go to Springsteen concerts. I've seen Bruce live on the west coast, on the east coast, in Canada, in Spain, in England and Ireland, in Norway, and to be honest, lots of other places. Annie and the financial advisor assure me I can afford it, so I do it. Once in a while Tony or Annie will accompany me, sometimes Mary will, sometimes I go alone, and at every concert, in every country, I look for Jersey. I never find him. When I'm alone, in an airplane, at home in Bozeman or driving through Montana, I find myself wondering about that miraculous Ranger football team from 1986, about their remarkable bond of loyalty and faith and about the transformation those games and that team brought to Whitehall. And when I wonder about those kids, that team and that transformation, I realize I've found Jersey.

Acknowledgements

Talk About a Dream is a work of fiction. There is no team in Montana called the Whitehall Rangers; in reality the Whitehall High School team is named the Trojans. In the book they are the Rangers to emphasize the point that what happens in this book never happened in real life. The Whitehall Rangers did not win a state high school football title and the Whitehall Trojans didn't either, although the Trojans did take second place in 1982.

Many of the Montana locations referenced in the book are real, and there truly is a town named Whitehall nestled in the Jefferson River Valley. The community newspaper is called the Whitehall Ledger, and while an occasional "real" Whitehall person shows up in the book – like John Kountz, for instance – almost everyone else is invented. Ted Schwinden was actually Governor of Montana during the time period the book narrative takes place, but if he ever visited Whitehall nothing even remotely close as described in the book took place. Quarterback Dave Dickson's fiery demeanor is modeled after former Griz quarterback Dave Dickenson. The main characters in *Talk About a Dream* are not based on real people, Whitehall or otherwise. They are fabrications created from imagination.

There are errors in the book about who in Whitehall owned what business when, or when what bridge was built or improved, or when what events took place in town. This is a work of fiction told in first person by a fabricated newspaper publisher, and no one is entitled to more errors of fact than a bogus newspaper owner.

The author's affection for Whitehall, small communities, rural newspapers and Montana's landscape and character is real, and it is hoped that affection is recognizable throughout the pages of the book.

The author would also like to thank many people instrumental in the production of this book. Whitehall teacher Holly Harper led the charge to combine the efforts of Whitehall High School students with the project of assisting the movie theatre purchase needed technology to remain open. Special thanks to my wife, Terri, who proofread many versions of the book and who worked tirelessly to get the book ready for publication. Thanks to everyone in who helped promote the book and helped fund-raise for the theater, thanks to the area businesses in Whitehall who also helped promote the book and help raise funds for the Star Theatre, and thanks to Kerry and Karen Sacry for their belief in this book, in the community of Whitehall and for making the commitment to keep the Star Theatre light shining.

Glenn Marx, June 2013

To Order Copies Of

Talk About A Dream

Cost:
$19.99 plus shipping & handling

To Order Online:
Go to the Whitehall Ledger's website at
http://www.whitehallledger.com

To Send Check:
WHS Interact Club, Save the Star
PO Box 1109
Whitehall, MT 59759
(see the Whitehall Ledger website above for shipping and handling costs before mailing check)